Hopes and
rekindled as
wishes c

Miracles in the
✳✳✳ *Village*

A fantastic collection brought to you
by Caroline Anderson, Josie Metcalfe,
Maggie Kingsley and
Margaret McDonagh

Miracles in the Village

CAROLINE ANDERSON
JOSIE METCALFE
MAGGIE KINGSLEY
MARGARET McDONAGH

MILLS & BOON

Mills & Boon, an imprint of Harlequin (UK) Limited, Eton House, 18-24 Paradise Road, Richmond, Surrey TW9 1SR

MIRACLES IN THE VILLAGE
© Harlequin Enterprises II B.V./S.à.r.l. 2011

Their Miracle Baby © Caroline Anderson 2008
Sheikh Surgeon Claims His Bride © Josie Metcalfe 2008
A Baby for Eve © Maggie Kingsley 2008
Dr Devereux's Proposal © Margaret McDonagh 2008

ISBN: 978 0 263 89717 3

025-0212

Harlequin (UK) policy is to use papers that are natural, renewable and recyclable products and made from wood grown in sustainable forests. The logging and manufacturing processes conform to the legal environmental regulations of the country of origin.

Printed and bound in Spain
by Blackprint CPI, Barcelona

Their Miracle Baby

CAROLINE ANDERSON

Caroline Anderson has the mind of a butterfly. She's been a nurse, a secretary, a teacher, run her own soft-furnishing business, and now she's settled on writing. She says, "I was looking for that elusive something. I finally realised it was variety, and now I have it in abundance. Every book brings new horizons and new friends, and in between books I have learned to be a juggler. My teacher husband John and I have two beautiful and talented daughters, Sarah and Hannah, umpteen pets, and several acres of Suffolk that nature tries to reclaim every time we turn our backs!" Caroline also writes for the Mills & Boon® Cherish™ series.

CHAPTER ONE

'DADDY!'

'Hello, pickle!' Mike scooped Sophie up into his arms and whirled her round, their laughter ringing round the yard and echoing off the old stone walls of the barn, bringing a lump to her throat.

These two adored each other, and now both their faces were lit up with a joy so infectious Fran couldn't help but smile.

'How's my favourite girl today?' he asked, hugging her tight and looking down into her beaming face.

'I'm fine— Daddy, where's Fran? I've got something really special to show her— Fran! Look!' she yelled, catching sight of her and waving madly.

She wriggled out of his arms, running across and throwing herself at Fran. She caught her little stepdaughter, hugging her close and laughing, kissing her bright, rosy cheek and holding out her hand for the little box Sophie was thrusting at her eagerly.

'It's a model—I made it at school!' she confided in a stage whisper. 'It's Daddy milking a cow—see, here's Amber, and this is Daddy, and this is the cluster...'

She pointed underneath the misshapen reddish blob that could just conceivably have been a cow, and there was a thing like a mangled grey spider stuck on her underside. She supposed if the blob could be Amber, then the spider could be a milking machine cluster. Why not? And as for Mike...!

'I'm going to give it to him for his birthday,' she went on, still whispering loud enough to wake the dead. 'We've got to wrap it. Have you got paper?'

Fran smiled and put the lid back on the box. 'I'm sure we've got paper,' she whispered back. 'It's lovely. Well done, darling. I'm sure he'll be really pleased.'

A flicker of doubt passed over Sophie's earnest little face. 'Do you think so? Amber was really hard to make.'

'I'm sure, but you've done it beautifully. He'll be so pleased. He loves everything you make for him. It makes him feel *really* special.'

Sophie brightened, her confidence restored, and whirling round she ran back to her beloved father and grabbed his hand. 'I want to go and see the cows— Oh, Brodie!' she said, breaking away again and dropping to her knees to cuddle the delighted collie who was lying on her back, grinning hideously and wagging her tail fit to break it. 'Hello, Brodie,' she crooned, bending right down and letting the dog wash her face with meticulous attention.

'Sophie, you mustn't let her do that!' Kirsten protested, but Sophie ignored her mother, laughing and hugging the dog while Brodie licked and licked and licked for England.

'Yeah, not your face, it's not a good idea,' Mike chipped in, backing Kirsten up simply because he just did. It was one of the many things Fran loved about him, the way he defended Sophie's mother's decisions to their daughter even if he didn't agree, and then discussed it with her rationally when Sophie wasn't around.

The fact that Brodie washed his face whenever it was in reach was neither here nor there! Now he held out his hand to Sophie and pulled her to her feet—and out of range of Brodie's tongue—with a grin.

'Come on, scamp, say goodbye to your mum and then let's go and see the cows. I'm sure they've missed you.'

Missed the treats, no doubt, because the six-year-old always seemed to have her little pockets bulging with pellets of feed, and she'd happily give it to them despite the cows' slippery noses and rough, rasping tongues. Nothing fazed her, and she was deliriously happy trailing round after her father and 'helping' him.

'Fran?' Sophie said, holding out her hand expectantly after they'd waved Kirsten off, but she shook her head. This was their time, precious and special to both of them, and she wouldn't intrude.

'I've got to make supper,' she said with a smile. 'You go with your father and say goodnight to the cows. I'll see you both soon.' And with a little wave she watched them head off towards the field where the cows were grazing, Mike shortening his stride to accommodate his little sprite, Sophie skipping and dancing beside him, chattering nineteen to the dozen while her pale blonde bunches bobbed and curled and flicked around her head.

They went round the corner out of sight, Brodie at their heels, and with a soft sigh Fran went back inside, the little cardboard box containing Mike's present in her hand. She opened the lid and stared down at the little lumps of modelling clay so carefully and lovingly squashed into shape, and her eyes filled. He was so lucky to have her. So very, very lucky.

If only it could happen to them.

They'd come so close—twice now.

It often happened, she'd been told. Miscarriages were common, and her first, three years ago—well, that had just been one of those things, they'd said. It probably wouldn't happen again.

And it hadn't, of course, because she hadn't conceived again, and so they'd undergone endless intrusive and humiliating tests, all of which had proved nothing except that there wasn't any obvious reason why they hadn't had a baby yet.

So they'd gone through the difficult and challenging process of a cycle of IVF, and she'd become pregnant, and then, just like before, she'd lost it.

Not unusual, they were told again, especially with IVF, possibly because the embryos weren't always as perfect as they might be with a normally conceived embryo, and this, it seemed, was probably what had happened to theirs.

All very logical, but she didn't feel logical about it, because there was nothing wrong with either of them, they just hadn't managed to make a healthy baby yet, and it was tearing her apart.

Looking on the bright side, they hadn't made an unhealthy one either, so if that was why the embryos had both failed, maybe it was for the best.

Small consolation.

Whatever the reason, she'd lost the embryos, and she wasn't sure she had the strength to go through it again. If she had another miscarriage…

And, anyway, they still had Sophie coming to visit them

and bringing so much sunshine into their lives. OK, it wasn't like having her own child, but Sophie was gorgeous, and she loved her to bits. Was it greedy to want more?

To want a child of their own who would come home from school bubbling with excitement and giving them some little blob of modelling clay to treasure?

She dragged in a breath, pressing her fist against the little knot of pain in her chest. Not now. She couldn't think about it now. Blinking hard, she put the little box in a safe place, opened the fridge and started pulling things out.

Supper. Practicalities. Forget the rest.

Just like the funny, amazing little present, she had to put her feelings in a box and put the lid on and put them all away.

It was the only way to survive.

They were sitting at the kitchen table.

Mike had finished milking on Saturday morning and he was hurrying back to join them for breakfast. Glancing through the window, expecting to see them cooking, he was surprised to see them seated side by side, Sophie's untamed blonde curls close to Fran's sleek, dark hair, and he could hear them laughing.

They were busy wrapping something that could well have been the little box Sophie had been brandishing yesterday so, instead of kicking off his boots and going in, Mike opened the door a crack to give them warning and said, 'Just going over to the shop to make sure everything's OK. Anything you need?'

'Daddy, go away, you can't see!' Sophie shrieked, plastering herself over the table.

'I'm not looking, I've got my eyes shut,' he said,

squashing a grin and screwing his eyes up tight. 'Want anything, Frankie?'

'Bacon?' she said, a smile in her voice. 'I thought we could have a nice cooked breakfast if you've finished milking.'

'OK. I'll be five minutes.' That should give them long enough to wrap whatever it was, he thought with the smile still tugging at his mouth.

'Fine.'

He went out, leaving Brodie behind to fuss over Sophie, and had a quick chat to his sister-in-law, Sarah, in the farm shop. She was just about to open up, and she threw him a smile as he went in.

'Hiya. How are you? Looking forward to tomorrow?'

'What—getting older, you mean? I can't wait.' He chuckled and picked out a packet of local dry-cured bacon. 'I've been sent to fetch breakfast,' he told her. 'You OK here? Need anything?'

'More blue cheese from the store, when you've got time. It's gone really well this week and we've only got half a wheel left.'

'I'll drop it in later,' he promised.

'Oh, and eggs? We've had a run on them—must be all those desperate women in Penhally making you a birthday cake in the hope of tempting you away from Fran!'

He chuckled again. 'Hardly. But I'll get Sophie on it right after breakfast. She likes collecting the eggs. We'll do it in the next hour or so, OK?'

'Fine. See you later.'

He sauntered back, whistling cheerfully so they could hear him coming and get the present out of the way, and when he opened the door a crack and called through it,

Sophie dashed over and opened it, her eyes twinkling mischievously.

'We're all finished. You can come in now,' she said primly, and he tweaked one of her curls and hugged her against his side.

'I'm glad to hear it. Give this to Fran, could you, sweetheart?'

She skipped across the kitchen with the bacon in her hand. Fran turned and met his eyes over her head, and they shared a smile.

'Here,' Sophie announced, handing it over, then sat down on the floor next to Brodie and sang, 'Bacon, bacon, bacon, we're having bacon! Do you want some?'

'Of course she does but she's not allowed,' Mike reminded her.

'Not even just a teeny, tiny, weeny little bit?'

'Not even a sniff.'

'Oh. Never mind, Brodie,' she said comfortingly, and cuddled the dog, who promptly rolled over and sprawled right in front of Fran.

'Come on, guys, out of the way,' she said patiently, and they decamped to the far end, Sophie propped up against the wall, Brodie propped up against her, both watching the bacon intently.

'Time to wash your hands,' Mike reminded her, washing his own and laying the table while Fran finished the cooking. He made a pot of coffee, poured some juice for Sophie and they settled down to eat.

Well, he and Fran did. Sophie couldn't even eat quietly, humming and jiggling while she ate, making appreciative noises and pretending that she wasn't sneaking bits of food down to Brodie, clamped firmly to her side.

'Brodie, go and lie down,' he said, and the dog, crestfallen, went and flopped apparently casually in a pool of sunshine and watched Sophie's every move.

Poor old thing. She adored Sophie, loving every moment of her visits, and she'd wander around like a lost soul after she'd gone, looking for her.

She wasn't allowed in the bedrooms but somehow, when Sophie was here, she seemed to find her way out of the kitchen door and up the stairs to the foot of her bed, and there she slept, one eye on the door and grinning manically every time they went in to tuck Sophie up, rolling onto her back and wiggling her tail, her melting amber eyes beseeching.

And getting away with it, because Sophie adored her and he couldn't see any harm in it, so they turned a blind eye, even to the point where they'd bathe Brodie before Sophie's visits. She'd been in there last night, and Mike had no doubt she'd be in there tonight, but he didn't care. Kirsten didn't approve, but she'd made her choice and she'd chosen to leave, and he'd moved on.

He'd met Fran four years ago when she'd come back to the village; they'd fallen in love on sight and were blissfully happy.

Or they had been.

If only they could crack this baby thing…

He put their plates in the dishwasher, bent and kissed Fran on the forehead and ushered Sophie towards the door. 'We've got to pick up eggs and take some cheese to the shop. Want to join us?'

Fran shook her head and smiled. 'I've got things to do. You go and have fun,' she told him, but the smile didn't go all the way to her eyes, and in their depths was something he couldn't bear.

He loved his present.

Sophie came creeping into their bedroom with the first rays of the sun, Brodie on her heels, and they ended up with her in the bed between them, with Brodie lying on Mike's legs and Sophie snuggled under his arm, watching in a dreadful mixture of excitement and trepidation as he slowly, carefully peeled the wrapping paper off and opened the box.

A frown creased his brow, and then a smile, and then a great big laugh as he hugged Sophie hard against his side and kissed her. 'It's me and Amber, isn't it?' he said, and Sophie turned to Fran with a huge grin before bouncing up and taking the models from Mike's hands and showing him the intricacies of her design.

'Look—see the cluster.' She showed him, turning Amber over. 'And you've got your hat on. It was meant to be red but I'd used up all the red making Amber and there wasn't enough, so you had to have pink.'

'Close enough,' he said, but Fran could see his mouth twitching and she had to bite her lip to keep the bubble of laughter inside.

'Do you like it?' Sophie asked, bouncing on the spot, and he reached out and hugged her again, his eyes suspiciously bright.

'I love it. Thank you, darling. It's really nice.'

'I was going to make Brodie too but Mrs Pearce said I

couldn't have any more clay, so you'll have to have her for Christmas.'

His lips twitched again. 'I'm sure she won't mind waiting.'

Sophie sat back on her heels. 'So can I help you milk the cows today?'

'I'm not doing it. My brother's doing it so I can have a lie-in,' he said, and Fran, glancing at the clock, stifled a sigh.

It was only five-thirty. So much for his lie-in! And Sophie was looking crestfallen. 'Does that mean I have to go back to bed?' she asked. 'Because I'm *wide* awake now.'

Mike wasn't. He looked exhausted, and without his usual alarm he might well have slept another couple of hours.

'I tell you what,' Fran said quickly. 'Why don't you and I go downstairs for a little while and see if we can find something to do while your daddy has a birthday lie-in, and then, when he's up, maybe we can go to the beach?'

'Brilliant! We can make sandcastles!' Sophie shrieked, leaping up and down on the bed until his present nearly fell off the edge. He made a grab for it, and Fran threw back the bedclothes and got up, holding out her hand to Sophie.

'Come on, you, I've got something I want us to do together.'

Sophie slid over the bed, bouncing on her bottom until her skinny little legs hung off the side. 'What?' she asked.

Fran bent over and whispered in her ear, 'We've got to make his birthday cake.'

Sophie's eyes sparkled. 'Can I help?'

'Of course. I'll need your help—lots of it.'

She spun round, kissed Mike and pulled the bedclothes back up round his chin. 'You go back to sleep, Daddy, for a nice long time,' she ordered. 'And don't come in the kitchen without knocking. We're going to be busy making a secret.'

He winked at her, and Fran ushered her away, throwing him a smile over her head as she closed the door.

'Dog!' he yelled, and she opened the door again, called Brodie and they went down to the kitchen and left him in peace.

'How many eggs?' Sophie asked, kneeling up on a chair at the table to help.

'Three.'

'Can I break them into the bowl?'

'No—break them into this cup, and we can check they're all right before we add them to the mixture, just in case.'

'Just in case what?'

Just in case she mashed the shell, Fran thought, but couldn't dent her pride. 'In case one's a bit funny,' she flannelled.

'Funny?' Sophie said, wrinkling her nose.

'Sometimes they smell a bit fishy or they have bits in.'

'And we don't want a fishy, bitty cake,' she said sagely, and Fran suppressed her smile.

'We certainly don't.'

'Can I measure the flour and the sugar and the butter?'

'Sure.'

It took longer—much longer—and they didn't use the mixer but a wooden spoon in a bowl, the way Fran's grandmother had always done it, because that way Sophie could be more involved and Mike got a longer lie-in. They grated the rind of an orange, and squeezed in some juice, and then, when it was all mixed together they spooned it into the tin, put it in the top oven of the Aga and set the timer.

'An hour? Really? That's *ages*! Can we make Daddy breakfast in bed?'

'We can make him breakfast in bed if you like, but not yet. He's tired, Sophie. He works very hard.'

Too hard, for too long, and the strain was beginning to tell. And no matter how badly she wanted to crawl back into bed beside him and go back to sleep herself, for now she had to entertain his daughter and keep her out of his way so he could rest.

'Want to help me make some things for the project I'm doing with my class?' she suggested, and Sophie, bless her, responded with her usual boundless enthusiasm.

If only Fran could say the same for herself...

'Bye-bye, sweetheart. Love you.'

'Don't forget I'm coming next Sunday for tea 'cos I'm going on holiday the next week!'

'I haven't forgotten. You take care.'

Fran watched as Mike kissed his little sprite of a daughter goodbye and closed the car door, lifting his hand to wave farewell. Sophie waved back, her hand just visible through the water streaming down the car window, and Fran waved too, her feelings mixed.

She adored Sophie; she was a lovely girl, sweet and bright, just like her mother to look at, and for that Fran was profoundly grateful. If she'd been the image of her father, the knife would be twisted every time she looked at her. As it was, it was easy enough most of the time to pretend she was just another little girl, just like the many little girls Fran taught all day.

But delightful though Sophie was, the very fact of her existence only served to underscore Fran's own failure to successfully carry a baby to full term.

Having Sophie to stay every other weekend, for a couple of weeks every holiday and at half-term once or twice a year was like a two-edged sword. When she was there, she brought sunshine and laughter into their lives, and after she'd gone, the house—a beautiful old house that should have been filled with the sound of children—rang with silence.

It might be better if she didn't come, Fran thought, and then shook her head. No. That was ridiculous. They both loved her to bits, and without her their lives would be immeasurably poorer. They'd had a lovely weekend, and even the rain today hadn't spoilt things, because by the time it had started they'd finished at the beach and were home, making sandwiches to go with Mike's birthday cake for tea.

And Sophie had been an absolute delight.

The car moved off across the streaming concrete yard, and Fran turned away from the cover of the doorway, steeling herself for the silence. Not that she had time to sit still and listen to it. She had a lot to do. Mike's parents and Joe and Sarah had joined them for tea, and the sitting room was smothered in plates and cups. Brodie went with her, tongue lashing, and cleared up the dropped birthday cake crumbs from the floor while she dealt with everything else.

She saw Mike's feet come into range as she was fishing for a fallen knife beside the sofa. There was a hole in the toe of his left sock, she noticed absently. Another failure in her wifely duties. She gave a muffled snort, and Mike dropped down onto his haunches beside her, his hand warm on her shoulder.

'You OK?'

Her fingers coaxed the knife closer. 'Of course. Why shouldn't I be?'

'I just— I thought you looked—'

'I'm fine, Mike,' she said firmly. 'I just have a lot to do and I'm a bit tired. *I* didn't get a lie-in.'

He sighed and stood up, and she could hear him scrubbing his hands through his damp hair in frustration. 'I'm sorry. I'll go and get the cows in, then. I'm late starting the milking.'

She straightened, the errant knife in hand at last, and threw him a tight smile. 'Good idea. I'll do supper for seven.'

'Don't bother to do much, I'm really not hungry after all the cake. Come, Brodie.'

And that was it. No offer of help. No thanks for his birthday tea, or having Sophie for the weekend.

No hug, no cuddle, no 'Don't worry, darling, it'll be all right.'

Not that she'd believe him, anyway. How could it be all right? They'd run out of time on the NHS, and she was wondering if she could psych herself up for another IVF cycle and failing miserably. Not that they could afford it, although the way things were going, she wasn't even sure Mike wanted a child with her. It was so much hassle and, despite his assurances, he seemed more than happy with just Sophie.

And why wouldn't he be? She was gorgeous.

Gorgeous, and his, and if she was honest Fran had to admit that she was simply jealous of his relationship with her. They'd spent hours together over the weekend, and every time she'd looked up they'd been there, giggling about something, Mike chasing her, catching her and throwing her up in the air, turning her upside down, leading her by the hand and showing her the chicks, showing her how to feed a calf—just being the doting, devoted father that he was, with Sophie right there being the doting, devoted daughter.

And every laugh, every hug, every smile had turned the knife a little more. Sure, Sophie spent time with her, and they'd had fun, but it wasn't the same as Sophie's relationship with Mike. That relationship was special, different, and Fran yearned for one like it.

Yearned and ached and wept for it.

She picked up a plate, catching it on the edge of the table, and it flew out of her fingers, clipped the edge of the hearth and shattered. She stared at it, at the wreckage of the plate, splintered into a thousand pieces, just like her dreams, and a sob rose in her throat.

She crushed it down, threw the bits back onto the tray and carried it through to the kitchen. She didn't have time to be sentimental and stupid. She had a pile of project work to mark before school tomorrow, and the house hadn't seen the vacuum cleaner in nearly a fortnight. Not that they'd been in it much. Mike was busy on the farm, she was busy with the end of the summer term coming up and lots of curriculum work to get through in the next week. And just as if that wasn't enough, they'd extended the farm shop in time for the summer influx of tourists and were run off their feet.

Which was just as well with the amount of money they'd sunk into that and the new cheese-making equipment, not to mention last year's investment in the ice-cream venture that her sister-in-law, Sarah, was running, but the result was that there weren't enough hours in the day.

So she needed to clean the kitchen, which was pointless since it was raining and Brodie coming in and out didn't help in the least, even if Mike wiped the dog's feet on an old towel, and she needed to clean the bathroom and their bedroom and change Sophie's sheets. That pretty much was it, because they hadn't had time to make the rest dirty.

Except for the sitting-room floor, of course, which now had crumbs, dog hair and bits of broken plate all over it.

She got the vacuum out and started in there.

'Hello, my lovely,' Mike murmured, wiping down Marigold's teats with a paper towel before attaching the cups to them. He rested his head against her flank for a moment, feeling the warmth of her side and the gentle movement of her breathing. She smelt safe and familiar. Nothing unexpected there, no emotional minefield, just a cow doing her job, as he was doing his.

He pulled the cluster down and slipped the cups over her teats, one at a time, the suction tugging them rhythmically, and watched in satisfaction as the milk started to flow in a steady, creamy stream.

Beautiful. He loved his Guernseys. Their milk was fantastic, the cheese and ice cream and clotted cream they made from it a lifesaver in the current dairy-farming climate. 'Clever girl,' he murmured, running his hand over her rump and patting it before moving on. Clever, uncomplicated, undemanding, a lovely old girl who still, after six calvings, delivered the goods better than any other cow. If only his own life were as straightforward.

Her daughter Mirabelle was next to her, her head in the trough, and he ran his hand over her udder and frowned. There was heat in the right front quarter, and when he tugged the teat down gently, she raised her head and lowed in protest.

She had mastitis. Damn. As if he didn't have enough to do.

'Sorry, sweetheart,' he murmured, and he wiped her other teats, attached the cluster to the three which were OK and then, taking advantage of the let-down reflex which the routine of the milking parlour always stimulated, with gentle, rhythmic movements he stripped out the infected quarter, discarding the milk. After dodging her disgruntled kick, he carefully inserted the nozzle of an intermammary tube of antibiotic ointment into the teat canal, squirted it into the udder and left her to finish.

The others were waiting patiently, the sound of their gentle mooing and soft, warm breath endlessly relaxing.

Funny. Most people who came to watch him milk, and it could be hundreds over the course of the summer, were fascinated from a distance, but thought it was smelly and dirty and couldn't understand why anybody in their right mind would want to get up at four-thirty in the morning and work right through till seven at night.

Including his ex-wife.

Kirsten had thought he was insane, but he loved it, and couldn't imagine doing anything else in the world. He could have been a vet, and he'd thought about it long and hard. He was clever enough, his school exam grades more than adequate for the entry requirements, but he'd gone instead to agricultural college because the farm was in his blood.

OK, it was hard work, but he was young and fit and it didn't hurt him. You had to do something with your waking hours, and the warmth of the animals and the relationship he had with them was all the reward he needed.

It was servicing the investment in the ice cream, clotted cream and cheese-making equipment and expanding the farm shop that made him tired and brought him stress, but that was only the other side of the coin, and he could deal with it.

Or he would be able to, if only Fran wasn't so stressed out herself.

He let the first batch of cows out and let the next ten in. It never ceased to amaze him the way they came in, all bar the odd one or two, in the same order, to the same places every time. It made his job that much easier.

Too easy, really. So easy that he had far too much time to think, and all he could think about was the look in Fran's eyes every time she saw him with Sophie. Which, when she was with them, was always. Sophie was his shadow, trailing him, helping with the calves and the chickens and the milking, asking endless questions, nagging him about having a pony, tasting the ice cream and chattering about the cheese, wanting to stir it and cut it and sieve it.

She was too small to reach right across the vat so he had to lift her and hold her, and she'd been known to drop the spoon into the vat. Not that it mattered if the paddles weren't turning, but if they were still at the mixing stage, he had to strip off to the waist, scrub his arm and plunge it nearly to the armpit in warm milk to fetch the spoon out so it didn't foul on the paddles.

Yes, she was a hazard, but he missed her now she was gone, and he knew Fran missed her too, although her presence just rubbed salt into the wound.

He sighed and let the last ten cows in. They were nearly all pregnant now. The last three had calved in the past six weeks, and it would soon be time to artificially inseminate them.

He was trying to build the herd on really strong genetic lines, and he'd got a young bull growing on his brother's farm which had excellent breeding and was showing promise. When he was mature, they'd see about using him, but until then they did it the clinical way, in the crush, with a syringe of frozen semen.

He gave a hollow laugh.

Not quite the same, not for the bull or the cows. He could empathise. He'd done his share of producing semen for his and Fran's fertility investigations and treatment, and it was the pits.

It was all the pits, the whole damn process. So many questions, so much personal intervention that in the end they'd felt like lab rats. He couldn't remember the last time he and Frankie had made love for the hell of it.

Not had sex, not timed it to coincide with her ovulation, or gone at it hammer and tongs for a fortnight in an attempt at quantity rather than quality, or done it out of duty and guilt because it had been months since they had, which was the current state of affairs, but made love in the real sense of the words, slowly, tenderly, just for the sheer joy of touching each other.

Or, come to that, clawed each other's clothes off in desperate haste to get at each other! There hadn't been any of that for ages.

Years. Two years? Three? Damn, so long he couldn't even remember what it had felt like. Certainly he hadn't touched her at all since the miscarriage in April.

He propped his head against Amber's flank and rubbed her side absently. The calf shifted under his hand, and he swallowed the sadness that welled in his throat. Would he ever feel his own baby like that, moving inside Fran, stretching and kicking and getting comfortable?

'You're getting a bit close, aren't you, girl? Last milking tonight, and tomorrow you can go and munch your head off in the meadow till you have your baby.'

She mooed, a soft, low sound of agreement, and he laughed and let them out.

He still wasn't finished. He'd milked them, but he had to flush the lines through and hose down the yard before he could go in for supper.

Not that he minded. The longer the better, really, because Fran would be in a foul mood and they'd eat their supper in an awkward, tense silence.

It was always the same after Sophie had been to stay.

'Mirabelle's got mastitis.'

'Oh. Badly?'

'No, just one quarter. I've given her a tube of antibiotic. It might be enough. I'll watch her.'

'Mmm.' Fran poked the cake crumbs around on the plate and pushed it away.

'Don't you want that?' he asked, and she shook her head.

'No. I've had too much cake.' Which was a lie. She'd hardly had any, but he wouldn't know that. She pushed the plate towards him. 'Here, finish it off. I know you're always starving.'

He picked up the almost untouched slice of cake and bit into it in silence while she cleared her plate away and put it in the dishwasher, then she heard the scrape of his chair against the tiles as he stood. 'That was lovely. Thanks.'

She took the plate from him. 'Don't lie,' she said with a pang of guilt for giving him such a scratch supper on his birthday. 'It was just a slice of cake, not a romantic candlelit dinner.'

The sort of dinner most wives would give their husbands on their birthdays. Shortly before they went to bed and made love...

A puzzled frown flickered across his face and was gone, leaving his eyes troubled. 'Fran, what's wrong?'

'Nothing,' she said, shutting down her runaway thoughts in case he could read them.

'That's not true. You didn't eat your cake just now, you hardly had anything this afternoon— And don't argue,' he added, as she opened her mouth. 'I saw you give that sandwich to the dog. And except for the time this morning when I was having my lie-in, you spent the whole weekend sending me off with Sophie and keeping out of the way. What the hell is it, love? Talk to me.'

She looked away, her conscience pricking. Had it been so obvious? She didn't want to hurt Sophie, but having her there...

'Frankie?'

She couldn't. It was a real Pandora's box and there was

no way she was opening it now. 'I'm fine. Just preoccupied. I've got a lot to do before tomorrow morning. You know what the end of the summer term is like—so many things to finish off.'

He just looked at her for a long moment, then turned away with a sigh. She watched him out of the corner of her eye, her peripheral vision picking up the moment he gave up. Damn her, then, she could almost hear him thinking. Damn her, if she wants to be like that.

'I'll be in the farm office,' he said. 'Don't wait up.'

And he went out, the dog at his heels, the door banging shut behind them. She felt the tears threaten, but swallowed them down, straightened her shoulders and got her class's project work out, spreading it out on the dining-room table and forcing herself to concentrate. The last thing she could afford to do was neglect her job and end up losing it. At the moment, with the farm overstretched because of the expansion, her income was the only thing keeping them afloat.

She gave a ragged little laugh. Perhaps it was just as well she wasn't pregnant.

CHAPTER TWO

IT WAS obviously going to be one of those weeks.

Mirabelle's mastitis had cleared up overnight, but Betsy had gone down with milk fever and needed IV calcium. Guernseys were prone to milk fever, and Betsy had had it before. And Mike should have been on the alert for it as she'd just calved, but his mind had been elsewhere.

Still, he'd caught her in time and given her the injection, so she'd made a rapid recovery. And he'd turned Amber out that morning to await the arrival of her calf. Her milk had dwindled to a halt, and it was time for her to rest and gather her strength. He'd have to take a walk up there later and check on them. They were near Ben and Lucy Carter's, grazing on the field by Tregorran House, the one with the barn where Lucy had had her baby at Christmas.

He could go with Fran when she got back from school— or perhaps not. It was a gorgeous day today, unlike yesterday, and no doubt Lucy would be out in the garden with the baby and would want to say hello.

He didn't think either of them needed that at the moment.

Fran had been moody for the past week, short with him

for no particular reason. And every time he tried to talk to her, she changed the subject. Whatever it was.

He went into the farm office and put a mug under the spout of the coffee-machine. It was one of those new pod ones, which meant he could have real coffee without fiddling around too much, and when reps from the whole-salers and farm shop outlets came to visit, he could give them decent coffee quickly that hadn't been stewing for hours. It also meant they didn't have to go into the house.

And recently, for some reason, he just didn't want to go into the house if Fran was around. She was always busy making something for school, and it was simpler to keep out of her way.

Not that that was going to sort anything out, but if he left her alone, she'd get over it. She always did, but usually quicker than this.

He was just taking the milk jug out of the little fridge when there was a tap on the door. Since it wasn't closed, knocking was a bit of a formality, but nevertheless he was surprised to see Nick Tremayne there.

'Hello, Nick,' he said, summoning up a smile. 'Come on in. Coffee?'

'Oh—yes, why not. Thanks.' He propped his hips against the battered old desk and Mike could feel the searching stare of those dark brown eyes burning into his back. They'd seen enough of their GP in the previous three years to know that Nick Tremayne never did anything without a reason, and Mike had no idea what it could be. Not unless Nick knew something that he didn't.

'So—what can I do for you?' he asked, turning round with the coffee in his hand and holding it out to Nick.

'Oh, nothing. I've just finished my visits and I was just passing, thought I'd have a look in the farm shop, pick something up for Ben and Lucy. You've got some interesting things now.'

'We try. The ice cream's going well, and the blue cheese is a runaway success. We can't keep up with the demand—but I'm damn sure you aren't here to talk about that.'

Nick's smile was wry. 'Am I so transparent?'

Mike just grunted, and Nick smiled again. 'OK. Point taken—but I really was just passing!' He hefted the farm-shop paper carrier in evidence. 'Ben's got a few days off and my daughter's invited me for lunch, and I didn't want to go empty-handed. And as I was here, I thought I'd just see if you were around. We haven't seen you recently—I wondered if you were both OK.'

Mike snorted softly and stared down into his coffee-cup, swirling the dark brew while he tried to work out how to reply. Honestly, he decided, and put the cup down.

'Not really. We haven't been since the miscarriage. Fran's preoccupied, her temper's short, she's lost all her sparkle—I don't know, she doesn't have anything to say to me any more, and I think it's pretty mutual. Frankly, Nick, I'm beginning to wonder if the strain of all this isn't going to be too much for our marriage.'

'Do you still love her?'

He hesitated, his eyes locked with Nick's, and then he looked away, scrubbing his hand through his hair and letting his breath out on a harsh sigh. 'Yes. Yes, I still love her. I just don't know if she still loves me.'

He swallowed hard, emotion suddenly choking him,

and Nick tutted softly and put his cup down as well. 'Time for a stroll?'

'Yeah. You going to Tregorran now?' Mike asked.

'I am.'

'I'll come with you. If you give me a lift there, I've got some stock to check and I'll walk back. It only takes five minutes across the fields.'

They pulled up on the drive at Tregorran House, and while Mike stood waiting by the car, Nick handed over the bag of shopping to Ben. 'There's some strawberry ice cream in there that needs to go in the freezer,' he said. 'Back in a minute. Mike's just going to show me something.'

A likely story, Mike thought with a mental snort, but he raised his hand and dredged up a smile for Ben. He liked his neighbours, and he was delighted they'd bought Nick's old family home, but it would have been easier if Ben hadn't come to the door with baby Annabel gurgling on his hip and rubbing salt into the wound.

'Mike, I'm glad I've seen you,' Ben said now, coming out onto the drive. 'I've been meaning to talk to you about something. Any chance we could have a chat some time?'

He nodded. 'Sure. Give me a call when you're not busy, or drop round. I'm usually about.' Mike gave him his mobile number and Ben keyed it into his own phone, then slipped it back into his pocket and smiled.

'Cheers. I'll call you.'

Ben waved, lifting the baby's chubby little hand as Mike himself had done with Sophie so many times, and Mike waved back to them both, his breath jamming in his throat as Annabel's face split into a cherubic smile, and he turned away.

Nick fell in beside him, and they went down the track at the side of the house and to the field at the side. It wasn't right on the cliff top, because that field had a footpath through it, part of the Cornish Coastal Path, and he didn't want his dry cows disturbed in their last few weeks of pregnancy by all the walkers.

'Here we are—my ladies-in-waiting,' he said to Nick, his eyes scanning the field to check that the six cows in there were all looking well. Amber came over to him, her gorgeous coat, fox-red splashed with white, gleaming with health in the summer sun, and he rubbed her poll and spoke softly to her for a moment.

'You love your farm, don't you?' Nick murmured, and Mike nodded.

'Can't imagine doing anything else, but it's a constant reminder of our own failure. With a dairy herd, all you do all the time is monitor their pregnancies and deliver their calves and manage their lactation. And it's impossible not to draw parallels.' He smiled, but he could feel it was off kilter. 'If we were livestock, Fran and I would be shot. It seems we're useless together. Giant pandas have more success.'

'That's not true. Fran's been pregnant before, and you achieved a pregnancy on your first cycle of IVF.'

'Yeah—which we also lost. We can't afford another cycle at the moment, and we've run out of NHS funding, so where do we go from here? It wouldn't be so damned frustrating if they could find anything *wrong* with us! But they can't, Nick. We're both well, there are no physical problems, we just can't seem to get it right. And right now I'm not sure I even want to, the way we are. Well, the way Fran is, anyway. I just can't get through to her at all.'

'But that's probably just a reaction to the miscarriage. Perhaps she needs to talk it through. Will she come to see me?'

Mike snorted again and shook his head. 'Not a chance. She might talk to Kate—woman to woman and all that.'

Nick's mouth tightened, and then he nodded. 'That could work. She knows Kate. It's an idea.'

One that was growing on Mike by the second. Kate was working as a midwife again now, and Fran had known her for years because of her son, Jem, who was at the school. Maybe she'd be able to get through to her. 'She could catch her at school,' he suggested, but Nick shook his head.

'Not really the place. But she could call in—maybe one day after school? On her way to see Ben and Lucy? Kate does drop by from time to time to cuddle the baby. I could make sure she doesn't have Jeremiah with her, and maybe you could make yourself unavailable?'

He laughed shortly. 'That won't be hard. I don't have a lot of time to hang around. By the time Fran's home, I'm usually milking so Kate should be able to talk to her undisturbed between four-thirty and six, and if I know she's going to be here, I can always drag it out.'

'Sure. Give me your mobile number. I'll let you know what she's planning so you're forewarned.'

He pulled out his phone and they swapped numbers, and then Mike turned his back on the cattle and stared out over the sea, which was flat and smooth and sparkling, the lazy swell scarcely visible. The surfers wouldn't be happy today, but the families with little children would be having a great time, just as they themselves had had with Sophie last weekend—just as they might one day be doing with another child of their own. His chest tightened with longing and he hauled in a breath and turned back to the GP.

'Thanks, Nick,' he said gruffly. 'I don't know if it'll do any good, but thanks for trying.'

'You're welcome. And you can call me whenever you want a chat, you know. Any time.'

Mike nodded, and they strolled back to the house in thoughtful silence. Nick went in, lifting his hand in farewell, and Mike nodded and set off back across the fields to the farm.

Fran would kill him for interfering, but he couldn't watch her falling apart any longer. He just hoped that Kate was able to reach her, because frankly he was at a loss, and if something didn't happen soon, the remains of their marriage would be unsalvageable.

He tried a little salvage that night.

They'd had supper, and for once they were sitting down together in front of the television. There was nothing on that either of them really seemed to want to watch, though, so he turned it off, found an easy-listening CD, soft and lazy and romantic, and instead of going back to his chair he went over to the sofa and sat down beside her, giving her shoulder an affectionate little rub.

'You OK, my love?'

She nodded, but she didn't meet his eyes and there wasn't a trace of a smile. 'Just tired. I'll be glad when the holidays come.'

'So will I. You can give me a hand—we'll try that new fresh curd cheese you've been talking about.'

Beneath his hand her shoulder drooped a little, then she

straightened up. 'Yes, we can do that. I might give Sarah a hand with the ice cream as well. See if we can get the raspberry one smoother. It's a bit too juicy and it tends to get ice crystals.'

'It's gorgeous. Maybe it just needs stirring for longer as it cools, and agitating more often. You've got it cracked with the strawberry, doing that. Maybe it just needs more of the same.'

'Maybe. We'll try a few things, see how we do.'

She stood up, moving away from him, and went out, coming back a moment later with a book. So much for cuddling up together on the sofa. He peered at the cover.

'Anything interesting?' he asked, and she lifted the book so he could see it.

'CBT—cognitive behaviour therapy. One of my pupils is having it, so I thought I'd read up a bit.'

And she curled up in the corner of the sofa again, opened the book and shut him out as effectively as if she'd left the room.

So *he* did.

He went upstairs, had a shower for the second time that day and came back down in a clean pair of jeans. He hadn't bothered with a T-shirt. It was still hot and, anyway, she'd never been able to keep her hands off him when he took his shirt off. All that rippling muscle, she'd say with a smoky laugh, and grab him.

But she didn't even look up.

The CD had finished, so he put the television back on and settled down to watch a repeat of something he hadn't enjoyed a lot the first time round.

Anything rather than be ignored.

* * *

What was happening to them?

She raised her eyes slightly from the book and let them dwell on his body. Long, lean and rangy, his muscles sleek and strong, not the muscles of a weightlifter but of a man who worked hard with his body, and it showed.

Lord, it showed, and there'd been a time not so very long ago when she would have got up and gone over to him and run her hand over that bare, deep chest with its scattering of dark hair, teasing the flat copper coins of his nipples until they were tight and pebbled under her fingertips. Then she'd run her hands down his ribcage, feeling the bones, the muscles, the heat of his body radiating out, warming her to her heart.

He would have pulled her onto his lap, his eyes laughing, and then the laughter would fade, and he'd kiss her, his hands exploring her body, searching out its secret places, driving her crazy with his sure, gentle touch.

What was that song about a lover with a slow hand? That was Mike—or it had been. Just lately he didn't seem to be interested, and if he had been, she wouldn't have. Just the thought of him touching her so intimately made her shrink away. She didn't think she could cope with the intimacy, baring her soul to him as well as her body. Not when her soul was hurting so much and her body had become public property with all the investigations. Even the idea of being touched there…

And he'd give her a lecture on getting too thin, which probably wasn't unjustified but wouldn't make her feel sexy. Right now, she didn't think anything would make her feel sexy.

Not that he'd tried recently. He'd been too busy, and

every night he was buried in the farm office until late. It was almost as if he was avoiding her. Hard to say, when she was so busy avoiding him, holding herself back because if she did that, if they didn't try, then it didn't hurt so much.

If you didn't try, you couldn't fail, could you?

The book—interesting under other circumstances—couldn't hold her attention, so she shut it and unfolded herself from the corner of the sofa and winced as the circulation returned to her foot. 'I'm going to have a bath,' she told him, limping for the door. 'Don't bother to wait up for me. I feel like a wallow.'

He flicked her an enigmatic look, nodded and turned his eyes back to the television, and swallowing down her disappointment she headed up the stairs.

'Kate, have you got a minute?'

She paused and glanced at Nick, then at the clock. 'Literally. I've got a meeting with Chloe—'

'It won't take long,' he said, holding open the door of his consulting room, and after a tiny hesitation she braced herself and went in, wondering what was coming as he shut the door behind them.

'I saw Mike Trevellyan yesterday.'

'Oh.' She felt the tension drain out of her shoulders and turned to face him. 'How are they?'

'Not sure. He's worried about Fran. They don't seem to be talking.'

She gave a soft snort. 'There must be something in the water.'

Nick's mouth tightened and he looked away, but not before his eyes flicked over her in contempt. 'You've had nearly ten years to talk to me about that, so don't get stroppy if I don't seem to be in a hurry to talk to you about it now.'

'That? It? We're talking about your son, Nick.'

'We don't know that.'

'We do.'

'It was just the once.'

She sighed and rolled her eyes. 'How many times have I heard that from a pregnant woman? And you only have to look at him. His eyes…'

A muscle worked in his jaw, and she gave up. For now. A gentle sigh eased out of her and she squared her shoulders. 'So—about Fran. What do you want me to do? She had a follow-up appointment with me after her miscarriage and she cancelled it. I don't know if I can get her into the surgery.'

'No, we thought of that. I've got Mike's mobile number. I thought if you could drop by there after school one day, when Fran's around and Mike's milking, maybe you could engineer the conversation.'

She stared at him in silence for a long moment, and eventually he turned and looked at her.

'Well? What do you think of it?'

'I think it's a conversation I should have without Jem—*your son*—since I'll have him with me after school.'

'Well, perhaps you could find someone to leave him with for an hour.'

'Mmm. His *father* springs to mind.'

His eyes widened with horror. 'I can't.'

'Well, then, neither can I,' she retorted. 'Not at short notice.'

'He must have school friends,' Nick said, looking a little desperate, but she wasn't going to back down.

'I'm sure he does—but I need to save them for emergencies, and my childminder's not feeling great at the moment so I can't ask her. Besides, Jem needs me. It's our time together—so if you want me to do this, and I agree it seems like a very good idea, then I think it would be an excellent opportunity for you to get to know him a little bit better. As his other parent.'

She watched him struggle, knew the moment he gave in. His jaw tightened, his eyes became shuttered and he gave a curt nod. 'Just don't let it become a habit.'

She laughed. 'What—dropping in on Fran?' she said, deliberately misunderstanding him. 'Hardly. She'll smell a rat before I get up the garden path! What am I supposed to tell her, Nick?'

'Tell her you're visiting Ben and Lucy. Tell her you're going to the farm shop and wondered how she was.'

'I'll tell her I was worried about her, because I am. I've been watching her at school, and a couple of times when she's been outside when I've picked Jem up, she's looked very tired. Don't worry, Nick,' she said soothingly, with only a trace of patronage. 'I'm sure I can manage to manoeuvre the conversation in the right direction.'

He shot her a blistering look and opened his mouth, then clearly thought better of it as a fleeting, rueful smile cracked his face just for a second. 'Thank you. When were you thinking of doing it?'

'Tonight? I can't tomorrow,' she said, thinking ahead. 'I've got a clinic, and on Thursday there's the school sports day, and Friday's the end of term.'

Nick nodded, a muscle working in his jaw. 'OK. I'll get Hazel to shift my patients to Dragan or Oliver. You can drop Jeremiah round to me on your way there, and I'll give him supper.'

'I'll do that. Now, if that's all...?'

'That's all,' he agreed, opening the door for her with something that could have been relief. Poor Nick, she thought as she walked away. He really, really didn't like this. The truth was obviously much too much to take, but that was tough.

He was going to have to get used to it, no matter how unpalatable—get used to the fact that ten years ago this summer, on the very night of the storm that had torn a hole in their community, while his father and brother had lain cooling in the mortuary and her husband's body was being sucked out to sea and shattered on the rocks, their frenzied, desperate coupling had given rise to a child.

And that child was their son.

She looked out of the window, across the bay to the headland where Nick had found her staring out to sea, her body drenched and buffeted by the wild storm, her eyes straining into the darkness. Not that there had been any hope. Even the coastguard had given up, at least for the night, but she hadn't been able to tear herself away.

So Nick had taken control—taken her back to her house, stripped off her sodden clothes, dried her—and then somehow, suddenly, everything had changed. It could have been put down to that old affirmation-of-life cliché, she thought, but it had been more than that. She'd loved him since she'd been fifteen, had wanted him for ever, and it had seemed entirely natural to turn to him for comfort.

And it seemed he had felt the same, because, laid bare by their emotions, when the world had been falling apart all around them and it had seemed as if they were the only people in the world left alive, they'd finally done what they'd come so close to before he'd gone to university and met Annabel. The timing had been awful, but maybe it had been because it was so awful that they'd been able to break through those barriers and reach for each other. And in that moment, when they'd both been too racked with grief and guilt to know what they were doing, they'd started another life.

Like it or not—and he clearly didn't—Nick Tremayne would have to acknowledge the result of their actions that night, and learn to live with it every day of his life, just like she had for the past ten years. After all, it had given her a son, a child she'd never thought she'd have, and he'd brought her so much joy.

So she'd learned to live with herself, with the shame she felt at having given in and taken comfort from Nick at that dreadful time, and she'd slowly, painfully, learned to forgive herself.

Now it was Nick's turn. He'd have to learn to live with himself, too, and maybe, with time, forgive himself.

And perhaps, in the end, he could even learn to love his son.

'Fran!'

She heard the knock, heard the voice calling and went to the window, leaning out and seeing Kate there, to her surprise. 'Kate, hi! Come in, the door's open. I'm just changing Sophie's sheets— Come on up, I'm nearly done.'

And then she wondered why on earth she'd said that,

because the house wasn't looking fantastic and Kate wasn't a close friend, not the sort of person who you just invited in—although maybe she was exactly the sort of person, she amended as Kate arrived in the bedroom with a smile, got hold of the other side of the quilt cover and helped her put it on.

'Thanks.'

'Pleasure. It's always easier with two.'

Fran plumped up the pillow and straightened up. 'I only did it yesterday, that's the frustrating thing, in time for Sophie's next visit, but the dog sneaked up here last night with filthy feet, and I didn't realise till this morning. So— what brings you here on a Tuesday afternoon?' she asked, finally voicing the question that had been in the forefront of her mind ever since she'd heard Kate calling her.

'Oh, I was just passing. I've been to see Ben and Lucy and I popped in at the farm shop. I thought I'd say hello and see how you are. It's always so busy at school and I haven't seen you for ages, not to chat to.'

Not since before the miscarriage but, then, you didn't really need antenatal care when there wasn't going to be any natal to worry about, Fran thought with a sharp stab of grief.

'I'm fine.'

She scooped up the washing and carried it downstairs, leaving Kate to follow. She ought to offer her a cup of tea, but that would open the door to all sorts of things she didn't want. A cosy chat. A more penetrating 'How are you'. A 'How are you really, now your dream's been snatched away' sort of 'How are you'.

But the teapot was there on the side of the Aga, and the kettle was next to it, and without being offered, Kate went over to it, lifted it and raised an eyebrow at Fran. 'Got time to give me a cup of tea?' she asked, and put like that, it would have been too rude to refuse.

She gave in.

'Of course. I'll make it.'

'No, you deal with the washing. I can make a cup of tea. I spend my life making tea and drinking it. That's what midwives do—didn't you know that?'

'Really? I thought they interfered.'

Kate met her eyes and smiled. So the gloves were off, their cards were on the table and they could both start being honest.

Kate lifted the hotplate cover and put the kettle on the hob. 'Fran, I haven't seen you for ages—not since the miscarriage. I'm worried about you,' she said gently.

Fran looked up from the washing machine, slammed the door on it and stood up. 'Don't be.'

'I am. You've got a lot of pressures on you. Sometimes talking them through can help.'

'Kate, I don't need counselling,' she said firmly and a little desperately.

'I never said you did. But a friend who understands the pressures you might be under and the choices open to you might be a help—a sounding board, someone to rant at that isn't your husband?'

Had Mike been talking?

'I don't rant at him.'

'But maybe you want to. Maybe you need to—not because he's done anything wrong but just because you need to rant, to let out your anger. It's all part of the grieving process, Fran. And you have to grieve for your baby.'

Fran swallowed. 'It was just a failed embryo—just like my other miscarriage. There was no baby.'

'But there was—there were two, and you loved them,' Kate said gently, and that was it. The dam burst, and Kate took the washing powder out of her hands, wrapped her arms firmly around her and held her tight. At first Fran could hardly breathe for the wave of pain, but then it got easier, just slightly, so she could actually drag in the air with which to sob.

And sob she did, cradled against Kate's comforting bosom, her hand smoothing rhythmically up and down her back, telling her without words that it would be all right.

'That's it, let it go,' Kate murmured, and when the tears had slowed to a trickle, when the pain had eased to a dull ache instead of the slice of a sword, Kate let her go, and she sat down at the table and groped for a tissue.

'Sorry—heavens, I must look a wreck,' Fran said, sniffing and patting her pockets until Kate handed her a clump of kitchen roll. She mopped her face, blew her nose, sniffed again and tried to smile. It was a wobbly effort, but it was rewarded by an answering smile and a mug of tea put in her hand.

When had Kate made it? In the few seconds she'd been mopping up? Must have. God, she was losing it.

'Thanks,' she said, wrapping her nerveless hands around the mug and hugging it close.

'Better now?'

She nodded, and Kate smiled sympathetically.

'Good. It always helps to get all that backed-up emotion out of the way. Helps you see things more clearly. Was that the first time?'

'Since April? Yes. Properly, like that, yes. I've always tried to stop it before, because it didn't help with the first miscarriage, and I cried so much then. Silly. I might have known it would come out in the end.'

'And Mike's too close to allow him to see it. Because he's hurting, too, and you don't want him to feel bad for you.'

'When did you become so clever?'

A fleeting shadow passed over Kate's face, and Fran was so preoccupied she nearly missed it. Not quite, though, but she had no idea what had prompted it, and Kate was smiling now.

'Oh, I'm not clever, Fran,' she said softly. 'Just human. Maybe I just try and put myself in someone else's shoes, and I know the difference Jem's made in my life, so it's not hard to imagine how I would feel if I'd been unable to have him.'

Fran didn't know what to say. She hadn't been in Penhally when Kate's husband had died, but she'd heard about it from her parents, and how sad it was that he couldn't have known that Kate had been pregnant after several years of marriage. But she didn't feel she could say anything about that now. It had been years ago, intensely private and nothing to do with her.

So she sipped her tea, and sniffed a bit more, and blew her nose again, and all the time Kate just sat there in a companionable silence and let her sift through her thoughts.

'Have you noticed,' Fran said finally, as the sifting came to a sort of conclusion, 'how just about everybody seems to be pregnant at the moment? I don't know if it's just because I'm hypersensitive, but there seems to be a plague of it right now, especially among the school mums. Every time I look up, there's another one.'

Kate nodded. 'And it hurts.'

'Oh, yes,' Fran said very softly. 'It really hurts. You have no idea how much I want a baby, Kate. It's like a biological ache, a real *pain* low down in my abdomen— No, not a pain, it's not that sharp, but a sort of dull awareness, an emptiness, a sort of *waiting*—does that sound crazy?'

'No,' Kate murmured. 'It doesn't sound crazy at all. I've heard it before, so many times.'

'The frantic ticking of my biological clock—except it's not ticking, is it? The spring's broken, or it needs oiling or something, but nobody can find out what exactly, and sort it out. And in the meantime we've run out of time on the NHS, we don't have any money to pay for another cycle of IVF privately, and even if we did, Mike's been so odd recently I don't even know if he *wants* a baby with me!'

Kate studied her tea thoughtfully. 'Do you want a baby with him?' she asked gently. 'Or do you just want a baby?'

That stopped her. She stared at Kate, opened her mouth to say, 'Of course I want a baby with him!' and then shut it again without saying a word, because suddenly she wasn't sure, and she felt her eyes fill again.

'I don't know,' she replied instead, looking down and twisting the tissue into knots. 'I really, really don't know.'

'Do you still love him?'

Again she opened her mouth, then shut it, then said softly, her confidence wavering, 'Yes. Yes, I do, but I don't know if I can live with him like this. And I don't know if he loves me any more.'

'Then you need to talk. You need to spend time together, find out if you've still got what it takes, because there's no point killing yourselves to have a baby together if you don't

in the end want to be together. If being with Mike, with or
without a child, is the first and most important thing in your
life, then go ahead and keep trying for a baby. But if it's
not, if the baby's more important than being together, then
you need to think very carefully before you go ahead. And
so does he.

'Think about it,' she went on. 'Talk to Mike. Take some
time together. And play, Fran. Take time out. The weather's
gorgeous now. As soon as you break up at the end of the
week, try and find some time away from the farm and all
its distractions. Is there any chance you can get away?'

She laughed, but with very little humour. 'Not exactly.
There's the milking, and the cheese making, and then we
share the weekends with Joe, so they each get one weekend
off in four. Well, Saturday afternoon and Sunday.'

'And when's your next one?'

'This weekend,' she said slowly. 'But Mike won't stop.
He'll just use the time to catch up on paperwork.'

'So stop him. Find a little hotel or a guest house or
something, and go away for the night.'

'I doubt if he'll wear that. Anyway, we've got Sophie
coming for tea on Sunday because she's away the next
weekend.'

'You can be back by teatime.' Kate stood up and put a hand
on Fran's shoulder. 'Try it. You've got nothing to lose. And
you might have everything to gain. And in the meantime, I've
heard some very interesting things about miscarriage and diet
and the relationship to damaged and defective sperm.'

Fran frowned. 'Are Mike's sperm defective? I don't
think they said anything about it at the fertility clinic—
well, not to me, anyway.'

Kate shook her head. 'Not particularly, according to the report from the clinic, but although there were a good number, a slightly higher proportion than one might hope for were defective or sluggish. That in itself might have been enough to cause your miscarriage, if it was a damaged sperm that fertilised the ovum. And this diet is supposed to reduce the numbers of defective sperm quite significantly, according to the study I've heard about. If you're going to try again, maybe you need to take a while to make friends again, and while you do that, you could try the diet to boost Mike's sperm production. It might as well be as good as it can be, and even if you decide not to go ahead and try again, it won't do either of you any harm.'

It sounded a good idea, but she wasn't sure she'd get it past Mike. 'Is it freaky?' she asked. 'I don't want to start giving him weird stuff. He'll ask questions or refuse to eat it. You know what men are like. And he's always starving.'

Kate laughed softly. 'Typical man, then—and, no, it's not freaky. It's more a supplement to his normal diet rather than any radical alteration. I can let you have all the details, if you like—why don't you come and see me tomorrow after school? I've got time, and we can go through it then properly.'

Fran nodded slowly. 'OK. Thanks. I will.'

And in the meantime, she'd try and talk him into going away. Just a few days, right away from the pressures of the farm.

She felt a shiver of something that could have been fear and could have been excitement. Maybe both. Probably.

She'd ask him tonight.

CHAPTER THREE

'THIS is ridiculous.'

Fran stared out across the yard. She couldn't see the farm office on the other side, but she could see the spill of light from the window, and she knew exactly what he'd be doing.

Avoiding her.

Night after night, week after week for months now.

It was becoming a pattern. He'd get up at the end of their evening meal, kiss her absently on the cheek and thank her, then go out, Brodie at his heels, to the farm office.

And he'd stay there, wrestling with the accounts and the endless paperwork, until nearly midnight. Sometimes she'd hear him come to bed, sometimes she wouldn't. And in the morning, when the alarm went at five, he'd get up and go into the bathroom and dress, then go out and do the milking.

On a good day, or at the weekend, she'd see him for breakfast before she went to work herself. On a bad day, and there were increasingly more of them, she wouldn't see him at all.

Tonight was no exception. He'd kissed her vaguely on her cheek, said, 'Don't wait up for me, I want to get those quota forms filled in,' and he had gone.

Well, she was sick of it.

Sick of not having a relationship, sick of not having anyone—not even the dog, for heaven's sake!—to talk to in the evenings, sick of going to bed alone. Even on his birthday.

No wonder Kirsten had left him.

She sighed and turned away from the window, sick, too, of staring out and willing him to come back in. It hadn't always been like this. At first, when they'd started going out together, he'd been able to find time for her, and after they'd married he'd been lovely. OK, he'd worked late and started early, but when he'd come to bed he would wake her, snuggling up, either for a cuddle or to make love to her, slowly, tenderly, languorously—or wildly, as if he couldn't get enough of her.

When had it changed? she asked herself, but she knew.

The miscarriage—the most recent one, three months ago.

That was when it had changed—when he'd withdrawn from her so completely. When she'd lost the baby she'd thought they'd been so thrilled about.

Except maybe she'd been wrong. Maybe he hadn't been thrilled at all. Maybe this last miscarriage had been a lucky escape, a narrow squeak in the midst of all the happy, fluffy stuff—choosing the colour of the paint for the nursery, discussing names, telling both sets of parents. Thank God they hadn't told Sophie, but they'd been waiting till after the three-month watershed, till it was safe.

Except it hadn't been.

She scrubbed away the sudden, unexpected tears and swallowed hard.

No. She wouldn't cry again. Not after all this time. She'd cried all over Kate today, embarrassingly, but she wasn't doing it again. It didn't help. She'd cried an ocean after the first miscarriage, and it hadn't done any good.

And neither had anything else they'd tried, because she still hadn't conceived again until they'd gone down the IVF route.

Of course, the opportunity wouldn't have gone amiss and, looking back on it, she realised that ever since the first miscarriage things had been different. She'd put it down to too much work and the pressure of the farm, but really he'd been avoiding her for years, she thought with shock, and she'd been more than happy to let him, because it meant she didn't have to confront her fears and feelings.

Well, not any more.

She stared out of the window again, and decided it was time to act. If she was going to save her marriage, she was going to have to fight for it—she just wished she knew what it was she was fighting…

'We can't go away!'

'Why not?'

Mike stared at her, puzzled by her sudden insistence, but maybe more puzzled by his own curious reluctance.

The truth was, with Joe already fixed to cover him for the coming weekend there was no reason at all why they couldn't go away. Sophie was coming on Sunday after-noon, but otherwise they were free—the animals were taken care of, and Brodie would be perfectly content down at Joe and Sarah's house with their two dogs. They spent a lot of time together anyway.

So there was no reason, no reasonable excuse he could give, and he wasn't sure why he wanted to get out of it, but he did.

'I've got a lot of paperwork.'

'You always have a lot of paperwork.'

'Yes, and it won't just go away because we have!'

'No, it won't,' she agreed. 'It'll still be there when we come back. Mike, nobody's going to die if you don't do the paperwork this weekend. We can do it together.'

'No. Fran, I can't go.'

'Or won't.'

He met her eyes, wondered what the hell was happening to them, and, abandoning his coffee, he walked out of the farm office and headed for the machinery store. 'I haven't got time to talk about this now,' he said shortly. 'I've got to get on. Brodie!'

And he walked away, haunted by the look of hurt in her eyes and kicking himself, but he couldn't imagine what the hell they'd do for the whole weekend.

He laughed bitterly. His own wife, the woman he loved, and he couldn't work out what they'd do alone together for a night? 'Hell, man, you're losing it,' he muttered, and Brodie nudged his hand, her face anxious.

'It's all right,' he said reassuringly, giving her a pat, but it wasn't. It was far from all right, and he didn't quite know how they'd ended up there.

He threw the chainsaw into the back of the pickup, loaded in the other tools he'd need for his day's work, opened the cab door for Brodie and followed her in, starting up the engine and getting out of the farmyard before Fran came up with any other excuses for—what? Finding time with him?

Was that really such a bad thing?

Yet just the other night, when he'd sat with her and tried to get through to her, she'd stonewalled him and got a book out. Well, let her run after him. Maybe she'd find she wanted him after all...

'So how did it go with Fran?'

Kate gave a 'so-so' shrug. 'Not sure, really. I think I gave her something to think about. She's coming in to see me at the end of the afternoon, before my clinic. I'm going to give her the details of that fertility-boosting diet I was telling you about, so that if they decide to go down the IVF route they're starting from the best possible position.'

'Do you think they will? IVF's not cheap and they've invested a lot in the farm recently. I don't know if they can afford it.'

'I don't know if they even want it,' Kate admitted quietly.

Nick sighed. 'It seems such a damn shame that they got pregnant and then she lost it.'

'But at least we know she can get pregnant, which is a good starting point.'

Nick nodded and pushed a hand through his hair, the fingers parting it, leaving it rumpled. It was greying now, pepper and salt, but still thick, and her fingers itched to feel it, to thread through it as his had, to see if it still felt as soft and heavy as before...

She was going crazy. She had no business thinking things like that. She had to get on.

'Just seems so tough, when the rest of the world seems to have babies at the drop of a hat.'

'Well, you would know,' she said, a touch bitterly, reminding herself of all the reasons why Nick was so very bad for her. 'And at least if and when *they* have a child, it'll know it was wanted.'

'My children are wanted!' he retorted.

'All of them?'

He coloured and turned away, staring out of the window and stabbing his hand through his hair again. 'We still don't know—'

'Yes, we do,' she said with quiet emphasis. 'James was sub-fertile. He'd had a test.'

Nick turned slowly and stared at her, his eyes carefully expressionless. 'So—he really is mine?'

She felt her heart kick. 'Yes, Nick. He really is. There's no doubt at all. Jem is your son.'

The colour seemed to drain from his face, and for a moment he just stood there, rooted to the spot. Then he swallowed, dragged in a breath, straightened his shoulders. 'Right. Um—got to get on.'

'That's it—run away.'

He stopped, paused, then started walking again, then paused once more with his hand on the doorhandle. 'I'm not running, Kate,' he said, defeat in his voice. 'There's no point. There's nowhere to go.'

And, opening the door, he strode out into the waiting room and left her there.

'Brodie, get out of the way! Come on. Stupid dog—what the hell are you doing?'

Brodie was tugging Mike's trousers, trying to get him to play, but he wasn't interested. He'd been clearing up fallen and dead timber all day, and he'd just found an old willow which had snapped halfway up the trunk but stayed attached, the top swinging down to make a ragged arch, but it was still hanging by a thick rope of twisted wood and bark, propped on a lower branch that had dug into the ground and broken its fall.

Under normal circumstances he'd get up the tree and cut it off at the trunk, but it was straddling the river, one end high in the air, the other, in a tangle of broken branches and twigs, sprawled across the ground on this side. There was no way to get to it without crossing the river, and he didn't have time to keep driving backwards and forwards over the nearest bridge.

And Joe had the forklift with the long reach for bringing in the hay and silage bales, otherwise he could have used that. No, he'd just have to tackle it from this side.

But it was big.

He'd tried levering it off the supporting branch with a smaller branch wedged under it and over another log, but he wasn't heavy enough to shift it. He couldn't leave it there, though, because it was unstable and if the wind got up again, it could fall—and the cattle had been grazing down here around it. So he had to shift it now, before the end of the day, so he could let the cows back into the field in safety.

He tried Joe again, but he wasn't answering his mobile. Probably couldn't hear it. Damn. And the dog was still begging for a game.

'Brodie, give it up,' he said crossly, and, picking up the chainsaw, he cut away a few more branches so he could roll the tree when it fell. But the dog was in the way, and he'd get her with the saw in a minute, so he put her in the cab and told her to stay, then went back to it.

'Right, you stubborn bloody thing,' he said, glaring at the tree, and touched the underside with the saw. It creaked, sagged a fraction.

Better.

He touched it again, but the tree was weaker than he'd thought, and the creaking was more ominous.

Too ominous.

He looked up, to where the fallen part of the tree was joined to the trunk on the other side of the river, and watched in horror as, almost in slow motion, the wood started to split away and flip up, freeing the hugely heavy upper section of the tree. It was going to fall, and he was right in its way.

He didn't have time to think. He didn't have time to do anything but turn and run, throwing the saw aside, and as he turned, he heard a loud crack and a sound like thunder, then a branch whipped round and felled him at the same time as the trunk rolled down and came to rest across his legs.

The pain was blinding, but the adrenalin was kicking in, his heart racing, and gradually the pain receded to a dull scream.

He lay motionless, waiting, listening, but apart from Brodie's frantic barking, there was silence. The tree had settled, and he could still feel his feet. And his legs. Hell, he could definitely feel his legs, especially the right one.

Well, the ankle really. The left one was OK, and he could even move it a little. It was in a bit of a hollow, but the right—there was no way he could move that, and no way he was going to try. Just lying there was agony.

So now what?

He was lying there, contemplating his very limited options and trying not to retch with the pain, when he felt the vibration of his phone against his hip. Great. It might be Joe. He'd be able to get him out of this mess. He wriggled around a little, gasping at the pain in his ankle and his ribs, and the tree creaked again and shifted in a little gust of wind, sending pain stabbing through him.

Hell! He'd thought it had settled! He tried again for the phone, and finally managed to get it out of his pocket. 'One missed call,' he read, and tapped the keys with a shaking thumb to bring up the number. Not Joe.

Ben Carter.

Well, it was a start. If that tree kept shifting, an emergency consultant might not be a bad man to have around. He called him back. 'Ben? It's Mike.'

'Mike, hi. I was just calling to have that chat—is this a good time?'

Mike gave a strangled laugh, his breath constricted by the branch over his back. 'Um…I've had better. Bit…um… stuck at the moment.'

'Oh, I'll call you later—'

'No! I mean—really stuck. I'm lying under a tree.'

There was a pause. 'As in lying under a tree on the grass, contemplating the meaning of life, or—?'

'Lying under a fallen tree that I was cutting up,' Mike finished for him. 'Sort of literally stuck. And I think my leg might be broken, and the tree's not stable.'

Just to underline that fact, the tree groaned again, and he felt sweat break out all over him. 'I'm down by the river—only a short way from you over the fields, but you'll need help. I'm trying to get hold of Joe, but maybe we need the fire brigade—they've got a few strong lads who could help shift this thing.'

'Tell me where to come, and I'll get them on their way, too,' Ben said, his voice all calm business, and Mike felt his confidence like a soothing hand.

'Out of your drive, turn left, down the hill to the river, then there's a track to the right. Follow it—shut the gates behind you—and you'll find me there. You'll see the pickup and hear the dog barking.'

'Right. Are you bleeding?'

He considered that for a second. 'I don't think so.'

'OK. Stay still, don't move and I'll be with you.'

'Like I can move,' he said, but the line was dead, and he tried Joe again, getting him this time. Joe's language was colourful, and he could hear the fear in his brother's voice, but he'd know what to do and how to get him out, and he could use the chainsaw.

They arrived simultaneously, Joe on the tractor, Ben in his BMW, grounding on the track, and Mike felt a stupid, stupid urge to cry with relief.

'Nice one, guys,' he said, cracking a grin, and Joe swore and knelt down beside him, reaching through the twigs covering him to squeeze his shoulder hard.

'Stupid bastard. This tree's huge, far too big to tackle alone—why didn't you call me?'

'I did. Several times. You weren't answering.'

Joe swore again. 'Sorry, I was clearing the auger. Right, let's have a look at this tree. If I could only get the tractor in here I could lift it off you with the forks, but there isn't enough room. The other trees are too close.'

'So what's plan B?'

Joe looked around. 'I'm going to get this branch off you first, so you can breathe better. Then we can get a closer look.'

'Great.' Mike grunted. 'Just make sure it's not holding up the tree.'

'It's not. There's a good-sized branch wedging it.'

'Good. Cut this one off, then, because I really can't breathe. The chainsaw's about somewhere.'

He got up, and Ben took his place, hands running confidently over Mike's body. 'Tell me what hurts.'

'My leg? My pride?'

'Idiot. Not your back? Only your legs?'

'No, my back's fine—well, in comparison to my legs. The right one, anyway—and, believe me, it's enough,' he said, fighting down bile and wondering how the hell Joe was going to get him out. The scream of the saw sounded, and the pressure on his back and ribs eased, but it didn't take away the other pain.

'What kind of pain is it?' Ben was asking. 'Sharp? Sickening? Dull? Raw? Tender?'

'No. More—excruciatingly sharp. And sickening, yeah.'

'Right. Sounds like a fracture.'

'Feels like it, but I'm not an expert.'

'Can you feel your foot?'

He gave a choked laugh. 'All too well.'

'That's good.'

Good? Mike snorted and turned his face down, resting his head on the back of his hand and closing his eyes. He felt sick—sick and scared. If he'd died, what would have happened to Fran? Or the farm? Joe couldn't cope alone, and his father was too old to want to start all over again. He'd just retired, handed over the reins to his sons and put his feet up.

That damn tree had better not fall any further, he thought, and, craning his neck, he saw Joe shifting logs, making a pile under the trunk so it couldn't roll any further and couldn't sag any more.

Or that was the theory, but it was so heavy it could probably shift the logs quite easily.

Then he heard a fire engine lumbering down the track, felt the ground tremble under the weight of it, and the tree shifted again. Just a fraction, but enough to make him swear and eye the pile of logs nervously. Would they hold?

'We need to clear these branches to get the airbags under it,' someone said, and he could hear people running, and then the sound of the saw, then the weight shifted again and he groaned as pain shafted up his leg.

'Stop! It's moving on him. He needs pain relief—where are the paramedics?' That was Ben.

'There's been a big pile-up. All the ambulances are out. They're having to send one from Plymouth. It'll be another twenty minutes, and I don't think we're going to be able to use the airbags. There isn't enough room to get them underneath without cutting off the branches, and they're supporting it. We need to get heavy-lifting gear and it'll take a while—it's at the pile-up too.'

Great. Sweat dribbled down his face and into a graze, stinging it. He turned his cheek against his sleeve to wipe it away and caught Ben's troubled eyes. He smiled reassuringly but for some reason it didn't work. Nothing to do with the tons of timber hovering over his body just waiting to crash the rest of the way down and kill him…

'Right. I'll get Nick.'

Mike heard Ben key in a number, then heard rapid instructions, and a hand came back on his shoulder. 'Nick's going to bring some drugs.'

'Excellent,' he mumbled. 'I love drugs. Drugs are good.' The tree creaked again, and he bit down on his hand and gave a grunt of pain as the fire crew started to shift whatever they could to prop the broken trunk.

'Fran, come on in, have a seat,' Kate said, her smile welcoming, and Fran sat down at the desk, her fingers knotted tightly together in her lap.

'Are you OK?'

She consciously relaxed her hands and smiled back. 'Fine. So—tell me about this diet.'

'I've got the details here for you.' Kate straightened up and reached for a sheet of paper, sliding it across the desk towards her. 'It's very simple—suggestions, really, for how to include certain things, trace elements and so on which, although probably present in your diet, might not be there in sufficient quantity.'

'Things?'

'Zinc, selenium, folic acid, vitamin C. You need Brazil nuts and shitake mushrooms and oysters—not together, obviously,' she said with a chuckle, and Fran smiled with relief.

'I wondered how I was going to work them in!' she said.

'Well, oysters are out of season at the moment, you'll have to wait until the end of October if you want local ones, but the mushrooms and Brazil nuts you can get any time. And fruit smoothies. Fruit and veg smoothies—do you eat a lot of fruit and veg?'

'I do. Mike's usually crunching an apple and he eats what I give him but he's not over-fond of salads so he tends to eat cooked veg. He drinks apple juice sometimes—does that count?'

'Not really, but it makes an excellent base for the smoothies, so make him smoothies with apple juice instead of giving him coffee—it's hot now, so you've got the perfect excuse. And you should both be avoiding having a high caffeine intake as well. It's been related to delayed conception, so avoid coffee if you can, and also colas, dark chocolate and black tea—that's not tea without milk, by the way, but any tea that isn't green, white, fruit or herbal. Oh, and cut out alcohol. It can reduce a man's sperm count by half.'

'Good grief. I don't mind that but I think he'll kill me if he can't have tea or coffee! Apart from the odd glass of wine and the occasional apple juice, that's all he drinks!'

'He'll love the smoothies. You can use the veg ones as chilled soups—lovely in the summer. And they'll do you good as well—boost your vitamin levels. If they help sperm production, they might have a beneficial effect on your ovaries, too. Just try, Fran. If it does nothing else, it'll improve your general health and make you feel much better. In fact, it'll do you a power of good to eat something nutritious. You've lost too much weight recently, and being underweight can harm your chances of conception—did you know that?'

She shook her head, wondering why they were having this conversation when Mike clearly didn't even want to spend one night—one miserable, solitary little night!—alone with her, without the dog or his daughter or the endless bloody paperwork to hide behind.

'Encourage him to take cool showers and not hot baths—does he have baths?' Kate went on.

'Sometimes—if he's been doing something very strenuous and he's aching. Usually he showers.'

'What about underpants? Does he wear loose boxers or

tight briefs? Because if they're too tight, the testicles can overheat and that can affect the sperm count as well. The whole design of the scrotum is to allow the testicles to be at a slightly lower temperature, but because we wear clothes and bundle them up nice and tight, they cook a bit. Of course, going commando is the best answer, but I can imagine he might object if you steal all his underwear.'

Fran chuckled. 'I'll just steal the tight stuff and tell him it was worn out. To be honest, as long as there's something in the drawer I don't think he'd care what it was. I can tell him I had a crisis with the washing machine or the dog ate it or something.'

Or she could just tell him the truth, but the whole thing was irrelevant at the moment. She was hardly going to get pregnant if they didn't—

'You need to eat lots of dairy, too,' Kate was saying, 'but be careful with the soft cheese and unpasteurised milk products if there's the slightest possibility you might be pregnant.'

A humourless little huff of laughter escaped from Fran's mouth. 'Chance'd be a fine thing.'

Kate clicked her tongue sympathetically. 'Did you broach the subject of going away?' she asked gently.

Fran laughed again, but it was just as bad as the last one and utterly unconvincing. She swallowed hard. 'He's— He hasn't got time.'

'Is that true?'

'Probably, but if he wanted to, he'd make time— wouldn't he?'

Kate smiled. 'Don't ask me. Men are a mystery.'

'Tell me about it,' Fran murmured.

'So do something romantic at home. Cook a nice meal, put something pretty on...'

'He'll think I've run up a credit card,' she said dryly, and then felt saddened that they'd come so far down the line that they'd come to this, her talking about her marriage to a woman she hardly knew, trying to gain insight into her husband's behaviour. Not to mention her own...

'Kate, sorry— Ah. Fran. I'm glad you're here,' Nick said, his face troubled. 'Um, I've had a call from Ben. Mike's got a bit of a problem. He was apparently cutting down a tree—'

'What?' The word came out soundlessly from lips suddenly numb. She felt the colour drain from her face, her limbs curiously heavy and her heart lumping with dread. She lifted a hand to her mouth. 'Not the chainsaw...'

'No—no, a branch rolled onto him and it's pinning his leg down. Ben's with him—thinks he's got a fracture but the ambulances are all out on a big RTA and it'll take them ages to get to him, so I'm going to pop over there with a bit of pain relief while the fire crew get the branch off him. I'm taking morphine, but I just wondered if we'd got Entonox, Kate.'

'Yes—I'll get it. And we'll come. Come on, Fran, I'll drive you.'

The props weren't working. The weight of the upper trunk was too great, and they couldn't shift enough wood to secure it. The fire crew was gathered round Mike, having a muttered conference that didn't inspire confidence. He just wanted to get the hell out, and he needed those drugs.

'I'm going to dig it out,' Joe said. 'If I undermine it,

under that leg and foot, we can ease him out. The other one's free.'

'Sounds like a plan,' he mumbled, but the fire officer in charge had other ideas.

'Sorry, I can't let you get that close,' he said.

Joe's reply was pithy and not in the least bit polite, and it made Mike smile. Seconds later he felt him digging, felt Joe's hands under his leg while Ben supported it, stripping away the shale that was digging into his shin, and then his foot moved a fraction and he let out a whimper as he felt his leg sliding down gradually, away from the weight of the trunk.

He bit down on his lip, knowing it was necessary to dig around his foot so he could wriggle free but not sure he could take it.

Not without pain relief, but Nick was there, bringing him Entonox. He knew about that—Kirsten had had it when she'd been in labour with Sophie, and he sucked greedily on the mouthpiece while Joe tunnelled away like a mole, shifting the stony soil away from his leg and foot while he tried not to yell. Nick was putting something in his hand—some kind of IV set—and then injecting something that made him feel woozy and light-headed.

'Whazat?' he mumbled.

'Morphine, and metaclopromide, to stop you feeling sick from the morphine.'

''S lovely,' he replied. It was. The pain was going, fading a bit, less global.

'Right, that's as good as it gets,' Joe said.

'OK.' That was Ben. 'Mike, can you get your legs out yourself? Just slowly and carefully.'

He took a deep breath of the Entonox, wriggled his left leg free, took another suck of the gas and tried to move.

Pain lanced through him despite the drugs, and he swore viciously, suddenly wide awake. 'I need a hand, guys,' he said, sweat beading on his brow. 'Just pull me out, nice and carefully. I can't do this myself.'

'It is free,' Ben said, feeling round his leg gently. 'We should be able to do it. It's a very unstable fracture, though, and I don't want to drag you. And you need a spinal board.'

'To hell with that. What I need is to get out of here now,' he muttered as the tree groaned again. He felt it shift against his calf, and yelled, 'Just get me—Joe and Nick maybe?—and he could feel Ben's hands on his leg, steadying it. On the count of three they pulled, he gasped and swore and bit hard on his lip, and then he was free, and they were dragging and lifting him away from the tree while everything went black for a second and he fought the urge to scream with the pain.

As they put him down and shifted him to his back, Fran's white, terrified face swam into view. He thought she was going to yell at him, but she just smiled a little shakily and said, 'I didn't know you knew half of those words.' And then with a last tortured groan the tree slipped and fell the last few feet with a thundering crash, and she burst into tears.

'What the *hell* were you doing down there on your own with the chainsaw?'

He gave a rueful smile, and Fran felt a terrible urge

to smack him. She'd hung on as long as she could, but the 'what the hell' question just wouldn't stay locked up any longer, and she sat by his bed in the hospital and clamped her hands together. So she didn't strangle him, or so they didn't shake?

She didn't know. She didn't care. All she cared about was that Mike was alive—damaged, but alive—and only because Ben, Joe and Nick had got him out when they had.

She and Kate had got there just as he had been yelling at them to pull him out, and she'd watched in horror as his face had blanched and he'd let fly a string of words she'd never heard him use before.

And then the trunk had dropped, right where he'd been lying, and one of the firemen had been lucky to duck out of the way of the flying branches.

It could have been so, so much worse.

Infinitely worse. Unimaginably worse—

'I've done the milking for you, you idle skiver—and can you stick to Monopoly and not pick-up-sticks in future?' Joe said, walking up behind her and saving him from the strangling he so surely deserved.

'Hi, Joe,' she said with a smile of welcome. 'Give your brother a hard time for me, could you? I'm just going to ring your mother again and let her know they've moved him.'

'She's here. She and Dad have just pulled into the car park. I told them where to come.'

Ensconced in his hospital bed, Mike groaned. 'Did you have to? They'll make such a fuss.'

'A fuss? *A fuss!*' Fran all but shrieked. 'I'll give you *fuss*,

Michael Trevellyan! If that tree had fallen a minute earlier—ten seconds, for heaven's sake—'

'Michael! Oh, my goodness, are you all right? We came as soon as we heard but we were on our way back from Plymouth and there was a huge tailback because of this accident—'

'I'm fine, Mum,' he said, grimacing as he caught sight of his father's stern face.

'How many times have I told you—?' Fran's father-in-law started, and Fran just smiled, stepped back and left them to it. She didn't need to strangle him. His parents would do it for her. In the meantime, she might go and get herself a cup of coffee.

'So how's the invalid?' Ben asked as she bumped into him at the ward entrance.

'Getting an earful from everyone,' Fran told Ben with a wry smile.

Ben smiled back, but his eyes were gentle with concern, and she felt hers fill again. 'You OK?' he asked, and she nodded, then shook her head, then shrugged a little helplessly and laughed, her traitorous eyes welling.

'I don't know. Yes. Maybe. At least he's alive.'

'He'll be fine. He'll be going to Theatre shortly to have it plated, and he'll be in for a couple of days, then they'll send him home in a cast to rest.'

'He'll be horrible. He'll be so bored,' Fran said with a sigh, and Ben raised an eyebrow.

'So entertain him,' he said with a smile. 'He'll be laid up and fizzing over with all that pent-up energy. I'm sure you'll be able to find something to do together to alleviate the boredom!'

She felt herself colour slightly, and found a smile. If only, she thought. 'I'll buy him a Sudoku book,' she said, and Ben chuckled.

'Yeah, right. Like that'll do it!' He tipped his head on one side. 'You going anywhere important?'

'Yes—to get a coffee,' she said, wondering if it mattered if she started Kate's diet a day later and deciding that today justified it. She could have lost Mike—so easily. And today had proved to her beyond any doubt that she wasn't ready to lose him. Not in any way. There was nothing like staring that dreadful possibility in the face to bring it home to her, so, yes, today justified a delay in the start of the diet, because at the moment whether or not they had a child was way down the list of her priorities.

And Mike—her beloved, darling, infuriating, broken Mike—was right at the top.

'Mind if I join you?' Ben was saying. 'I was just about to make a drink when I called him, and I still haven't had one yet. I'll even treat you to a chocolate muffin.'

She laughed. 'You truly know the way to a woman's heart,' she replied, and wondered when she and Mike had last laughed like that, about nothing in particular, just for the sake of laughing. Ages. A lifetime.

But they would again. She'd make sure of it…

CHAPTER FOUR

THEY were sending him home on Friday, and he couldn't get out of hospital quickly enough.

Not that he'd really known that much about it for the first twenty-four hours, because he'd been in so much pain he'd been drugged up to the eyeballs.

It was the bottom of his fibula where it joined the tibia on the outside of his ankle—the lateral maleolus, or some such bone—that had sheared off, and his fibula was fractured again just above the ankle joint. Such a skinny little bone to cause so much pain, although the ligaments between the two bones hadn't ripped. This, apparently, was a good thing, or it would have been ages before he could bear weight.

Even so, he'd have to be in a cast for weeks.

Fabulous. In the summer, when he relied on the longer hours of daylight to do all those endless jobs about the farm that he couldn't simply do in the dark. Hedging, fencing, repairing the fabric of the buildings—cutting up fallen trees?

But on the bright side, luckily the skin hadn't broken. It seemed a very slight thing to worry about, considering they'd had to cut it open anyway, but apparently it made a great difference to the sort of repair they could do, and it meant it could be plated and screwed, and he didn't have to have an external fixator.

Thank God, because there was no way he could work on the farm with a metal frame on the outside of his leg and pins going through into the bone, carrying filth and infection right into the heart of the injury. And, anyway, even the sight of them made him feel sick. There were several people in the orthopaedic ward with them on, and others in traction, even one screwed into a special revolving frame, bolts into his head and shoulders and hips and legs...

Hideous. God only knows what it must feel like to be in there, he thought, but the man didn't seem to be aware of too much. That had to be a good thing—probably the only good thing, if the drawn faces of his relatives were anything to go by.

He glanced across at the man. On second thoughts, maybe it wasn't a good thing. He discovered he was extremely grateful he wasn't in so bad a way that he wasn't aware of his surroundings, never mind his ankle.

Although he felt all too aware of it most of the time, and he was desperate for a good night's sleep in his own bed, with soft cotton sheets, their lovely down duvet and his own pillow.

And Fran.

God, he missed her. She'd been in to visit him each evening, but it wasn't enough, and he couldn't believe he'd been so reluctant to go away with her this coming weekend for the night. He'd give his eye teeth for the chance to do it now, he thought, lying there waiting for someone to come and discharge him.

And then Ben strolled in, hitched his hip onto the edge of the bed and grinned. 'Want to cut loose?'

'Oh, do I ever!' he said fervently. 'Got the power to spring me?'

'Absolutely. Well, not really, but I've just seen your consultant and he's happy to lose you. They're just filling in the paperwork, and I thought, as I've got the afternoon off, I'd give you a lift—unless you're organised?'

He shook his head. 'No, not at all. I was going to ring my father or my brother, but I haven't done that yet. I'm supposed to be getting a lesson on my crutches.'

'Yeah, the physio's on her way. I'll get them to give me a call when you're done, and I'll get you out of here.'

'You're a star. Cheers.'

'My pleasure.'

It took another hour, but finally he was ready to go, and Ben came up, put him into a wheelchair and trundled him out into the fresh air. He dragged in a great lungful of it, closed his eyes and sighed hugely. 'Oh, that feels so good. You can't imagine what it's like when you're used to being outside all the time, to be cooped up in there without feeling the wind in your hair and the sun on your face. I just kept telling myself I was lucky not to be six feet under.'

'Shouldn't think you needed to,' Ben said dryly, pushing him through the car park to his BMW. 'I would have thought you'd got Fran doing that for you, on the minute every minute. She was beside herself, you know, when she realised how dangerous it might have been.'

Mike gave a rusty chuckle. 'She wasn't alone. When I heard that tree go—well, let's just say I won't be taking chances like that again.'

'Good. I'm glad to hear it, and I'm sure she will be. Right, shift across and I'll get rid of the wheels while you settle yourself.'

Easier said than done, he realised. God, how could anything so simple be so profoundly awkward? It took him ages, while Ben stood holding the wheelchair and telling him to take his time.

But so much? Finally there, he slumped back in the seat, his skin breaking out in a cold sweat, and concentrated on getting his breath back. Not easy with his ribs screaming in protest.

He was shocked at how hard he'd found it, how even such a comparatively minor injury could have taken such a toll on him. And once he was at home, he'd have to go up and down stairs. How the hell was he going to manage that? And bathing, for crying out loud. He'd have to shower with his leg in a bin bag.

He gave the cast a jaundiced look and wondered for the umpteenth time how he could have been so stupid. It was going to be weeks before he was fixed—months, even. Certainly a couple of weeks before he could do anything even remotely useful on the farm. Even the dreaded paperwork would be too much for him at the moment.

He swore under his breath, hauled his broken leg into the car, swung the comparatively uninjured one in beside it and eyed the bruises with disgust.

Pity he couldn't have worn trousers to hide them a bit, but he didn't have any that would go over the cast, so he was wearing shorts and a T-shirt and his Technicolor injuries were all on display.

Well, not quite all of them. His body under the clothes

was also black and blue all over, a million points of pain and mutilation. He'd caught a glimpse of the bruises over his cracked ribs in the bathroom mirror this morning and had nearly had a fit. Fran would take one look at him in the nude and run, if she had any sense. Probably just as well, because he didn't have the strength to argue with her about how stupid he'd been and just now she wasn't wasting a single opportunity to lecture him.

He closed his eyes and dropped his head back against the seat. He just wanted her to come home and hug him. He'd missed her so much, and his family had all been in telling him off, so their visiting times had hardly been cosy, intimate occasions.

'Come on, Ben,' he muttered. 'Take me home.'

As if he'd heard him, Ben opened the driver's door, slid behind the wheel and shot him a smile. 'Sorry about that. Somebody wanted the chair and then couldn't manage to get her husband into it. As he was having a heart attack, I didn't feel I could leave them.'

'Of course not,' Mike said, trying for a smile and probably producing a grimace.

'Right, let's get you home.'

He hadn't heard anything so good in ages.

'Mike?'

Fran ran lightly up the stairs, crept down the landing and pushed open the bedroom door, tiptoeing round the bed so she could see his face.

He was fast asleep, his lashes dark crescents against his cheeks. He looked pale under his tan, drained of warmth, and she bit her lip and blinked back tears. He looked awful. Washed out and exhausted, and it made her want to cry.

She'd been fighting the urge since it had happened, moaning at him about being stupid when all she'd really wanted to do was curl up in his arms and howl her eyes out.

She backed away, meaning to leave him alone, but her foot hit the creaky board and his lids fluttered open, those gorgeous brown eyes fixed on hers.

'Hi.'

'Hi,' she replied softly, perching carefully on the edge of the bed and giving him a shaky smile. 'Welcome home.'

His answering smile was tired but contented. 'Thanks. It's good to be back.'

'How long have you been home?'

He glanced at his watch. 'Two hours? Ben gave me a lift.'

'Ben?' she echoed, surprised. 'That was kind of him. I thought Joe or your father would do it.'

Mike shrugged. 'He was there, he offered, and they were busy.'

'Can I get you anything—a drink?'

He shook his head, his eyes intense. 'Not yet. The first thing I want is a hug from my wife without an audience.'

'Oh, Mike...'

She kicked off her shoes, lifted the quilt and slid carefully under it, turning towards him as his arms reached for her and he gathered her up against his chest with a sigh. She breathed deeply, drawing in the scent of him, a strange mixture of hospital and warm, earthy man, and she squeezed her eyes shut and slid her arms carefully round him and hugged him.

He grunted, and she froze, lifting her arms away. 'Mike?'

'It's OK. I've got a few bruised ribs.'

She lifted the quilt back and propped herself up, staring down at the vicious bruises over his side and back, a huge spreading stain of vivid, deepest purple where the branch had fallen on him, the bruises so many they'd all run together in a great blotchy sheet. She hadn't seen them before, because he'd been in a T-shirt and boxers in the hospital, but now, with his T-shirt removed and just the boxers on, she could see them, and they brought tears to her eyes.

'Bruised?' she questioned sceptically, a give-away shake in her voice. 'Is that what you call it? Just…bruised?'

His smile was a little crooked. 'Well, the odd rib might be cracked.'

She shut her eyes again and lay down, keeping her arms well away from his ribs, one hand lightly resting on his shoulder, her face cradled against his chest. It rose and fell slowly, then stopped, and she looked up and saw his lips pressed hard together.

'What is it? Are you OK? Where do you hurt?' she asked, panicking, and he turned his head and stared at her, his eyes raw with emotion.

'It's just so good to be home—to hold you,' he said, and she was stunned to hear a catch in his voice. 'I've missed you.'

'Oh, Mike…' She broke off, the words dammed up behind the tears, and she lifted a hand to his cheek, letting it linger as she feathered a kiss over his lips. 'I've missed you, too,' she said, knowing that they weren't just talking about this last two nights but the months and months before, the aching void since things had been good between them, natural and relaxed and just plain happy.

A sob broke free, and his arms tightened around her,

easing her closer. 'Don't cry,' he murmured gruffly. 'I can't bear it when you cry. It tears me apart.'

'You could have died,' she whispered, her chest shuddering, and his arms squeezed tighter.

'But I didn't, and I'm home now. Stay with me, just for a while. Dad's here, doing the milking, and Joe and Sarah have still got Brodie—it's just us, Fran, and we don't have to do anything or be anywhere. So stay with me. Let me hold you—just for a little while.'

It had been so long since he'd held her that she'd have been happy to stay there for ever. He didn't need to talk her into it. She tilted her head and kissed him again. 'Just for a while,' she agreed, and, closing her eyes, let herself relax against him.

She was asleep.

It felt so good to hold her after all this time, but he needed the bathroom, and he didn't think he could get up without help. He couldn't bear to disturb her, though.

Not that they could stay there for long, because he could hear his mother moving around in the kitchen, and his father would have finished milking now. With a sigh he bent his head and brushed his lips against her cheek.

'Wake up, darling,' he murmured.

'Mmm,' she said, snuggling closer and ignoring him.

'Fran, I need a pee and I can't get up when you're holding me.' He probably couldn't get up at all, but they'd cross that bridge when they got to it.

She eased away, lifting herself up on one arm and turning back the quilt, her eyes widening as he sat up with his back towards her and she saw the full extent of his bruises. Her lips pressed together but she didn't say a word, just slid out of bed and came round to his side, moving the quilt the rest of the way off him and helping him shuffle forwards to the edge of the bed.

'Stay there for a moment, give yourself time,' she said, and handed him a clean T-shirt. 'Here, put this on. You don't want to frighten your mother to death.' When he'd carefully eased his way into it, trying not to wince, she gave him his crutches. 'OK?'

He nodded, shifted his weight to his left foot and the crutches and stood up carefully. Hell. He was still wobbly, and she was so tiny that if he started to go he'd crush her.

He gave it another second, then tried a step. Fran reached up, steadying him by the shoulders as he adjusted his weight and swung slowly forwards on the crutches. OK. So far, so good. He took another step, then another, and he was at the bathroom door in a few more steps without incident.

'Can you manage?' she asked, and only his pride made him say yes.

'I'll be fine,' he assured her with more confidence than he felt.

'OK. I'll go and put the kettle on.'

'Great. I could kill a decent cup of tea,' he said. Shutting the bathroom door, he leant on it quickly before he fell over. Damn.

Triple damn with a cherry on top.

He eyed the loo in disgust. Who on earth had decided to put it right on the other side of the bathroom?

'How is he?'

Fran shook her head, sat down at the kitchen table and

smiled unsteadily at his mother, still ridiculously close to tears after watching him struggle to the bathroom. 'OK, I suppose, but he's very sore. I didn't realise— I thought it was just his legs, but it's everywhere. He says he might have a cracked rib.'

Joy nodded. 'Joseph said there was a big branch across his back. He was lucky—'

She broke off, biting her lip, and Fran realised she wasn't the only one who'd been through hell. And it was so stupid!

But she wasn't going to fight with him any more about it, or tell him off. He was well aware of how close he'd come—he had to be, he wasn't an idiot. Although how anyone as clever as him could be so frustratingly dense was incredible.

His father, Russell, came in, followed by Sarah and Brodie, and then Joe, shucking off his overalls and grinning at her.

'You look a bit rumpled,' he said, and she ran a hand through her hair and smiled self-consciously, colour warming her cheeks.

'I just lay down next to him for a minute and fell asleep,' she said, oddly embarrassed to have been caught napping with her own husband, but Sarah hugged her as if she understood.

'Are you OK?'

'I am now he's home. He's in the loo—I must go and help him back to bed.'

But he was there, in the doorway, as white as a sheet and fending off Brodie with one hand while he leant heavily against the doorframe.

'So where's that tea, then?' he said, cracking a smile. 'I don't know, five of you in the kitchen and the kettle isn't even on.'

'We were just debating on the slowest and most painful way to kill you,' Joe said mildly, scrubbing his hands in the sink. 'I've cleared the slurry pit.'

'I can tell—I can smell it on you,' Mike said, wrinkling his nose.

'The lengths some people will go to to get out of the worst jobs,' Joe quipped, and, shaking his hands, he wiped them on his jeans and gave his brother a crooked smile. 'Take a pew, for God's sake, before you fall down.'

He pulled a chair out, steered his brother towards it and propped his broken leg on another chair while Joy put the kettle on. Fran moved to his side, laying her hand gently on his shoulder, afraid to hurt him until her mental map of his bruises was more accurate, but he just tilted his head and smiled at her, covered her hand with his and squeezed her fingers.

In the busy, crowded kitchen you would have thought such a tiny gesture would go unnoticed, but suddenly you could have heard a pin drop. Everyone stopped talking and stared at them, then looked away, finding things to do, a burst of conversation ending the brief, deafening silence.

Was it really so strange that she should go to him, that he should touch her, that his entire family had stopped in their tracks and stared?

Evidently it was.

Mike, looking up at her, hadn't even noticed, but she had, and it made her wish they'd all go away. Their marriage felt so fragile at the moment; they needed to work on it, to find out if they had anything left, to piece together, slowly and painstakingly, the fragments of their love, and she wasn't sure she could do that under the penetrating gaze of their relations.

Because what if, like Humpty Dumpty, they couldn't put it together again? If, at the end, they found there simply weren't enough pieces left to make it work…?

They had to make it work. Anything else was unthinkable. And so, burying her natural reticence, she bent her head and kissed him. It was the merest touch of her lips to his, but it was a sign, and a promise, and his eyes met hers and held them for a long moment. Then he squeezed her hand again where it rested on his shoulder, and the world started to breathe once more…

CHAPTER FIVE

'SHALL I sleep in the spare room?'

Mike looked up, frowning, but Fran's eyes were unreadable. 'You don't have to do that.'

'I didn't want to crowd you. With your foot—if I hit it in the night, I might hurt you.'

'You won't hurt me. It's all pinned and plated, Fran—it's not going anywhere. You're more likely to stub your toe on the cast.'

'But what about your ribs? If I shift around…'

'You won't. You never disturb me. Anyway,' he added, sure that there was more to it than just concern about hurting him but not knowing what, or how to deal with it, just that he had to keep her with him come hell or high water, 'what if I need to get up in the night? I might need help.'

For the longest moment she hesitated, then with a tiny, almost imperceptible sigh her shoulders sagged in defeat and she nodded.

'You're right. I'll try and keep out of your way.'

'You're not in my way,' he said, feeling a wave of relief at her submission. He'd really thought she was going to sleep in another room, and it had scared the living daylights out of him.

It was the thin end of the wedge, the beginning of the end, and for all they were hovering on the brink, he couldn't let it go that far. Not yet. Not now. Hopefully not ever.

He was curiously reluctant to let her out of reach, even though he'd actively avoided her for months. But he'd better not scare her off. Shucking off his dressing-gown and letting the new, loose boxers she'd got him that fitted over his cast fall down around his ankles, he kicked them carefully away and lay down, wondering if he could find a position that didn't hurt his leg and then deciding that it was his leg and not the position that hurt, and it wouldn't frankly matter if he hung the damn thing out of the window...

'You haven't had your painkillers, have you?' she said, and he wondered if she was a mind-reader.

'I didn't think I needed them,' he lied. He knew perfectly well he needed them, but they made everything blurred at the edges and he was worried he'd say or do something—

What? Something affectionate? Romantic?

Desperate?

Damn. Perhaps he should have kept the boxers on.

She handed him the pills and a glass of water, and he swallowed them down. What the hell. He'd just lie with his back to her and keep his hands to himself and his mouth shut, and hopefully he'd be asleep soon...

He was restless.

Fran lay awake beside him, keeping a careful distance and wondering how much pain he was in.

A lot. He must be. She'd seen the X-rays, seen the metal

framework holding his leg together, seen the screws that went right into the bones…

It made her feel sick just to think about it, sick and scared and as if she wanted to gather him up against her and hold him close, to ease it, to take away the pain in any way she could.

Except she couldn't take it away, of course, and, besides, he'd lain down with his back firmly towards her, discouraging any repeat of their earlier cuddle. But then he mumbled something in his sleep, and she reached out a hand and laid it gently on his side, and he sighed softly and went quiet.

Comforted by her presence? She felt a tear leak out of the corner of one eye. She'd missed him so much. He'd only been gone two nights, but they'd been lonely and endless. Crazy when, apart from their earlier hug, they'd hardly even touched each other by accident in bed recently, never mind deliberately, but nevertheless she'd missed his presence there.

He murmured again, and she moved closer, curling her body behind his and snuggling up, her hand resting lightly on his hip, afraid to wake him. But the painkillers must be keeping him under because he didn't stir, just sighed and relaxed against her, the tension she hadn't even been aware of seeping out of him, and she felt her own tension dissipate into the night.

Her eyes drifting shut, she laid her cheek against his shoulder and fell asleep…

He woke to find her curled around him.

It was his leg that had woken him—that and the ribs he

was lying on—and he really needed to turn over, but she was in the way and he couldn't bear to wake her.

She'd move away—he knew that, knew she must have ended up lying against him by accident, because, God knows, apart from their cuddle when she'd got home from work and the briefest of brief kisses in the kitchen, if there'd been a way to avoid it she hadn't touched him in ages. There could have been chainlink fencing down the middle of the bed since April for all the difference it would have made, they'd kept so strictly to their own sides of the bed.

He straightened his leg a fraction and, as if she'd read his mind again, she shifted away, giving him room.

'You OK?'

'Mmm. Just need to move my leg.'

'Sorry.' She scooted across to the far side of the bed, and he rolled carefully over towards her.

'Better?'

'Mmm,' he said again. Better, but too far from her. He lifted a hand, almost reached for her, then, letting his breath out on a silent sigh, he lowered his hand back to the mattress. No. Too dangerous. He didn't trust himself, and the last thing he wanted to do was drive her away.

He shifted a fraction, trying to get comfortable, and listened to the sound of her breathing. It took her ages to fall asleep again, and he wondered if she was listening to him breathe as well, so he deliberately slowed his respiration rate down and after a few more minutes he heard a subtle change in hers as she slid into sleep.

But it wasn't a happy sleep. She was restless, murmuring, and he reached out a hand. Should he?

Yes.

This time, he let himself touch her, let his fingers curl over the slender, fragile curve of her shoulder, and with a contented little sigh she wriggled backwards until she was touching him, the soft roundness of her bottom brushing his thighs, her back against his chest, and she relaxed again.

Lucky her. He didn't. He couldn't.

It had been so long since he'd touched her. She was wearing a nightshirt, not much more than a long T-shirt, and it had ridden up so that the soft, bare skin of her bottom was against his legs, silky smooth and unbelievably arousing; he ached to rest his hand on her thigh, to slide it up and round her slender, tiny waist, up over her ribs, curling his fingers round to cup one of her small, firm breasts in his palm—

His body reacted instantly, and he felt his erection brush against her, sending shockwaves racing through him. Dear God, he wanted her. Wanted to hold her, touch her, bury himself in her, but he couldn't. Couldn't risk it. Couldn't put her in that position again.

He shifted his hips, pulling back away from her, but she followed him, her bottom bumping against his penis, and then he heard a soft gasp as she came suddenly, instantly awake.

Fran froze.

What the hell was she doing? Snuggling against him, her back against his chest, her bottom spooned—oh, lord. She couldn't move away. If she moved, he might know she was awake, and if she didn't…

If she didn't, and he reached out for her again, wanted to make love to her—could she do that? Let him? After so long, she really wasn't sure, wasn't sure at all that she could let him touch her, kiss her…

She felt the brush of his erection again, felt the stillness in his body and knew he was awake. Awake, and aroused, and waiting for her to make the next move.

Oh, dear God. She couldn't deal with this. Her emotions were too close to the surface, and if he touched her, all hell might break loose. So she faked a mumble, shifted away, rolling onto her front with her head turned away from him, and after an endless moment she heard him sigh.

Had she fooled him? She closed her eyes, squeezing them shut against the threatening tears, and after a few more minutes she heard the rustle of the quilt, felt the mattress shift and heard him grunt with pain as he sat up.

What was she to do? Pretend he'd disturbed her and get up and help him? Stay put with her eyes closed and listen out for him until he'd got down the corridor to the bathroom?

He was naked. If he was still aroused...

She stayed put, her ears straining as he picked up the crutches, took a step, swore softly and moved again. The bedroom door was open and as he went unsteadily down the corridor, she turned her head and watched him until he was in the bathroom.

The door closed softly, and she dropped her face into the pillow and sighed. What now? Pretend she'd been asleep? If she was a decent wife she'd get up and make him a drink, but that would mean talking to him, and she felt awkward—gauche and nervous and oddly apprehensive. What if he said something about it?

What if he knew she'd been awake?

Oh, why on earth had she wriggled up against him? Because she had, of course. She'd been right on her side of the bed after he'd rolled towards her, and when she'd woken, she'd been slap in the middle, her bottom rammed firmly up against him—as in, Sit on my lap and we'll talk about the first thing that comes up, she thought, and groaned with embarrassment.

No wonder he'd had an erection. He'd have to be dead not to react to that, whether he'd wanted her or not. He was a relatively young man after all, fit and healthy and in the prime of his life. And it had been literally months since they'd made love. After such a long time, he'd surely react to anything female.

He came back to bed, and she heard the crackle of the pill packet, heard the swallow as he took his painkillers, felt the mattress dip slightly as he lay down with a muffled groan.

She cracked an eye open. He was lying on his back, staring at the ceiling with one arm flung up over his head.

'Fran?'

His voice was soft, little more than a breath, but she ignored it, afraid to answer, afraid to open that Pandora's box.

After an age, he sighed quietly, the arm settling over his eyes, and eventually a soft snore heralded his slide into sleep.

She wasn't so lucky. Every cell of her body was aware of him, every breath he took, every slight shift, every grunt. She daren't relax, daren't go to sleep in case she ended up curling into his side. So she lay awake, staring at the ceiling and listening to him breathe, until the sky lightened and she could creep away...

Mike woke alone.

Odd, that. He was always the first to wake, the first to get up, the last to come to bed. He was *never* alone in bed.

He hated it.

He had no idea where Fran was, what she was doing, and how she'd greet him when he finally caught up with her.

He thought back to the night, to the way she'd recoiled from him, pretending to be asleep and rolling away from him—because she *had* pretended, she *had* been awake, and in the end he'd had to get up and move around or he'd have screamed with frustration.

So he'd gone to the bathroom, and the pain in his leg had dealt with his untimely arousal, and he'd gone back to bed and stared at the ceiling for ages while Fran had lain rigid beside him and feigned sleep. Again.

He swore, softly and comprehensively. Where on earth did they go from here?

The kitchen would be a good start. He could hear voices, and he got up, slowly and carefully, and struggled into his boxers. He didn't bother with his dressing-gown. It was hot today, and he needed a shower. Maybe Joe was about.

He made his way slowly and carefully downstairs, shuffling down on his bottom because he'd been warned in no uncertain terms not to put any weight through his leg yet— not that he needed warning. Even resting it on the floor made it ache like hell.

The kitchen, when he eventually got there, was rammed again. It had obviously become Party Central since his accident, he decided, and discovered that he was relieved, because otherwise he'd have to deal with Fran without anyone to run interference.

Except she wasn't there.

'Morning.'

They looked up, Joe and his father from breakfast, his mother from the sink, Sarah from sorting a pile of vegetables by the fridge. 'Hi,' she said. 'Fran's gone over to the shop to get some fruit. Joe, shove up, let him sit down. Want a cup of tea, Mike?'

'Um—thanks,' he said, sinking gratefully into the chair Joe had vacated and stretching his leg out cautiously. Brodie propped herself against the other one and gazed soulfully up at him as if she couldn't understand why he'd deserted her. He rubbed her behind her ears, and she washed his hand, her eyes still on him anxiously. Sarah brought his tea over, set it down and stared at him open-mouthed.

'Wow,' she said, and his brother grunted.

'That's my brother you're eyeing up,' he reminded her, and she laughed.

'Really? I thought he was a refugee from a film set. The last time I saw bruises like that was a post-mortem in a forensic science drama. Impressive. You ought to take photos.'

'Don't overdo the sympathy,' Mike said, but he was smiling, knowing that in her way Sarah was telling him how sorry she was that he was hurt. 'Any more of that bacon, Mum?'

She dragged her eyes from his side and tried for a smile. 'Coming up. Want it in a sandwich?'

'Lovely. With an egg in it. You're a star.'

And then Fran was back, with a box full of fruit, and he stared at it in surprise. 'Is that all close to its sell-by date?' he asked. They often got a surplus of one kind of fruit or another, but not normally so much at once unless it had been over-ordered, and they tried not to do that. It dented profits.

But to his surprise she coloured a little and put the box down on the side. 'There was a lot and I just thought it looked nice,' she said, avoiding his eyes. 'Fruit's good for you, and I've got some cheese and yoghurt as well. You need all those vitamins and minerals to help you mend and build your strength up.'

What for? he thought. What have you got in mind for me? Because it's clearly not sex…

He felt his body reacting at the thought, and regretted leaving his dressing-gown upstairs, but his mother put the sandwich down in front of him and he leant forwards, giving himself a bit of privacy until he got his crazed libido under control. Hell, he must be nuts, but all he could think about was her bottom, soft and warm and snuggled up to him…

She bent over, putting the fruit in the fridge, and he was treated to the curve in question, her jeans, loose now since she'd lost weight, pulling taut as she bent and giving him a tempting view of the very part of her that was giving him so much trouble.

He yanked his eyes off her and concentrated on not dribbling the softly fried egg down his chest.

'You around for a while?' he asked Joe around a mouthful of sandwich.

'Why?'

'I need a shower.'

Joe arched a brow. 'Long time since we shared a shower,' he said dryly, and Mike felt himself colour.

'I don't want to share it with you, you jackass. I need someone to grab me when I fall over, and Fran's too little. I'd squash her.'

Joe looked disbelieving, but he shrugged and nodded. 'I can give you a hand. Be more fun with Fran, though.'

He felt himself colour again, his neck reddening, and his

hands itched to strangle Joe. Not that his brother realised he was being tactless. How could he? Only they knew their marriage was in tatters.

'Don't tease him, Joe,' their mother said gently, and Mike heard something else in her tone. A warning? A warning to tread softly?

So maybe their problems weren't as private as he'd thought.

Damn.

He pushed the plate away. 'That was lovely, Mum. Thanks. Right, Joe, are you ready? I don't want to hold you up, I know you've got loads to do.'

'Tell me about it,' Joe said, dropping his mug into the sink and handing his brother the crutches. 'Come on, then, Hopalong, let's get you scrubbed. Pity we haven't still got the sheep-dip.'

'Ha-ha. I need a bin bag and some elastic bands,' he said, and while Joe found those, he headed upstairs the same way he'd come down.

He turned the shower on, got the temperature right and then Joe trussed his leg up like a turkey and he swung round into the bath, getting awkwardly to his feet and pulling the shower curtain closed. 'So how are we going to manage this, Joe?' he asked.

'Hell, you want me to wash you?' Joe asked in disbelief.

'Not the shower—the farm,' Mike retorted, struggling with the soap and wondering if a little help *wouldn't* go amiss.

There was a heavy sigh from Joe, and the curtain twitched back a little. 'We'll cope, bro. You get yourself right. Don't worry about the farm. Dad's quite enjoying having a bit to do with it again, and at least the weather's nice.'

'Yeah—and Mum was probably planning all sorts of work on their house in the next few weeks and it won't get done.'

'It doesn't matter. There's always another day. Want a hand with your hair?'

'No, I'm fine,' he lied, struggling to scrub it with one elbow propped against the tiles so he didn't lose his balance. He rinsed it quickly, swilled the water over his body one last time and turned off the taps. 'Might need a hand getting out,' he confessed, and Joe steadied him while he sat on the edge and swivelled round, grunting with the pain in his side.

'Your ribs OK?' Joe asked, giving him a searching look.

'Not really, but what are you going to do about it? What I could really do with is a good night's sleep. I couldn't get comfortable last night.'

Except when I was snuggled up to Fran, he thought, but didn't voice it. Too much information, and he didn't want to think about it when he was stark naked. His body was all too keen to betray him at the moment.

Joe towelled off his back and leg, took the bin bag off his cast and washed his toes carefully with a flannel, then looked round. 'Got any clean boxers?'

'In the bedroom. It doesn't matter, I'll go like this.'

'What, and shock Mum rigid? You've grown up a bit since she changed your last nappy.'

'Well, then, hopefully she won't be foolish enough to be in my bedroom.'

She wasn't. Fran was, bending over the laundry basket, and he grabbed another pair of new boxers out of the drawer, struggled into them and then lay back under cover of the quilt to get his breath.

'You OK now?'

He nodded. 'Thanks, Joe. You go and get on. I'm sorry to hold you up—and I'm sorry about all this...' He waved in the general direction of his leg, and Joe shot him a wry grin.

'Could have been a whole lot worse, big bro,' he said softly, and left them.

Alone.

Fran stood up, washing in her arms, and eyed him warily. 'Are you OK? You have to go to the fracture clinic in a bit.'

He nodded. 'Can you take me?'

'Of course I can,' she said, frowning slightly. 'I need to put the washing on. Can you manage to dress yourself?'

He nodded again, not wanting to make her do anything intimate for him—not if it was so repugnant to her—and her recoil in the night couldn't have been clearer. 'I'll be fine. I'll come down in a little while,' he said.

'Take your painkillers first,' she advised, and left the room as if it was on fire.

The fracture clinic seemed happy with him.

He told them he was having trouble getting comfortable, and they gave him some advice for propping up his leg in the night—advice which Fran was relieved to know would make it impossible for her to end up snuggled on his lap, thank goodness, because he'd have to lie on his back. At least it didn't seem to be swelling, so long as he kept it propped up, and that seemed to be what worried them most.

She drove him home, and when they were almost

there, he asked her to drive down to the river. 'I want to
see it,' he said.

'What, the tree?' she asked, a cold shiver of dread
running over her. 'Whatever for?'

'To know how big an idiot I was?'

She gave a strangled little laugh. 'Oh, I can tell you that.'

'I thought you had,' he pointed out. 'But I want to see
for myself.'

So she detoured, turning left instead of right and running
down past Tregorran House to the gate at the bottom of the
hill, opening it and driving along the river until they
reached the fallen tree.

'Here you go,' she said. 'The crime scene.'

He opened the door, got out with difficulty and swung
himself over to the tree on his crutches, standing there and
staring down at it for an age.

He could see the depression where Joe had dug away
the ground under his leg. It was about five feet from where
the tree had ended up—which would put it right across the
back of his shoulders, maybe even his head. Whatever, he
wouldn't have survived it.

He felt goose-bumps coming up all over him, and he
gave a sudden shiver.

Fran took his arm. 'Come on, Mike. You've seen
enough,' she said softly, and he looked at her and realised
she was as white as a sheet.

Poor Fran. He wanted to hug her. Was it wise?

'Ah, hell,' he muttered, and turned back to the Land
Rover. He couldn't hug her, could he, with the crutches
hanging on his arms? And anyway, she probably wouldn't

want it. He got back in, swung his legs in—he was getting
good at it now, although his ribs still hurt like hell to do it—
and Fran shut the door.

She walked round the bonnet, giving the tree one last
wary look, and slid behind the wheel, starting the engine
and heading back towards the road.

'I'm sorry.'

She shot him a startled look. 'What for?'

'Being so bloody stupid. Scaring the living daylights out
of you. Making you come back here when you obviously
didn't want to. Take your pick.'

She sighed softly and gave him a hesitant little smile.
'Idiot. Put your seat belt on. I don't want you flying
through the windscreen if we meet a lunatic tourist. We've
all got enough to worry about at the moment.'

He fastened his seat belt obediently, tried to find a comfortable position against the backrest as they jolted down
the track and then sighed with relief when they hit the flat,
even surface of the road again. They were home in
moments, and he slid down out of the Land Rover and
swung himself towards the back door.

'Gosh, it's hot,' Fran said, following him in. 'Fancy a
drink?'

'Coffee would be good.'

There was a second's hesitation, then she said, 'Oh. I
was thinking more of something cold—a fruit smoothie?
Use up some of that lovely fruit I sorted out this morning.'

He would rather have had a coffee, but she was right,
the fruit needed to be used up and with all the painkillers
he was on, if he didn't have fruit his system would grind
to a halt. 'Sounds good,' he lied, and eased himself into a

chair. Brodie wasn't around—gone off with Joe and Sarah, probably, so it was just him and Fran and a rather awkward tension between them which he'd never felt before.

She peeled and chopped the fruit—strawberries, a chunk of melon, two bananas and a handful of blueberries—threw in a good glug of locally sourced apple juice and turned on the liquidiser.

At least it drowned out the silence, he thought, and then she handed him a glass of purplish mush, clinked hers against it and said, 'Welcome home, Mike.'

What could he do? He picked up the glass, took a breath and sipped, then frowned at it. 'This is really nice,' he said, surprised, and she smiled—in relief?

'Good. Drink up, and you can go and have a lie-down. You look tired.'

He was, and, curiously, what he wanted more than anything was to ask her to join him, but he didn't think he could. Not easily. Not after last night.

So he drank up, took some more painkillers and went to bed.

Alone.

CHAPTER SIX

HE SLEPT most of that day, and the night was made easier by the stack of pillows under and around his leg, propping it up and protecting his toes from the pressure of the quilt. Not that he needed it, because it was hot, and in the end they abandoned it in favour of a sheet.

But then it grew cooler, the wind picking up a little, and because their bedroom was on a corner and there was a cross-draught from the windows, Fran found herself snuggling closer to him for warmth.

Only her head and shoulders, her body carefully kept out of reach, but he slid his arm round her and held her, and together they slept the rest of the night till the fingers of light crept over the horizon and woke them.

Well, woke her. And when she looked up, Mike was watching her, his eyes curiously intent, and her heart thumped.

'Want a drink?' she asked him, easing away and stretching out the kinks in her neck.

'Mmm. Tea would be nice.'

She hesitated. 'How about juice? It's quicker and it won't keep you awake.'

He gave a short laugh. 'Fran, I've slept for nearly eighteen hours straight, apart from waking up for supper. I don't think sleep's an issue.'

'OK.'

She slipped out of bed and went down to the kitchen, foraging in the back of the cupboard for the decaf tea bags she'd bought for them. 'Oh, Brodie, it would be so much easier if I could tell him what I was doing and why, but I don't know if I can. What do you think he'll say?'

And that was the trouble, of course. Mike was avoiding her, she was avoiding him, and they just weren't talking. Not that they ever had, really. Maybe that was the trouble, but once the lid was off that box…

'I can't talk to him, Brodie. Not about getting pregnant again. Not until I know how he feels about me.' And, of course, without talking to him, she never would.

'So—what are we going to do today?'

Mike dragged his eyes from the window and looked at her. They were in the sitting room overlooking the garden and the sea in the distance, the church and lighthouse just visible on the horizon.

'I don't know. You tell me,' he said, wondering if he sounded like a spoilt brat. He felt like one. If it wasn't for the physical impossibility, he would have stamped his foot, but because he couldn't he just ground his teeth and crossed his arms over his chest, drumming his fingers on the other arm.

God, he *hated* the inactivity! Hated sitting still, being unable to do anything, just—sitting, for heaven's sake! He *never* sat! Well, not unless he was in front of the computer, filling in endless farm returns and tweaking the farm-shop website. Maybe he should do that.

'How about going for a drive?'

He thought about it, but his ribs probably weren't up to being jostled and he'd quickly discovered that if he didn't have his foot up, the cast got uncomfortably tight. Although comfort wasn't really a word he could have used truthfully and it was all a matter of degree.

'We could play Scrabble.'

Fran stared at him. 'You hate Scrabble.'

'Not as much as I hate lying here doing nothing. Got any better ideas?'

She looked away, and he was stunned to see a warm sweep of colour brush over her cheeks. Fran, blushing? She got up hastily and crouched down, rummaging in the cupboard where the games were kept, and by the time she straightened up her colour had returned to normal.

She still didn't look at him, though, and he was fascinated. Fascinated, and very curious, and strangely a little edgy.

'If I move the coffee-table over by you, can you manage on that?' she asked.

'I'll give it a try.'

It worked. Sort of. It was a little low, but that was fine, because every time she leant over to put her letters down on the board, he got a view straight down the V of her T-shirt, and it was worth every second of the discomfort he felt when he put his own letters down.

Especially when she realised it was hurting him and started taking the letters from him and putting them down for him. So he got twice as many opportunities to see the soft, warm shadow between her breasts.

The effect was predictable, and he shifted a little on the sofa, pretending it was to do with his ribs but actually trying to ease the tension in his boxers.

'Grackle? You can't have that!' she said. 'It doesn't exist.'

'Want a bet?'

'What is it, then?'

'It's a type of mynah bird.'

She sat back and stared at him. 'Really?'

'Look it up.'

'And lose my go? No way. I know you and animals.' She added the score, and he leant over and shifted one of the letters to expose the coloured square.

'Don't forget it's on a double word score,' he pointed out, and she scribbled out the score and wrote the correct one in.

'I'm not going to let you win,' she said fiercely, scowling at her letters and checking the board. 'You always win—even though you hate it, you always win.' She put down 'lathe', and he added an 'r' to it and got another double word score.

'Don't sulk,' he teased, and she glared at him, then laughed and threw a letter at him.

'Don't gloat, then! I was going to do that when I got an "r".'

'You should have hung on.'

'No doubt.' She shuffled her letters, grinned and hung 'runcible' on the 'r' of 'lather', getting a triple word score and a bonus for using all her letters.

'Runcible? You can't have that, it's not a proper word!' he protested.

'Yes, it is.'

'Rubbish. It's Edward Lear—he has a runcible spoon in "The Owl and the Pussycat"—"They dined on mince and slices of quince which they ate with a runcible spoon." It's just nonsense.'

'*And* a runcible cat in "The Pobble Who Has No Toes",' she said, and quoted back at him, '"He has gone to fish, for his Aunt Jobiska's runcible cat with crimson whiskers." I rest my case,' she said smugly.

He tried not to laugh. 'It's not in the dictionary.'

'Oh, yes, it is.'

'I bet it isn't.'

'What do you bet?'

He took a slow breath, his eyes locked with hers. 'A kiss.'

She coloured, and then looked away and laughed a little oddly. 'You're on.' And she handed him the dictionary.

Except he didn't take it. He caught her wrist, gave it a gentle tug and toppled her towards him. She gave a little shriek and grabbed the back of the sofa with her free hand so she didn't fall on him, but his nose ended up in her cleavage, and he turned his head and brushed his lips against the soft, shadowed skin.

She caught her breath and straightened, sinking down onto the edge of the sofa, and their eyes locked. Slowly, carefully, he leant forwards, stifling the groan as his ribs pinched, and touched his mouth to hers.

For an endless, aching second she was still, then she moved away. 'Uh-uh,' she said, her voice over-bright and her smile pinned in place. 'You have to win a kiss, and you haven't looked it up yet.' And she stood up and moved back to the other side of the coffee-table and safety.

He found it—of course. She was never so definite if she wasn't sure about something, and he'd bet she'd looked it up recently when they'd been doing Lear at school.

'See? It's a three-pronged fork with a curved edge on one side.'

'Shame,' he said softly, closing the dictionary, and her eyes flew up and met his, then slid away again, but he'd had his kiss. Sort of. And it had left him aching for more.

He wanted to drag her off to bed, kiss her senseless and drive out this reluctance of hers, but he had a feeling it wouldn't and, anyway, it was as much as he could do to drag himself there, never mind an unwilling woman.

Besides, he didn't want to. Not if it meant her going through hell again with another failed pregnancy somewhere down the line because of him.

He reached out, letters in hand, but she tutted and put another word down before him. 'My turn,' she pointed out. 'You forfeited your turn when you looked in the dictionary.'

He gave up trying and let her win, as much as anything because he couldn't sit there any longer and look down her cleavage at something he wasn't able to touch…

Sophie came later, running into the sitting room with her eyes wide with worry and fascination. 'Wow, you've got a proper cast!' she said in awe. 'Can I draw a picture on it?'

'Sure—when I've had a hug.'

'Mind his ribs, darling,' Fran warned her. 'He's a bit sore.'

Her eyes widened. 'Will I hurt you if I hug you?' she asked, nibbling her lip, and he shook his head and pulled her up onto his lap, snuggling her close on his right side, the side that didn't have the bruises. Well, not so many, anyway, and he needed a cuddle from his little girl.

She wriggled down tighter, burrowing under his arm, and then lay almost motionless, even breathing carefully in case she hurt him. It made him want to laugh and cry at the same time, and he hugged her gently.

'So—are you all ready for your holiday?' he said, and she shuffled round so she could see him, gently kneeing him in the groin as she did so. He grabbed her leg and held it still, and over her shoulder he could see Fran biting her lip and trying not to laugh.

'Yup. I've packed my things already. I want to see Nessie again. Last time we went to Scotland we saw Nessie,' she said. 'Didn't we, Mummy?'

Kirsten smiled. 'Well, there were some ripples on Loch Ness that might have been caused by an animal, but they could have been the wind.'

'It was Nessie, I know it was,' Sophie said adamantly. 'And we had haggis. I'm not eating *that* again!' She pulled a face, and Mike chuckled.

'Didn't you like it?'

'It was dis*gust*ing!' she said. 'All greasy and smelly and made of a sheep's *stomach*! It was horrid. But we had lots of shortbread and I like that. Mummy says we can go back to the shop we bought it from and get some more. Oh, and we're going up Ben Nevis again! We walked halfway up last time, to the little lake, and Andrew had to carry me down 'cos I had bendy legs, but I'm bigger now. Maybe we'll even get to the top!'

He smothered the laugh and hugged her again. 'Poor old Andrew! Let's hope you make it both ways this time. Coming down's always the hardest bit.' He knew—he'd carried Sophie down his fair share of hills over the years, and it got your knees like nothing else. 'Hey, how about some cake? I know Fran's brought some over from the shop and I'm getting really hungry.'

'Good idea,' Fran said with a smile. 'Come on, guys, let's go and make tea for Mike.' She held out her hand to Sophie, who slithered over his chest, grabbed her hand and cuddled up to her side.

'Can I make him banana sandwiches?'

'I expect so.' Fran chuckled, and Mike listened to them making their way towards the kitchen and smiled at Kirsten.

'Sounds like you'll have a busy holiday.'

'Well, we will if she has anything to do with it, but we all love Scotland and Andrew's parents spoil her to death. So— are you OK to have her for the week when we get back?'

'Fine. Make it Sunday afternoon, can you? I should be able to help out in the shop over the weekend by then, and I feel I ought to be pulling my weight.'

'Sunday's fine. It'll give me time to unpack and wash her stuff.' She stared at his leg. 'I'm sorry about your accident.'

He shrugged. 'I was being stupid.'

'So I gather. And I always thought you were clever. Maybe we should get Sophie screened for the reckless gene.'

He snorted. 'So rude.'

'You asked for it.' She stopped smiling and perched on the edge of the sofa. 'Actually, I've got something to tell you.'

He looked up into her face, and his heart sank. He knew, before she opened her mouth, what she was going to say.

'When's it due?' he asked.

She frowned, then said sadly, 'Is it so obvious?'

He nodded. 'I've seen that look in your eyes before, don't forget. So when is it? February? March?'

'February—the very end. We haven't told Sophie yet, but I wanted to warn you, because of Fran and—well, you know.'

Yes, he knew. What he didn't know was how on earth he was going to tell Fran. He dredged up a smile. 'Congratulations, Kirsten,' he said softly, and, drawing her down, he hugged her gently and brushed a kiss against her cheek. 'I hope it all goes well for you. Sophie's dying for a little brother or sister and we don't seem to be getting any closer to achieving that for her, so I'm really pleased for you.'

She blinked hard and smiled. 'Thank you. I know it isn't easy for you.'

'Mummy—Mummy! It's a chocolate fudge cake! Absolutely my favourite! And I've made some banana sandwiches, and Fran's made a huge pot of tea—she's bringing it on a tray.'

'How lovely—I'll help her,' Kirsten said, standing up and giving him another slightly worried smile. 'Mike, are you sure you're OK about it?'

'About what?' Sophie asked, bouncing around the room with the dog on her heels.

'Having you for the week once you're back,' he said quickly. 'I think if Fran's OK with it, we could have you from the weekend after next? I should get a walking cast so I might be a bit more mobile by then. And we're pushed on the farm at the moment, because one of the shop ladies is off on holiday, so we'll have you from Sunday afternoon, perhaps? Then we'll have plenty of time to hear about your holiday.'

Kirsten shot him a grateful look for his hasty intervention. 'That would be fine. I'll bring her over—we'll go and talk to Fran now and sort out the times,' she said, and went out to help with the tea things.

Sophie went too, dithering and skipping and chatting to Brodie as she went, and Mike laid his head back against the sofa and closed his eyes.

Pregnant.

Hell. It was going to kill Fran—and he was going to have to strike the fatal blow…

Mike seemed much more comfortable with the new cast.

Maybe it was because his leg was starting to recover from the insult of the fracture and the repair, or maybe he was giving in and taking the painkillers regularly and not trying to be heroic.

Whatever, he was sleeping better, and that meant Fran was too.

Just as well, she thought, because with him out of action, now she was on holiday from school she was doing as much as she could on the farm to help out. She didn't do the milking—Russell seemed more than happy to do that, and she didn't like to stop him. She sensed that he missed the farm, and also that he needed to be needed, something that Mike wasn't very good at understanding.

He was so busy trying to take the pressure off his father that sometimes she wondered if they'd taken too much too soon, but it was certainly back on now, and Russell seemed to be thriving on it.

And Joy was helping in the farm shop, as usual, and so Fran ended up making the cheese.

She didn't mind. It was quite therapeutic, really, and because of the tight timings—adding the starter culture once the milk was the right temperature, then stirring it, then leaving it, then adding the rennet, and the mould if it was to be a blue cheese, then cutting it, then scooping out the curds into the strainers, and all the time checking the temperature of the various processes, washing out the vats, scrubbing down the tables, sterilising everything, endlessly hosing the floor and brushing it clean—there was no time to think and yet the steady rhythm of the work was curiously restful.

There was all the work in the cheese stores as well, turning and salting and testing, and then packaging the cheeses for sale, either in wheels or cut into wedges and shrink-wrapped.

It all took time, and as they were so busy with the summer tourist influx it kept her well out of Mike's way, but it was quite hard physical work, and she was feeling drained this week. Just because it was another thing, another turn of the screw at a time when things were already tough enough, she'd started her period on Sunday evening, and although she *knew* she couldn't be pregnant— well, after all, how could she without any contact with Mike?—nevertheless it still made her feel down.

She'd just finished a long session of salting and turning in the blue cheese store on Thursday and was cooking their supper when she saw Ben heading towards the house with a book in his hand. She went to the door and opened it with a smile. 'Hi, Ben!' she said, and he smiled back.

'Hello, Fran. Is Mike in? I've got something for him.'

'Yes—go on through. He's in the sitting room. He's bored to death. He'll be delighted to see you. Want a cup of tea?'

He shook his head. 'No, I won't hold you up, I can see you're cooking. I'll just go and have a chat for a few minutes.'

'If you're sure?'

'I'm sure. You carry on, I won't be long.'

* * *

'Is the invalid up for a visit?'

Ben was standing in the doorway, and Mike chuckled and shifted up the sofa, propping himself up against the backrest and moving his leg into a more comfortable position.

'Absolutely. Come on in, make yourself at home.'

'So how are you?'

'Oh, you know—bored, sore, frustrated with the cease-less inactivity…'

'Peachy, then.'

'Oh, utterly.'

Ben grinned and dropped into the armchair opposite. 'Thought so. I've brought you a book—it's an autobiogra-phy I've just finished reading. The guy was unfortunate enough to become one of my patients and he gave it to me. Nice man. I thought you might enjoy it. It's quite funny and very touching—he used to be a farmer.'

He slid it over the coffee-table and Mike picked it up, flicked through the pictures and put it down. 'Thanks. I've heard about it—if I'd thought I'd have the time, I would have bought a copy, so I'll enjoy reading it. God knows, there's not much else to do at the moment.'

Ben chuckled. 'I can imagine. So when did they change your cast?'

'Tuesday. It doesn't seem to be swelling too much, so they were happy to do it. I have to say it looked pretty grim.'

Ben nodded. 'I expect it's black.'

'Mmm—like this,' he said, lifting up his T-shirt and making Ben wince.

'That's a goody. You were lucky your chest didn't cave

in. You could have had a flail segment there and it would have made it much more exciting.'

Mike groaned. 'No, thanks. It was quite exciting enough. In fact, I'm not sure I've thanked you for coming to my rescue.' He tipped his head on one side. 'Actually, I seem to remember you rang me at a rather opportune moment for that chat, and you never did say what it was about.'

'Oh, that. It's nothing to worry about—it'll keep.'

'Well, if it's nothing to worry about, bring it on, frankly, because all I've had to do for the last week is sit here and worry about all the things I should be doing and can't, and how much work this has put on everybody else, and how far behind we'll be if I can't get all the summer jobs done—so, please, if it's something to think about that isn't a worry, tell me!'

Ben laughed and sat back, studying him for a moment. 'OK. It's about the field in front of the house. Well, all round it, really, but especially the bit between the house and the road. It's not huge, but when we had the christening you let us use it for parking, and it was hugely helpful. The drive's really not big enough if we have more than one visitor, and if we had that field, we could extend the parking at the front and make a bit more of a garden on that side of the house. And if you got really carried away and wanted to sell the bit between us and the clifftop, and maybe a little strip round each side too…?'

Mike thought about it for a moment, then nodded slowly. 'It would make a lot of sense for you, but we tend to move the cattle through from one side of you to the other along that field, and if you've got the whole section from the cliff to the road, we'd have to move them on the lane, and we try to avoid that. And it wouldn't help you with access to the beach—I take it you've found out how steep it is there? You can't walk down.'

'No, I know. It was just an idea. It's the other bit, really, that's the most significant, and Lucy's decided she loves gardening—takes after her grandmother, I think, and she really wants to expand it. She says I only want it so I can have a little red tractor mower and drive around on it, pretending to be a farmer—'

Mike laughed out loud at that. 'Any time you want to play at being a farmer, give us a shout and you can get up at five and do the milking.'

Ben grinned. 'I'll stick with the mower,' he replied. 'So—think about it, ask Joe what he thinks. There's no rush, and we certainly don't want to put any pressure on you, but if the land's going begging, we'd be more than happy to pay you amenity rates. We'd have to get it valued to make it fair.'

Amenity rates? They doubled the price of agricultural land, sometimes more than doubled it. And the land Ben was talking about wasn't in any way fundamental to the running of the farm. They had plenty of grazing, and certainly the area between the house and the road was only ever grazed just to keep it down. It wasn't good enough for hay, it wasn't big enough for crops and the most sensible thing would be to sell it to the Carters.

And, God knows, cash at the moment was tight.

'Have you got a plan of the plot?'

'Not here,' Ben said. 'I have at home. Want me to draw it up so you can see?'

'Or I can walk over it with you.'

Ben arched a brow ironically, and Mike sighed. 'Well, drive, then. I can get Joe to bring me up. We could all talk it over on site. I'll speak to him and Dad first.'

'Do that. And now I'm going to leave you in peace. Fran was cooking something that smelled really gorgeous, and I don't want to be responsible for ruining your supper. Enjoy the book—and drop in when you're next in the hospital. The fracture clinic's right next to A and E, and if I've got time, I'll stop for a coffee with you.'

'I'll do that,' Mike promised.

Ben went out, and he could hear his voice in the kitchen, talking to Fran for a moment before the back door shut.

So Ben wanted to buy the land.

And if he did, Joe and Sarah would get enough money to refit their kitchen, which was absolutely falling apart, and he and Fran—they'd have enough money, he thought, the realisation slowly dawning, to pay for another cycle of IVF.

He swallowed. If Fran felt brave enough to go for it. And if she did, he'd have to find the strength from somewhere to support her when it all went wrong.

Assuming she even wanted a baby with him any more. Right now, he wasn't sure she did. He didn't know what was going on in her head, and that made life with her an absolute minefield.

And to make matters worse, Sophie was coming back on Sunday week and he still hadn't worked out how to tell Fran that Kirsten was pregnant.

Oh, damn.

CHAPTER SEVEN

THERE was only one way to do this, Mike decided, and that was to tell Fran straight.

So he did—eventually.

She'd prepared a lovely meal—chilled watercress and tomato soup with basil and garlic croutons, a really tasty chicken dish in a creamy blue cheese sauce with shiitake mushrooms on a bed of wild rice served with the freshest, crunchiest runner beans out of their own garden, and then a fabulous fruit salad rammed with fresh summer fruits topped with a dollop of clotted cream. It was streets away from the usual food they ate, when she was up to her eyes in schoolwork and he was milking until six-thirty and then fighting with the paperwork. He didn't care if it was geared to helping his leg mend, it was gorgeous, and he scraped the last dribble of cream off the edge of the bowl and pushed it away with a sigh of regret.

'That was delicious, darling, thank you,' he said with a smile, and she smiled back and took his plate.

'You're welcome,' she said.

It would have been easier if he hadn't felt so guilty because he was about to wreck it all by telling her about

Kirsten. In fact, he was so preoccupied with working out how to do it he was surprised she hadn't picked up on it.

But apparently she hadn't, because she cleared the table, loaded the dishwasher and topped up his glass of apple juice without commenting on his silence.

He wished he didn't have to do this. Telling her about the baby was going to spoil their evening, and good times between them were so few and far between. She'd made a real effort tonight—did he *really* have to say anything to spoil it?

Yes, because otherwise Sophie would come next weekend and if she knew she was bound to say something, and he owed Fran a few days to get used to the idea without having to pretend enthusiasm to a delighted little girl who was finally having her dream realised.

But not now. Later, perhaps. When they'd gone to bed. When he could lie there and hold her, and hug her when she cried—because she would, of course. She was bound to, and if she was already in his arms, maybe she wouldn't run away and cry in private.

Although he hated it when she cried, he hated even more the idea that she'd run away and do it in a corner somewhere, like a wounded animal. That he really, *really* couldn't bear.

'Coffee?' he suggested.

She hesitated, then smiled. 'OK. Just a little one. I don't want to keep you awake.'

He'd love her to keep him awake, but that wasn't what she was talking about, and, anyway, there was still this whole pregnancy minefield.

Oh, hell. Life was so incredibly complicated.

'What's wrong, Mike? You've been frowning all evening.'

He turned towards her in the darkness. With the bedroom

curtains open, as they always were, he could just about make out her features, but he couldn't read her expression. That was a definite disadvantage of doing this in the dark, but it was more intimate, easier to say the things that would hurt her so badly.

'Nothing's wrong, exactly,' he said, not knowing where to start. He reached out and found her hand, curling his fingers round it and squeezing gently. 'It's just—Kirsten's…'

He let it hang, and after a few seconds she sucked in her breath and he knew she'd worked it out.

'When?' she said, her voice almost inaudible.

He ached to gather her into his arms. 'February,' he told her, although he couldn't see that it made any difference, but it had been his first question, too, and he supposed it was only natural, part of the process of establishing just when the changes would start to show. Soon, he thought, remembering Kirsten's first pregnancy.

Fran's fingers tightened on his, and he squeezed back and didn't let go.

'Does Sophie know?' she asked eventually, her voice hollow.

'I don't know. She didn't when Kirsten told me.'

'When did she tell you?'

'On Sunday.'

'Sunday?' she exclaimed, pulling her fingers away. 'But—it's Thursday!'

'I know,' he said heavily. 'I didn't know how to tell you.'

'Oh, Mike, that's silly,' she said, her voice more normal now—or was it? 'It's lovely for them. And Sophie will be delighted.'

'Are you going to be OK with it?' he asked, wishing to God he could read her face. If only he'd done this in daylight....

'I'll live. It was always going to happen, Mike.' But this time there was a little wobble in her voice, and without thinking about it, because if he did he'd talk himself out of it, he reached out and gathered her against his chest.

For a moment she resisted, then he felt her chest hitch, and her arms slid round him and she squeezed him tight. Right over his cracked ribs, but he stifled the groan and held her, running his hands gently up and down over her back to comfort her.

'I'm so sorry,' he murmured, and she sniffed and her chest jerked again, but she wouldn't let the tears fall, wouldn't give way to them.

Damn, she was so ridiculously *brave*! If only she'd cry—let it out, let him hold her while she worked through all her feelings, but she wouldn't, and he could understand that. He wouldn't lie and cry in her arms either. It was just all too revealing.

'I knew it would happen,' she said finally. 'I mean, why not? Everyone else in the world seems to be pregnant.'

Everyone but her. He knew that, knew without a shadow of a doubt that she wasn't pregnant because she'd had a period this week. Not that it made any difference without the means to conceive, but it must just rub it in when something like this happened.

And she'd been in a foul mood earlier in the week, distant and unapproachable, and he didn't know if she was still angry with him about the accident or unhappy because she wasn't pregnant again or if it was just PMT.

In the good old days, if she'd been grumpy like this he

would have made a wisecrack about her hormones. Not now. He knew better now, because PMT was an indicator of just how monumentally unsuccessful they were being in the baby department, and frankly it just wasn't funny.

He pressed a kiss to her hair, and she snuggled closer, letting him hold her. He wasn't really comfortable. He should have had his leg up on a pillow, but it wasn't as bad as it had been and for now it wasn't his priority.

Fran was, and he wasn't going to do anything that might make her leave his arms. He wished he knew what to say, how to comfort her, but he didn't, so he just held her, and after an age she fell asleep.

It was hot—too hot to lie so close—and he shifted slightly, easing away from her and stretching his leg out, wishing he'd propped it up on the pillows first before they'd started this conversation.

She'd rolled to her side away from him, and he shifted to face her, hunting for a better position. It wasn't, but his good leg brushed hers, and she wriggled back towards him, seeking him out in her sleep the way she always did if things were tough.

The way she always *had*, he corrected himself, and let his arm circle her waist, drawing her back more firmly against his chest. To hell with the heat. She needed him, and it was little enough to do for her.

Even if the feel of her soft, warm body in his arms was killing him…

Fran woke to Mike's arm around her, his fingers curled gently around her breast, the insistent nudge of his erection against her bottom.

Heat speared through her, flooding her with a fierce, desperate need, a hollow ache that only he could fill. It was so long since she'd felt it, felt anything at all except empty and cold. And she wanted him—wanted the old Mike, the man who laughed and chased her around until she let him catch her, who made love to her, tormenting her until she was sobbing with need, then taking her with a wild and uncontrolled passion that left her spent and boneless in his arms.

Where was that man? Gone for ever? Or was he still here? If she only had the courage to reach out…

'Mike?' she whispered.

For a moment he said nothing, so she almost wondered if he was asleep, but he was too still, too silent, and then he spoke, his voice gruff and low.

'I'm sorry. It's just— I'll move.'

'No!'

The word was out before she could stop it, and he froze again. 'Fran, please. I can't do this. Can't lie here night after night, wanting you like this, and—'

'Wanting me?' she breathed, stunned. Turning, she stared at him in the moonlight. 'Do you want me? I thought you didn't.'

'Of course I want you,' he whispered roughly. 'I'll always want you.'

'But—you've been avoiding me. Going over to the farm office, telling me not to wait up, getting out of bed in the morning without waking me.'

'I've always done that. I never wake you that early.'

'Not like this, Mike. Not like this, so I thought you didn't love me any more.'

'Oh, Frankie, of course I love you.' He sighed. 'I just…'

'Just can't bring yourself to touch me?' she said, her voice hollow to her ears—hollow and empty, like her heart.

'No! How could you think that?'

'Then why are you avoiding me?' she wailed softly, ridiculously, all but inviting him to make love to her when she couldn't even contemplate his intimate touch.

He sighed again, his hand coming up, the knuckles grazing her cheek with infinite tenderness. 'It's not that I can't bring myself to touch you, Fran. It's—oh, hell, much more complicated than that.'

'Then tell me! Talk to me, Mike!'

He didn't answer, but she could hear the cogs turning, feel the tension radiating out of him.

'Mike?'

'Frankie, I'm no good with words. I'm a farmer, for God's sake. I don't talk about my feelings.'

'Why?' she asked. 'Why not? Dammit, I'm not enjoying this either, but we *have* to talk. Our marriage is in tatters, we're falling apart and I'm trying here, really trying to get through to you, to sort it out, to find out if we've still got anything, and I can't do that on my own! I can't lay myself bare, wide open to you—not on my own! You have to do it too, Mike. You *have* to tell me how you feel. You *have* to share. Please…'

Her voice cracked, and with a ragged sigh he reached out and found her hands in the darkness, gripping them so tight she nearly cried out, but she wasn't letting go, not now, when they were so close…

'It's not that I can't bring myself to touch you,' he said gruffly. 'Far from it. It's more that—I daren't.'

'Daren't?' she breathed. 'Why ever not?'

He hesitated an age, then said, so softly she could hardly hear him, 'In case you get pregnant.'

She froze with shock. So she was right, she thought numbly, her eyes searching his but unable to read them in the shadows. Her voice cracking, she said desperately, 'I knew you didn't want a child with me—'

'Oh, Frankie, no!' He reached out, wrapped her in his arms, dragged her against his chest with a groan of protest. 'Of course I want a child with you. But every time you're pregnant, every time you lose it—I just can't bear to watch you go through that, sweetheart—not again. I can't bear watching you fall apart, seeing what I've done to you destroying you—'

'What you've done?' She pushed away, tilting her head so she could look into his eyes, her hand cradling his face. 'Mike, don't be silly! You've done nothing to me.'

'Except get you pregnant with dodgy sperm.'

'We don't know that. It could be my eggs. Maybe they're dodgy. What makes you think it's you? There's nothing dodgy about Sophie.'

'Maybe she was a one-off. My lucky break. And anyway, you've been avoiding me, too,' he added softly. 'Sometimes, when I've reached the end of my tether and I really, really needed you, you've turned away, reading a book or going to have a bath or—I don't know, almost anything rather than be alone with me. I've even wondered…'

'Wondered what?' she asked, when the silence stretched on.

'If there was someone else.'

'Mike! You know I wouldn't!'

'I know. I do know. Or I know you wouldn't have an

affair, at least, but—you can't stop yourself falling in love, Frankie. And if there's someone else—someone you'd rather be with— I know you don't want me to touch you. I've felt you recoil…'

'When?'

'The other night?'

'Oh, Mike.' She felt tears fill her eyes, felt the anguish in his voice cut through her like a knife. 'It wasn't that.'

'What, then? What is it that makes you flinch away from me as if I'm somehow…repugnant to you?'

'Oh, darling, you're not. Not at all. It's just—I feel like a medical investigation. As if so many people have looked at me there, touched me, talked about me—as if the part of me that had belonged to us is suddenly public property. And I don't know if I could bear for you to touch me, or if it'll just bring it all back—' She broke off, biting her lip, then went on unsteadily, 'Mike, I don't know if I can respond to you any more. I don't know if it hasn't just killed it for me, and I'm scared to find out.'

His breath sighed against her face, warm and reassuring. 'Oh, Frankie. Oh, my love—what's happened to us?' he whispered, folding her against his chest again and rocking her. She could still feel the brush of his erection, but softer now, less urgent, and as he cradled her so her confidence grew, her need to hold him, to touch him building until finally she found the courage to reach out.

'Mike?' Her voice was soft, gently questioning, and her hand stroked against his shadowed jaw, the rasp of stubble unbearably erotic against her palm. Leaning in to him, she brushed her lips lightly against his, tentatively, not sure of her reception or how she'd react if he took it further than this, but he wasn't going to let her find out.

He drew back, taking her hand and turning his face into it, pressing a kiss against her palm. 'No,' he said softly. 'Not tonight. Not when you're still unsure—still not ready.'

'I am,' she lied, but he knew her better than that. So much better. And he was right, of course. She wasn't ready, and maybe he wasn't either. They still had a long way to go, a lot to unravel, much to talk through.

And for a man who didn't talk and a woman usually too shy to reveal her inner self, it was going to be uphill all the way.

They slept in each other's arms, only waking to the sound of his family in the kitchen at seven.

She groaned, and he chuckled and hugged her closer to his chest. 'Maybe they'll cook us breakfast,' he suggested.

'And maybe I should be up and helping them, not lying here with you and—' She broke off, and he let her go.

Lying here with him and—what? Wanting him, the way he wanted her? God, he hoped so, because a few more nights of persistent arousal was going to give him a serious medical problem.

But what if she didn't? What if she never wanted him, couldn't ever bear his touch? What if all the investigations had turned her off so thoroughly that they never made love again?

The thought took his breath away.

'Coming down?' she asked, and he shook his head.

'I'll have a shower first.'

'Need a hand?'

'No,' he said firmly. Not to have a cold shower. And it

would need a bucket of ice to settle him down after last night. He watched her as she walked down to the bathroom, the nightshirt hitched up slightly by the clothes she'd scooped up to take with her, revealing an incredibly tempting glimpse of the crease below her left buttock as she walked.

The softly shadowed fold did nothing to help his state of arousal, and with a groan he shut his eyes and dragged his mind to something dull. Anything. The paperwork? Farm records?

Funny how his mind had emptied, how he couldn't think of a single thing except that soft shadow and the warm, silky feel of her skin…

She was busy all day, out on the farm, and he was driven crazy. He started to read the book Ben had given him, but it couldn't hold his attention. Not against such fierce competition.

And he was getting so unfit it was driving him mad.

He went into the kitchen, poked about in the larder and found an unopened bag of rice. That might do the trick. He sat down on one of the chairs, draped the rice bag over his cast and did some lower-leg lifts until his thigh and abdominal muscles were burning. Then he shifted onto his right hip and lifted the leg up and in towards the centre, over and over, then stood up and held on to the sink and lifted his leg out sideways until the muscles round his hip were screaming in protest.

He looked at the clock and sighed. Ten minutes. Barely that, and he was cream-crackered. Still, it was a start.

He put the kettle on, then went to the freezer and hunted around for the packet of coffee. Funny, he had been sure there'd been one in here, but he couldn't find it. Oh, well. He picked up his crutches and went slowly over to the farm office. Joe was in there with his father, and he stuck a coffee-pod in the machine and put a mug under the spout.

'So how are things?' Mike asked while he waited for the coffee.

'OK. How about you?'

'Bored to death. Doing exercises so my leg doesn't wither and drop off. Why?'

'I'm going to cut up that tree,' his brother said. 'Want to come and keep an eye on me?'

'I can't do anything.'

'You can dial 999 when I cut my leg off,' Joe pointed out dryly, and Russell snorted.

'I hate to point this out to you two but I can't run the entire farm alone without either of my suicidally reckless sons.'

'Don't worry, Dad, I'll look after him,' Mike assured him. 'And tell Fran not to worry about lunch, we'll grab something from the shop.'

He drained his coffee—the first decent one for days, he realised—and climbed into the cab of the pickup with Joe. Maybe if he was careful he could stack some of the logs...

'Cheers. You've been a real help—hope you haven't overdone it.'

'I'm fine. It was good to get some fresh air,' Mike told Joe, and slapped his shoulder. 'Right, I'm going in. No doubt I'll get a lecture. I'll see you later.'

He went into the kitchen and sniffed appreciatively.

'Wow, that smells good.'

'It's more than you deserve,' Fran growled, but when she

turned she was smiling and he hobbled over to her, stashed his crutches in the corner of the worktop and hugged her.

'I was sensible. I was just going crazy, stuck in the house, sweetheart.'

'I know.' Her arms were round him, holding him close, and she felt so good he could have stayed there for ever, but she pushed him away and told him to wash.

'You've got ten minutes before supper,' she said. 'And I want you clean and presentable. We're eating in the dining room.'

He peered through the door on the way past and did a mild double-take. Candles?

He yelled back, 'Give me fifteen minutes. I'm having a shower.'

A nice hot one, followed by a shave and a slosh of the citrusy cologne she'd given him for Christmas two years ago. He contemplated the cast with disfavour, pulled on a fresh pair of the baggy boxers, then his favourite aqua-blue soft cotton shirt and his decent shorts—his dress shorts? he thought with a chuckle—and went downstairs.

Wow.

She'd said clean and presentable, but she hadn't expected him to go to so much trouble. He was even wearing aftershave!

She was wearing a sundress—she'd changed into it after she'd finished turning the cheeses and had a shower, and she'd been out in the garden picking fresh herbs and dead-heading the roses. She could feel the warmth in her shoulders, even though she'd been out of the sun at midday, but it had obviously been enough.

Now, though, looking at him in his shorts and that lovely shirt, which did incredible things to his fabulous chocolate-brown eyes, she wished she'd made more effort—put on a touch of make-up, her best underwear—

She cut herself off. This was supper for her husband. Nothing more. Nothing huge. They were going to eat, and they were going to talk and make friends again. And if tonight went like last night, he wouldn't let it go any further.

'Anything I can do?'

'Yes—sit down in the dining room and light the candles. I know it's not dark yet, but it's gloomy in there.'

'You're an old romantic, do you know that?' he murmured softly, right behind her. Feathering a kiss over her bare shoulder, he stumped out, the clatter of his crutches almost drowned out by the beating of her heart.

Brodie was looking hopeful, but she was banned. 'Sorry, sweetheart, two's company and all that,' she said, and shut the dog out.

They had oysters to start with. Not Falmouth oysters, because they were out of season, but imported oysters that she'd found on the supermarket fish counter. Normally she wouldn't have dreamed of buying anything so unlocal, out of season and environmentally unsound, but they were on the list, they were reputedly an aphrodisiac and, besides, Mike loved them and he deserved a treat.

'I can't believe we're having oysters,' he said, raising his eyebrows.

'They were on special offer,' she lied, and wondered how many more lies she'd have to tell him before the end of the meal.

He squeezed lemon juice over them and sucked one off the shell. 'Mmm,' he said. 'Not bad. The Fal ones are fresher.'

'Well, they would be. They've only come fifty miles.'

He chuckled. 'Fair point. These are still good, though. Thanks.'

'Pleasure.'

'So—are they part of this diet you've got me on?' he asked casually. 'Because, if so, I think I like it. And I should certainly heal fast.' He looked up, laughing, and was arrested by the guilty look on her face. 'Fran?' he said, slowly lowering the next shell to the plate untouched. What the hell was going on?

She swallowed and knotted her fingers together. She always did that when she was nervous—but why?

'Talk to me,' he said, and she looked up and met his eyes, her own filled with remorse, and he *knew*—he just knew—that she was hiding something. 'It's nothing to do with my leg healing, is it?' he said slowly. 'So what's it all about?'

She got up and went out, coming back seconds later with a folded sheet of paper. She handed it to him, and he opened it and scanned it.

'Fertility-boosting diet?' he said, noticing all the things that were on it that should have rung alarm bells. The lack of tea and coffee, the extra fruit, the smoothies, the raw veg soups, the lack of alcohol—not that they drank much, but if she was going to this much trouble they'd usually share a bottle of wine, but there was fruit juice by their plates, and a jug of water on the table.

He lifted his head and met her wary and slightly defiant eyes. 'Fran?'

'I saw Kate—about the baby thing. She discussed our diet with me.'

She looked guilty, and he had a feeling they'd talked about a lot more than diet. Good, because he'd wanted her to have someone to talk to, but he'd never dreamt she wouldn't discuss things like this with him.

'Why didn't you say anything?' he said, hurt and puzzled that she'd felt the need to lie—*lie, for heaven's sake!*—about something so uncontroversial and trivial. Or was it? Was it that she hadn't been sure if he wanted a child with her? She'd said that last night—did she really believe he didn't? If so, maybe that was why she'd been reluctant to get it out in the open.

'She said it wouldn't hurt to try it, to improve our diet, to get fitter—and then, if we decided we wanted to go ahead and try again for a baby, we'd be in the best possible position.'

He felt a flicker of fear for her, dread that yet again she'd be faced with crippling disappointment or a gut-shredding loss that would leave her devastated.

'If?' he said softly.

Her eyes flicked back to his. 'I wasn't sure if you wanted one—if you didn't feel it was just a lot of angst and hassle, if Sophie wasn't enough for you.'

'This isn't about me, Fran, it's about you, and if you want a baby.'

'I do—but I want yours. And I need you to want it, too. And right now I'm not sure you do.'

He sighed. 'It's not so urgent for me,' he pointed out. 'I've got Sophie, and my clock's not ticking the way yours is. And anyway...' he scanned the paper again, noted the section about boosting sperm production and reducing

DNA damage '…if you want a baby, maybe you'd be better off with someone else.'

'What?'

Her soft, shocked exclamation tore at him, but he went on regardless. 'Maybe, if you want a healthy baby, you'd be safer trying with someone who hasn't already got you pregnant twice with an embryo that was probably flawed.'

'We don't know that that was you!'

'We know that some of the sperm were damaged—that the motility was down a little, that they weren't all perfect.'

'But—everyone's are like that, Mike! It's perfectly normal to have a proportion of sperm that aren't a hundred per cent. It could just as easily have been something to do with the IVF process.'

'Not the first time.'

'Mike, miscarriage is really common,' she said, repeating to him all the things he'd told her again and again, trying to encourage her, to give her confidence to try again, but it sounded as hollow now as it had when he'd said it, and he felt the burden of guilt settle firmly on his shoulders.

'But if it is me,' he said quietly. 'If it is my fault, then I may not be able to give you a baby, Fran. And how many times are you prepared to try? How many miscarriages are you going to go through before you give up? And what if— just consider, for a moment—what if we have a baby that you *should* have miscarried but didn't? A baby nature would normally have rejected as unviable? What if we have a baby with problems—physical or mental disabilities, developmental problems—what then, Fran? Will you be able to forgive yourself for not choosing a better partner? Will you be able to forgive *me*? Because I'm not sure I could.'

She stared at him for an age. 'That could happen to anyone at any time. Are you telling me if we had a disabled baby you couldn't love it?'

'Of course not!' He didn't even have to stop and think about that one. In fact, for a while now he'd been on the point of suggesting to Fran that they adopt a child with special needs, but he'd held back, not ready to concede defeat in the fight for their own child until she was. But she didn't know that, didn't realise that he'd considered it, and now she thought he just couldn't hack it if they had a child with problems.

'Of course not,' he said again. 'But I don't know if I could forgive myself for bringing a child into the world if I had a fair idea that that child would be damaged in some way because of my contribution to its existence. And if that was the case, maybe it would be better to adopt. That's all I meant. Nothing more sinister. And if it *is* me—'

'But I don't want anybody else's baby,' she said with a certainty that brought a lump to his throat. 'I want yours, Mike—and if I can't have yours, then I don't want one at all. We've got Sophie. That's enough. We should be grateful and concentrate on loving her.'

Her voice cracked, and he was up and round the table in a second, his crutches abandoned, hauling her into his arms and cradling her against his chest, unable to bear the desolate look in her eyes. 'Don't give up,' he said gruffly, his eyes prickling. 'We'll take our time, try the diet, have some more tests. And then—if you want to, if you think you can cope with it—we'll try the IVF again.'

'But we can't afford it, Mike, so it's pointless,' she said, her voice clogged with tears.

'Maybe we can,' he told her. 'Ben and Lucy want to buy some of our land around their house. Joe and I are going to have a look at it at the weekend. Ben's talking about paying amenity rates—that's about double what it's worth, at least. I don't want to fleece them, but it'll add significantly to the value of their property, and Joe and Sarah want to do their kitchen—and it would mean we could afford to try again. If you want to.'

She looked up at him, her eyes uncertain, and as he watched, a flicker of hope came to life. 'Really?'

'Really.'

She smiled slightly. 'You'd better sit down and finish your oysters, then,' she said with a return of her old spirit, 'because we've got baked sea bass and new potatoes and mangetout, followed by hazelnut meringue ice cream with mango coulis and chocolate Brazil nuts with decaf coffee to finish up.'

'And then?'

She smiled again, and he could see a pulse beating in her throat.

'Then we go to bed.'

CHAPTER EIGHT

It was the longest meal of his life.

He didn't want it. Every mouthful, delicious though it undoubtedly was, was just another step on the path to the bedroom, and the anticipation was killing him.

Not just the anticipation, though. There was also the fear of failure, of letting down.

What if he rushed her—if, while she was still uneasy about her body, he was too fast for her, in too much of a hurry for his own satisfaction that he left her behind?

No. He couldn't. Not tonight, when it was clearly so significant in the salvation of a marriage he'd realised he wanted more than anything else in the world.

So he ate his meal slowly, mouthful by mouthful, and he talked to her about what he and Joe had done that day down by the river, and they laughed about him taking the saw from Joe and cutting up the part that had trapped him into tiny little bits.

'It's just matchsticks now,' he said, and she laughed again.

'That'll teach it,' she said, and then her laughter faded. 'I was so scared,' she confessed. 'When I saw you trapped under it, when they were just about to pull you out and I saw it shift—I knew it was going, and I thought I was going to lose you.'

'But you didn't.'

'No—but it came too close, Mike. It scared me. It was bad enough that you were injured, without having to watch you die—' She broke off, her eyes filling, and he felt a lump in his throat.

'Well, it didn't happen, and I'm fine.'

'Only because they got you out in the nick of time. Just because you're big and tough, you think nothing can hurt you.'

'You think I'm tough?' he asked, flexing his muscles and flirting with her for the first time in years, and she laughed again, softly.

'You look pretty tough to me.'

Her eyes strayed over him, and he felt the heat building until he thought he'd scream with frustration. But he didn't scream, and he didn't leap to his feet and drag her upstairs. Not that he could, unless he sat down and dragged her up backwards!

Instead they stayed in the dining room for their coffee, but he didn't eat any of the chocolate Brazils. He was full enough—and with the workout he had in mind, he didn't want to be over-full. Even by one mouthful.

And then, at last, it was finished.

The sun was setting, the last fingers of the day pulling back and leaving them alone in the candlelight.

He met her eyes—they were wary, a little nervous, but unflinching, her lips parted, the breath easing in and out of the top of her chest, rapid and unsteady.

It was time.

He pushed back his chair and stood, holding out a hand to her. 'Come to bed with me,' he said softly, and she got to her feet, taking his hand, her eyes locked with his.

'I ought to clear the table,' she said, giving it a guilty glance, but he cupped her chin and turned her back towards him, his fingers gentle.

'Later,' he murmured. 'It'll keep.'

Still she hesitated, killing him, and then she gave a tiny nod, as if she'd made the decision, and, letting go of his hand, she passed him his crutches and headed for the door.

'You go on up. I'll let the dog out,' she said.

He paused. 'Don't be long.'

'I won't.'

He wanted to stay with her, didn't trust her not to change her mind and run away, but by the time he was finished in the bathroom, he could hear her calling the dog in, locking the door, running up the stairs.

Running?

He opened the bathroom door and she was standing there, backlit by the landing light, looking just like the girl he'd fallen in love with, and he smiled.

'Five minutes,' he said, and she smiled back.

'Five minutes,' she agreed.

Lord, she was so nervous!

She'd never felt like this with him, not even the first time, but that had been then and this was now, and so much had happened.

She cleaned her teeth, washed her face and stared at herself in the mirror, wishing she had a gorgeous silk night-dress she could put on, or some really fabulous underwear—something to bolster her confidence and take his eyes off the fact that she was so thin.

But she didn't. Because she hadn't expected things to go so far tonight, she was wearing a pretty but still fairly ordinary bra and a pair of lacy knickers, not very new and not overly glamorous even at the beginning, and a sundress which with the best will in the world was very simple.

But at least it covered her.

Oh, help.

She was so scared that her whole body was shaking. What if she froze at the crucial moment? What if she just couldn't *let* him?

She looked herself in the eye, took a steadying breath and straightened her shoulders.

'You can do it, Fran,' she told herself firmly. 'You can do it.'

He was standing by the window, watching the sun go down.

The room was tinted pink from its last rays, and he held out his hand to her.

'Come here,' he ordered softly, and she went to his side, standing in front of him with his arms around her and his head close to hers. She could feel his heartbeat against her back, feel the steady, solid pounding of it as the sun slipped down into the distant sea, melting away in a flare of crimson and gold.

Then he turned her in his arms, staring down at her, his eyes serious.

'I love you, Francesca,' he said quietly. 'You mean everything to me. You're the reason I get up in the morning, and the reason I come to bed at night. You make the sun shine for me, put colour into everything I do. But if this—my love, our marriage, being here with me—isn't what you want, then I'll let you go. All I'm asking for is one last night, one last chance to put things right between us. Can you give me that? Give me this chance?'

She couldn't believe it. This man, who never showed his feelings, certainly never spoke about them, was baring his soul to her in words that brought tears to her eyes.

And nothing—*nothing*—could have convinced her more that their marriage was worth saving.

She couldn't speak, couldn't find any words to match his, so instead, swallowing the tears and stepping back, she held out her hand to him.

He took it, squeezed it, then swung himself over to the bed, less awkward now on his crutches, and propped them up against the wall, then took her hand again and drew her close.

'I love you,' he breathed, bending his head and touching his lips lightly to hers. She parted her lips but he eased away, cradling her close, pressing soft, breathy kisses to her hair, her temple, her cheek, his lips grazing her skin like the wings of an angel.

She let her head fall over to one side, giving him access to the incredibly sensitive skin of her throat, and she felt the hot trail of his breath as his lips traced slowly down to the hollow at the bottom, the rasp of stubble unbearably erotic.

She could feel her heart beating there, his lips pressed softly to the pulse point. A little cry rose in her throat, and he must have felt it vibrate under his lips because he moved then, lifting his head, staring down into her eyes as if he was trying to read her soul.

He ought to be able to. It was there for him to read, everything she was, everything she felt for him laid out there for him to see.

And maybe he did, because he smiled then, a tiny flicker of encouragement, before his mouth lowered again and he captured her lips with his. She opened to him on a sigh, and this time he settled his mouth against hers, his arms tightening, supporting her as his kiss grew bolder, deepening until she thought her knees would go out from under her.

But he had her, held close against his heart, and finally he lifted his head and stared down at her again.

'I want you, Fran,' he said unsteadily. 'I need you. Not just tonight, but every night, for the rest of our lives. I need you more than I need to breathe.'

'Oh, Mike,' she whispered, the tears that had threatened earlier finally spilling over. 'I need you, too. I love you—so very, very much. I just don't know if I can be the woman you want.'

'You are the woman I want,' he said, his voice vibrating with sincerity, 'and if you can't do this—if you really don't want to, then you're still the woman I want. I still love you. Whatever happens, I'll always love you.'

'I can do this,' she said, her doubts dissolving like mist in the sunshine, leaving her certain. 'Make love to me, Mike. I've missed you so, so much.'

He gave a ragged, broken groan, and his mouth came down on hers hard, seeking, demanding her response, and she rose up on tiptoe, threaded her fingers through his hair and kissed him right back, her tongue tangling with his, stroking, suckling, pleading until he dragged his mouth away and reached for the hem of her dress, pulling it over her head and throwing it aside, his eyes settling on her hungrily.

The bra was gone in a second, then he pushed her back onto the mattress, one hand capturing hers and holding them over her head, the other cupping her heat, his fingers curling hot against her, slipping under the edge of the lace and tracing the soft, aching flesh that wept for his touch.

'Mike, please...' she gasped, and he straightened and stripped them away, leaving her there exposed to his eyes. The bedroom light was off, but the landing light was on and she knew he could see her clearly. Knew by the way his eyes darkened, the way his lips parted and the air hissed out of them.

He grasped her thighs, kneeling, awkward in the cast, and laying hot, open-mouthed kisses from her knee slowly, slowly up her thigh, so near and yet so far...

'Mike, please!'

He looked up, his eyes black. 'Not yet,' he said tightly. Turning his attention to the other leg, his tongue teased the trembling, quivering flesh behind her knee, the soft graze of his stubble torture as he worked his way slowly up her thigh until at last, finally, he was there, his mouth closing over her...

'Mike!'

She felt the tremors start, felt the sensation build as his tongue flicked against her, and then she felt his fingers there, thrusting into her in time with his tongue, and her body arched, a scream leaving her throat as wave after wave of sensation crashed through her, leaving her shaking and stunned in its wake.

'Mike?'

'I'm here,' he growled, his voice rough with need, and she felt a button ping off his shirt and flick against her skin.

He struggled out of the shorts, swearing as they caught on the cast, and then he was beside her, dragging her up the bed and taking her in his arms. With a shuddering sigh he drew her tighter against him, taking her mouth in a wild, desperate kiss that she thought would never end.

It did, finally, but only because he'd moved on, his breath hot against her throat, his lips parted, nipping, nibbling, his tongue like fire licking over her, leaving her shaking and wild with a need every bit as desperate as his own.

Her hands clung to him, plunging into his hair, holding him against her as his chin grazed her chest, her breasts, tormenting her, his breath sighing over her skin until finally, when she thought she would have to scream if he left it another second, his mouth closed hotly over a nipple and she did scream, a sobbing scream of need and frustration satisfied at last.

Except not, because it just made it all much worse, and the need was building again, another need, much greater, and she bucked against him, feeling the hard, urgent thrust of his erection against her thigh. And tonight she was ready for it.

More than ready.

'Mike, please,' she sobbed, her hands dragging at him, and with a fractured groan he shifted over her, settling against the intense, liquid heat, the fire he'd lit in her burning recklessly out of control as he stared down into her eyes and drove deeply into her.

'Oh, God, Fran, I love you,' he said brokenly, and then he started to move, the long, slow thrusts driving her higher, higher, until with a sobbing cry she felt her body tighten around him and sensation flooded her again. He drove into her one last time, then stiffened against her, a great groan torn from his chest as his body convulsed with the devastating power of his release, and then with a ragged sob he rolled to the side, taking her with him, cradling her against his heart as if he'd never let her go...

He held her all night.

She woke towards dawn, and he made love to her again, slowly, tenderly, afraid he'd hurt or frighten her, but she clung to him, her breathy sighs sweet music to his ears, and as she curled against him to sleep again, there was a smile on her face.

He didn't smile. He was too close to tears, too moved to speak. He just held her, thankful for the chance, hoping that the future wouldn't prove too much for them but a little more confident now that they would make it.

They had to, because without her he would be nothing.

Fran woke again later, the sun well up, and found Mike gone.

She could hear his voice in the kitchen, and she slipped out of bed, hot colour scorching her cheeks as she saw the trail of underwear strewn across the floor. She scooped it up, showered and dressed quickly and went downstairs.

'Hi, Fran,' Joe said, and then did a mild double-take before turning away, just a fraction too slowly to hide his smile.

She felt the heat climb her cheeks again and went over to the kettle. 'Any tea in the pot?' she asked brightly.

'I should make some fresh,' Joy said. 'It's been there a while. I would have brought you up a cup but Mike said to let you sleep.'

'Mmm,' she said, filling the kettle and avoiding Mike's eye. They hadn't exchanged a word since last night, and she felt ludicrously self-conscious and aware, her body still humming from his touch. If she looked at him…

'How about a fruit smoothie?'

Oh, lord. He was right behind her, his body big and powerful and radiating heat. He rested his hand on her hip, and she leant against him, wondering what his family would make of their closeness and deciding it was none of their business. 'OK,' she said, surprised by his suggestion as well as his closeness. 'Want one?'

'Please.'

She met his eyes, saw the unspoken message and smiled. So he was engaging with this diet, taking it seriously, even though she knew he was afraid for her in case it all went wrong again. She went up on tiptoe, brushed a kiss over his lips and then pulled a selection of fruit out of the fridge.

'Two smoothies coming up,' she said lightly. Chopping the fruit, she wondered how long his family were going to hang around before they left them in peace so they could go back to bed and carry on where they'd left off…

It was a glorious few days.

Fran absconded from the farm, taking Mike to get his cast changed again and his stitches removed. The skin had healed well, and the swelling had subsided a lot, so they put on a lightweight walking cast and told him to start bearing weight.

Which meant they could do more, and so they did. They drove down to Penhally and had lunch in the Smugglers, then sat on the harbour wall in the sunshine and watched the children crabbing off the jetty, and then they went home and went back to bed and made love until the racket in the kitchen told them that milking was over and Joe was returning Brodie to them.

She pulled on her clothes and went down, Mike following her a few moments later when he'd dressed himself more slowly, and if the family was studiously avoiding looking at them, she didn't care, because she'd got her husband back, the man she'd loved for years and thought she'd lost, and she wasn't going to be ashamed of spending time with him in their own home.

Even if it was the afternoon!

'Can you guys manage without us for a day or so?' Mike asked, coming up behind her and wrapping his arms round her, the declaration so blatant they couldn't fail to understand it.

In unison they chorused, 'Of course!'

'Going anywhere nice?' Sarah asked.

Joe started to say something and got her elbow in the ribs for his pains, and Joy and Russell just looked at each other and smiled.

'We might take a run down to Falmouth if the weather stays fair,' Mike said. 'Don't really know. We haven't made any plans, but as I can't really do anything and Fran hasn't had a holiday for ages, we thought we might just take off for a night or so. Could you hang on to Brodie till Sunday?'

'Sure.' Joe nodded. 'Got a hotel in mind?'

Fran felt Mike shrug. 'No plans. We'll see where the road takes us.'

In the end they found a fabulous hotel right on the clifftop with spectacular views of the rugged Cornish coast, and booked in for two nights, taking advantage of a late cancellation, and spent most of the day in bed, making love slowly and lazily, getting to know each other again—and talking.

Talking like they'd never talked before, talking about anything and everything.

Everything except the whole baby thing. That was taboo, a sort of tacit avoidance, because at the end of the day all that really mattered was that they loved each other. Anything else was just the icing on the cake.

And then, relaxed and comfortable with each other, closer than they'd ever been, they went home because Sophie was coming, and Mike broke the taboo.

'Will you be OK?' he asked, and she smiled, realising with surprise that she would.

'I'll be fine,' she told him. 'And I'm looking forward to seeing her again.'

Sophie was fizzing with excitement, of course, because Kirsten and Andrew had told her about the baby and she was utterly obsessed with the prospect. She talked about it non-stop, her holiday hardly getting a mention, and Fran thought it was just as well she was OK with it, because if this had happened before she and Mike had spent the last few days together in their glorious idyll, it would have been intolerable.

But then Sophie snuggled up to her that evening, her restless little body finally still, and said, 'I wish you could have a baby too, 'cos then I could have a baby in *both* my homes!'

It was the 'homes' that did it for Fran. The fact that Sophie still considered this to be her home, even though she and her mother had moved out of it years ago and she now had another home, nearly moved Fran to tears. She hugged the little girl tighter, looking up and meeting Mike's eyes and giving him a supporting smile, because his mouth had pressed together and his eyes were over-bright.

'That would be nice, wouldn't it, Mike?' she said. 'We'll have to think about it.'

'Maybe one day, sweetheart,' he said softly, looking at Sophie, but Fran felt his words were for her. 'And, anyway, you might like coming here and having a bit of peace at night without the baby crying,' he added, this time definitely to his daughter, and her nose wrinkled.

'Babies do cry a lot, don't they? And they smell. Suzie's mum's got a baby and she had to change his nappy the other day when I was there and it was *really* smelly!'

Fran chuckled and hugged her again, then stood up. 'Come on, young lady, it's time for bed.'

'Oh, do I have to? I haven't seen you for *ages*!'

'It's only two days longer than usual, so don't give us that rubbish,' Mike said with a laugh, standing up and scooping his daughter off the sofa and throwing her over his shoulder. He winced as his ribs twinged, but Fran handed him the crutch he was using as a stick and he hobbled out of the room, Sophie draped over his shoulder and giggling.

'Mike, are you sure you're OK to put her to bed, or do you want me to do it?' Fran asked as he limped away.

'I can do it. I'm fine,' he assured her. Sliding Sophie down to the floor at the bottom of the stairs, he clapped his hands behind her and chased her up. She won easily, because he still found the stairs hard, but she heard him stumping along the landing, a great roar and a little shriek echoing back down the stairs, and Fran hoped he wasn't doing too much for his ankle.

Whatever, she thought. He was a grown man, he knew if it hurt or not and she wasn't his mother. He had one of those already, making more than enough fuss over him, so she really didn't need to join in.

She went into the kitchen and made them some fennel tea, letting it brew while she loaded the dishwasher, and by the time she'd finished he was down. 'All tucked up?'

'Mmm.' He came up behind her, put his arms round her and sniffed. 'Smells interesting.'

'Fennel tea,' she said, turning her head to look at him, and his eyes narrowed suspiciously.

'Really?'

'Really. Try it, it's really refreshing.'

He looked doubtful, but then his eyes twinkled mischievously. 'One condition.'

'What's that?'

'I get a reward for drinking it.'

'Such as?'

He smiled lazily. 'Oh—I'm sure you can work it out.' He bent his head and brushed a feather-soft kiss over her shoulder, trailing his lips up the side of her neck and nibbling her ear with his lips.

'Michael Trevellyan, behave,' she said, giggling and swatting him away, but her knees were like jelly and her heart was pounding and she could feel her body responding to his instantly.

'I don't want to,' he said, suddenly serious. 'I've missed this, Fran. It's been too long. Come here.'

And he turned her into his arms, stepped forwards so he

trapped her between the cupboards and his long, hard body and, wedging his thigh between hers, he took her mouth in a kiss that surely would have set the kitchen on fire if the phone hadn't rung to interrupt them.

'Rats,' he said mildly, easing away from her, his eyes blazing with promise. 'Remember where we got to.' And he picked up the phone. 'Trevellyan.'

He winked at her, then said, 'Sure. That'll be fine. I'll have Sophie with me, but she's no trouble.' His eyes flicked to Fran's, his gaze assessing, the mischief gone, and he said, 'That would be lovely. Thanks. I'll check with Fran and get back to you if there's a problem. See you tomorrow—two? Fine.'

He put the phone down. 'That was Ben Carter,' he said, and she thought his voice sounded a little wary. 'He's got a couple of days off, and they've invited us for a barbeque tomorrow. He wants to look over the land with me, show me where he's talking about so I can discuss it with Joe later.'

And, of course, the baby would be there. 'That's nice,' she said, summoning a smile, and it was, of course. It would be lovely. Annabel was gorgeous, and she couldn't isolate herself from everyone just in case she ever encountered a baby. She taught the reception class of a primary school, for heaven's sake! She was surrounded by babies and toddlers and pregnant women at every turn.

And just because, for now at least, she wasn't able to join them, it didn't mean she wanted to avoid them.

'You really OK with it?'

She smiled again, a bit more convincingly. 'Yes, Mike. I'm OK with it. It'll be lovely. Stop worrying. I can cope—I have to. And Sophie will be in her element. She'll be able to tell Lucy all about the new baby that's coming and practise on Annabel. Why don't you ring them back and say yes? I'll make a salad and we can take some steaks and burgers from the farm shop. It'll be fun.'

And if she told herself that enough times, maybe she'd believe it…

CHAPTER NINE

IT WAS an absolutely gorgeous day, and Sophie was up with the larks, bursting into their bedroom and clambering onto the bed, effectively putting an end to their early-morning cuddle.

Especially as the dog came too, trampling all over them and lashing Mike with her tongue.

Fran ducked under the bedclothes with a little shriek, Mike yelled at Brodie and told her to get down, then he must have grabbed Sophie because she started to giggle hysterically.

'No, no, stop!' she screamed, then there was a yelp from Mike, and Fran emerged from the bedclothes to find him sitting up and holding his ribs, his mouth open as he gasped with pain.

'I only tickled him back,' Sophie said, her eyes flooding with tears, and Mike reached out and tucked her under his right arm, well away from the damaged ribs, and kissed the top of her head as she burrowed into him, sobbing heartbrokenly.

'It's OK, sweetheart, don't cry, I'm fine,' he said softly. 'It wasn't you, it was because I jumped. You didn't hurt me.'

Her head came out from his side and she stared up at him soulfully. 'Are you sure?'

'I'm sure. Come here.'

So she snuggled back into his side and, reaching out her hand, caught hold of Fran and tugged her over, pulling her into the cuddle, too.

'That's better,' she said, and for a few minutes they all lay there quietly until Sophie's natural ebullience returned. 'So— what are we going to do today? Can we go to the beach?'

'Not while your dad's got his cast on,' Fran said, saving him from having to tell her. 'Anyway, we're doing something much more exciting. We're going to see Ben and Lucy Carter, just down the road at Tregorran House, and they've got a little baby girl called Annabel. I expect you'll be able to play with her.'

Sophie wriggled round and looked up at Fran, eyes sparkling. 'Is she very new?'

'Not very. She was born on Christmas Eve, but she's still pretty tiny. She can't do a lot, but you can play peep-bo with her and teach her how to play with her toys, I expect.'

'Can I hold her?'

'I don't know. Maybe.'

'That means no,' Sophie said with an exaggerated sigh.

'No, it means maybe,' Fran reiterated, 'and it depends on Lucy.'

'That's not till this afternoon, though,' Mike put in, 'so what do you want to do this morning?'

'Go riding,' Sophie said promptly. 'Can I? Please? Mummy said you might let me.'

Mike met Fran's eyes. 'Got any other plans?'

She shook her head. 'No. I've got things to do here, like

picking up the eggs and mucking out the chickens, and they might need a hand in the farm shop, but if I get up early and get on with it—since I already seem to be awake,' she added, wriggling her fingers into Sophie's ribs and making her giggle, 'I might as well get on. Why don't you two have a bit of a rest and make some breakfast for me? And by the time you've done that, I'll have finished with the chickens. And I'll take Brodie with me, she could do with a bit of a run. It might be late enough then to ring the stables and see if they can fit you in.'

They could, and they set off at a quarter to eleven, Sophie fizzing with excitement. They turned into the stableyard and pulled up, and she was out of the door and hopping from foot to foot with impatience while Mike sorted out his crutches.

'Come on, you, hold my hand and let's go and find Georgina,' Fran said to her, and Sophie slipped her hand into Fran's and all but dragged her over to where a few fat little ponies were tied up to a rail by the stables. Children were milling around them, brushing and fussing over them, and the ponies stood patiently and tolerated it with what Fran felt was very good grace.

'Hi, Sophie, haven't seen you for a while,' Georgina Somers said, coming over and smiling at them. 'You're looking well, unlike your dad—he's been in the wars, hasn't he?'

'He broke his leg,' Sophie said, a little unnecessarily as Mike hobbled towards them in his cast, leaning heavily on one crutch and grinning.

'Really?' Georgina teased, then flashed a smile at Mike which might have made Fran jealous if she hadn't been loved so very thoroughly by him the night before. 'The wounded soldier. I heard about your accident. Good to see you up and about.'

'Good to be up and about. They gave me a walking cast the other day—it's so much better, but I must say I'm a bit scared about my toes. I'm used to steel toecaps, and I feel a bit vulnerable.'

'Mmm. I did when I broke my leg. Right, Sophie, let's get you a hat sorted out and then pop you up on your pony. You're riding Bracken today.'

'Oh, goody, I love Bracken! He's really nice.'

'She says that about every one of them,' Mike murmured as Georgina took Sophie to get her hat. 'She'd love us to buy her one—that's the trouble with bringing her here, we'll have nothing else for the rest of the week, and there's no way she's having a pony part time, it just isn't fair. Apart from anything else, I've got more than enough to do without pooh-picking and grooming and changing rugs and so forth, and that's never the end, is it? There's always another one, and then another one, because the first is too small and then the next one will be lonely and then you can't get rid of the old one and it just goes on. I know so many farmers who're overrun with their children's first ponies and they just can't get rid of them.'

Fran chuckled. 'Sounds to me like a done job,' she teased, but he shook his head.

'No way, Fran. To tell you the truth, I don't really like her riding. It's dangerous, and the odd ride from time to time is OK, but all the time? She's only six—it's too risky. So I'm just going to keep saying no to her own pony and letting her come here instead. She's too precious to us.'

She was. Fran watched her skipping out of the tack room in a body protector and a hat with a shocking pink silk cover on it, looking utterly delectable, and she felt her eyes fill.

'I have to keep her safe, Fran,' Mike said, and she heard the little catch in his voice.

'Don't worry. I'll back you up.'

His hand found hers and squeezed. 'Thanks.'

The lesson passed without incident. Well, more or less. One little girl ended up on her bottom in the sand school, but she was all right and got up laughing, and another ended up in tears because her pony ran off with her and wouldn't stop, and a boy wanted to change ponies because his wouldn't go, and Georgina refused and told him that when he gave the pony the correct cues, it would understand. And of course, eventually, when he got it right, the pony trotted forwards nicely and Fran suppressed a smile.

'Know him?'

'Oh, yes. I know most of them. He's a bit of a bully. It's nice to see something big enough and stubborn enough to beat him. Take him down a peg or two. It'll do him good.'

'OK, everybody, that's it now. Give your ponies a nice big pat and take them back out and tie them up. Well done, all of you.'

Georgina opened the gate, and the ponies filed out.

'That was so cool! Daddy, can I have a pony? I really, *really* want one!' Sophie said, the pleading starting before she'd even dismounted, and Mike rolled his eyes at Fran and gave a hollow laugh.

'Kids,' he said under his breath. 'Do we really need another one?'

Fran stopped in her tracks, and after another step Mike came to a halt and turned back to her, his face stricken.

'Oh, hell, Fran, I didn't mean that! Darling, I'm sorry.'

'It's OK,' she said, struggling to find a smile. 'I know it was a joke.'

'No, it was a stupid, thoughtless remark—I'm so, so sorry, Fran. I don't know what I was thinking about.'

She shook her head. 'Not here, Mike. Not now. I'm fine—really. Just let it go.'

But it put a dampener on the drive back and, while Sophie chattered happily about the pony and how she wanted one of her own and what she was going to call it, Mike stared straight ahead, and Fran tried to concentrate on driving and wondered just how much of a joke it really had been, and how much he'd meant it.

Many a true word is spoken in jest, she thought. Maybe he really doesn't want another child after all and he's just playing along with me out of pity? It would explain the way he'd kept his distance all these last months, and although he'd said it was because he was afraid of getting her pregnant again, that he couldn't bear the possibility of her having another miscarriage, maybe that was just an excuse, something legitimate he could use to hide his real feelings behind.

They got back to the farm, and Joy was just coming out of the farm shop as they pulled up.

'Grannie!' Sophie yelled. Sliding out of the car, she ran over to her grandmother and started telling her about her riding lesson.

Mike opened the car door and swung round, eased himself out and hobbled over to his mother. 'Are you busy?'

'No, not at all. Why?'

'Just wondered if you'd like to spend a little time with Sophie—who, incidentally, knows she's not having a pony of her own, so don't let her try and talk you round—while I have a bit of a rest? And Fran's got some things to do, so if you don't mind?'

Fran watched them, heard his words, saw his mother nod agreement and look up, meeting her eyes with concern.

'Is everything OK?' she was asking, but Fran couldn't take any more. She turned away and, locking the car, went into the house, leaving Mike to follow her.

He couldn't believe he'd said that.

Of all the crass, stupid remarks!

He limped into the house, calling her name, and found her eventually in their bedroom, stripping the bed with fierce concentration, her movements almost savage. He went over to her, took her hands in his, held them against his heart.

'Frankie, talk to me.'

'No, you talk to *me*,' she cried, wrenching her hands away and stripping off the pillow case with enough force to tear it. 'You tell *me* what you really feel, what you really want. Because I thought I knew, and then I suddenly realised that maybe I didn't know at all, maybe you don't really want a baby with me despite all the stuff you've said over the last few days, and I have to *know*, Mike,' she said, throwing down the pillow with a ragged sob. '*I have to know!*'

Her eyes were filled with tears, and with a rough sigh he hauled her up against his chest and hugged her tight. 'I want a baby,' he said emphatically. 'I want your baby. Our baby. And what I said was just a knee-jerk reaction to kids in general, and nothing to do with us. I know it was stupid, but I thought—Frankie, I thought we'd sorted this out? Thought you knew how I felt. Of course I want a baby. You know I do.'

'No, I don't, Mike,' she said, her body still and unresponsive in his arms. 'I really don't, not any more.'

'Oh, God.' He sighed, and let her go, frustration at his stupidity making him want to scream. He paced away, then turned back to her, scrubbing his hands through his hair. 'How can I prove it?' he asked desperately.

'Let me try again,' she said. 'I know you said you couldn't bear the thought of me having a miscarriage, but it isn't you that has to bear it. It's me. So let me. Or, at least, let's think about it, because for the last few days we haven't talked about it at all, and I want to, in the context of our relationship now. Not what it's been, but what it is now. I know you love me. I know you want me. But I need the truth from you about this, Mike. I need to know that you really, really want a child with me, not that you're just going along with me, humouring me. Indulging me.'

'I'm not,' he said instantly. 'Never. I want a baby with you, Fran. I've said it over and over again. I know what it means to you, how it's tearing you apart, but it means a lot to me, too. It's not just for you. I want a child as well—a child who'll live here with us, a child to share every moment of our lives, not just the odd weekend. I adore Sophie, and I wish she could be here with us more, but if I'd stayed with Kirsten I would have wanted more children. Sophie shouldn't be alone, and this house needs kids, Fran. Either ours or somebody else's. And if we can't have a baby of our own, then I'd like to adopt one—or more. Maybe disabled in some way, a child nobody wants. Not necessarily a pretty little baby but a real person with needs that maybe, with enough love, we could meet. The farm's a wonderful place to be a child, and nature has a way of healing all sorts of hurts. This would be a good place to let that happen.

'So, yes, I do want a child. With you. And I'll do whatever it takes, for as long as you want to try. And failing that, I'd like to adopt, because I want to be a full-time father. I love being a father. It's part of who I am, and I want to share it with you. Does that answer your questions?'

She stared at him, then gave a scratchy little laugh. 'Pity I wrecked the bed,' she said, 'because I could just do with lying down in it with you and having a really big cuddle.'

'Oh, you idiot,' he said, his voice cracking. Limping quickly back to her, he grabbed the pillows off the floor, shoved the quilt out of the way and lay down, pulling her down after him. 'Come here,' he said gruffly. Wrapping his arms round her, he sighed deeply and pressed a kiss to her forehead. 'I'm sorry,' he murmured. 'Forgive me?'

She tilted her head back and smiled. 'I forgive you. Actually, I more than forgive you. Maybe I need to push you more often, because you get really honest then, and tell me all the things you've been keeping to yourself. Like this adoption business. How long have you been thinking about that?'

He shrugged. 'I don't know. Ages. Years, probably. Since I married Kirsten.'

'Then let's do it. If I have a baby, great. If I don't—well, we'll do as you said. Maybe do it anyway.'

He looked down at her, saw new determination in her

eyes and kissed her. 'One thing at a time,' he cautioned, and she smiled.

'It's all right, Mike,' she said. 'You won't wake up one morning and find we're running a children's home, but it's something to think about. Something for the future.'

She settled her head down on his chest. 'Now go to sleep. We've only got a short time before we have to get ready to go to the Carters'.'

'Seems a shame to waste it,' he murmured, and she lifted her head again and looked up at him.

'Are we making up for lost time?' she asked.

He chuckled. 'Is that a problem?'

'No problem,' she said, and kissed him.

The baby was gorgeous.

Sophie was captivated, and when the men wandered off to look at the fields, Fran asked Lucy if there was anything she could do to help and ended up with Annabel in her arms.

'Oh, that's better. She can pull your hair instead of mine,' Lucy said with a laugh, kissing the baby's nose and making her giggle deliciously. She clapped her chubby hands in delight, and Fran caught one of them and blew a raspberry on it, making her giggle even harder.

'I want to blow a raspberry,' Sophie said, and Fran crouched down so Sophie could reach, and the baby giggled again and grabbed Sophie's curls.

'Ouch!' Sophie said with a laugh, gently pulling her hair out of Annabel's fingers. She danced over to Lucy and said, eyes sparkling, 'I'm going to have a baby too!'

'Oh!' Lucy spun round, her eyes also sparkling, and

said, 'Oh, Fran, that's so lovely, because so am I! When's yours due?'

Oh, lord. 'Um…it's not me, it's Kirsten—Sophie's mother,' she explained, wondering if everything today was going to be destined to floor her, 'but congratulations! That's really lovely for you.'

'Oh, well—it's a bit quick. Fran, I'm really sorry,' she added, her eyes conveying her regret.

'It's a shame it's not you and Daddy,' Sophie chipped in, looking up at her with wistful eyes. 'That would have been so nice.'

Wouldn't it just? Fran thought, and banished it. She was going to enjoy herself this afternoon. One thing at a time, Mike had said, and she was starting now, having a lovely cuddle with little Annabel to fill her achingly empty arms.

'But perhaps you could have one too,' Sophie went on, as relentless as ever. 'Daddy said maybe one day, so maybe it could be a *soon* maybe instead of a never maybe. He usually means never, though. Like the pony. He said maybe once, when I was four, but now he just says no.'

Lucy laughed a little awkwardly. 'I think a baby's a bit different, Sophie. I'm sure Fran and your father will have a baby when it's right for them.'

'What if it's never right?'

'Then you'll have your mother's new baby anyway,' Fran pointed out. 'And, like your father said, it might be nice to come to us and have a bit of peace.'

Lucy rolled her eyes. 'Amen to that,' she said fervently. 'This one still doesn't always go through the night and by the time she does, I expect I'll have the other one.'

A shadow fell across the room, and Mike and Ben walked into the kitchen.

'All right, girls?' Mike asked, scanning their faces and picking up on the atmosphere.

'Fine,' Fran said.

But then Sophie opened her mouth and said, 'Guess what, Daddy? Lucy's having another baby!'

'So—what do you think about the fields, Mike?' Lucy asked.

They'd finished eating, Annabel had been put down for a nap and Sophie was standing on the other side of the track, talking to Amber through the fence. The adults were all sitting round in the shade, sipping a nicely chilled rosé.

'Oh, I think we should be able to do something,' he said, very conscious of the need for money so they could afford another IVF cycle, and yet wondering how they could possibly charge the Carters the going rate for a bit of land that was little more than useless to the farm.

'You're having a fit of conscience,' Ben said astutely, narrowing his eyes. 'Don't. We want it, you've got it—it's called supply and demand, Mike.'

'I think we need an independent valuation,' he said, wondering if he was shooting himself in the foot and if they'd end up without the land and with not enough money to do anything. Not that losing the land mattered, because the bit the Carters were most interested in was essentially worthless to the farm. And that was the problem, of course. Oh, damn.

'I'll get the auctioneer who sold us the house to have a look, shall I?' Ben said. 'Unless you've got a better suggestion?'

'No, he's fine. He's the man, I would have said.'

'Well, we'll do that, then,' Ben said, picking up the wine bottle. 'Top-up?'

Mike shook his head. 'No. I'm still on painkillers. I shouldn't, really,' he lied, although he had taken one the night before after chasing Sophie up the stairs, so it wasn't really a total lie.

'Fran?'

She shook her head. 'No, I'm fine, Ben, thank you. It was lovely.' She looked at Mike. 'We ought to go, darling. I promised Sarah I'd give her a hand to restock the shelves in the shop, and Sophie could do with a bath. She's covered in cow slobber.'

'Right. Ben, I'll have a chat to Joe—I might see him tonight. He's doing the milking. I'll talk to you when we've got the valuation.'

They took their leave, Sophie reluctant to drag herself away from Amber and wanting to stay until Annabel woke up. But Mike bribed her with the promise of hot chocolate in the bath, and Fran drove them home and went over to the farm shop, leaving Mike to deal with Sophie.

He was clearing up the bathroom while Sophie was getting into her pyjamas when Joe called up the stairs.

'Sophie, come down when you're ready,' he said, sticking his head round the door, and he hobbled downstairs to the kitchen.

'Hi. I'm glad you popped in. We've been with Ben and Lucy, and he's walked me over the fields and shown me what he wants. I've got the plans.'

'OK.'

He looked at his brother's face, wondering what was wrong. Something, that was for sure, because Joe was looking troubled. 'What is it? Don't tell me we've got foot and mouth or something, because I don't want to know.'

'No!' Joe laughed awkwardly. 'No, it's nothing like that. It's just—oh, hell, bro, I don't know how to tell you, so I'm just going to say it. Sarah's pregnant.'

Oh, God, not another one. Mike stood motionless for a second, then forced his face into a smile. 'That's really great news,' he said, but his voice sounded hollow and Joe couldn't fail to notice.

He didn't. He said something very rude, and then added, 'You don't have to lie. I know what this news means to you, and I'm so sorry. It wasn't really planned, but actually we're thrilled to bits—or we would be, if it wasn't for you guys.'

'You *be* thrilled to bits,' Mike said gruffly, grabbing his brother and hugging him hard. 'It's fantastic news, and I really, really am pleased for you. Just because we're having trouble, it doesn't mean nobody else in the county can have a baby.'

'But it's not just us, is it?' Joe said quietly. 'Sarah told me Kirsten's pregnant.'

'And Lucy,' Mike said flatly. 'But, hey, that's life. We're all the right age, it's bound to happen. Anyway, we're talking about maybe trying the IVF again. That's why I want to talk to you about this land. We're getting the agent who sold the house to have a look and value it, but I don't know what we should ask.'

'How about splitting the difference between agricultural rates and what it would add to the value of their house?' Joe suggested. 'That would seem fair. And if it isn't enough, we don't have to refit the kitchen. It all works—

and with the baby coming, I don't know if we'll want that much upheaval. You could have it all.'

'That's not fair.'

'Life isn't. Sometimes it sucks. And if you need help, you just have to ask. This is more important than the kitchen, and the clock's ticking, Mike. We don't want Fran to run out of time because we want some fancy new cupboards and a bigger fridge.' He glanced at his watch. 'Got to go, I've still got to feed the calves again before I can stop. Let me know if there's any news on the valuation.'

'Will do. And tell Sarah congratulations for me.'

Joe nodded and went out, leaving Mike alone with his thoughts. Not a happy place to be. He couldn't believe it was happening again.

It was going to kill Fran. And once again he was going to have to be the one to tell her.

'Everything all right, Fran?'

His eyes held hers for a second then slid away, something that could have been guilt lurking in their depths, and Fran stared at him, her heart breaking. He knew. He actually knew, and he hadn't said anything! He'd been upstairs putting Sophie to bed when she'd come back from helping Sarah, and just when she'd needed him, he hadn't been there.

And now she discovered that he'd already known, and he hadn't told her. Just when she'd thought there were no secrets. Why hadn't he told her?

'Oh, just peachy,' she said flatly.

'Fran, I'm sorry,' he began, but she cut him off.

'How long have you known?'

He sighed. 'About half an hour,' he said heavily, taking the wind out of her sails. 'Joe told me while Sophie was getting her pyjamas on. I'm really sorry, darling.'

And he was, she could see that. His throat was working, his eyes were sad and he held out his arms to her. She walked into them, laid her head on his chest and sighed, the fight going out of her and leaving only sadness.

'I'm sorry, too,' she said. 'Sorry I jumped down your throat. I thought you'd been keeping it from me for a while.'

'No. So I take it Sarah told you?'

She gave a strangled little laugh. 'Not exactly. I found some coffee that was past its sell-by date and handed it to her, commenting on the lovely smell, and she dropped it and ran. Bit of a give-away, really.'

He rubbed her shoulders with his hand, the other hand lying lightly in the small of her back and holding her against him comfortingly.

'I'm sorry. If I'd known, I would have told you, given you some warning.'

She sighed and eased out of his arms. 'Don't be silly. You can't protect me from every pregnant woman in Cornwall, Mike.' Although there did seem to be an extraordinary number of them. It just seemed so hard, when they wanted a baby so much, and they hadn't done anything wrong. Surely they *deserved* a baby of their own as much as anyone else?

She looked up and met Mike's worried eyes and smiled, but the honeymoon was over, and the yearning was back in spades.

Mike saw the change in her eyes, saw the fragile happiness of the past few days recede and the longing take its place, and he felt a flicker of dread return.

Damn. He'd hoped for longer to build on their relationship, more time to celebrate the joy they'd found in each other, to cement the foundations of their marriage before they'd had to face this.

And now it had all caught up with them again.

It came to a head later, after they'd made love and were lying in each other's arms. He was stroking her, his hand running lightly up and down her spine, and he could feel the tension in her, the determination in every line of her body, and he knew it was coming.

Her voice was just a murmur. 'Mike?'

'Mmm?'

'I want to try again,' she said softly.

He didn't pretend not to understand. 'Maybe we should persevere with this diet for another few months,' he suggested, stalling because he couldn't bear to lose this newfound closeness, and he was afraid that when they started the awful business of the injections and whatever all over again, that was exactly what would happen. 'Really give it time to work.'

'Maybe. I'll talk to Kate,' she said, but although she was lying still against him, he could sense the restlessness in her, the urge to do something *now*, and he knew she wouldn't be stalled, that this was it.

'Fran?' he prompted. 'Talk to me.'

She shifted slightly, sighed. 'Oh, Mike, I want a baby—I *need* a baby—and I can't afford to waste time. I'm thirty-four—my clock's ticking. I'm getting old for this, and if we can get the money from Ben and Lucy—I think we have to try.'

He sighed softly and drew her closer. She was right. She was getting on, in reproductive terms, and if her system was starting to shut down, they didn't have the luxury of waiting. But it wasn't easy.

'Are you sure, my love?' he said quietly. 'It's so hard on you—the hormones made you so sick before, the headaches…'

'I don't mind,' she said, her voice soft but firm. 'I can do this, Mike. I'm not looking forward to it, and I won't pretend I'm not scared that it'll all go wrong again, but I'll do it, and if it ends in a baby, I'd go through it ten times. Fifty.'

Oh, lord. So much courage. He'd seen what it had done to her, the side-effects of the treatment, the indignity and invasion of personal space—it had nearly cost them their marriage, and then when she'd lost it…

'Mike?'

Her voice was tentative now, seeking reassurance, and he pressed his lips to her hair and held her close. 'I'm here,' he promised. 'I'll always be here. There's not much else I can do to help you, but I can do that. I can be here for you, and support you, and we'll do whatever you feel you can bear.'

He just hoped Ben's surveyor came up with the goods.

CHAPTER TEN

'I'VE got Fran and Mike Trevellyan coming in to see me on Monday.'

Nick cocked his head on one side and raised a brow slightly. 'Any idea why?'

'They didn't say, but I suspect they want to talk about trying another cycle of IVF,' Kate said. 'You know I gave Fran the fertility-boosting diet sheet and lots of other advice and information?'

'Mmm—that was the day of his accident, wasn't it? They'll need longer that that. It was only a few weeks ago—three, wasn't it?'

'Something like that. It's certainly not long enough to have made a great deal of difference, and if they want to go ahead I'll encourage them to wait a bit longer, but I don't know if that's what they want.'

'Well, we know she's not pregnant,' Nick told her, lounging back in his chair and fiddling with his pen. 'Lucy told me she made a bit of a faux pas the other day—Sophie said she was going to have a baby brother or sister and Lucy assumed it was Mike and Fran having the baby and congratulated Fran, but it turned out it's Sophie's mother, Kirsten. Lucy felt dreadful.'

'I can imagine. Poor Fran.' Kate sighed softly. 'She said to me last time how it was funny that everyone seemed to be pregnant. And now Lucy and Kirsten are pregnant as well. Oh, dear.'

'And Joe and Sarah, although I don't know if Mike and Fran know that yet.'

Kate sat down, deeply troubled. 'I hope this isn't going to push them into a hasty decision.'

'Hardly hasty. They've been trying for years.'

'But they weren't ready, Nick. Only weeks ago when she came to see me their marriage was in ruins.'

'Well, not now. Not according to Lucy. They were there on Monday for a barbeque, and she said the air between them was sizzling.'

'Interesting.' Kate frowned. 'So maybe they just want to chat through the next stage in the process.'

'What time are they coming? I could drop in if I'm free.'

She gave a dry chuckle. 'I think I can manage to counsel a couple trying for a baby rather better than you,' she pointed out.

'Why do you say that?' he protested, bristling, and she gave him a wry look.

'Because I spent six years trying to have a baby and so I know where they're coming from?' she said softly. 'Because—correct me if I'm wrong—not one of your four children was planned or anticipated in any way, and infertility just doesn't even cross your mind? And neither, apparently, does your fertility, so if it's all the same with you, I'll handle the Trevellyans my way. And if you're very good, I'll tell you what it's all about.'

She got up and walked out, his growl of frustration clearly audible, then his barked 'Shut the door, then!' followed her down the corridor.

'Pretty please,' she said, sticking her head back round it, and got a sour look for her pains.

'I can't believe you think I'd be so bad at this,' he muttered, scowling. Oh, dear, poor Nick. He obviously felt insulted, but she didn't care. Her feelings were all with Mike and Fran, and Nick was big enough and ugly enough to take care of himself.

'Get over it,' she advised, and shut the door.

It was the longest week of Fran's life.

Well, no, it wasn't. Waiting to hear that she was pregnant after their IVF at the beginning of the year had been dreadful. This, waiting for their appointment with Kate to find out when they could start the process again, was different, but she felt so impatient to be getting on with it that every day dragged.

Mike was doing a bit more on the farm now, serving in the farm shop and doing the dreaded paperwork, but he didn't start at stupid o'clock in the morning and he wasn't coming to bed late, so they had plenty of time together to reinforce their new-found closeness.

With his gentleness and passion he'd repossessed her body from the grip of the medical profession, and their relationship was stronger and better than it had ever been. And it would have been wonderful if it wasn't for the suspense.

A few things broke it up. Amber had her calf, and

Sophie was there and saw it born, something Mike had no problem with and Kirsten was annoyed about.

'It's nature—she needs to know,' he said when Sophie was out of earshot.

'And I'm pregnant, and I don't want all sorts of embarrassing questions!' Kirsten protested. 'I can hear them all now— Oh, God, I could kill you sometimes, Mike.'

'Feel free to try,' he said blandly. 'She's my daughter, too, and I grew up knowing where babies come from. It didn't do me any harm. It was just one of those things. Better to know from the start than to be totally grossed out by the idea when you're twelve or so.'

'But to *see* it!'

'It was lovely,' Fran chipped in in his defence. 'She was captivated. Believe me, Kirsten, I teach in a rural area, and the kids that see animals reproduce have a much greater acceptance of sexual matters and their parents' subsequent pregnancies than those who don't. They just accept it as normal and natural and part of everyday life.'

'And what about my pregnancy? Did she say anything? Anything about my baby and where it's going to come from?'

'Actually, yes,' Mike confessed, looking a little uncomfortable. 'She asked if you'd stood up too when you had her, or if you were lying down, and what you'd do with the new baby.'

Kirsten closed her eyes and made a tiny screaming sound. 'And?'

'And I said people were all different, and it depended on how you felt at the time. I told her you walked round and round till the end then lay down to have her, but you might not feel like doing that with this baby.'

She groaned. 'Too much information, Mike. She doesn't need it at her age.'

Mike opened his mouth, then shut it, and Fran wondered if he'd thought better of telling Kirsten how fascinated Sophie had been with the afterbirth and the fact that Amber had eaten it. But then Sophie came back into the room with Brodie in tow and the subject was swiftly dropped.

'All ready to go?' Kirsten said, and Sophie nodded reluctantly.

'I want to stay and see Amber's calf some more. She's really cute—she's called Ama—something.'

'Amaryllis,' Mike supplied. 'And she'll still be cute when you come next time. Maybe cuter, because Amber will let you get closer. Right, come on, into the car. Your mother's in a hurry and we've got to go out.'

'Where are you going?' Sophie asked.

'The memorial service at the church in Penhally,' Mike told her. 'You remember, I told you about it. Lots of people died in a storm, and it was ten years ago today, so we're all gathering together to remember them.'

'That was four years before I was born,' Sophie said, counting on her fingers. 'That's *ages* ago.'

Not for the people who were still grieving, Fran thought, and wondered how Kate Althorp and the Tremayne family would be feeling. Had they moved on?

'We'd better go,' she said to Mike as soon as Kirsten and Sophie had gone.

There was standing room only, and Kate would rather have been outside with the majority of the villagers than trapped inside the pretty little church. At least outside she could look out to sea and communicate with James somehow, instead of being trapped inside this box with thoughts and feelings that were too painful to contemplate in public.

So she shut them down, sat quietly and still, and remembered him for the good man and loyal husband he'd been. She didn't let herself think about Nick, sitting with the rest of his family in the pew to her right, there to remember his father and brother. And she certainly didn't let herself think about that night ten years ago.

Reverend Kenner was leading the service, and when he read out the names of those lost, Jem leant closer to her, his hand in hers. For comfort, or to comfort her? She wasn't sure any more. He was growing up, turning into a fine young man, and James would have been proud of him.

Except, of course, the boy who was here to mourn his father wasn't that man's son at all.

Dear lord, it was so complicated. So sad and veiled in secrecy. She squeezed his hand, and he squeezed back.

Did he have the right to know who his real father was? She had no idea. No idea at all if it was better to mourn a man who had been a hero than to know that the man who really was your father was refusing to acknowledge your existence in his life.

The service moved outside and down to the beach, and as she and Jem stood on the rocks and threw their wreaths into the water and watched them carried away, as James had been, she blinked away threatening tears and straightened her shoulders.

They didn't need Nick in their lives. They could manage without him.

And if sometimes, at night, she still cried herself to

sleep for the love of a man she had no business loving, that was between her and her maker.

'Hello! Come on in and sit down. How are you, Mike?'

He gave a dry chuckle. 'Better than the last time you saw me,' he said, and Kate laughed.

'Yes, I think I'd probably agree. And Fran. How are you?'

Fran smiled, not knowing quite where to start and what to say. 'Um—good,' she said in the end, because it was true. She felt good—a bit sick with nerves, because now they'd decided to go for this, she was having to face all her demons all over again, but she could do it.

She reached out, and Mike took her hand, folding it in his and holding it tight. 'Um…we wanted to talk to you about the IVF. Trying again. We've spent a lot of time talking…' Her voice faltered, but she could feel Mike's fingers tightening on hers, and out of the corner of her eye she could see his reassuring smile.

'Anyway,' she said, firming her voice, 'we've been talking and thinking and we've been sticking to the diet and all the other things you said—the boxers and the showers and so on—and—'

'Boxers?' Mike said, frowning in puzzlement, then the light dawned. 'I thought they were because of the cast,' he murmured, but she could see a smile lurking in his eyes, and she smiled back.

'Sorry. And the coffee and alcohol and so on have all been strictly rationed.'

'And are you feeling better?' Kate asked, looking at them both.

'Probably, yes,' Mike said, looking thoughtful. 'I'm

sleeping better, but that could be all sorts of things. Less pressure, we're talking again—all sorts. And I feel energetic and optimistic, but again that could be because I'm not killing myself on the farm.'

'Looks like your broken leg's been quite useful, then,' Kate said with a smile, and turned to Fran. 'How do you feel?'

'Scared. Sick. Dreading the injections and all the intrusive stuff, but…' She shrugged and tried for a smile. 'Generally better. Like Mike. Sleeping better, more energy, happier—but there are lots of reasons for that.'

Kate smiled again. 'I'm so glad you're both happier,' she said quietly. 'An unhappy relationship is never a good start to this journey, and I must say from my point of view you both look light years better.'

'We feel it, and we were wondering if you could check us over,' Mike said. 'You know, run a ruler over us and make sure everything's up to scratch before we start again.'

'Of course. You probably haven't given the diet and the other changes long enough yet, but if you really feel you can't wait, we can start getting ready for the process of referral. You'll have to go to a different centre for private treatment, but we can run a lot of the preliminary checks from here, to rule out anything that's going to make them send you away. I'll need blood from both of you, so can you roll your sleeves up? That's great.'

She put a strap round Fran's arm, slid a needle into the vein and took several vials of blood from it, then, giving Fran the swab to press down on the vein, she repeated the process with Mike. 'You aren't still on painkillers or anything, are you?' she asked him, and he shook his head.

'I'm not on anything at the moment. Neither of us are.'

'Not even caffeine,' Fran said, giving him a rueful smile. 'I think that's probably been the hardest for him.'

'It's nothing,' he said, pressing down on the swab. 'Not compared to what's at stake.'

'Indeed. Right, let's weigh you both.'

She noted down their weights, commenting on the fact that Fran had put on three much-needed kilos, and took their blood pressure.

'OK. That's that. And I'll need a urine sample from each of you to make sure you haven't got diabetes or any sub-clinical infections, and you know what we're going to want from you,' she said, sliding a little pot across the desk to Mike with a smile.

He gave a wry laugh. 'Oh, yes. Do I ever. My favourite bit.' He pushed the ominous little pot around, picked it up and tossed it in the air, then said, with a tension in his voice that probably only Fran would have noticed, 'Will they be able to check for damaged sperm? Because if there's any likelihood that it was my sperm quality that caused Fran to miscarry, I want to do something about it before we try again.'

Kate's smile was reassuring. 'Of course. If there's a significant number of non-swimmers or sluggish ones, they'll have a closer look. It might be that you have to persevere with the diet for longer, or there might be something more significant wrong, although I doubt it. That would have been spotted before, I'm sure, and if you remember they never did find anything significantly wrong with either of you last time. But let's get the first tests out of the way and see what they come up with before we worry about what's next.'

'And then if everything comes back all right?' Fran asked, feeling the tension ratchet up a notch.

'Then we refer you to the clinic in Exeter, and they take over from us.' She finished labelling all the bottles of blood, slipped them into the plastic sleeves, filled in the various request forms and looked up. 'The semen sample needs to be as fresh as possible, so I would do it at the hospital, Mike, preferably near the beginning of the working day,' she said. 'Would you have time to do it this morning?'

He nodded, and Fran's heart hitched.

'Then I'll give you all this stuff to take to the lab as well,' she said, handing over all the blood samples and request envelopes, together with the urine sample bottles. 'The sooner they get them, the better the results. And I'll see you next week when they're all back—I'll give you a call when they're in.'

She smiled and pushed back her chair, stood up and shook their hands and opened the door. 'Good luck. I'll see you next week.'

'I can't believe I've got to go into that ghastly room again,' Mike muttered as they walked down the corridor towards the path lab. 'It's just awful, Fran—even thinking about it's enough to put me off. The girly magazines and the smutty videos—it's just horrible.' He suppressed a shudder, and then without warning she got hold of his arm and yanked him through a doorway.

'What the hell are you doing?' he asked as she shut the door and turned on the light. 'Fran? Why are we in the loo?'

She pushed him against the wall, took the pot out of her

handbag and put in on the basin, then reached for his zip. He grabbed it and held her away from him, unable to stop the splutter of laughter that rose in his chest.

'Fran, stop it! We can't do this here!' he hissed.

'Why not? Why ever not?'

'Because it's a public toilet!'

'Don't be silly, it's a single cubicle off the corridor and it's a lot more private than that dreadful room. Now, stop fighting.'

She pinned his hands out of the way, grabbed his zip and slid it down, reaching inside and curling her fingers round him.

Dear God. He was already hard, the thought of her touching him enough to bring him to the edge even though they were both still laughing. But then she moved her hand, the firm, rhythmic strokes enough to bring him to his knees, and he dropped his head forwards on his chest and stared down at her, her hand curled round him, her lip caught between her teeth, her pupils darkening as she looked up and met his eyes.

'God, you are so sexy, Trevellyan,' she muttered, flicking her nail across the tip of his penis, and he fisted his hands in her T-shirt and closed his eyes.

'I'm going to come any second if you do that,' he said through gritted teeth, and she gave a sexy little chuckle.

'I thought that was the general idea,' she said, and reached for the pot…

'Kate? It's Jan, at the fertility clinic. We've got a lot of results here from some patients of yours, Francesca and Michael Trevellyan. I think they were probably for you and

I'll send them through to you straight away, but I thought you'd want to know the results anyway.'

'Of course,' Kate said, surprised to feel a little kick of apprehension. 'I was going to chase them up, it's been over a week now. OK, fire away. I've got a pen.' She listened, frowned, raised her eyebrows and jotted down all the information. 'Really? Thanks, Jan. I'll pass all that on,' she said. Cutting the connection, she dialled the Trevellyans' number.

'Fran? It's Kate. Are you both in? I've got your results, and I was just about to leave the surgery. I thought I might drop by on my way to collect Jem from my mother and have a chat about what happens next.'

'Oh. Um…yes, sure,' Fran said, sounding instantly worried. 'We'll be here. Mike's in the office. I'll get him.'

'I'll be with you in ten minutes,' Kate said, and replaced the phone in its cradle.

'Mike?'

He glanced up at Fran and got straight to his feet, one look enough to know something was going on. 'What is it?' he asked, his chest tight with dread.

'I don't know. Kate's coming to see us. She's got our results.'

He felt his heart lurch and went over to her, gathering her in his arms and hugging her tight.

'We can handle this, Frankie,' he said softly. 'Whatever it is. Come on, let's go into the house and wait for her. I take it she's coming here now?'

'Yes. She said she'd be ten minutes. Mike, I feel sick.'

'Me, too,' he said. 'Come on.'

* * *

She would have fallen down without his support. They left the door open, standing there in the kitchen facing it, him behind her, his hands on her shoulders, steadying her, and so when Kate came in they couldn't see her face because the light was behind her.

'Well, I'll get straight to the point,' Kate said. 'It wasn't the news I was expecting to give you, but we aren't going to be referring you for the IVF programme.'

'No!' Fran wailed, her knees threatening to buckle, and she felt Mike's arms tighten round her.

'Fran, no,' Kate said hurriedly, and Fran couldn't work out why on earth she was smiling. 'It's not bad news! You can't have the IVF because you don't need it. You're pregnant, Fran,' she said, and her smile widened. 'Congratulations, both of you. You're going to have a baby.'

Fran stared at her for an age, numb with shock, and then with a fractured little sob she turned and fell into Mike's waiting arms...

They talked for hours.

Once Fran had stopped crying, of course, and they realised that Kate had left.

She was sitting on Mike's lap, one arm round his neck and his hand resting lightly over their baby, and she said softly, 'It's going to be OK this time, Mike. I feel so different. Much sicker. I thought it was just fright, but of course it isn't. My period is two days overdue, and I feel really different. And tired, but I thought that was just you keeping me awake half the night.'

He chuckled and tilted his head back, smiling up at her tenderly. 'You're to take care of yourself,' he said. 'Nothing silly. No unpasteurised milk or soft cheese or any of the other things—and no cheesemaking either. I can do that with a bin bag on my foot. And I'm sure Kate will give you a huge list of dos and don'ts.'

'I'm sure she will.' His hair had flopped forwards, and she lifted it back with her fingers and smoothed it out of the way so she could see his eyes. 'I don't want to tell Sophie yet, though,' she said, not wanting to acknowledge the possibility of failure but all too aware that it might lurk round the corner for them. After all it had before, twice.

'It'll be fine. Third time lucky, Fran,' he murmured. 'But I agree, we won't tell her yet. We won't tell anyone. Not till you're past the three-month mark.'

'I lost both the others at eight weeks,' she reminded him sadly.

His arm tightened. 'I know.'

'Three weeks and five days to go.'

'We'll make it,' he assured her, his voice quietly confident. 'And even if we don't, we've still got each other. As far as I'm concerned, that makes me the luckiest man alive. The rest is just the icing on the cake.'

She rested her head against his and sighed. 'I'm so lucky to have you,' she said softly. 'Have I told you recently how much I love you?'

He chuckled. 'Only about ten times today, but feel free to do it again.'

The phone rang, and she hung on to his neck and reached over, grabbing it from the charger without leaving Mike's lap. 'Hello? Oh, hi, Ben. Yes, he's here. I'll hand you over.'

She gave Mike the phone, and after a brief conversation he hung up and smiled at her. 'The valuer's been.'

'And?'

'If we'd ended up having to go the IVF route, we'd have had more than enough, but Joe and Sarah can do their kitchen, and Mum and Dad can change the car. And we can put the money on one side and spend it on something later. We're going to make it this time, Fran,' he said with conviction. 'I know we will.'

'We can spend it on the nursery,' she said, allowing a little bloom of hope. 'The house could do with a bit of decorating, and the heating's not great.'

He laughed. 'Don't get too carried away,' he said, and then kissed her. 'Time for bed?'

'Sounds good,' she said.

He lay watching her sleep, a little knot of fear in his chest. They had to make it. If she lost this baby…

Then he'd cope, he told himself firmly. If Fran had the courage to do this, then he had to find the courage to support her if it all went wrong. And they'd have the money put on one side for the IVF, should they need it. Please, God, it wouldn't be necessary…

Fran thought The Day would never come.

That was how she'd started thinking about it—with capital letters, because it seemed so huge, so important, so very far away that somehow nothing else would do.

Her pregnancy was a nightmare. Not because anything went wrong, because it didn't. She got through it, day by day, hour by hour, focusing on the end, planning for the magical day when she could bring her baby home, but somehow not daring to believe that it would ever happen.

The eight-week deadline passed.

Safely.

She gave a shaky sigh of relief when she reached nine weeks and realised she was probably over that hurdle. The next danger point was twelve weeks, and she got through that, too.

Then she had a scan—an image of her baby, just a tiny curl of a thing, but with an unwavering heartbeat.

'Oh, Mike,' she said, clinging to him and staring mesmerised at the screen, not knowing whether to laugh or cry. So she did both, and so did Mike, and they were given a photo to keep.

Their first, in the album she started with a trembling hope.

Then at twenty weeks she had her second scan, and another photo for the album.

'Do you want to know what sex it is?'

She looked at Mike for guidance, and he shrugged, passing the ball back to her.

'I don't care, so long as everything's all right,' he said, and she smiled.

'No, then,' she said. 'We'll wait and see.'

And then she kicked herself, because they started decorating the nursery, the little room off their bedroom that had always been the nursery, where Mike and Joe had slept for the first year of their lives, where their father, Russell, had slept, and so on back for generations. And because they didn't know the sex of the baby, they didn't know what colour to paint it.

'Yellow?' Mike offered. 'That's sunny and sort of neutral.'

'It makes them look jaundiced,' Fran said doubtfully, and he chuckled.

'Not daffodil yellow. Something softer. A pale creamy primrose?'

So that was how it ended up, a lovely soft colour, and when she was thirty-six weeks, they bought a cot. They didn't assemble it, though. It was as if, by tacit agreement, they didn't want to push their luck. So it stayed in the room, propped up behind the door, and for the next three weeks they didn't look at it.

It was as if they were holding their breath, but every night Mike would hold her in his arms, cuddled together like spoons in a drawer, with his big, strong hand splayed tenderly over the baby, soothing it with gentle strokes when it kicked and squirmed.

It had hiccups, too, which made them chuckle once they realised it was nothing to worry about.

And then Fran woke one morning tired and grumpy, and the house was a tip. So she cleaned it, furiously, from end to end, which frankly would have been stupidly ambitious when she hadn't been pregnant, she thought in a rare pause when she'd changed their sheets and vacuumed the bedroom floor, but she just had to do it, because the baby was coming soon and it couldn't be brought back to a place hanging with cobwebs.

Well, one cobweb, and it wasn't exactly hanging, but it was soon banished with a flick of the feather duster, and after another half-hour the dining table was gleaming, the old mahogany nourished within an inch of its life.

And she ached. Lord, how she ached! She straightened

up, the beeswax in her hand, and arched her back. She'd done too much, she thought. Much too much.

Time to sit down for a while.

Except she couldn't sit down, because it was so horrendously uncomfortable suddenly, and then she had one of those lightbulb moments and couldn't believe she'd been so stupid. She'd watched Brodie do just the same thing only two weeks ago, dragging her bedding round and round to get it comfortable, before finally settling down and giving birth to three puppies.

And she hadn't even realised she was doing the same thing!

She phoned Mike on his mobile. 'Um, can you come?'

'Sure—is supper ready?'

'Not exactly.'

He must have picked up on the tone of her voice, because he swore softly and she could hear him running. 'I'm on my way,' he said, and five minutes later he burst into the kitchen and found her standing leaning over the sink, a pool at her feet, panting.

'Fran?'

'Mind the floor,' she warned, worried he'd slip.

'What have you spilt?'

'I haven't. My waters have broken.'

'Oh, God.' He went pale, then lifted her out of the way and scrubbed his hands. 'I'd better take you to hospital now. Are you having contractions?'

'Um, sort of— Ah-h-h!'

It poleaxed her. It was the first time she'd felt anything other than a horrendous ache, but this was different. This was strong, and powerful, much bigger than her, and it took her over completely.

'Fran?'

'Bed,' she said through gritted teeth. 'Now.'

And Mike peered down at her, stopped flapping and turned into the father, stockman and one-time-maybe vet that he was, scooped her up and carried her up the stairs.

He dumped her on the edge of the bed, grabbed the plastic sheet they'd had for Sophie out of the airing cupboard, spread it over the mattress, covered it in thick, soft towels and lifted her into the middle of it.

She couldn't move, couldn't do anything to help him, but she didn't need to. He was doing fine, his smile reassuring, his hands slow and steady and confident as he stripped off her wet underwear.

'In a bit of a hurry, I think,' he said, rubbing her back gently and smiling at her.

She suddenly realised why the livestock trusted him so much, why his cows were so content and relaxed around him.

'I've called an ambulance,' he told her, but they both knew she wasn't going anywhere till she'd had the baby, and she felt a great peace steal over her. Generations of his family had been born here, in this room, and their baby would be the next in line.

'Help me out of my clothes,' she said, struggling to get out of them. She didn't know why, she just wanted to get rid of them, get rid of anything that wasn't natural, anything tight, anything constricting that would come between her and nature, because nature was taking her over and she was following her instincts blindly.

Mike eased the dress over her head, pulled off her

T-shirt, unclipped her bra and took it off, then drew her naked body into his arms and held her, rubbing her back through another contraction.

'I need to push,' she said a minute later, shoving him out of the way and struggling to her knees. 'Now!'

She couldn't have done it without him. She locked her hands around the back of his neck and hung on him, whimpering, and he knelt there in front of her and cradled her, then turned her so she was lying over the pillows, hanging on to the headboard for dear life while he concentrated at the business end, and as the baby let out a lusty howl, she turned and sagged back onto the bed, her empty arms outstretched.

Mike lifted their son, slippery and shuddering with rage, and put him into her waiting arms. 'It's a boy,' he said, his voice unsteady, and his hand came out, trembling, and he brushed the back of his knuckles gently over the soft, soft skin. 'We've got a boy, Fran. A son.' And his tears welled over and splashed onto her hand.

She stared down at them, the tears he'd shed, and the child they'd made together, the child they'd feared they'd never have, and she looked up at him, her own eyes flooded with tears.

'Come here,' she said, and he covered them both with the quilt, lay down beside them and drew them into his arms. The baby was nuzzling now, and she looked up at Mike helplessly. 'I don't know how to do this,' she confessed.

'Yes, you do. Remember the classes?'

And wrapping his big hand round his son's tiny head, he steered him in the right direction, brushed his cheek against her nipple, and as his mouth opened instinctively, Mike pressed him firmly against her and she felt the baby start to suckle.

'Oh! It's so strong!' she whispered, and stared down at him in wonder. 'Oh, Mike. He's beautiful.'

'He is. Incredible. Amazing. Our little miracle.'

His tiny fingers were splayed over Fran's breast, the transparent nails so small she could barely see them, but he was strong, a real fighter. He was suckling hard, his tiny rosebud mouth making little sucking noises, and she looked up at Mike and laughed softly.

'He's got his father's appetite,' she said, and Mike chuckled and hugged her closer.

'We haven't talked about names,' she said, remembering their reluctance to take that much for granted.

'Sophie has,' he confessed with a groan. 'She's been nagging me. She's had hundreds of ideas, but her favourite seems to be Thomas.'

'Thomas. I like that. Thomas Trevellyan. Sounds good.'

'I think so.'

She stroked his tiny cheek. 'I think we ought to let your sister name you, little man, don't you? She'll be so excited. You have to tell her, Mike.'

'Not until we've got you sorted out,' he said, easing away from her. 'The ambulance is here. I'll talk to her later.'

'Daddy!'

'Hello, pickle!' Mike scooped Sophie up into his arms and hugged her. 'How's my favourite girl?'

'I'm fine—Daddy, where's Fran? I've got something really special to show her. Fran! Look!' she yelled, catching sight of her. Fran hugged her close and took the little box Sophie was thrusting at her eagerly.

'It's a model—I made it at school!' she said. 'Look, it's Brodie and her puppies!'

'So it is,' Fran said, smiling down at the little model nestling in its bed of cotton wool. 'It's lovely. Give it to your daddy, then.'

'It's not for him, it's for the baby. Can I see him? I'm dying to see him. I can't believe Mummy made me wait *two whole days*!'

She was beside herself with excitement and, taking her by the hand, Fran looked up at Kirsten, still in the car. 'Coming in?'

She shook her head and smiled. 'I'll see him when I pick her up on Sunday,' she said, and drove away, leaving them with Sophie.

Fran led her through the kitchen, past Brodie and her three little puppies all snuggled up together in her basket, into the sitting room to where Sophie's brand-new little brother was lying sleeping in his crib.

'Oh, he's tiny!' she said in a stage whisper. 'Much smaller than Millie. Daddy, he's just like you! All that black hair—and he's got your nose!'

'Poor kid,' Mike said with a proud grin, wrapping his arms round Fran and hugging her close.

'There's nothing wrong with your nose,' Fran told him, turning and kissing the tip of it with a smile. 'Nothing at all. And there won't be anything wrong with Thomas's either. It's just a bit squashed, but I'm sure he'll grow into it.'

'I'm sure he will,' Mike said, staring down at his son

with an expression of wonder and love so profound it brought tears to Fran's eyes.

'Can I hold him?'

'Of course. Sit down.'

Sophie sat on the sofa, with Fran next to her just in case, and Mike slipped his big hands gently under his son's small body and lifted him, resting him carefully on Sophie's lap.

'Hello, Thomas,' she whispered, and kissed her little brother gently on his forehead. His eyes fluttered open and he stared at her, and they were both transfixed.

It was magical, Fran thought as Mike sat down beyond Sophie and put his arm around them all. Perfect.

Then Sophie looked up, her eyes shining and her smile as bright as the sun, and said, 'We're a proper family now.'

And Brodie, wandering in to see what was going on, rested her head on Sophie's knee and thumped her tail in agreement…

Sheikh Surgeon Claims His Bride

JOSIE METCALFE

Josie Metcalfe lives in Cornwall with her long-suffering husband. They have four children. When she was an army brat, frequently on the move, books became the only friends that came with her wherever she went. Now that she writes them herself she is making new friends, and hates saying goodbye at the end of a book—but there are always more characters in her head, clamouring for attention until she can't wait to tell their stories.

PROLOGUE

THE pain was unrelenting, but Zayed was almost used to that by now.

What hurt his pride was to admit that, by this time in the evening, he had little chance of disguising the unevenness in his stride as he made his way down to the stretch of water-smoothed sand at the edge of Penhally Bay.

Anyway, there was nothing he could do to switch off the agony that came with the end of a busy day, other than taking large doses of analgesia, and he wasn't going to start down that path. If using those means to relieve his pain left him unfit to take care of one of his little ones, there would be no point to his existence.

He swore softly as his foot caught on the roughness of the granite steps and forced himself to concentrate a little harder. At least, at this time of an August evening, with the sun sliding towards the ocean, there were few people around to notice if he stumbled about like a drunk.

He smiled wryly at the thought, unable to remember the last time he'd tasted alcohol. It must have been back in the days when he'd been in medical school, indulging in that brief spell of belated teenage rebellion...before his world had become such a dangerous place, before everything had finally spiralled out of control.

'But Penhally isn't such a bad place to end up,' he murmured as he paused long enough to scan his surroundings, the perfect picture postcard of a Cornish fishing village. It had been only fairly recently that the influx of summer visitors drawn to the better-than-average surfing beach had expanded the place into quite a thriving little town. He'd first visited the area one summer, in his other life, and the serenity of this little place, where almost every building looked out towards the vastness of the ocean, had called to him.

Perhaps that was because it was so unlike his own country. 'Apart from the sand, of course,' he added with a half-hearted chuckle, glad that there was no one at this end of the beach to hear him talking to himself.

He leant forward to deposit his towel in the sand and the renewed stab of pain was enough to take his breath away for several seconds while he waited for it to subside.

'Stupid!' he hissed as he stripped off his cotton shirt and trousers and started the stretching routine that began every visit to the beach, knowing that it didn't matter how careful he was, by the time he finished, every nerve and muscle would be screaming for him to stop.

It was a great temptation to give in to it—it would be so much easier not to put himself through this agony. But that way his mobility and stamina would never improve, and that was unacceptable. If he didn't make the fullest recovery possible, then he wouldn't be able to help the children who needed him so badly.

Anyway, the pain was a necessary part of his life. It was a reminder…a penance…a payment he had to make for the fact that he had survived while Leika, Kashif and so many others…

Zayed deliberately blocked the thought before it went any further. His nightmares were vivid enough without allowing himself to recall those events by day as well.

It was enough for him to know that he was guilty of having allowed them to die. The pain he felt could never be enough to balance the loss of everything he'd once held most dear.

'*That* is one of the good things about coming back to Penhally,' Emily murmured aloud, mesmerised by the changing colours in the streaks of cloud against the horizon while she waited for the sun to sink into the sea at the end of another perfect summer's day.

And *there* was another benefit to coming back to her home town, she added silently as a good-looking man stepped into view on the sand and proceeded to strip his clothing off.

'Oh, yes!' she breathed as the last golden rays outlined each new vista, from broad shoulders and a wide chest decorated with an intriguing swathe of dark silky-looking hair to a tautly muscled belly and slim hips, all covered by darkly tanned skin. 'That is *definitely* a good reason for living near a beach.'

As she watched, he began an obviously well-practised routine of stretches before progressing to a seriously strenuous workout. For just a moment she wondered if he was putting on a show for her benefit, but there was no way that he could know she was there. This little alcove at the base of the rocks was one of the first places to be thrown into shadow as evening began to fall, and had been a favourite spot of hers ever since she'd come to live with her grandmother in her teens.

It wasn't until the man finally turned to walk into the sea that she noticed that he was limping fairly heavily, and her professional interest was raised. Had he injured himself during that punishing drill he'd just put himself through, or could the disability itself be the reason for the routine?

The light level had fallen too much by now for her to see any evidence of an injury, and while he had probably come to the beach at this time so that he could have some solitude, the idea of leaving anyone to swim alone when they might get into difficulties and need assistance wasn't something she could contemplate.

'Well, it's no hardship to sit here a bit longer,' she murmured. The air was still warm and even though a playful breeze had started up as the sun began to go down, she was perfectly sheltered where she was. Then, of course, there was the fact that she would have a second chance to look at that beautiful body when whoever he was finally emerged from the water.

In the meantime, she had some serious thinking to do and a mountain of guilt to come to terms with.

She'd been away for such a long time while she'd gone through her arduous medical training and had only realised that it had been far too long when a visit had revealed the dreadful secret her grandmother had been hiding.

'I didn't want you to come home just to watch me die, not when you had all those exams to take,' she'd explained stubbornly when Emily had arrived for a long weekend visit to give her the latest good news in person.

She'd been so looking forward to seeing Beabea's face

when she told her that she'd just been offered the plum job she'd been after at St Piran's Hospital. Admittedly, it was only a six-month placement, but she had high hopes that there might be a permanent position she could apply for at the end of that time.

The taste of triumph had turned to ashes in her mouth when she'd realised just how little time she had left with the only family she possessed in the world.

With her grandmother's permission, she'd spoken to the oncologist at St Piran's the next day, hoping against hope that there was room for some glimmer of optimism—an operation, perhaps, or chemotherapy—but, if anything, the prognosis was worse than she'd thought.

'She could have several months, but I really think it's unlikely,' the kindly man had said, leaving Emily feeling sick to her stomach. 'With this sort of thing, the patient is usually fairly well, despite the devastation going on inside, right up until the last couple of weeks. That's the point when she'll need to come into hospital or transfer into a hospice—somewhere where they'll be able to monitor the pain medication, because she'll need it by then.'

'If she's put on PCA, couldn't I take care of her at home?' Emily had pleaded, knowing just how much her grandmother loved her little cottage. The place was full of years of love and so many happy memories, and if she was put on a morphine pump for patient-controlled pain relief, Emily wouldn't have to worry that she wasn't giving her grandmother the correct dose.

'You could, initially,' he'd agreed. 'But we've found that it's often far too stressful for the patient to stay at home right to the end, knowing that their relatives are having to do so much for them and watching them die by inches. In the end, the two of you will find that you'll know when it's time to make the move, for both your sakes.'

And in the meantime, Emily had started her new job under Mr Breyley and had obtained permission to spend her off-duty hours far further away than the immediate vicinity of St Piran's.

Their little system had worked well, with Emily taking care of her grandmother's needs before she drove the hour to St Piran's, knowing that Beabea still had many friends in the Penhally area, including several in the medical profession in one capacity or another, who would be dropping in throughout the time she herself was away on duty.

And while her grandmother slept for longer stretches each day, Emily took herself off for walks along the harbour, past the Penhally Arms and the Anchor Hotel. Each time she glanced in she saw that holidaymakers and locals alike were enjoying themselves, and it seemed somehow wrong that they were oblivious of the life-and-death battle that was going on just around the corner.

A time or two she'd sat at the café on the end of the row, sipping a long frothy latte while she watched the holidaymakers leaning on the parapet of the bridge, who were watching the waters of the river Lanson hurrying on the final stretch of their journey to the sea.

She'd stood there a time or two herself, gazing down at the chuckling, purling waters tumbling over the rocks while she'd pondered on the timelessness of the view. So little had changed from the first time she'd balanced on the parapet on her stomach as a teenager, risking a painful dunking if she'd gone head first over the edge. And yet, even though the stones and the water hadn't changed, everything else had.

She was a different person from that teenager, a doctor, now, with the job of her dreams. And her grandmother, who had always seemed so ageless that she might live for ever, was now a shrunken old lady with thin grey hair and papery skin and barely enough energy to breathe.

In fact, apart from working under Mr Breyley, which was everything she'd hoped for and more, the one bright spot in her day was if she managed to make it to the beach to complete her mind-numbing run along the hard-packed sand before her mystery man arrived.

Several times she'd been tempted to speak to him, to let him know that she was there and to get her first good look at his face, but that would have spoilt the fantasies she'd been weaving about him, especially if she found out that he was only someone she'd gone to school with.

Then there was the fact that he might see her as some sort of voyeur, hiding in the rocks while she watched him put himself through his nightly torment, but she could always counter that accusation by pointing out that she was doing nothing more than acting as an unofficial lifeguard. Not that she thought that would cut much ice with a man who seemed so driven and so utterly self-contained. In fact, his focus seemed so intense that she found it difficult to imagine that he was the sort who would ever relax enough to reveal a softer side to his nature.

'But that won't stop me imagining one,' Emily murmured as he set off into the water again lit only by the dying rays of the sun.

Today she'd really needed the distraction of watching him, to take her mind off the fact that she'd spent the afternoon settling her grandmother into her room up in the new hospice wing of the nursing home up on Penhally Heights.

The oncologist had been right after all. She'd been utterly determined to take care of her grandmother herself, even if it meant arranging to take some time off from her job. But in the end they had both agreed that it was finally time for Beabea to move out of the bedroom that had been hers ever since the day she'd moved into it as a new bride, more than fifty years ago.

'And as soon as my mystery man stops punishing himself, it will be time to go back to the cottage and get some sleep,' she told herself, although she didn't like the prospect of going back there knowing that she was going to be completely alone in the little stone cottage for the very first time.

At least she had a great job to go to in the morning, and she might hear some more gossip about that foreign surgeon who had been setting up a specialist paediatric surgical unit at St Piran's.

The buzz had been all around her ever since she'd started working for Mr Breyley at the opposite end of the dedicated paediatric block, and when she had time, she was going to take a walk upstairs to take a look at the set-up that had everybody talking. After all, paediatric surgery had been her other choice for her specialty and she hadn't finally decided which way she was going to go at the end of her six months with Mr Breyley if she *wasn't* offered the chance of a permanent post.

CHAPTER ONE

EMILY paused silently in the shadows outside the recently expanded specialist paediatric surgical unit and fell in love.

Well, she'd needed something good to happen after the shock she'd received down in her own department.

She'd barely stuck her head inside the door when Mr Breyley's secretary had beckoned her into the office.

'I'm sorry he's not here to tell you about it himself, Dr Livingston,' the rather austere-looking woman had said with a slightly frazzled glance around at the haphazard piles of paper littering her normally pristine desk. Then she had unbent enough to murmur, confidentially, 'He and his wife flew out to New Zealand this morning. Their first grandchild is on the way. He was diagnosed with transposition of the great arteries *in utero* and is arriving prematurely, so they wanted to be there for their daughter…at least, until the corrective surgery's over and done with.'

'Completely understandable,' Emily had agreed, even as panic had started to set in. Was she about to lose her job? With Mr Breyley on the other side of the world, she had lost her mentor and tutor. The hospital would be unlikely to be able to find someone of his calibre available at short notice.

Then there was the fact that it hadn't only been the job that had brought her back to Penhally. Of course, it had been a terrific step up on her career path, and the fact that it had been within easy travelling distance of Beabea had been a bonus. But now that her grandmother's condition was rapidly worsening and now she'd transferred to the hospice, the last thing Emily wanted was to have to move away, perhaps to the other end of the country for a comparable post.

She just couldn't do that. She needed to be here, in the hospital closest to Penhally, so that she could spend as much of these last precious days with her grandmother as she could. Also, there was the fact that transferring to another hospital at short notice, and so soon after starting a placement, could look bad on her CV. Anyway, there was no guarantee that she would find a comparable post either.

With the likelihood that her perfect job was going to vanish into thin air, there were other worries to be considered, too.

It was highly unlikely that the hospital would be willing to keep paying her salary until they appointed a new surgical consultant to take her on and, no matter how much she wanted to spend time with Beabea, she couldn't afford to take an expensive break, either financially or professionally.

But she had so little time left to be with her grandmother and didn't want to waste any of it travelling endless hours to and fro.

'However,' the senior consultant's secretary continued, breaking into her endlessly circling thoughts, suddenly all efficiency, 'before he left, Mr Breyley had another look at the application forms you sent in when you applied for the post on his firm. He'd remembered that you'd noted an interest in the field of paediatric orthopaedics as well, so he took your references to have a word with Mr Khalil about the situation. Anyway, he has persuaded Mr Khalil to let you join his team *pro tem*, to see whether you fit in.'

Emily blinked a bit at that. It was amazing that Mr Breyley had found time to consider her situation when he must have been desperate to start his journey to New Zealand, but she really wasn't certain that she liked the sound of his arrangements for her. It almost made her sound like some substandard piece of equipment being dumped on an unwilling recipient.

Mr Breyley was an acknowledged expert in his field and had thought her good enough to join *his* team. And considering the fact that her record throughout her training had been second to none, it was almost an insult that this Mr Khalil had needed to be persuaded to take her on, even temporarily.

'I'm sorry I can't be more specific,' the harried secretary continued, apparently oblivious to Emily's chagrin at being treated as an unwanted parcel, 'but Mr Khalil said to tell you that he'd either be in his office or in Paediatric Intensive Care.'

So here she was, on a mission to find Mr Khalil and see if she could discover why he thought *his* requirements so much higher than Mr Breyley's when he was choosing new team members.

She'd started off her search at his office and found a stunningly beautiful woman with an intriguing accent manning the desk.

'He is not available at the moment, and he will be

starting his surgical list at ten this morning,' she informed
Emily coolly, as kohl-lined dark eyes flicked dismissively over her from head to toe.

Emily stifled a wry grin. It was obvious that her simple
summer cotton clothes had been found seriously wanting
in the elegance stakes.

Well, that was just too bad. She'd long ago decided that
spending half of her time in baggy surgical scrubs, with
something that looked like a pair of paper knickers on her
head, meant that there wasn't a lot of point in trying to
impress her colleagues with anything other than her
medical capabilities.

'My name is Dr Livingston,' she informed her quietly.
'I'm the new member of Mr Khalil's team and need to
know where to find him as soon as possible.'

'But…you're a *woman*!' she exclaimed, and grabbed
for some paperwork on the top of her immaculately tidy
desk. 'We are expecting a Dr Emil Livingston, and Emil
is a man's name, no?'

'Emil is a man's name, yes,' Emily agreed, almost
giggling when she found herself mimicking the woman's speech patterns. There was just something about
these effortlessly flawless women that rubbed her up the
wrong way, probably the fact that she would have to
starve herself for weeks…*months*…to wear anything
like the size zero designer clothes this secretary was
wearing, in spite of the fact that she tried to force herself
to go for a run each day. 'But my name is Emily, with
a "y", but without the corresponding chromosome.'

'Excuse me?'

Emily stifled a sigh as she glanced at her watch, for-
going any effort at an explanation of her attempt at humour.

'If you could just tell me where I can find Mr Khalil, I would be very grateful.' It wouldn't do anything to impress her new boss if she was any later reporting for work, and she really needed to impress him if he was to allow her to join his team properly until Mr Breyley returned from New Zealand. For Beabea's sake, she really needed this job.

'He will be up in PICU with the Hananis...the parents of a child who will have surgery this morning. I will ring him to tell you are coming.'

'Don't bother interrupting him while he's talking,' Emily said quickly, loath to draw any extra attention to her tardiness. 'I'll find him easily enough when I get there.'

Except she hadn't found him yet.

She'd run up several flights of steps, right to the top of the hospital where the recently expanded and refurbished PICU was situated just round the corner from the brand-new surgery suite she'd caught a glimpse of when she'd come for her interview.

She'd had to knock for admittance to the ward, not privy to the code to unlock the door yet.

'I'm Dr Livingston, the new member of Mr Khalil's team,' she announced, hoping she didn't sound too winded, but taking the stairs instead of the lift was one of the habits she'd had to adopt if she was to stand a hope of keeping her weight under control.

'Welcome!' the staff nurse said with a smile as she swung the door wide. 'We had no idea we were going to be getting a woman on one of our paediatric surgical teams. I'm Jenna Stanbury.'

She, at least, had looked pleased to see her, Emily noted as she was led into the unit. Several heads looked up from what they were doing and smiled vaguely in her direction.

'I'm afraid that Tamsin...Sister Rush...has shut herself in her office with strict instructions only to be disturbed in case of fire or flood while she fights with a mountain of paperwork,' Jenna said apologetically.

'Actually, I've been trying to catch up with Mr Khalil,' she said with a grimace when she caught sight of the time on a clock shaped like a cat with a long tail swishing rhythmically to count off the seconds. At this rate she was going to be fired for poor time-keeping before she even started work.

'Don't panic,' Jenna soothed. 'The last time I saw Mr Khalil, he was going into the interview room with the Hananis to explain exactly what's going to happen during their son's operation. I sent one of the juniors in a little while ago with a tray of coffee, so you've probably got time to have a bit of a walk around while you catch your breath. Don't forget infection control procedures...he's very hot on that.'

'I'm glad to hear it,' Emily said as she reached for the gel dispenser. 'It's bad enough when an adult gets a hospital-acquired infection, but when it's a sick child...' She was pleased that her new boss was as keen on good hygiene as she was. That was one thing they had in common already.

She made her way around the unit to familiarise herself with the layout, hoping that it would soon be a second home to her. It was an environment that she felt comfortable in, where post-operative patients would be continuously supervised by batteries of monitors and their needs taken care of by highly trained specialist nurses while they began their recovery after surgery.

And there he was.

Oh, she had no idea *who* he was, just that he was the most beautiful man she'd ever seen, with thick dark hair cut short to combat an obvious tendency to curl, dark lustrous eyes with more than a hint of the exotic about them, surrounded as they were by the thickest, longest eyelashes she'd ever seen on a man. But the most beautiful thing about him was the way he was smiling as he was leaning over the equally beautiful child in an isolette, spending precious time with him while he was awake.

She watched him as he tenderly stroked an elegant, long-fingered hand over soft dark curls, smiling again as he murmured softly.

Her heart clenched at the sight of that smile and the way it lit those beautiful dark eyes from within. This was a man who loved his child and wasn't ashamed who knew it, and something inside her ached that she'd never known such unconditional love from anyone other than her grandmother.

She didn't know whether she'd made a sound or whether her presence in the doorway had finally registered on him, but suddenly *she* was the focus of those dark eyes…and they weren't smiling any more.

'Who are you? Do not come any closer,' he ordered in a voice soft enough not to startle the little child at his side, but with the obvious stamp of authority in every exotically accented syllable. 'What are you doing here? Do you wish to speak with me?'

'If you are Mr Khalil, yes, I do,' she said with a crushing sense of disappointment adding a crisp edge to the words. Where was the warm, caring father with his dark eyes full of love that she'd just lost her heart to? This man was something else entirely, the expression in his eyes almost cold enough to freeze her in her tracks in spite of the glorious Cornish summer day outside.

'And you are…?'

He was obviously a man of few words, she thought as she took his nod as permission to approach, his commanding presence growing more overwhelming the closer she came.

For the first time since she'd embarked on her medical career she actually found herself wanting to step back from a challenge, but that wasn't her way…had *never* been her way, from the day when a brusque social worker had dumped her unceremoniously on her grandmother when she'd been rescued from her parents' crushed car.

Deliberately, she straightened her shoulders and forced herself to meet that obsidian gaze, noticing for the first time that his face was marked with the evidence of deep-seated suffering, the eyes that had been so expressive such a short while ago now showing absolutely no emotion.

It took another second for her brain to compute all the other information it was receiving about the tall, lean man facing her from less than an arm's span away—the arms that were bare to the elbow in compliance with the latest infection control policy, darkly tanned skin and even darker hair on well-muscled forearms, the taut skin of his freshly-shaven cheeks, the crisp freshness of his plain white shirt startling against the natural tan of his soap-scented skin.

His collar was open, in line with the hospital's no-ties

policy, and she could see a dark, delicious hollow at the base of his throat and the prominent knobs of the ends of his collar-bones and, just in the deepest part of the V of his shirt opening, a dark tangle of silky-looking hair that seemed impossibly intimate, hinting at what she might reveal if she were to reach out and unfasten more of those small white buttons.

'Well?' he said shortly, and she felt the warmth surge up into her cheeks with the realisation that for the first time in her life she'd been so busy looking at him that she'd completely forgotten to answer his question.

'I—I understand that Mr Breyley told you about me before he left for New Zealand. I'm Emily Livingston, the new member of your team,' she said, and to prove just how scrambled her brain had become in his presence, she completely forgot about infection control and held her hand out to him.

CHAPTER TWO

ZAYED blinked at the announcement that *this* was his newest colleague, so startled that he only just remembered in time not to reach for the slender hand hovering in mid-air.

One half of his brain was wondering whether anyone had remembered to tell her how strict he was about maintaining hygiene around his patients.

'You should be a *man*!' he exclaimed, while the other half of his brain busied itself with taking in the perfection of her barely sun-kissed, peaches-and-cream complexion and the blonde hair wound tidily away in an attempt to make her look professional. Then there was the lushness of her gently rounded body clad in the simplest of clothing that struck the first spark of sexual interest he'd felt in far too long.

Not that he would ever do anything about it. He couldn't.

'My secretary took down the details,' he continued, forcing both halves of his brain to work together so that his voice came out far more harshly than he'd intended.

'I know,' she said calmly, and an intriguing hint of a smile hovered at the corners of a mouth that didn't seem to have a trace of artifice deepening its soft rose colour.

'She'd left the "y" off the end of my name and added it to my chromosomes.'

He almost chuckled at the clever play on ideas, strangely delighted when he realised that there was more to this woman than met the eye, but he ruthlessly subdued the unexpected impulse. Any attraction that he felt for her would be nothing more than a momentary aberration…it could never be more than that, not since…

'Well, if "xx" is willing to work as hard as "xy", I will have no cause for complaint,' he said shortly, the old pain and the never-ending guilt gripping him anew even as he tried to banish the bitter memories from his mind.

'In that case, where do you want me to start?' she offered, and he felt a strange sense of disappointment when he saw the way she'd deliberately switched off any warmth in her expression, but what else did he expect when he'd been so cold with her?

A demanding cry behind him drew his attention before he could answer her question.

'Come and meet Abir,' he invited, and was puzzled by the arrested expression on her face, those startling green eyes of hers wide with what looked almost like surprise as they travelled from his mouth to his own eyes and back again.

He frowned, wondering what on earth was the matter with the woman as he gestured towards the child in the plastic isolette.

'He was delivered by emergency Caesarean when his mother went into full eclampsia, but there were no adverse after-effects. Both mother and child were doing well…until she noticed that his head was not like the heads of the babies of her friends.'

By this time they'd reached the isolette and he broke off to murmur a few soothing words to the fractious infant before he continued.

'Her doctor was not really sure what was the matter with the child, and there was no paediatric specialist nearby, so as she was the sister of a…friend…' he prevaricated, avoiding specifying the real connection between Abir's family and his own, 'I was asked to see the child.'

He ran his hand over the child's head, mourning the fact that all this silky dark hair would be gone in a matter of minutes now, as he was prepared for the life-changing surgery. He refused to let himself remember cradling another little head, little knowing just how short that precious life would be.

Abir had settled under his touch, his big dark eyes gazing up at the two of them with that strange solemnity that he sometimes saw in these little ones.

'If you would like to clean your hands, you could make an examination of Abir,' he invited, and stepped aside slightly to gesture towards the child, inviting Dr Emily Livingston to make her own assessment of Abir's condition.

'I used antibacterial gel on my hands just before I stepped inside the room,' she said, then startled him by blushing softly. 'And apart from trying to shake hands with you, I haven't touched anything since then.'

'So…' He repeated his gesture towards the infant, who seemed almost as captivated by the woman's blonde hair as *he* was.

'Hello, Abir. Haven't you got beautiful big brown eyes?' she crooned as she bent down to bring her head almost to the same level as the child's. She reached out a slender hand to stroke a gentle finger over the back of a chubby little fist and smiled when the little one immediately grabbed it and held on tightly.

'That's a clever boy,' she praised as she began to stroke her other hand over the silky dark hair covering the unusually shaped skull, her voice taking on an almost sing-song quality that clearly mesmerised the child.

The tone of her voice stayed the same as she continued speaking softly to the little one so that it was a couple of seconds before Zayed realised that she was now speaking to him.

'Without seeing any X-rays, I'm assuming that this is craniosynostosis, with some of the cranial sutures fusing before birth,' she said with an air of steady confidence in her diagnosis that impressed him no end. Her fingertips were gently tracing the lines where the joins between the plates of the skull were already showing pronounced abnormal ridges. 'Is there a genetic component here— any history of Crouzon or Apert in the family, for example?'

'An uncle and a cousin,' he confirmed. 'But we only found that out when we started questioning the rest of the family. As neither of the affected members has survived, their disfigurement meant that they are rarely mentioned any more, and especially not in front of a pregnant woman.'

'For fear her baby will "catch" the problem?' she asked with a smile in the baby's direction that had him gracing her with an answering open-mouthed, gummy grin.

'That sort of superstition still lingers in some of the more remote villages in Cornwall, too,' she continued, this time smiling directly up at him as though sharing a particularly delicious secret as she added, 'At one time, it even included redheads being banned from visiting.'

'And what would be your preferred treatment modality?' He wouldn't allow himself to be beguiled by a pair of sparkling green eyes. There was no point.

'Surgery, of course, to excise the affected bone,' she answered, so promptly that he wasn't sure whether it was her own decision or one based on the fact she'd already been told about the impending surgery.

'Because?' he probed with unexpected intensity, suddenly needing her to be able to justify her assertion, although he had no idea why.

'Because otherwise the fact that the bones had already fused before he was born will mean that there's no room for expansion and his brain will end up terribly damaged. If I remember correctly, a linear craniotomy and excision of the affected sutures is most effective when performed in the first three months of life,' she added.

She was looking down into those big brown eyes, and he suddenly knew that she had recognised the gleam of intelligence already lighting them, too, and understood just what a tragedy it would be if that spark were crushed out of existence.

'What are the potential hazards of the operation?' He forced himself to ignore the sudden feeling of connection with her by concentrating on the specifics of the procedure. This was the sort of detail that he would hope she knew backwards, forwards and inside out, having taken her latest exams so recently.

There was a sudden flash of concern in her eyes, as though she was genuinely concerned that he might not be sufficiently satisfied with her answers to give her the placement on his team. But surely he'd been mistaken. She would only have been informed of Mr Breyley's departure when she'd arrived at the hospital that morning. It wasn't as if this position was one that she desperately wanted or that she'd had time to become nervous about a make-or-break interview…or was it?

There was something about the tension in her feminine frame that told him there *was* a burning need in her to gain his approval for the placement, that there was something inside her that meant she would work every bit as hard in his department as she had in his colleague's.

So, was there another reason why she wanted the job, a personal reason, completely separate from her career aspirations?

Perhaps she particularly wanted to stay in this part of the country, between the wild desolation of the moors and the rugged majesty of the coast. Perhaps she had family here, or a boyfriend she wanted to be close to.

He was almost grateful for the fact that she began speaking, able to ignore the sudden unexpected clutch of disappointment in his gut at the thought that some undeserving man had the right to wrap that beautiful body in his arms. He had absolutely no right to feel anything for this woman other than the need for her to be the best junior she could be.

'During surgery, there's the possibility of hypovolaemic shock, especially in such a young patient,' she announced with a slight quiver in her voice that belied her apparent confidence. 'There's also the chance that there might be dural tears unrecognised during the procedure that can cause cerebrospinal fluid leaks. They could leave a pathway open for infection. There could also be epidural or subdural haematoma due to surgical trauma. Post-operatively,' she continued swiftly, almost as fluently as though she were reading word for word from the relevant specialist text, 'there will be facial swelling, of course, especially around the eyes. That usually resolves in the first few weeks, but the improvement in the head shape is almost immediate.'

'And have you observed such surgery?' He was careful not to reveal just how impressed he was. Not only had she made a correct diagnosis of a relatively rare condition, but had obviously recalled, verbatim, everything she had read about it.

'Only in my teaching hospital's video library,' she admitted. 'I've always been interested in paediatric orthopaedics.'

'In that case, we just have enough time to introduce you to Abir's parents before it's time to scrub,' he announced, suddenly eager to see how well this young woman would acquit herself in an operating theatre.

As if they were obeying some invisible signal, that was the precise moment that the Hananis chose to emerge from the interview room.

Zayed led the way towards them, touched by the matched pairs of reddened eyes that were clear evidence that both parents had obviously given in to a bout of tears in his absence.

'Dr Emily Livingston, these are Abir's parents, Meera and...'

Further introductions seemed unnecessary as the newest member of his team stepped forward to take the young mother's hands in hers.

'You have a beautiful baby,' Emily said simply, as though she'd guessed that neither of the child's parents had a detailed command of English. 'I will do everything I can to help make him well.'

Athar Hanani threw Zayed a puzzled frown, obviously needing some clarification of the situation.

'Dr Livingston will be in the operating theatre with me, assisting me while I'm operating on Abir,' he said, and when the young man switched to his own language to question the presence of a doctor who was a female, Zayed was glad that Emily couldn't understand this clear evidence of his countryman's chauvinism.

Before he could find the words to set the record straight, it was Meera who did the job for him, rounding on her husband and berating him for failing to see that the young woman doctor obviously cared about their son already.

'I put my son, Abir Hanani, in your hands,' she said to the green-eyed woman, reverting to English and wiping away the worried expression Zayed's new junior had been wearing while the sharp-edged conversation had whirled incomprehensibly around her.

'I am honoured by your trust,' Emily said, and her smile almost seemed to light up the corridor.

An hour later, Emily's concentration on the operative procedure was broken again by her conviction that Zayed Khalil was in pain.

The doctor in her had belatedly tallied the fact that there had been a slight hitch in his stride the first time he strode away from her along the corridor. At the time, she'd been full of a mixture of trepidation and excitement that she would shortly be assisting in a major surgical procedure; she'd also been slightly distracted by her sympathy for the terrified parents. It wasn't until the first time she noticed that Zayed seemed to be shuffling constantly from one foot to the other that she deliberately started to take notice.

Even as she marvelled at the fact that a live human brain was only millimetres away, under the softly gleaming dura, she found herself speculating that the handsome surgeon probably maintained his impressively fit physique by some form of vigorous exercise. Had he overdone the exercise last time? Or was the marked hitch in his stride the result of an accident in his youth—perhaps the spur that had set him on course towards his career in orthopaedics?

Suddenly, she realised that this was a very similar train of thought to one that she'd had not so very long ago; that this was the second man with impaired gait she'd met since her return to Penhally...although she could hardly say that she'd *met* the man on the beach, only ogled him from her shadowy hideaway among the rocks. Whereas Zayed Khalil...

Well, she couldn't really imagine this man standing on a beach as the last of the sunset faded around him while he pushed his body harder and harder to perform such a punishing workout. His preference would probably be some high-tech gym now that he was an important surgeon. And, besides, his position at St Piran's meant that he would have to live within a relatively short distance of the hospital. The other man definitely had to live somewhere close to Penhally, otherwise he wouldn't be able to turn up at the beach at roughly the same time each evening.

And if by some impossible fluke of coincidence they happened to be one and the same person...

Well, they aren't, and that's that, she told herself crossly as the surgeon shifted position yet again.

Afterwards, Emily told herself it was just her impatience with her silent speculation that took the brake off her tongue but, whatever it was, she couldn't believe it when she heard herself saying, 'If your back aches, you might try taking those clogs off for a while.'

There was an instant deathly hush in the operating theatre and she was certain that her mask was nowhere near large enough to hide the fiery blush that swept all the way up her throat and face until it reached her hairline under her disposable hat.

'I beg your pardon?' His eyes were almost black, as were the eyebrows that were raised so high that they nearly reached the hat covering his close-cropped hair.

In for a penny, in for a pound, she could hear her grandmother saying, and she tipped her chin up an inch before she repeated her suggestion.

'I said, if your back aches, you might try taking off your clogs and going barefoot...you could put disposable hats over your feet if you're worried about contamination.'

This time the silence seemed to stretch for ever, filled only by the rhythmic bleeps and hisses of the monitors and anaesthetic regulators.

When she was beginning to wonder if she was going to be thrown out of the theatre for breaking his concentration, he gave one swift nod.

'It is worth trying,' he said, and in an instant there was a nurse on her knees beside him, giving a nervous giggle as she pulled a bright blue plastic hat over each of his elegant long feet before she took his theatre clogs away.

Without another word, the operation continued as seamlessly as though the last couple of minutes had never happened, the second strip of misshapen bone carefully cut out of the skull so that the prematurely fused sutures were removed entirely.

Emily was utterly absorbed in the procedure, even more so now that she was assisting than when she had merely looked at a tape.

The brutal part was over and, hopefully, would never need repeating. Now it only remained to irrigate, check for leaks and close before he'd finished. She was quite looking forward to finding out if his suturing technique was as meticulous as every other one she'd observed when he suddenly stepped back from the table.

'Taking the clogs off helped for a while,' he announced in a slightly rough-edged voice as he stripped off first one glove and then the other, somehow managing to tuck one inside the other without getting any fluids on either hand. 'But now I will watch while you complete the process.'

From the electric atmosphere in the theatre Emily knew that something momentous had just happened, but she couldn't allow it to break her concentration, not if she was going to do herself and little Abir justice.

'You might want to rest your best feature on an anaesthetist's stool while I close,' she said, as she positioned herself in his place at the table and held her hand out for the gently warmed saline, hoping her tone was matter-of-fact enough not to wound his ego. 'I'll probably take rather longer over this than you would.'

She almost chuckled when she heard Zayed murmur

'rest your best feature' in obvious amazement, and allowed herself just a couple of seconds to reflect on whether she'd spoken nothing less than the truth. The ubiquitous pale green scrubs he was wearing might be the most shapeless garments in existence, but when they were washed after every use, they soon became thin, and all it had needed was for the man to lean forward over his patient for every lean, tight curve of his muscular buttocks and thighs to be lovingly outlined.

Then it was time to switch her concentration up to full power as she thoroughly irrigated both operating fields to ensure that there were no bony fragments left inside the skull, then a minute inspection of the dura to check for any inadvertent tears. Of course, there weren't any, and the way was clear for closing the initial incisions.

'Clips or sutures?' said the voice with a delicious hint of accent even in those few words.

'I prefer sutures for areas that will be on constant show, even on a scalp where they will hopefully be covered by hair,' she explained, pausing before she inserted the first one in case he had any objections to her decision.

Although she'd been conscious that those dark eyes were watching her every move, the fact had been reassuring rather than intimidating. It had been an amazing experience to be allowed to do such a sensitive part of the procedure on her very first morning on his team. Mr Breyley had allowed her to do little more than close for weeks before he'd allowed her to lead on more routine procedures, and even then he'd hovered over her, poised to take over at the first sign that things hadn't been to his liking.

'I am sure he will thank you if he eventually goes

bald,' her new mentor said dryly, and she concentrated on drawing the edges of the incisions together with as neat a row of sutures as she could manage.

'Are you happy to supervise his transfer to Intensive Care?' he asked as she positioned protective dressings over her handiwork while the anaesthetic was reversed.

'You're going to have a word with his parents?' Her quick glance in his direction told her that even sitting down for the last part of the operation hadn't relieved his pain, if the tension around his eyes was any indication. What on earth had the man done to himself?

'The waiting is awful, so I'll just let them know that the operation went well,' he explained, already on his way to the door, adding over his shoulder, 'And tell them that they'll be able to see him in PICU in—what—twenty minutes?'

'Maybe half an hour, to give us time to get him settled properly?' Emily glanced up at the experienced nurse who would be accompanying Abir on the short journey from the operating theatre to the nearby unit, and received a confirming nod.

'That will give us long enough to put some bandages on and clean his little face up a bit,' the older woman said. 'Although we're not going to be able to do anything to disguise his swollen eyes. Poor little mite looks as if he's not even going to be able to open them when he comes round.'

'Thank goodness that's one of the less important side-effects of the procedure…one that will sort itself out,' Emily murmured, even as she winced at Abir's appearance. 'But he does look as if he's gone several rounds with a prizefighter, and lost.'

After transferring him to Intensive Care she reassured herself that he was receiving the right levels of sedation and pain medication. Then there was the post-operative paperwork to take care of, so it was nearly an hour before she was able to think about the sudden detour her career had taken. And as for finding time to hunt down a cup of coffee and something to put in her rumbling stomach...

'Forget it,' she muttered as she hurried towards the out-patients clinic in response to her first bleep.

'Mr Khalil has been called down to Accident and Emergency, and he is very particular about his clinics starting on time,' snapped the heavily accented voice of his disapproving secretary. 'Some of his patients have travelled a very long way to see him.'

Unspoken, but hovering in the air like a bad smell, were the words 'and they won't be happy to see someone as insignificant as *you* when they walk in the room', but there was nothing Emily could do about that. All she could do was dive in at the deep end and hope that she didn't drown before he arrived.

Her heart nearly stopped when she stuck her head round the doorway to the waiting area and realised that the majority of the people waiting there were probably going to have as little command of English as the Hananis.

'Don't panic,' said a reassuringly Cornish voice behind her. 'I've put out the call for an interpreter, just in case.'

'Were my thoughts *that* obvious?' Emily asked as she turned to find a pair of dark eyes smiling up at her from a motherly body in a uniform that could have done with being a size larger.

'Not your thoughts, maid, but the look on your face

told me you were about to head for the nearest hideyhole.'
She chuckled richly. 'So, shall we make a start? I'm
Keren Sandercock, by the way.'

'I'm very pleased to meet you. As you've probably
gathered, I'm Emily Livingston, the newest member of
Mr Khalil's firm.' She gulped. 'I know it will slow everything down, but could you possibly give me a couple of
minutes with each file before you show the patient in?'
she suggested.

'I can do better than that,' Keren said with a smile. 'I
can introduce you to each of the patients and tell you all
about them. Save you all that time trying to decipher the
notes.' She winked slyly. 'He might be the most wonderful surgeon and the best looking man at St Piran's but his
writing's atrocious. And anyway, I've been part of this
unit ever since Mr Khalil set it up so I've already met them
all.'

'What do you mean, *he set it up*?' Emily hurried in her
wake and found herself obeying instantly when Keren
pointed briskly at the gel dispenser.

'You mean you've joined the madhouse without
knowing anything about what's going on here? You'm
brave, maid.' She chuckled richly again and hitched one
ample hip on the corner of a desk that was already
groaning under a mountainous pile of files. 'Well, here's
the potted version. Mr Khalil was given permission to set
up this paediatric orthopaedic unit on the understanding
that he is free to treat children from his own country who
would otherwise not be able to get any help. Of course,
he also treats patients from the area around St Piran's, but
his special interest is the ones who wouldn't have a hope
of getting any surgery if he didn't bring them over here.'

Emily was speechless, but before she could find the words to ask how she hadn't heard a word about what was going on here, there was a brisk tap at the door.

'Why are you not started?' demanded a heavily accented voice, and Emily didn't need to turn round to know exactly who had just marched into the room, neither did she need to see the sour expression on Keren's face to know that the other woman shared her feelings about Zayed Khalil's secretary.

Start as you mean to go on, she could hear her grandmother's voice advising her when she began each new project, and she whirled sharply to face the intruder.

'Out!' she ordered firmly, flinging one hand out with a finger pointing directly at the door. 'And you will *never* come into my room again without waiting to be invited. Is that clear?'

'It is not *your* room,' she sneered. 'It is *Zayed's* room. *He* is the consultant.'

'And that is all the more reason why a *secretary* should never enter without an invitation,' Emily insisted. 'What goes on in this room is private and confidential and you will *not* walk in again like that or I will report your unprofessional conduct to Mr Khalil. So, unless you have brought me some important paperwork pertaining to one of the patients waiting outside, anything you have to say to me can be communicated by telephone. Please, leave. Now.'

'Good for you, maid,' Keren murmured as the elegant fashion plate flounced out of the room, shutting the door sharply in her wake as she no doubt muttered imprecations through clenched teeth. 'She needed telling, but I'm afraid you've made yourself an enemy there, especially as she's angling to marry our gorgeous consultant.'

Emily's instant pang of dismay was followed by a silent admission that the two of them would look perfect together, tall and dark-haired with the same deep gold skin...

For heaven's sake! What did it matter what he did in his private life? She had a roomful of patients to see.

'Well, now that we've got rid of her, perhaps we should start on the clinic,' Keren continued briskly as she picked the top file off the pile. 'We're a couple of minutes early, but I can't see any of them complaining about that. Now, your first customer is Ameera Khan. She's here for her final check-up before she returns home. Her operation was fairly simple and straightforward—the correction of a break which had gone untreated and had set badly, leaving her with limited movement in her right arm.'

Emily tipped the X-rays out of the accompanying envelope and slid the first set under the clips at the top of the view box. She winced when she saw the way the original break had healed so that virtually no rotational movement had been possible. The second set had obviously been taken shortly after surgery had been completed, with plates and screws much in evidence to hold everything back in the correct position while it healed. The final set had that morning's date printed at the top and showed good progression in the healing process.

Meanwhile, Keren had flipped open the file and when the first thing Emily saw was a set of photographs of a solemn-eyed child cradling her twisted arm with a hopeless expression on her face, she could understand exactly why her new boss had been determined to help.

'Can you show Ameera in?' she asked while she scanned the notes as quickly as she could, looking for any problems that might have been noted at the time of the operation. There was nothing untoward—in fact, this was the sort of simple problem that should never have necessitated a child having to travel to a strange country for treatment...unless her own was so impoverished that even the most basic facilities were unavailable.

The little girl who came bouncing in through the door looked nothing like the sad-eyed waif in the photos, and the young woman who accompanied her was having trouble keeping up with her, especially as she was heavily pregnant.

'This is Mrs Khan,' Keren began the introductions. 'And this is Dr Emily Livingston, who is working with Mr Khalil. She would love to see how strong and straight your arm is, Ameera.'

The interpreter had slipped into the room almost unseen behind the woman and child and, as Keren spoke, translated her words into a mixture of incomprehensible sounds that sounded almost like spoken music.

Without any hesitation, the little girl tugged her sleeve up to reveal a scar so neat that, in time, it would probably become almost unnoticeable.

It didn't take long for Emily to gain her trust, especially when she discovered that the youngster was ticklish, and it was very satisfying to note that every test she performed confirmed that the prognosis was excellent.

'It is good, yes?' her mother asked, clearly worried about her daughter.

'Yes. It is good,' Emily confirmed with a broad smile. The flaking skin that was the result of the time spent in a cast would soon disappear, and the way Ameera eagerly

completed every task Emily had set her spoke well for
her regaining her full range of motion in time, even if
structured physiotherapy wouldn't be available once she
returned to her own country. 'I just wish I could take
another photo to put in the file.'

'But you can!' Keren exclaimed as she hurried across
to a cupboard at the other side of the room. 'I'm sorry,
but I completely forgot to give you the camera.'

'Ah!' the little girl exclaimed when she saw what
Keren was fetching. She obviously knew what was
expected of her and pulled her sleeve up again, this time
proudly showing off her straight arm with a broad smile.

'Thank you so much,' her mother said, her dark eyes
glittering with the threat of happy tears. 'Everybody.
Thank you so much for Ameera arm.'

'You'd better go away before you make us all cry,'
Keren said, and when the interpreter translated what she'd
said, everybody gave a watery laugh.

'It's a good job I didn't have time to put any mascara
on after my shower,' Emily muttered wryly after the door
closed behind them. 'If they're all going to be like that
one, I'd have ended up with a bad case of panda eyes.'

'Maid, that's why mine is waterproof,' Keren confided.
'If it isn't the successes like Ameera tugging at your
heartstrings when you see them put right, it's the parents
arriving with their kids, terrified that no one's going to
be able to do anything to help.'

Emily suggested that she show the next patient in,
suddenly conscious that being close to Beabea wasn't the
only reason why she wanted Zayed Khalil to confirm her
position on his team.

In little more than half a day she'd been allowed to

assist in an operation that would change a tiny child's life expectation and had seen a little girl's hopeless expression change to one filled with the joys of being alive. And neither would have been possible without the unit to which she was now attached, and the man whose determination had driven its inception.

CHAPTER THREE

SHE'D been wrong about the hair on his chest, she thought as she drove towards Penhally that evening, grateful that she hadn't been asked to be on duty this evening.

She hoped that Mr Breyley had explained the special circumstances that had led him to absolve her from staying within easy reach of the hospital while her grandmother was so ill, but she certainly hadn't felt up to discussing the matter with her new boss—at least, not until she'd sorted her head out and relegated her crazy awareness of the man to its proper place.

A blush heated her cheeks at the realisation that she'd actually been...what was the current term?...checking her new boss out while he'd been bending over Abir's head on the operating table.

That was something she'd never done before, never been interested in doing, if the truth be told, but when Zayed Khalil had leant forward over Abir and the V of his top had gaped forward...

'Well, I could hardly help seeing, unless I closed my eyes,' she muttered defensively, and even that wouldn't have erased the image once it had been imprinted on her retinas.

She'd wondered about his chest when she'd seen the

hint of dark hair at the opening of his shirt, and had speculated about the amount of body hair he would display if she were ever to see him naked.

'Well, it certainly isn't a mean scattering of wiry hairs,' she said with a strange sense of satisfaction, even as her body sizzled with heat at the idea of seeing the man totally naked. Mean was the last word she would use to describe the thick, dark pelt that had covered him as far as she could see down the front of his scrub top. As for whether it was wiry… She snorted aloud at the thought that she might ever have the opportunity to find out.

'As if!' she scoffed at the idea of ever becoming familiar enough with the man to run her fingers over the dark swells of his pectorals, trailing them through the thick silky-looking strands until she found the flat coppery discs of his male nipples and—

'Enough!' she snapped into the privacy of her little car, and leant forward to flick the radio on, loudly. 'The last thing I need is to arrive at the home looking all hot and bothered.' Her grandmother may be just weeks away from the end of her life but she certainly hadn't lost her keen eyesight or her unfailing instinct for when there was something on Emily's mind.

'So, how's the job going?' Beabea asked, almost before Emily had settled into the chair beside her bed. 'Are you still enjoying it as much as you thought you would?'

Emily smiled wryly at the fact that her grandmother had picked the one topic that she would rather not have talked about, at least until she'd banished those strange new feelings of awareness that were plaguing her.

'By the time I got to work this morning, Mr Breyley was on his way to New Zealand,' she announced, hoping that the ramifications of her side-tracked job would fill the time until Beabea's next round of medication made her too drowsy to pick up anything untoward.

The story of the consultant's concerned dash to the other side of the world so that he and his wife could be there for their daughter and new grandchild was like meat and drink to a woman who knew almost everything that happened within a fifty-mile radius of Penhally. It was testimony to the fogging effect of the analgesics that it was some time later before she suddenly realised what a disastrous effect it might have on her granddaughter's employment.

'But your job!' she exclaimed breathlessly. 'If he's gone away, does this mean that you're going to have to move away? Oh, Emily! And you've only just moved back, and I was so enjoying being able to see you each day…'

'Hush, Beabea, it's not a problem,' she soothed, squeezing her grandmother's hand gently, almost afraid that she might shatter the delicate bones. 'Before he left, Mr Breyley organised another job for me in the interim, until he comes back.'

'What sort of job? There can't be two posts for the same work, surely?' She was still fretting.

'Not exactly the same, no,' Emily conceded. 'But I've certainly fallen on my feet with the new post. It's paediatric orthopaedics and I went into Theatre this morning and the consultant actually let me assist.'

'On your first day in the job?' Beabea was understandably amazed. She'd had to listen patiently at the beginning of Emily's time on Mr Breyley's firm while she had moaned about wanting to do more than observe and do endless paperwork and legwork.

'On my very first day,' she agreed with a triumphant grin. 'It was an operation on a little boy. The bones of his skull had fused too soon and we had to—'

'Don't tell me any of the gory stuff,' Beabea warned with a grimace. 'I don't like thinking about it when it's happening to little ones. It's bad enough when it's adults. At least they can understand what's happening and why.'

'Softy,' Emily teased. 'But I know what you mean. I hate the idea that they'll be in pain so I always double-check their medication.'

'But you say this new man let you assist. Does that mean passing the tools or instruments or whatever they're called, or—'

'No. There's a member of theatre staff who does that. I was allowed to irrigate the incision—'

'Irrigate? That sounds like something I'd do in the garden,' Beabea teased, and Emily's heart lifted that she was in good enough spirits to joke.

'Then I stitched everything up and put the dressings on before he was transferred to Intensive Care.'

'And what did the consultant think of your work?' Beabea quizzed, and Emily felt the swift tide of heat flood into her cheeks. She was so grateful that there was a knock at the door before she could find an answer that wouldn't reveal her own thoughts about the consultant.

'Am I intruding?' said an unexpected male voice, and a greying head appeared round the edge of the door.

'Dr Tremayne!' Beabea exclaimed, and Emily was amused that her grandmother sounded almost flustered. Well, for an older man he wasn't bad looking, she supposed, and for a woman of her grandmother's generation, the idea of a good-looking younger man seeing her in her bed was probably plenty of reason for embarrassment.

'I was just visiting a couple of patients and thought I'd call in on one of my favourite ladies—unless it's inconvenient. I can always come back another time.'

'Not at all!' Beabea exclaimed, her cheeks several shades pinker. 'Emily, can you get another chair for Dr Tremayne? This is my granddaughter, Emily Livingston— *Dr* Emily Livingston,' she amended with evident pride. 'She's working at St Piran's.'

'Is she now?' His dark brown eyes twinkled at Emily but didn't cause so much as a twinge of reaction. 'She hardly looks old enough and definitely looks far too pretty to toil away in a hospital. Are you sure you aren't harbouring a longing to train as a GP and move back to Penhally?'

'There isn't a lot of call for paediatric orthopaedic surgery in Penhally,' she pointed out politely. 'And I'm thoroughly enjoying working with Mr Khalil in the unit he's set up to operate on the children he flies in from his own country.'

Uh-oh! she thought as she saw the distinct spark of interest in her grandmother's eyes. She had definitely said far more than she'd intended, and it was time to beat a hasty retreat before she was subjected to an embarrassing grilling in front of the GP.

She stood up and gestured towards the chair she'd been using. 'If you'll excuse me, I'll just go and see if there's any possibility of an extra cup of tea while you talk to my grandmother.'

'There's no need to leave on my account,' he began, but she made her escape and hurried down the corridor, suddenly overwhelmed anew by the significance of the GP's visit.

It had been bad enough when she had been taking care of Beabea in her little cottage. But at least there, any professional medical visits from Dr Tremayne and the health visitors and nurses had taken place while she had been at work. Any adjustments to her medication had already been made by the time she'd returned.

Nick Tremayne was obviously a caring doctor who was concerned enough about his elderly patient to visit frequently and spend time making sure she was comfortable, but to actually be in the room while they discussed her worsening pain and, God forbid, speculated on how much worse it would get, was more than Emily could deal with.

This was her grandmother, the last member of her family left alive. Once she was gone, Emily would be totally alone in the world and she didn't think she could cope with talking about how little time there was left.

'I'm not really thirsty, dear,' Beabea said when she returned with a little tray, and her voice bore the slurring that told Emily that she'd received a recent boost of medication. 'I'm feeling quite tired. Perhaps I'll have a little sleep. Thank you for coming, Doctor. I'll see you…see you…'

Emily felt the threat of tears burning her eyes.

Not so long ago, Beabea would have been impatiently waiting for the man to go so that she could ask endless questions about the interesting situation her granddaughter had skated over earlier. It was a measure of the rapid progression of the disease that all she'd wanted to do was drift off to sleep.

'I promise we'll do our best to keep her discomfort to a minimum,' Nick Tremayne reassured her quietly. 'We pride ourselves on making a dreadful situation as easy as possible for both patient and family, but if you have any concerns or need to speak to me at any time…'

'Thank you,' she whispered, 'but nothing can really make it any easier when you're losing the only person in the world who…' Her throat closed up completely and she was unable to utter another sound.

To her utter mortification, the tears started to stream down her cheeks and with one last despairing look at the precious figure slumped against the mountain of pillows, she fled from the room.

It wasn't very far from the front door of the nursing home to the steps from Mevagissey Road down onto the beach and Emily made it at a flat-out run, uncaring for once whether anyone saw her tear-stained cheeks or not.

Once on the beach, she kicked off her shoes and made for the hard-packed sand at the water's edge, knowing that she desperately needed the physical exertion of a long run to get herself under control again.

There were still a number of surfers taking advantage of the waves ramped up by the evening's onshore wind, but they seemed every bit as oblivious to her presence as she was to theirs once she hit her stride.

She had no idea how long she pounded backwards and forwards, but eventually the fact that her legs were shaking with a combination of exhaustion and lack of food slowed her pace and forced her to take refuge in her usual spot among the rocks at the base of the cliff.

Almost before she'd settled herself into her little haven she caught sight of her mystery man making his way to his usual spot, as if he'd been waiting for everybody to leave the foreshore.

As on every other occasion, he began with a series of stretches and warm-up exercises before he started to push himself further and harder than ever.

Even in the depths of her own misery Emily could see that there was something different this time. It was almost as though he couldn't find his usual rhythm, or perhaps the injury that had given him the limp was more painful than usual. Whatever it was, she could tell that he was struggling, but she had a feeling that he was so stubborn that he would be more likely to do himself further damage than give in to the disability, no matter how temporary it was.

The harder he tried the more concerned she became, until all her concentration was on what he was doing rather than on the misery that had driven her down to the beach so precipitately.

Even as she watched, he faltered and nearly fell, only just managing to stay on his feet, then, with a despairing shout towards the last of the sunset he sank to the sand.

For several minutes he sat hunched over, the very picture of disheartened male ego. She felt so sorry that all his efforts over the last few days seemed to have been for nothing, and for the sake of that dented ego would happily have remained out of sight if he'd simply left the beach when he'd recovered.

As it was, she was still watching him when he gathered up his belongings, but when he went to straighten up, something went wrong and he virtually collapsed onto the sand again with a hoarse cry.

'Dammit, what have you done to yourself now?' she demanded under her breath. One half of her wanted to hurry across to offer her help, but she was almost certain it would be refused—there weren't many men who would willingly accept physical assistance from a woman.

So she stayed where she was, her gaze riveted to him as she waited for him to make a successful attempt at getting to his feet.

Only it didn't happen, even though he tried twice more.

'Enough is enough,' she growled when he started to make a third attempt, even though she could see clearly that he must be suffering from some sort of muscular spasm in his back or his leg. She snatched a quick breath for courage, hoping that whoever it was would have the sense to accept the helping hand she was about to offer.

'Hang on a minute,' she called as she stepped out from the shadows at the base of the cliff. 'Let me give you a bit of support so you don't hurt yourself any further.'

She broke into a jog and arrived at the man's side just as he turned to look up at her from his crumpled position on the sand.

'Zayed! I mean Mr Khalil,' she hastily corrected herself when she recognised his unmistakable face in spite of the encroaching dusk.

'What are *you* doing here?' he snapped, for all the world like a trapped and wounded beast.

Emily recoiled from his harsh tone, but she'd suffered much worse from patients during her training and survived.

'I live not far away, in one of the cottages in the old part of Penhally,' she explained simply, sticking to plain facts. 'I was visiting my grandmother and came for a run on the beach.'

His frown was disbelieving until his eyes dropped to her bare feet and the sand-encrusted hems of her trousers.

'In that case, if you have finished your run, you can go home to your cottage and leave me in peace.'

'To leave you sitting on the beach all night in pain?' she challenged. 'I don't think so. If you remember, I've taken the Hippocratic oath, too. Now, where does it hurt? What have you done to yourself?'

He stayed stubbornly silent for such a long time that Emily began to think that he really was going to refuse her help.

Finally, when there was so little light remaining that it was only the paleness of the silvery sand that showed her where he was, he cleared his throat.

'I have had reconstructive surgery after an injury,' he admitted in a voice that clearly contained disgust at his own weakness.

It was very easy for Emily to read between the lines, especially since she'd seen the stubborn way he'd been determined to struggle on in Theatre that day.

'And at a guess, you've been pushing yourself to get fit on top of days filled with a punishing regime of surgery and assessments as well as late nights and early mornings in Intensive Care.' She shook her head in disbelief at what he'd been putting himself through, before realising that he wouldn't be able to see it. 'You were already hurting earlier on today. What on earth made you think you were in a fit state to come down here and push yourself like this?'

Without giving herself time to think about the advisability of what she was doing, she stepped behind him and knelt in the sand to put one hand on each of his shoulders.

'Where is the pain worst?' she demanded, refusing to let herself think about the warmth of his oiled-satin skin as she ran both thumbs up his neck, one on each side of his cervical vertebrae.

Emily could feel the tension in every one of his muscles, but whether that was as the result of the pain or because she was touching him she didn't know. All she knew was that she needed to help him if she could…and if he would let her.

'Relax,' she urged as she began to gently massage the knotted muscles at the base of his skull. 'Is it too painful to bend your knees up and rest your forehead on them?'

Relax?

Zayed stifled a groan as he contemplated his alternatives: humiliate himself by attempting to crawl off the beach on his hands and knees or pillowing his head on his stacked forearms and letting her continue.

Didn't the woman know she was asking for the impossible? He hadn't been relaxed since he'd looked up from Abir's bedside and seen her standing in the doorway.

She'd been like a ray of sunshine with her blonde hair and pale summery clothes sprinkled with flowers, and as for those eyes…their limpid green had seemed cool and soothing as they'd taken his measure across the room, even as they'd sparked something impossible deep inside him.

Impossible?

Yes, he reminded himself bitterly.

She was nothing like Zuleika, and even if she had been, he was not free to do anything about this unwelcome attraction. He would never be free of the guilt.

'It is not necessary,' he argued brusquely, hating the weakness that made this unavoidable, then gave in to the inevitable and settled his head on his arms.

'Yes, it is,' she countered, 'unless you're prepared to spend the night on the beach. And the local police will be around in a while on their patrol to check for drunken kids, and worse.'

'Worse?' he repeated, hazily aware that his brain function appeared to be strangely sluggish. All he seemed to be able to concentrate on was the musical sound of her voice, the light floral scent that was swirled around him by the sea breeze and the fact that she was touching him as if she actually cared about his pain.

'Drugs,' she said, and for a moment he couldn't remember what they'd been talking about.

Was she recommending analgesia for his pain or…?

'In some of Cornwall's coastal towns it's quite common, particularly during the summer holidays,' she continued, even as he was still trying to marshal all the reasons why blunting his physical and mental responses wasn't a good idea. 'So far, Penhally seems to have escaped, but that's probably because, in spite of the influx of holiday-makers each year, it's essentially the same close-knit community it's always been, with everyone looking out for each other…and keeping an eye on each other.'

He agreed with her assessment of the special charm of Penhally and its inhabitants. It was a major reason why, when he'd decided to set up a unit dedicated to the less fortunate of his little people, he'd wanted it to be close to this area. And when the big house up on the cliff had become available…

Ah, it was so hard to follow a single train of thought.

The things she was doing to his muscles with those clever fingers, searching out each knot in turn and concentrating on it until it finally loosened. It almost seemed as if she had magic in her hands so that, for the first time since he'd rejected the mind-numbing effects of the analgesics his surgeons had prescribed, he was free of the gnawing pain.

'What happened?' she asked, her voice so soft that it was barely audible over the rhythmic susurration of the waves over the sand.

Immediately, he felt himself grow tense.

There was no way that he could tell this woman about the violence and destruction that had resulted in his injuries. For all that she was a professional woman, there was something essentially innocent about her that would probably be destroyed if she were to hear of the chaos and misery that he had brought down on his family and friends.

'I'm not asking what caused your original injury,' she hurried to add, almost as if she was able to read his reluctance through her fingertips. 'I meant, what happened today to set this off? You're not usually this bad.'

'How do you know I am not always like this?' he asked, grateful that she wasn't trying to pry. 'We only met for the first time this morning. Perhaps I am always this crippled.'

It was her turn to tense up, her fingers ceasing their painful but ultimately soothing ministrations.

He heard her mutter something under her breath but before he could summon up the energy to turn and face her she began speaking.

'It's true that we met this morning when I came to the

unit for the first time, but…well, I've seen you before, several times. Here, on the beach.'

The final words emerged in a rush, as though there was something shameful about them. He shook his head. It was more likely that she was making things up for some reason of her own.

'That is impossible. I never come down here until the beach is empty. I deliberately leave it until the light is fading, but I would have seen you.'

'Not when I'm sitting in the shadows at the base of the cliff,' she said firmly, her fingers taking up their rhythm again. 'There's a place in between the jumble of rocks behind us where I used to come as a child…my thinking place, I used to call it. I discovered it shortly after I came to live with my grandmother.'

'So, while I have been thinking I have the beach to myself, you have been…' He paused, tempted to say spying, but that was a harsh word for someone who'd accidentally ended up sharing a public space.

'I've been watching over you, I suppose,' she confessed, sounding rather uncomfortable about making the admission.

'Watching over me?' He hadn't needed anyone to do that since he'd moved to Cornwall. It had only been in Xandar that he'd had to be surrounded by armed security. And even then it hadn't prevented the dissidents from…

'Surely you realise how dangerous it can be to swim alone,' she rebuked him sternly. 'Especially when you've been pushing your body the way you do. And to do it in the dark is just asking for trouble. If you got cramp, or—'

'So you appointed yourself my unofficial lifeguard,' he said wryly, not quite certain how he felt about the idea, or about the fact that she hadn't said something about it sooner. After all, they'd been working together for most of the day. Surely she could have said something about seeing him on the beach at Penhally.

'Actually, I didn't know who you were until a few minutes ago,' she admitted, much to his surprise. 'Because you only ever came down here at sunset, you were always silhouetted against the sky, so I never saw your face.'

'But, when you saw me at St Piran's…'

'If you'd taken your clothes off, I might have recognised you,' she joked, but the image her words planted in his head made their present situation seem far too intimate, with her hands touching his naked back.

And he didn't even have the option of walking away from her because he wasn't yet certain that he could make it to his feet unaided.

'So, what *did* happen today to get your back in such a painful mess, unless…does it just do this every so often without provocation?' she asked, returning to her question, and he grabbed the topic like a drowning man grabbing a lifeline.

'There was provocation,' he said wryly. 'I made the mistake of picking one of the patients up.'

'But you do that all the time.' She sounded puzzled. 'I've seen you, when you're examining them. You don't just ask the parents to put them on the couch and examine them like a bug under a microscope—you make friends with them and put them at their ease.'

'Until I forgot to take my mask off and the patient panicked,' he told her, while a strange feeling of warmth spread through him at the approval he heard in her voice. 'He fought me and I nearly dropped him—'

'And overloaded your back,' she finished for him. 'No wonder it was killing you while you were operating on Abir. You should have rescheduled the surgery until you'd recovered.'

As if anything was that easy.

He suddenly realised that he'd been sitting there for far too long, lazing like an overfed cat while his responsibilities piled up around him, responsibilities that someone as happy-go-lucky as Emily Livingston couldn't possibly understand. She probably didn't have anything more pressing on her mind than picking up the threads of the social life she'd left behind when she'd left Penhally to go to medical school.

He grabbed his scant belongings and surged to his feet, amazed that he was actually able to do it without the vicious stab of agony that usually accompanied such precipitate activity.

'Would you have wanted to be the one to tell Meera and Athar Hanani that the surgery they had been steeling themselves for—the nightmare of having the head of their baby son cut open and part of his skull removed—was not going to happen today because the surgeon had a pain in his back?'

'Oh, but I didn't mean—'

'Go back to your cosy little cottage, Dr Livingston,' he interrupted rudely as anger froze all the soft warmth that spending time with this woman had created. 'I will not be requiring your self-imposed offices as lifeguard tonight, so you can leave with your conscience clear.'

As he strode away from her he heard a brief sound of distress carried on the salty breeze but deliberately ignored it, ignored, too, the manners that had been drilled into him from infancy that demanded he should thank her for what she had tried to do for him.

He couldn't permit himself to register the fact that for the first time since the explosion his stride was almost perfectly even, or that the warmth of her hands seemed to linger in every cell of his back under the shirt he'd tugged on over his head.

All he could allow himself to think was that he should have known that someone who looked as beautiful as she did couldn't possibly understand the imperatives of duty and responsibility that were the only way he could assuage the crushing guilt he bore.

In fact, someone like Emily was the last person he needed in his life or on his team. She had been a distraction today, with her soft blonde hair and sparkling green eyes, her womanly body and her ready smile, and he couldn't afford any distractions.

'She will have to go,' he said firmly, startling a couple perusing the menu outside the door of the Anchor Hotel. He could feel their concerned eyes boring into his back for several moments as he continued past the parade of shops towards the promontory where the lifeboat station dominated that side of the bay.

'I will call her into my office and tell her that it would be better if she looked for a position in her original specialty,' he muttered as he passed Penhally Bay Surgery and Althorp's boatyard, and had to fight down a pang of remorse that he wouldn't get to watch her fledgling but meticulous surgical technique again.

He'd been so impressed when she'd apparently stepped up to the table without a trace of nerves, in spite of the fact that her involvement in the surgery had come completely out of the blue. She was good, and with the right guidance, had the potential to be excellent. It was a shame that…

That what? he challenged himself as he finally reached his car. That she was too beautiful and he was too susceptible? That certainly wasn't her fault. And neither was the fact that he'd just jumped down her throat for suggesting that he hadn't been in a fit state to perform Abir's surgery.

She was probably right, but he'd grown so accustomed to working through the pain that he just hadn't realised how bad it was going to get until he had already been in trouble.

He swore viciously under his breath when he finally admitted that he wasn't going to enjoy what he was going to have to do in the morning, glad that since he was using his own language there was almost no likelihood that anyone would be able to understand him.

CHAPTER FOUR

'YOU'RE from Penhally, aren't you?' asked Nance Penwarden, one of the newer members of staff recruited to the unit who almost seemed to have been waiting for her to step inside the door the next morning.

She was an older woman, who had returned to nursing as a way of supporting herself and her children after the breakdown of her marriage.

'I grew up there, but I've only just returned after going away to train,' Emily confirmed. 'Why do you ask?'

'Oh, it's just that we had one of the Penhally GPs in this morning—Dr Tremayne? He called in to see one of his patients who had to come in to our unit after emergency surgery as a result of an accident on the family farm—his pelvis was fractured and had to be stabilised,' she added briefly, before hurrying on. 'Dr Tremayne stayed with the parents for a while, explaining everything and calming them down, then he asked me to show him around the unit and he ended up spending some time talking to some of our older children.'

Her smile was slightly embarrassed and Emily suddenly wondered if one of the reasons why she'd returned to such a demanding profession had been the possibility of looking for a replacement for her husband.

'He was really good with them, really patient,' she continued. 'He spent ages answering questions and… well, you wouldn't happen to know if he's married, would you?' she asked in a sudden rush, and Emily's suspicion was largely confirmed.

'He was married and has several children…three, I think, and all grown up…but I'm almost certain that he's a widower now.' Emily had heard a rumour going around Penhally about some sort of a connection between Nick Tremayne and Kate Althorp, but she wasn't one to spread gossip. Neither did she really have time for this conversation when there were patients to see, and especially with Zayed stalking towards her with a steely expression on his face.

'Dr Livingston, would you come into my office, please,' Zayed said, with a rough edge to his voice that had Emily wondering whether he'd had as little sleep as she had, last night.

'Certainly, Mr Khalil,' she replied formally and stepped away from the side of Abir's cot, pausing only to give Meera a reassuring smile as she left the room.

In his long-legged wake she only had time to throw a glance at the pile of files with which she'd been hoping to familiarise herself this morning. With the outpatients and referral clinics yesterday, to say nothing of Abir's surgery, she hadn't really had much time to take in the specifics of each of the unit's little charges.

That was why she'd driven in to St Piran's a couple of hours before her shift was due to start, but she still hadn't arrived before the man who had dominated almost every one of her thoughts for the last twenty-four hours.

No, actually it had been far longer than that, she realised as she followed him along the brightly decorated corridor towards his office. She hadn't recognised it at the time, but it had been in his persona as the intensely focused man on the beach that he'd first set her hormones humming.

That had been a first for her.

She'd never believed that she was so shallow that she would allow a muscular body or a handsome face to dictate her attraction to a man. But Zayed had that, and more—a keen intellect, a caring heart and a sense of responsibility that…

Oh, who was she trying to kid? It hadn't been his intellect that she'd been dreaming about so heatedly. It had been the feel of his skin under her hands, the way the swells and curves of his hard-won muscles had filled her palms and the subtle smell of musk that had lingered even after she'd made her way to Beabea's cottage.

'Take a seat, please,' he demanded quietly, dragging her instantly away from her mental images of the bronzed figure silhouetted against the sunset to the professional man in front of her.

Not that it completely drove the thoughts away. How could it when she could see the same lean, powerful body, albeit this time clothed in pale coffee-coloured trousers and a dark bronze shirt that brought out unexpected gleams of gold in those beautiful dark eyes?

His face was every bit as handsome as the first time she'd seen it, but after watching it at intervals for the last twenty-four hours she felt as if she was actually getting to read some of the emotions that were going on behind the 'official' look he seemed to hide behind sometimes.

There was something about his expression this morning that she hadn't seen before...an uneasiness that sent warning prickles up the back of her neck, especially when he couldn't seem to decide whether to perch one hip on the corner of his desk or retreat to the plush-looking chair behind it.

It couldn't be that something had gone wrong with Abir's recovery. Before she'd set off for the hospital that morning she'd spoken to the anaesthetist who'd been first on call last night, as well as the nurse who'd been specialling him. Both had been very pleased with the way his little body had coped with the trauma of such major surgery, in spite of the fact that he was still very heavily sedated.

And it had only been moments ago that she'd been standing beside his high-tech cot, surrounded by the clicks and bleeps of all the monitors, keen to reread his notes and hold Meera Hanani's hand reassuringly, even while she knew that nothing less than holding her baby son in her arms, whole and healthy, was ever going to be reassurance enough.

As for any problems with the other patients she'd seen yesterday, she hadn't had time to get to the pile of case notes so she had no idea what would have put such a buttoned-down expression on his 'eminent consultant' face.

So, was it something she'd done...or failed to do?

For goodness' sake! Guessing just wasn't her way, she thought impatiently.

'Is there a problem?' she demanded forthrightly, just

as the possibility that he was trying to find the words to give her the sack exploded into her brain.

'I am afraid… There is something…'

He made two false starts and she nearly growled with anxiety, suddenly realising just how much she did *not* want to lose this job.

It wasn't just that she needed to stay close to her grandmother, although that was essential to her plans for the foreseeable future. No, it was the blinding revelation that, much as she had been enjoying the work she'd been doing in Mr Breyley's unit, there was something so much *more* in what she'd seen and done yesterday.

And it wasn't just that her new boss was the most good-looking, sexiest…

Enough! she chided herself fiercely, knowing those sorts of thoughts were totally inappropriate, especially with her job on the line.

'I am sorry,' he said gruffly, and her worst fears were confirmed.

'Why?' she gulped, feeling too sick to be able to voice all the questions she wanted to ask.

Why did he want to sack her?

Why wasn't he willing to give her a second chance?

Why couldn't he…?

'I must apologise because I was unnecessarily rude and abrupt last night, and I completely forgot my manners. I totally forgot to thank you for your help.'

Emily was left floundering like a fish out of water, almost certain that her mouth was gaping like a fish's, too.

'You're *not* sacking me?' She hardly dared to believe it. She'd been so sure that…

'*Sacking* you? What on earth for?' he demanded, but

she noticed that he hadn't quite been able to bring himself to meet her eyes.

So he *had* considered it, she realised with a sudden heaviness inside her and a panicked feeling as if she'd only just realised how close her feet were to the edge of an unstable cliff.

Who would have thought that it would matter this much to her that she might never get to work with him again?

Still, he'd obviously changed his mind, the more optimistic side of her nature pointed out firmly. And that meant that she had more time to show him how good a doctor she could be, more time to make herself indispensable to him.

'You know as well as I do that you proved yourself more than competent in Theatre yesterday,' he continued, that deep, slightly husky voice sounding almost musical with the liquid syllables borrowed from his own tongue. And as for the unexpected praise…she could already feel a wash of heat sweeping up her throat and into her face.

'As for your help on the beach,' he continued, and it was his turn to sound almost embarrassed this time, 'I am not absolutely sure what you did, but I was able to walk all the way to the car park near the lifeboat station without having to stop, and the improvement seems to have held this morning, too. So I really do owe you my gratitude.'

'I'm glad you're feeling easier, and you're welcome,' she said, tempted to allow a broad grin to creep from ear to ear. Utter relief took the brakes off her tongue. 'So, are we going into Theatre again today? Will you be letting me assist again?'

'Have I created a monster?' he murmured, but she

could see from the gleam in his eyes that he approved of her enthusiasm. 'We will be welcoming some new patients this afternoon. They flew into Heathrow airport from Xandar overnight and will be transferring by plane down to St Mawgan where they will be met by a translator and medical staff for the last part of the journey.'

'Let me guess who will be in charge of documenting their admission,' Emily grumbled, screwing her nose up at the sheer volume of paperwork that was always involved.

'You will also be in charge of leading the case conference session when all the different disciplines get their heads together,' he announced quietly, taking her breath away completely.

'This is a test isn't it?' she said nervously, guessing that at the very least there would probably be a top-flight surgeon from the plastics department as well as the anaesthetist at that meeting.

'Why not look at it as more of a challenge?' he suggested. 'You will have three patients with various problems and you will need to pull together their case histories, such as they are, and put together an up-to-date picture of their problems, their needs and at least one possible course of treatment.'

'Will that include blood work and X-rays?' She barely glanced up from the rapid notes she was taking, her heart already pumping at the task ahead.

'Of course. Everything we will need to make an informed decision about the best way to proceed. And in the meantime,' he added, 'do not forget to keep an eye on Abir. I am not expecting any problems, but Meera is delighted that you have been in to visit him. I am certain she appreciates the fact that you are a woman. Xandar is currently ruled by some very traditional men who continue to make it very difficult for women to feel comfortable in the company of men who are not their husbands or close family members.'

'She must be feeling very isolated over here,' Emily said, her heart going out to the young woman all over again. It must be so hard for her to be going through this while she was so far away from the support of her friends and family. 'That must make the whole situation even more fraught for her if she doesn't like to ask questions for fear of offending.'

'Exactly so,' he said quietly, 'and the language barrier just makes things even more difficult.'

'I shall have to learn some of your language,' Emily announced with a sudden flash of inspiration. 'Even if I can only manage a few words of greeting, it would be better than nothing. Would you teach me?'

He seemed almost as startled as she was to hear the request coming out of her mouth, but before she could hastily retract it, he was answering.

'Of course, if you are really interested in learning. But it is not one of the easiest languages,' he warned.

'So, you don't think I'll be fluent by the end of my time on the unit?' she teased as a bubble of excitement grew inside her. The idea of learning his language had been a spur-of-the-moment idea but the more she thought about it, the more she liked it, not least because it would mean she would have an excuse to spend more time in his company.

And how stupid was that? she berated herself once she was out of his presence. Ever since she'd first seen him on the beach there had been something about the man that had drawn her like a magnet. And now that she was working with him, the attraction seemed to be growing stronger so that all she could think about in his presence was the next time she would be with him. And as for her dreams last night, after the interlude on the darkening beach when she'd come to know the textures and warmth of his back as intimately as her own, well, they'd been enough to have her waking up that morning needing a cold shower to cool off.

'Dr Livingston, where is Mr Khalil? I must see him immediately,' announced an imperious voice that dragged her away from her vivid memories with a snap.

Of course it was Nasima Osman, his beautiful secretary, as immaculately dressed as ever and with such perfect hair and make-up that it must take her hours to get ready for work each day.

'He's just gone into the little conference room to talk with the parents of one of the patients, but he left strict instructions that he didn't want to be disturbed,' Emily told her with a glance towards the door, and was horrified when the arrogant young woman immediately headed towards it.

'Don't!' Emily cautioned sharply, but Nasima whirled on one slender heel to face her with an expression that reminded Emily of a spitting cat.

'His "do not disturb" only refers to *you*,' she announced haughtily. '*I* am *always* welcome,' and she turned back to open the forbidden door with a flourish.

'*Out! Now!*' Zayed snapped, his dark eyes angry as they met Emily's across the intervening yards. 'I told you I was *not* to be disturbed.'

'But, Zayed,' the young woman simpered. 'I have brought you a message that—'

'It can wait,' he growled, his impatience only too clear, as was the fact that he was blaming Emily for the interruption. 'Or give it to Emily. But shut that door *now*.'

The young woman pulled the door shut with a pout and a deliberately loud bang, then started to flounce her way out of the unit.

'What about the message?' Emily reminded her.

'I would not give any message to *you*,' Nasima snapped rudely. 'I will give it only to Zayed when he comes to me.'

'Suit yourself,' Emily murmured to the slender departing back, but she may as well have saved her breath. Anyway, the young woman's pettiness didn't matter when measured against the fact that she'd deliberately interrupted Zayed's meeting.

Emily knew just how important the conversation going on in that room was. Those poor parents were being faced with a terrible choice and the last thing they needed was to be disturbed.

Repeatedly she replayed the expression of annoyance on Zayed's face and wondered if she should have done more, if there had been any way she could have stopped his secretary from barging in like that.

'Zayed... Ah, Mr Khalil,' she corrected herself hurriedly when he finally emerged from the interview room, shocked to discover that she'd worked for Mr Breyley for almost a month without ever wondering whether she could call him by his first name, whereas, in her head, she was already calling this man Zayed after a single day.

'In a minute, please,' he said stiffly as he strode straight past her to his office and closed the door.

Her heart sank. He obviously thought it was her fault that he'd been interrupted, and if she were to say anything, it would look as if she was trying to shift the blame.

Still, it was important that she tried to set the record straight. She didn't want him to think that she would flagrantly flout a direct request, so she went to stand outside his door, determined to catch him before he was called elsewhere.

She could hear the low rumble of his voice behind the door and even though she wasn't deliberately listening to what he was saying, she quickly realised that there was no point even in trying. As his voice took on a louder, angrier note she could tell that he was speaking in his own language and she wouldn't have understood a word.

Suddenly the door was snatched open and his secretary emerged looking much less than her perfect self, with her heavy eye make-up smudged and her flawless olive-toned skin blotchy with a mixture of tears and temper.

'You!' she snarled when she saw Emily waiting there, then let loose with what was obviously a flood of invective.

'Enough! Go!' Zayed ordered icily, his expression looking as if had been carved from Cornish granite.

Emily's heart stuttered at the thought of having that much anger directed at her, but stood her ground. She knew she hadn't done anything wrong, but...

'Emily.' The edge to his voice made all her nerves jangle while she waited for the verdict but, instead of inviting her into his office to detail his displeasure, she actually saw the slightest lifting of his ire. 'There has been a mix-up in the arrangements, so the two of us will have to go to St Mawgan to meet the plane. We will need to leave in half an hour. In the meantime, would you contact the human resources department and ask them to find me a half-competent secretary? I have fired my previous one for misconduct…oh, and for being a totally useless secretary!'

Her head was whirling as he turned and disappeared into his office again, but she had no time to contemplate the recent turn of events.

Her hand hovered over the phone at the reception desk but she wasn't certain who to contact. She'd only been at St Piran's for a month so had no idea how to go about requesting staff.

'Problem?' asked Jenna Stanbury as she consulted the long printed list of numbers for the various hospital departments.

'I need to get in contact with Human Resources in a hurry,' Emily said, concentrating so hard on her search that she didn't consider how that would sound to someone else.

'Oh, Emily! You're not leaving us already!' Jenna exclaimed, seeming genuinely upset by the idea. 'What happened? Is it anything I can sort out for you?'

'No, it's not for me,' Emily reassured her, feeling quite heartened that her new colleague was disappointed at the thought of her departure. 'Zayed…Mr Khalil…asked me to find him a competent secretary.'

'A secretary?' Jenna's eyes grew round and a broad grin spread over her face. 'Whooee! You mean the fashion plate's been given the boot, without getting her hooks into him? Thank goodness for that. She's nowhere near good enough for him.'

'Not that you're biased or anything.' Emma chuckled, glad to know that she wasn't the only one who would be glad to see the back of the woman. 'Now, tell me how to find her replacement, quick, or she might have to stay.'

It was amazing how the mention of Zayed Khalil's name seemed to smooth everyone's feathers. All Emily had to do was say that he was the one needing a secretary in a hurry and the woman on the other end of the phone sounded as if she was falling over herself to find him someone competent.

'It's unlikely that I'll be able to find a bilingual one at such short notice,' she warned. 'Did he want to wait while I track one down or does he need someone straight away?'

'He definitely needs someone today,' Emily stressed, determined that there would be no possibility of a certain person having a chance to talk herself back into the job. 'The sooner the better, because we're expecting three new patients to fly into St Mawgan and we'll have to leave to collect them in under half an hour. If you've any idea of the amount of paperwork they'll be bringing with them—'

'Say no more,' the woman interrupted decisively. 'I'll do my best for him, even if I have to juggle some of the other secretarial staff around.'

'All sorted?' Jenna asked eagerly, when Emily had put the phone down.

'I hope so. She seemed to want to be helpful. Now all I've got to do is find out what I need to do to collect patients from the airport.'

'There should be preliminary files on them, if Madam hasn't made a complete mess of the system,' Jenna said with a grimace as she tried to access the information on the computer. 'Most of them are referred by their own physicians in Xandar, so there's a whole heap of stuff sent over to persuade Zayed to take them on.'

'Wouldn't it be better if they were treated in Xandar?' Emily asked. 'It would save them the stress and expense of having to travel thousands of miles to a strange country.'

'It would, if they had somewhere suitable to perform the operations and someone of Zayed's calibre willing to do the procedures,' Jenna said sombrely. 'Most of the ones who come over here are the children of the poorer people, the ones who live out in the more remote regions who wouldn't have the money to pay for the treatment even if they could get to it.'

'But…' That didn't make sense. 'If they're too poor to get the treatment in their own country, how can they possibly afford to come all the way to Cornwall?'

'They have a wealthy benefactor who pays for them,' Jenna said simply, then flicked a deliberate glance in the direction of Zayed's office door.

'Zayed?' Emily breathed, shocked to discover this whole new layer to the man's character.

'It's not generally known,' Jenna warned. 'He prefers that people just think he works here, not that he actually funds the unit personally.'

'Wow! A man with deep pockets.' She couldn't imagine how much such a set-up must cost.

'Very deep, hence his little gold-digger secretary.'

'That explains a lot, but it doesn't do anything towards getting ready to collect the new patients,' Emily pointed out.

'Well, just hang on a minute and I'll have some details printed out for you,' Jenna promised.

She was as good as her word, and by the time Zayed emerged from his office again, Emily had three neat files of basic information prepared and waiting.

'Ready?' he asked as he strode towards her, shrugging his shoulders to settle his suit jacket perfectly into position.

'Ready,' she agreed, reaching for the files even as her eyes greedily took in the way the width of his shoulders filled out the smooth pale fabric and the way the cut of the suit emphasised his lean waist and long legs.

There was no way her own summery skirt and top could compare with his elegance but, then, having heard what Jenna had told her about the man, there really was no comparison between the two of them on any level. He was obviously a very wealthy man while she was still paying off the debts she'd amassed during her training. He was sophisticated and had travelled widely while the furthest she'd ever gone had been to London. He was doubtless accustomed to lobster thermidor prepared in a Michelin-starred restaurant while she was far more familiar with fish and chips wrapped in paper and eaten on the beach in Penhally.

This was no time for a pity party for one, she reminded herself as she followed him, his long strides meaning that she almost had to jog to keep up with him. Anyway, what did it matter that the two of them had nothing in common? There was never any likelihood that there would be anything more than a professional relationship between them, no matter what her hormones wanted.

'You are thinking deep thoughts,' he commented as he

bypassed the waiting ambulances and made for a sleek silver car.

'Aren't we going in the ambulance?' She hastily avoided the topic of her thoughts. There was no way she was going to tell him that she'd been thinking about the impossibility that he would ever be interested in her in a personal way.

'There are three ambulances,' he said with a gesture towards the three long-wheelbase estate cars that had been specially adapted for use as ambulances. 'Each one has a driver and a paramedic and there is room for the patient to be on a stretcher, in a wheelchair or sitting in an ordinary seat. There is also room for the parents to travel with their child, but there is no room for any extra bodies.'

'So, why do we need to go?' Emily asked as she made a mental note to find the time to take a closer look at those ambulances. From what she could see, as the three vehicles pulled out in convoy, each interior had been very carefully planned so that the paramedic would still be able to take proper care of his patient even while they were on the move. It would be interesting to find out how well they did the job and whether there were any drawbacks in comparison with the bigger box-on-wheels ambulances.

Zayed made an impatient sound as the three vehicles disappeared round the corner, not making any attempt to follow them, even though the engine of his car was already quietly purring. 'I will be there to act as translator and to provide any medical help that the paramedics are not qualified to administer.'

'So, what is my role?' she asked, wondering what he was waiting for.

'You are here to see how the organisation of these transfers is supposed to work, and to come up with any improvements that you can think of—and to provide protection.'

'Protection?' She blinked in surprise. 'From what?'

He nodded towards something he was watching over his shoulder and she glanced across to see the scowling figure of his ex-secretary making her way towards them with a large wheeled suitcase and a bulging shoulder-bag.

'We are giving Nasima a lift to the airport so that she can make the connection with a flight from Heathrow,' he said as he released his seat belt. 'She will be back in Xandar before midnight,' he added with what sounded suspiciously like relief, then got out of the car to stow her luggage.

Emily knew the exact second the young woman saw her sitting in the front of Zayed's car, and if looks could have shot poison, she would have been writhing in her death throes.

The journey took a little over half an hour and was one of the most uncomfortable journeys Emily had ever taken. Not because of the car or its driver, because both were excellent. No, it was the sullen black cloud sitting in the back seat that cast a pall over the journey, in spite of the fact that their route was taking them through some of the most beautiful Cornish countryside on a perfect golden September day.

At intervals, Nasima would mutter under her breath, but obviously not quietly enough to disguise what she was saying if Zayed's stony face was any indication. Finally, he broke his silence, and Emily didn't need to understand a single word of the quietly spoken tirade to know that he was reading his former secretary the Riot Act.

It was a very chastened-looking woman who climbed out of the car at the airport and her tear-filled eyes as she gazed up at Zayed and her rapidly moving mouth told Emily that she was making an impassioned plea to be allowed to stay, but to no avail. Zayed silently unloaded her luggage onto a trolley, handed her a piece of paper that looked like an email flight confirmation and gestured towards the door.

The last Emily saw of Nasima Osman was the hate-filled glare sent her way before she turned and stalked into the building.

'I am sorry about that,' Zayed said as he settled himself back into the driving seat and started the engine. 'Her parents are friends of my family. They were concerned for her safety when she said she wanted to work abroad and when they heard I was setting up the unit in Penhally they asked me to…'

'Take her under your wing?' Emily suggested when he paused.

'Exactly,' he agreed. 'Except she was not happy to come somewhere so far away from the bright city lights and she seemed to think…'

He paused again and Emily was intrigued to see a wash of colour darken the high slash of his cheekbones. She almost chuckled aloud when she realised that he was embarrassed, but decided to spare his blushes.

'She decided that if she couldn't have the social life she wanted, you were going to be the consolation prize.'

Did he choke or was that a laugh, swiftly stifled?

'Something like that,' he admitted, but he seemed inordinately pleased that they'd reached the designated parking area for picking up incoming passengers. 'Do you want to stay with the car or…?'

'I won't learn very much about the way you organise things from here,' she pointed out as she released her seat belt and slid out of the sinfully comfortable leather seat. Once more she found herself trying to keep up with those long legs as he strode towards the plate-glass doors.

At the last moment he seemed to realise that she wasn't with him and paused to allow her to catch up.

'I am sorry,' he said with a rueful grin.

'It's all right for you people who can leap tall buildings at a single bound, but us mere mortals have to work a little harder at it,' she grumbled. 'I've always wished I was taller, then I wouldn't have to work so hard to keep the weight off because it wouldn't show so much.'

'You do not need to lose any weight!' he exclaimed. 'Your body is exactly right for…' He stopped abruptly, as though he'd only just realised what he was saying.

This time there was no mistaking the dark colour that flooded his face and Emily almost felt sorry for him. Almost, because she couldn't help being absurdly delighted that he'd said something so complimentary.

'I am sorry. It is not my place to make personal comments,' he said formally, and laughter bubbled out of her.

'Oh, *please*, don't apologise! That's the nicest thing anyone's ever said about me. When you're only five feet six and tend towards…shall we call it chubbiness…the compliments are rather few and far between.'

'Then the men you know are all idiots,' he growled. 'A real woman is not a handful of bones covered in skin. She has curves and softness so that when she holds her child…' He shut his mouth with a snap then muttered something under his breath before saying, 'I am sorry,' again and gesturing for her to precede him into the arrivals hall.

Emily knew that her smile must be stretching from ear to ear but she really didn't care—in fact, crazy as it sounded for someone of thirty years of age, her feet hardly felt as if they were touching the ground because Zayed had just said that a real woman should have curves and softness and he thought her body was exactly right.

CHAPTER FIVE

THE rest of that week soon disabused Emily of the idea that Zayed had any special interest in her.

He kept up a brutal pace.

She knew that he arrived at St Piran's in the early hours of the morning to deal with the unending office work entailed in the organisation of such a specialist unit, because he was always there before she arrived for her shift. He then continued through a twelve-hour shift of ward rounds, consultations, assessments and operations, and in between all that he still managed to find time to speak to worried parents and play with the children or just give them a comforting cuddle.

The only time she could be almost certain that he wouldn't be involved right up to his neck at the hospital was in the early evening, when the sun slid down over the western horizon. Then, unless there had been some sort of emergency on the ward or he'd been called down to consult in A and E, she knew she would probably be able to find him down on the wave-flattened sand on the beach in Penhally.

It was totally self-deluding, she knew, but that was when she'd come to think of him as *hers*, and of that time as their special time together, even though he never so much as glanced in her direction.

It had started the very evening after his back had seized up on him.

As usual, she'd been to visit Beabea, but as her disease was progressing, she was alert for less and less time as the morphine kicked in. Rather than sit there staring at the visible signs that her beloved grandmother was fading away in front of her eyes, Emily had taken to running from the hospice unit down to the beach.

She was honest enough to admit to herself that it wasn't just displacement activity so that she could switch off from what was happening up in that almost silent room. It had rapidly become an essential part of her day to see that tall, tanned figure stride down onto the sand and strip off to begin his self-imposed routine.

Today was no different.

She'd actually caught herself clock-watching when it had looked as if she might have to stay late, and her concern wasn't just that she might not arrive until Beabea was already asleep. But here she was, once more sitting in the shadows among the rocks, with her pulse tripping with crazy excitement at the prospect of seeing the man she'd been working with all day.

'So, this is where you hide,' said a familiar voice, and she almost leapt out of her skin.

'Zayed!' she squeaked when he loomed over her, silhouetted against a spectacular peach and lavender sunset, then coloured even more furiously when she realised that once again she'd actually used his given name to his face.

'I saw you looking at your watch earlier today, just after you had been holding Abir, and then you disappeared,' he complained. 'I was not certain whether you were on late duty this evening or whether you would be here as my guardian.'

Emily suddenly realised that she'd never explained the special dispensation she'd been granted by Mr Breyley and felt a sharp pang of concern that her current freedom from on-call duties might not continue.

'I'm sorry, Mr Khalil, I should have told you about that,' she started to babble, her brain totally scrambled by the possibility that she might not be able to visit Beabea for days if the arrangement were rescinded. 'Mr Breyley arranged that I should be allowed to live so far away from St Piran's so that I would be able to visit my grandmother. That's why I'm not on the on-call roster at the moment, but when…as soon as…'

'Hush, hush! Calm yourself,' he soothed in exactly the same way that he calmed their little patients when everything became too much for them. 'There was obviously some good reason why the arrangement was made this way, and I have no complaints about the work you do when you are on duty. Now…' His tone of voice changed completely. 'Are you just going to watch me or are you going to do some exercise, too?'

Emily's emotions were in complete turmoil.

She didn't think she would ever be able to talk about her grandmother's illness and her inevitable loss without choking up, but at the same time the fact that this handsome, charismatic man seemed to be inviting her to keep him company this evening was enough to double her pulse rate in seconds.

'Have you already been running?' he asked, as if she weren't standing there with her mouth hanging open and her eyes glued to the expanse of taut male flesh he was uncovering right in front of her.

'Uh, n-not yet,' she managed to stammer, finally managing to drag her covetous gaze away. She could remember all too clearly just what that skin and those muscles felt like and her fingertips were tingling with the desire to touch them again.

'Well, then, if you go for your run now, you could join me when I am ready for my swim,' he suggested. 'You do swim, do you not?'

Emily rolled her eyes. 'Beabea never allowed me down to the beach by myself until I could prove that I could swim well enough. Then I completed a lifesaving course so I could be useful if anyone else got into difficulties. The lifeguards can't be on duty twenty-four hours a day.'

'And that is why you insisted on watching over me when I was breaking all the rules,' he said with a nod of comprehension, but Emily wasn't going to tell him that it wasn't only the fact that he'd gone in to swim on his own that had prompted her to wait for him to emerge that first evening. There was no way she would be admitting that it had also been the prospect of catching another glimpse of that beautifully sculpted body.

Emily had set off for her first trip to the end of the beach when she wondered whether it would be a good idea to go swimming with Zayed after all.

Although he'd seemed perfectly friendly so far this evening, she had definitely been aware that he'd created a deliberate distance between the two of them after their last encounter.

Had he resented her presence here? After all, Penhally

was a rather long way to go if he only wanted to find a beach to do his exercises and finish up with a swim. It might be that he'd deliberately come this far so that there was less likelihood of bumping into anyone who would recognise him.

There was also the isolation factor.

This late in the season there were far fewer holiday-makers about, especially the school or university students who might linger on the beach that much later in the day. This would almost guarantee that he wouldn't have an audience while he pushed himself to the limit to regain his strength and flexibility.

He certainly wasn't struggling so much this evening, she noticed as she passed him for the third time, only now allowing herself to notice that, as she was sticking to the very edge of the firm sand, she was between him and the dying sun and was therefore not limited to seeing him as a silhouette. In fact, this was the clearest view she'd ever had of him, apart from the glimpse of firm male flesh she was treated to when he leaned forward in his V-necked scrubs.

Just then he turned to pick up his towel and as she got her first good look at the injury that had made his struggles so necessary, she almost tripped over her own feet.

Dear Lord, what *had* happened to him?

She'd felt the irregularity of his skin when she'd been working out the knots in his muscles—she hadn't been able to avoid feeling it—but in the poor light she'd never realised just how livid the scarring had been, or how extensive.

'It was an explosion,' he said suddenly, and she was horrified to realise that she'd been standing there staring at his injuries.

'That would explain the type of scarring,' she said, finally managing to grab hold of a little of the control she'd learned during her training. 'Did you need a great deal of surgery and skin grafts?'

'Not as much as I might have done if the spinal cord had been severed,' he said prosaically, and the image of such a vital man being confined to a wheelchair made her shudder.

She wanted to know more. In fact, she wanted to know everything there was to know about this man, but before she could formulate the next question he was gesturing towards the sea.

'Ready to swim?' he invited.

She actually put both hands to the hem of her top, ready to strip it off over her head, before she remembered the reason why she couldn't.

'I'm not wearing a costume under my clothes,' she said with a grimace, and the feeling of disappointment was immediate. If she'd thought about it earlier, she could have run back to Beabea's cottage to change. It had been so long since she'd swum with anyone, and the thought of sharing this stretch of the sea with him was…

'You are wearing sports clothes under those things, are you not?' he asked, gesturing towards the casual clothing she'd donned before she'd left the hospital. 'Can you not swim in those?'

'Why not?' she exclaimed with a grin when she suddenly remembered that her sports bra and pants were the sort of utilitarian shape that wouldn't look unlike a modest bikini.

Before she could second-guess herself and realise that she was exposing far more than she ought to the man, she stripped her cotton knit top over her head and shoved the drawstring trousers over her hips to pool around her ankles.

With the sort of burning awareness that told her he was watching her every step, she sprinted for the water. Barely waiting for the waves to reach above her knees, she dived through the next line of surf and came up with her arm already poised for the first fierce stroke.

It was some time before she realised that Zayed had stopped swimming and was now standing in the fading light on the beach.

This time he'd been the one standing guard while she'd ploughed backwards and forwards across the mouth of the bay until her muscles began to quiver in a way that told her she'd regret this in the morning.

'I hadn't realised just how much I'd missed that. Have you been waiting a long time?' she asked, panting as she splashed her way through the shallows towards him. It was only when he didn't reply that she looked a little more closely and realised that he seemed to be transfixed by her appearance…her almost naked appearance as the waning light rendered her coffee-coloured clothing all but invisible against her tanned skin, and the cool sea breeze puckered her nipples into tight little beads.

'Here,' he said gruffly, holding out his own towel in her direction, then dragged his gaze away to stare fixedly towards the fading horizon.

Emily's breath caught in her throat as she stepped close enough to take the nubby fabric from him to wrap it around her shoulders, wishing she was able to see his expression more clearly.

For just a second it had seemed as if there had been something almost…almost predatory in those dark eyes as they'd skimmed over her, and the thought that he'd been looking at her with sexual intent sent an atavistic thrill right through her that was waking all sorts of primitive responses.

'Why do you…?'

'What is it…?'

They both hurried into speech to fill the uncomfortable silence stretching between them, and both halted at the same time.

'What did you want to know?' he offered as he pulled the edges of his shirt together and began to button away the sight of that impressive chest.

'Oh, I just wondered…' What *had* she been thinking about while her body had still been reacting to the thought that he might have liked what he'd seen? Oh, yes. 'Why do you come all the way to Penhally to swim? Is it because it's far enough from St Piran's so that you're unlikely to bump into someone who'd recognise you?'

'If that was the reason, it obviously did not work,' he said wryly. 'But, actually, it is because it is convenient for me as I have a house up there.' He gestured towards the far end of the beach, to the cliffs beyond Penhally Bay.

Emily knew the area he meant and knew the sort of houses that had been built up there.

'The view must be spectacular,' she said, even as she silently acknowledged that only someone wealthy enough to set up a specialist unit would be able to afford one of those houses. They were a far cry from Beabea's little cottage.

'And what is it that has you hurrying to Penhally every day?' he asked as he accepted the neatly folded towel from her and tucked it under one arm. 'I saw you looking at your watch today, just after it was time for you to leave. Do you have a man waiting impatiently for you to come—?'

The shrill sound of a mobile phone cut through his unexpectedly personal question and Emily reached for it, recognising the ring tone. She caught sight of the name of the person ringing her and her heart suddenly leapt into her mouth.

'Hello?' she said, breathless with dread.

'Hello, Emily, love.' Her grandmother's gentle voice filled her ear with the reassurance that she hadn't gone yet. 'Staff Nurse let me use her phone to tell you that I'm awake if you want to visit. I didn't know if you might have given up on me and gone back—'

'Of course I want to see you,' Emily cut in. 'I've just been for a swim on the beach down below you, but it won't take long for me to get there. Five minutes. Ten at the most.'

She ended the call and turned to the silent shadow standing beside her with a smile. 'That's the reason why I hurry to Penhally every day.'

'Your boyfriend expects you to stop what you are doing to come when he calls?' he asked, and in the darkness his voice sounded almost disapproving.

'No.' She chuckled. 'That wasn't a demanding boyfriend. That was my grandmother.' She was struck by the sudden urge to introduce the two of them to each other. It would be interesting to see what Beabea made of the man who'd begun to fill her every waking thought. 'Would you like to walk up with me to visit her? She had to move into the hospice a few days ago and...'

'The hospice? She is ill?' She was almost certain he'd intended refusing the invitation until that moment.

'She has inoperable cancer,' Emily told him, the words no easier to say than the first time she'd ever said them. 'She's unlikely to live until October.'

'Surely she will not want a stranger to intrude upon her?' They were walking while they were talking and she could see his expression a little better now that they were climbing closer to the lights along Harbour Road, well enough to see that he was intrigued.

'Beabea has never met a stranger,' she said with a chuckle. 'It has never mattered to her whether someone is a duke or a dustman—she is just fascinated by people and always finds a way to put them at their ease.'

'Even now, when she is—?'

'Especially now,' Emily broke in, preventing him from saying the hateful words. 'She has been complaining that she hasn't had enough visitors to make life interesting. I think she would definitely find *you* interesting.'

He laughed aloud, the sound bouncing merrily back at them from the row of houses that faced out towards the sea. 'In that case, how can I refuse the invitation?'

'Beabea? Are you still awake?' Emily called gently as she stuck her head round the door.

'Come in, Emily, dear,' her grandmother invited. 'I'm sorry I was asleep when you came earlier. They had to change the dose on that dratted pump thing. I have no intention of sleeping my last few days away if I can help it.'

'Are you feeling up to a visitor?' Emily asked, every nerve aware of Zayed's presence in the corridor behind her as she stepped forward to give her grandmother a gentle hug.

'Of course I am, dear.' Her faded blue eyes brightened at the prospect, even though she was now barely strong enough to lift her hand in an automatic gesture to check that her soft silvery curls were tidy. 'I hope you've brought someone entertaining.'

'I do not know how entertaining I will be, but it is an honour to meet the grandmother of Emily,' Zayed said as he stepped into the room and walked forward to offer his hand. 'I am Zayed Khalil and I work with your grand-daughter at St Piran's Hospital.' He bent low over Beabea's hand and Emily saw delight sparkle in her eyes even as she took his measure.

'Emily has spoken of you,' she said after several long seconds of the sort of silence that would have had Emily shuffling her feet when she'd been younger. Zayed stoically stood his ground and seemed to have no difficulty meeting her grandmother's direct gaze until she gave a single nod and a smile.

'I am very pleased to meet you,' she said, and Emily could hardly blame her for sounding almost coquettish in the face of Zayed at his most charming. 'But she completely forgot to tell me how handsome you are,' Beabea added, and Emily cringed.

'Perhaps Emily does not think I am handsome,' Zayed retorted with a sideways glance and an unrepentant grin at Emily's blazing face

Her grandmother snorted. 'I didn't bring up a stupid grandchild,' Beabea told him sternly. 'She knows a good man when she sees one.'

It was something that she'd heard her grandmother say a thousand times over the years, but it was the first time Emily had ever seen it bring such a look of sadness to a man's face. And she had absolutely no idea why. Zayed *was* a handsome man and he was also a good man, otherwise he would never have thought about setting up the unit at St Piran's and working the hours he did to take care of his little charges.

And as for the way he was gently teasing her grandmother, bringing a touch of colour to cheeks that had been grey and lifeless for so many weeks…well, if that wasn't a mark of a good-natured man, Emily didn't know what was.

Within moments, Zayed had been invited to perch on the edge of Beabea's bed and was being given the third degree. All Emily had to do was stay in the background, listening quietly to learn that he'd been born and brought up in Xandar and had returned there after he'd completed his medical training, only leaving in the wake of the most recent wave of atrocities.

'I remember,' her grandmother said thoughtfully. 'There was a series of explosions, wasn't there? Several prominent people were killed when one of the more reactionary groups tried to make a point.'

'There is nothing wrong with your memory,' Zayed said, and Emily was sure that some odd sort of understanding seemed to pass between the two of them, but then Beabea was back in full flow again.

'So, where are you living now?' she demanded. 'In one of those dreadful little flats they put up for the single staff who have to live close enough to reach the hospital when they're on call?'

'Thankfully, no,' he said with a grimace. 'Because my unit is largely privately funded, I have been able to set many of the rules myself, including employing enough staff so that the on-call times are not too onerous. This means that I am able to live in my house in Penhally most of the time and travel backwards and forwards to the hospital.'

'You have a house in Penhally?' Beabea's tone was one of disgust that she'd missed out on this prime piece of gossip. 'Where? Do you know the name of the person who lived there before you?'

Emily suddenly blessed the inspiration that had prompted her to bring Zayed to visit her grandmother. In just these few short minutes she was hearing the answer to all the questions she'd been wanting to ask but hadn't dared to for fear of seeming too inquisitive.

'The house is up on the cliffs on the other side of Penhally, looking out across the water, like your room here. And as for the person who lived there before, he was one of the doctors who worked at the surgery down in the town. An Italian, I think, by the name of Marcus…'

'Marco,' her grandmother corrected him swiftly. 'Marco Avanti. He and his wife have gone back to Italy. But…if you're living in Marco's house, that means that you're the person who's set up that special unit for the children.'

'I told you all about the unit, Beabea,' Emily cut in, wondering if this confusion was a sign that it was time for the two of them to leave her in peace. If the morphine pump had recently delivered her next dose of analgesia, it wouldn't be long before she fell asleep again. 'Do you remember? Mr Khalil was kind enough to take me onto his team when Mr Breyley had to fly out to New Zealand.'

'Ah, yes! I meant to ask you about that. How is that

little grandchild of his doing?' Beabea was momentarily distracted. 'How soon after the baby was born were they going to have to operate?'

'He phoned St Piran's to tell us that the operation has already been done,' Emily told her with a smile. 'They've detached all the faulty plumbing around the heart and put it all back where it should have been in the first place, and everything's looking good now.'

'Thank goodness for that,' her grandmother said with a nod of satisfaction. 'But I still want to know about this rehabilitation place of yours, young man. The gossip says that there are dozens of children up there, living a life of luxury with gold taps and marble floors and people to wait on them hand, foot and finger.'

'And I'm sure your language has just as many sayings about those who listen to gossip as mine does,' he said with a laugh.

'So, what *is* the truth, then?' Beabea pressed him.

'The truth is that it *was* a very luxurious house,' he admitted, 'but it was the position and the space and the possibility of converting it to my requirements that made me buy it. I knew I was going to need somewhere suitable for my little patients to go when they were well enough to leave St Piran's but not yet well enough to travel back to Xandar, and it had the added benefit of a wide view of the sea and proximity to the beach, which is something none of these children have ever seen or experienced before.'

'And the life of luxury with gold taps and servants?'

'A figment of the imagination, I am sorry to say. The servants are really nursing and physiotherapy staff, and they are there to take care of the children and to show their parents how to continue the work when they return home.' He threw a quizzical glance in Emily's direction. 'Perhaps Emily could bring you over for a visit, so that you can tell all your friends about the real story.'

'I would love to,' Beabea said, but smiled a little sadly. 'Unfortunately, I think my visiting days are over, and I wouldn't like to upset your little patients if they saw such a sick old lady. But that doesn't mean that Emily can't come in my place,' she suggested, just a shade too brightly for Emily's liking. 'Then she could tell me all about it instead.'

'Beabea,' Emily began, embarrassed that Zayed might feel that he'd been forced into inviting her.

'I would be delighted to show Emily around,' he interrupted swiftly. 'In fact, I will be going on there this evening, when you have had enough of our company. Perhaps she will want to go with me then?'

CHAPTER SIX

As EMILY led the way out to her car a few minutes later, Zayed was still marvelling at the elderly woman's strength and determination, even though her body was failing her.

In those first few seconds when he'd stepped into the room it had felt very much like the times when he'd been called to stand under the eagle eye of his own grandmother, and he'd felt the same crazy conviction that she could read his mind and the same boyish need to fidget.

Then she'd silently nodded and smiled at him, and it had almost felt like some sort of blessing.

He was glad that he hadn't been tempted to underestimate the woman's intelligence, especially when the conversation had turned to his home country. Who would have thought that an elderly woman dying of cancer in the depths of Cornwall would have such accurate recall of the potentially catastrophic happenings in Xandar, a country so many thousands of miles away? And who would have believed that she would have so accurately connected those events with his own life?

He was only grateful that she hadn't questioned him about those dark times in front of Emily. It was some sort of relief to be working with someone who didn't know all the details and wouldn't be tempted to pity him for all he'd lost. Pity was one emotion that he couldn't bear, not when he didn't deserve it.

If it hadn't been for him…

'If you'd rather I didn't go to your house, just say so,' Emily said suddenly. 'Beabea did rather Shanghai you into making the invitation.'

By that time they had made their way around the curve of Penhally harbour wall and the row of shops, cafés and hotels that faced the tightly enclosed bay. They were approaching the turning for the car park by the lifeboat station by the time she finally broke the silence in her little car.

'Do you not want to see where the children go when they leave the hospital?' He was suddenly disappointed that she might not want the guided tour he'd been looking forward to. There was something about her sheer enthusiasm for everything she did that seemed to lift the spirits of everyone around her, and he certainly wasn't immune.

'Of course I want to see it!' she exclaimed impatiently, and he had to suppress a satisfied smile at the thought that he was coming to know her so well. 'Apart from anything else,' she continued as she pulled neatly to the kerb, 'Beabea would never forgive me if I didn't come back to her with all the details.'

'Why do you call her Beabea?' He'd been curious ever since he'd heard the name. 'Is it the Cornish word for grandmother?'

'No.' She chuckled, a delightful sound that wrapped intimately around him in the semi-darkness of her car. 'If I remember rightly, grandmother is *henvamm* or *henvammow*.'

'So, why Beabea?' he persisted.

'Because her name is Beatrice,' Emily said simply, then decided to give him the full explanation. 'At the time I came to live with her, she had two friends... twins...who always did everything together, but one was always half a beat behind the other. So when they called her Bea, it sounded as if they were saying Beabea. I imitated them and it just stuck.'

'Do they still call her Beabea?'

'No.' She sighed. 'They're both gone now; so many of her lifelong friends have gone. That's one of the reasons why she's so delighted when I bring her visitors.'

Zayed thought about his own family—the remnants of it, at least—and suddenly realised just how long it had been since he'd seen them. His grandfather and the collection of great-aunts had all been well when he'd last seen them, but who knew what toll the years had taken? Any one of them could be in the same situation as Emily's grandmother.

Not that he could do anything about it. He was the very last person they would want to see on their doorstep.

'So, do you want me to drive you up to the house, or shall I follow you?' Emily asked, and he realised with a start of surprise that he must have been sitting lost in his thoughts for several minutes.

'You could follow me up there,' he suggested, releasing his seat belt and unfolding himself from the cramped position, grateful to find that his back hadn't seized up in the time since he'd climbed into her little car. 'Then you will have transportation to escape when you are too bored.'

'I'm still not certain I should be going *anywhere* when I look such a mess,' she complained with a despairing flick at the damp tangled ends of her hair. 'I haven't even got a comb with me and it looks like a rat's nest…a *salty* rat's nest. I should have stopped off at the cottage on the way past and done something about it.'

'You will not find any of the patients complaining,' he promised as he ducked back down to look at her, lit only by the courtesy light inside the car. 'Most of them will probably think you are some kind of exotic sea creature with your long wavy hair and your green eyes.'

He wasn't immune either. She looked perfectly stunning without a scrap of cosmetics on her skin, fresh and youthful and…and everything he had no right to be looking at.

'If you're sure?' she said doubtfully.

'I *am* sure.' He closed the car door to stride across the car park to his own vehicle.

It only took a few minutes to turn up past the surgery and climb the hill onto the top of the cliffs, and from there it was a relatively short run to the driveway leading to the strikingly modern house with the commanding view over both town and sea.

The security lights came on as soon as they approached the house and he signalled for Emily to draw up beside him, close to the front entrance.

'A word of warning,' he said as he reached for the door, suddenly unaccountably nervous about taking her inside. For some crazy reason, it really mattered what this young woman thought of the facility he was setting up here. 'Because they have a sleep in the middle of the day, not all of the children will be in bed yet, and it can be a little noisy.'

'A *little* noisy?' Emily echoed a few minutes later when she could almost hear herself think, again.

When Zayed had opened the door there had been a couple of seconds of absolute silence as everyone had looked to see who had arrived, and then the place had erupted into chaos, with every child shrieking for attention at the same time, each one with a smile from ear to ear as soon as they saw him.

Emily realised that she may just as well have been invisible as far as his little charges were concerned, and she slipped in quietly and closed the door, quite content to stand to one side and watch what was happening.

Those who were mobile had mobbed him and he'd rapidly disappeared under a maul of bodies, arms and legs, many sporting casts of varying lengths and colours. Those unable to join in had been forced to shout for attention in what was obviously a regular occurrence, while a scattering of their carers and parents looked on indulgently.

For a moment Emily had been worried that the children might be in danger of re-injuring themselves until she saw just how gently Zayed was treating them in spite of his blood-curdling growls.

'He should have children of his own…lots of children,' said a middle-aged woman who was obviously from Xandar, too, her accent full of the same liquid syllables as her countrymen that Emily had met on the unit at St Piran's. 'Taking care of other people's children is good but it will never fill the empty space inside him.'

Emily had an instant vision of dark-haired children with cheeky grins and the same gold-shot dark eyes that she saw over Zayed's mask every day, then ruthlessly shut the images away, refusing to let herself think about his eventual children. There was so little likelihood that they would be her children, too, that the thought of him surrounded by them was sharp enough to cause a physical pain around her heart.

'I am Reza Saleh,' the woman introduced herself, and settled herself comfortably against the wall beside Emily. 'I was one of those who worked with Zayed in our own country, before tragedy struck. Then, when I heard he needed staff over here in Penhally...' She shrugged eloquently. 'I learned English so I can come here to help him.'

'Reza! Come and save me from these terrible children!' Zayed called, then used exactly the same inflection when he said something in his own language, so it wasn't just the children's hilarity that told her he'd said the same thing again.

'Time for bed, children,' Reza said firmly with a clap of her hands, and copied Zayed in translating the order to their little charges.

'Not bed! No!' called several voices, obviously not tired of their game yet.

'No bed, no story,' Reza decreed in no-nonsense tones, and the children clearly understood that threat without the need for any translation.

Zayed was still helping the last of the children to their feet when someone caught sight of Emily for the first time.

Within seconds they were all staring at her as though she were an alien from another planet, their sudden silence erupting into a welter of incomprehensible questions.

'OK! OK!' Zayed called, putting both hands up in the air to call for silence as he made his way across to her. To her surprise he took her hand in his to lead her forward into their midst, then apparently forgot to let go because she ended up standing there surrounded by inquisitive children and adults with the warm strength of his hand wrapped around hers.

'This is Emily Livingston,' he said slowly and clearly, while she tried to work out exactly why it felt so right to stand there like that. 'She is a doctor at the hospital. She helps me to fix bones.' He repeated the simple sentences in their language to make sure they had all understood, but one little girl began shaking her head.

'No! No dotor!' she insisted, wide-eyed, then reverted to her own tongue for several impassioned sentences.

Several of the adults chuckled, including Zayed.

'What did she say?' Emily demanded softly.

'That you are too beautiful to be a doctor,' he said with a definite twinkle in his dark eyes. 'That you are really a princess who will wave your magic over them to make them well.'

'If only it were that easy,' Emily murmured, even as her pulse responded to his expression. 'Hello,' she said to the little girl, finally forcing herself to break the connection between their hands so that she could crouch down to bring them to more or less the same height. 'My name is Emily. What is your name?'

This time it was Reza who translated for her, and supplied the dark-haired moppet's name in return.

'This is Leela, and I don't think she'll ever believe you're not a princess,' she said with a grin. 'Just look around the room and see if there are any other people here with blonde hair and green eyes.'

Blonde hair full of dried seawater so that it was as stiff as baler twine and green eyes with the most attractive dark shadows under them, either from too many hours spent worrying about Beabea or from too many nights spent dreaming about a certain dark-eyed consultant, to say nothing about coping with a demanding job.

Most attractive, she thought wryly, except that to one little girl, it was obviously good enough.

Reza clapped her hands again. 'Bed or no story,' she reminded her little charges, but little Leela wasn't going to be hurried, planting herself right in front of Emily to pose an urgent question.

'Leela has decided that she wants *you* to tell them the story tonight,' Zayed informed her with a grin as he gently lifted the little girl up to his shoulder.

Emily was barely aware that her feet were automatically taking her in his wake. 'Me? I can't tell them a story. I don't know any stories.'

'Oh, I am sure you will think of something,' he said airily as he led the way into what looked like an extremely well-appointed paediatric ward, albeit one that would have the most fantastic panoramic views once the sun came up in the morning.

'This is amazing,' Emily breathed as she looked around. There was everything any of the children might need to make life easier while they were hampered by casts and frames, but the decoration of the room and the colourful bedding and piles of toys gave it a very different feeling. And with the combination of the high staffing level and parents eager to do anything they could to help, it wasn't long before everyone was in pyjamas and nightdresses and smelling of toothpaste.

'Story,' Leela said eagerly, as she held up a slim book for Emily to see.

'"*The Little Mermaid*",' she read on the cover, and

when she heard Zayed choking back laughter she knew where that suggestion had come from. 'Oh, I'm sure we can think of something else.'

'You do not want to tell the story of the little mermaid who falls in love with the handsome prince?'

Emily had an uncomfortable feeling that it wouldn't just be a story in a book if she didn't get herself under better control. Seeing him by Abir's cot that first morning had definitely had an unexpected effect on her heart, but learning about this other side to the man had pushed her dangerously close to falling in love with him.

For all the good it would do her, she admitted wryly. He was definitely every inch the elegant gentleman good enough to be a prince, but she was a long way from being the mermaid he would fall in love with.

Anyway, that sort of thing only happened in fairy-tales.

Looking at the books on the bookshelf, her eyes fell on several old favourites from her own childhood and she exclaimed with delight before pausing for a moment, wondering how on earth she was going to tell any story when she couldn't speak a word of the children's language.

'There is a problem?' Zayed asked when she scanned the titles, some in English and some in Arabic, and her shoulders slumped when she realised that the task would be all but impossible.

'There are so many wonderful stories, but I have no way of telling any of them,' she mourned.

'So simplify the story and tell it to me, and I will translate it for them,' Zayed suggested. 'Come. Sit here and begin.'

Emily hesitated when he beckoned her towards the seat

beside him, knowing she ought to be sensible, but the temptation to be that close to him was suddenly too great to resist.

'Leela is very insistent that you read this one,' Reza said with a twinkle in her eye as she handed Emily the copy of *The Little Mermaid*.

The picture on the cover was the traditional one with the fish's tail replacing the young woman's legs, but Emily was sure she'd never noticed before that she was shown with long blonde hair curling over her shoulders to disguise the fact that she wasn't wearing a bikini, or that she was quite so well endowed.

'You also swim like a mermaid,' said a husky voice in her ear, and Emily turned shocked eyes towards a face that was suddenly as full of mischief as one of their young audience.

Was he implying that she had looked like the illustration, too, down on the beach this evening?

And if ever there was an inappropriate thought to have when surrounded by a dozen sharp-eyed strangers…

'Once upon a time…' Emily began, firmly refusing to acknowledge Zayed's presence beside her in anything other than his current role as translator.

Several pages in, she had the sneaking suspicion that his translations bore little relationship to what she was reading, especially when most of them were greeted with gales of laughter.

Leela seemed to be the only one who didn't appreciate his version and there was a decidedly militant look on her little face when she finally closed the book that told Emily that the story definitely hadn't ended the way she wanted it to.

'No! No!' she insisted even as the rest of their audience was applauding.

The sparkle of tears in those big dark eyes was more than Emily could stand.

'What is she saying?' she demanded, turning to face Zayed when Leela voiced her vehement disapproval. 'Why is she so upset?'

Zayed had the grace to look a little sheepish. 'She is not happy that I...took a few liberties with the story.'

'So, what does she want? Shall I start reading again?' Emily offered.

'It is not so much the story that is the problem,' he admitted. 'It is the ending.'

'I don't understand. What ending? There is only one ending.'

There was a hint of colour tingeing his cheeks as the little girl stood right in front of him, obviously telling him in great detail where he'd gone wrong.

'She says that the prince has to fall in love with the mermaid and give her a kiss so they can live happily ever after.'

'And that wasn't the way you translated it.' Emily could all too easily understand the reason for all the laughter before. She fixed him with a stern gaze, then suggested sweetly, 'So, tell the story that way, Mr Consultant. It's not worth upsetting her just before she goes to bed.'

If anything, his embarrassment deepened and Emily suddenly became aware that the two of them were the focus of some hilarity from their adult audience, too, and not a little horrified fascination.

'I *have* tried to tell her, but she has convinced herself that you are the mermaid princess and that I should...'

Emily stared at him when the full import of what he *wasn't* saying poured over her.

Suddenly she was very aware of the fact that their bodies were touching from shoulder to knee and could almost swear that she could feel the temperature rising around them. Any hotter, and the settee would burst into flames.

She couldn't drag her eyes away from his, totally aware of everything from the sinful dark length of each individual eyelash to the way his pupils were dilating in evidence of his own awareness.

This was crazy. There was absolutely nothing between the two of them other than their professional relationship, but as the seconds stretched out it felt like something else entirely, and she didn't know whether to laugh or run away and hide.

What she did know was that all of a sudden she couldn't wait to see what Zayed was going to do. Was he going to find some other way of calming Leela down, or was he actually going to lean over and press his lips to hers…an act that she was almost certain would be forbidden in his own country.

One dark eyebrow rose, almost as if he'd read her thoughts, and a wicked smile teased the corner of his mouth as he reached for her hand.

'Oh, beautiful mermaid princess,' he intoned, then turned to Leela, obviously providing the enthralled youngster with her own personal translation, as though the rest of the room wasn't waiting breathlessly to see what would unfold.

'I am the handsome prince and I have found you at last,' he continued, staring soulfully into her eyes with enough simulated heat to set her tangled, salty hair on fire before switching the expression off to break into translation mode.

'Tell me you will give me your hand and we will live happily ever after,' he finished with a dramatic flourish, bringing her hand up to his lips to press a kiss to the backs of her fingers.

Emily barely heard his voice as he translated his final declaration. All she was aware of was the lingering heat and unexpected softness of his mouth where it had touched her.

'It is *your* turn,' he muttered out of the corner of his mouth, his eyes sparkling with glee, almost as if he knew how badly he'd scrambled her nerves.

'Oh, handsome prince, of course you can have my hand,' she said with a simpering smile and fluttering eyelashes, only to add under her breath, 'As long as you remember to give it back before I need it to drive home.'

It felt good to see him fighting laughter as he announced to the room, 'She said yes!' in both languages, and to be a part of the happy cheers that greeted the announcement.

And it wasn't just the memory of Leela's satisfied little face that had her feeling good when it was time to take her leave. This time she'd spent with Zayed had convinced her that underneath the driven professional persona he showed to the rest of the world, there was a gentle, generous man who would make a wonderful husband and father.

'Are you sure you don't want a cup of coffee before you leave?' he offered, as he stood with her by the front door.

The house behind them was largely silent now, with all the children safely tucked up in their beds even if they weren't all asleep yet. Most of the staff and parents had either gathered in the kitchen for a restorative cup of tea or coffee or had retired to their rooms, too, knowing that the morning would bring another exhausting, activity-filled day.

'I'd better not,' she said, even as a large part of her was aching to spend even a little more time with him. 'I wouldn't want to be late for work in the morning or my boss wouldn't be very happy.'

'He is a slave driver?' Zayed asked, and the smile in his voice told her he'd quickly understood that she was teasing him.

'Actually, no, he isn't,' she said honestly, keen to give credit where it was due. 'He's an excellent boss and works harder than anyone on his team.'

Emily caught her breath and bit her tongue sharply, suddenly conscious of the extra warmth that had infused the words. She'd only recently become aware of the feelings that had been growing since the first time she'd seen him. Had she betrayed too much?

'Well, now that he knows about your home situation, you can be sure that he will not have a problem if you should have to leave suddenly to be with your grand-mother.'

If there was anything he could have said that would have been more calculated to bring tears to her eyes, Emily didn't know what it was.

'Thank you for that,' she said, and had to blink hard. 'But the oncologist was fairly certain of the course that her illness would take and how long…' Her throat closed up, filled with the huge lump of misery that was never far away.

'Ah, Emily, you know as well as I do that with any disease process there are no certainties,' he reminded her, and reached for her hand just as he had when they had been sitting side by side not long ago. 'Just know that I will understand if you need extra time to be with her. She is a lovely lady.'

'Thank you,' she managed to whisper, and had to force herself to retrieve her hand from his warm strength and step away. It was far too tempting to stay where she was and hibernate within the cocoon of his consideration. 'I'll see you in the morning,' she murmured as she opened the car door and slid into her seat, when all she wanted to do was walk back to him and wrap her arms around him in the hope that he would wrap his around her.

'Idiot!' she berated herself as she made her way down the hill, passing the turning that would have taken her towards Penhally Bay Surgery and the lifeboat station until she came to her grandmother's cottage.

She switched off the engine then realised that she would far rather turn round and drive back up the hill than go into the darkened house that had been a haven for most of her life. It seemed somehow sad and abandoned now that she knew Beabea wasn't in there waiting to hear about her day; now that she knew that her grandmother would never be coming back to her little cottage again.

Zayed made one last soft-footed tour through the house as everyone settled down for the night, wondering idly what its wealthy former owner would make of the place.

The basic structure was unchanged, but where the rooms had looked spacious and luxurious before, now some of them almost resembled a cross between boarding-school dormitories and an old-fashioned hospital ward, albeit one with all the latest high-tech gadgetry.

The kitchen where he'd helped himself to a last cup of wickedly strong coffee could have rivalled the best in any of the local hotels and…

'Stop wasting time,' he growled into the silence of the one room that was exclusively his as he leant wearily back against the door. 'There is no point in trying to picture the place through her eyes. She has already told you that she is impressed. And as for the way she was with the children…'

That was the biggest problem, he admitted honestly. The children.

There had been something that had felt so *right* when the two of them had been sharing the storytelling this evening. It had felt to him almost as if they had been playacting at being parents, and he could see that it had been affecting her every bit as much. And when he had sensed how reluctant she had been to leave…

'That can*not* be allowed to happen,' he growled fiercely as he kicked off his soft shoes and padded barefoot across the emptiness of the sparsely furnished room towards the bed. 'She is a talented doctor who could go far. She does not need any involvement in my life, except as a member of staff.'

But even though he said the words aloud, it didn't stop the thoughts from circling inside his head. Like the intriguing fact that she might be a highly intelligent and dedicated doctor with a lovely rapport with children of all ages, but it almost seemed as if in other ways she was an innocent.

It was all too easy to remember the smiles she'd bestowed on Abir and their other little charges at St Piran's, and Leela and the others this evening, but it was also dangerously easy to imagine them being directed his way as he discovered exactly what it would take to make her pulse race and the stunning green of her eyes darken with arousal.

'As if that could ever happen!' he scoffed bitterly, dismissing the impossible image of Emily Livingston cradling a dark-haired baby against the pale skin of her breast and smiling up at him as the greedy mouth suckled her.

'Been there, done that,' he whispered, with a pang of renewed agony for everything he'd lost, knowing that he could never replace it.

And that was why there was absolutely no point in allowing himself to dream that Emily could ever be a permanent part of his life. There was no way he could ask her to give up her obvious natural desire for eventual motherhood, even if he could guarantee her safety, and there was no way he could ever allow himself to be the cause of her destruction.

He already had far too much blood on his hands.

CHAPTER SEVEN

SOMETHING had changed, but she had no idea why.

Emily clicked her safety belt in position and started the engine before she leant back in her seat and stared up at Zayed's house thoughtfully, trying to pinpoint what was different and when it had happened.

It was nearly a week since that first visit to his house but the magical feeling of being somehow connected to the man may as well have been the last remembered wisps of a dream for all the evidence she'd seen of it since then.

Oh, she was made perfectly welcome by everyone else, and gave them all endless entertainment as she tried to learn enough of their language to be able to communicate in the simplest way with them. Her story-telling was much in demand, too, but, much to her disappointment, since that first day Zayed's role as interpreter had been taken over by Reza or one of the other staff.

In fact, it was almost as if Zayed was deliberately distancing himself from her, just when she'd realised…

'Oh, damn!' Emily breathed when the enormity of her feelings suddenly overwhelmed her.

All she had to do was picture the first moment she'd

seen Zayed—the handsome man she'd watched smiling down at Abir—or recall his delighted grin when he'd been submerged under a pile of wriggling children, or the gentle concern he'd shown for Beabea, to know that she *had* completely lost her heart.

'I'm in love with him,' she whispered, saying those special words aloud for the very first time in her life.

And now that she'd made the admission, simple honesty meant that she would also have to admit that the feeling had been growing with every day they worked together and with every new facet she discovered of this complex man's personality.

Unfortunately, that same honesty compelled her to acknowledge that the emotion would be completely wasted on the man because there was so little chance that her feelings would be returned. It wouldn't matter how much she loved him or for how long because it just wasn't going to be reciprocated, not while he was haunted by shadows from his past.

Whatever had happened in his former life to drive him out of his own country seemed to have been dreadful enough to close off the essential part of him that would ever be able to love her in return.

Emily put the car in gear and set off down the driveway with a heavy heart.

It would have been wonderful if the realisation that she'd finally fallen in love could be accompanied with the knowledge that she was loved in return, but that wasn't the case.

Zayed Khalil might be—*was*—the embodiment of everything she'd ever dreamed of in a life's partner…hard working, honest, intelligent, handsome, caring…but the last few days had confirmed, without a word needing to be spoken, that he was interested in only one thing—operating on his little patients and seeing them returned to their parents whole and healthy.

Just this week, Emily had assisted while he'd done his utmost to correct clubbed feet that should have been dealt with years earlier, and had given a new cheekbone and eye socket, to replace one eaten away by disease, to a little girl who had believed she would always be too ugly to have any friends.

She'd been given an enormous boost in confidence when he'd offered a quiet word of approval when she'd closed at the end of a particularly harrowing mixed-discipline operation to repair the results of a child on a bicycle who had strayed into the path of a reversing tractor, but as she let herself into Beabea's darkened cottage it was time for her to admit the painful truth.

She may be the important second pair of hands when she was with him at the operating table, and the second pair of eyes when they were checking on the patients in post-op and ICU, but she could just as well be a particularly sophisticated robot for all the response Zayed had to her on a personal level.

'Did I do something wrong?' she murmured as she stood in front of the fridge and tried to summon up some enthusiasm for eating.

If anything, she would have expected him to withdraw from her after she'd worked on his painful muscles and ligaments down on the beach. If he was going to distance himself from her, that would have been the one time that she'd obviously stepped over the boundaries between his exalted status and her far lowlier one.

And yet… She shook her head when she realised that he hadn't completely withdrawn from all contact with her because Beabea had told her that he'd been back several times to visit her.

At first, Emily had wondered if the visits had been a figment of her grandmother's mind under the influence of the strong painkillers, but when Nick Tremayne had mentioned bumping into her boss the last time she'd encountered him at Beabea's bedside, she'd realised that it must be true.

So why would he visit an elderly lady in the final stages of terminal cancer while he avoided spending any but the most essential time with her granddaughter?

Unless… An awful thought suddenly made her feel so ill that she abandoned the sandwich she'd just constructed as though it was contaminated with deadly bacteria.

Had she inadvertently revealed the strength of her feelings towards him? Had he realised that she was falling in love with him before even she had recognised it? Had he been so horrified by the unwelcome thought that he'd immediately done the only thing available to him—put as much distance between them as possible?

Her face felt hot with embarrassment but her body was cold and clammy as though she was going into shock.

What could she do about the situation to make it less…uncomfortable?

'Well, resigning isn't an option,' she said aloud, and found her determination bolstered by hearing the words. 'I'm not doing anything that might make visiting Beabea any more complicated. And, anyway, I like the job and I know I'm learning so much from him.'

That was one thing she *could* admit—Zayed was a

generous and gifted teacher, probably one of the best she'd had since she'd started her medical training.

'And I'm pathetic,' she admitted softly, not liking the truth of those words quite so much. 'He obviously doesn't want any sort of relationship with me beyond our professional one, but I still want to be near him.'

So, how was she going to deal with the situation?

'Well, I'm certainly not going to be skulking around in the shadows to stay out of his sight,' she said firmly. 'I am who I am, and if he doesn't like it, tough!'

She would still be doing her work to the best of her ability and she had no intention of cutting back on her visits to the children and staff at his house. And as for her visits to the beach…?

'Well, it was *my* beach before it was his,' she said, then giggled when she realised just how childish that sounded.

But it was true. She'd been going to that beach ever since she'd come to live with Beabea, and no taciturn surgeon was going to drive her away.

'Besides, if he insists on going swimming when there's no one else about to keep an eye on his safety, then he's just going to have to put up with me being there.' And it would be her private, guilty pleasure to look at that taut, tanned body and dream of what might have been, if only…

Anyway, the trips to the beach would end soon enough. They were halfway through September already, and the evenings were starting to draw in. All too soon it would be dark by the time they finished work at St Piran's and made the journey across to the coast to Penhally, and she didn't think that even Zayed would be foolish enough to swim alone in the dark in winter.

'And if he tries it, I'll bring Beabea's big torch down

and use it like the lifeboat men's searchlight,' she declared, just before a jaw-cracking yawn overtook her.

It didn't take long to get ready for bed, but even when she was comfortably ensconced with a large mug of hot chocolate and a fresh sandwich, her brain wouldn't let the topic go.

All she had to do was think about seeing Zayed in the unit the next morning and a whole squadron of butterflies tried to steal her appetite.

'Enough of this nonsense!' she said, drawing on the determination that had got her through the first crippling weeks of loneliness when she'd left the cosy familiar world of Penhally for medical school, and had fired her to do her utmost to make her grandmother proud of her.

'First of all, much as it injures my pride and my heart, I've got to accept that there's never going to be anything personal between us.' The bald words *did* hurt, but they were necessary if she was going to be able to do her job properly.

'Secondly…what?' She took a bite of her sandwich and savoured the tang of the locally made cheese complemented to perfection with slices of the last of Beabea's home-grown tomatoes. The only thing that could have made it better was if it had been between two slices of Beabea's home-made bread, but that was already a thing of the past.

Tears burned her eyes but she refused to let them fall. There would be plenty of time for that later, when the worst finally happened. For now, it was important that she work out what sort of relationship she could have with Zayed as the one she wanted was impossible.

'Friends?' she suggested tentatively, and paused while

the idea grew like a plant from a single tiny seed. 'Yes. Why not friends?' The word wasn't nearly so tentative the second time as she visualised a return of the fledgling camaraderie that had been such a good part of their first few days of working together.

Was it possible?

'Well, I won't know unless I try,' she declared, and smiled when she heard an echo of Beabea's voice in the words.

She was still smiling when she turned out the light and settled under the covers, comforted by the realisation that for the rest of her life there would be moments when advice her grandmother had given her or even just a turn of phrase would bring memories of the wonderful woman back to her.

It would never be the same as having her grandmother there in her life, but at least it wouldn't feel as if she'd lost her completely.

The next morning Emily implemented her plan, breezing into the unit with a cheery greeting for each member of staff she encountered.

'Shirley! I love the new hairstyle,' she said to Zayed's new secretary, meaning every word of it. The motherly woman was one of the old school, and had apparently been letting herself slide slowly towards retirement until she'd been sent at short notice to replace Nasima Osman, when her predecessor had been fired and sent back to Xandar.

It was amazing what difference a few days of working for someone who appreciated her meticulous approach to her job had made to her…or was it the fact that Zayed's dark eyes lighting up his handsome face had reminded her that she wasn't just a secretary but a woman, too?

'Good morning, Zayed,' she said equally cheerfully, even though the fact that he'd refused to meet her eyes had embedded the barb of disappointment a little deeper in her heart. 'How was Reza's migraine? Did the tablets work for her?'

She hardly left him enough time to confirm that Reza was back on form before she was off again and hailing the children's favourite staff nurse. 'Jenna, how did the birthday party go? Was Steve surprised when he found the whole family there?'

Emily was relieved when Jenna drew her along to the office to check some details in a file, chattering all the while about the surprise party she'd arranged for her husband's birthday. She didn't think she could have kept the 'bright and breezy' front up for very much longer knowing that a certain pair of dark eyes were boring into her back with an all-too-familiar intensity. She could almost hear his thoughts as he registered the fact that she was behaving differently, today. Perhaps he was trying to work it all out, to decide what she was up to.

'Well, let him wonder,' she said under her breath as another busy shift got under way. 'He's made it clear that he's not interested in being a lover or a husband, but that doesn't mean that I can't have him as a friend.'

'Abir looks so much better today,' Emily said to the Hananis, laboriously trying out one of the sentences she'd been taught last night.

And it was true. He did look much better, the swelling around his eyes all but gone and his mischievous nature already asserting itself.

In fact, if it weren't for the thick protective bandages

still swathed around his head, you would hardly know that the little boy would have had no chance of a normal life before he'd come into Zayed's care at St Piran's Hospital.

'How he is looking is no much important,' Meera Hanani said fiercely, trying out some of the English she'd been equally determined to learn. 'Abir is my son, so he always look good to me. Now his head is good, too, *everything* is good.'

A little gurgle drew their attention down to the bright eyes twinkling up at them and the gummy grin that had become a permanent feature since he'd recovered from the immediate trauma of the operation.

'Yes, it is good,' Emily agreed. 'But now he looks like his daddy again, so this is good too.'

'Very good,' Meera agreed with a shy smile in Athar's direction. She said something to her husband in their own language but it was spoken far too quickly for Emily to understand with her limited vocabulary. Whatever it was, the two of them shared a soft-eyed smile before Meera turned to her and continued. 'We have a baby again.'

Emily frowned slightly, not quite certain what she meant. Was she saying that she felt as if Abir was theirs again?

'More baby,' Meera said, and touched a hand to her waist, and Emily felt the smile bloom across her face.

'Congratulations, both of you!' she exclaimed in delight, spontaneously wrapping an arm around each of them. 'I'm so happy for you.'

It was only later, when she was sitting surrounded by several piles of paperwork, that she allowed herself to explore the sudden pang of jealousy that had struck her when she'd heard the Hananis' news.

It was crazy for her to feel envious of them after all they'd been through in the last couple of months. They were due for a bit of good news, and she really was delighted for them, but…

'Has my biological clock suddenly started ticking?' she wondered, only realising that she'd voiced the question aloud when Jenna answered her.

'Working with Zayed Khalil is enough to get anyone's biological clock ticking.' She laughed. 'Isn't he just the sexiest man you've ever met?'

'Sexier than Colin Firth in Pride and Prejudice?' Emily challenged, knowing from a previous conversation that he was one of Jenna's all-time favourite actors and hoping desperately that she wasn't blushing.

'Ah! Now you're talking!' the staff nurse sighed then looked thoughtful. 'Actually, they both have that same dark brooding quality to them, and the feeling that, once they fall in love, there's nothing they wouldn't do for the woman in their life.'

'And does your Steve know you feel like this?' Emily teased. 'Doesn't he feel jealous?'

'Nah!' Jenna laughed. 'He knows that I might go starry-eyed over some actor—or our illustrious consultant—but Steve's the one I go to bed with.'

'So he's confident you're not pining for the unobtainable?' Unlike me, she added silently.

'Definitely not pining,' Jenna said with a saucy wink. 'How about you?'

Could the woman read her mind? Was it obvious to everyone that she'd fallen in love with Zayed? Would the gossip be all around the hospital by lunchtime?

'Colin Firth's OK, I suppose. He's a pretty good actor,

and he was just right as Mr Darcy, but he doesn't really ring any bells for me,' she invented hastily, knowing that any slight of her hero would distract Jenna from pursuing the topic in Zayed's direction.

'*OK?* He's far more than OK,' she said as she sniffed in disgust and sailed out of the room. 'Some people just don't have any taste' was her parting shot as the door swung shut behind her.

'Oh, but they do,' Emily murmured softly as she forced her eyes back to the open file in front of her, in spite of the image of Zayed imprinted in her brain. 'Impeccable taste.'

'Is there a problem?' the man in question asked, and Emily found herself fighting a blush again. Rather than turning towards him and have him question the heat in her face, she focused on the information she was adding to Abir's file.

'It's not a problem yet, but it's something that will need to be checked in about nine months' time,' she said as she completed her notes.

'Nine months? That is very specific,' he commented as he hitched one hip on the corner of the table. 'So, what is it that will need investigation?'

'Read for yourself,' she said, and handed him the file with a smile, looking forward to seeing his delight.

Except it wasn't delight that crossed his face when he read the fact that Meera Hanani was pregnant again. It looked far more like…pain.

And then the expression was gone, wiped away as if it had never appeared, leaving the stoic, apparently emotionless man behind.

'I will make sure that the baby can be checked after it

is born,' he said flatly, without any evidence of pleasure in the young couple's news, and Emily couldn't help staring at him in consternation. This wasn't the same man who had smiled down at Abir that first morning, or the one who had allowed the children to swarm all over him as soon as he'd set foot inside his house.

What on earth had happened since then to change him so much? And how could she ever ask him?

Once again, the answer came down to friendship, she decided as she swiftly stripped off her clothes to don theatre scrubs a little later. If she could show him that being friends wasn't a threat—could even be enjoyable—then perhaps he would relax enough to tell her about the demons that beset him.

'Our patient is Raquia Khan,' Zayed said to the assembled staff as soon as she joined him at the table, and despite the fact that he was all professional detachment, just the sound of his voice was enough to send a shiver up her spine. 'Raquia is a twin. The delivery of her brother was straightforward but Raquia suffered considerable trauma due to malpresentation, receiving a broken clavicle…' He stroked the slightly misshapen collar-bone with a gloved finger and Emily couldn't take her eyes off the gentle movement '…and a broken radius and ulna.'

It was obvious that both bones in the little forearm were considerably deformed, as though they had simply been left to heal without being positioned correctly.

'Unfortunately, the injuries were apparently completely overlooked by the midwife, who was more concerned with the survival of the mother and her son.' There was an edge to his voice as he recounted the details and Emily was glad to hear it—it was proof that he wasn't as detached as he would have them think. But was it enough to allow herself to hope that she might be able to get through to him?

'This has left Raquia without the full range of rotational movement in her arm as the bones cannot slide properly past each other,' he continued after a moment, once more the cool, calm professional. 'Today we will re-break both bones in her arm and position them correctly, using titanium screws and plates where necessary. Because this arm is considerably shorter than the other, we may have to use bone grafts to fill in and speed up the repair process, but this should not be difficult.'

'Won't there be a problem with her skin?' asked one of the newer trainee theatre staff, her face almost purple with embarrassment as everyone looked across at her. 'Will it stretch enough for you to lengthen it that far?'

'That is a good question,' Zayed said with a smile that was evident even behind the camouflaging mask, immediately putting her at ease. 'In some cases—for example, a little boy we had in the unit a couple of months ago— we would have to attach the two ends of the bone to a frame and wind them apart day by day to lengthen the bone gradually to the right length. With Raquia that will not be necessary because, although the difference looks great, it is not too far for her skin to accommodate.'

'How do you know?' Emily was beginning to suspect that the young trainee was deliberately attracting Zayed's attention to herself...or was that her own jealousy talking?

'Obviously, I wasn't given green eyes without a reason,' she muttered under her breath, glad that her mask disguised the fact that she was speaking...except when she glanced up it was to see a pair of dark eyes watching her intently, with a hint of a smile in their glittering depths.

'Years of experience tell me so,' Zayed answered. 'But that does not mean that sometimes we do not have to change what we intend to do when we start the operation. So, if we need to use a fixator, we will do so, but I do not expect it will be necessary today.'

And he was right in his assessment. Raquia's surgery went as smoothly as anyone could have wished, and although her arm looked badly bruised by the end of the operation and would look even worse during the next couple of days, that would be largely hidden from view by the dressings. Then, once the stitches were ready for removal, any residual discolouration would have time to disappear by the time the full cast was removed.

'If you would like to close, Emily, I will go to talk to the parents of Raquia.'

Emily was becoming quite accustomed to being left to complete the process and took it as a mark of his confidence in her growing skills that he would sometimes even leave the room for a short while. In this case, she could understand that he would want to put Raquia's parents' minds at rest. They had been feeling so guilty that their daughter hadn't received the care she'd needed, even though they had a ready-made excuse in the fact that they lived so many miles from the nearest hospital.

Zayed left the room on silent feet and as Emily bent to her task, she wondered if she was the only one who had noticed that he had performed more than half of the surgery without his clogs on. He certainly seemed to be less uncomfortable during the more lengthy procedures these days, but whether that was due to her suggestion that he go barefoot or proof that his injuries were finally improving was something else she couldn't ask him—at least, not unless they were friends rather than professional colleagues.

'Have you been to see your grandmother this evening?'

Zayed's husky voice reached Emily over the rhythmic flow and hiss of the waves across the silvery sand but she wasn't surprised to hear him speak. She seemed to have developed some sort of sixth sense that told her whenever he was nearby, and even though she hadn't seen him come onto the beach, she'd somehow known he was there. She wasn't even surprised that he'd learned how to find her secret thinking place among the jumbled rocks.

'I went as soon as I got to Penhally,' she confirmed with a brief glance in his direction, her spirits the lowest they'd ever been. 'She was asleep when I got there and only woke up for a few minutes before she dropped off again.'

'Is this not what you would want?' he asked softly, perching on a nearby rock as though prepared to stay for a while. 'Would you prefer that she was awake and in pain?'

'No! No, of course I wouldn't,' she protested, then flung up her hands. 'Oh, just ignore me. I'm feeling disgustingly sorry for myself. I should be glad that she's not in any discomfort and all I can do is complain that she's not alert enough to talk to me.'

'But this is understandable, too,' he said, his soft words eddying around the two of them in the fitful breeze. 'You have the feeling of time running out and the need to hear any last words of wisdom, the need to hear once more that you are loved and to say that you love in return.'

'That's exactly the way it is. How did you know?' she demanded.

'I lost my grandmother, too, and I can remember.' There was a slightly hollow sound to his voice, as though part of him was lost in thoughts and memories.

'It is the ones you lose without warning that are worst,' he added suddenly, almost as though the words had been torn out of him against his will. 'Then there is no chance to apologise for the things you failed to do, no time for a final declaration of love.'

He shook himself, as though suddenly realising where he was and who he was speaking to, and stood up.

'I came to deliver an invitation,' he said formally. 'It is the birthday of Jasmine Mohatar and she has asked if you will come to take a piece of birthday cake with us. And Reza has said that *I* will get no cake if I do not bring you.'

Emily laughed aloud. She could just imagine Reza delivering that sort of ultimatum, despite the fact that Zayed was her employer.

'I would be delighted to have some of Jasmine's cake. How is her spine progressing?' It was the first time Emily had ever seen TB in a spine, outside pictures in medical textbooks, and she'd quickly realised just how vital it was to support the weakened structure during the treatment phase so that it wouldn't collapse before new bone could be laid down.

'There will be no miracles in one night,' he said as the two of them set off across the sand towards the steps that led to the car park at the top of the cliff. 'As you know, the treatment of the tuberculosis will take a year or more, and it will take at least that long for her body to grow new bone.'

'How much longer will she stay in Penhally? Does she need to be over here the whole time she's in treatment and recovery?' She could only imagine how disruptive that would be to the rest of the Mohatar family. So far, every member who'd been tested to see if they, too, had TB, had been negative, but all their lives must have been thrown into disorder when Jasmine had needed to come to Penhally for the treatment she'd needed.

On a purely practical level, it was much more difficult to deal with Jasmine than most of the other patients due to the infectious nature of the disease she'd contracted. And barrier nursing was time-consuming and could end up being costly...although she knew that Zayed wouldn't let that be a consideration. As far as he was concerned, the only criterion would be that none of the other patients should be put at risk while he completed Jasmine's treatment.

'I have been in contact with an old colleague in Xandar,' Zayed said, and she noticed that his accent became just a little stronger when he spoke of his own country.

Was there also a hint of longing in his voice?

Did he miss the familiar heat and the sights and sounds he'd grown up with?

Were there people he was longing to see?

Would he eventually leave Cornwall to return there, leaving others to continue his work at St Piran's and at his house on the outskirts of Penhally, leaving her to mourn the man she'd never forget?

'If I can set everything up, he will supervise the continuing treatment of Jasmine when she returns to Xandar, and will send me reports of her progress. That way, she will be close to her family and will be able to see her brothers so she does not become a stranger to them.'

'How soon will she be able to go?' Emily asked eagerly. 'She was in tears today because her baby brother has learned to walk while she's been away and she missed seeing it, and now it's her birthday and she can't share her cake with them.'

'She will probably be able to leave by the end of the week, if all goes well, but her parents must be willing to take her for her treatment without fail, or the TB may become resistant.'

'Well, if you speak to the father while I take the mother to one side, we should be able to impress on each of them how deadly that could be…for the whole family.'

She stood aside while he unlocked his car then slid onto the supple leather seat, slightly disappointed that there would be no leisurely walk along Harbour Road to get to his usual parking place. Making the journey by car left her with far too little time to spend with him, especially if she was going to try to find ways to build a friendship between the two of them.

'How is your own back these days?' she asked, as a tentative idea began to form.

'A little better, thank you,' he said, politeness itself.

'Good enough to go surfing?' she suggested, as she hid her superstitiously crossed fingers under the folds of her skirt.

'*Surfing?* I do not think so,' he said, clearly appalled by the idea.

'You make it sound as if I'd invited you to parade along Harbour Road naked!' she teased. 'What's wrong with surfing? It's done all around the world by everyone from little children to their grandparents. *I* do it, too.'

'I do not think this would be appropriate,' he demurred. 'I have seen the people who surf during the summer with their baggy, garish clothing and their—'

'Oh, don't be so stuffy, Zayed!' she broke in impatiently. 'Relax a bit and enjoy life. If you were any stiffer, I could use *you* as a surfboard.'

CHAPTER EIGHT

STIFF enough to use as a surfboard? If only that were true, Zayed thought bitterly.

Ever since the explosion there had been what his consultant had euphemistically called 'no activity' in that important part of his male anatomy.

Was it a fitting punishment for his failures as a husband?

Perhaps.

But it was just one more reason why he could never allow anything personal to develop between himself and Emily, no matter how much his soul yearned for just a little of her sunshine in his life.

At first his surgeon had thought that his inability to perform was the result of his traumatic injuries, especially when he'd spent several days convinced that the paralysis was going to be permanent. But then he'd regained the use of his legs and the man had been distraught to have to tell him that he had absolutely no idea why the rest of his system hadn't returned to normal function.

The thud of Emily's car door closing snapped him out of his useless musings and he followed her to the front door.

'They here!' shrieked one little voice, and the mayhem that announcement caused was instantaneous.

He was aware that Emily wisely stood aside while he allowed himself to be besieged by all those eager little recuperating bodies, carefully staging his spectacular fall so that none of the children was bumped or jostled.

As if they would care! All they were interested in was seeing how many of them could sit on his chest or any other part of his anatomy they could pin down while he pretended to struggle mightily.

And all the time he was overwhelmingly aware that Emily was watching everything that was going on.

What was she thinking?

Was her attention nothing more than concern that he might cause a setback in one of the children's recovery? Was she dismayed that he could so easily abandon the proper gravitas of his position?

A quick glance in her direction between the flailing limbs told him that this, at least, wasn't true, not if the wistful smile was any indication. She looked almost as if she would like to join in the mêlée, or…or what?

Suddenly he wasn't quite so sure that he'd been making the right decisions in his life recently, and it was all the fault of this beautiful woman.

Oh, he knew that there could never be anything sexual between them, but what if she could accept…?

No! It wouldn't be fair to ask her to condemn herself to a life without bearing children. She would be so good at loving them and taking care of them. And he already knew, from meeting her grandmother, that Emily wasn't the sort of woman to be satisfied with anything less than the dreams she'd set her heart on.

That meant that offering her nothing more than friendship would be…

'Impossible!' he declared aloud, and startled the giggling children into wary silence.

'You are all impossible,' he said, this time with what he hoped was a wolfish grin as he pretended to take bites out of each of them. 'And now it is time for you to get ready for bed.'

'Not bed. Story first!' declared an emphatic little voice, and this time his grin was genuine.

'OK, Leela. Story it is,' he conceded when they all joined in the demand, and sighed with relief when the last little body crawled off him.

'Are you all right?' That could only be Emily's voice, filled with concern, as was the hand that she offered to help him lever himself to his feet. It was such a slender, soft little hand but already showing the skill that would make her a superb surgeon…and with enough hidden strength to counteract the weight of a full-grown man.

'I am all right,' he confirmed, his voice sharper than it should have been as he tried to ignore the urge to hang onto that brief connection.

'I was only concerned that the children might have hurt you,' she explained quietly, and he realised that even though she clearly thought he was rebuffing her concern, she was keeping her voice below the level of volume of the children's excited chatter. 'The children are getting stronger and fitter—and putting on weight and muscle with all the physiotherapy and special food they're getting—and they might not realise that they were—'

'It is all right Emily,' he soothed, and allowed himself a brief touch of her hand. 'I understand what you are saying, but I was not hurt. Rather, it is I who worry that I might hurt them.'

Her smile made his heart kick hard in his chest. 'You would never hurt a child,' she declared confidently. 'In fact, I've never met a man who would make a more perfect father. Reza thinks you should have a whole houseful of children of your own.'

Her praise was like a kick to another portion of his anatomy and all the more painful for the knowledge that it wasn't true…could never be true.

'Not so,' he said gruffly, the words having to be forced from his throat with the realisation that it was time for an overdue conversation.

The situation had never arisen before because he'd never allowed any of his other colleagues to get past their professional relationship, but there had been something different about Emily right from the first time he'd set eyes on her.

And just now there had been a light in her eyes and a lightening in her voice that had told him she wasn't any more immune to it than he was, but it couldn't go on, couldn't go any further, not when there was no future in it for either of them.

'I need to speak to you,' he said, and only realised how grim he'd sounded when he saw the worried way her eyes widened, their soothing green darkening with concern.

'Of course,' she said, her voice calm in spite of the fact that he knew from the frantic pounding at her slender throat that her pulse rate had just doubled. 'When? In the morning at the hospital?'

That would be the more professional choice. It would

help him to put a necessary distance between them, but the morning was far too many sleepless hours away. Perhaps, once he'd told her the whole dreadful story, she would stop haunting his dreams.

'No. Tonight,' he decided, 'after the children have had their story.'

He silently cursed his own cowardice, but he wanted to have one last happy memory to counteract the terrible emptiness that would be left once he'd pushed her completely out of his life.

It would be better for both of them if he could dismiss her from the unit, too, but that was impossible. Not only did he need her growing skill to achieve what he wanted for their little charges, but he wouldn't do something so destructive to her career. She didn't deserve it, not when any problems between them were his fault.

'Come in,' he invited an hour later after a story time that had been, if anything, more fun than ever before. Had that been because he knew it was probably the last?

Zayed turned to close the door behind her and surprised a look of blank shock on Emily's face as she took her first look around his private space.

He scanned the room and only then realised just what a bleak place it was.

There was a bed, of course, and a wardrobe for his clothing, and a desk for his computer, which was liberally piled with paperwork, but apart from that virtually nothing, certainly nothing decorative—no little oasis of exotic sun-baked Xandar transported to a Cornish cliff-top home or anything of a personal nature—and having seen her grandmother's collection of family photos, he knew instinctively that those were what she'd been expecting to see.

'Would you prefer to take the chair by the desk or sit on the bed?' Those were the only two options in his barren private space and he cursed at the way his own pulse responded to the wash of colour that swept up her face when she glanced at the place where he slept. With difficulty, he forced himself to focus on the fact that the blush only went to confirm his initial assessment of her— that even at thirty years of age she wasn't the sort of woman who was accustomed to spending much time in men's bedrooms.

'Um, the chair, please,' she said, and scurried across to stake her claim.

He almost smiled at the way she avoided looking at his bed, but that was the only light moment there could be in this room. By the time he'd finished talking to her, he'd be surprised if she even wanted to stay on his team, no matter how much damage it would do to her career.

But where to start?

He'd never spoken to anyone in Cornwall about what had happened in Xandar and it was almost impossible now to separate the events from the terrible guilt and the pain of loss.

'Why don't you have any photos of your family?' Emily asked, then bit her lip as though worried that she'd overstepped the invisible boundaries he'd set up around himself. He could have blessed her for supplying him with the perfect place to start his confession.

'Because…they remind me,' he said haltingly, any fluency gone as he tried to find the words to explain the inexplicable. 'And it is already hard enough, living with the memories.'

'But that's what they're for…so that you don't forget

all the happy times,' she said eagerly, and he almost resented her for her naiveté.

'Even if the memories are of guilt and loss?' he demanded harshly. 'Even if all they remind you of is the fact that, once upon a time, you had everything you could want and you had been so careless of it that you had lost it all?'

The memories were all around him now—no need for photographs—and he could almost hear the screams and smell the tang of blood under the choking blanket of explosives and dust.

'It was my job to protect them,' he said, barely aware that she was there and yet knowing that he had to continue so that she would know...would know everything. 'I should have stopped her from being there, from bringing him with her...especially when there had been so many warnings. But she was so determined to be there for the opening ceremony...said that after all the hours it had taken me away from my family she had a *right* to be there...'

He shook his head, unable to continue, and to his horror felt the swift slide of tears down his face.

Embarrassed by his lack of control, he whirled away from her and dragged both hands over his face but that couldn't stop them now that the dam had been breached.

'I am sorry for this,' he muttered brokenly, but he needn't have bothered because suddenly she was there, right in front of him, and in her eyes he saw not condemnation or pity but a deep well of empathy that he would never deserve.

'Sit down,' she urged, guiding him to the bed she'd rejected just a few minutes ago, then stood close beside him and cradled his head against her as though he were one of the children now sleeping peacefully around them.

It took some time before the heart-wrenching sobs finally died away but Emily still hadn't worked out the best way to approach their aftermath.

Like any proud man, Zayed would be mortified to have broken down in front of her unless she handled the situation just right.

But what *was* just right?

She had so little experience that she could very well make everything much worse, especially as she had little idea what had actually happened. His words had been so broken, wrenched out of the nightmare scenes playing inside his head. All she was really certain of was that he'd lost his family in some disaster and was convinced that it had been his fault that they'd died.

Well, the only way to be sure that she wasn't going to rip open even more wounds was to wait until he'd recovered himself and ask him to explain.

'I'm sorry,' he said hoarsely. 'That was not supposed to happen.' He tried to pull away from her but she deliberately tightened her arm around his shoulders.

'There's no need to apologise for tears,' she said firmly. 'They're just a physiological fact of life, like sneezing or yawning. A manifestation of the body's need for some sort of cathartic release that—'

'All right, Emily, thank you for the lecture, but—'

'But I need to know something,' she interrupted quickly, afraid that if she gave him too much time he'd retire behind those barricades that kept the world at bay. 'What happened? Down on the beach you said it was an explosion that caused your injuries, but you didn't say what caused the explosion. Was it during an earthquake, or some other sort of disaster?'

'Would that it had been something as innocent as an earthquake,' he said, and drew in a shuddering sigh before sitting silent for so long that she began to think he'd changed his mind about talking to her.

Finally, he tipped his face up to hers and she could have cried herself when she saw the mixture of pain and guilt that dulled his eyes.

'If you want to hear the whole depressing story, you had better sit down,' he suggested wearily, and gestured towards the almost clinically neat bedding beside him. 'It is not something that can be done in a moment or two.'

He seemed so reluctant that she almost offered to leave instead, but something inside her knew that he needed the relief of speaking about what had happened. And if he regretted it in the morning, he could always console himself that she would be leaving in a matter of months.

'In Xandar, my family is…powerful,' he began, and as ever when he spoke of his home country she noticed that his accent grew stronger, the syllables flowing like exotic honey from his tongue. 'Even before I started my medical training it was obvious that the poorer people did not have access to the medical services they needed for their children. So I was determined to build a place where specialist doctors could come from many countries to treat the children who had no help and teach us what we needed to know about their care.'

'Like the one at St Piran's? A special unit that can call on all the different specialties within the hospital, depending on the needs of a particular patient?'

'Exactly so. It was the unit I planned in Xandar on which my department at St Piran's is based. Unfortunately,' he continued, with a visible darkening of his expression, 'there are in my country some who would keep things as they have always been and who refuse to accept that modern medicine—even when it is delivered by women—is a good thing.'

'And your unit was actually built?' He'd said something about an opening ceremony, so…

'Not only the unit,' he said with a hint of pride, 'but also the start of a series of clinics throughout the country so that little ones could be seen more quickly and easily than having to travel all the way to the capital. Then only if an operation was necessary would the family have the expense of that journey.'

'And the explosion?' She hated to push him to recall such distressing events, but she was discovering that she needed to know what had happened to the man she loved every bit as much as he needed to tell her.

'The world believes that it was caused by a group of rabid fundamentalists—those who object to all things that come from outside the traditions of our country.'

'But?' It was anger she had heard in his voice just then, fierce and raw.

'None of these groups claimed responsibility for the atrocity, the way they usually do, and there were other people who had their own reasons…' He shook his head. 'It is complicated…politics…but I believe that it was someone who used the threats by the fundamentalists to hide their own agenda. And they almost succeeded… except *I* didn't die. It was my wife and son who were destroyed because I didn't protect them.'

'*Didn't* protect them or *couldn't* protect them?' she asked, remembering the fact that he'd been badly injured, too.

'There can be no difference because I failed them. They died that day and I lived,' he said, voicing the torment that sounded as if it would never leave him.

It was almost as though a light bulb switched on inside her head.

'And is this why you hold yourself aloof from everyone…why you won't let anyone get close to you?'

'Why would anyone want to?' he asked, those broad shoulders slumping in the closest she'd ever seen him come to defeat. 'I am a man who has nothing to give… who deserves nothing…because I have not proved myself worthy.'

Those lean fingers she'd watched, mesmerised while they'd performed their magic for his little patients, were knotted into white-knuckled fists now.

Emily wanted so very much to reach across and soothe those fists with gentle fingers, but she knew he was in no mood to accept such a gesture from her.

'So, in Xandar there's no such thing as someone being granted a second chance?' she asked quietly, knowing he was intelligent enough to get her point.

'Of course there is, if the person deserves a second chance,' he retorted. 'But how can I have a second chance when they never will?' His dark eyes almost burned her with their intensity as he continued.

'Leika was twenty-four when she died, young and beautiful and with so much life in her.'

'Leika?' Jealousy sank its claws deep into her soul.

'Zuleika,' he clarified. 'She was my wife, chosen for

me by my family to cement a political alliance, and the price I had to pay for agreement to my plan for the specialist unit.'

The fact that Zayed was important enough to Xandar that he could be coerced into such a match was almost irrelevant to Emily when all she felt was a selfish relief that it hadn't been a love match between them.

'Neither of us really wanted to marry,' he continued in a low voice full of regret. 'Leika wanted to pursue a career in law, specialising in what are called *women's issues*, so when Kashif was born a year later, she almost resented him because everyone expected her to do the traditional thing…the *right* thing…and give up her work to stay home with him.'

'So when the unit was going to open—the unit that her marriage had allowed—she was determined to be there,' Emily said, reading between the lines.

'And when the explosion came, I couldn't save them.' His dark eyes were full of torment as they stared right through her, and she knew that he was seeing the horrors in his memory instead. 'I'm a doctor but I couldn't do anything for them. I just…just lay there and watched them die, right in front of me.'

Probably because you were too badly injured to get to them, she reflected, knowing with absolute certainty that he would have done everything in his power to help them if he'd been able.

Not that she could say any of that, she knew as she allowed her eyes to drift around his room again.

The barrenness of his surroundings was still a shock. When he'd invited her into his private space, she'd been expecting to see a little bit of Xandar transported to

Penhally. Fabrics with a rich variety of textures and colours, perhaps even the luxury of silk on his bed. She certainly hadn't imagined this…this monk's cell.

And when she'd mentioned the lack of family photos, she'd actually seen him shut down to avoid the pain, but hadn't known why until now.

Except…she didn't really understand.

'Why did you decide to travel so far away…to cut yourself off from the rest of your family?' she demanded. 'When Beabea…when the time comes…I'll be completely alone in the world. I'd give anything to know that there were other people who were going to be there for me… uncles and aunts and cousins who would be feeling the same loss when she's not there any more.'

'There are reasons,' he began stiffly.

'I'm sure there are, but why punish yourself unnecessarily?' she demanded, her own heart aching for his loss and wishing she could ease it for him. '*You* didn't set the explosion, so why are *you* feeling guilty and putting yourself in exile? You should be in Xandar, showing those fundamentalists—or whoever it was that did it—that they aren't going to win. You should be organising the rebuilding of the unit for all those children that need it…all the Abirs and Neelas and Jasmines who can't come to a small unit in Cornwall, no matter how good it is.'

Emily believed so passionately in what she was saying that Zayed could almost see sparks flying off her as she took him to task.

She was an amazing woman, so open and generous… and magnificent in her fierceness.

If they had met in another place, another time…another life, he would have done everything in his power to make her his, because with a woman like her at his side there was nothing he couldn't accomplish.

Just look at all the things she managed to cram into each and every day.

Not content with a busy and demanding career, she was arriving early for her shift each day to spend extra time with their little patients so that their bewildered parents would be relaxed enough with her to voice their fears. Then she was hurrying back to Penhally to spend time with her grandmother, often returning several times during the evening to take advantage of the increasingly brief spells between her morphine-induced sleep.

She hadn't even bothered to ask for permission to visit his home after that first time, simply assuming that she would be welcome to join in the nightly mayhem of story time and lingering long enough to give every child a moment or two of gentle attention, playing with them and cuddling them while they settled down for the night so that their parents and carers could have time for a little adult conversation.

And then there was her determination to be present on the beach each evening to watch over him.

He sighed inwardly, still unable to work out how he felt about that insistence.

His male pride wanted to be offended that she was implying that he might be unable to take care of himself, even as his common sense told him that it was taking unnecessary risks to swim alone, no matter that the beach at Penhally was hardly a remote location.

The one emotion that he hadn't allowed himself to examine was the feeling of pleasure that came over him at the thought that she might care enough about him as an individual to be concerned about his safety, and that was crazy.

The last thing he should want was for Emily to grow to care about him, knowing that he couldn't offer her anything in return. He just didn't have it in him any more and she was a person who deserved the best of everything.

So, even though she was sitting on his bed, close enough to touch, close enough to breathe in the sweet musky scent of her body that never completely disappeared even under the tang of sea water, even though he would like nothing more than to pull her into his arms and never let her go, he had to try to keep a professional distance between them, for both their sakes.

But that didn't mean that he could help himself from loving the way she related to every one of the children, and the quietly steadfast way she showed her love and care for her grandmother, even though having to watch her die by inches was devastating her.

The last couple of days he'd even timed his departure from St Piran's so that he could follow her to the hospice, then waited out of sight until she emerged to make her way to the beach with the few stray tears that escaped her steely control already streaking her cheeks.

He'd discovered by accident just how close she was to tears after each visit and wanted to be there for her, but unless she granted it to him, he had no right to intrude on her private misery.

'Zayed?' The uncertain tone in her voice and the shadows that were gathering rapidly in the room were the only things that told him that he'd allowed the silence to stretch between them for far too long.

'I am sorry,' he said. 'Your words made me think and my thoughts took me in many directions…the explosion…the unit…your grandmother.'

'Oh, I forgot!' she exclaimed. 'Beabea asked particularly if you would come to visit her tonight. She seemed fairly insistent but, of course, only if you have the time. It might mean waiting until she wakes up because she's pretty much drifting in and out at the moment, and—'

'Emily, it is all right. I would be honoured to visit her again,' he interrupted with a smile. He enjoyed her grandmother's spiky sense of humour, which even terminal cancer couldn't take away. It didn't matter that he felt wary of the keen way she watched him each time he visited, as though she were dissecting him right to the bone. He wouldn't have been at all surprised if she possessed the facility for reading minds, the way his own grandmother had seemed to.

'When did you want to go?' he asked, relieved to have a chance to draw some sort of a line under their emotionally fraught conversation this evening. He had never spoken of those events to anyone before and the painful experience had left him feeling drained and on edge.

Then there was the danger that the longer he spent in Emily's company, the more likely it would become that he'd make a slip and reveal how he really felt about her. 'We could leave now, if you like,' he offered, hoping he didn't sound too eager.

The expression in those clear green eyes told him that she knew exactly why he was so keen to go, and left him with the uncomfortable feeling that yet again he was guilty of cowardice.

* * *

His first look at her grandmother's face told him that the end was very close and for a moment he wondered whether he ought to excuse himself and leave the room to give the two of them some precious private time together.

Then she opened her eyes and fixed him with a surprisingly alert gaze, almost as if she'd known what he was thinking.

'Come…closer,' she mouthed faintly, beckoning with a single skeletal finger to make the point.

When he would have demurred, directing Emily to stand closer instead, a glimmer of the fire he'd seen so often in her granddaughter's eyes flashed at him, telling him without words that *he* was the one she wanted to talk to first.

She started to speak, but her voice was so insubstantial that he could barely hear it.

Frustrated, she stabbed an imperious finger into the bedclothes, letting him know in no uncertain terms that she wanted him to sit close beside her.

'You…' she breathed when he leaned as close as he could without crowding her, concerned that she was already struggling for breath, even with the assistance of supplemental oxygen. 'You are…a good man,' she declared in a way that forbade him to argue with her, no matter how much he might want to set the record straight. 'You've…been hurt…' she continued laboriously, 'been sad…but it's time…'

'Time?' He knew that Emily hadn't had a chance to tell her grandmother anything of their conversation this evening, and was uncomfortable with the idea that the older woman could tell so much about him. Perhaps she *could* read his mind, but he certainly couldn't read hers.

'Time…to forgive…yourself,' she whispered. 'Time… to go on…with your life.' She fumbled for his hand, her own feeling almost as weightless as a baby bird in his as she trapped his gaze with a fierce intensity that he wouldn't have believed she was still capable of. 'Promise me…' she said. 'You must promise…you will…take care of…my Emily…'

Those simple words sent fear flooding through him, choking him so that he couldn't utter a single word to deny her.

But he couldn't be responsible for taking care of Emily. It wasn't right that she should ask him. He couldn't take care of anyone—he'd already proved that when he'd let Leika and Kashif die.

'Promise me…' she demanded with all the energy she could summon, and suddenly he knew that, no matter how much he wanted to…no matter how much he should…he couldn't refuse what might be her dying wish.

'I promise,' he said, even as despair crept into his soul with the realisation that he had just vowed to do the impossible.

CHAPTER NINE

BEABEA beckoned Emily to her then and, regardless of the fact that it meant she was almost plastered against Zayed's side, she hurried forward and leant as close as she could.

'I...love you...darling girl,' she managed, but Emily could tell that it was becoming harder and harder for her to form the words. She seemed to be so desperately tired that everything was becoming a real struggle.

'I know, Beabea,' she reassured her, stroking the tissue-paper-fine skin on the back of her hand and trying to ignore the unhealthy yellow colour of the jaundice that signalled the severity of her liver failure. 'I've always known. And I love you, too. Now, you get a good night's sleep and we can talk again in the morning.'

She bent to press a kiss to her grandmother's cheek and when she straightened up, she noticed that those faded blue eyes were focusing first on Zayed's face, then on hers.

A sweet smile just lifted the corners of her mouth as she closed her eyes.

'No more...talk...I've said...all that needed...to be

said,' she managed with what sounded almost like satisfaction before her hand relaxed its grip in Emily's.

'She's asleep,' Zayed whispered, and Emily realised that her sudden panic must have shown in her face. 'Her heart is still beating,' he pointed out, indicating the pulse still beating at her grandmother's throat. But not for long, was the silent rider that he didn't need to say aloud.

Emily waited until they were outside the hospice wing, standing by their respective cars, before she tackled him about the private conversation he'd had with her grandmother.

'Beabea was speaking so softly that I couldn't hear what she was saying to you,' she said, suddenly realising that she sounded quite stiff with the resentment that he'd taken up some of her precious time with her grandmother. 'What were the two of you talking about?'

Zayed's eyes looked almost black in the shadows this far away from the security lights and his expression was totally unreadable as she waited for him to speak.

Instead, there was a sudden call from the door they'd only recently exited.

'Emily!' called the sister on night duty who had only just wished them goodnight as they'd passed her desk. She beckoned. 'You'd better come in, quickly. Your grandmother's taken a turn for the worse.'

'Beabea!' Emily exclaimed frantically as she whirled and started to run.

It was a short corridor but it felt as if the faster she ran the further away her grandmother's door became until Zayed caught her hand and ran beside her.

Emily wasn't quite sure how he came to be beside her or how she came to be holding his hand so tightly, but she was very aware that having Zayed with her was her only comfort at that moment.

Unfortunately, by the time they hurried through the door they were just in time to see the nurse release her grandmother's wrist with a shake of her head.

'I'm so sorry,' she said, and seemed genuinely upset that the end had come so quickly—just moments after Emily had left her grandmother sleeping peacefully. 'She was a lovely lady.'

Emily's legs refused to hold her for a second and she was even more grateful that Zayed was there willing to lend his strength to lower her safely into the familiar chair at the side of Beabea's bed.

At first glance Beabea didn't look any different to the way she'd been when Emily had glanced back at her from the doorway just minutes ago. But there *was* a difference—in some indefinable way it was obvious that her grandmother just wasn't *there* any more.

Emily had expected to cry bitterly when this moment finally arrived, but she was too stunned for tears, overwhelmingly aware of an enormous feeling of loss and emptiness.

'Emily? You are all right?' Zayed asked gently, his arm tightening supportively around her shoulders. 'Do you want me to drive you home?'

Home? *That* nearly broke through the strangely echoing distance that had appeared between her and the rest of the world.

The little cottage that she'd shared with her grandmother ever since her parents had died was *Beabea's* home, and now that she was gone, it felt to Emily almost as if *she* didn't have a home any more.

'I can't leave yet,' she said in a voice that felt as if it scratched her throat on the way out. 'There are the formalities to see to and…and…'

'Shh,' he soothed, as if he knew she was just seconds away from flying apart into a million pieces. 'First you just need to sit here quietly with your grandmother to say your last farewell.'

He was so understanding of the churning chaos inside her that she only just held onto her control, but the dark shadows in his eyes reminded her that the reason why he knew what she needed was because he had suffered so much worse.

At least Beabea's life had been long and full. Zayed's son had hardly begun to live when his life had been snuffed out like an ephemeral candle flame.

'I'll be fine,' she said, and hoped that the smile she managed looked a little more convincing than it felt. But she had to try. It wasn't fair, after all the sadness he'd suffered, for him to be burdened with her unhappiness, too. It could only bring back the memories that haunted him. 'I expect that someone on the staff here will have telephoned the surgery for someone to certify the death. Once that's over, I'll go home.'

'Are you sure that is what you want? I do not mind waiting with you,' he offered, and sounded as if he really meant it.

She was so tempted to accept, knowing that just to have him by her side would make everything so much more bearable, but Beabea hadn't raised her to be a coward.

'I'm sure,' she said quietly, and he nodded, accepting her decision.

'Ring me on my mobile to tell me when you leave,' he suggested, and when he took that first step away from her she was already wishing she could change her mind, especially when he added, 'If you want me to come over, I will come—so you are not alone.'

'Dr Tremayne's arrived,' Nan Yelland murmured softly, and Emily blinked. She'd completely lost track of time while she'd been sitting there, her mind wandering over so many happy memories in the years since she'd come to live with Beabea.

'What time is it?' she asked, her voice sounding as rusty as if it hadn't been used in a long time.

'Nearly three o'clock,' said a male voice in the doorway.

For just a second her heart leapt with the hope that it would be Zayed standing there, but it was only the very tired and rumpled figure of Nick Tremayne.

Emily smiled at him, feeling a sense of rightness that he should be the one to see Beabea for the last time. He'd been her GP ever since he'd started the practice in Penhally and her grandmother had always had a great deal of faith in him. It just wouldn't have been the same if a stranger had performed this last duty.

'I'm sorry I couldn't get here any earlier, my dear,' he said, as he placed his bag very precisely on the bedside table and released the locks. It only took him a second to find the relevant paperwork. 'There was an accident out at the junction of Penhally View and Dunheved Road. Youngsters going too fast and one didn't make the corner.' He looked up with a wry twist to his mouth. 'You'd think local lads would grow up knowing that you can never win in an argument with a Cornish stone hedge.'

'Was anyone hurt?' Emily seized on the topic to take her mind off the fact that he was treating her grandmother so impersonally. Although he was being perfectly respectful, it seemed almost as if she was no longer a person to him any more, just a routine job to be done.

Did it seem that way simply because he was exhausted at the end of a long, traumatic day or was it perhaps a defence mechanism, his way of dealing with seeing his patients when they were no longer alive, by shutting a part of himself away inside?

Would she ever be able to do that if they lost one of their little charges? Would that be the way she could cope with the feeling that she should have been able to do something more for them?

'The passenger was trapped and it took a while to cut him free,' he continued. 'He'll probably be on crutches for a while when they get his leg reassembled, but the driver was unconscious at the scene—a depressed skull fracture. We'll just have to wait and see what St Piran's can do with him. If it's as bad as it looked, he might never come out of ICU, even if he makes it out of Theatre.'

The sharp click of locks drew her attention to the fact that he'd just closed his oversized briefcase again.

'I've done the necessary,' he said as he turned towards her. 'Of course, you know that there'll be no need for a post-mortem. It wasn't as if her death was unexpected or that the cause is in any doubt.'

'No.' Somehow Emily forced her voice to work. 'Thank you for coming out so late,' she added, the manners that Beabea had always insisted on a totally automatic part of her life even when everything else had been turned on its head.

'Nan told me you were sitting with her and I couldn't leave you here all night.' He reached out an avuncular hand to pat her on the shoulder. 'She was a lovely lady and it was always a pleasure to see her. I'm sure you'll feel better when you've had a good cry, my dear. Just concentrate on the fact that she'd had a good innings—and that she was tremendously proud of you—but if you'd like me to organise some grief counselling…'

'I don't think so,' she said firmly, not seeing the point. No amount of counselling would bring her grandmother back and she would rather deal with this loss the same way she'd dealt with the loss of her parents—in her own way and in her own time.

Still, it was kind of the man to spare the time to talk to her like this, especially when he must be longing to get back home to his bed. But all Emily could think was that it was wasted on her when she would far rather that it was Zayed comforting her. And it could have been, except she'd been stupid enough to send him away.

The sky's always darkest just before the dawn, she could hear Beabea's voice saying as she drove slowly down the driveway, but it seemed as if this night was never going to end in the bright promise of a new day.

She halted at the junction with Mevagissey Road, knowing she ought to turn left to go back to the cottage, but suddenly she couldn't face going there.

There was only one place she could go while her emotions were in such turmoil and that was her secret thinking place on the beach, the hidden nook among the rocks that had played host to almost every decision she'd ever made about her life—whether she really cared at thirteen years of age that stuck-up Melanie Philp didn't want to be her best friend any more; whether to cut her waist-length hair really short before her school leavers' Ball to make herself look more grown-up and ready for the big wide world; whether to specialise in paediatrics or surgery, and so many other milestones, great and small.

She parked her car at the top of the cliff in the car park near the steps and made her way down to the beach, glad of the thick cardigan she'd grabbed off the back seat. September was going fast and even though the weather was still beautifully warm by day, at this time of the morning, she could feel that autumn was not so far away.

Beabea had always said that autumn was her favourite time of the year, the season that showed the fulfilment of all the promise of spring and the burgeoning of summer in harvests of fruit and vegetables to sustain them through the winter. She'd especially loved the fabulous displays of colour as the deciduous trees began to shut down for their winter rest.

'I'm sorry you missed the leaves turning colour,' she whispered into the breeze, her heart heavy at the thought that she'd never again come home to a kitchen table covered in a display of brilliantly hued leaves that her grandmother had collected on her walk that day. But even though she hated the thought that she was now all alone in the world, she couldn't in all conscience have wanted Beabea to linger long enough to see the leaves one last time, not with the level of medication it had taken at the end to control her pain.

'Emily,' said the voice she most wanted to hear, and

she closed her eyes tightly against the imagined sound, wishing it were real and regretting again that she'd sent Zayed away.

Why had it seemed so important that she show the world that she had the strength to deal with this loss alone? Why couldn't she simply have admitted just how good it would have felt to lean on him and borrow his strength for a little while?

She was sitting here feeling frozen inside, hardly daring to allow herself to imagine what the days and weeks ahead would be like because she was afraid to.

There! She'd admitted it.

It was all very good saying that she'd coped with loss before and had dealt with it, but the last time she'd had Beabea there to hold her while she'd fallen apart and put herself back together. This time she would have no one because she'd sent away the only person she wanted near her.

In fact, she needed him to be with her so much that a moment ago she had even imagined that she'd heard his voice swirling around her in the chill of the early morning breeze.

'Emily?' The sound of those liquid syllables couldn't belong to anyone else, and she opened her eyes to peer eagerly into the darkness, knowing with a sudden leap of joy that Zayed had come to find her. Was there enough light for him to be able to find this place again? Would he be able to find her in the darkness?

'Zayed. I'm here,' she managed with a rusty croak to her voice as tears of relief began to threaten. She couldn't even get to her feet as the events of the last few hours finally overwhelmed her. 'I'm here,' she repeated, but he was already there in front of her, darker than the darkness surrounding them, arms strong and shoulders broad as he wrapped them around her and invited her to rest her head against him.

'Oh, Zayed,' she whimpered as she burrowed into him, finally knowing that she had found a safe refuge before the storm broke, and with that thought the tears started to fall.

Even as he wondered what on earth he was supposed to say to her, Zayed ignored the brief flash of panic and simply tightened his hold on the sobbing woman in his arms.

There was no sign now of the dedicated young doctor eager to learn everything he could teach her, or of the empathetic young woman who voluntarily spent her time visiting the convalescent children in his house. This was the young girl whose parents were already long gone and who had just lost the only close relative she had left in the world.

When he hadn't been able to wait any longer for her to contact him, he'd driven back to the hospice to discover that her car wasn't there any more. As he'd already established that it wasn't parked at the cottage, there was only one other place he knew to look.

And, just as he'd guessed, she'd been here in her special place, probably doing nothing more than staring blindly out to sea, feeling numb with disbelief that her beloved Beabea had gone.

He pressed his cheek gently to her head, easily able to empathise with her grief even as he drew in the fresh herbal scent of her shampoo mixed with the underlying essence that was pure Emily.

In his head he could admit just how much he was drawn to her…had been drawn to her from the first time he'd caught sight of her.

To have her in his arms like this, even in such devastating circumstances, was almost enough to make him feel whole again—for all the good it could ever do him.

If he were into self-delusion, he might dream that she could be satisfied with someone who would never really be a whole man again, but why would she?

Emily Livingston was a woman with the whole world at her fingertips, talented, intelligent, beautiful and able to take her pick of any man she wanted. It certainly hadn't escaped his notice that she had every single man in the department lusting after her, to say nothing of the less faithful married ones. Not that she paid any of them any attention, far less accepted their invitations.

What chance would a man who wasn't even a countryman of hers have with a woman so quintessentially English?

A sudden smile flicked across his face when he replayed that last thought. It was a good job that he hadn't voiced it aloud or he would have been shot down in flames.

Not English! Cornish! she would have corrected him proudly. *And don't you forget it!*

'I'm sorry,' hiccuped that same voice from somewhere under his chin. 'I didn't mean to blubber all over you.'

'You may *blubber* all you like,' he invited. 'You know it is an important part of the grieving process.' But it seemed as though the storm was beginning to abate.

'Did you?' she asked when she finally broke the silence again.

'Did I what?' Had he missed a part of the conversation while he'd examined…and dismissed…the idea of asking her to accompany him back to his country? Even if she were to agree to the idea, how long would it be before she realised that she didn't want to stay with a man without honour; the sort of coward who had let his wife and son die without doing a thing to save them; the sort of man who had fled his country and the never-ending nightmares without doing his utmost to bring justice down on the murderers who'd killed his family.

'Did you cry when you grieved?' she asked softly, but the question had all the impact of the original explosion.

It completely short-circuited his thought processes so that he couldn't brush it aside the way he'd done in the past. This time the only thing that came out of his mouth was the raw, unvarnished truth.

'No, I did not cry, because I did not have the right,' he admitted hoarsely. 'How could I play the wronged husband robbed of his family when it was so much my fault that they died?'

He heard the sharp hiss of her indrawn breath and steeled himself to feel her withdraw from him in disgust.

She did pull back a little way but only so that she could glare up at him in the half-light of the early dawn with eyes that reminded him of those of an angry cat.

'So you set the explosion, did you?' she challenged. 'You invited your wife and child to stand there while you detonated it and then you deliberately did nothing to save their lives?'

'No, I did not make the bomb or detonate it,' he said, impatient that she was deliberately misunderstanding him. 'But they died because I did not do anything to save them.'

'Because you yourself were seriously injured,' she broke in sharply, but he dismissed that argument the way he always did. He was a doctor with the skill to save lives, therefore he should have been able to save his wife and child. 'And has anything been done to track down the people who perpetrated this atrocity?' she continued, apparently only too happy to ignore her own problems by occupying her thoughts with his.

'That would be difficult, considering the ones who caused it are the ones who would be charged with investigating it,' he fired back hotly, and could have cursed aloud at his indiscretion.

'You mean, you *know* who killed them?' she demanded incredulously. 'And they are not in prison?'

He closed his eyes and counted to twenty, then again backwards to one, but still the only thing that felt right was to tell her everything—that his was a family divided, with an uncle who had craved power enough to try to wipe out any opposition, including his own brother, while conveniently placing the blame on fundamentalist extremists.

'Is there any way of proving this?' she asked, and his heart swelled with unaccustomed elation when he realised that her outrage was clearly on his behalf—he could tell that just by looking at her as the sun started to peep over the horizon.

'Not unless I go back to Xandar and confront him,' he said. 'And then, only if he didn't arrange to have me killed before I could do it.'

'But then? Would you be free to stay in Xandar and set up another department for your little patients?'

'That would be irrelevant because I will not be going

back,' he said firmly, suddenly struck by the realisation that this time it wasn't the situation in Xandar that was ruling his decision but the fact that going back to take on such a project would mean breaking the promise he'd made to Emily's grandmother.

And if there was one thing he hated doing, it was breaking promises.

He'd been brought up to be an honourable man, and even though his bride had been chosen for him for political reasons, he'd had every intention of laying down his life to protect her and any family they had. So the fact that they'd died while he lived felt like an indelible stain on his character.

Except…would the promise wrung out of him by Emily's grandmother be a way to lessen that stain? If he were to succeed at taking care of the grieving woman in his arms, would he be able to hold his head up again? Would it be the second chance that Emily had spoken of?

The two situations were not in the least similar. Xandar and all its political turmoil was so very different from peaceful Cornwall, and Leika had been the wife chosen for him, while Emily…

He paused in his thoughts, wondering exactly how he should categorise the person who had brought sunshine into his life just by entering it.

If he were being fanciful, he could say that she, too, had been chosen for him, by her grandmother, placed in his care by an unbreakable promise.

And just why did that thought fill him with dismay and set his pulse racing with excitement at the same time?

'I'm dreading going home,' Emily admitted in a small

voice still thick with the threat of tears. 'It was bad enough when Beabea moved to the hospice, but at least she was still almost within sight of the cottage. Now…'

'So come to live with me instead,' Zayed heard himself say with a sense of disbelief.

'*Live with me…*' Emily's heart stood still as those words wrapped around her, then it started beating again at twice the pace.

'You want us to live together?' The suggestion was so unexpected that she was having difficulty believing that she'd heard him correctly.

'Would that be so bad?' he asked. 'You have already said that you do not want to go to your own home and you seem to enjoy yourself at mine.'

'But that's not what you just said,' she pointed out, scared by her bravery but needing to have everything spelt out in words of one syllable. Her heart was involved here, and she'd already had it broken enough times for one lifetime. 'You invited me to live with you, so I need to know whether that was some sort of proposal or…' Emily could feel her cheeks burning with the fear that she was making a monumental fool of herself.

'I should warn you,' she continued without giving him time to reply, 'just because Beabea's gone, it doesn't mean that I'm going to…to drop my standards.'

That didn't mean that she wasn't tempted to, she admitted silently. Zayed was everything she wanted and she'd fallen deeply in love with him in the short time she'd known him, but she could never be happy with anything less than marriage.

Then there was the fact that he was still carrying so much baggage…so much unwarranted guilt.

'Drop your standards?' he repeated with a frown that was easily visible now that the light was strengthening behind the cliff at their backs, making the sea look as if it stretched away from them like a rippled silver sheet all the way to the horizon.

'It wouldn't feel right to move in with a man without the benefit of marriage,' she said, and cringed when she heard how prim and proper she sounded.

He stiffened against her and she had an awful feeling that she knew exactly what he was going to say when he finally broke the uncomfortable silence.

'I am sorry, Emily, but I had not thought to marry again because I have nothing to offer a woman.'

'Nothing to offer?' This time it was her turn to look puzzled as she leant back far enough to focus directly on his face. 'What do you mean, nothing to offer? You're an intelligent, hard-working man who also happens to be extremely good-looking, and you do a difficult job extremely well.'

'Thank you for that testimonial,' he said wryly, 'but there is one thing that can never be changed, no matter how much you might want to.' The harsh tone of his words drew her eyes up to his to see that dreadful empty look return. She wanted to reach up to cradle his cheek in her hand but somehow knew that this was not a time when he would be comfortable accepting gestures of caring.

'The explosion did not just injure my back,' he continued gruffly. 'The surgeons were convinced that the situation would improve but it looks as if the condition is permanent.'

'Condition?' She could feel the tension tightening still further in his body and knew he would rather be up on his feet and striding around on the sand than sitting here among the rocks with an argumentative, weepy woman in his arms.

'I can never have another child,' he said bluntly, the words exploding out of him. 'It appears that some connections from my spine to my…my masculinity…have been damaged.'

'And you think I would only marry a man if he could give me a child?' she exclaimed as she leapt to her feet, uncertain whether to be insulted that he might think that of her or sad that the idea would have occurred to him in the first place. 'I would never even think to do that because, to me, a child is just the *byproduct* of a marriage. A wonderful byproduct, if you are lucky enough, but the most important people in any marriage will always be the two people who make their vows.'

He rose more slowly and she wondered guiltily whether that time spent with her weight pressing down on him might have stressed his injuries and put back his recovery programme. But one look at his expression told her that the ever-present pain in his back was the last thing on his mind.

It was obvious that he had serious reservations about where the two of them went from here, but she refused to be embarrassed about her assumption that he was making some kind of proposal. If she hadn't, they wouldn't be having this conversation and she'd never have learned about the hidden consequences of his injuries.

'We both need time to think about this,' she said firmly,

even though she already knew exactly what she wanted. It was desperately sad that he would never be able to have a child of his own, because the more she'd seen of him the more she'd realised that he would have been a perfect father.

But even if it meant she could never have a child of her own, she would count herself lucky if she had Zayed by her side for the rest of her life.

'In the meantime, there's work and plenty of it waiting for us at St Piran's,' she declared.

'Not for you. Not today,' he said with a shake of his head. He held out one lean hand in invitation to accompany him back up the steps to the car park at the top of the cliff.

Emily held back a moment, finding that she was dreading the start of the new day and loath to end this 'time out of time' together.

Behind him, she could see the first of the early-bird surfers paddling out to catch their first wave of the morning, oblivious to the events of the night that had changed her life for ever.

Zayed turned to follow her gaze, watching the first figure leap agilely to its feet to guide the board so that it received the full force of the incoming wave, before he flicked a glance in her direction. 'And you think you could teach me to do that?' he said in tones of disbelief.

'It's possible, even for someone of your great age,' she teased, but the mention of age brought back other memories that spoiled her enjoyment of the tranquil scene.

'What will you do today?' he asked as they climbed the cliff, and the thought that he would soon be going to work while she was condemned to spend the time alone was depressing.

'There are my grandmother's things to deal with,' she said, dreading the task. 'Perhaps if I do it while I'm still numb from losing her, it won't hurt quite so much.' And anyway she needed time to get her head straight and…

'Do you need company for this?' he offered, and she felt her eyes grow wide with surprise. 'I will be useful for carrying things, even if I can not make any decisions about the possessions of your grandmother. Only you can do this.'

'But you need to go to work.' She should have bitten her tongue rather than give him a cast-iron reason to leave her to it, especially when his suggestion had made the awful day seem briefly brighter.

'I have left a message at the unit to say that I will be away for the day,' he said with the calm assurance of a man who was obviously accustomed to command. How had she not seen this before? It would have been a giant clue to the fact that he was something more than an ordinary man who had worked his way up to his current position at St Piran's.

'They can call me if there is any urgency,' he added, 'but I do not expect that there will be any problems. All our little ones are stable and the next intake is not due for a couple more days.'

Reassured that he already had everything organised, Emily accepted his offer with something suspiciously like excitement. She found herself glancing into her mirror all the way along Harbour Road to check that he was following her towards the cottage, and realised she was behaving with all the sophistication of a smitten teenager.

She'd parked her car and locked it and was walking

back to join him by his much more stylish vehicle when they heard shouting coming from further along the harbour.

'That sounds as if it's coming from somewhere near the surgery,' Emily suggested with a frown as she glanced in that direction. 'We don't usually get drunken disturbances at this time of day…in fact, September is usually a fairly quiet month once the children have all gone back to school. It's unlikely to be anyone hoping to break in for drugs—not in broad daylight.'

She had her keys in her hand ready to unlock the front door when there was a loud bang and a scream. Then they both heard someone shout, 'Fire,' and without a second's hesitation they both began to run.

CHAPTER TEN

'IT's Althorp's,' Emily called as soon as they were close enough to work out where the noise and smoke were coming from. 'The boatyard,' she clarified when she remembered that Zayed might not know the names of the various businesses along Harbour Road.

The mental image of the business, mainly constructed of time-weathered timber and probably containing dozens of drums of flammable paints and chemicals needed for the building and refurbishing of boats of all sorts, was enough to make her shudder.

There could be any number of boats in there too, from simple wooden dinghies to cruisers worth hundreds of thousands of pounds. Any fire would spread frighteningly fast with so much combustible material around.

She was beginning to pant by now but even though she was running on the road in unsuitable footwear after a night of no sleep and too much emotion, the adrenaline surging through her system lent wings to her feet.

There had been several more explosions since that first one and as she got closer she could see that the flames were already leaping above roof height and scattering burning embers in all directions.

But her first thought wasn't about the destruction of property, no matter how historic it was to Penhally. She was far more concerned about the possibility that some of the boat-builders might already have started work, and if there were people trapped in that inferno…

Zayed was already silently cursing the fact that that his injuries were slowing him down.

There had been a time when Emily would never have been able to outrun him, but today he had to bear the frustration of watching her gradually pulling away from him as she sprinted towards the heavy smoke that had started billowing out across the road towards the harbour.

And then he was there, right in front of the gaping wooden doors to the yard when the wind momentarily lifted the thick smoke, and it was like looking into the mouth of hell.

Instantly, Zayed was catapulted right back to the explosion that had killed Leika and Kashif and had come close to ending his own life.

For several interminable seconds he was paralysed with remembered terror as he relived the realisation that he couldn't even stretch his hand out far enough to touch them.

Then there was another explosion, louder than all the rest, and the shock wave sent Emily reeling back into him, sending both of them to the ground.

Immediately he was helping her to her feet but when he tried to push her behind him to protect her from the flying debris, she grabbed his arm and pointed at the dark outline of a figure trying to make his way into the yard.

'Dammit, *no!*' she screamed over the roar of the flames that were consuming everything in their path as she leapt forward to grab hold of the figure. 'It's only a bloody boat!'

He reached for the man's other arm before it could land the blow that would force Emily to let go, and suddenly they were both struggling to hang on, fighting to hold onto the smouldering clothing and the powerfully built person inside it to prevent him trying to enter the death trap that the yard had become.

Zayed twisted one of the man's arms up behind his back to help Emily to restrain him from his intention of trying to save his precious boat from the flames.

What he knew he would rather be doing than keeping the ungrateful individual from risking his life was grabbing Emily into his arms and taking her as far away from danger as possible.

'Let me go!' the man roared, his eyes wild as he saw the flames spreading with nightmare speed. 'I'm going to lose everything.'

'A boat can be replaced with money,' Zayed shouted right in the man's face, automatically noting that several blisters had formed down one cheek. 'People cannot!'

'It's not just a boat,' the man argued, fighting like a demon, and for a brief second Zayed wondered if it was worth risking permanent damage to his back to restrain a man intent on such lunacy. 'That's my whole life going up in there,' he continued. 'The yard, the sail loft, other people's boats…'

With the sound of the fire engines arriving, all the

fight suddenly went out of him and he allowed Zayed and Emily to direct him to the paramedic already parked a safe distance away on the other side of Penhally Bay Surgery next door.

'Are you all right?' Zayed demanded, as he and Emily were bustled aside to leave the firemen space to get their equipment functioning as quickly as possible.

It was obvious that there wasn't going to be much of Althorp's left to save, even once the powerful hoses started pouring thousands of gallons of water onto the inferno. The blaze had become so fierce so quickly that very little in there had stood a chance, not the buildings or the craft, large or small.

'I'm all right,' Emily reassured him, her eyes fixed in awful fascination on the destruction taking place right in front of them.

They were standing by the far corner of the surgery now, but the heat was still reaching them. Even so, Zayed was confident that the granite that formed the surgery's stone walls was solid enough to be unaffected. The paintwork on the side closest to the fire was another matter. That would probably already be showing evidence of scorching and blistering.

Nick Tremayne was standing just a few feet away, his face creased by a deeply concerned frown. He was probably noting just how much work would need to be done before the winter came, but, considering the ferocity of the fire and its proximity to the surgery, they'd got off very lightly.

The woman who came to join him in his vigil was another matter entirely. With tears streaming down her face, it was clear that she was distraught by the destruction of the yard.

'That's Kate Althorp,' Emily told him quietly. 'Her husband was a partner in the business before he died in the big storm a few years ago.'

'Oh, Nick, look at it.' Kate was sobbing, oblivious to their attention, and they saw the older man put a consoling arm around her shoulders. 'This was Jem's inheritance, and there's nothing left of it.'

'Shh! Kate, everything will be all right,' Nick said soothingly, as Zayed took a look around to see that the emergency services were now fully in charge of the scene. 'Either the business can be rebuilt with the insurance money or…perhaps you and John would be interested in selling the site to the practice—for parking, initially, but with the new estates going up around Penhally, we'll obviously be needing to expand in the future, take on more staff, perhaps put in a full-time physio. That way, you won't have to worry about money for…for Jem's schooling or…'

His voice and the concern in it faded into the distance as Zayed led Emily away, only realising as he wrapped an arm around her shoulders that both of them were shaking in the aftermath of the event.

'Are you sure you are all right?' he demanded, suddenly realising just how much this woman's safety meant to him. 'You were not hurt when that man—'

'Poor John,' Emily said softly. 'The boatyard has been in his family for years and years.'

'But everyone is out of danger, and the fire will soon be under control, yes?'

Emily was quiet for a moment before she replied, then stopped almost in the middle of the pavement in front of Beabea's cottage to gaze up at him. 'Oh, I hope everyone is all right, Zayed.' She paused for a moment and he could tell from the little frown pulling her brows together that she was trying to decide whether to continue. Or was it a question she wanted to ask?

'Did it bring everything back?' she demanded softly, concern clear in those beautiful green eyes. 'The explosions? It must have been…'

'Yes,' he admitted, remembering his utter paralysis for just those few seconds. 'For a moment it was almost like being back there, at the hospital in Xandar, and I was sure I would not be able to move to help anyone.'

'But you could and you did, because *this* time you weren't one of the injured ones,' she declared firmly, obviously determined to stress the fact that had finally been driven home to him in that moment.

'I know this now,' he admitted, with a new sense of peace spreading through him. 'But I will probably always feel sad that I was not able to do anything for Leika and Kashif, even if I could not have saved their lives.'

'Well, you helped me stop John Althorp from risking his,' she pointed out as she sorted through her key ring for the front door key. 'I couldn't have held him much longer on my own, not when he was so determined to go back into the yard.'

She paused when the door swung open, looking back over her shoulder to ask, 'Are you sure you want to do this? It's mostly going to be a long and boring job and I'm probably going to weep buckets when I come across all the little mementos Beabea kept.'

Zayed stared at this special woman who had come into his life and was suddenly overwhelmed with the knowledge that she was the one person with whom he wanted to spend the rest of his days.

He desperately wanted the chance to spend every one of those days doing his best to make her happy, even if he couldn't give her the children she deserved. Perhaps she could learn to be content with a constant stream of other people's children to care for.

'Emily, will you marry me?' he asked with his heart in his mouth.

'Wha—what did you say?' she stammered, her eyes wide and a dark forest green as she gazed up at him, clearly every bit as shocked as he was to hear the words he'd just said.

'I said, "Emily, will you marry me?"' he repeated firmly, as a feeling of excitement flooded through him at the knowledge that everything in his life was going to be different from this day on. It was almost a feeling of dizziness mixed with the sensation that that he might float right up off the granite front doorstep at any second, a feeling that, for the first time in his life, the world held endless possibilities.

'Why?' she asked faintly. 'Why do you want to marry me? Is it just because I said I wouldn't live with you? Because if it is…'

'No, Emily!' He felt a smile spreading over his face. 'I respect you for that, but it is not why I am asking you to marry me. I am discovering that, for me, there is really only one reason to propose to a woman and that is because I have fallen in love with her and can not imagine my life without her.'

He was glad to see that the shock was lessening a little but her eyes were still wide with disbelief when he took her in his arms for the second time that day. But this time it wasn't to comfort her as she mourned her grandmother but to kiss the mouth that had been fascinating him for weeks.

Zayed's mouth was everything she had dreamed it would be and more, and she couldn't help the whimper that escaped when he took it away far too soon.

She needed that close connection to him, now more than ever. When that explosion had knocked them off their feet, she'd suddenly realised just how vulnerable the two of them were, standing in front of that raging inferno, and that Zayed might not be lucky a second time. The thought that she might lose him before she'd ever told him that she loved him had squeezed a tight fist around her heart and stopped the breath in her throat.

In that moment she had recognised the essential truth that, even if he wasn't ready to commit to marriage, she would rather be with him than without him. Even as they were walking back to the cottage, she'd been trying to find the words to tell him that, if he still wanted her to, she was ready to accept his invitation to move in with him.

Except she hadn't needed to compromise her principles, because that same explosion had apparently been an epiphany for Zayed, too, and there in the hallway of her grandmother's cottage, after a sleepless night and smelling of smoke, he'd asked her to marry him.

Suddenly she found herself chuckling at the incongruousness of the setting.

'You think it is funny that I ask you to marry me?' Zayed demanded, trying to sound outraged, but her response to his kiss must already have told him what her answer would be.

'I think it's wonderful that you've asked me,' she reassured him. 'I was only laughing because Penhally is surrounded by some of the most beautiful scenery in the world and you chose the hallway of my grandmother's cottage to propose.'

'So, what would you prefer?' he challenged. 'For me to take you out for a perfect meal first? Or perhaps I should put you in the car and take you further along the coast to find some sand dunes, then put up a Cornish version of a Bedouin tent so that I can ask you properly?'

Emily was laughing out loud now, the happiness bubbling out of her, but Zayed hadn't finished.

'How about if I promise to take you out into the desert when we go to visit Xandar and propose to you properly?' he suggested, his eyes very dark and solemn, and her laughter quickly died away.

'You're serious?' she demanded, knowing just what a huge step this was for him. 'You're really going back to visit Xandar?'

'Initially, it would be a visit, but only if you will be coming with me,' he said firmly. 'Then, when I have put the evidence in front of those who will deal with the one who I believe was ultimately responsible for the death of my wife and son, perhaps we can start to make plans for a new hospital unit for the little ones…but only if you decide you would like to live in Xandar.'

'Ah, Zayed,' she breathed, loving him all the more for the way he was going to face his demons, but before she could accept his proposal he was speaking again.

'Do not give me an answer now,' he said, with a fierce light of excitement filling his dark eyes with sparks of golden fire. 'Wait until we are in Xandar. You will come with me to my country?'

'Of course I'll come with you,' she agreed, loving this new facet to his character. She didn't need elaborate, romantic scene-setting to tell him that she loved him and wanted to accept his proposal. Neither did she need to see Xandar to know that if she was with him she would love it, too, especially if they were going to be working on those plans together.

His eyes lit up and he tugged her back into his arms. 'Ah, we have so much to do today, Emily,' he said, full of bubbling enthusiasm. 'We must decide what to do about the things of your grandmother, make arrangements for someone to take our places in the unit, and then contact my friends in Xandar to prepare them for our visit. But first I need one more kiss before we start to work.'

'Where are we going?' Emily demanded as her horse followed Zayed's out into the apparently endless sand dunes.

'Not much further,' he promised, his accent more pronounced than ever since they'd arrived in his homeland.

'You said that five minutes ago,' she reminded him, but she didn't really mind how long the journey took. This was like something out of a fantasy. Just two weeks ago they'd been in Penhally, feeling the heat of the fire as Althorp's yard had burnt to the ground. Today she was swathed in fine white cotton to ward off the heat of the burning desert sun in Xandar.

And then they rounded the curve of a dune and she knew exactly where he'd brought her and why.

'A Bedouin tent?' she asked with a tremulous smile as he lifted her off the pretty little mare.

'The Xandar equivalent,' he admitted, as he held out a hand to help her dismount and invite her into the shady interior. 'If you would like to make yourself comfortable, I will bring you something to eat and drink.'

In a move that had quickly become automatic, Emily stepped out of her shoes by the doorway and trod across a thick, smooth richly patterned carpet that could only be made of silk.

The cushions piled around the low table were covered in silk, too, and in every opulent lustrous shade imaginable.

'Do I sit on them or lie down?' she murmured uncertainly to herself.

'Whichever you prefer,' he said softly from right behind her as he relieved her of the voluminous robe that had protected her from the heat. Underneath she wore a simple garment, a gift from Zayed in the finest silk, that drifted and clung to her body with the slightest breeze.

When she'd donned it, she'd been almost embarrassed by how much it revealed, but here, alone with Zayed and seeing the gleam it brought to his eyes, it seemed to bring out the sensual side to her nature.

'Would you like something to eat…some fruit, perhaps? Or can I get you a drink?'

Either would have been lovely, but in spite of the fact that he'd obviously enjoyed himself creating the romantic fantasy he'd described on the day of the fire in Penhally, she could tell that he had something else on his mind.

For just a second she allowed insecurity to persuade

her that he was regretting bringing her to Xandar, but she knew that wasn't true.

In fact, just today he'd been overjoyed to tell her that the uncle who had been so hungry for power that he had tried to engineer the death of Zayed's entire family had finally been arrested and imprisoned, and was awaiting trial.

'Zayed, what's the matter?' she asked. 'Is there a problem with setting up the replacement unit at the hospital?'

His immediate smile was reassurance enough.

'Not at all,' he declared confidently. 'Everything is going to plan without a hitch since the Hananis and their influential family got together with some of the other parents to tell everyone about what we've done for their children.'

He sank slightly gingerly onto the pile of cushions beside her and she wondered if she ought to suggest massaging his back to relieve the stiffness. It would probably take a while before his body became accustomed to riding again, but she had every confidence that he would eventually regain most of his mobility.

'Emily, even the most hard line of the traditionalists were won over by all those successful operations, and especially by all the good things the families had to say about my new colleague, despite the fact that she is a woman. They have made it a source of national pride that as soon as the unit is completed, these operations will all be able to take place in Xandar from now on.'

My new colleague. There was something almost possessive about the way he'd said those words that had sent a shiver of joy through her, but she couldn't ignore the shadow she'd seen in his eyes.

'So what *is* the problem?' she pressed, knowing that neither of them would be able to relax and enjoy this romantic idyll until they'd discussed whatever it was.

'While you were getting ready to ride with me, I caught an item on the international news,' he said reluctantly.

'And?' she prompted with a slight frown, wondering what sort of news would put that concerned expression in those gold-shot dark eyes.

'It seems that when we left Cornwall, the beautiful weather did not last. There were pictures showing that there has been a flash flood in Penhally.'

'A flood? In Penhally, itself? Was anybody hurt?' The images of all the people she knew in the town, friends and neighbours right from the first day she'd come to live with her grandmother, flickered before her eyes. 'How much damage was done?'

'I did not hear anything about any injuries, but I did see…' He hesitated briefly before continuing. 'I am sorry, Emily, but I recognised it from the pictures taken from the helicopters. The house of your grandmother was one of those that were flooded.'

'Oh, no!' Emily felt the hot press of tears burning her eyes at the thought that a lifetime's memories had probably been washed away in a matter of seconds.

None of her belongings would have been damaged because they'd all been removed and put in temporary storage before she and Zayed had left for Xandar. But the house itself, with its solid stone walls and Delabole slate roof and the ancient floorboards polished over the decades to a lustrous dark honey colour, to say nothing of all the memories attached to every nook and cranny…all that could have been destroyed in the blink of an eye.

And then there would be the aftermath.

She'd seen enough of what had happened after the Boscastle and Crackington Haven floods at first hand to know that by the time the flood damage had been cleared and the repairs had been completed, it would seem like a completely different cottage.

For a moment it felt as if a hand squeezed tightly around her heart when she realised that, with her job at St Piran's ably filled by one of Zayed's colleagues, there would now be nothing left to go back to in Penhally.

But, then, why would she want to go back there when everything she wanted was here in Xandar?

'Zayed, it's all right,' she reassured him, reaching up a hand to cup his cheek. 'It's always sad when something is destroyed, but it's only a house several thousand miles away. And as you said when the boatyard went up in flames, it can be replaced with money if I ever wanted to go back to Penhally. It's people that are important, people that are irreplaceable.'

'You are certainly irreplaceable,' he said seriously as he knelt beside her, and she suddenly realised that the moment she'd been waiting for had come. 'You have become the other half of my soul, Emily Livingston, and now that I have brought you out into the desert in the country of my birth, it is time for you to give me your answer. Will you marry me so that my soul can be whole again?'

'Oh, Zayed, yes! Of course I'll marry you,' she said as she held her arms out towards him. 'You're the other half of my soul, too, and I'll need you for the rest of my life.'

'Ah, Emily, my Emily,' he murmured as he took her in his arms and their lips met for the first time since he'd kissed her in the hallway of Beabea's cottage.

Their kisses quickly became heated after their self-imposed abstinence and Emily had no objection when Zayed began to explore the willing body beneath the garment he'd given her. How could she when she was equally eager to explore the smooth skin and taut muscles of the body she hadn't touched since that night on the beach in Penhally?

Suddenly Zayed rolled away from her, putting far too many brightly coloured cushions between them as he gazed at her in a strange mixture of disbelief and hope.

'What's the matter, Zayed? Did I do something wrong?' She felt the heat of a blush sweep up her throat and into her face. 'I'm afraid I haven't had very much experience at this sort of thing, so you'll have to tell me what you—'

'Ah, Emily, my Emily, I love your innocence. It will almost be a shame to destroy it, but…' He rolled back towards her again and took her hand in his.

'Since we have been kissing and I have been exploring your body, I have made the discovery that my surgeon did not know everything,' he said with a gleam in his eyes. 'He did not know that when my Emily accepted my proposal and kissed me, she would revive the part of me that the doctors could not.'

Emily's blush grew fiercer still when she followed his downward glance and realised what he was talking about, but she quickly decided that this was no time for maidenly modesty.

'Hmm. This could be a problem,' she said seriously, and had to stifle a laugh when Zayed's face fell.

'A problem?' he echoed uncertainly.

'Well, we aren't married yet, so Beabea wouldn't approve if we were to...take advantage of the situation. But...' She deliberately drew the word out, loving the fact that this powerful man was completely in her thrall for the moment.

'But?' he prompted, completely unable to hide his eagerness.

'But just in case there's the slightest chance that your doctors were right and this may never happen again,' she suggested, 'perhaps...'

'Perhaps?' he pressed impatiently and she marvelled at his control. She was also looking forward to the moment when that control broke.

This, she realised with a burgeoning sense of her own power as a woman, *this* could be the most wonderful game between them, and it was one that could have as many variations as there were hours to their lives.

'Perhaps we ought to take advantage of it while we can?' she hinted, and finally lost control of the happy smile she'd been hiding.

'Ah-h! I was not expecting this to happen, so I have brought nothing with me to protect you,' he groaned, holding back when all she was longing for was to finally learn what it was to be completely possessed by the man she loved. It was something that she'd believed his injuries had robbed them of and she thought she'd schooled herself to accept that this would never happen, but she'd never thought that they would be this fortunate.

'I don't need to be protected,' she told him eagerly, as a quick mental calculation of dates sent an arrow of excitement through her.

She'd been teasing him, but they both knew that there was very little likelihood that his prowess would only have returned for this one occasion. Still, could they really be so lucky as to conceive a child in the first time they came together?

'I would never need to be protected from you,' she whispered as she raised her arms to allow him to slide her silky covering away, feeling powerful and womanly when she saw the gleam in his eyes as they travelled over her nakedness for the first time. 'I just need to know that I have your love as you have mine.'

'Ah, my Emily, you have it,' he said. 'You have my love, my heart, my soul and my body…for ever!' And he made them one.

* * * *

A Baby for Eve

MAGGIE KINGSLEY

Maggie Kingsley says she can't remember a time when she didn't want to be a writer, but she put her dream on hold and decided to "be sensible" and become a teacher instead. Five years at the chalk face was enough to convince her she wasn't cut out for it, and she "escaped" to work for a major charity. Unfortunately—or fortunately!—a back injury ended her career and, when she and her family moved to a remote cottage in the north of Scotland, it was her family who nagged her into attempting to make her dream a reality. Combining a love of romantic fiction with a knowledge of medicine gleaned from the many professionals in her family, Maggie says she can't now imagine ever being able to have so much fun legally doing anything else!

This book is dedicated to five extremely talented and generous writing friends: Kate Hardy, Jessica Matthews, Margaret McDonagh, Alison Roberts and Jennifer Taylor. Without their encouragement I can truthfully say this book would never have been finished.

CHAPTER ONE

A WRY smile curved Eve Dwyer's lips as the door of St Mark's Church creaked open then closed again. Somebody was cutting it fine. Very fine. Another five minutes and the wedding ceremony would have begun, and curiously she glanced over her shoulder to see who the latecomer might be only for the smile on her face to freeze.

It was him. His thick black hair might be lightly flecked with grey now, and there were deep lines on his forehead that hadn't been there twenty years ago, but Eve would have recognised the man walking rapidly towards an empty seat near the front of the church anywhere. Tom Cornish was back in Penhally Bay and, if she hadn't been sitting in the middle of a packed pew, surrounded by her colleagues from the village's medical practice, Eve would have taken to her heels and run.

'Good heavens,' Kate Althorp, the village's senior midwife, whispered from Eve's left. 'Is that who I think it is?'

Other people were muttering the same thing, Eve noticed, seeing the number of heads suddenly craning in Tom's direction, the nudges people were giving their neighbours. Not the younger members of the congregation. They wouldn't remember a Dr Tom Cornish but those aged over forty-five certainly did, and not very kindly if the frowns on some faces were anything to go by.

'Is that who?' Lauren Nightingale asked from Eve's right, but Kate didn't have time to answer the physiotherapist.

The organist had launched into the wedding march, which meant the bride had arrived. A bride Tom Cornish wouldn't have known from a cake of soap, Eve thought, gripping her order of service card so tightly that the embossed card bent beneath her fingers. Both Alison Myers and her bridegroom, Jack Tremayne, would have been children when Tom had last been in Penhally Bay so why was he here, and why had he come back when he'd always sworn he never would?

'Doesn't Alison look lovely?' Lauren sighed as the girl walked past them, radiant in a simple long gown of cream satin.

Alison did, but any enjoyment Eve might have felt in the occasion had gone. The flowers in the church, which had smelt so sweet just a few minutes ago, now seemed cloying. The crush of bodies, which had once felt so companionable, now simply felt oppressive, and even the sight of Jack and Alison's small sons, walking solemnly down the aisle behind Alison, failed to give her pleasure.

'Eve, are you OK?'

Kate was gazing curiously at her, and Eve faked a smile.

'I'm fine,' she murmured. 'It's just a bit…crowded.'

The midwife chuckled. 'Penhally loves a wedding. A christening's good, but a wedding is the only thing guaranteed to get the whole village out.'

But not Tom Cornish, Eve thought, stiffening slightly as she saw him half turn in his seat. Tom who had once said marriage was a prison he had no intention of ever inhabiting. Tom who'd said he wanted to be free, to travel, and was damned if he was going to rot away in the village in which he had been born.

'Oh, aren't they sweet?' Lauren exclaimed as Alison's three-year-old son, Sam, and Jack's equally young son, Freddie, held out the red velvet cushions they were carrying so everyone could see the wedding rings sitting on them.

'Yes,' was all Eve could manage as a collective sigh of approval ran round the congregation.

Why was Tom here—*why*? She'd read in a medical magazine a few years back that he'd been appointed head of operations at Deltaron, the world-famous international rescue team, so he should have been somewhere abroad, helping the victims of some disaster, not sitting in the front pew of St Mark's, resurrecting all her old heartache, and anger, and pain.

'Eve, are you *quite* sure you're OK?' Kate whispered, the worry in her eyes rekindling.

'I…I have a bit of a headache, that's all,' Eve lied. 'It's the flowers—the perfume—strong smells always give me a headache.'

Kate looked partially convinced. Not wholly convinced, but at least partially, and Eve gripped her order of service card even tighter.

Pull yourself together, she told herself as the service continued and she found her eyes continually straying away from the young couple standing in front of Reverend Kenner towards Tom. For God's sake, you're forty-two years old, not a girl any more. Tom probably won't even remember you, far less recognise you, so pull yourself together, but she couldn't. No matter how often she told herself she was being stupid, overreacting, all she wanted was to leave. Immediately.

'Eve, you look terrible,' Kate murmured when Jack and Alison had walked back down the aisle as man and wife, and everyone in the congregation began to get to their feet. 'I have some paracetamol in my bag—'

'Air,' Eve muttered. 'I just… I need some fresh air.'

And to get as far away from here as I can before Tom sees me, she added mentally as she hurried to the church door and out into the sunshine. She wasn't tall—just five feet five—so, if she was quick, she could lose herself amongst the congregation, then hurry down Harbour Road and go home. She'd tell everyone at the practice on Monday she'd had a migraine, and her colleagues would understand, she knew they would. All she had to do was keep walking, not look back, and—

'*Eve Dwyer*. By all that's wonderful, it's you, isn't it?'

His voice hadn't changed at all, Eve thought as she came to a halt, moistening lips that had suddenly gone dry. It was as deep and mellow as it had always been, still with that faint trace of Cornish burr, and she wanted to pretend she hadn't heard him, but she couldn't.

'Eve Dwyer,' Tom repeated, shaking his head in clear disbelief as she turned slowly to face him. 'I never expected to run into you within minutes of coming back to Penhally. It's Tom Cornish,' he added a little uncertainly when she stared up at him, completely unable to say a word. 'Don't tell me you've forgotten me?'

How could I? she wanted to reply, but she didn't.

'Of course I remember you, Tom,' she said instead. 'You're…you're looking well.'

He was. Up close, she could see he was heavier now than he had been at twenty-four but on him the extra weight looked good, and the grey in his hair, and the lines on his forehead, gave his face a strength it hadn't possessed before, but it was his eyes that took her breath away.

For years those startlingly green eyes had plagued her dreams, teasing her, laughing at her, and she'd told herself that time and absence had created an unreal image of him, but they were every bit as green as she had remembered, and every bit as potent, and she had to swallow, hard.

'So…'

'So…'

They'd spoken together, and she felt a tingle of heat darken her cheeks.

'I didn't realise you knew Alison and Jack,' she said to fill the silence.

'Who?' He frowned.

'The couple whose wedding you've just been at,' she declared, moving swiftly to one side so the people who were still leaving the church could get past her.

'Never met either of them in my life,' he said.

'Then why come to their wedding?' she asked in confusion.

'I arrived in Penhally just before twelve o'clock, found the place deserted, and when I asked at the shop I was told everybody was probably here.'

Which still didn't explain why he'd come.

'Tom—'

'Tom Cornish.' Kate beamed. 'What in the world brings you back to Penhally? I thought you were still in the States.'

For a second Tom stared blankly at the midwife, clearly trying to place her, then grinned. 'Kate Templar, right?'

'Kate Althorp now, Tom.' She laughed. 'Have been for years.'

And he hadn't answered Kate's question either, Eve thought.

'Are you coming to the reception?' Kate continued, waving to Reverend Kenner as he hurried towards his car. 'It's a buffet at The Smugglers' Inn so there'll be plenty of food, and I'm sure Alison and Jack would be delighted to meet you.'

'And I'm sure Tom has better things to do than go to a reception that will be packed with doctors and nurses who'll only end up talking shop,' Eve said quickly, and saw one of Tom's eyebrows lift.

'I can talk shop,' he said. 'I'm a doctor, too, remember, so I can talk shop with the best of them.'

'Yes, but—'

'Afraid I might embarrass you by smashing up the furniture, getting drunk and insulting all your friends?' he said dryly, and she crimsoned.

'Of course not,' she protested, though, in truth, she wasn't one hundred per cent sure about the insults. 'I just thought…'

She came to a halt. A small hand had slipped into hers. A hand that belonged to a little girl with long blonde hair who was staring up at her eagerly. 'Tassie, sweetheart. Where in the world did you spring from?'

'I've been out here since the wedding started,' the ten-year-old replied. 'Sitting on the wall, listening to the music.'

'Oh, Tassie, love, why didn't you come inside the church?' Eve exclaimed, her gaze taking in the girl's thin and worn T-shirt and her shabby cotton trousers, which weren't nearly warm enough to withstand the cool of the early October day. 'There's quite a breeze blowing in from the harbour—'

'Don't feel the cold,' Tassie interrupted, 'and I'm not really wearing the right sort of clothes for a wedding. Her dress is pretty, isn't it?' she added, gazing wistfully towards the lychgate where Alison and Jack were having their photographs taken.

'Yes, it's very pretty,' Eve murmured, her heart twisting slightly at the envy she could see in the little girl's brown eyes. Eyes which had always seemed too large for her thin face even when she'd been a toddler. 'Tassie, does your mother know you're here?'

'She said I was to get out from under her feet, so I did. She won't be worried.'

Amanda Lovelace probably wouldn't, Eve thought with a sigh, but that wasn't the point.

'Tassie—'

'I was wondering whether I could come to the reception?' the girl interrupted. 'I heard Mrs Althorp say there would be lots of food, so could I come? I won't be any trouble—I promise.'

Eve's heart sank. Normally she couldn't refuse Tassie anything. The child had so few treats in her life, but she didn't want to go to the reception. She didn't want to go anywhere but home.

'Tassie, the reception's not really for children,' she began. 'It's more a grown-up thing.'

'Nonsense!' Kate exclaimed. 'My son Jem will be there and he's only nine. And Alison's son Sam and Jack's son Freddie are both going, and they're only three, so I'm sure Tassie would enjoy it.'

'Perhaps,' Eve declared, 'but I really don't think—'

'Oh, I do, most definitely,' Tom interrupted. 'If Tom Cornish can be given an invitation then I think this half-pint should have one, too.'

'But her mother won't know where she is,' Eve protested, all too aware she was losing this argument, but determined to give it one last try. 'She'll be worried.'

Tom delved into his pocket and produced his mobile phone.

'Not if we use the wonders of modern technology,' he declared. 'Give her a quick call, and then I'll get to take two beautiful women out to lunch.'

Tassie giggled, and Eve sighed inwardly. There was nothing left to say—no argument she could come up with—and when she reluctantly took the phone Kate beamed.

'That's settled, then,' the midwife said as Eve made her call then handed back the phone to Tom. 'Tom, Eve can show you how to get to The Smugglers' Inn if you've forgotten where it is, and…' She stopped in mid-sentence as a dull, metallic thud suddenly split the air followed by the sound of breaking glass. 'What the…?'

'Sounds like someone's just backed into something,' Tom observed.

'And no prizes for guessing who the "someone" is.' Kate groaned as Lauren clambered out of her car, her hand pressed to her mouth.

'Oh, come on, be fair, Kate,' Eve protested. 'The cars are parked really close to one another. Whose car did she hit?'

Kate frowned. 'Don't know. It's a metallic blue Range Rover, not from around here by its number plate, so my guess is it belongs to some flash holidaymaker.'

Tom cleared his throat. 'I'm afraid I'm the flash holiday-maker, so who is the "she" who has just reversed into my car?'

Kate looked uncomfortably at Eve, and Eve bit her lip.

'Lauren. She's our practice physiotherapist, and a really lovely woman, but quite dreadfully accident prone.'

And currently absolutely mortified, Eve thought as Lauren hurried towards them, her cheeks scarlet, her eyes worried.

'I was certain I had enough space to reverse,' she exclaimed, 'absolutely certain, but... Does anyone know who owns the blue Range Rover?'

'Tom does,' Eve replied. 'Tom, this is Lauren Nightingale.'

'Not Florence?' he said, and Eve rolled her eyes.

'Tom, Lauren must have heard that joke about a million times.'

'A million and one now, actually,' Lauren said, 'but that's not the point. I'm so sorry about your car—'

'From the looks of it, your Renault's come off worse,' Tom interrupted, gazing critically at his car, then at Lauren's. 'You've scraped quite a bit of paintwork off your tail, whereas you've only broken my indicator light cover.'

'Which I will pay for,' Lauren insisted, digging into her bag. 'I have my insurance certificate in here—'

'Look, how about I simply send you the bill for the repair, and we don't involve our insurance companies at all?' Tom suggested. 'That way you won't lose your no-claims bonus.'

'Are you sure?' Lauren said uncertainly, and, when Tom nodded, she extracted a notebook and a pen from her bag. 'You'll need my address for the bill. It's Gatehouse Cottage. That's—'

'The cottage at the bottom of the drive that leads to the Manor House.' Tom smiled when the physiotherapist looked at him in surprise. 'I was born in Penhally, lived here for the first twenty-four years of my life, so I know where everything is.'

'Where are you staying so I can contact you?' Lauren asked.

'The Anchor Hotel,' Tom replied, taking the notebook and pen from Lauren, 'but I won't be there long so you'd better have my London address.'

His London address. So he didn't live in the States any more, Eve thought as she watched him scribble in Lauren's notebook, and he wasn't going to be staying in The Anchor for long, but did that mean he was moving back into his old home in Penhally, or what?

'You're staying at The Anchor Hotel?' Kate said before Eve could ask the questions she so desperately wanted the answers to. 'Very posh.'

'You mean, you're amazed they let anyone called Cornish through the door?' Tom said with an edge, and Kate coloured deeply.

'Of course I didn't mean that!' she exclaimed. 'I just meant...'

Her voice trailed away into awkward, embarrassed silence, and Eve came to her rescue.

'Kate, shouldn't you be making tracks for The Smugglers'?' she said. 'Alison and Jack headed off a few minutes ago, and they must be wondering where you are.'

'Oh. Right,' the midwife declared with a grateful smile and, as she and Lauren both headed for their cars, Eve turned to Tom, her expression sad.

'So, it still pushes all your buttons, does it, even after all these years?'

Tom's face tightened.

'Only in Penhally,' he said, then forced a smile as he noticed Tassie gazing up at him in obvious confusion. 'Well, half-pint, what are we waiting for? If we don't get to the reception fast all the best food will have gone.'

'Are we going in your car?' the little girl asked. 'The one that got hit?'

'We can walk,' Eve said hurriedly. 'The Smugglers' isn't far—just up the road.'

'We drive,' Tom insisted. 'If I'm taking two gorgeous women out to lunch then we go in style, even if my car is missing one indicator light cover.'

Walking would be better, Eve thought. Tassie would leap about as she always did, pointing things out to Tom, which would mean she wouldn't have to talk to him, but she could hardly insist on them walking. Tom would wonder why, and if Tom was the same man she had known—and she strongly suspected he was—he would badger and badger her until she told him.

'In style it is, then,' she declared, striding determinedly towards his car before she lost her nerve.

'Can I sit in the front?' Tassie asked, hopping excitedly from one foot to the other, her fine blonde hair flying about her shoulders, and Tom shook his head.

'Surely you know royalty always rides in the back behind the chauffeur?' he replied.

'But I'm not royalty,' the little girl pointed out, and Tom smiled the smile Eve knew could charm the birds off the trees.

'Today you are,' he said, helping Tassie up into the Range Rover. 'So, where to, ma'am?'

'Smugglers' Inn, as quick as you can, driver,' Tassie declared with an imperious air that was completely ruined when she dissolved into a fit of giggles.

'That was kind,' Eve murmured, as she got into the front seat, and Tom slipped into the driver's seat beside her.

'It's only manners to open a door for a lady,' he replied, and Eve shook her head.

'I meant it was kind of you to be so nice to Tassie.'

'She's a nice kid.'

'Not everyone sees that,' Eve observed, then managed a smile when Tom stared at her curiously. 'Do you honestly remember where everything in Penhally is, or do you want directions for The Smugglers'?'

'I haven't forgotten anything about Penhally,' he said abruptly, then grimaced as a slight frown creased Eve's forehead. 'Sorry. An hour back in the place, and already I'm defensive. No, I don't need directions,' he added as he drove out of the car park and turned left. 'The Smugglers' is at the top of Mevagissey Road.'

Odd, she thought as he drove north, that he should remember that. They'd never been to the inn when they'd been younger. It had been too expensive for them when he'd just qualified as a doctor and she'd just finished her nurse's training, and yet he'd remembered where it was. What else did he remember? she wondered, but she didn't want to go down that particular memory lane. It was fraught with too many dangers, too many complications.

'How long have you lived in London?' she said, deliberately changing the conversation. 'I mean, I thought you were still in the States,' she continued as he glanced across at her, 'but you gave Lauren a London address.'

'I haven't lived in the States for the past ten years,' he replied. 'I have a flat in London now, and an apartment in Lausanne overlooking Lake Geneva.'

'Sounds—'

'Posh?' he finished for her dryly, and she shook her head at him.

'Lovely—I was going to say lovely,' she said, and Tom shrugged.

'They're just places I stay in between trips, not proper homes. Homes have people you love in them. Wives, children.'

Don't ask, she thought as she stared out the windscreen at the trees flashing by. Trees that were beginning to lose their leaves under a sky that was as blue as only a Cornish sky could be. She didn't need to know, and it was better if she didn't, but she couldn't help herself.

'You're not married, then?' she said, glancing across at him.

'Nope,' he replied, braking slightly to avoid the rabbit that had dashed out in front of them. 'Never found anyone prepared to put up with the kind of erratic work patterns my job demands. At least, not for any length of time.' His green eyes met hers. 'What about you?'

She shifted her gaze back at the trees.

'No, I'm not married.' She took a deep breath. 'Tom, are you planning on coming back to Penhally to stay, or…?'

'I'm only here until Monday. I have things to do—sort out—then I'll be off again.'

A surge of relief engulfed her. Monday. This was Saturday. She could cope with that. If she should accidentally meet him again tomorrow, she'd be pleasant and friendly, talk about everything and nothing. She'd managed to keep silent for all these years so she could keep quiet for one more day because what good would it do to tell him? Telling him wouldn't change anything, alter anything, make it less painful.

'Eve?'

He was staring curiously at her, and she managed to smile.

'I read in a magazine a while back that you'd been made head of rescue operations at Deltaron,' she said. 'You must be very pleased.'

'Yeah, well, it's certainly a whole different ball game when your desk is the one the buck stops on. What about you?' he asked. 'Still nursing?'

She nodded.

'I actually just started work in Penhally last month,' she said. 'Before that I worked in Truro and Newquay, but Alison—the girl you don't know whose wedding you were just at,' she added, and saw Tom smile, 'is pregnant so I've temporarily taken over her position as practice nurse in the Penhally surgery.'

'Which means if she comes back after her maternity leave, you'll be out of a job,' Tom observed.

'Not for long,' she said briskly. 'There's a big shortage of nurses in the UK so I'll get something else pretty fast.'

'But you'd rather work here, in your home village.'

It was a statement, not a question, and her lips curved wryly.

'Well, you always did say I had no imagination.'

'Did I say that?' He shook his head. 'God, I had a big mouth when I was twenty-four, didn't I?'

'Uh-huh,' she replied, and he laughed. 'Actually, although you don't know Alison or Jack,' she continued, 'you do know Jack's father. It's Nick Tremayne.'

'Nick Tremayne, the doctor?' Tom declared.

'The very same,' Eve answered. 'He's the senior partner in the Penhally surgery now, and my boss.'

'Are you telling me I've just been to the wedding of the *son* of somebody I went to med school with?' Tom groaned. 'God, but now you've made me feel old.'

Eve chuckled. 'Do you remember when we thought anyone older than forty was decrepit?'

'And anyone over fifty might just as well be dead.' He nodded. 'Shows how little we knew, doesn't it?' His eyes met hers again. 'Eve—'

'Are we almost there yet?' Tassie chipped in from the back of the car. 'I'm *starving*.'

'In other words, quit with the talking,' Tom said ruefully, 'and drive faster.'

'Something like that.' The little girl giggled and, as Tom grinned across at Eve, and her own lips curved in response, her heart contracted.

No, she told herself. *No*. The past is past, nobody can ever go back, and if you allow yourself to be sucked back into his world he'll only hurt you again, and this time you might not survive.

'What's wrong?' Tom asked, his green eyes suddenly puzzled, and Eve shook her head.

'Just hungry, like Tassie.'

'Eve—'

'We're here!' Tassie interrupted with a shriek as the grey-stoned façade of The Smugglers' Inn suddenly came into view. 'And look at all the cars. I hope there's room inside for us.'

And I hope it's standing room only, Eve thought, so I can hide myself in the crush, but Tom must have read her mind because as she got out of the car he took her arm firmly in his.

'Now we eat, and socialise, right?' he declared.

'You go ahead,' Eve replied. 'I just need…'

She waved vaguely in the direction of the door leading to the ladies' cloakroom, but it didn't do her any good.

'We'll wait for you, won't we, Tassie?' Tom said, and Tassie beamed, leaving Eve with nothing to do but obediently disappear into the ladies' cloakroom.

At least it was empty, she thought with relief as she walked in. Company was the last thing she wanted right now, and quickly she washed her hands then pulled her hairbrush out of her handbag. Lord, but she looked awful. White face, panic-stricken brown eyes, her shoulder-length brown hair slightly windswept, and…

Forty-two, she thought bleakly as she gazed at her reflection in the mirror over the sink. I look forty-two. OK, so that wasn't old, but nothing could alter the fact that she was heavier than she'd been at twenty-two, that there were faint lines at the corner of her eyes, and her hair wouldn't be brown if Vicki at the hairdresser's didn't tint it every six weeks.

Impatiently, she dragged her hairbrush through her hair. What did it matter if she didn't look twenty-two any more?

Because I would like to have looked as I did when he last saw me, her heart sighed as her eyes met those in the mirror. Because it would have shown him what he lost when he walked away from me, and it was stupid to feel that way. Stupid.

'Feeling any better now?'

Eve whirled round to see Kate Althorp standing behind her, and forced a smile.

'Much,' she lied, and Kate shot her a shrewd glance as she ran some water into a sink and began washing her hands.

'It must have been quite a shock to see Tom again.'

'A surprise,' Eve said firmly. 'It was a surprise, that's all, seeing him back in Penhally.'

'Yes, but you and he were quite close before he went to the States, weren't you?'

Close. What an, oh, so very British, euphemistic way of saying 'lovers', Eve thought wryly, and of course Kate would remember she and Tom had spent that summer together. Kate was in her forties, too, and nothing stayed a secret for long in Penhally unless you really worked at it, and Tom hadn't given a damn about what people thought.

'Kate, I was twenty-two, he was twenty-four,' Eve declared, injecting as much careless indifference into her voice as she could. 'We shared a short summer romance, that's all.'

'Which wouldn't make it any the less painful when it ended,' Kate Althorp said gently.

The midwife saw too much—way too much—and Eve picked up her hairbrush again.

'Water under the bridge years ago,' she said. 'We've both gone our separate ways since then, led very different lives.'

Or at least Tom had, Eve thought as Kate looked for a moment as though she'd like to say something, then dried her hands on a paper towel and left the cloakroom. Tom had gone off to the States, full of determination to succeed, and he had, whereas she…

She squeezed her eyes shut. He was not going to do this to her. She had spent all these years rebuilding her life into something to be proud of, something that mattered, and she was not going to let his presence tear it all down, make it seem worthless.

'Enough, Eve,' she said as she opened her eyes and gazed at her reflection again. 'The past is past. Don't resurrect it.'

Except it wasn't that easy, she realised as she walked out of the cloakroom, and found Tom and Tassie waiting for her, grinning like a pair of conspirators.

'Tassie was convinced you'd slipped down the toilet,' Tom declared. 'I told her we'd give you another five minutes, then I'd go over the top in my capacity as head of rescue operations at Deltaron.'

'Promises, promises,' Eve said lightly, and Tom's grin widened.

'You think I wouldn't—or couldn't?' he replied.

'I think we should eat,' she said firmly, refusing to be drawn, but he knew what she was doing.

She could see it in the glint in his eyes. The familiar half daring, half challenging glint which had appeared in the past whenever he'd been about to do, or say, something completely outrageous, and a faint unease stirred in her. An unease which must have shown on her face because he smiled.

'I'm a mature man now, Eve,' he declared. 'No fights, no arguments, I promise.'

And he was as good as his word.

For the next hour Tom charmed his way round the crowded room as only he could when he wanted to. Of course it helped that most of the people at the reception were newcomers to the village, but even when some of the older villagers cut him dead he didn't rise to the bait. He simply moved away with a wry smile to gently reassure Lauren about his car, then make Chloe Mackinnon, the village's other midwife, laugh as her fiancé, Dr Fawkner, stood by, watching protectively.

'He's changed, hasn't he?' Kate observed, nodding towards Tom who was now engaged in an animated discussion about fund-holding practices with Dr Lovak.

'Tom always could string more than two words together, you know,' Eve said more caustically than she'd intended, and Kate's eyebrows rose.

'I never thought he couldn't,' the midwife replied. 'Just as you also know I never thought he got a fair deal in Penhally.'

'Still won't, judging by the reaction of some people,' Eve said, nodding across to a small group of villagers who were throwing deep frowns in Tom's direction.

'People have long memories and old prejudices. I'm not saying they're right,' Kate continued as Eve opened her mouth to interrupt. 'In fact, the longer I've lived, the less inclined I've become to judge anyone, but don't forget Tom has friends here, too, as well as detractors.'

Name one, apart from yourself, Eve was tempted to say, but she didn't.

'I must get Tassie home,' she said instead. 'She's beginning to look tired.'

Tom clearly wasn't because the minute Eve began to make her way through the throng he was instantly at her side.

'Trying to run out on me, are you?' he said, and she shook her head at him.

'It's time I took Tassie home,' she replied, sidestepping quickly as Freddie and Sam dashed past them, slipping and sliding on the polished wooden floor, whooping at the top of their lungs.

'Regular little bundles of fun, aren't they?' Tom said with amusement as the youngsters scampered off.

'You used to hate kids,' Eve reminded him. 'Said they should all be kept indoors by their parents until they were teenagers.'

'Yeah, well…' Tom glanced back at the two boys. 'Do you ever find yourself wishing you'd had children?'

Eve stared fixedly at the wedding cake sitting on the table by the window.

'No point in wishing, Tom,' she said. 'It's better to deal with the here and now.'

'I guess so,' he said, then smiled and waved to Tassie. 'But I still think I'd like to have kids.'

'And I think it's way past time Tassie went home,' Eve said through a throat so tight it hurt.

'Eve—'

'Well, well, well. If it isn't Tom Cornish. And what brings Penhally's local-boy-made-good back to Cornwall?'

Eve glanced over her shoulder to see Nick Tremayne standing behind them, and smiled.

'Tom,' she began, 'this is—'

'Nick Tremayne.' Tom grinned. 'No need for an introduction, Eve. I would have recognised this old reprobate anywhere. Good to see you again, Nick, and still doctoring, I hear.'

'And you're still globetrotting with Deltaron if all I've read about you is true,' Nick replied with no smile at all.

'You've been following my career?' Tom said lightly, but Eve could see a slightly puzzled look in his eyes. 'I'm flattered.'

'Oh, even in a sleepy little backwater like Penhally, we have the internet and satellite television now,' Nick replied, 'which means I'm all too aware of your exploits.'

'Tom is just back for a short visit,' Eve said, glancing from Tom to Nick, then back again uncertainly. Lord, but the animosity emanating from Nick was so patent it could have flash-frozen fish. 'He's leaving on Monday.'

'Back to singlehandedly, heroically saving the world, I presume?' Nick declared, and what little smile there had been left on Tom's face disappeared completely.

'If you want heroes, Nick, then it's the people who live in the countries my team and I go into to help who deserve that title,' he said tersely. 'They're the ones who have to tackle the long-term effects of any disaster.'

'I couldn't agree more,' Nick observed, 'but they don't get

the credit, do they? Because they get left with the boring, tedious stuff, like rebuilding their country, while you swan off on yet another photo opportunity.'

'Now, just a minute,' Tom began, his face darkening, and Eve caught hold of his sleeve quickly.

'Tom, we really *do* have to get Tassie home,' she said. 'She's very tired, and I told Amanda we'd make sure she wouldn't be too late back.'

For a moment she didn't think he was going to come with her. He certainly didn't look as though he wanted to as he glared at Nick, and Nick glared back, then he nodded reluctantly.

'Right,' he said, then added, 'See you around, Nick,' before he strode out of the room, leaving Eve and Tassie with nothing to do but hurry after him.

'I thought you said you and Nick Tremayne were friends?' Eve protested when she caught up with him in the car park.

'I thought we were, too,' Tom replied, 'but I've clearly done something to rattle his cage. Any idea what?'

'None at all,' Eve said. 'He can certainly be a bit brusque at times, but he's not normally so…so…'

'In your face?' Tom shook his head as he helped Tassie clamber into his Range Rover. 'Kate Althorp sure had a lucky escape.'

'From what?' Eve asked in confusion.

'From marrying him. Don't you remember how close Kate and Nick were at school?' he continued as Eve looked at him in surprise. 'Everyone was certain they'd get married.'

'Well, they didn't,' Eve replied. 'Kate married James Althorp.'

'So I gathered.' Tom frowned as he switched on his ignition. 'Which I have to say I find surprising. Don't get me wrong,' he added. 'James was a nice enough bloke, but I'd have thought he was a bit too laid back for Kate, which only goes to show you never can tell. Nick married that girl he met at med school, didn't he? Anne…Isabel…'

'Annabel.'

'Yeah, that was her name. Nice girl, she was, too, as I recall.'

'She died nearly three years ago now,' Eve replied. 'Her appendix ruptured and because she'd taken aspirin she bled out and there was nothing anyone could do.'

'I'm sorry about that,' Tom declared, 'but I still reckon Kate had a lucky escape.'

But Nick isn't normally like that, Eve thought with a frown, as Tom drove them down the winding road back into the village. The senior partner could certainly be sharp and cutting if he felt people weren't pulling their weight, but she'd never seen him verbally attack somebody for no reason, and yet that was exactly what he'd done this afternoon.

'Where does Tassie live?' Tom asked as they drove down Harbour Road.

'Just off Morwenna Road, but if you drop us at the post office we can walk from there,' Eve replied.

'But that will still leave you quite a distance to walk,' Tom protested.

'All to the good,' Eve said calmly. 'I need some exercise after what I've eaten.'

'But—'

'Drop us at the post office, Tom.'

He sighed but, after he'd crossed the Harbour Bridge, he obediently pulled up at the post office.

'Thanks for the ride, mister,' Tassie said when she and Eve got out of his car, and he smiled and ruffled her hair.

'Could you make yourself scarce for a couple of minutes, half-pint?' he said. 'I need to talk to Eve.'

'Tom, Tassie really does have to go home,' Eve began as the girl obediently skipped down the road for a few yards, then waited. 'The wind's getting up, and she's not dressed for the weather—'

'I was wondering whether you'd like to come out with me

tomorrow?' he interrupted. 'We could have lunch, and you could show me the sights of Penhally.'

'Tom, you were born here, you know what the sights are,' she protested.

'There's bound to have been some changes—new developments—since I was last here,' he argued back, 'and I thought—perhaps for old times' sake?'

She didn't want to do anything for old times' sake. Two postcards, that's all he'd sent her after he'd left for America. One from New York, saying he was homesick and lonely, and another one from California six months later, saying he'd applied for a job with Deltaron. After that, there'd been nothing. Not a card, or a letter, or a phone call, for the past twenty years during which she'd got on with her life, and if it hadn't been the life she'd planned, dreamed of, it had been a satisfying life, and now he was back, and she didn't want him to be back.

'I'm sorry,' she said firmly. 'I have things to do tomorrow.'

'Please.'

If he had been smiling at her with that old gotta-love-me smile she would never have wavered, but he wasn't smiling. In fact, he looked uncharacteristically unsure, uncertain, and Tom Cornish had never been unsure of anything in his life.

'I can't do lunch,' she said hesitantly. *Won't, more like*. 'As I said, I have things to do tomorrow.'

'Half a day is better than none,' he said. 'Do you still live in Polkerris Road with your parents? I'll pick you up at two o'clock—'

'Three o'clock,' she interrupted. 'And I'll meet you outside your hotel.'

He looked disappointed, then he nodded.

'OK, three o'clock it is,' he said, then to her surprise he added quickly, 'You will come, won't you?'

The uncertainty was back in his eyes, big time, and a slight frown creased her forehead.

'I said I'd come,' she pointed out, 'and I will.'

Though God knows why, she thought as she joined Tassie and the two of them began walking down the road together.

'He's nice,' Tassie observed, hopping from one paving stone to the next in some sort of elaborate game only she understood.

'Tom can be very nice when he wants to be,' Eve replied noncommittally.

'He told me you and he were best friends when you were younger,' Tassie continued with her usual directness, and Eve manufactured a smile.

'It was a long time ago, Tassie.'

'He still likes you. I can tell. In fact,' the girl added, 'I bet if we turn round right now he'll be watching you from outside the post office.'

'Tassie,' Eve began in consternation, but the girl had already stopped and was looking over her shoulder.

'Told you so,' Tassie said.

'He's watching us?' Eve said faintly.

'See for yourself if you don't believe me,' Tassie declared, and Eve shook her head, feeling her cheeks prickle with heat.

'I've got to get you home.'

'Chicken.' Tassie laughed.

Self-preservation, more like, Eve thought, walking on determinedly. I don't owe him anything, not after all these years.

But you've still agreed to meet him tomorrow afternoon, haven't you? a little voice mocked at the back of her mind, and she groaned inwardly.

She must have been out of her mind.

CHAPTER TWO

IT WAS strange, Tom thought as he leant back against the grey-stoned wall of the Anchor Hotel and breathed in deeply. He'd been all around the world in the course of his work, and yet no air had ever smelt quite the same as the air did in Penhally Bay.

And nobody had ever looked quite like Eve Dwyer, he decided when he heard the faint sound of footsteps in the distance, and turned to see her walking down Fisherman's Row towards him wearing a cherry-red sweater and a russet-coloured skirt, her brown hair gleaming in the early October sunshine.

Lord, but she'd scarcely changed at all. She still had the same cloud of brown hair, the same long, curly eyelashes, and even the same two dimples which peeked out when she smiled. Perhaps she was slightly curvier now than she had been when at twenty-two, but it suited her. It suited her a lot, he decided as his gaze swept over her appreciatively.

'Am I late?' she said, her brown eyes apologetic when she drew level with him.

He shook his head, and breathed in deeply again.

'You know, I think I would recognise Penhally air even if I was blindfolded.'

'You mean the pong of old seaweed and fish?' she said, her eyes dancing.

'I meant the tang of the sea, as you very well know,' he said severely, then his lips curved. 'And there was me thinking you'd still be a romantic.'

The light in her eyes disappeared, and a shadow replaced it.

'Gave up on romance a long time ago, Tom. So…' She spread her hands wide. 'Where do you want to start?'

'Start?' He echoed, still puzzling over what she'd said about giving up on romance.

'You said you wanted a tour of Penhally,' she reminded him. 'So, do you want to go north towards the lighthouse first, or down to the lifeboat station?'

'The lighthouse, I think,' he said. 'You always used to go there when you wanted to think, didn't you?'

She shot him a surprised glance.

'What an odd thing to remember,' she said.

'Oh, my mind's a regular ragbag of odd bits of information,' he replied lightly as she crossed the Harbour Bridge back into Fisherman's Row and he fell into step beside her.

'Of course, not many fishermen live in Fisherman's Row any more,' she declared. 'In fact, there aren't many fishermen left in Penhally full stop. Too few fish to catch nowadays, and too many quotas, to make it a viable way of life.' She waved to a dark-haired young woman who had come out of one of the cottages to scoop up a ginger cat. 'That's Chloe MacKinnon. You met her yesterday at Alison and Jack's reception.'

'Midwife like Kate, yes?' Tom frowned. 'Works in the village practice, and is currently engaged to, and living with, Oliver Fawkner?'

'That's the one,' Eve said as the woman waved back and disappeared into her house. 'You met Oliver at the reception, too.'

'I remember.' Tom nodded, then chuckled. 'You know, if one of the local midwives and a practice doctor had been living together when I was last in Penhally, they'd have been tarred and feathered then run out of town.'

'Times change even in Penhally, at least for some things,' she murmured, and before he could say anything she pointed across the harbour to where a pretty cottage sat high on the hill. 'That's where Kate lives. Her house must have one of the best views in Penhally.'

'Right,' he said, shooting her a puzzled glance.

'Dr Lovak used to live in Fisherman's Row,' Eve continued as they walked past the library and into Harbour Road, 'but he and his wife, Melinda, moved out into the country in the summer. I guess with a baby coming they wanted more space.'

Tom was sure they did, but talking about where the members of the village practice lived was not exactly what he'd had in mind when he'd asked Eve to meet him today, and if she was going to spend the whole afternoon pointing out the homes of her colleagues it was going to be a very long afternoon indeed.

'Eve—'

'I'm sorry,' she broke in, turning to face him, her expression contrite. 'I know I'm babbling a load of boring drivel, but the thing is…' She lifted her shoulders helplessly. 'We don't know each other any more, and I don't know what to say, or talk to you about. I know we were…close…in the past, but—'

'Us meeting again is fast turning into your worst date ever,' he finished for her, and she coloured.

'Maybe not quite that bad, but we're practically strangers now, Tom, so why did you ask to see me again—what was the point?'

Good question, he thought, but how could he tell her that part of him had hoped to find her happily married so he could finally squash the dream that had haunted him for years—that he could somehow go back, change things—while the other part had hoped she was still single so he might be given another chance at happiness.

She would say he wasn't making any sense, and maybe he wasn't. Maybe nobody could—or should—ever try to go back.

'Look, I won't take offence if you just want to give this up, and go back to your hotel,' Eve continued.

If her eyes hadn't met his when she'd spoken he might have been tempted to accept her suggestion, but, lord, she really was as lovely as he'd remembered, and how could he have forgotten her eyes weren't simply brown, but had tiny flecks of green in them? Because he'd forced himself to forget, he thought with a sigh, spent so many years trying not to remember, until a year ago, when…

Don't go there, his mind warned. It's better not to go there.

'Tom?'

She looked awkward and uncomfortable, and he forced a smile.

'Of course I don't want to go back to the hotel,' he said. 'Leastways, not until you've pointed out Nick's house and I've thrown a brick through his window.'

She gave a small choke of laughter. 'I thought you said you were a mature man now?'

'OK, I'll see if I can capture some greenfly and let them loose on his roses instead,' he said, and when she laughed out loud he linked his arm with hers, and began walking again. 'Eve, I know it's been a long time since we last met,' he continued, 'but it simply means we've a lot of catching up to do. And speaking of catching up,' he added when she said nothing, 'are you *quite* sure you don't know why Nick appears to consider me dog meat?'

'I thought you might know the answer to that,' she observed, and he shook his head.

'I knew him at school, and met him a couple of times when I went to med school, but he was a few years older than me, and his friends tended to be the more studious type, whereas mine…' He grinned down at her. 'Tended to be a little rowdier.'

'I bet they were,' Eve said dryly.

'How many kids does Nick have?' Tom asked, and Eve smiled as they reached the end of Harbour Road and turned towards the lighthouse.

'He and Annabel had three of a family. Lucy and Jack, who are twins, and Edward. They're all doctors.'

Tom pulled a face. 'All of them! I don't think I'd want any kids of mine becoming medics, would you?'

He'd said the wrong thing. He didn't know why, or how, but her face had suddenly closed up completely, and he longed to hug her, or say something totally outrageous to bring the smile back onto her face, but no words occurred to him, and as for hugging her... In the past he wouldn't have thought twice, but even thinking about doing it now made him feel ridiculously awkward, as though it would be too forward which was crazy when he remembered what they'd once meant to one another.

'Odd time of day for a church service,' he said, deliberately changing the subject as they passed the church and the sound of enthusiastic singing drifted out.

'It's not a service,' Eve replied. 'Reverend Kenner runs a club for the village youngsters on Sunday afternoons. Daniel's a nice man. A good one, too.'

'Single, is he?' Tom said, feeling a spurt of something that crazily felt almost like jealousy.

'Daniel's a widower like Nick, with a seventeen-year-old daughter.'

And she didn't look any happier, Tom thought as they walked on to the lighthouse. In fact, she looked even more strained and, in desperation, he pointed out to sea to where the wreck of the seventeenth century Spanish galleon, the *Corazón del Oro*, had lain for the past four hundred years.

'Remember when we wished we could dive down there, find loads of gold coins, and make our fortune?'

'Except neither of us could swim, so it was a bit of a non-starter,' she replied. 'Still can't swim, which is a dreadful admission for somebody who lives by the sea. What about you?'

'I had to learn for my work so they sent me on a course and, believe me, being in a class of five-year-olds when you're twenty-four, and five feet ten inches tall, doesn't do a lot for your ego.'

Her lips twitched. 'You're making that up.'

'Scout's honour,' he protested, and she laughed.

'Tom, you were thrown out of the Scouts for disruptive behaviour when you were thirteen.'

'OK, so maybe I was,' he said, relieved to see her smile again, 'but I honestly was stuck in a kids' class. My boss reckoned it would concentrate my mind wonderfully, and it did. I always wondered why your dad didn't teach you to swim, what with him being a sailor.'

'He was too busy trying to make a living. My mum wanted me to learn, but you had to pay for lessons, and...' She shrugged. 'Money was always tight when I was a kid.'

'Are they still alive—your mum and dad?' he asked, as they turned and began walking back from the lighthouse.

She shook her head.

'My dad died of cancer fifteen years ago. Never would give up his cigarettes, though Mum nagged him like crazy about it. My mum died of a heart attack five years ago.'

'I'm sorry,' he said gently. 'I know they were apoplectic that summer when we started dating, but I liked them.'

'So did I,' she murmured, and Tom swore under his breath.

Hell, but she had that look on her face again. That bleak, almost haunted look as though he had conjured up memories that would have been better left buried.

'Look, why don't we go down to the beach?' he said quickly. 'Have a walk along the sand.'

'I'm not really dressed for it, Tom,' she replied, pointing down at her shoes. 'My heels will get stuck.'

'Then take your shoes off,' he said. 'Take off your stockings, too, and you can paddle if you want.'

'Tom, it's October,' she said. 'It's too cold to paddle.'

'Rubbish,' he said, steering her firmly towards the steps that led down to the beach. 'It's a gorgeous day.'

It was, too, Eve thought as she stared up at the sky. Seagulls were wheeling and diving overhead, their white feathers standing out in sharp contrast to the clear blue sky, and there was a deceptive warmth in the air despite the fact that it was October. Soon it would change. Soon it would be winter and the green-blue sea would become grey and stormy, sending breakers crashing onto the white sand, and only the very toughest would walk along the shore, but today there was enough heat in the day to make it pleasant.

'If you hurry up,' Tom continued as he sat down on the top step, and began pulling off his shoes and socks, and rolling up his trousers, 'we'll have the beach to ourselves—just the way you used to like it.'

How had he remembered that? she thought with surprise, and he'd also remembered she used to sit at the foot of the light-house when she wanted to think. They were such little things—such inconsequential things—and yet he'd remembered, and the water did look tempting, so very tempting, but she could just imagine what the gossipmongers would say if somebody saw her.

Eve Dwyer went paddling with that Tom Cornish yesterday. Paddling, *and with that Tom Cornish.*

'Tom, maybe we should just go back into the village,' she began, and his green eyes danced as he looked up at her.

'Eve, I'm not suggesting we go skinny-dipping. Though I'm game if you are.'

Her lips curved in spite of herself.

'In your dreams,' she said.

'Chicken.'

He was the second person to have called her that in twenty-four hours, and she discovered she didn't like it. She didn't like it one bit. OK, so skinny-dipping was completely out of the question but, hell's bells, even in Penhally she could surely paddle if she wanted to, and she discovered she wanted to.

'OK, move over,' she said, and he slid across the step so she could sit down beside him.

'So, are we paddling, or skinny-dipping?' he said, and, when she gave him a hard stare, his eyes glinted. 'Pity. I was kind of looking forward to shocking the good people of Penhally.'

'I bet you were,' she said dryly as she unbuckled the straps of her shoes and slipped them off. 'Right. Turn your back while I take off my stockings,' she added, and when his mouth fell open, she said, 'I'm not having you staring at my thighs, and making snarky comments about cellulite, so turn your back.'

'I don't even know what cellulite is,' he protested, but he did as she asked, and when she eventually stuffed her tights into her skirt pocket and stood up, he said, 'You're an idiot—you know that, don't you?'

'Probably,' she agreed, picking up her shoes by their straps, and walking down the steps. 'So, are we walking or not?'

He shook his head at her as he followed her down the steps.

'You didn't used to be so shy,' he observed, and a stain of colour spread across her cheeks.

He was laughing at her, she knew he was, remembering all the times he'd seen her completely naked, and she bit her lip, waiting for him to point that out, but he didn't.

'I don't think I'll ever forget you dancing and singing on this beach,' he said instead, completely surprising her. 'It was the height of summer—the place was packed with tourists, and families from the village—and suddenly you began singing that Whitney Houston song at the top of your lungs.'

'"I wanna to dance with somebody"!' she exclaimed with a choke of laughter. 'I'd forgotten all about that. I got into such a row with my mother after Audrey Baxter told her I'd made a public spectacle of myself.'

'Audrey Baxter would say that,' he replied with feeling as they began walking along the beach.

'And you told me I had no taste,' she reminded him. 'That if I wanted to sing, then I should have sung one of Bruce Springsteen's songs because he was the only singer worth listening to.'

'Still is,' he insisted, and when she rolled her eyes he laughed, and said, 'Do you still have that dress?'

'What dress?' she said in confusion.

'The red dress you wore that day. It had a big wide skirt, and puffy sleeves, and when I first went to the States I couldn't turn on the radio without hearing Chris de Burgh singing "The Lady in Red", and every time I heard it I thought of you, singing on this beach.'

'Did you?' she said faintly, and he nodded.

'You wouldn't believe how homesick I got whenever they played that song.'

But not homesick enough to write to me, or phone me, she thought, but she didn't say that.

'I'm afraid I threw the dress out years ago,' she said instead.

'Pity,' he murmured, picking up a pebble and sending it skimming across the water in front of them. 'I always liked that dress, and the little red boots you used to wear.'

'My *pixie boots*!' she exclaimed. 'I'd forgotten all about them, too. I *loved* those boots. Couldn't wear them now, of course.'

'Yes, you could. You've still got great legs. Great figure, too,' he added.

'Not that good,' she said, feeling the wash of colour on her cheeks return as his gaze swept over her. 'Years ago I could eat whatever I wanted and never put on a kilo. Now I just have to look at a cream cake, and, pouf, on goes the weight.'

He grinned. 'Well, you're looking good from where I'm standing.'

So was he, she thought. With the sun on his face, and the

wind ruffling his hair, he looked exactly like the town bad boy he'd been all those years ago, whereas she…

What had she been back then?

Naïve, yes. Trusting, most definitely, but mostly so full of dreams, and hopes, and plans. Tom had been the same, but her dreams hadn't been the same as his. He'd wanted to get as far away from Penhally as he could, to live a life of adventure and excitement, and she… She'd simply wanted him.

'Let's have some fun,' he'd said when he'd come back to Penhally as a fully qualified doctor that summer, and she'd been so happy because he'd finally asked her out that she'd chosen not to believe him when he'd told her he would be heading for the States at the end of September.

He'll change his mind, she'd told herself, and for four wonderful, glorious months they'd walked, and talked—lord, how they'd talked—and they'd made love. She'd been a virgin when they'd first started going out and he'd teased her about it, said a woman could have just as much fun as a man without fear of the consequences, and she'd gone on the Pill to be safe, and then after four far too short months he had left.

'What are you thinking about?'

She looked up to see him gazing at her quizzically, and managed a smile.

'I was just wondering where the last twenty years had gone,' she said. 'Sometimes it seems like a lifetime, doesn't it, and sometimes just a few months.'

'And I can't believe you're still single,' he observed. 'The men in Penhally must be either blind, or stupid, or both.'

'I almost got married once,' she replied, kicking the sand in front of her so it sprayed out as they walked, 'but…'

'It didn't feel right?'

'Something like that. What about you?' she asked. 'Were you never tempted to take the plunge?'

'I've had a couple of semi-serious relationships, but…' He

shrugged. 'My work makes it difficult because I never know where I'm going to be from one day to the next.'

'Maybe you're just not the marrying kind,' she said. 'Some people aren't.'

He stared out to sea, then back at her, and to her surprise he looked suddenly wistful, almost sad.

'And maybe I simply got my priorities all wrong.'

His eyes were fixed on hers, refusing to allow her to look away, and her heart gave an uncomfortable thump. This conversation was getting too personal, way too personal, and she had to change it. Now.

'Last one to reach the end of the beach is a wimp,' she said, and, before he could reply, she was off and running, her bare feet flying over the sand, her skirt billowing above her knees, her shoes swinging from her hand.

From behind her she heard him shout a spluttered protest, but she didn't stop. She just kept on running and when she heard his footsteps begin to thud behind her she suddenly, and inexplicably, began to laugh.

To laugh like the girl she'd once been. The carefree young girl who had once sung on a beach, feeling nothing but the joy of being alive, and she knew she probably looked like a demented lunatic, but she didn't care. For this moment—for just this one moment—with her hair streaming in the breeze, and the taste of the sun and the sea on her lips, she felt like that girl again, and it was wonderful.

'You *cheated*!' he exclaimed when he caught up with her, and grasped her by the waist, spinning her round so fast she had to catch hold of his shirt to prevent herself from toppling over.

'Sore loser,' she threw back at him, laughing breathlessly as she pushed her hair away from her face. 'You've been spending far too much time behind a desk.'

'Too much time…?' His eyes narrowed. 'I'll make you pay for that remark, Eve Dwyer.'

'Oh, no, you won't,' she said, turning to run again, and he made a grab for her, and she jumped back to escape him, only to let out a yell as she ended up ankle deep in the sea. 'Oh, my God, it's *freezing*.'

'Serves you right.' Tom laughed but, when she scooped up some water and threw it at him, he splashed into the water after her. 'Play rough, would you? OK, you deserve a complete ducking for that.'

'You wouldn't,' she cried, trying to evade him, but he caught her round the waist again and swept her up into his arms.

'You think?' he said, deliberately lowering her towards the water, and she shrieked and threw her arms round his neck.

'Tom, no!'

He grinned. 'OK, if you don't want to be ducked, you'll need to pay a forfeit, and I think you know what that forfeit is, don't you?'

A kiss. The forfeit had always been a kiss when they'd dated and, as Eve stared up into his, oh, so familiar face, she realised with a stab of pain that even after all that had happened, even after all the heartache and desolation, she wanted to kiss him, and the thought appalled her.

'Tom, let me go,' she said, but he didn't hear the strain in her voice.

'Nope, not a chance,' he said. 'The forfeit, or the sea. Your choice.'

'Tom, *please*.'

'Make a decision—make a decision,' he insisted as he whirled her round in his arms, but she didn't have to.

She had suddenly seen what he hadn't, and she tugged desperately on his sleeve.

'Tom, we have company.'

'Company?' he repeated, then swore under his breath as he followed her gaze. 'Oh, wonderful. Bloody wonderful. Is that who I think it is?'

'I'm afraid so,' Eve said, through gritted teeth, and when Tom quickly put her down she splashed out of the sea, feeling completely ridiculous and stupid, as Audrey Baxter walked towards them.

'Tom Cornish,' Audrey declared the minute she drew level with them, her faded brown eyes alive with curiosity and speculation. 'My heavens, but I never thought to see you in Penhally again.'

'Us bad pennies have a nasty habit of turning up again, don't we, Mrs Baxter?' he replied dryly.

'Oh, I wouldn't call you a bad penny, Tom,' Audrey declared. 'You were a little wild, to be sure—'

'I think the words you used to shout after me when I was a teenager were, "You're heading straight to hell in a handcart, Tom Cornish".'

Audrey patted her steel-grey curls and shook her head at him reprovingly.

'That was a long time ago, Tom.' She shifted her gaze to Eve, making her all too aware that her hair must be sticking out all over the place, and the hem of her skirt was wet. 'I see you and Nurse Dwyer are getting reacquainted.'

Tom moved up the beach a step. 'We are, but now I'm afraid we have to be going.'

'I thought you might have come back to Penhally two years ago, Tom, when your father died,' Audrey continued. 'I know you didn't always get on—'

'And I think your dog's looking for you,' Tom interrupted, pointing to the brindle and white greyhound which was splashing in the water further up the beach.

'Looking for crabs, more like,' Audrey replied. 'He loves them.'

'Indeed,' Tom declared, 'and now if you'll excuse us…'

But Audrey wasn't about to let him leave so easily.

'I hear your father left you his house in Trelissa Road?' she called after him, and Tom turned slowly to face her, his expression tight.

'What a very knowledgeable little community Penhally is,' he said, the sarcasm in his voice so plain that even Audrey couldn't miss it, and Eve grabbed his hand quickly, not caring that Audrey's eyes followed her action.

'Tom, we really do have to be going,' she insisted, and determinedly she urged him back up the beach, but it wasn't over as far as he was concerned.

'Nothing changes, does it?' he spat out when they reached the steps leading off the beach, and he glanced over his shoulder to see Audrey was watching them. 'Twenty damn years, and nothing changes. I could be the Prime Minister of Britain, and in Penhally I'd still be Tom Cornish, that drunkard, Frank Cornish's, son who no decent family ever wanted their daughter dating.'

'Tom—'

'If you're going to say Audrey meant no harm, you can save your breath,' he interrupted, sitting down on the step and beginning to drag on his socks, heedless of the fact that his feet were still covered in sand. 'And if you were going to ask me why I didn't come back for my father's funeral, you can save your breath on that one, too.'

'I know why you didn't come back, Tom,' she said gently, 'and Audrey… There's no question she can be an interfering busybody, but your father's dead and gone. Don't let him keep hurting you.'

'He left me his house, Eve,' he said furiously. 'After years of battering me from pillar to post until I was big enough to hit him back and make it count, he had the gall to leave me his house.'

'Maybe…' She shrugged helplessly. 'Maybe he was trying to make amends, at the end?'

'If I believed that for one second,' he retorted, 'I'd go round and torch the bloody place myself. No guilt gift can ever make up for the fact he hated me from the day I was born. Time and time again, he'd tell me of all the things he could have done—would have done—if my mother hadn't become pregnant, and her family hadn't forced him into marrying her, and when she died he hated me even more.'

'I know,' she said, sitting down beside him, aching at the pain she saw in his face, feeling a different kind of pain in herself, but he rounded on her furiously.

'No, you don't. You have *no* idea of what it's like to live with a man whose dreams you've shattered. No idea to feel, even as a seven-year-old child, that it would have been better if you'd never been born.'

She opened her mouth, then closed it again.

'I'm sorry,' she murmured. 'You're right. I don't know.'

Silently she brushed the sand from her feet, then pushed her feet into her shoes, but when she made to stand up he put out his hand to stop her.

'You've forgotten your stockings.'

'Doesn't matter,' she replied, and, for a second he said nothing, then he thrust his fingers through his hair, and she saw his hands were shaking.

'I'm sorry,' he said, his voice so strained it almost broke. 'So sorry for yelling at you.'

'It's all right,' she said.

'It's not,' he declared. 'I shouldn't have taken it out on you, and I'm sorry, too, that Audrey saw you in my arms. I know what this place is like—the gossip, the innuendo…'

'It's *all right*, Tom,' she insisted, and saw a small smile creep onto his lips.

'I've always created trouble for you, haven't I?' he said.

'Of course you haven't,' she lied. 'And now, come on,' she added, 'or we'll be completing this tour of Penhally by moonlight.'

'Which would really set the local tongues wagging, wouldn't it?' he declared as he fell into step beside her. 'Audrey—'

'Forget her,' Eve ordered as they began walking back down Harbour Road, and he shook his head.

'This is a professional observation, not a personal one,' he replied. 'Her colour's very high.'

'She has angina, and she's hopeless about remembering to use her glyceryl trinitrate spray. "I keep forgetting, Nurse Dwyer",' Eve continued in a perfect imitation of Audrey's voice. 'I don't think she realises, or will accept, how serious her condition is.'

'Denial can be a form of self-protection when people are scared,' Tom observed, kicking a pebble at his feet so that it ricocheted down the street in front of them. 'If they don't think about it, it hasn't happened.'

It was true, Eve thought, but denial had never worked for her. All the denying, and pretending in the world, had never made it go away for her, and when they reached Harbour Bridge she came to a halt.

'Tom, why did you come back?' she asked. 'You always said you wouldn't, so why are you here?'

For a moment she didn't think he was going to answer, then he shrugged.

'My dad's solicitor has been bending my ear about the house, wanting to know whether I want to sell it, or rent it out.'

'You didn't have to come back to Penhally for that,' she pointed out. 'You could just have told him over the phone.'

'I suppose,' he murmured as he stared down at the river Lanson flowing gently under the bridge beneath them, then he grinned. 'OK, you've rumbled me. I thought it might be interesting to see Penhally again.'

He wasn't telling her the truth. She didn't know how she knew that, but she did.

'Tom—'

'What happened to the cinema?' he interrupted. 'It used to be up there, in Gull Close, didn't it, on the right-hand side of the river?'

'It was on the left-hand side of the river, in Bridge Street, but it closed down years ago,' she replied, all too aware that he was changing the subject, but she had secrets so she supposed he was entitled to secrets, too. 'People gradually stopped wanting to go so much once they had television in their own homes.'

'I took you to see *RoboCop*.'

'No, you didn't.'

'I did, too,' he insisted as they began walking again. 'I remember us kissing in the back row.'

'Must have been someone else. Come to think of it,' she added wryly, 'it undoubtedly *was* someone else considering you were Penhally's answer to Casanova.'

'I was not,' he replied, the grin reappearing on his face.

'Yes, you were!' she exclaimed. 'Even when we were at school, every girl fancied you like mad despite you having the most dreadful reputation.'

'You didn't.'

Oh, but I did, I *did*, she thought, but you never noticed me. It was only when you came back from med school that summer that you realised I was alive.

'That's the Penhally Bay Surgery,' she continued, deliberately changing the conversation, and Tom let out a low whistle as his gaze took in the large building to the left of the Serpentine Steps.

'I remember when the doctor's surgery was that pokey little place in Morwenna Road,' he observed.

'Nick's made big changes since he took over the practice,' Eve replied. 'And he's making even more, as you can see,' she added, pointing to the scaffolding at the back of the surgery. 'In less than a week Lauren will have a state-of-the-art physiotherapy suite, and we'll have an X-ray room, and even more consulting rooms.'

'Well, he may have grown into a grumpy old so-and-so,' Tom said, 'but at least he wants the best for his patients.'

'He does,' Eve said, 'but you haven't told me anything about yourself, your work with Deltaron.'

'Not much to tell,' he said.

'There's bound to be,' she said, but he wasn't listening to her. He was already crossing the road, heading for the children's play park and playing field. 'Tom, where are you going?'

'I fancy a swing,' he shouted back, and though she shook her head she followed him.

'Big kid,' she said when she'd caught up with him.

'You'd better believe it,' he replied, then frowned slightly as he looked up at the new houses on the hill, then down at the older buildings clustered round the harbour. 'It's odd, but it seems so much smaller than I remembered it.'

'Hicksville. That's what you used to call Penhally,' she said. '"There's a whole world out there, Eve, and I want to see it, be a part of it."'

'Did I say that?' he said dryly. 'Yeah, well, I guess I always was a stupid kid.'

She stared at him for a second, then sat down on the swing next to his.

'Tom, what's wr—?'

'You wanted to know about my work with Deltaron,' he interrupted. 'There's almost fifty of us in the organisation, but normally we'll send in around fourteen people who are specialists in the sorts of conditions we're likely to encounter.'

'What sort of specialists?' she asked.

'Let's say we're going into an earthquake situation,' he declared. 'In that case, we'd want people who are familiar with the construction of buildings, plus experts in flammable and explosive materials, electricians, pilots, plumbers and medics.'

'And when you go into a disaster area, you're in charge.'

'Yup,' he said. 'I decide where we start looking for survivors, and I decide when we quit. When there's no point in looking any more.'

A harshness had crept into his voice, and his eyes… They had become bleak, empty, and desolate.

'It must be heart-breaking at times,' she suggested tentatively, and saw his jaw tighten.

'Bleeding hearts need not apply, that's for sure.'

'Tom…' She put her hand on his arm. 'Tom, are you OK?'

He stood up abruptly, letting the swing bang back against his calves, and faked a smile.

'Couldn't be better,' he said, 'and isn't that your little friend?'

For a second Eve continued to stare at him, then she glanced in the direction of his gaze, and saw Tassie running along the road, her blonde hair flying.

'She'll be going home,' she said. 'Tom, are you quite sure you're—?'

'What's the connection between you two?'

'None,' she said, getting to her feet, and leading the way out of the play park, 'apart from the fact I've taken an interest in her since she was about four years old. Her mother, Amanda… She's had to bring up five of a family virtually on her own so I help out by looking after Tassie one day a week.'

'Isn't there a Mr Lovelace?'

'He's in prison at the moment for petty theft. I'm afraid it always is petty theft with him, or selling on stolen goods.' Eve sighed. 'The whole family are completely out of control, including Tassie's twin brother, Terry, but Gary Lovelace is the worst. Seventeen years old, and already a complete and utter waste of space.'

Tom's eyebrows rose.

'It's not like you to write off someone when they're so young.'

Eve struggled with herself for a moment, then blurted out, 'Do you remember me telling you Reverend Kenner had a daughter? Well, she's pregnant, Tom. Rachel is just seventeen years old, and pregnant by Gary Lovelace.'

'Accidents happen, Eve,' Tom declared. 'You know that.'

'This was no accident,' she retorted. 'Rachel told Chloe MacKinnon it wasn't. Gary deliberately went after Rachel because he thought it would be fun to play around with the minister's daughter. What kind of boy does that, Tom? He's no job—no desire to get one—just hangs about with his friends… He—'

'Sounds exactly like I was at his age,' Tom interrupted, and Eve shook her head vehemently.

'You were nothing like Gary.'

'Hell, Eve, I was *exactly* like Gary,' Tom protested. 'God knows what would have become of me if it hadn't been for Gertie Stanbury.'

'Our old headmistress?' Eve exclaimed. 'What did she have to do with anything?'

'Do you remember the day when the bicycle sheds burned down at school, and I swore blind I didn't do it? Well, I did, and Gertie knew I did though she couldn't prove it. She called me into her office and said, "Cornish, you can either spend the rest of your life destroying things, or you can make something of yourself. Your father—and most of Penhally—have written you off, but you've got brains and ability, so are you going to prove your father and Penhally right, or show them they're wrong?"'

Eve shook her head in amazement. 'You never told me any of this.'

'Well, it was hardly my finest hour,' Tom said wryly. 'I was furious with Gertie—thought she was an interfering old bat, to be honest—but when I went home that night, and found my father lying dead drunk as usual on the sitting-room floor, I suddenly realised I was going to be him in a few years if I didn't knuckle down at school, and get some qualifications.'

'Which is what I want Tassie to do,' she declared, 'to get some qualifications. She's such a bright child, Tom, and Gertrude has been helping her by lending her books—'

'Gertie Stanbury is still alive?'

'Very much so.' Eve nodded. 'She thinks Tassie is clever enough to win a scholarship to the Lady Joan Mercer's Boarding School in Devon which would be wonderful because though Amanda wants what's best for Tassie she'll never be able to afford to let her stay on at school once she reaches leaving age.'

'And if she does go to this school?'

Eve smiled.

'At the moment Tassie wants to become a doctor. Of course, she'll probably change her mind, but if I can get her into Lady Joan's, and she studies hard, the world will be her oyster.'

A slight frown appeared on Tom's forehead.

'You do realise if you send Tassie off to this private boarding school, she'll lose her own family?'

'Of course she won't.'

'She will,' Tom insisted. 'She'll have nothing in common with them, could even end up looking down on them, while they'll simply think she's got above herself.'

'You're saying I'm wrong—I shouldn't encourage her,' Eve exclaimed, anger rising in her.

'I'm saying…' Tom stopped and rubbed the back of his neck awkwardly with his fingers. 'I'm saying Tassie's not your daughter, Eve.'

'I know that.' Eve flared. 'I know she isn't mine, but what's so wrong about me wanting her to have every opportunity?'

'Nothing,' Tom replied gently, 'just so long as she, and her mother, and you, understand it will come at a price.'

He was wrong, Eve thought furiously as she gazed at him. Tassie wouldn't lose her family, and when she thought of all the things the girl would gain…

'I have to go,' she said, her voice tight as she stepped back from him.

'Already?' he protested. 'But I thought we could have dinner together.'

'I can't.'

'Then what about tomorrow?' he declared. 'We could drive up to Newquay—'

'You're leaving tomorrow,' she reminded him, 'and I have to work.'

'Couldn't you ask for a few days off?' he demanded. 'Even just one day?'

It was clearly important to him that she said yes, but she had no intention of saying yes. She'd agreed to today but even during the few short hours they'd spent together he'd unsettled her so much, and she'd had enough unsettling.

'Tom, I can't,' she said. 'I've only just started work at the practice so it would hardly look professional if I took time off.'

'Then this is goodbye,' he said, making it a statement, not a question, and she stuck out her hand.

'It's been nice seeing you again, Tom.'

'Eve…'

He'd taken her hand in his, his eyes intent, earnest, and he was clearly hoping she would change her mind, but he was too late. Twenty years too late, and she pulled her hand free.

'Goodbye, Tom,' she said.

And she walked away from him, and she didn't look back.

CHAPTER THREE

'SOPHIE, tell me this isn't true?' Eve declared, gazing in horror at the sullen teenager.

'Look, I just miscalculated my insulin dose, OK?' Sophie Banks retorted belligerently. 'That's why my blood-sugar levels are all haywire today. I just made a *mistake*.'

'Mistake, my foot!' Sophie's mother exclaimed, her face tight, her eyes angry. 'I thought it was strange the way she kept rushing off to the bathroom, even wondered if she'd perhaps caught a chill, and then I heard her—bold as brass—on the phone to her friend last night, talking about this internet site she'd found—'

'You had no right to listen in to my private phone calls,' Sophie declared, outrage plain in her voice. 'I don't listen to yours—'

'Sophie, I know you weren't happy when you started putting on weight after your diabetes was diagnosed,' Eve interrupted quickly, seeing the mother and daughter round on one another, 'but skipping, or lessening your dosage in order to excrete more urine and stay thin is a recipe for disaster.'

'None of my clothes fit any more,' the teenager protested. 'I look *gross*.'

Or like a perfectly normal fifteen-year-old, Eve thought, but there was no point in saying that.

'Sophie, your weight gain is purely temporary,' she said instead. 'Once we get your blood-sugar levels under control, your weight will return to what it was before.'

'Yeah, right,' Sophie muttered under her breath, and Eve sat forward in her seat.

'This internet site you found,' she declared. 'Did it tell you that not only would you lose weight if you manipulated your insulin doses, you could also damage your eyes, and develop hypoglycaemia?'

'One mistake,' the girl said mutinously. 'All I did was make one lousy miscalculation, and now you all think I have a problem. I don't have a problem.'

Eve didn't believe her. Alison had warned her before she'd gone off on her maternity leave that Sophie seemed more interested in her weight loss than the fact she had diabetes, and when she'd tested the girl's blood-sugar levels this morning they'd been appalling. She didn't doubt for a second that Sophie had been deliberately skipping doses but warning the girl that she was, quite literally, dicing with death would achieve nothing. To a teenager, death was something that happened to other people, elderly people.

'I'm going to have a word with Dr Tremayne,' she declared. 'I'm sorry, Sophie,' she continued as the girl let out a hiss of irritation, 'but your temporary weight gain is clearly worrying you, so I think you should see an endocrinologist who will be able to advise you on your diet.'

And who will also be considerably more experienced than I am in dealing with eating disorders and diabetes, Eve added mentally.

Mrs Banks shot her daughter a that-will-sort-you-out-young-lady look, but, instead of getting to her feet and leaving as Eve had expected, the mother suddenly cleared her throat, her eyes sparkling with keen interest.

'I happened to meet Audrey Baxter on my way down to the surgery this morning, Nurse, and she said—'

Here it comes, Eve thought grimly. I thought I might have got away with it, but here it comes.

'She saw you and Tom Cornish on the beach yesterday.'

'That's right,' Eve said with the biggest smile she could muster. 'Now, as regards Sophie,' she continued determinedly. 'Hopefully, she won't have to wait long to see the endocrinologist, but until she gets an appointment I'd like to see her twice a week from now on to check on her blood-sugar levels.'

That Mrs Banks considered her a singularly disappointing source of information was plain. That she was itching to delve deeper into Tom Cornish's presence was even plainer but, unlike Audrey Baxter, Mrs Banks clearly possessed some scruples because she got to her feet, albeit reluctantly.

'We'll see you on Thursday, then, Nurse,' she said, then trooped out of Eve's consulting room, with Sophie trailing belligerently behind her, and Eve sighed wearily as she closed the teenager's folder.

Well, what did you expect? a little voice whispered in her mind. *When Audrey saw you in Tom's arms she was bound to spread the word, wasn't she?*

Yes, but couldn't she have kept quiet, just for once? she thought wistfully.

Fat chance in Penhally, Eve.

She could almost hear Tom saying that, and a smile curved her lips for a second then faded.

He'd be on his way to London now, back to the new life he'd made for himself, and their trip down memory lane was over. And that was all it had been, she reminded herself. One sunny October afternoon spent reminiscing about their youth although it had been strange how much Tom had wanted to look back. The Tom she had known had been forever planning, scheming, looking to the future, but this Tom… And he had no need to look back. He had it all right now, in the present.

'Eve, Mrs Baxter came in for a repeat prescription this morning,' Nick declared as he stuck his head round her examination-room door, 'and her BP's haywire again.'

'Like Sophie Banks's blood-sugar levels,' she replied, and when she told him what she suspected the teenager of doing Nick shook his head.

'Of all the stupid… What is it with women nowadays that so many of you want to look like stick insects?'

'I suppose it's the models we see in magazines and on television,' Eve observed. 'They're all extremely thin.'

'Idiots, the lot of them,' Nick declared. 'I'll send a letter to the endocrinology department right away, but you'd better keep an eye on her. The last thing we want is her going hypoglycaemic on us. Can you fit Mrs Baxter into your Thursday clinic, to check her BP for me again?'

'Unfortunately, yes,' Eve said dryly, and a rare smile appeared on Nick's lips.

'I know she can be a nosy old bat at times, but there's no malice in her.' The senior partner half withdrew, then paused. 'Tom gone, has he?'

The question sounded casual, indifferent, but Eve wasn't deceived.

'He left this morning,' she replied. 'Back to London, or it could have been Switzerland. I didn't ask.'

'Right.' Nick nodded, then seemed to come to a decision. 'It's better this way, Eve. It might not seem like it at the moment, but the past is simply that. Something over, done with, and attempting to recapture it can only be a mistake, especially—' his eyes met hers '—in the circumstances.'

He remembered, she thought, staring up at him, drymouthed. It had been one consultation all those years ago. Nick had been her GP even then while working in a practice in a town nearby. He must have seen hundreds of patients since, and yet he remembered, and not just remembered, had put two and two together and come up with the right answer. Not the whole answer, not the complete answer, but the right one.

'Nick...'

'Practice meeting in ten minutes, OK?'

She dredged up a smile, but when he'd gone she shut her eyes tightly. She should have gone to another doctor. She had, at the beginning. At the beginning she'd gone up to Bude because she hadn't wanted anyone to know, but then she'd caught an infection, and she'd had to go to Nick. A prescription for antibiotics, had been all she'd asked for, and when he'd examined her he hadn't said anything so she'd thought he hadn't realised, but he had. For all these years he'd known, and she couldn't bear the fact he'd known.

'Eve, do you have Stephanie Richards's file?'

Eve looked up with difficulty to see Kate standing in her doorway, and shook her head. 'Sorry, no, I don't.'

'Blast.' The midwife frowned. 'She's been on the phone—panicking again—and I thought I'd drop in on her after the practice meeting, but I wanted to check what her BP was the last time it was taken.'

'Can't help you—sorry. Maybe Dragan has the file,' Eve declared, and Kate tilted her head to one side.

'You OK?'

Eve didn't feel OK. She'd tossed and turned last night, her dreams plagued by memories she didn't want to have, and now to discover Nick knew...

'I'm fine,' she managed. 'And we,' she added, glancing down at her watch, and picking up her folders, 'had better get our skates on, or Nick will have our guts for garters for being late.'

He didn't. In fact, when Kate and Eve arrived in his consulting room, Nick was poring over plans laid out on his desk with Dragan Lovak, Oliver Fawkner, Chloe and Lauren.

'So, I should be able to move into my new physiotherapy unit by the end of the week?' Eve heard Lauren declare. 'Excellent.'

'Is Dr Devereux having one of the new consulting rooms when he arrives?' Oliver asked, and, when Nick nodded, the young doctor grinned. 'Which means Lauren will have the French charmer not only living next door to her, but also working beside her.'

'He's rented the Manor House, Oliver,' Lauren protested. 'That hardly makes him living "next door" to me.'

'Maybe you could drop in on him with a pot of soup when he arrives, make him feel welcome,' he replied slyly, and the physiotherapist shook her head at him.

'And maybe I won't.'

'And maybe we should remember this is a post-practice meeting, and not a dating agency,' Nick declared, rolling up the plans on his desk.

The consulting room became instantly silent, and Eve saw Oliver roll his eyes at Chloe, while Lauren exchanged a resigned look with Dragan. Only Kate was frowning quite openly at Nick, but he was completely ignoring her, and Eve sighed inwardly. Good doctor though Nick was, he really did need to lighten up. Tom would have handled the situation quite differently. He would have understood that sometimes they all needed to be a bit silly to relieve the stress of their jobs, but Nick either couldn't—or wouldn't—see it.

'OK, let's get down to business,' Nick continued. 'Eve, are your influenza inoculation clinics ready to roll next week?'

She nodded. 'I noticed from Alison's notes that the practice only had a 67 per cent take up rate last year.'

'Getting people to come in is proving difficult,' he conceded, 'but it *is* worthwhile particularly for those at high risk, like the elderly and those who suffer from asthma and bronchitis. We can't afford to ship them all off to drier climates for the winter.'

To places like Switzerland, Eve thought. It had a drier climate, despite the snow it got in winter. Tom had said he had a home overlooking Lake Geneva. She'd never been there—had never been abroad, full stop. She'd always meant to travel, but somehow—

'How's her BP?'

Eve felt a hot wash of colour creep over her cheeks. Dragan was gazing at her expectantly, and she didn't have a clue what he was talking about, and it was all Tom's fault. She had to get him out of her thoughts. He had gone, and he wasn't ever going to come back, so she had to stop this, and stop it now.

'I'm sorry,' she was forced to say, 'but whose BP are you talking about?'

She felt, rather than saw, Nick stiffen with disapproval, but Dragan merely smiled.

'My mind is always a bit of a sieve on Monday mornings, too,' he declared kindly. 'Lizzie Chamberlain. I saw her coming out of your room, and she looked decidedly stressed.'

'She is,' Eve replied, smiling gratefully at him. 'Her blood pressure is still way too high, but she's so worried about her mother. I know you all felt Lizzie needed a break, that nursing her mother was making her ill, but she's got it into her head that by agreeing to her mum temporarily going into the Harbour View Nursing Home she's abandoned her.'

'I have to say Mrs Chamberlain isn't doing nearly as well in there as I'd hoped,' Dragan admitted. 'I thought she might see it as a mini-holiday, but the last time I saw her she seemed very lethargic, and not really interested in anything.'

'It's a Catch-22 situation,' Eve observed. 'Nursing someone with Parkinson's is exhausting, but if Lizzie's feeling guilty, as she obviously is…'

'Would you like me to drop in on Mrs Chamberlain?' Lauren declared. 'I'm on home visits today, and I could see her before I call in on Harry Biscombe in Gow Court. It wouldn't be a bother.'

Both Eve and Dragan nodded their agreement and, to Eve's relief, Oliver then launched into an account of the patients he'd seen that morning, leaving her with nothing to do but simply appear interested.

And she *was* interested, she told herself as she constantly found her mind wandering. She loved her work—always had done—so why did she feel all unsettled, and shaken up, like leaves in an autumn gale, or the flakes of snow in a snow globe, tumbling everywhere?

Because Tom came back, her mind whispered, and unconsciously she shook her head. It was over. It had been over a long time ago.

'No prizes for guessing who he's phoning.' Chloe chuckled when they all trooped out of Nick's consulting room, and Dragan immediately extracted his mobile phone from his pocket.

'I think it's sweet the way he keeps checking on Melinda, to see if she's OK,' Kate protested.

'Melinda doesn't,' Chloe said as Dragan disappeared into his room. 'I think the words, "He's driving me crazy" were the ones she used last week when she came in for her prenatal check-up. In fact, she's actually started turning off her mobile so she can get some peace and quiet.'

'No—really?' Kate laughed. 'Well, I'm off. I'll be in Bridge Street, if anyone needs me, reassuring Stephanie Richards—yet again—that her symptoms are perfectly normal, and she'll have a lovely, healthy baby in a couple of weeks' time.'

'And I'll be home if I'm needed,' Chloe declared, then shook her head as Oliver's eyes lit up. 'Defrosting the fridge, so you can forget any ideas about slipping home for a cup of coffee.'

'Coffee wasn't what I had in mind, babe,' he murmured, and the midwife chuckled, and he laughed and, as they walked away together, Eve felt her heart twist slightly.

The young couple were so much in love. Tom hadn't been in love with her, she thought sadly as she tightened her grip on the pile of folders she was carrying and started walking towards Reception.

'Let's have fun' was all he'd said that summer, and for him their romance had simply been that, a bit of fun, whereas for her... She had loved him so much, and when he'd left, when he hadn't phoned, had sent her only those two postcards, she'd felt as though her heart had been ripped out and trampled on.

'Oh, damn, blast and bloody hell!' she exclaimed as she rounded the corner and cannoned straight into someone coming the other way, sending the folders she was holding clattering to the floor.

'Language, Nurse Dwyer, *language*.'

It couldn't be, she thought, feeling her heart give an almighty leap, but as she looked up and met a pair of sparkling green eyes she saw that it was.

'You're not supposed to be here,' she blurted out before she could stop herself, and Tom grinned.

'Decided to stay on for a few more days. Thought I'd let the local garage mend my broken indicator light, make it easier for your physio.'

Pathetic, she thought as she stared up at him, wondering how he could possibly manage to look quite so heart-tinglingly handsome in an old, threadbare blue sweater and a pair of jeans. That was the most pathetic reason for staying on in Penhally she'd ever heard, but she had no intention of calling him on it. Calling him on it might mean he'd give her the real reason, and something told her she was better off not knowing the real reason.

'I'm afraid Lauren isn't here,' she said, getting down on her hands and knees to begin retrieving the files. 'She's just gone out on her home visits.'

'I didn't want to see Lauren,' he replied, hunkering down beside her. 'I wanted to see you.'

'Me?' she said faintly.

'I wondered if you'd like to come out to lunch with me?'

'Lunch?' she repeated, and his green eyes twinkled.

'As in food. A substance which sustains every living thing,' he said.

'I know what lunch is,' she protested. 'I just…' Absently, she reached for the last file, just as Tom did, too, and when their hands touched she snatched hers away quickly, all too aware that a disconcerting crackle of heat had raced up her arm. 'I just…'

'Is there a problem here?'

Eve glanced over her shoulder to see Nick standing behind her, his expression colder and stonier than she'd ever seen it.

'No problem,' she mumbled. 'Tom…he's decided to stay on for a few more days.'

'So I see,' Nick replied.

'I was also hoping to entice Eve out to lunch,' Tom declared. 'You do allow your staff to have lunch, I presume?'

'Naturally,' Nick said, his voice every bit as tight as Tom's. 'But it's my staff's choice as to who they eat that lunch with.'

And frankly I'd be happier if Eve had lunch with Genghis Khan.

Nick didn't say those words, he didn't have to. His whole body language said it for him, and although Eve now knew why the senior partner was being so antagonistic towards Tom, she didn't need—or want—him protecting her.

'It's all right, Nick,' she said, and for a second she thought the senior partner might actually argue with her, then he nodded and walked abruptly away.

'What *is* it with that guy?' Tom demanded. 'We haven't seen one another in years, and yet every time we meet it's obvious he'd dearly like to stick a knife in me.'

'Personality clash, maybe?' Eve suggested evasively. 'Give me a couple of minutes to offload these with Hazel,' she continued quickly, indicating the folders in her arms, 'and to change out of my uniform, and I'll be right with you.'

And it would be only a few minutes, she thought as she

handed the folders to their practice manager. Any longer, and she dreaded to think what Nick might come back and say.

But it wasn't Nick who was uppermost in her mind when she went into the ladies' cloakroom to change out of her uniform and saw how flushed her cheeks were, how bright her eyes. She should have looked angry, horrified, because Tom hadn't left, but the truth was she looked more alive than she had in years, and she closed her eyes to shut out the image.

What was happening to her? Just two short days ago she'd had a life. OK, so maybe it hadn't been the world's most exciting life, but she'd had her patients, and Tassie, and she'd been in control and content, and yet now…

She couldn't still have feelings for Tom, not after all these years. He'd left her without a second's thought, and though she'd been heartbroken for a long time she'd eventually picked up the pieces of her life, had dated other men. Dammit, she'd even got engaged once.

But you broke off the engagement, her mind whispered.

Only because I realised it was a mistake, she argued back. That it would be wrong to marry someone, and keep secrets from him. It wasn't because I still had feelings for Tom.

Oh, really? Her mind laughed, and she gripped the edge of the sink tightly.

Somehow, some way, she had to pull herself together. Somehow, some way, she had to keep her emotions in check, because she couldn't go down that road again, Nick had been right about that. Recapturing the past would mean resurrecting it, and she couldn't do that, not ever.

'Eve, we were just talking about you,' Dragan said when Eve emerged from the ladies' cloakroom to find him and Tom laughing about something.

'Saying something nice, I hope?' Eve said lightly, and Dragan smiled.

'Tom was telling me about his home in Lausanne, and I was

saying he must take you there some time. It's a beautiful part of Switzerland.'

'You know it?' Eve asked, deliberately sidestepping the suggestion that she would want Tom to take her anywhere.

'I do, indeed,' Dragan observed. 'When I was young, my family and I went there a couple of times for holidays before... Before everything changed.'

A shadow had appeared in his eyes, and Eve knew the Croatian doctor was remembering happier times when his homeland hadn't been torn by war, when all of his family had been safe, and alive.

'Dragan,' she began hesitantly, and he shook his head and forced a smile.

'Sometimes it's good to remember the past, and sometimes it's not,' he said. 'But you must let Tom take you to Switzerland. It truly is a beautiful place.'

'I'm sure it is,' Eve said, then added quickly when she saw Tom open his mouth, clearly intending to interrupt, 'How's Melinda?'

'Tired,' Dragan admitted. 'Tired of waiting, tired of looking—she says—like a hot-air balloon that's about to go pop.'

Eve laughed.

'At least she hasn't got much longer to go,' she said. 'Just two more weeks, and then you'll be a proud papa.'

'Do you know whether it's a boy or a girl?' Tom asked, and Dragan shook his head.

'Melinda and I didn't want to know. We wanted it to be a surprise. And speaking of surprises,' he added, glancing at his watch, and letting out a muttered oath, 'if I don't get my home visits started the only surprise will be me managing to have them finished by midnight.'

'Brave man,' Tom observed as Dragan hurried away, 'coming to the UK, making himself a new life in a foreign land.'

'It wasn't easy for him—not at first,' Eve replied, 'but then he met Melinda, and…' She smiled. 'The rest, as they say, is history.'

'What I don't understand is why I keep feeling I know him from somewhere,' Tom said. 'I thought the same thing when I met him and his wife at the reception on Saturday, but I can't for the life of me figure out why.'

And I'm not about to jog your memory, Eve thought as she slipped on her jacket, and led the way out of the surgery. Melinda and Dragan had endured more than enough harassment back in April when their photographs had been plastered all over the newspapers, and they were entitled to some privacy.

'Where do you want to have lunch?' she said, deliberately changing the subject.

'I thought maybe The Grape Seed.'

'I'm afraid it closed down years ago,' she replied as they began walking up the road past the surfing and souvenir shops, skirting the puddles left from the thunderstorm that had deluged the village earlier that morning. 'When Mr Forrest retired, his son didn't want to take it over, so it became an estate agent's.'

'Damn!' Tom exclaimed. 'I loved The Grape Seed. Remember when you could choose all those different sorts of salad dishes, like grated carrot mixed with coconut, curried eggs, and pasta salad with tuna, and we thought we were the height of sophistication?'

Eve smiled and nodded, but she wished he'd stop this. She didn't want to keep dwelling on the past. It was over, gone.

'We could have lunch at the Anchor?' she suggested, and he shook his head.

'Too stuffy. I always feel as though they're itching to check my pockets for cutlery after I eat there.'

She let out a small snort of laughter.

'We could just buy some tortilla wraps, and eat them down by the harbour,' she said, then glanced up at the sky. 'And, then again, perhaps not. I think it's going to rain again.'

And it would be yet more heavy rain. The sea might currently be a sheet of near-Mediterranean blue, and the houses and steep roads that made up Penhally Bay might be standing out in sharp relief against the cliffs behind, but she could see another band of black clouds gathering over the cliffs.

'What's that café like?' Tom asked, inclining his head towards it.

'They do very nice soups, and puddings, and if you want something a bit more substantial—'

'*Lovak!*' Tom exclaimed, coming to a sudden halt in the middle of the pavement. 'Melinda and Dragan *Lovak*. She's that European princess. The one who gave up her throne to marry the Croatian refugee.'

Eve sighed. 'So it reached the London newspapers, did it?'

'It reached *every* newspaper, Eve.' Tom shook his head in disbelief. 'I should have recognised them immediately.'

Eve wished he hadn't recognised the couple at all.

'Tom, as far as Melinda is concerned, she's Mrs Lovak, the local vet, and a soon-to-be mum,' she said. 'And as far as Dragan is concerned, he's simply one of the Penhally doctors.'

'I can see why,' Tom observed. 'I wouldn't want my past splashed all over the papers. You'd be OK with your blameless history, but me…' He laughed. 'I doubt if my bosses would be overjoyed to learn I burned down bicycle sheds when I was at school.'

And he'd somehow put his foot in it again, Tom thought as he saw Eve's face set. He'd only been making a joke at his own expense, and yet the shutters had quite clearly come down and he could almost feel her physically withdrawing from him.

'Is Dragan taking paternity leave after his wife's given birth?' he continued quickly. 'I know I would be if I were in his shoes.'

'Yes, he's taking paternity leave.'

And that hadn't helped at all, he realised, seeing her face set into even more rigid lines. *OK, change the subject*, he told himself. *Talk about something else—somebody else.*

'I met your minister on the way down here—Reverend Kenner,' he declared. 'He had his daughter, Rachel, with him. Nice kid. When's her baby due?'

'December.'

Which didn't seem to please Eve any more than his comments about Dragan and Melinda had, he thought with a sigh.

'Look, I know you're not happy about the situation,' he said. 'Her being only being seventeen, and Gary Lovelace being the father, but I've always been a very firm advocate of a woman's right to choose. She didn't have to go ahead and have the baby, Eve. She could have opted for a termination, but she didn't. Her decision, her choice, and I admire her for it.'

Eve clearly didn't if her complete silence as she led the way into the café was anything to go by, and Tom groaned as he followed her.

Hell, was he always going to be fated to somehow inadvertently say the wrong thing? Maybe he should just have gone back to London this morning, but he hadn't wanted to leave, hadn't wanted the last words they'd exchanged to have been remote and distant ones.

And was that the only reason you didn't want to leave? his mind whispered, and he sighed.

He wished it was. It would have made things so much easier, but he'd spent the last twenty years of his life trying to convince himself he'd done the right thing only to have that illusion blown straight out of the water the minute he'd seen her again. All it had taken was one smile from her and the great weight that had been lying on his heart for so long had suddenly lifted and the world no longer seemed such a dark and empty place.

But how to tell her this? he wondered as they sat down at a table, and both picked up a menu. How to confess he'd made a mistake all those years ago?

'Eve—'

'I'll have the carrot and coriander soup, then lemon meringue pie, please,' she told the smiling waitress who had appeared at their table.

'The same for me,' Tom said, not bothering to look at the menu. He glanced around at the café as the waitress bustled away. 'Nice place,' he continued awkwardly. 'I'm surprised we're the only customers.'

'They'll be closing at the end of the week,' Eve replied. 'They haven't gone bankrupt, or anything,' she added. 'A lot of the restaurants, and most of the craft and gift shops, in Penhally close down at the end of the summer. It's not really viable for them to stay open over the winter.'

'Right,' he said, then cleared his throat. 'I want to apologise to you for what I said about Tassie yesterday. I don't know the family—don't even know the girl—so I spoke out of turn.'

'Yes, you did.'

Which pretty well finished that as a topic of conversation, he thought.

'It's raining again,' he ventured, as he stared out of the café window looking for inspiration. 'And the Lanson's running pretty high.'

'We had a lot of rain this morning,' Eve replied. 'We often do in October.'

And I'm dying a death here, Tom thought ruefully, if we're reduced to talking about the weather. Hell's teeth, it shouldn't be this hard to start a conversation, and keep it going. All he had to do was not mention Tassie Lovelace, Melinda and Dragan Lovak, Rachel Kenner or Eve's parents, and surely he'd be on safe ground.

'*Dirty Dancing*,' he said quickly. 'I've just remembered the film I took you to see at the old La Scala was *Dirty Dancing*, and you made me see it three times because you had a thing about Patrick Swayze.'

'It wasn't so much Patrick Swayze,' Eve said as the waitress appeared with their soup. 'It was more… I think I liked the film because it was about trying to fulfil your dreams.'

'Don't tell me you actually sit down and watch it when it comes on TV?' He laughed, and saw her jaw set as she picked up her spoon.

'No. I don't.'

OK, he thought. Let's try something else.

'Do you remember—?'

'Stop it, Tom.'

Her large brown eyes were unexpectedly hard, and he gazed at her in confusion. 'Stop what?'

'All these reminiscences, this trip down memory lane. We're not in our twenties any more. We've both moved on, we're different people now.'

'I don't think you've changed very much from the person I once knew,' he said with a smile, and she shook her head.

'You didn't even know me twenty years ago, Tom, not really.'

'Of course I did,' he protested, then glanced over his shoulder to see where their waitress was. 'Hell, Eve, we were lovers. If anybody knows you, it's me.'

'You might have known my body,' she said quietly. 'But you didn't know me.'

'You're talking in riddles,' he replied. 'Of course I knew you. Just as I also feel…' He lowered his voice still further. 'The old attraction between us… It's still there, isn't it?'

A peal of thunder had rung out, followed by a jagged fork of lightning, but Eve ignored them both and put down her spoon, cynicism and anger plain in her eyes.

'What you're feeling is a desire for the past, Tom,' she replied, 'for when your life was simpler. It's isn't me you want back. It's your youth.'

Was she right? he wondered as he stared back at her and unconsciously he shook his head. It was more than that, so much more than that.

'If you're saying I want to be young again, then the answer's no,' he replied. 'If I could go back, knowing what I know now, that would be different, but to go back to the thoughtless man I was then…' He reached out and clasped her hand. 'All I do know is I never forgot you.'

'Your never forgetting me didn't extend to you keeping in touch, did it?' she exclaimed, pulling her hand free, and he winced at the hardness in her voice. 'Two postcards, Tom. Two lousy, miserable postcards. One saying you were lonely, the other saying you had applied for a job with Deltaron, and then nothing.'

'I meant to write,' he began hesitantly, 'but the longer I was away, the more—'

'You forgot about me?' she finished for him, and he dragged his fingers through his hair.

'No,' he protested. 'I just thought—as the years passed— you'd be bound to be married—have a family.'

'And now you've discovered I'm not, you think it might be nice to try to pick up where you left off,' she said, her voice brittle. 'Well, you can forget it, Tom.'

'Eve—'

'Something wrong with the soup?' the waitress interrupted, appearing without warning at their table, and glancing from Eve's scarcely touched bowl to Tom's.

'It's lovely—perfect,' Tom said with an effort.

'Better than the weather.' The waitress laughed as another peal of thunder rang out and rain began bouncing onto the street outside, filling the drains and gullies so quickly they started to overflow.

'Eve, I didn't come back to resurrect the past,' Tom said the second the waitress had gone. 'I came back for two reasons. One I can tell you about, the other…' He shook his head. 'I can't tell you that, not just yet.'

'Then tell me the one reason you can,' she said, folding her arms across her chest with a look on her face that said all too plainly, you'd better make this good.

'I came back because…' He took an uneven breath. 'I wanted to see if I could still feel anything. Even if all I felt in Penhally was the old resentment, the old hatred, at least it would mean I could still feel *something*.'

Eve gazed at him, open-mouthed. Whatever she had been expecting him to say, it hadn't been that.

'I…I don't understand,' she faltered, and Tom pushed his soup away.

'Eve, during the years I've worked for Deltaron, I've witnessed the most wonderful—amazing—acts of courage and self-sacrifice. I've seen men and women tear at rubble with their bare hands in a desperate attempt to rescue people they've never met, but I've also seen men and women trample on children— babies—crushing them into the mud, in order to save themselves or to grab a crust of bread.'

'I suppose disasters always bring out both the best, and the worst, in people,' she said awkwardly, and his lips twisted into a bitter smile.

'It also breeds indifference, Eve. I was in New Orleans, and Colombia, and Phuket. Horrendous, all of them, but they got help because they made the headlines, whereas in so many places—too many places—I've had to watch people die because the food, and the shelter, and the medicine never came.'

'Tom—'

'Jean Paul Sartre, the French philosopher, said Hell was other people. He was wrong, Eve. Hell is people ceasing to care.'

'But you care,' she protested, seeing the desolation in his face. 'You wouldn't be doing the job you're doing if you didn't.'

'But the trouble is…' He picked up his spoon and put it down again. 'I'm ceasing to care. Ceasing to feel anything. So a hundred people were killed a month ago, a thousand the month before that. Maybe they're better off dead rather than being rescued by my men simply to survive for another month, or a year, only to be hit by yet another catastrophe, yet another disaster, and lose more loved ones.'

It was so dark outside the café now it could almost have been night, and vaguely Eve was aware of people scurrying past the café window, hurrying to get out of the rain, but what she was most aware of was the bleak, raw despair in Tom's face. Never had she seen such utter desolation on someone's face before and, as she stared at him, she suddenly realised she was feeling an emotion she would never have believed she would ever feel for him, and it wasn't attraction, or anger, or hatred. It was pity.

'Tom, you can't—you mustn't—think like that,' she said quickly, but he didn't seem to hear her.

'So many children orphaned, Eve,' he murmured. 'So many babies, sitting in cots all over the world, who are given enough food and water to live on, but no love, no affection, because there's simply too many of them, and every year their numbers increase.'

'Tom—'

'Maybe Nick was right,' he continued with a shuddering sigh. 'Maybe my whole working life has been nothing but a series of photo opportunities.'

She caught hold of his hand and held it tightly.

'Nick was wrong,' she protested. 'Your work is vitally important.'

'Yeah, right,' he said, with a smile that tore at her heart. 'Dr Tom Cornish, head of operations for Deltaron, the big cheese, the head honcho, but, when it comes right down to it, you're the one who's made something of your life.'

'But you've made a wonderful success of your life,' she said, even more confused. 'I'm just a nurse, Tom, whereas you... There are people alive today who wouldn't be if you hadn't rescued them.'

'But at the end of the day, it's you people remember, isn't it?' he said, turning her hand over in his, and staring down at it. 'You're that nice, kind, sympathetic nurse at the surgery. The one who holds people's hands when they're scared, the one who gives them a cuddle when they need it.'

The misery in his face was palpable and she had to swallow hard before she could answer him.

'Tom, people remember you,' she declared, her voice uneven. 'You're the man who arrives whenever there's an emergency, the man who helps. What you do, it's what you always wanted to do—so how has it all gone wrong? I can see how constantly facing so much death and destruction must wear you down, but what's happened to make you feel your work—your whole life—has been pointless?'

He didn't get a chance to reply. Another peal of thunder rumbled overhead, the lights in the café flickered and went out, and the waitress bustled towards them.

'Thought as much,' she said with resignation. 'Sorry, folks, but I'm not going to be able to give you your puddings.'

'It doesn't matter,' Tom said, getting abruptly to his feet and extracting his wallet. 'We've discovered we're not very hungry.'

'I'd get home as quickly as you can if I were you,' the waitress declared as she took Tom's money. 'The Lanson's running higher than I've ever seen it.' She glanced at Eve's light jacket, and Tom's sweater and jeans. 'You'd better borrow these umbrellas or you'll both be soaked in seconds.'

The waitress was right, Eve realised when she and Tom left the café. Not only was the rain—if anything—even heavier, the Lanson was now lapping ominously close to the top of its banks.

'I don't like this,' Tom murmured as he stared at it. 'Look at the colour of the river, Eve. It's almost black, and can you smell it? That's earth—lots and lots of earth. We have to get back to the surgery, and phone the emergency services, because I think this means trouble. Big trouble.'

'The Lanson's breached its banks before,' Eve protested. 'See, people are already putting sandbags round their doors, and boarding up their shop windows. OK, so we'll probably get an inch or two of water on the pavements, but once this thunder-storm's over—'

'Eve, we have to get away from here *now*,' he interrupted.

He was overreacting, Eve told herself, shivering slightly as more thunder and lightning split the sky. Yes, the river was high—incredibly high—and it smelt and looked odd, but calling the emergency services was far too extreme.

'Tom—'

He didn't even acknowledge she had spoken. He was already hustling her down the road, but, just as they reached the bottom of Harbour Road, they both came to a halt as a sound shattered the air. A bomb or a gas explosion, was Eve's immediate thought, but the sound was immediately followed by a roar. A terrible, screaming roar that made her look over her shoulder and what she saw made her heart stop.

'Tom.' She whispered. 'Oh, my God, Tom, *look*!'

A torrent of water was cascading out of Bridge Street, com-pletely engulfing Harbour Bridge. Engulfing it in a raging, nine-foot-high torrent of black water in which dustbins were being tossed like toys before being spat out into the harbour, and when Tom grabbed her hand she didn't hesitate for a second. She began to run.

CHAPTER FOUR

'HAS a gas main exploded?' Hazel, the practice manager, exclaimed, her face white with shock, as Tom and Eve raced into the surgery. 'I heard this awful sound, then our landline went dead, and I've been trying to get the police on my mobile—'

'Where's Nick?' Tom demanded, cutting right across the practice manager without compunction.

'He's not here,' Hazel replied. 'Kate rang about fifteen minutes ago, saying she wasn't happy about Stephanie Richards, so he went to help her.'

'Who's Stephanie Richards?' Tom asked, looking from Eve to Hazel, but it was Eve who answered.

'Mum-to-be, due date the 20th of this month. Her boyfriend walked out on her when he discovered she was pregnant, and she's not had an easy pregnancy. She…' Eve swallowed convulsively. 'Tom… She lives in Bridge Street.'

'Not the best place to be at the moment,' Tom said evenly, and Eve let out a cry that was halfway between a sob and a laugh.

'Not the best place?' she repeated. 'Tom, you saw that water—'

'What the hell was that noise?' Oliver interrupted as he came running out of his consulting room. 'I was ploughing through my paperwork, listening to the rain bouncing off the roof, then it sounded as though a bomb had gone off.'

'The river Lanson's broken its banks,' Tom declared, 'and, at a rough guess, I'd say it's running nine feet higher than it should be.'

'Nine *feet*?'

'Oliver, it was awful—truly awful!' Eve exclaimed, as the young doctor stared at her, open-mouthed. 'One minute the Harbour Bridge was there, and the next…'

'You mean, the bridge has collapsed?' Oliver gasped, and Eve shook her head helplessly.

'I don't know. It might still be there, under the water, but…' She clasped her hands together to try to stop them shaking. 'Tom—Kate and Nick, and the people who live in Gull Close and Bridge Street like Gertrude Stanbury, Audrey Baxter—we have to help them. That water…'

'I know,' Tom said, his gaze steady, his voice calm, 'but we both also know we haven't a hope in hell of getting up either of those streets. Hazel, phone Nick on his mobile—'

'I can't, Tom,' the practice manager interrupted. 'Bridge Street, Gull Close and Penhally Heights—they're all blind spots as far as mobiles are concerned. I could try reaching them by radio, but if they've left their handsets in their cars…'

'We'd be better off using smoke signals,' Tom finished for her grimly. 'OK, Oliver, as Nick isn't here, you're in charge.'

'No,' the young doctor declared immediately. 'Absolutely not. Hell, Tom, you're head of operations at Deltaron. If anyone has the expertise for a situation like this, it's you.'

That Tom didn't want to be in charge was plain. A shadow had crossed his face, making him look, Eve thought, suddenly every one of his forty-four years, but Oliver was right. Only Tom had experience of dealing with this sort of situation, and whatever had happened to him, whatever he had witnessed that had made him feel he had wasted his life, it didn't alter the fact that they needed him.

'Tom?' Eve said hesitantly, and saw a small muscle clench in his cheek, then he nodded.

'All right, but one thing has to be understood,' he said. 'If I'm in charge then whatever I decide we go with, no argument, no discussion. Even if you don't like my decision—feel it's the wrong one—my decision stands.'

'I hardly think any of us are going to query your judgment,' Oliver said, and when Eve and Hazel nodded their agreement, Tom's lips curved slightly.

'I'll remind you of that later,' he said, then turned to Hazel. 'Phone the coastguard, the fire brigade, and keep phoning the police. Tell them the Lanson's broken its banks, and we need help now.' He glanced at his watch. 'It's just after two o'clock, which means the kids will still be in school. Oliver, phone both the primary and secondary schools, tell them not to let any of the children go home. Eve, I need a map of the village—the more detailed the better.'

Eve scarcely heard him. Try as she may, she couldn't forget the wall of surging, churning water, and when she thought of Audrey, and Gertrude, the people who might have been walking down those two streets… And Tassie. Her heart clutched and twisted inside her. Tassie was always calling in on Gertrude to borrow books. What if she was there, in Gull Close, trapped?

She won't be, her mind insisted. It's a school day, so Tassie will be in school, safe, and, as she felt a surge of relief course through her, she dug her fingernails deep into the palms of her hands, hating herself for feeling such relief when so many others were in danger.

'Eve, we can stand here worrying, or we can do something, and right now I need that map.'

She looked up to find Tom's gaze on her, and though there was understanding in his green eyes, there was impatience in them, too, and with an effort she straightened her shoulders.

'There's an aerial photograph of Penhally in the waiting room,' she said. 'Would that be any use?'

'Perfect,' Tom replied. 'Absolutely perfect.'

'Tom, how can this have happened?' she said as she followed him into the waiting room. 'We've had violent thunderstorms before, but never anything like this.'

'My guess is the thunderstorm earlier this morning caused something to collapse further up the hill, forming a dam,' Tom replied as he took the photograph off the wall. 'Then, when we had the second thunderstorm, the sound we heard was the dam breaking. I can't think of anything else which would cause such a volume of water to travel down at such speed.'

'Schools alerted,' Oliver announced when Tom and Eve returned to Reception, 'and I've phoned St Piran Hospital, warned them to be on standby for possible casualties.'

'The firemen are on their way,' Hazel chipped in, 'but whether they'll be able to get here is another matter. Roads seem to be flooded everywhere. The coastguard have scrambled their helicopter, and the Royal Navy are sending three more.'

'What about the police?' Tom demanded, and Hazel shook her head.

'All of their mobile phone numbers seemed to be permanently engaged. Not surprising, really, under the circumstances.'

'Keep phoning them,' Tom said. 'They need to start evacuating people in case that water spreads, and we have to find somewhere safer, too.'

'But surely we're safe here?' Eve protested. 'The water was racing straight out of Bridge Street into the harbour.'

'We need to be higher, much higher,' Tom insisted. 'Do either of the schools have a generator?'

'The high school does,' Hazel replied.

'Then the high school would be the best place for us to relocate to, and it would also be perfect for the villagers living on the west side of the Lanson to assemble,' Tom observed. 'For the people who live east of the river...' He squinted at the aerial photograph. 'The Smugglers' is the highest, and there's also fields behind it where a helicopter could land. Would there be anybody at the inn at this time of day?'

'Tony—the owner,' Eve replied. 'He's always there, and I know he'd be more than willing to help, but won't we need a medic on site in case someone comes in injured?'

'Dragan,' Tom said. 'He was going out on home visits today, wasn't he, so where's he likely to be?'

Eve picked up the home-visits notebook, and scanned it quickly.

'At a guess, I'd say he should have reached Mrs Young at Penhally Heights by now.'

'Excellent.' Tom nodded. 'Oliver...' The young doctor wasn't listening. He was punching numbers into his mobile phone, and with a flash of irritation Tom turned to Hazel. 'Phone Tony at The Smugglers', explain the situation, and then see if you get Dragan. If you do, tell him not to attempt to come back into the town, but to head for The Smugglers'. Where's your physio? Laurie—'

'Lauren,' Eve corrected him. 'She said she was dropping in on Mrs Chamberlain at Harbour View, then going on to Gow Court.'

'Where's Gow Court on this photograph?' Tom asked, and Eve pointed to it.

'It's a newly built sheltered housing complex, in this small cul-de-sac running off from Trelawney Rise.'

'Which means, if Lauren's already left the nursing home, and is on her way to Gow Court,' Tom murmured, 'she'll either be driving down Penhally View, then into Polkerris Road, and on to Gow Court, or...'

'She could have taken the quicker route down Bridge Street,' Eve said.

Tom's eyes met hers, blank, unreadable.

'Then let's hope she's taken the scenic route,' he said evenly. 'Hazel—'

'Chloe's not answering, Eve,' Oliver exclaimed in frustration. 'I've rung her over and over, and she's not picking up the phone.'

'Maybe she's asleep,' Eve declared, seeing the worry on the young doctor's face. 'Maybe she had to go out,' she continued, only to realise too late that this hadn't been the wisest wise thing to say. 'I mean—'

'I've left a message on Dragan's mobile, telling him to make for The Smugglers',' Hazel interrupted. 'I've also got Chief Constable D'Ancey on my mobile. Do you want me to tell him we've agreed on two places of safety—the high school and The Smugglers'?'

Tom nodded, and turned back to Eve. 'Does Gow Court have wardens as it's a sheltered housing complex?'

'Carol and Florry Ford,' Eve replied.

'Phone them. If Lauren's there, tell her to make straight for the school hall.'

Eve didn't say, *But what if she isn't there?* But Tom must have realised she was thinking it, because as she picked up her mobile he smiled encouragingly at her.

'One step at a time, Eve,' he said, and she managed to smile back, but she felt less like smiling when she couldn't get a reply from Gow Court, and her smile disappeared completely when the lights in the surgery began to flicker.

'I'm surprised that hasn't happened before,' Hazel observed. 'Our emergency generator will kick in but…'

'It's time for us to move,' Tom finished for her. 'Where's your radio equipment?' he continued, and when Eve led him through to the back of Hazel's office to show him, he let out a low whistle. 'I'll say one thing for Nick, he hasn't stinted on anything. OK, we need to take this, and every piece of movable medical equipment we think we might need up to the school hall. Where's Oliver?'

As though on cue, the young doctor appeared behind them, his face white with worry.

'Chloe's still not answering,' he said. 'Where is she—*where the hell is she*?'

'Oliver, you have my permission to keep phoning your fiancée,' Tom exclaimed, not bothering to hide his irritation, 'but can you do it while you're also carrying some medical equipment out to your car?'

Oliver opened his mouth, then closed it again, and grimly picked up two of their portable defibrillators and disappeared with them.

'Tom, he's worried about Chloe,' Eve said awkwardly. 'He loves her.'

'And as far as we know she's safe, whereas a lot of people in Penhally aren't,' Tom retorted, 'so can we start moving things to the hall, or are we going to wait until the Lanson is lapping round our ankles?'

He was right, Eve knew he was. Speed was of the essence, but she wished he'd been a little kinder, a little gentler, with Oliver. She would have been frantic, too, if she'd been in the young doctor's shoes, and it didn't surprise her when she saw Oliver constantly checking his phone as they moved their portable medical equipment out to their cars, and he was still attempting to contact Chloe when they were carrying it through the rain and into the school.

'She said she was going to spend the whole afternoon at home, Eve,' Oliver muttered when they began setting up the radio equipment in the small office leading off from the school hall. 'You heard her. That's where she said she would be, so *why* isn't she answering the phone?'

Eve wished she knew. She wished, even more, that she could find some words of comfort to give to the young man, but she couldn't think of anything to say apart from, *She'll be all right*, and there was no point in saying that. Oliver would quite rightly turn round and demand to know how the hell she knew, so she simply squeezed his arm, and tried to look as reassuring as she could as they finished connecting all the radio equipment.

'OK, this radio must never be left unattended,' Tom declared when he joined them. 'When our mobile batteries run out—as they assuredly will—it's going to be our only means of contacting the outside world. We'll take it in rotas, but somebody needs to be by the radio at all times.'

'I'll take the first shift,' Eve said quickly. 'I mean, I haven't exactly been of much use up until now,' she added as Hazel hurried off in answer to Oliver's beckoning wave, 'so can I take the first shift on the radio?'

'Of course you can,' Tom said, 'but what do you mean, you haven't been much use?'

Eve shrugged helplessly.

'Hazel... She's been so efficient, on the ball, and I...I just keep seeing that wall of water, thinking if anyone was walking down Bridge Street, or Gull Close, when the dam broke...'

'Considering how heavy the rain was beforehand, I should imagine most people would have hurried indoors, don't you?' he said, and she forced a smile.

'I suppose so,' she said, then bit her lip. 'How do you do it—manage to stay so calm?'

'Because it's my job,' he answered simply. 'Running around like a headless chicken isn't going to get me anywhere.'

'No,' she muttered. 'Sorry. Memo to self. Stop behaving like a headless chicken. It's just...' She shivered involuntarily as the sky outside the office window lit up with lightning. 'I'm so cold, Tom. I don't know why, but I'm so cold, and I can't seem to get warm.'

He walked towards her, and before she knew what was happening he had wrapped his arms around her.

'Shock,' he said. 'What you're suffering from is shock.'

'Is that a professional diagnosis, Dr Cornish?' she said, resting her forehead on his chest, and holding onto him because he felt warm and solid, and so very good.

'Absolutely,' he murmured into her hair. 'Are your feet dry?'

She jerked her head up to look at him. 'What?'

'Wet feet make you feel cold, and cold hands made you feel downright miserable.'

'What medical textbook did that come out off?' she said, chuckling a little unevenly.

'The Dr Tom Cornish book of medical symptoms,' he said. 'It's never ever wrong.'

She put her head back on his chest, needing his warmth, his closeness.

'Tom…I'm scared—so very scared.'

'Glad to hear it,' he said to her surprise. 'A healthy dose of fear means you're not going to be tempted to do anything stupid.'

'I've got more than a healthy dose of fear at the moment, believe me,' Eve said with feeling, 'and yet you… Doesn't anything scare you?'

'Lots of things. Spiders the size of dinner plates, crocs, boa constrictors.'

She shuddered.

'You must think I'm such a wimp,' she mumbled, and to her surprise he tilted her chin so she had to face him.

'I think you're wonderful. I always have done.'

There was tenderness in his face. An unutterable tenderness that made her heart clutch, and desperately she tried to remember all the years they'd been apart, the times when she'd been so unhappy, the reasons why she'd hated him, but all she was aware of was that—stupidly—crazily—she wanted to stay in his arms for ever.

'Do you ever wonder what would have happened if I hadn't

gone to the States?' he said as though he'd read her mind, and she tried to avoid his gaze but couldn't.

'I think it's too late for regrets, Tom,' she said, feeling her throat tighten.

'Is it?' he said. 'Eve—this flood—if anything should happen to me—'

'Don't say that,' she ordered, quickly putting her fingers to his lips to silence him, feeling a chill wrap itself round her heart at his words. 'We're safe here. Nothing is going to happen to either of us.'

'But suppose it did,' he declared. 'I just want you to know—'

Whatever he had been about to say was lost as their radio crackled into life, and a deep, male, Irish voice suddenly rang out.

'Is that idle bastard, Tom Cornish, sitting on his backside somewhere nearby?' the disembodied voice said, and Tom turned quickly towards the radio with a broad smile.

'Hey, Mad Mitch,' he said, releasing Eve to pick up the handset and press the respond button. 'What the hell are you doing there?'

A booming laugh echoed down the radio.

'Well, the Navy contacted Deltaron, said Penhally was in a bit of bother, and asked if we could help. The boys and I hummed and hawed because there was a football match on the television, but when they said our contact was someone called Tom Cornish, we knew there couldn't be two lazy buggers by that name so here we are.'

'Who in the world is that?' Eve whispered, and Tom grinned.

'Michael Finnegan, known to everyone at Deltaron as Mad Mitch because he'll fly when no sane man would.'

Another guffaw came over the radio.

'Nice to know I'm appreciated, Tom, but maybe you ought to get your lady friend to show you how to use the mute button in case I hear something I shouldn't. I tell you, mate, they could put you in a men-only changing room, and you'd still manage to find a woman.'

'He's just kidding,' Tom said, colouring slightly as Eve's eyebrows rose. 'Where are you, Mitch?'

'Coming into Penhally over the sea, and let me tell you it's horrendous out here. Rain's just running off my blades, and visibility's virtually nil. All I'm picking up is what my strobes are hitting. I've been told to head for two streets called Bridge Street and Gull Close, but, if the floodwater's as bad as we've been led to believe, you know what that could mean. OAO until we're closer to you.'

'What did he mean by, "you know what that could mean"?' Eve asked as the radio went dead.

'At the moment, the water's flowing down Bridge Street and Gull Close, and out to sea,' Tom replied. 'What Mitch is worried about is if it encounters a blockage.'

'Is that likely?' Oliver asked as he joined them.

'If buildings start to come down, then, yes, it is,' Tom declared. 'All we need is a large enough fall of masonry and the water will have to find some other way out.'

'So, what you're saying is, nowhere in Penhally is safe?' Oliver exclaimed.

'Harbour View should be OK as it's high above the village, as should the two schools, and The Smugglers',' Tom replied, 'but other than that… Yes, I guess that's pretty much what I'm saying.'

'But isn't there something you can do if a building collapses?' Oliver faltered. 'Some way you can divert the water, make it flow elsewhere?'

'In an open environment there are things I could try, but in the middle of a village…' Tom shook his head. 'All we can do is hope and pray.'

'Is anyone there?'

The voice on the radio was faint, but unmistakably that of Kate Althorp, and quickly Eve lifted the handset.

'Kate, I'm here,' she said. 'Where are you?'

'Nick, are you sure this damn thing works?' she heard the midwife demand. 'All I'm getting is a lot of crackles.'

'Kate, you need to press the red button,' Eve said. 'Once you press that, you'll be able to hear me.'

'Oh. Right. Eve, is that you?' Kate said. 'Thank God. I thought… Never mind what I thought. OK, I know this is probably a non-starter,' the midwife continued, 'but we really could do with some help here. Stephanie's in labour, and it's a breech. We've no electricity, scarcely any equipment except what's in our medical bags, and we can't leave because there's about three feet of water downstairs.'

Eve glanced across at Tom, and he took the receiver from her, and sat down.

'Kate, it's Tom Cornish here. Where are you in Bridge Street?'

'Number sixteen. Luckily, it's a two-storey building, so we're upstairs, but…' They heard the midwife take a quick, and unsteady intake of breath. 'The building is shaking rather ominously, and Stephanie really does need to get to hospital, and the faster the better.'

'Can you hang a white pillowcase—something visible like that—out of the window of the room you're in so the choppers know where you are?' Tom asked.

'We can do that,' Kate replied. 'But, Tom…' The midwife took another uneven breath. 'We really do need help.'

'I know,' he said softly, then flipped the off button on the handset.

'Kate must be terrified,' Eve said as she saw him change the frequency on the radio, and knew he was trying to contact his colleague, Mad Mitch. 'Her husband—James—he drowned ten years ago, trying to rescue children who were cut off by the tide. Kate's always been scared of water, and if anything should happen to her… Her son's only nine, Tom.'

'I *know*,' Tom flared, then shook his head when Eve flinched. 'Sorry—sorry. Mitch, are you there, and if you are, where are you?'

'I'm over the harbour, Tom, and this is a bad one,' the Irish pilot declared. 'I've been talking to the coastguard pilot, and the Navy blokes, and we're all agreed. We're going to have to fly in singly, and do a snatch and grab. The access into Penhally over the harbour is too narrow, and if our blades collide…'

'Mitch, we have a woman in labour in Bridge Street,' Tom declared. 'She has two medics with her, but they've no electricity, and she needs to be in hospital pronto.'

'I hear you, Tom, but I can see people on roofs, people hanging out of windows. Men, women, children, and… Holy mackerel, part of a building's just gone. It looks like a hotel, but…' There was silence, then Mitch spoke again. 'Bob says that according to his map it's the Anchor Hotel, and the water's now spreading into…' There was another silence. 'Fisherman's Row. Bob says the water's now in Fisherman's Row.'

Eve heard Oliver's sharp intake of breath, but Tom ignored him.

'Mitch, can you see any people in danger of drowning?' he asked with a calmness that Eve could only wonder at.

'Hell, mate, I can see people everywhere in danger of drowning,' the pilot replied, and Tom's eyes met Eve's, then Oliver's.

'OK, save any children you see first,' he said.

'But, Tom,' Oliver protested. 'Chloe—'

'I repeat, Mitch,' Tom declared. 'Save any children you see first.'

Deliberately he cut the radio connection, and Oliver stared wordlessly at him for a second, then straightened up.

'I…I have to go,' he said with difficulty. 'Chloe…she's in Fisherman's Row.'

'You're going nowhere,' Tom declared, swinging round in his seat, as Oliver made for the office door. 'Number one, you'll never get across the Lanson, and, number two, we need you here.'

'Chloe needs me more,' Oliver said tightly, and Tom shook his head, his face impassive.

'No, she doesn't,' he said. 'If she's not in the house, she's safe. If she *is* in the house, the only people who will be able to rescue her are the helicopter winch men.'

'But you said they were to rescue children first. Chloe—'

'You put me in charge,' Tom declared, his voice level, flat, 'and you said you would accept whatever decision I made. My decision is they lift any children they see first, and you are to stay here. It's a question of priorities, Oliver.'

'A lifeboat, then,' Oliver said, dragging his fingers through his hair in desperation as, overhead, they all heard the drum of helicopter blades. 'Can't you at least ask them to launch the lifeboat?'

'Oliver, the water's running too fast for a lifeboat to make any kind of headway,' Tom protested, 'and I can't—I won't—order men to put their lives at risk for one woman.'

'I notice you're not out there endangering yourself with the men you profess to care so much about.' Oliver flared. 'You're sitting in here, all nice and warm and comfortable.'

A flash of anger appeared on Tom's face and when he got to his feet Eve instantly moved between the two men.

'Oliver—Tom—please,' she protested, but neither were listening to her.

'If I were a pilot, I'd be up there, doing my damnedest to save people,' Tom said with difficulty, 'but I'm not a pilot. When the water ebbs I'll be out there with my men, but until then I'm doing what you asked me to do—co-ordinating, and organising this operation.'

'And that's all this is to you, isn't it, just another operation?' Oliver said, fury and fear mixed on his face. 'You don't give a damn about Chloe. To you, she isn't even a person, she's just a statistic, a nameless, faceless nobody.'

'Oliver…' Tom's mouth compressed for a second, and when he eventually spoke his voice was strained. 'Believe me, this is as hard for me as it is for you, but I have to prioritise.'

'And if Chloe dies?' Oliver exclaimed, and Eve saw Tom's eyes darken.

'I'm sorry, Oliver.'

'Sorry?' Oliver echoed in anguish. 'You're *sorry*? How do you live with yourself, Cornish—how do you sleep nights?'

'I live with myself because making hard decisions is what I'm paid for, and as for sleeping…' Tom's lips curved into a bitter parody of a smile. 'I actually sleep very badly, if you want the God's honest truth, but I'm still not ordering the lifeboat to put to sea, and I want you to go back into the hall and see if there are any people needing your medical services.'

For a moment Oliver looked as though he intended to argue, then his jaw set and he strode out of the small office, banging the door behind him, and Eve turned awkwardly to Tom.

'Tom, what Oliver said… He didn't mean it, not really.'

'I know,' he murmured, sitting down again, and turning his attention back to the radio. 'But there honestly isn't anything I can do but hope Chloe either isn't in the house, or when the water started to come in she had the sense to head for the attic.'

He sounded drained. Completely, and utterly drained, and for a moment she hesitated then walked up behind him and put her arms round him.

'It's hard to believe, isn't it,' she said, 'that a little over an hour ago we were walking up the street, discussing where we would have lunch, and you said not the Anchor Hotel because you felt they always suspected you of stealing their cutlery?'

He gave a husky chuckle.

'Yeah, well, this afternoon's the day they stopped needing to worry about their cutlery.'

She gazed out of the office window, seeing nothing but darkness illuminated by the strobe lights of a hovering helicopter.

'Is it always like this, Tom? The rescue missions you and your men go out on. Are they always like this?'

'Pretty much,' he replied and, as she held him tighter, she felt his head fall back against her chest.

'How do you stand it?' she said. 'How can you bear it?'

'Because I have to,' he said quietly. 'It's my job, what I signed up for, what I agreed to do. I know Oliver thinks I'm a completely unfeeling bastard, but children always come first in a disaster, and to launch the lifeboat, risk the lives of eight— ten—men in conditions I know would be suicide…'

'Tom…'

She didn't get a chance to say any more. The office door opened and, when Chief Constable Lachlan D'Ancey appeared, she stepped away from Tom quickly.

'I picked up the emergency message on my car radio,' the policeman gasped, pulling off his cap and sending rain drops scattering everywhere, 'so I knew it was going to be bad, but I never thought it would be as bad as this. I've got men out sand-bagging Harbour Road, the council have brought in diggers, but nothing is stopping it from spreading.'

'Have you closed the roads into Penhally?' Tom asked. 'The last thing we want is people returning from work, adding to the chaos.'

'We've blockaded all the roads, and I can tell you it's holy murder out there. The word's already gone out that Penhally's in a bad way, and husbands—wives—are trying to get back into the village to find their loved ones. Luckily, a lot of the stay-at-home mums, and the elderly, seem to have taken police advice and made their way towards either Smugglers' or here, but we've no way of knowing just how many people are out there, trapped.'

'Lauren's just rung in,' Hazel declared as she appeared behind Chief Constable D'Ancey. 'She made it to Gow Court, and she's now going to try to make her way to the school hall.'

'Any word from Dragan?' Eve asked, and the practice manager shook her head.

'I'm guessing he's still out of range, and it's taking him a little while to get to The Smugglers'.'

But surely not this long, Eve thought, but she didn't say it and neither, she noticed, did Tom.

'I'd better get back outside,' Chief Constable D'Ancey declared, 'see what's happening.' His eyes met Tom's. 'Any orders—instructions—advice?'

'How about praying it stops raining?' Tom replied as another deluge began to bounce off the school roof, and the policeman smiled wryly.

'I doubt if I have a direct line to the Big Man upstairs, but I'll do my best.'

He didn't linger, and when he had gone, Hazel turned to Eve apologetically.

'Could you have a word with Lizzie Chamberlain? I've told her time and time again that Harbour View is probably the safest place in Penhally for her mother to be at the moment, but she's stressing like crazy.'

Eve glanced across at Tom enquiringly, and he nodded.

'Take a break—you deserve one,' he said, and Hazel rolled her eyes as she led the way out of the office.

'I don't think anyone could call this a break,' she muttered. 'Lizzie is a wonderful woman, and I admire her no end for all the work she does with abandoned animals but if her BP isn't through the roof mine certainly is after listening to her for the last half-hour.'

Eve chuckled, but it didn't take her long to discover that the practice manager wasn't exaggerating. Lizzie had worked herself into a complete panic attack, and eventually Eve had to concede defeat and call Oliver over to give her a sedative.

'I very much doubt she'll be the only one who cracks tonight,' Oliver declared, his face tight, strained. 'Look around you, Eve, see how crowded the place is, and yet there's scarcely a sound.'

The young doctor was right. Everywhere Eve looked she could see people sitting either in silent huddles, white-faced with shock, holding onto their families, or sitting alone, and those who were sitting alone watched the school-hall door constantly, clearly desperately hoping the next person who came in would be one of their loved ones.

'Eve…'

She knew what Oliver was going to say, just as she also knew she had no words of comfort to give him, but she was saved from saying anything when a familiar figure appeared beside her.

'Amanda, I'm so pleased to see you,' she said, turning towards Tassie's mother with relief. 'I was hoping you and your family would come here. Is there anything you need—anything I can get you?'

'We're fine, Eve,' Mrs Lovelace replied. 'A nice policeman told us to bring some food with us so we're not going to starve, but…' She glanced in the direction of her family. 'Do you think we'll have to stay long? My boys are getting a bit restless.'

They would, Eve thought as she stared at Amanda's children. The woman's three sons were looking as truculent and surly as ever, while Kelly, Amanda's eldest daughter, appeared to be painting her fingernails with an air of unutterable boredom.

'Where's Tassie?' she asked.

'Tassie?' Amanda repeated. 'But, I thought… I mean, isn't she with you?'

'No, she's not with me,' Eve said, seeing a flash of fear cross the woman's face, and knowing her own face had just mirrored it. 'Wasn't she at school today?'

'She said she didn't feel well—'

'Skiving, more like,' Tassie's twin brother Terry muttered sullenly, but his mother ignored him.

'She said she felt a bit better after lunch, and when she asked if she could go for a walk I thought she meant she was coming down to see you.'

'No, she didn't come to see me,' Eve said, fighting to stay calm, but knowing she was losing the battle. 'Have you talked to any of her friends—asked if they've seen her?'

'Nobody's seen her, Eve,' Amanda protested, panic plain now in her voice. 'You don't think—? You know how she liked to borrow books from Miss Stanbury—you don't think she could have gone to…to Gull Close?'

Please, God, no, Eve thought, as she stared wordlessly at Tassie's mother. Please, God, don't let Tassie be there, not there, and blindly she turned and hurried towards the office, her heart hammering.

'Tom—'

He held up his hand to silence her as she rushed in.

'OK, Mitch,' he said. 'Can you give me an update when you're closer to Stephanie Richards's house?'

'Will do,' the pilot replied. 'OAO.'

'Tom, Amanda doesn't know where Tassie is,' Eve said before he'd even hit the cut button on his handset. 'She wasn't at school today—she didn't feel well—but she went for a walk after lunch, and no one's seen her since.'

'And?' he said, getting stiffly to his feet.

'You have to find her,' she declared, wondering why he was suddenly being so unnecessarily dense. 'She must be out there somewhere so you have to find her.'

'The chopper pilots are picking up everyone who looks as though they're in trouble so hopefully they'll see her.'

'And that's *it*?' she protested, her voice rising despite her best efforts to prevent it. 'That's all you're going to do—*hope* Tassie is seen by somebody? Tom, she's just a little girl, just ten years old, and if she's trapped somewhere she's going to be terrified out of her mind.'

'As will be a lot of people at the moment,' he murmured, and

she grabbed hold of the front of his sweater, knowing she undoubtedly looked wild-eyed and deranged but she didn't care.

'Please, Tom, you have to do something. Get your friend—
Mad Mitch—back on the radio, tell him what Tassie looks
like—'

'For God's sake, Eve, the only lights out there are the helicopter search lights,' Tom flared. 'The pilots will scour all the
rooftops, but I can't—and won't—order them to look for one
specific child. While they're doing that, other men, women and
children could drown.'

'*I don't care!*' Eve cried, then took an unsteady breath when
Tom stared at her in shocked astonishment. 'I'm sorry—I don't
mean that—not really, but this is Tassie, Tom. *Tassie.*'

'Eve—'

'Tom—if you're there, mate, we have a problem.'

Tom eased Eve's fingers from his sweater and picked up the
handset.

'What's wrong, Mitch?'

'I'm over Bridge Street, and can see the white pillowcase
you mentioned for the woman who's giving birth, but, Tom, I
can't take a woman in labour out of that small window. When
the baby's arrived, we can do a scoop and run, but a woman in
labour, over that water, I'm sorry, but I can't.'

'I understand,' Tom said. 'Mitch—'

'I have to go, mate. I can see a couple of kids—one about
two, the other about three—sitting with a woman astride one
of the roofs in Bridge Street, and there's a blonde-haired girl of
about nine hanging out of an attic window in Gull Close.'

'*Tassie,*' Eve breathed. 'Tom, that'll be Tassie. Tell him to
pick her up first—please tell him to pick her up first.'

Tom gazed at her for a long moment, then hit the 'talk'
button on his handset.

'Pick up the youngsters on the roof and their mother first,
Mitch.'

'*No!*' Eve exclaimed. 'Tom—'

'The child hanging out of a window in Gull Close is safe for the moment, Eve,' he replied, 'but those kids on the roof have no shelter, no protection. If one of them slips—'

'But—'

'It's a question of priorities, Eve.'

'You keep saying that,' she said, feeling tears begin to trickle down her cheeks, and she rubbed them away roughly with the back of her hand. 'Like…like it's some sort of justification.'

He caught her by the shoulders, his face dark, and forced her to look up at him.

'It's the only justification I have, Eve. Can't you see that?'

'Then I'll go and help her,' she said blindly. 'If you can't— won't—I have to. I'm not going to let her down. I'm not going to abandon her the way I—' She bit off the rest of what she'd been about to say. 'She's a little girl, Tom, just a little girl, out there in the dark, and she must be terrified.'

'Eve, you are not leaving this hall.'

'I have to—don't you see that?' she cried. 'I can't live with another twenty years of regret, spend another twenty years wishing I'd done things differently.'

'Eve, you're talking nonsense,' Tom declared, giving her shoulders a little shake. 'You have never let anybody down in your life.'

'But I have, I have,' she insisted, knowing she was crying in earnest now, that her words were coming out choked with sobs. 'And I won't do that again. I *can't,* Tom.'

'Eve, you're not making any sense. Who did you let down?'

She could see the complete bewilderment in his face, and she didn't want to tell him. She'd always sworn she never would, but if she told him maybe he'd understand, maybe he would send people to help Tassie, and she took a ragged breath.

'Our baby, Tom. I let our baby down.'

He stared at her blankly.

'Eve, we don't have a baby. Look, shock can play strange tricks, affect people differently. I'll get Oliver—'

'Listen to me, Tom,' she interrupted, clutching hold of him, 'you have to listen to me. I didn't realise I was pregnant until a month after you left for America. I hadn't been feeling well, and I thought it was simply something I'd eaten until I was talking to one of the midwives at the practice I was working at in Newquay, and the penny dropped.'

'But…' He shook his head. 'You can't have been pregnant. You were on the Pill. You told me so.'

'Maybe it took longer to begin working on me—maybe it just didn't work properly—I don't know,' she protested. 'But I took one of the pregnancy kits from the surgery I was working in, and when it came up positive I thought it was a mistake— was so sure it must be a mistake—that I went up to Truro and bought another one, and…'

'It came up positive, too?'

She nodded. 'I was pregnant, Tom.'

'And you had a miscarriage,' Tom said, grasping both of her hands tightly in his. 'Oh, hell, Eve, if I'd only known, had been there with you.'

'I didn't have a miscarriage, Tom.'

'You mean…' His eyes searched hers, and she saw amazement followed by dawning delight appear in them. 'You mean, I have a son or a daughter? Eve, that is—'

'You don't have a son or a daughter, Tom,' she interrupted, her voice uneven. 'I…I had an abortion.'

CHAPTER FIVE

HE DIDN'T believe her. She could see the disbelief and denial in his face, knew he was expecting her to suddenly smile and say, 'I didn't mean that,' but as she continued to stare silently back at him, she saw his incredulous expression gradually turn into one of shocked horror.

'You had an abortion?' he said hoarsely. 'You aborted our child?'

'I didn't want to do it, Tom,' she said, returning the pressure of his fingers, willing him to believe her. 'If there had been any other way—if I could somehow have kept the baby—but I couldn't, and believe me there hasn't been a day since then when I haven't regretted what I did.'

'You had an abortion,' he repeated as though by saying it he could somehow make it untrue.

'Yes,' she whispered, and he let go of her hands, and stepped back from her, revulsion flooding his face.

'How *could* you have done that?' he demanded. 'How *could* you have taken the life of an innocent child and just thrown it away?'

His words and his expression cut her to the bone but, as she stared back at him, saw the disgust in his eyes, it wasn't pain she felt, it was anger. A blind, furious anger that he could judge her so easily, and so instantly.

'You think,' she said, her voice shaking so much she could hardly get the words out, 'you think I just did the test, and thought, Oh, good heavens, I'm pregnant, now that's really inconvenient, but never mind, I'll *get rid of it*?'

'I don't know what you thought,' he threw back at her. 'How can I when I don't feel like I know you at all? All these years and you said nothing. All these years when I could have had a son or a daughter, but you chose to go ahead…to…without telling me… It was my child, too, Eve.'

'A child you wouldn't have wanted—not then,' she cried, her heart thumping so hard she was sure he must hear it. 'Time and time again, that summer, you told me you didn't want to be tied down, didn't want a wife, or a family, wanted to be free, to make something of your life.'

'You didn't give me the chance to say whether I wanted our baby or not,' he declared, his face twisted with fury and anguish. 'You just decided, without a word, a call…'

'*How* could I have contacted you, Tom?' she protested. '"I'm off to the States," you said, and then I got a postcard from New York, and another one from California saying you were applying for a job with Deltaron, but you never even bothered to tell me whether you'd got the job. All I knew—guessed—was you were somewhere in America. Well, America is a pretty big place, Tom.'

'You…you could have phoned the offices of Deltaron,' he said defensively. 'They would have told you where I was.'

'And if I'd done that—turned up on your doorstep—and said, "I'm pregnant, Tom," how would you have felt?' she demanded. 'What would you have done?'

'I would…I could have offered to help,' he said, beginning to pace backwards and forwards across the small office, his face a tight mask of anger, his green eyes blazing. 'OK, so maybe I wasn't making very much money then, but I could have sent you something every month to help you take care of the baby.'

'And resented me and the child for the rest of our lives for putting you in that position.'

He whirled round at her, his face so contorted that she involuntarily took a step back.

'How *dare* you say that?' he exclaimed. 'I would *never* have resented my child. You know how I feel about children.'

'I know how you feel now,' she countered, bunching her hands into tight fists at her sides, 'but that wasn't how you felt when we were young.'

'Eve—'

'You wanted freedom. "No emotional baggage", that's what you said you wanted, and if I'd told you about the baby… Do you think I wanted you to hate him or her as much as your father hated and resented you?'

'So, it's my fault, now, is it?' he flared.

'Tom—'

'Eve—Oliver—is anyone there?'

Dragan's voice crackled over the radio, insistent, concerned, and when Tom made no move to answer it Eve shakily lifted the handset, and hit the reply button.

'I…I hear you, Dragan,' she said with difficulty. 'Where are you?'

'The Smugglers' Inn, as per instructions. I gather things are pretty bad in Penhally?'

Eve glanced across at Tom's rigid back.

'You could say that,' she replied.

'Well, I'm sorry to add to your troubles, but I need a helicopter asap,' Dragan continued. 'Tony, at the Smugglers', has apparently been experiencing chest pains for the past month, but he's been ignoring them, thinking they were due to indigestion, but the pain's so bad even he can't ignore it. Chloe says—'

'Chloe's there?' Eve interrupted quickly.

'She was visiting Rachel Kenner at the manse when the word to evacuate went out, so she and Rachel came here. Why?'

'She hasn't had her mobile switched on, and Oliver's been a bit worried about her,' she said. *Which had to be the biggest understatement of the year.* 'You think Tony's having a heart attack?'

'His BP's 130 over 90, his skin's sweaty, and the pain's radiating from his chest down his left arm and up into his jaw, so I think we can safely say he's having a heart attack,' Dragan replied. 'I've given him nitro to relieve the pain, and Chloe's started an IV line of morphine, but he needs hospital, Eve, and fast.'

Out of the corner of her eye, Eve could see Tom holding out his hand for the handset, and she gave it to him.

'I'll get one of the Navy guys to Smugglers' Inn right away, Dragan,' he declared. 'Could somebody put out a light, or a flare, to show the chopper where you are?'

There was a distant murmur of conversation from Dragan's side of the connection, and then Dragan's voice rang out.

'We're on it, Tom, but can you be quick? Tony's not in good shape.'

Tom handed the handset back to Eve, then picked up their spare.

'Keep him on the radio,' he said abruptly. 'I can page the Navy with this, and then give him an ETA.'

Eve nodded.

'Is Melinda all right, Dragan?' she said, turning back to the radio.

'Would you believe she's actually watching what's happening in Penhally on television?' the Croatian doctor replied. 'She said she couldn't believe it when part of The Anchor collapsed.'

'Someone's been filming this?' Eve gasped, and heard the Croatian doctor give a wry chuckle.

'Eve, people would film a car crash if they thought they could make a quick buck out of it.'

'Tell him the ETA for the helicopter is five minutes,' Tom declared.

'No need to tell me,' Dragan said. 'I heard it myself. Thanks, Tom, and now I'd better go,' he added. 'There's quite a crowd gathering here, and some of them are panicking pretty badly.'

'Tell Melinda to stay where she is when you next talk to her,' Eve said. 'And tell her not to do anything stupid, like going out to check her animals.'

'I've already told her that,' Dragan replied. 'Got an earful back for my pains, of course, but when I first heard about what was happening in Penhally, all I could think was, Please, God, don't let her be there. Just the thought of losing her, and the baby…'

'I know,' Eve said softly, and heard Tom draw in a ragged breath behind her, but she didn't turn round, couldn't. 'Call us if there's anything else you need, OK?'

She heard Dragan's muttered assent but, after she'd switched off the reply button, she stared at the radio equipment for a long moment before she hesitantly turned towards Tom.

'That's good news,' she said. 'About Chloe, I mean.'

He nodded, but he didn't meet her gaze.

'Tom…' She moistened her lips. 'Tom…'

'I'll tell Mitch to pick Tassie up next.'

'Thank you,' she said, wishing he would look at her, wishing she could touch him, but not daring to. 'Tom—'

'You'd better tell Oliver about his fiancée.'

His face was cold and forbidding, but she couldn't leave it like this—simply couldn't—and hesitantly she took a step towards him.

'Tom, about our baby,' she said, her voice choked, and he made a convulsive movement with his arm, clearly warning her not to say anything else, but she couldn't remain silent. 'Tom, you cannot possibly regret what I did more than I do.'

'You *think*?' he exclaimed, his green eyes dark, pain-filled. 'Tom… *Please*.'

The raw pain in her face tore at his heart, and part of him wanted to go to her, to hold her and comfort her, but the other part—the part inside him that hurt so much—never wanted to see her ever again.

'Just go, Eve,' he said. 'Just…*go.*'

She did. She walked stiffly out of the office, but, when she'd closed the door quietly behind her, he let his breath out in a long, shuddering gasp of pain.

How could she have done that? he wondered. She'd said she'd had no choice, but other women were single mothers, other women had brought up—were bringing up—children on their own, and for her to have…

A son. He might have had a son he could have taught how to play football, taken to matches, joked with, laughed with, advised so he wouldn't make the same mistakes he had. Or a daughter. He squeezed his eyes shut, but that didn't stop him seeing her in his mind's eye, a smaller version of Eve with big brown eyes, and a cloud of dark hair.

How could she just have gone ahead and had an abortion? He'd thought he'd known her. He'd thought in the mêlée of death and destruction that his life had become, she was the one constant, the one calm haven, and to discover she'd…

'Eve… Oh, sorry,' Hazel declared as she stuck her head round the office door. 'Where's Eve?'

'She…' Tom stared at the radio equipment, deliberately avoiding the practice manager's eye. 'She's with Oliver.'

'Oh. Right,' Hazel said. 'It's just Amanda Lovelace—she's very worried about her daughter, and she seems to be under the impression Eve knows something, or can do something.'

'Tell Mrs Lovelace we think we know where Tassie is.'

'You mean she's safe—she's been picked up?' Hazel said.

'No, she hasn't been picked up, not yet,' he replied.

'But—'

'Hazel, I'm not God,' he snapped, then held up his hands

apologetically when the practice manager blinked. 'Sorry—
I...I'm sorry.'

'It's OK,' Hazel said, her face softening with understanding.
'I'll be as encouraging as I can to Amanda, without being too
specific.'

He nodded but, when the practice manager had disappeared,
he bit down hard on his lip to quell the sob he could feel welling
in his throat.

To think he'd told Eve just a few short hours ago that one of
the reasons he'd come back to Penhally had been to see if he
could still feel anything. Well, by God, he knew he could. He
was caring so much right now he felt as though he would die of
it, and, desperately, he glanced around the silent office, searching for some way to release the anger and despair he felt, but
there was no way, and he knew there wasn't. Nothing could ease
what he felt inside. Nothing could remove the knowledge that
he could have had a son, or a daughter, and that Eve had taken
that from him. Taken it without asking him, or even telling him
what she'd done.

How could she have told you? a small voice whispered at
the back of his mind, but he didn't listen to it, didn't want to.
All he wanted was the pain to go away, for him never to have
known, because the knowledge was tearing him apart.

'Eve, are you there?'

Tom swore as Nick's voice rang out on the radio. The senior
partner was the last person he wanted to talk to right now, but
he couldn't ignore the voice.

'It's me, Nick,' he said, flicking on the handset.

'Oh. Right.'

Nick's clipped tone said it all, and a horrible suspicion
suddenly crept into Tom's mind. Could Eve had gone to Nick,
all those years ago, asked him to authorise her request for a termination, and that was why Nick always looked at him as
though he was something unmentionable stuck to the bottom

of his shoe? It would have made more sense for her to have gone outside the area, to a doctor she didn't know, but, then, he didn't know anything with any certainty any more.

'St Piran's?'

Tom stared blankly at the radio equipment. Nick had clearly asked him something, but he hadn't been listening.

'Sorry, Nick, interference on the line,' Tom lied. 'Can you say that again?'

'I said,' Nick declared with clear impatience, 'that Stephanie's just given birth to a boy, and she really needs to be in hospital so we'd appreciate the appearance of a helicopter as quickly as possible.'

Despite everything, Tom could not prevent a wry smile from curving his lips at the senior partner's peremptory tone. When Nick said, 'Jump', he clearly expected people to obey irrespective of the circumstances.

'You're a priority two, Nick, if that's any consolation,' he said, then hit the talk button so he could speak to Mitch.

'Did you hear that?' Nick said, turning to Kate as he put down his handset. 'We're a priority two.'

'Good to know we're somewhere on the list,' Kate said with a wobbly smile, 'especially as our torches aren't going to last much longer.'

Nick nodded, then frowned.

'I feel so damned useless, stuck in here,' he protested. 'All my patients are out there, and I'm trapped in here and about as much use as a chocolate fireguard.'

'Stephanie Richards didn't think you were useless,' Kate pointed out. 'A breech birth isn't easy to pull off even with every surgical piece of equipment known to mankind, but you did it with just what was in your bag.'

Nick shook his head. 'Flattery will get you nowhere.'

'Not flattery,' she said. 'You're a good doctor, Nick, you

always were, and…' She came to a halt as the building swayed slightly. 'I wish it wouldn't do that.'

'Stop fretting,' Nick replied. 'This building's made of good Cornish stone. It can withstand worse than this.'

'Right,' Kate said without conviction, then flushed when Nick shook his head at her again. 'Sorry. I'm not doing positive and upbeat very well, am I? Trouble is, I'm a coward when it comes to water.' She took a shaky breath. 'Bad memories.'

'Nothing's going to happen to us, Kate,' Nick said gently, and she forced a smile.

''Course it won't.' She bent down to tuck a blanket round the young mother and her baby. 'Strange to think Stephanie was right all along. She kept saying she felt something was wrong, and I kept thinking, Here she goes again, panicking. And yet she was right.'

'I hardly think she can have known she was going to have a breech birth,' Nick observed, and Kate rolled her eyes.

'Must you be so pedantic, Nick? I didn't mean she knew she was going to have a breech birth. I just meant sometimes mums-to-be have a sixth sense about whether things are right, or not.' She gazed down at the sleeping young mother. 'Actually, although she doesn't know it yet, this is when the really hard bit starts, and it's going to be doubly difficult for her as she'll have to bring up the baby on her own.'

'She'll cope,' Nick said firmly. 'It never ceases to amaze me how strong women are, and she'll cope.'

Kate nodded, and cleared her throat.

'Do you think Jem's all right?'

Nick's eyes met hers, calm, unreadable.

'I should imagine they've kept all the kids in school,' he said, 'and, as both the high school and the primary school are up on a hill, he'll be fine.'

'Yes,' Kate said, more in an attempt to convince herself than in actual agreement. 'It's just he's like me—not keen on water.'

'Nothing's going to happen to him, Kate.'

'No, of course not,' she said with an effort. 'Do you think it will be Tom who will come with the helicopter?'

'God, I hope not.' Nick groaned. 'That would be all I'd need. The mighty Tom Cornish winching me out of a window.'

Kate tilted her head, and gazed at him speculatively. 'You seriously dislike him, don't you?'

'Yes.'

'Care to share the reason?'

'Can't,' Nick said tightly. 'Patient confidentiality.'

'It's got something to do with Eve Dwyer, hasn't it?' Kate pressed. 'She looked as though she'd seen a ghost when he turned up at Alison and Jack's wedding.'

'Kate—'

'Nick, given that we're both medical professionals, and we could well be dependent on Tom to rescue us,' Kate exclaimed, 'don't you think I have the right to know what he did that has made you dislike him so much?'

For a second she saw indecision warring with professionalism on Nick's face, then he sighed.

'Eve came to me twenty years ago, asking for a prescription for antibiotics. She told me she had a vaginal infection. Well, there was no way I was going to prescribe anything without examining her first, so I did. She'd had an abortion, Eve.'

'And you think Tom was the father?' Kate said calmly.

'Kate, it was common knowledge twenty years ago that they were lovers.'

'You mean it was Penhally gossip, twenty years ago,' Kate replied dryly, and Nick looked irritated.

'She wasn't going out with anyone else at the time, so I think we can safely say he fathered her baby. And what did he do? He skipped off to the US, leaving Eve to deal with it.'

'He might not have known she was pregnant when he left,' Kate protested. 'He might only have found out later.'

'He didn't come back, though, did he?' Nick countered. 'And what kind of man does that?'

'Nick—'

'Kate, I was just nineteen when Annabel and I got married, and I was a father to twins soon after. I don't know how Annabel and I survived those early years, never knowing where the next meal was coming from, always panic-stricken that we wouldn't be able to pay the rent, but I would never have suggested she have an abortion.'

'Nick…' Gently, Kate put her hand on his arm. 'Things are seldom black and white, right or wrong, and who are we to judge? Our haloes are hardly shiny bright. Ten years ago—'

'I don't want to talk about this,' Nick interrupted, throwing her hand off, and walking towards the window, but Kate followed him.

'Nick, we might die tonight,' she said, 'and I don't want to die with what I need to say to you—what I've wanted to say to you for the past ten years—left unsaid.'

His face contorted, and for a second she thought he was going to refuse to listen to her, then his shoulders slumped.

'Do you have any idea how much I deeply regret that night?' he said hoarsely as he stared out of the window into the blackness. 'It should never have happened, and I blame myself entirely.'

'Nick, it takes two to make love, and I didn't push you away,' Kate said softly. 'I could have done—should have done—and yet I didn't. I wanted you that night as much as you wanted me, and when I heard James had died…' She closed her eyes, then opened them again. 'I knew it was a punishment. That God had taken my husband from me to punish me.'

'Oh, Kate…'

'No, please, let me finish,' she insisted as he turned towards her, his face taut. 'We made love that night. You were unfaithful to your wife, and I was unfaithful to my husband, and it was wrong—so very wrong—and when I discovered I was pregnant…'

'Are you telling me you actually considered having an abortion?' Nick said, horror plain in his voice, and tears appeared in Kate's eyes.

'Maybe I should have done. It would certainly have made everything easier for us both, wouldn't it, with no living reminder of what we'd done, but despite all the guilt I've felt over the years, all the torment…' Kate's voice broke. 'As God is my witness, even though I know I will be damned for all eternity for saying this, I can't—and won't ever—regret having him.'

Nick reached out and jerkily clasped her hands in his.

'Kate, if there is a God, he would never condemn you, but what I can't forgive myself for—will never be able to forgive myself for—is cheating on Annabel that night, betraying my marriage vows.'

'And you think I can forgive myself for betraying James?' Kate demanded. 'You think I'm saying that because Jem has brought me so much happiness, his birth justified what we did? I'm not saying that, Nick, I would never say that, but…'

'But?' he prompted, and she could see the uncertainty in his eyes, and the pain.

'We can't undo it, Nick. We will both have to live with our guilt until the day we die, and if by some miracle we're spared tonight then what I want—what I hope—is for us both to perhaps be able to move on, move forward. Not forgetting what we did—we won't ever be able to—but living with it, accepting it, and for you—maybe in time—to let Jem become a part of your life.'

'Kate…'

His voice was deep, strained, but she didn't get a chance to find out what he'd been about to say. A light suddenly appeared at the window, followed by the sound of a gloved hand knocking against it.

'You have a woman and a newborn in here?' the winch man asked when Nick opened the window, and, when Nick nodded, the winch man grinned. 'Then your helicopter awaits, and Tom Cornish sends his compliments.'

'He would,' Nick said darkly.

'And Chloe really is safe?' Oliver declared for what felt, to Eve, like the hundredth time, and she nodded.

'Yes, she really is safe,' she said.

'No thanks to Tom,' the young doctor muttered as he gazed out over the crowded school hall, then flushed when he saw Eve's expression. 'I'm sorry, but he didn't exactly help, did he?'

'Oliver, it's not his fault only one helicopter can fly into Penhally at a time because the entrance to the harbour is so narrow,' she protested. 'It's not his fault the water's rushing so high and fast it would be suicide to launch a boat. What else could he have done—what would you have done if you'd been in his shoes?'

'Saved the woman I loved first,' he said simply, and Eve managed a smile.

'Which is why neither you nor I would make very good heads of operations at Deltaron,' she said. 'We can't see the bigger picture.'

'I'd rather keep my ability to feel, to care,' Oliver declared, and, as Eve caught sight of Tom coming out of the small office, her smile died.

'Tom has the ability to feel, Oliver,' she murmured, 'and to care, very deeply.'

And to hate, she thought, feeling her heart contract as Tom's gaze stopped momentarily on her without expression, then moved away.

'Eve?'

Oliver looked concerned, puzzled, and she forced her smile back into place.

'How's everyone doing?' she said.

'Those who have their families with them are obviously coping better than the others.'

'Are…?' Eve swallowed hard. 'Are there many missing?'

'We don't know,' Oliver admitted. 'What with half the village being here, the other half at The Smugglers', and some people away at work… Chief Constable D'Ancey has put the number missing at around eighteen, but that's purely guesswork.'

'*Eighteen?*' Eve echoed in horror, and Oliver squeezed her hand.

'It's guesswork only, Eve. We'll know better when it's daylight, when the water starts to go down. Hopefully, nobody is lost at all, and people are just sheltering where they can.'

'Lizzie Chamberlain's looking a little better,' she observed, and Oliver nodded.

'She should do, considering the size of sedative I gave her. Amanda Lovelace is understandably in a bit of a state, but she point blank refuses to let me give her anything.'

And Tom was talking to her, Eve noticed. He was bending down towards Tassie's mother, then suddenly she saw Amanda's face light up, and she was gripping his hand tightly, and he was shaking his head, his cheeks darkening slightly, at whatever she'd said.

Could this mean Tassie was on her way? She prayed the girl was. She prayed, too, that Gertrude Stanbury had survived. The elderly school teacher was a determined, spunky woman, but she was crippled with arthritis, and though Tassie was agile enough to have reached the attic she couldn't see how Gertrude could possibly have managed to clamber up there.

'Is…is Tassie safe?' Eve said hesitantly as Tom passed her, and he paused, but he didn't look at her.

'Mitch has picked both her and Gertie Stanbury up. He's going to drop them on the playing fields, and the police will bring them here.'

Eve closed her eyes tightly.

'Thank you,' she whispered. 'Thank you.'

'Nick knows, doesn't he?'

Eve's eyes flew open. 'What?'

Tom caught her by the arm, and steered her none too gently back into the school office.

'Nick—you went to Nick, didn't you, when you decided you weren't going to have the baby?'

'No— I— No,' she faltered. 'I went up to Bude when I discovered I was pregnant. I had…I had it done there.'

'But Nick knows.'

Tom's face was tight with barely suppressed anger, and she wished she could lie, but there was no point.

'He knows I had an abortion,' she said. 'I didn't realise until quite recently that he knew—had guessed—but I caught an infection afterwards, so I had to go to him for antibiotics and he must have guessed then.'

'Which is why he thinks I'm scum,' Tom said. 'He thinks I walked out on you when you were pregnant, forced you into having the abortion.'

'Why would he think that?' she protested. 'Why would he even suspect you were the father?'

'Oh, give me credit for some intelligence,' Tom said, his voice harsh, bitter. 'You and I were an item that summer so he had to suspect it was me, didn't he?'

'Tom—'

'What else haven't you told me?' he said, talking right over her. 'What else don't I know?'

'You know everything now,' she said wretchedly. 'You're the only one who does. No one else. I told no one else.'

'Couldn't your parents have helped?' he demanded. 'I know they didn't have much money, but—'

'They didn't know either.'

He stared at her blankly.

'They didn't know? But—'

'Tom, you know what my parents were like,' she cried. 'My dad—he was a kind man, a generous man, but he disapproved of me even going out with you. He would have said I'd made my bed, and I had to lie in it, and my mum… She would have wanted to help, but this was twenty years ago, and her first thought would have been, What will the neighbours say?'

'So, you kept this from them,' he said, 'just as you kept it from me.'

'And I paid for it, Tom,' she said, her voice thick with unshed tears. 'Because I couldn't tell them, because they never knew they could have been grandparents, it got harder and harder for me to face them so I visited them less and less, so I lost my parents, too. I didn't just lose my baby, I lost my parents, too.'

'But you didn't have to,' he protested. 'Even twenty years ago, women had babies without being married, without their parents' approval.'

'Tom, I'd only just qualified as a nurse, and you know what the wages were like back then,' she said, willing him to understand. 'I thought of adoption, but what was I going to live on while I was pregnant, unable to work? I was twenty-two, Tom, and I was scared witless. I couldn't see any other way out.'

'If you didn't want it—'

'Don't…don't you *dare* say that to me,' she said, her voice breaking on a sob. 'Don't you *dare* say I didn't want my baby. I would have given anything to have kept that baby.'

'Except given birth to it.'

'I *loved* you, Tom,' she replied, feeling her heart splinter with absolute loneliness at the coldness in his voice. 'I loved you back in school even when you and your friends used to shout "Starchy Dwyer" after me in the corridor. And when I discovered I was pregnant, knew there was a part of you growing inside me, I wanted to keep your baby so badly, but I couldn't—I *couldn't*.'

'So you just…you just…'

'Took the easy way out,' she finished for him. 'That's what you're accusing me of, isn't it, taking the easy way out?'

'Perhaps not the easy way out,' he muttered, hot colour darkening his cheeks. 'Maybe that was the wrong thing to say.'

'You want to know how easy it is to have an abortion, Tom?' she said, her voice every bit as hard as his now. 'Then maybe I should tell you. Maybe I should tell you *exactly* how easy it is to have an abortion.'

'I know what the procedure involves,' he said, turning his back on her, and she came after him, and grabbed his arm.

'Maybe you do—medically,' she said, forcing him round to face her. 'But you don't know what it's like emotionally. You don't know what it's like to sit in a waiting room full of women where nobody makes eye contact, and nobody talks, because you all know why you're there, and you're all locked inside your own private little hell.'

'Eve, I don't want to hear this,' he said, pulling his arm free and walking away from her, but she followed him.

'And the nurses,' she continued, 'maybe it was my imagination, but I felt—I thought—that all I could see in their eyes were the unspoken words, "You should have known better. You should have been sensible, should have used a condom, or been on the Pill," and I wanted to yell at them that I had been on the Pill, that this wasn't supposed to have happened, but I didn't say anything because I knew...' Her lips trembled. 'I knew if I started yelling I would never stop.'

He turned to face her, his face white, taut. 'Look, if I've implied—'

'And all the time you're sitting in the waiting room you're thinking, you're thinking...' She choked down a sob. 'That you can still change your mind, you don't have to go through with this, you can still change my mind, but you know you won't because you've been through all the options in your head a thousand times, and you know there isn't anything else you can do.'

'Eve—please—I don't want to hear any more,' he said, his voice cold.

He clearly didn't, she realised as she met his gaze and saw no sympathy or compassion at all in his green eyes, only complete condemnation, and, as tears began to trickle down her cheeks, she felt as empty and as utterly alone as she had felt all those years ago.

'Maybe you don't want to know, Tom, but there's one thing you should know,' she said, wiping her face with a shaking hand. 'Afterwards, when it's done, and the doctor says you can leave, they tell you it's over, but it isn't over because what you don't know—what no one tells you—is that abortion doesn't end anything. It simply starts something else.'

'I don't know what you mean,' Tom said harshly, and Eve shook her head.

'I know you don't,' she said, 'because, you see, nobody warns you that from then on you'll live a lifetime of regret. Nobody tells you you'll discover that the world is full of babies and pregnant women, and every pregnant woman you see, every…every baby you see, will remind you of what you did—what you gave up.'

'Eve—'

'And it never goes away, Tom,' she said. 'Oh, gradually, you pick up the pieces, learn somehow to go on, but it can't ever go away because there are all these dates, you see. The day when he or she would have had their first birthday, the day they would have started school, and all…' She took a ragged breath. 'All the Christmases you never share with them.'

'Eve, I—'

'You implied I took the easy way out, Tom,' she said, catching his gaze, refusing to allow him to look away. 'Well, you tell me whether you think it's been easy for me.'

He opened his mouth to reply, but, before he could say anything, Hazel had appeared, her eyes shining.

'Eve, someone's just arrived I know you'll be delighted to see,' the practice manager declared.

Quickly Eve hurried out into the school hall and when Tom followed her he saw her glance around, expectant, hopeful, and then the hall door opened, and Tassie raced in. For a second Eve's face lit up with a blinding smile but, as she held out her arms, and Tassie raced straight past her towards her mother, Tom saw her smile slide slowly sideways. Slide—just for an instant—into an expression of hurt, and then into an accepting, rueful, wistful yearning that tugged at his heart.

Tassie wasn't simply a child Eve was trying to help. Tassie was the child Eve had never had, the child she had lost.

Not lost, a small voice reminded him. Didn't want, but the small voice held no conviction. In truth, it never had. It had been his own guilt which had made him stand coldly by while Eve had poured out all her anguish and suffering. His own guilt which had kept him aloof from her, because she had been right.

He wouldn't have wanted a child when he'd been twenty-four. All the plans he'd had then, his aims, his dreams… He would have seen a child as an encumbrance, something he had been saddled with, and what kind of life would that child have had, with him rejecting her or him, giving money perhaps but even then grudgingly? He would have been his father all over again, not in the violence—never in the violence—but in the resentment, the feeling of having been cheated out of the life he had wanted, dreamt of.

Savagely, he bit his lip. How could he have accused her of taking the easy way out? She'd taken the hardest decision any woman could ever make, taken it alone, had had to live with it alone, carrying the knowledge, and the pain, for twenty years, and what had he done? He'd watched impassively as she'd broken her heart all over again in telling him. He'd been wrong—so wrong—and somehow he had to tell her that, but how could he get her to listen to him after what he had said, what he'd accused her of?

'I don't believe it,' Gertrude Stanbury declared, as she walked towards him, leaning heavily on the arm of a young policeman. 'I wondered when the pilot said he'd been sent by a Dr Cornish, but I didn't believe it really could be you, not after all these years. It's good to see you again, lad.'

'It's good to see you, too, Miss Stanbury,' he managed to reply. 'I understand you and young Tassie have had quite an afternoon.'

The old lady chuckled.

'You could say that,' she said. 'In fact, I wouldn't be here at all if it hadn't been for the girl. I told her I'd never get up into the attic—that she was to save herself—but she refused to take no for an answer, and somehow, between the two of us, she got me up there.'

'Would you like something hot to drink, Miss Stanbury?' Eve asked as she joined them. 'We've tea—coffee—cocoa…'

'Cocoa,' Miss Stanbury said firmly, 'and a seat if one's available. The young man who winched me out of my house was most kind, and reassuring, but dangling above Penhally, held only by a harness and a stranger's arms, is not my idea of a fun time out.'

Eve laughed. Gently, she and Tom helped the elderly lady across the hall, but once Eve had settled Gertrude into a seat, she straightened up and there was no laughter in her face, only an unreadable blankness.

'I expect you'll be wanting to get back to the radio, Tom,' she said.

The finality in her voice was plain and he knew, as he watched her walk away to get Gertrude cocoa, that he had been dismissed as effectively as if she'd actually closed a door on him, and he deserved it. Twice in her life he had let her down. Twice he hadn't been there for her when it had really mattered, and this last time…

'Whatever it is, lad, I'm sure you'll sort it.'

He glanced down to see Gertrude staring up at him, her small face oddly understanding, and shook his head.

'I don't think I can this time, Miss Stanbury,' he said. 'I think this time I've screwed up big time.'

CHAPTER SIX

THE sun was shining. It was unbelievable, Eve thought as she stared up into the cloudless blue sky, but the sun was actually shining and as long as she kept looking up she could almost believe that the devastating flood which had hit Penhally yesterday had never happened. Almost, but not quite.

'I suspected it might look pretty bad this morning,' Kate murmured, 'but I never for one minute…'

The midwife's voice trailed away into silence and Eve could understand her difficulty. Yesterday Penhally had been a picture-perfect village, full of people going about their daily business, but this morning the area around the harbour looked as though some malevolent giant had taken a hammer and smashed his way through the buildings, heaping boulders, trees, telephone poles and dustbins onto roofs, and tearing up roads and pavements in his relentless march onwards.

'I'm amazed the surgery wasn't touched, or any of our homes, apart from poor Chloe and Oliver's,' Eve observed. 'They're going to stay with Lauren, aren't they, until their house can be dried out?'

'*If* it can be dried out,' Kate said dubiously. 'Tom says all the houses can be made habitable again but when you look at this…I know the Lanson's flowing within its banks again, and somehow the Harbour Bridge is still intact, but one of Tom's men told me all of the houses have at least three feet of water and mud in them.'

'I suppose Tom's the expert,' Eve said uncertainly, though she had to admit she couldn't see how anyone could ever live in Bridge Street or Gull Close again either.

'I'm just so glad Tom is here,' Kate continued. 'I wouldn't have a clue about how to begin searching for the people who are missing, would you?'

Eve shook her head as she glanced over to where Tom was deep in conversation with Nick, Chief Constable D'Ancey and a group of men dressed in coveralls emblazoned with the Deltaron insignia. It wasn't a task she would have liked and, judging by the expression on Nick's face, Tom's suggestions weren't meeting with his approval, whereas Tom…

She shifted her gaze quickly towards some of the shopkeepers who were standing in dazed huddles outside their ruined shops. She didn't know what Tom was thinking, didn't want to be anywhere near him for fear he would look at her with the same condemnation and disgust as he had done yesterday.

'How's Stephanie Richards?' she asked, deliberately changing the subject.

'She and her son are doing very well,' Kate replied, 'though goodness knows where they're going to stay when they're discharged from hospital.'

'Oliver said the owners of the Penhally Paradise Caravan Park have offered some of their caravans as temporary accommodation for people who can't go back to their homes,' Eve observed. 'And Tony has offered the use of some of the bedrooms at Smugglers' Inn.'

'Did you hear he was still giving out orders while they were carrying him out to the helicopter?' The midwife shook her head. 'The man was having a heart attack, for God's sake, and yet he was still giving out orders.'

Eve laughed. 'One of a kind, Tony.'

'So is Tom.'

Kate's gaze was fixed on her, and Eve couldn't meet the midwife's eyes.

'He's certainly a good organiser,' she said noncommittally, and Kate sighed.

'Eve, whatever happened in the past, let it go. You can't alter it—change it—so let it go.'

'What has Nick been say—?'

'This has nothing to do with Nick,' Kate interrupted as Eve's eyes shot to hers in alarm, 'this is just me talking to you, one woman to another. We've all made mistakes—me, more than most—but you have to forgive yourself your mistakes or they will simply corrode your present and your future.'

Which was easy for Kate to say, Eve thought as her gaze went back to Tom, but she couldn't forgive herself. She had learned to live with what she'd done, but she had never forgiven herself and she never would. Tom hadn't resurrected the old pain. He had simply ripped off the unhealed scab, exposing the old wound for the ugliness it was.

'Which of you two lovelies is Eve Dwyer?'

A tall man, with flaming red hair and a bushy beard, was gazing at them quizzically, and Eve managed a smile.

'I'm Eve Dwyer.'

The man's eyebrows rose.

'Do I know you?' he asked. 'Your voice sounds strangely familiar.'

She recognised his voice, too. It was Mad Mitch or, to be more accurate, Michael Flannery, the pilot from the radio last night.

'I'm the woman Tom found in the men-only changing room,' she said before she could stop herself, and the pilot threw back his head, and laughed.

'Pleased to meet you in the flesh, so to speak,' he said. 'Tom would like a word.'

'With me?' Eve said faintly.

'With you.' The pilot nodded. 'He has a suggestion to make, and your boss isn't very happy about it.'

Kate's eyes gleamed.

'Now, this I want to hear,' she said, and carefully the midwife followed Eve over the rubble-strewn pavement towards where Tom was standing.

'So, what you're basically saying is, according to your engineer, most of the shops and houses should be habitable once the water and silt have been pumped out, but the Anchor Hotel is a writeoff?' they heard Chief Constable D'Ancey declare.

'I'm afraid so,' Tom replied. 'For the moment I'd recommend you erect scaffolding to ensure no more of it comes down, but after that I'd say you're pretty well definitely looking at a demolition job.'

'When are people going to be allowed back into their homes to collect their personal possessions?' Nick demanded. 'The police can't watch every house, and people are becoming understandably twitchy about their valuables.'

'They'll become considerably twitchier if they're electrocuted,' Tom said dryly. 'The electricity company isn't sure all power has been disconnected to the village, and until they are nobody enters any house apart from me and my men.'

'Yes, but—'

'Nick, if you want to be useful, go and open up the surgery,' Tom interrupted. 'With all this polluted water lying about I should imagine you'll be inundated with people requiring tetanus injections.'

'I don't take orders—'

'I've the press at my heels wanting to come into Penhally to take photographs,' Chief Constable D'Ancey declared, cutting across Nick who shot him a fulsome look. 'They're also very keen to do an interview with you.'

'I've more important things to do than give interviews,' Tom said tightly, 'and neither do I want photographers scrambling over the rubble in search of a story. Keep them out.'

Eve saw Nick's lip curl as the chief constable hurried off to forestall the members of the press. So, too, she noticed, had Tom, and quickly she cleared her throat.

'Mitch said you had a suggestion to make to me?' she said, and Tom nodded.

'At the moment, I'm the only medic on the rescue team,' he declared. 'We have spare medi-bags but they're no use without someone who knows how to use the contents, and I wondered if you'd like to help.'

'And *I* have said,' Nick exclaimed, 'if another medic is required then Oliver or I will volunteer. Eve is not a qualified rescue worker, or a doctor.'

'But she's a fully qualified nurse, and she's small, and there may be areas that only someone small will be able to get into,' Tom said, his voice calm but with an unmistakable hint of steel beneath it. 'And I would like Eve to help, if she's willing.'

'Eve is a member of my staff, and I will not agree to this,' Nick retorted.

'I don't think it's a question of whether you agree or not,' Tom began. 'Eve—'

'Can make up her own mind, thank you very much,' she interrupted, 'so would the two of you both park your testosterone to one side for the moment, and concentrate on what's really important?'

Tom's jaw dropped, Mitch Flannery smothered a wry chuckle, and Nick looked absolutely furious, but Kate laughed.

'Well said, Eve,' she declared. 'Nick, it's Eve's decision,' she continued quickly as the senior partner opened his mouth, clearly intending to continue the argument. 'If she wants to volunteer then surely it's her choice, not yours.'

Eve didn't have the faintest idea of what she might be volunteering for but she didn't care. All that mattered to her was that Tom had specifically asked for her. She hadn't expected him to—was amazed that he had—and if he was holding out any kind of olive branch she had no intention of rejecting it.

'I want to help,' she said firmly, and saw Tom's lips curve into a hesitant smile, a smile she returned equally tentatively.

'I am Eve's boss,' Nick declared angrily, 'and I still don't think—'

'I know you don't, Nick,' Kate interrupted, 'but right now we have a surgery to open.'

And, with a backward wink at Eve, the midwife towed a clearly reluctant Nick away leaving Eve standing awkwardly beside Tom and Mitch Flannery.

'Do we know how many people we're looking for?' she asked.

'Thankfully only three people still haven't been accounted for,' Tom replied. 'Reverend Kenner, Audrey Baxter and Sophie Banks.'

'Sophie?' Eve gasped. 'But—'

'She should have been at school.' Tom nodded. 'Her mother thought she was, and so she didn't worry about her, thinking she was safe with the other kids, and the school weren't concerned because they thought Sophie had been told to take the day off after she'd been to the surgery to see you.'

'And Reverend Kenner and Audrey Baxter?' Eve said.

'A neighbour saw Mrs Baxter leaving her house just before the river broke its banks,' Mitch Flannery declared. 'Reverend Kenner appeared to be trying to persuade her to go back into her house but, since then, there's been no sign of either of them.'

'Mitch, do we have any protective coveralls and thermals that would fit Eve?' Tom said, his gaze taking in her jeans, sweater and sturdy boots.

'I doubt we've anything small enough,' the pilot said dubiously. 'Gregory's our shortest man, but even he's a good four inches taller than this lass.'

Gregory was.

'If you laugh at me, you're a dead man,' Eve warned a little later, when Mitch led her back to Tom and she saw his lips twitch as his gaze took in her rolled-up sleeves and trouser legs.

'Would I laugh?' he protested, and she nodded.

'Without a second's thought,' she said, and heard Mitch guffaw.

'Keeper, Tom,' the pilot observed. 'Trust me, this one's a keeper.'

'A keeper of what?' Eve said in confusion but, for an answer, Tom placed a string round her neck with a whistle at the end.

'Blow once on this if you spot somebody alive, and blow twice if you see a body. It's standard rescue procedure,' he continued as she stared down at the whistle.

'Right,' she said, swallowing hard, and praying she would only have to blow once on the whistle as Tom called for his men's attention.

'Does everyone have a thermal imaging camera?' he asked and, when his question was greeted with a series of nods, he added, 'OK, Mitch, I want you and your men to survey Bridge Street. Gregory, you and your team will do Gull Close, Frank, you take Harbour Road. I'll do Fisherman's Row, and if anyone spots any signs of life, it's the usual drill.'

Obediently, the men split themselves into four groups but, as Tom began to move off, Eve tentatively put her hand on his arm.

'Why, Tom?'

To her relief he didn't pretend to misunderstand her.

'Because—as I said—you're a qualified nurse, and small, and because…' He lifted his shoulders awkwardly. 'Yesterday, I said some totally unforgivable things to you, and apologising… You know I'm not good with words. If you want cutting and cruel, then I was taught by the best, but saying I'm sorry…'

'You don't have to say anything,' she said softly, and saw a muscle clench in his cheek.

'I do, but now's not the time to discuss it. I just wanted you to know…' He bit his lip. 'Asking for you, I hoped maybe you might see…'

'An olive branch?' she said. 'Seen, and accepted, Tom. Now, tell me how these thermal imaging cameras work.'

For a second he gazed at her silently, then he smiled.

'You're something else, Eve Dwyer.'

'Lippy, irritating, argumentative—yeah, I know,' she said lightly, unnerved by the intensity of his gaze, 'and you still haven't told me what a thermal imaging camera does.'

His smile widened.

'They detect and produce images of radiation, and since infrared radiation is emitted by all objects based on their temperatures, warm objects stand out well against cool backgrounds so humans and other warm-blooded animals become easily visible whether it's day or night.'

'Clever,' she said with admiration.

'Very.' He nodded, then his smile faded. 'Of course they can only pick up images of living things.'

'You think…' She swallowed. 'You think they might all be dead?'

'I think we have to be prepared for that given the silence.'

'The silence?' she repeated.

'Eve, if you were trapped, what would you be doing?'

'I'd be… Oh, I see,' she said with dawning comprehension. 'I'd be yelling my head off to attract attention, but nobody's yelling.'

'Exactly.'

She hoped he was wrong. She hoped it even more as the morning crept by with a painstaking slowness she found frustrating as Tom and his men scanned every square foot of rubble in Fisherman's Row with their cameras, and then checked and double-checked the results with a sound detector and fibreoptic probe.

'You thought a rescue operation would be a lot more exciting,' he observed with a slight smile, correctly reading her mind when he ordered his men to take a break. 'With people rushing from place to place.'

She coloured. 'I suppose so.'

'Sometimes it's like that,' he admitted. 'If a lot of people are trapped you can come upon them quite quickly, but when it's just three we have to take it slowly in case we miss something, plus there are a lot of potential hazards. Standing water can be electrically charged from underground or downed power lines, and we don't know how much untreated raw sewage there is in the water, not to mention the biohazards of dead animals, rotting food and liquid petroleum gases.'

She shivered as she stared up at the water line which showed how high the floodwater had reached in Fisherman's Row, and she knew it had been even higher in Bridge Street and Gull Close.

'I don't know how you can do this over and over again.'

'Somebody has to,' Tom observed.

'I know, but…'

She shivered again and, as though on cue, one of Tom's men appeared carrying a tray of steaming white polystyrene cups.

'What's this?' she asked, screwing up her nose after she'd taken a sip.

'Hot water, with three sugars,' the man replied, and she grimaced.

'I'd rather have a coffee,' she observed, and Tom grinned.

'Wouldn't we all, but both coffee and tea have caffeine in them, and that's a no-no because caffeine dehydrates you, and as we're all dehydrating rather a lot because we're sweating we don't want to add to it.'

'I'd still rather have a coffee,' she said with feeling as she sipped the hot water. 'Do you suppose…?' She came to a halt, seeing a dog appear at the top of Fisherman's Row. 'Tom, isn't that Foxy—Audrey's dog?'

He nodded as his eyes followed hers.

'Which would suggest Audrey is somewhere nearby. Dogs have a much more highly developed sense of smell than we do, and... Oh, hell.'

'What?' Eve said, in confusion, seeing Tom throw down his polystyrene cup, his face grim.

'He's pawing at the rubble by the Anchor Hotel. I think we may have found Audrey.'

They'd also found Reverend Kenner, too.

'My guess is the lady lost her footing when the river burst its banks,' Mitch declared. 'The reverend was holding her round the waist, so I'd say he was trying to keep her head above water, and then the outer wall of the hotel came down on them.'

Foxy was howling at the top of his lungs, desperately trying to get to his mistress, and Eve turned away quickly, not wanting anyone to see the tears that had filled her eyes at the sight of the two covered bodies lying on stretchers, but an arm came round her shoulders instantly.

'I shouldn't have asked you to do this,' Tom murmured. 'I'll get Mitch to take you back to the surgery.'

'No,' Eve insisted, wiping her sleeve across her eyes. 'Sophie is still missing so I'm not giving up. I just need...' Her voice became suspended, and she took a ragged breath. 'Why, Tom? Daniel Kenner... He was such a good man, such a kind man, and now Rachel has no father, her child will have no grandfather, and Audrey... Yes, she was a gossip, but to die like that... Why do some people live, and some people die, Tom?'

'An old Buddhist monk once told me that for some people it's simply their time,' Tom said, drawing her closer.

'It isn't for everyone—not always,' she said with difficulty, and she knew he understood what she meant because she felt his chin come to rest on the top of her head.

'Sufficient unto the day, Eve,' he said, his voice as uneven as hers. 'Sometimes that's all any of us can hold on to.'

'Tom, I…' She looked up at him, begging him to believe her, to understand. 'I didn't want to do it. Our baby. I truly didn't want to do it.'

'I know,' he said, his voice thick. Gently, he smoothed her hair back from her face with his fingers. 'Eve…' A loud blast from a whistle rent the air, and he turned towards it immediately. 'Someone's found a live one.'

He and Mitch were off and running before Eve could say anything, and by the time she'd caught up with them near the top of Bridge Street they were already deep in conversation with the man Tom had called Gregory.

'Is it Sophie?' she asked breathlessly as she stumbled to a halt beside them.

'Yes.'

Something about Tom's tone made her heart clutch.

'But I thought— One blast of the whistle—doesn't that mean she's alive?' she said.

'She is, but she's in big trouble,' Tom replied.

'I have glucagon in here,' Eve said, opening the medi-bag that Mitch had given her. 'If her blood-sugar levels are too low, and she's become hypoglycaemic—'

'She had the presence of mind to keep taking her glucagon, at least at the beginning,' Tom interrupted, 'but she was spending her day off school hiding out in one of the concrete sheds at the back of Bridge Street. That's why it's taken us so long to find her because Mitch and his men were concentrating on scanning the houses first.'

'And?' Eve demanded, wishing he would get to the point.

'When the shed flooded, part of it came down trapping Sophie by her leg.'

And not just trapping her by the leg, Eve realised when she followed the men down the narrow alley way to get to the back of the houses in Bridge Street. The piece of concrete had also come down at a right angle so all that was visible of the teenager was her head and upper body, and only somebody small would have any chance of being able to crawl close enough to her to assess her medical condition.

'It will have to be me, won't it?' Eve declared, cutting right across Mitch and Tom as they discussed how Tom might reach the girl. 'Look, you said one of the reasons you wanted me was because I'm a fully qualified nurse, and I'm small,' she continued, seeing Tom's eyebrows snap down, 'so it has to be me, doesn't it?'

'But if the rest of the shed comes down…' Tom said, indecision plain on his face.

'Tom, the longer we stand here debating this, the more likely it is that it *will* come down,' she said.

'She's right, Tom,' Mitch declared, and Eve saw Tom's eyebrows knit together still further.

'OK,' he said with clear reluctance, 'but if the shed begins to move I want your promise you'll get out of there.'

'I promise,' Eve said.

'Show me your hands.'

'What?'

'Eve, I know you've got your fingers crossed behind your back,' he declared, 'so let me see your hands when you promise.'

'OK—OK—I promise, no fingers crossed, and now can we get on with this?' she exclaimed, but she didn't feel anything like as confident when she began crawling under the concrete to get to the teenager.

Not only was the space a lot smaller than it looked, the water was filthy, and when she felt something brush against her leg and realised it was a dead rat, it took all of her self-control not to scuttle back out and run screaming from the building.

'Are you OK?' Tom called when she let out a gasp and Eve gritted her teeth until they hurt.

'Fine,' she said, but she felt even less fine after she'd examined the teenager.

Sophie was barely conscious and didn't even seem to be aware she was there and with a temperature of 91°F, and a GCS of 3-3-4, the girl was very ill indeed.

'I think she must be losing a lot of blood from her leg,' Eve said, and saw Tom shake his head.

'I think she's losing some, but not enough to cause those Glasgow coma scale results,' he replied. 'My guess is the main problem is she's been lying in freezing water for the past twenty-one hours.'

'A thermic lance,' Mitch declared. 'It's the only way, Tom.'

'What's a thermic lance?' Eve asked, glancing from Mitch to Tom, and it was Tom who answered.

'Basically, it's a long iron tube packed with a mixture of iron and aluminum rods. We feed oxygen through the tube, and when it's lit, it produces an intense flame that can cut through steel and concrete, but...'

'But?' Eve prompted.

'I don't know whether it will be able to cut through fast enough,' Tom said, 'and if it does whether the two halves will split away from her leg or impact down on her.'

'Tom, if we don't do something soon I think the question of what way the concrete might fall will be academic,' Eve replied. 'Her temperature's falling all the time.'

'OK, we use the thermic lance,' he said. 'Try to keep her awake, Eve. Sing to her—talk to her—but somehow keep her awake.'

It was easier said than done, Eve thought as Tom and Mitch began using the thermic lance to cut through the concrete that was pinning Sophie to the floor. Never had time seemed to pass so slowly as she crouched beneath the concrete, talking about everything and nothing while Sophie became increasingly unresponsive.

'Tom, her pulse ox is 80, her temperature's now 88, and she's not shivering any more,' Eve reported.

Because Sophie was developing hypothermia.

Neither she nor Tom said it, but they both knew it, and if Sophie's temperature continued to fall she'd start developing cardiac arrhythmias, then her heart would begin to fibrillate, and if her temperature slipped below 82°F there would be no way back for her.

'Fifteen minutes,' Tom replied in answer to Eve's unspoken question. 'We should be through the concrete in fifteen minutes.'

'Tom, I don't think she's going to hold on for fifteen minutes,' Eve said, and he let out a colourful oath.

'I know,' he exclaimed, 'but my only other alternative is to amputate her leg, and she's a kid, Eve, just a kid.'

But Sophie was going to die if she stayed in this water for much longer, Eve thought, and her feelings must have been all too apparent, because Tom thrust a dirt-grimed hand through his hair.

'Five minutes, Eve. Five minutes, and if we're no further forward, we amputate.'

She nodded and, as the seconds ticked by, she prayed as she had never prayed before. Prayed that the concrete would split in two soon. Prayed that Sophie would survive because there was no guarantee, no matter what they did, that she would. The girl was virtually comatose now, and her lips were beginning to turn blue which was a sure sign of cyanosis.

'It's moving, Tom,' Mitch shouted. 'The bloody thing's finally moving!'

Without a word Tom immediately crawled as far under the concrete as he could get, and Eve knew why. If the concrete fell on them he intended taking the full brunt of the fall, and her heart stopped for a second at the thought of him being crushed, of him dying in front of her eyes, and then—miraculously—

she saw a rush of bubbles in the water and Sophie sagged in her arms.

'She's free—I think she's free,' she declared, holding onto the girl for all she was worth, and Tom scrambled to his feet and splashed through the water towards her.

'Mitch, where's your chopper?' he demanded as he gripped Sophie under the armpits.

'The playing fields,' the pilot replied.

'Crank it up. This girl needs a hospital, and fast.'

Mitch couldn't have been faster. Within a short time he had Sophie and Tom airborne and in less than half an hour the girl was being admitted to St Piran's Hospital.

'Tom and his men—they're quite something, aren't they?' Lauren said when Eve told her about it later. 'It's not a job I'd like to do, but if I was ever in trouble I'd want the men from Deltaron coming over the horizon.'

And especially Tom, Eve thought as she helped the physiotherapist ensure that those who had sheltered in the school hall last night, and those who had taken refuge in The Smugglers', had all been allocated temporary accommodation in order to leave the hall free for Tom's men. He must have been exhausted when Mitch brought him back to Penhally but he'd stopped only long enough to tell them that the A and E consultant was hopeful Sophie would make a complete recovery and then he'd gone back out onto the streets with his men.

'I just wish I could find somewhere other than Harbour View for Miss Stanbury to stay in temporarily,' Lauren continued. 'There's no room left at The Smugglers', and I've put my foot down over a caravan, but she's such an independent woman, and staying in the nursing-home even for a short time... The last thing I want is her losing confidence in her ability to cope.'

'Who's losing confidence?'

Eve turned quickly at the familiar voice, and try as she may she couldn't prevent her heart lifting when she saw Tom smiling down at her.

'It's Miss Stanbury,' Lauren said, and after she'd explained the situation Tom shook his head.

'Not a nursing-home, not for Gertie. She can stay in my father's house in Trelissa Road. It's fully furnished, so she'll be quite snug and comfortable until her own home dries out.'

'Are you sure?' Lauren declared. 'I mean, lovely lady though Miss Stanbury is, I don't know what she would be like to share a house with and you'll be staying in your father's house yourself, won't you, now that the Anchor Hotel is uninhabitable?'

'Actually I won't,' he replied. 'I've made other arrangements.'

'Really?' Lauren exclaimed and, when Tom nodded, she beamed. 'Then you must come and tell her about your kind offer. She'll be so grateful.'

'Can't you tell her?' he said, already beginning to back awkwardly towards the school-hall door. 'I'm a bit tired—thought I might just head off, grab some sleep.'

He was out of the hall before Lauren could say anything else, and Eve laughed when she caught up with him.

'You fraud,' she declared. 'You just don't like people thanking you, do you?'

To her surprise, a faint wash of colour appeared on his cheeks.

'Not really, no.'

'And what are these other arrangements you've made?' she demanded, and saw Tom give a shamefaced grin.

'None, to be honest, but I can think of nothing I'd like less than staying in my father's old house, plus Gertie did me a good turn in the past and I figure it's time I repaid the debt. I can sleep in the hall with my men. It's no big deal, Eve,' he continued as she began to protest. 'I'll be perfectly fine.'

'I'm sure you will but not when there's an alternative,' she said firmly. 'My house has two bedrooms and you're more than welcome to use one of them. If…if you want to, that is,' she added, feeling her cheeks heat up when he stared at her in obvious surprise.

'I'd love to,' he said, 'but have you considered what people might say?'

'Tom, half of Penhally is covered in mud, silt and boulders. Half of the population are either sleeping with friends, or in a caravan, or at The Smugglers'. If anyone has the time or the energy to check up on where you're staying, then they need to get a life.'

He laughed.

'Well, if you're sure?'

'I'm sure,' she said. 'I can't offer you much to eat, but…' Her gaze took in his dirt-smeared face and hair, and bloodshot and weary eyes. 'I can offer you a bath.'

'You can heat water?' he said, his eyes lighting up, and she nodded.

'My dad installed a generator years back. He said he didn't much care if he couldn't watch TV when we had a power cut, but he was damned if he was going to sit in the dark, unable to have a bath.' She took a deep breath. 'I only have one condition to make.'

Tom grinned. 'Don't use all the hot water?'

She smiled. 'OK, two conditions. Don't use all the hot water, and…' Her smile faded. 'We don't talk about…about the baby. I know you want to,' she added quickly, seeing a flash of pain in his eyes, 'and I know we have to but, please, not tonight.'

He looked at her for a long moment, then smiled slightly crookedly.

'OK, not tonight,' he said.

'How do you feel now?' Eve asked when Tom joined her some time later in her small sitting room.

'A lot cleaner, that's for sure,' he said. 'I used some of your shampoo—I hope that was OK. Unfortunately you don't seem to have a razor so I couldn't get rid of this,' he added, rubbing his hand over the stubble on his chin, 'which means you'll have to put up with me looking scruffy.'

Or downright sexy, she thought, and stamped on the thought quickly as she put another log on the fire.

'Lauren and Chloe organised a clothes and general toiletries collection today for the people who can't get back into their homes,' she said. 'I should have thought to ask them to make up a bag for you, but I'm afraid I forgot you must have lost everything in the Anchor.'

'It doesn't matter,' he said dismissively. 'I've my wallet and my car keys. Everything else can be replaced.' He looked round awkwardly. 'Is there anything I can do—something to help?'

Aside from trying not to look quite so big, or so very immediate? she thought, but she didn't say that.

'Not really,' she said instead. 'I thought I would just heat up some soup, put it into a couple of mugs, and we could have it in here. It's warmer by the fire than in the kitchen.'

'Sounds good to me.' He nodded. 'Has Rachel Kenner been told about her father?'

'Nick went to see her this afternoon. As you can imagine…' Eve shook her head. 'It wasn't very pleasant, but Rachel's aunt and uncle have come over from Plymouth to stay with her. Audrey had no immediate family, but she had a sister who lives in Devon and we're trying to trace her.'

He sat down on the sofa and let his head fall back against it.

'God, but I'm tired.'

He looked tired. He also looked rumpled, and sloppy, and more attractive than any man had any right to be, and she put another log on the fire even though it didn't need it.

'When do you think they'll be able to restore the electricity to the village?' she asked.

'Perhaps tomorrow. Then we can send in the fire brigade to begin draining the houses, and my work will be done.'

And I'll leave.

He hadn't said the words, he didn't need to, and of course he would leave. He was only still here in Penhally because of the flood so it had been stupid of her heart to dip at his words but she couldn't deny it had dipped.

'Eve?'

He was gazing at her questioningly, and she forced herself to smile.

'I'll get the soup,' she said, but when she went into the kitchen she leant against the table and closed her eyes.

How had he managed to slip so easily back into her life? She'd always sworn she'd never let him get close to her again and yet, within the space of a few short days, it was almost as though he'd never been away, but he was going to leave again as he'd done before, and she was going to be alone again as she had been before.

Which was how it had to be, she told herself. Yes, she felt the old attraction—he had been right about that—but there was too much hurt and pain between them now and, even if he could eventually forgive her for what she had done, he had his life, and she had hers, and their time was past.

Except it wasn't that easy, she realised, when she went back into the sitting room with their soup and she found him fast asleep on the sofa.

Twenty years. It had been twenty years since they'd last met, and yet she only had to see him like this, his face so tired in the firelight, his hair still damp from his bath, his eyelashes dark against his skin, and she wanted him all over again. Wanted to go to him, to wrap her arms around him, to have him hold her as he used to.

You can't go back, Eve, her heart whispered, and yet before she could stop herself she had carefully put the soup down on the mantelpiece, and just as carefully stretched out her hand, meaning only to smooth his hair back from his forehead, but he was a light sleeper and his eyes flew open with a start.

'I'm sorry,' she said awkwardly, backing up a step. 'I didn't mean to wake you.'

'It's just as well you did,' he said ruefully. 'I never could fall asleep in a chair without waking up with an infernal crick in my neck.'

'Snap.' She laughed as she handed him a mug of soup, but to her surprise he didn't join in her laughter.

Instead, he stared down at his soup, then up at her.

'I'm thinking of resigning from Deltaron, Eve. Maybe going into general practice.'

Her mouth fell open, then she shook her head.

'Tom, you'd be bored witless in under a week,' she protested. 'You're used to immediacy, constant change. I know you said you were worried you were ceasing to care but, believe me, GP work is not for you.'

'Perhaps not,' he murmured, his face all dark planes and shadows in the firelight. 'But… I used to get such a buzz from the danger, Eve, from pitting myself against the elements—fire, flood, earthquake—and yet now… All the time I'm thinking, What if I get it wrong, make a mistake, miscalculate?'

'You haven't yet.'

His face darkened still further.

'I have.'

His voice was so low she barely heard him, and for a second she hesitated then she sat down on the sofa beside him.

'What happened, Tom?'

She didn't think he was going to answer, then he put his soup down on the floor beside him and gripped his knees.

'We were sent to India last year to help out after a very bad earthquake. The village we were assigned to had been pretty well flattened, but one house was still standing, and we could hear people calling for help from inside it. I knew…' Tom took in an uneven breath. 'I knew the house was unstable, that it could go at any minute, but I could hear kids crying so I took the gamble it would hold.'

She reached out and laced one of her hands with his, and held it tightly.

'Go on,' she said.

'Charlie Dobbs, the other medic on the team, and I went in,' he continued with an effort. 'We'd just reached the kids—I had actually caught hold of one of their hands—and the house collapsed. I was pulled out alive, but Charlie, the people, the kids, they were all killed.'

'It wasn't your fault, Tom,' she said softly. 'You were trying to give them a chance, and Charlie… He would have known the risks, just as you did.'

'That's what the head of Deltaron said,' he declared, his eyes desolate, 'but I keep thinking if I'd done it differently, maybe tried to shore up the house, maybe waited…'

'You did what you thought was right at the time, Tom,' she said, hating to see the torment in his eyes. 'That's all anybody can do.'

'I went to Charlie's funeral,' he continued as though she hadn't spoken. 'Deltaron flew his body back to the States, so I went to his funeral and there was nobody there but me and the minister. He had no brothers or sisters, and his parents were both dead, so it was just me and the minister standing at the graveside, and I thought…' He swallowed. 'I thought, One day that's going to be me.'

'No, it won't,' she insisted, but he shook his head.

'It will, Eve. I've given my whole life to the company, just as Charlie did, so one day I'll be buried with no one there to mourn me, nobody who cares enough about me to come and say goodbye.'

'I'll come, Tom,' she said, her lip trembling. 'You wouldn't be alone. I'd come.'

'But you wouldn't know, Eve,' he said, his eyes meeting hers, dark and empty. 'You'd be here in Penhally, and I could be anywhere in the world.'

'Tom—'

'Eve, there's something I have to tell you,' he interrupted. 'Something I want you to know. Do you remember when I said I had two reasons for coming back to Penhally? Well, the other reason…' He came to a halt with a muttered oath as his mobile phone began to ring, and impatiently he pulled it from his pocket, checked the caller ID, then punched the answer button. 'Mitch, this had better be important,' he said.

It clearly was, Eve thought as she watched the frown lines on Tom's forehead deepen at whatever the pilot was saying, and when the call was over Tom immediately got to his feet.

'Bad news?' she said uncertainly.

'They've found a fractured gas main in Gull Close,' he replied. 'I have to go.'

'But you're exhausted,' she protested, 'and you're not an engineer. Can't somebody else deal with it?'

'I'm the boss, Eve, so I have to be there. Don't wait up for me. I don't know how long I'm going to be.'

'Right,' she said, then added quickly before she could stop herself, 'Be careful.'

'I fully intend to,' he said with a small smile, 'because we have a conversation to finish, and I intend finishing it.'

And, to her surprise, he bent down and kissed her lightly on the forehead, then strode out of her sitting room, leaving her gazing open-mouthed after him.

CHAPTER SEVEN

THE WAITING room was crammed to overflowing with press people, and each and every one of them seemed to be armed with a camera, a notebook and an apparently unending supply of stupid questions.

'I wonder how long it's going to be before Nick hits someone,' Dragan murmured as he and Eve stood outside in the surgery corridor watching Tom, Nick, and Chief Constable D'Ancey field questions.

'I should imagine just until one of those reporters asks him—yet again—whether he's sure there's only been two fatalities,' Eve said dryly.

'Or maybe until someone asks him for yet another photograph of him and Tom shaking hands,' Dragan declared, and Eve let out a small choke of laughter.

'Yup, I reckon that would probably do it.'

'Ghouls,' Dragan said with distaste. 'The whole pack of them are nothing but ghouls. The paparazzi came out in droves when they found out about Melinda and me, but this…' He shook his head. 'I don't know how Tom keeps his temper when you consider how many of these press conferences he must have taken part in.'

'I suppose because he has to,' Eve murmured, glancing back into the waiting room and seeing Tom wearily rotate his shoulders, his face a carefully arranged expressionless mask. 'I think Tom has learned to do a lot of things because he has to.'

Including having to accept he wasn't God, she thought sadly, with all the attendant heartbreak that knowledge could bring.

'Looks like Nick's just reached breaking point,' Dragan said when the senior partner suddenly stood up, his face dark and stormy. 'Yup, he's reached it, and I think he's actually passed it.'

The senior partner had. With an angry nod at Chief Constable D'Ancey, Nick strode out of the waiting room without a backward glance and, when he went into his consulting room, he slammed the door so hard it shuddered.

'It doesn't look as though Nick has enjoyed his encounter with the members of the press, does it?' Kate said, her eyes dancing as she joined them.

'Perhaps it will teach him to have a little more sympathy for Tom in future,' Eve replied before she could stop herself, and the midwife laughed.

'We can but hope,' she said. 'Do you think we might be able to get on with afternoon surgery soon?' she continued as the press began to file out of the waiting room. 'I know the press is entitled to a story, but we've told them all we know, and what we need now is to try to get back to some sort of normality, and that means seeing patients.'

'I couldn't agree more,' Dragan replied, 'and in that spirit I'll be in my consulting room if anyone wants me.'

'And I'll be in my examination room,' Kate declared as Dragan disappeared, 'hoping at least some of my mums-to-be manage to make it down for their prenatal check-ups.'

'Is the embargo on evening home visits still in place?' Eve asked, and Kate sighed.

'Nick is adamant that unless it's an emergency none of us are to be out after dark, and he's even more against it since Lauren took a tumble yesterday. I know it makes sense,' Kate continued. 'Some of the pavements and roads in Penhally are lethal, but I have quite a few my mums-to-be who can't come in during the day because they're at work.'

'Do you think…?' Eve began, then stopped. Chloe and Oliver were walking down the corridor towards them and it was obvious from the woman's stricken countenance that something was badly wrong. 'Chloe, are you all right?'

'She insisted I take her down to Fisherman's Row this morning,' Oliver replied, 'and she's a bit upset by what she saw.'

'Chloe, your home can be repaired,' Eve said quickly. 'Tom said once all the mud and silt have been pumped out—'

'It's not the house,' Chloe interrupted. 'That's just bricks and mortar, but Cyclops and Pirate… Eve, there's no sign of them, anywhere.'

'Cats have nine lives, babe, you know that,' her fiancé said, putting his arm around her and giving her a hug. 'They're probably just hiding out some place, too scared to come home.'

'Truly?' Chloe said, and, when Oliver nodded, she gave a wobbly smile. 'You think I'm being stupid, don't you?'

'Babe, you could never be stupid,' he said gently. 'They'll be fine. I know they will.'

But he wasn't, Eve knew, as Chloe and Kate hurried away to start their afternoon clinic, and she knew why. The water level in Oliver and Chloe's home must have reached nine feet at the flood's height, and neither Cyclops nor Pirate were robust cats.

'What's the matter with Chloe?' Tom asked as he joined them. 'She looks as though she's lost a pound and found a penny.'

'It's her cats,' Eve replied and, after she'd explained, Tom frowned.

'So, Cyclops is a ginger cat and only has one eye, and Pirate is white with a black patch over one eye. OK, I'll ask my men to keep a special watch out for them.'

'Yeah, right,' Oliver muttered, but Tom heard him.

'Oliver, I know your opinion of me is about as low as it can be,' he said without heat, 'but when I make a promise I keep it.'

'Right,' Oliver said, his cheeks darkening slightly. 'Sorry,' he added, but as Tom turned to go, the junior doctor held out his hand to stay him. 'Look, I truly am sorry, Tom, and not just for the cats. On the night of the flood, I said some pretty appalling things to you—'

'Forget it,' Tom interrupted.

'Yes, but—'

'Forget it,' Tom repeated. 'We were all a bit fraught that night, and if someone I loved had been missing I would have behaved exactly as you did.'

'Yes, well…' Oliver thrust his fingers through his hair awkwardly. 'It's good of you to say so, and considerably more than I deserve. If your men do find the cats, and they're dead, could you tell me first? I don't want Chloe to see them looking… messed up. She…' His shoulders lifted helplessly. 'They mean so much to her, you see.'

'Not a problem,' Tom replied but, after Oliver had gone, Eve folded her arms across her chest and shook her head at him.

'He owes you a much bigger apology than that,' she said, and saw one corner of Tom's mouth lift.

'Eve, people say things in the heat of the moment, and I have broad enough shoulders and a thick enough skin to cope with it. Oliver was worried sick about Chloe that night, and if I'd been in his shoes I would probably have said a hell of a lot more.'

'Even so,' she protested, 'I still feel—'

'Plus, I hardly think I'm in a position to criticise somebody else's thoughtless words, do you?' he interrupted.

His eyes were fixed on her, and she felt a faint wash of colour creep across her cheeks.

'Tom…'

'I know.' He nodded. 'Not here, not now, but we're going to have to talk about it some time, Eve.'

She knew they would, but she didn't want to talk about it because talking changed nothing, altered nothing. Talking simply meant she had to relive it again, and she'd relived it so often in her mind—regretted it so often.

'Do you know what's going to happen to Audrey's dog, Foxy?' she said, deliberately changing the subject, and knew from the way Tom shook his head that he wasn't deceived for a second.

'The RSPCA is looking after him at the moment,' he replied, 'but to be honest they're a bit worried about him. He's not eaten anything since they picked him up, and there's no doubt he's going to be difficult to rehome because people generally want puppies, not older dogs. I'd take him myself, but the RSPCA say he's wary of men, plus a dog really shouldn't have a globe-trotting owner. Maybe if I had a wife, a family…'

His words hung in the air between them, and Eve plucked at a loose thread on her sleeve.

'I hope you find someone one day, Tom,' she murmured. 'You deserve to be happy.'

'But you don't think you do.'

The unexpectedness of his comment completely threw her.

'Of—of course I deserve to be happy,' she stammered, 'and I *am* happy. I have my work, and Tassie, and…' Desperately she tried to think of something else that made her happy but to her dismay her mind seemed suddenly blank. 'I'm *happy*, Tom.'

'Eve, you need more in your life than your work, and looking after someone else's child once a week,' he said gently, 'but until you let go of the past, move on, you're not going to believe that. You're going to continue to keep people at arm's length because you don't think you're entitled to happiness.'

'I— You—you're talking nonsense,' she said vehemently. 'You're making it sound as though—'

She didn't get an opportunity to finish what she'd been about to say. Dragan had appeared, looking white-faced and tense.

'I've just had a phone call from Melinda,' he said unevenly. 'Her waters have broken. She's having the baby, Eve, and it's two weeks early.'

'Which is no time at all,' she said soothingly. 'In fact, she probably got her dates wrong—it's not uncommon.'

'Right,' he said, though Eve doubted whether he'd actually heard her. 'I need to go to her, but I have surgery this afternoon— My patients—'

'I'll take your place,' Tom interrupted. 'I'm a fully qualified doctor, remember, and I'm sure Nick wouldn't object.'

To Eve's amazement the senior partner didn't. He simply gave Tom a long, appraising stare, then nodded.

'Just so long as you realise what you're letting yourself in for,' he said. 'General practice is not for everyone.'

'Then it's OK if I go?' Dragan said, clearly anxious to leave, and Nick gave him a gentle push with his finger.

'Of course you can go, you idiot. Give Melinda my best, and try not to faint. It reflects badly on the practice.'

Quickly, Dragan strode to the door, then came back and gripped Tom's hands.

'Bog te blagoslovio!' the Croatian doctor exclaimed. *'Hvala*, Tom. I just want to say—*hvala.'*

'Do you have any idea what he said?' Tom asked, bemused, when Dragan had rushed away.

'I imagine he was thanking you,' Eve declared, 'but I'm afraid I can't give you an exact translation as I don't speak Croatian.'

Tom grinned. 'In which case he could have been telling me in no uncertain terms to…um…remove myself.'

'Maybe somebody should,' she muttered, and walked off to her examination room, but Tom came after her.

'Eve, what I said earlier—about you needing to move on— I'm sorry if you feel I spoke out of turn.'

If, she thought angrily. How dared he imply—suggest—she was some lonely, unhappy woman, stuck in the past, who had spent the last twenty years punishing herself for what she'd done? She may not be able to forgive herself, but she'd created a full life, a satisfying life, and she was on her own through choice. Not everyone met someone they wanted to spend the rest of their life with. A lot of luck was involved, like being in the right place at the right time.

Like you and Tom, her heart whispered, and she crushed down the thought immediately.

'As you appear to make a habit of speaking out of turn, I don't suppose I should be surprised,' she said tightly.

'Eve, I was only speaking as I see it,' he protested, and she shook her head.

'Isn't that what people with big mouths, and even bigger egos, usually say to justify sticking their noses into other people's business?'

He opened his mouth, then closed it again.

'Fair point,' he declared. 'In future I will button my lip whenever I feel the urge to make any kind of observation.'

'You couldn't button your lip if your life depended on it!' she exclaimed, and saw his eyes twinkle.

'No, but I'm prepared to swear anything to get back into your good graces.'

He was gazing at her with a quite ludicrously hangdog expression, and anger warred with amusement inside her for a moment and amusement won.

'You're impossible, Tom Cornish. You know that, don't you?' she said.

'Yup.' He grinned. 'But I got you to laugh.'

'I don't think you're going to be laughing by the end of this afternoon,' she observed. 'In fact… Look, are you sure you know what you're doing—volunteering to take Dragan's clinic?'

He groaned. 'Not you, too. It's bad enough having Nick doubt my professional capabilities—'

'It's not your professional capabilities I'm worried about,' she interrupted, 'and I don't think it's what Nick is concerned about either. It's been a long time since you've met "ordinary" members of the public, Tom, and I think you're in for quite an eye-opener.'

Tom rolled his eyes with exasperation, but it didn't take him long to discover both she and Nick were right. He could tolerate the stream of people he saw that afternoon who had met with unfortunate accidents due to the uneven roads and pavements, but what he found impossible to cope with were the people who appeared to have blithely ignored every health leaflet Nick had sent out, and now felt distinctly aggrieved because they weren't feeling well.

'Is it my imagination or is the entire world populated by complete idiots?' he demanded, by the end of the afternoon. 'There's been a flood, the water supply has been contaminated, Nick has issued leaflets advising people to drink bottled water, and yet what do some people do?'

'You tell me,' Eve said, her lips twitching as her gaze took in his distinctly frazzled expression.

'They drink water out of the tap,' Tom retorted. 'They come in here, saying, "I thought it looked all right, Doctor, and now I've got a fever, and a really bad headache." Well, of course they have. The prats have contracted Weil's disease.'

'And did you tell them they were prats?' Eve asked, controlling the laughter she could feel bubbling up inside her with difficulty.

'No, but it was a close-run thing,' he admitted. 'And do you know how many people I saw this afternoon who decided it would be a whiz bang idea to light a camp stove to speed up the drying out of their houses?' he continued. '*Three*, Eve. That's three idiots who now have carbon-monoxide poisoning because they were too lazy, or too dim, to read the warning leaflets which specifically said the fumes from charcoal were deadly.'

'Oh, dear,' she said unevenly, and he gave her a hard stare.

'It is *not* funny, Eve.'

'The illnesses certainly aren't, but your face sure is,' she said with a peal of laughter. 'I'm sorry, Tom. It's not fair of me to mock,' she continued as his eyebrows snapped together, 'but Nick and I did try to warn you that general practice wasn't for you.'

He thrust his fingers through his hair, making it stand out all over the place, then smiled reluctantly.

'OK—all right—so you were both right, and I was wrong. Maybe becoming a GP would be a bad career move for me.'

'If you were on the verge of strangling the patients you saw after just one afternoon, then it sure would be,' she replied. 'Deltaron is where you belong, Tom. I think you need a break—a long holiday—but I think Deltaron is where you're meant to be.'

'But only if I get myself a life outside my work, just as you should.'

The smile on her face disappeared.

'I thought we agreed this subject was a no-go area?'

'Can't blame a bloke from trying.' He grinned, and she shook her head at him.

'You're completely incorrigible.'

'I think that was one of the nicer things Gertie Stanbury used to say about me when I was at school,' he replied. 'In fact—'

'The very person I wanted to see,' Lauren interrupted as she came out of her physiotherapy room and saw them. 'Tom, I have Miss Stanbury with me, and she'd very much like to thank you personally for the loan of your house.'

That he didn't want to be thanked was plain. In fact, he had the look of a man who would have preferred to have his toenails pulled out, but Eve wasn't going to let him get away with it, at least not this time.

'Tom, if she wants to thank you, you have to let her,' she

declared, and she saw reluctance and unwillingness war with each other on his face for a second, then he sighed.

'OK—all right,' he said.

'And I dare you to call her Gertie to her face,' Eve added in an undertone as she followed him down the corridor.

'Are you kidding?' he protested. 'I want to live to be fifty.'

Eve didn't think the elderly lady would have cared what Tom called her. She was far too overwhelmed by his generosity.

'It's almost like being at home,' she said, her small face wreathed in smiles, 'and I can't thank you enough for allowing me to stay there. I just hope I'm not inconveniencing you.'

'Not in the slightest,' Tom insisted. 'Stay for as long as you like, and most definitely until your own home is habitable again.'

'Amanda Lovelace drove me round to Gull Close this morning,' Gertrude continued. 'Seeing it… I can't believe Tassie and I got out of there alive.'

'It's not going to always look like that, Miss Stanbury,' Tom said softly, seeing the stricken look that had suddenly appeared in her eyes. 'Once the fire brigade has pumped out the water, and it's been dried out, you'll soon have it looking as it did before.'

'I just wish I'd thought to take my papers and photographs with me when I went up into the attic,' she said. 'When I looked in the window, they were all there—floating about in the water.'

'Miss Stanbury—'

'I know—I know,' she interrupted as Tom looked at her with concern. 'The most important thing is Tassie and I are here to tell the tale. As for my photographs, papers…' Her lip trembled slightly, and she firmed it. 'Not important.'

Tom hunkered down on his heels in front of her, his green eyes soft with understanding.

'You haven't lost them,' he said. 'If this was the summer we could air-dry them for you in a trice but at the moment what we need is a freezer. If we can find someone with a big freezer, all we need to do is to pop your photographs and papers in, freeze them, and they can be air-dried when the weather is better.'

'And that will work?' Gertrude declared, and Eve could see hope stirring in the elderly lady's eyes.

'Yup,' Tom said, and Gertrude shook her head in amazement.

'The wonders of modern technology.'

'Nah.' Tom grinned. 'Knowledge gained from a misspent youth.'

Gertrude chuckled wryly.

'You haven't changed a bit, Tom Cornish,' she declared. 'You're just the same lippy, opinionated, and—' she stretched out and caught hold of one of his hands, and gripped it firmly in her own frail one '—downright kind and decent human being you always were.'

'And there was me thinking I had you fooled,' Tom said, his cheeks darkening, and Gertrude shook her head.

'Not for a minute, lad. Not for one single minute.'

'That was kind of you,' Eve said when she and Tom left the surgery some time later.

'I wasn't lying to Gertie,' Tom replied, taking hold of her elbow to steer her round the rubble in Harbour Road. 'She might not be able to save all of her photographs and private papers, but she should be able to salvage most.'

'I didn't mean that,' Eve said. 'I meant the way you talked to her. You've a good heart, Tom.'

'Anyone else would have done the same,' he said dismissively, but she could see the embarrassment back on his face again, and stared at him curiously.

'Why does gratitude make you so uncomfortable?' she said, and to her surprise he didn't meet her gaze.

'I guess…' Tom took an awkward breath. 'Maybe it's because my father always battered it into me when I was a kid that nobody does anything for nothing. "There's no such thing as a free lunch, Tom." That was one of his favourite sayings, so I suppose I find it hard to believe people are on the level.'

'Gertrude is, and she knows you are,' she said softly.

'I'd rather you did,' he said, turning to face her, and it was her turn to look away.

'Your promise didn't last very long,' she said.

'Yeah, well, never trust a Cornish.'

She could hear the laughter in his voice, and shook her head.

'Ain't that the truth,' she replied. 'Tony at The Smugglers' has huge freezers. I bet he'd offer to help Gertrude in an instant.'

'I understand he's doing very well in hospital,' Tom said, and Eve couldn't help but laugh.

'You mean, you've heard he's giving the staff merry hell, demanding to be discharged.'

'I heard that, too.' Tom grinned. 'I'm afraid he's going to have to take things a lot easier from now on whether he wants to or not.'

'I think this flood is going to change quite a few people's lives.' Eve sighed.

'I'm hoping so.'

His words were innocuous enough, but she wasn't deceived for a second.

'I thought we agreed—'

His green eyes met hers.

'You can run, Eve, but you can't hide.'

He was right, she thought, and his words became even more prophetic after they'd reached her cottage and she made them both a simple meal of pasta Bolognese. Every time she looked up his gaze was on her, thoughtful, pensive. Every time she tried to start a conversation, he answered her in monosyllables and she knew why. He was waiting. Waiting for her to talk about the baby, and though she knew they had to talk about it, she didn't want to see his eyes darken again with pain or to relive the decision she'd made all those years ago.

'Would you like anything else to eat?' she said hopefully after she'd gathered up their empty plates. 'I have cheese and biscuits, and I managed to get some fruit from the corner shop. Goodness knows how it survived the flood, but it did.'

'No, thank you,' he replied.

'A coffee, then?' she suggested, knowing her voice was beginning to sound slightly panic-stricken but quite unable to control it. 'It's only instant but—'

'I don't want a coffee, thank you,' he interrupted. 'What I want is to talk to you.'

'Tom, I'm really tired,' she said quickly. 'In fact, I thought I might actually have an early night.'

He got to his feet, took the plates from her hands and put them back on the table.

'Eve, I could get a call at any time from Deltaron,' he declared, 'and I don't want to leave Penhally without us having spoken about…about our child.'

He was right about the call, and she knew from his set expression he wasn't going to take no for an answer, but when she walked over to the sofa she sat down wearily.

'Tom, what is there left for us to say?' she murmured. 'I was pregnant, I decided I couldn't have the baby, I had an abortion. I know you must hate me for what I did—'

'I don't hate you,' he interrupted, sitting down beside her. 'Maybe I thought I did, when you first told me—when I thought of the son or daughter I could have had—but those thoughts were the thoughts of the man I am now. The man I was all those years ago would have felt only relief that you didn't have the baby.'

'Relief?' she echoed, and he took a deep breath.

She had opened her heart to him, told him everything, and she deserved the same truth from him no matter how badly it reflected upon him.

'Eve, I'm ashamed to admit it, but if I'm honest—and I want

to be completely honest with you—I wouldn't have wanted a baby, not then. I had this wonderful career, you see,' he continued, his mouth twisting into an ironic and bitter smile. 'I was Dr Tom Cornish, all set to conquer the world, and a baby… I would have seen a baby as an encumbrance, that I was being trapped into a responsibility I didn't want to have, just as my father was.'

'And now you wish I hadn't done it,' she murmured, pleating and unpleating her fingers, 'but I can't undo it, Tom, no matter how much I might want to. I was weak all those years ago, took the easy way out, just as you said I did.'

'Weak?' he exclaimed. 'Eve, you took the hardest decision anyone can ever make, and you took it alone. When I think of you going to the clinic by yourself…' He shook his head. 'No one should have to go through that alone, and yet you did. You were the one who possessed the strength all those years ago, not me.'

'It wasn't strength, Tom, it was cowardice,' she said, her voice raw, harsh. 'I was so desperate. Desperate and scared that I wouldn't be able to cope, and I wish—I so wish—I could go back, and do things differently, but all the wishing in the world isn't going to make that happen.'

Awkwardly, he half reached for her, but he didn't know whether she would reject his touch—not want it—so he clasped her hand in his instead.

'If anyone's to blame for what happened, it's me,' he insisted. 'You should have felt you could come to me, and the fact you didn't… I let you down, Eve. Me.'

'I don't even know whether we had a son or a daughter, Tom,' she said, her lips trembling. 'I felt—I don't know why— it was a little girl, but one of the nurses… She said it wasn't a baby, not a real baby, just a collection of cells. But it was a baby, Tom. Our baby—and I killed it.'

He felt his heart twist with pain, but what deepened the pain, intensified it, were the tears he could see shimmering in her eyes, tears he knew were going to fall at any moment, and holding her hand was not enough—not nearly enough—and he put his arm around her, drawing her close.

'Don't, Eve, *don't*,' he begged, hating to see her suffering, but she misunderstood him.

'It's the truth, Tom,' she said. 'I did it. It was my decision, not yours. Mine, and I want so much to say I'm sorry to our daughter, but I can't. There's not even a grave I can stand beside so I won't ever be able to tell our baby that I'm sorry, and sometimes…'

The tears in her eyes overflowed, and Tom put his other arm round her, and held her tightly, his own throat constricted.

'Eve, listen to me,' he said into her hair. 'If we had made love ten years ago, and you'd discovered you were pregnant, would you have had an abortion?'

'Of course I wouldn't,' she said into his chest.

'Why not?' he said, knowing full well what her answer would be, but knowing, too, that he had to make her say it, see it.

'Because I had a good job ten years ago,' she exclaimed, 'and a flat of my own in Newquay!'

'None of which you had when you were twenty-two. Eve…' He clasped her face between his hands and forced her to look at him. 'You did what you thought was right twenty years ago, and now you have to forgive yourself, to move on, and believe you're entitled to a future, to happiness.'

'I don't know if I can,' she said brokenly.

He smoothed her hair back from her damp cheeks.

'You asked me—oh, it seems a lifetime ago now—why I came back to Penhally. I said I could give you one reason, but not the other—not then. Well, I can give you that other reason now. I came back because I've never stopped loving you.'

She stared at him in open-mouthed amazement for a full minute, then drew back from him.

'You're asking me to believe you've been in love with me for the past twenty years?' she exclaimed.

'Is that so very surprising?' he said.

It clearly was to her, he thought, seeing her shake her head, and her words confirmed it.

'Tom, if you'd truly felt like that you would have kept in touch,' she protested, 'but you never phoned, or wrote, or made any attempt to see me.'

'Because I was the one who walked away,' he said, willing her to believe him. 'I was the one who'd said I didn't want to be tied down, didn't want a wife or a family. You would have been quite within your rights to say, *On your bike, Tom Cornish*, and, as the years passed, I told myself you must be married, so I thought—I felt—I couldn't come back.'

'And you've been pining for me for the last twenty years?' she said, not bothering to hide her cynicism. 'I don't think so, Tom.'

'No, I haven't been pining for you for the last twenty years,' he admitted, 'but, because I made the biggest mistake of my life, I have spent those years trying to convince myself that the image I had of you couldn't be a real one, that no one could be so special, or different.'

'I'm not different, or special, Tom,' she said.

'You are, and because you are I kept on dating, and dating, and…' He broke off awkwardly, with a crooked smile and a gesture of dismissal. 'When none of my relationships worked out, I finally had to admit what I'd known all along. That I was looking for someone like you, and there wasn't anyone like you, there never could be.'

'So you came back to Penhally hoping to find me unhappily married, or divorced, so you could become involved with me again?' she said, outrage plain in her voice, and he swore under his breath.

Hell, was he never going to be able to find the right words to say to her? Was he doomed always to screw things up, and he was screwing things up, big time, because he see her barriers going up, and he couldn't lose her a second time, simply couldn't.

'It wasn't like that,' he said vehemently. 'I thought…' He grasped her hands before she could draw back, and held onto them. 'Part of me hoped to find you happily married because I thought—if you were—I might finally be able to move on, to bury the dream I had of somehow undoing the mistake I'd made, and the other part…I thought if you were still single that maybe…you and I…maybe we could try again.'

Her eyes met his, and he could read nothing of what she was thinking in them, and then she cleared her throat.

'Tom, have you thought that what you've been wanting back for all these years isn't me, but your youth and your dreams, and I can't give you that. No one can.'

'You said that to me before,' he said, willing her to see the truth in his eyes, 'but it isn't that, I know it isn't. Since we parted there's never been anybody in my life like you. There have been other women—I won't deny that—but it was always you. Nobody ever came anywhere close to you.'

Gently, she slipped her hands free from his.

'Even if I believed that, Tom,' she murmured. 'Even if what you say is true, we can't go back. You know we can't.'

'Why not?' he said.

It was a good question and one Eve wasn't entirely sure she could answer. She knew nobody had ever touched her heart the way he had, but she also knew no one had ever hurt her quite so much either, and to go down that road again, risk everything again…

'Tom, we're not the same people any more, and our worlds—they're too different, too far apart.'

'Then I'll give up working for Deltaron, and come back to Penhally,' he said. 'I'm getting too old to be traipsing around the world anyway, and after what happened last year in India—'

'And what would you do in Penhally?' she interrupted. 'This afternoon must have proved to you beyond a shadow of a doubt you'll never make a country GP, and Penhally… There are too many bad memories for you here. You'd never feel you belonged.'

'Then you could come to London with me,' he declared. 'Or there's my flat in Lausanne. You'd love Switzerland, Eve. It's a beautiful country, and if you wanted to continue nursing you'd easily find work there.'

He looked so desperate, so anxious, and she didn't want to hurt him, but she knew she must.

'Tom, my home is here,' she said. 'And to uproot myself from everything I know, from everyone I know on the strength of…'

'A whim?' he finished for her. 'It's not a whim, Eve, it's a question of trust. A question of whether you believe me when I say I love you and I always will.'

He made it sound so easy, so simple, but he'd made it sound easy and simple all those years ago, too.

'Let's have fun,' he'd said, and she'd thought they'd get married, raise a family in Penhally, and within a few short months her dreams and hopes had all been left lying shattered in the dust.

'I can't, Tom. And you're assuming too much,' she continued as he tried to interrupt. 'Assuming I still feel the same way about you.'

He reached out and gently cupped her cheek with his hand. 'Don't you?'

His eyes were deep and green and dark, and she shivered at the intensity she could see in them and, when he traced her neck with the fingers of his other hand, she shivered even more.

'It's still there, isn't it?' he continued, his voice suddenly deep, husky. 'What you used to feel for me, it's still there?'

'No,' she said, trying to sound firm but unfortunately her voice wobbled.

'Then, if I kiss you, you'll feel nothing?'

He didn't even need to kiss her, she thought. She could already feel herself melting, responding to him, wanting to touch him, to hold him, but she also knew nothing had been resolved between them, and it never could.

'Tom…I don't…I…'

'I'll take that as a yes,' he said, and bent his head towards her, and before she could say anything his lips met hers and she was lost.

Lost on a tide of need and longing. Lost in a sea of old memories, and sensations, and she slid her arms up his back to bring him closer, heard him groan against her mouth as he deepened the kiss, and he threaded his fingers through her hair so she couldn't escape, and she didn't want to escape.

'I have dreamt about doing this for so long,' he said, his breathing ragged. 'Wanted it, longed for it, and now you're here, in my arms, and it's right, so right.'

It felt right to her, too, as he smothered her face and neck with kisses, and when he slid his hands up under her sweater, and she felt the heat of his fingers through the lace of her bra, she arched against him, feeling her nipples harden instantly. It would be so easy to let go, she thought with a sigh as he drew her closer to him, and she felt his heart beating rapidly against hers, felt a heat begin to spread out deep and low in her stomach. It would be so easy simply to enjoy the moment, and it had been so long since she'd been in a man's arms, so long since she'd made love, but though her body and her heart spoke loudly, her head spoke louder still.

Nothing has changed, her mind warned, nothing *can* change. In a few days' time—probably less—he'll be gone, and then what? Then you'll be left with even more regret, even more memories to hurt you. With a sob, she pulled herself free from his arms and stood up.

'I can't,' she cried. 'I'm sorry, but I can't do this.'

'Eve—'

'I'm scared, Tom.'

'Of me?' he said in horror, and she shook her head as she wrapped her arms around herself.

'Of what will happen to me if I let you get close again. I can't go down that road and have you leave me again. I can't.'

'Why would you think I'd leave you?' he demanded.

'Because you always do,' she said, her voice trembling. 'You make me feel special, and different, and then you leave.'

'Eve, I *love* you,' he protested, reaching for her only to see her back away. 'I want us to be together for always. Can't you believe that?'

'I want to—I truly want to,' she said, 'but I can't risk it—I *can't*, Tom.'

'Eve, listen to me—'

'No,' she interrupted. 'No,' she repeated. 'You'll just talk me round like you always could. Go back to your world, Tom, and I'll stay in my own little one. I know it's not an exciting place like yours, and maybe…maybe it's not always completely fulfilling, but it's safe. It's never going to let me down, or walk away from me, and I have to have that kind of certainty, don't you see?'

'I can give you certainty,' he protested. 'Eve—'

'No, Tom,' she said, and before he could stop her she'd fled, and he swore long, and low, and fluently.

CHAPTER EIGHT

'DOES anybody else have anything to add, or can I call this practice meeting to a close?' Nick said, leaning back in his chair.

'Has anyone heard anything from the hospital about Melinda?' Eve asked.

Nick shook his head.

'Dragan phoned Chloe a couple of hours ago, said he was hoping it wouldn't be too much longer, but we haven't heard anything since.'

'That must be—what?—nineteen hours now?' Oliver said.

'It's not unusual for first babies to take a while to arrive,' Chloe said calmly. 'I'm sure there's no need to worry.'

'I wouldn't tell Dragan that.' Her fiancé grinned. 'I bet the poor bloke's got no fingernails left.'

'I'm surprised Tom had any hair left after he took over Dragan's surgery yesterday afternoon.' Kate laughed. 'I see you didn't take up his offer to help out this morning, Nick.'

'I thought he'd suffered enough,' the senior partner said with a rare smile, 'though I have to say, with Dragan shortly going on paternity leave, I wish Dr Devereux was arriving sooner.'

'We'll manage, boss,' Oliver declared, and Nick's smile widened.

'I'll hold you to that.'

'Where is Tom this morning?' Chloe asked, and to Eve's dismay all eyes in Nick's consulting room turned to her.

'I don't know,' she said uncomfortably. 'He got a call this morning at breakfast, and I haven't seen him since.'

A breakfast that had been eaten in a strained, awkward silence with neither of them saying anything. A breakfast she'd eaten at breakneck speed, all too aware he was watching her every move.

'Sorry to interrupt,' Hazel declared to Eve's relief as she appeared at Nick's consulting-room door, 'but Mrs Banks is here, Eve, and she'd like a word with you.'

'With me?' Eve said in surprise.

The practice manager nodded, and Eve glanced across at Nick.

'I don't think we have anything else to discuss, do we?' the senior partner said, and, when everyone shook their heads, he said, 'you'd better see what she wants, Eve.'

Eve thought she'd better, too, though she couldn't imagine what Mrs Banks might want to talk to her about unless it was how Sophie was getting on in hospital.

It wasn't.

'I simply had to come in and thank you personally, Nurse,' Mrs Banks declared the minute she sat down in Eve's examination room. 'Dr Tremayne told me what you did for my Sophie, how she probably wouldn't have survived if it hadn't been for you, and I'll never forget it.'

'It's not me you should be thanking, Mrs Banks,' Eve replied with a smile. 'Dr Cornish, and his pilot, Michael Flannery, were the real heroes of the hour.'

'Yes, but they get paid to rescue people, you don't,' Sophie's mother said dismissively.

Eve stared, open-mouthed, at the woman sitting opposite her, then straightened in her seat.

'Dr Cornish and Michael Flannery may—as you say—be paid for the job they do,' she said, fighting to control her mounting anger with difficulty, 'but there are precious few people in the world who would be willing to put their own lives on the line every time they go into work. It takes a very special man—or woman—to join a rescue service, Mrs Banks.'

'Granted,' Sophie's mother observed, 'but Dr Cornish… Well, he always was a bit wild, reckless, and as for his father—'

'I'm afraid you'll have to excuse me,' Eve interrupted, getting abruptly to her feet and pointedly walking over to her examination-room door and opening it. 'I'm on a tight schedule this morning.'

She wasn't. In truth, she was actually finished for the day, but she knew if she sat in the same room as Mrs Banks for even a minute longer she wouldn't be responsible for her actions.

'Oh—of course,' Mrs Banks declared uncertainly. 'I know how busy you professionals are, but I felt I couldn't let another day go past without thanking you.'

Eve wished Sophie's mother hadn't said anything at all as the woman left.

How could Mrs Banks be so blinkered, so stupid? she wondered. Tom and Mitch might be paid for their work, but how could that possibly make their actions less courageous, less admirable?

She shook her head as she began gathering up the folders on her desk. And to think this was the village Tom had said he would be prepared to come back and live in. A village where people would never let him forget his origins or his youthful behaviour. He must have been insane.

Or very deeply in love with you, her heart whispered, and she bit her lip.

Part of her desperately wanted to believe he'd meant what he'd said. Part of her wondered if perhaps, this time, they might both be able to get it right, but she knew the part that wondered was her heart. Her heart which had deceived her all those years ago, telling he would change his mind, and stay in Penhally instead of going to the US, so she mustn't listen to it, she told herself as she picked up the last folder and strode down to

Reception to find Amanda Lovelace deep in conversation with their practice manager. This time she had to listen to her head. This time she had to be sensible because if it all went wrong again she knew she would never recover.

'Hello, there, Amanda,' she said, forcing a smile to her lips. 'I hope this isn't a medical visit?'

'Not at all,' Tassie's mother replied. 'Hazel loaned me a little portable gas stove to cook on while the electricity was off, and now it's back on again I thought I'd better return it.'

'How's Tassie?' Eve asked. 'None the worse, I hope, for her adventure?'

'She's fine. And talking about Tassie,' Amanda continued, steering Eve away from the reception desk, 'I just want to say thank you. Thank you *so* much.'

'For what?' Eve said in confusion, and Tassie's mother tapped the side of her nose and winked.

'You don't have to pretend, Eve. I have to say I wasn't very happy when Dr Cornish first suggested it—felt I couldn't be beholden—and I know he doesn't want thanks, or for anyone to know—he was most insistent about that—but I had to thank you because I'm guessing you came up with the idea.'

'Amanda, I don't know what—'

'I have to go,' Tassie's mother interrupted. 'I heard on the way down here that there might be a delivery of bread today at the corner shop, and you can bet your life it will all be sold out in ten minutes.'

'But, Amanda…'

She was too late. After giving her a big hug, Tassie's mother bustled away, leaving Eve standing in the centre of the waiting room with a puzzled frown. A frown that deepened when Tom strode through the surgery door.

'Whatever it was, I didn't do it.' He grinned as he saw her expression.

'You obviously did something,' she observed, 'because I have just had the weirdest conversation with Amanda Lovelace.'

'Ah,' he said.

'Yes, "ah".' She nodded. 'Care to elaborate?'

'Nothing to elaborate on,' he replied lightly but when she saw a tell-tale wash of embarrassed colour begin to creep across his cheeks, she folded her arms across her chest.

'Tom, you have two choices. Either you tell me what you've done, and how it involves Amanda, or I'll go round to her house this afternoon and ask her myself.'

He sighed, then guided her towards the waiting-room chairs furthest away from the reception desk.

'You know how you and Gertie are very keen for Tassie to apply for a scholarship to go to the Lady Joan Mercer's Boarding School in Devon?' he said.

'And you're dead against it,' Eve replied.

'Not against it,' he countered. 'Just worried about the possible long-term consequences for Tassie and her family. Well, I've been making discreet enquiries about Penhally High School, and it seems to be as good a school as it was in our day.'

'And?' Eve prompted.

'I've arranged with Mrs Lovelace to pay her a monthly allowance so she can afford to allow Tassie to stay on at the local school for as long as she wants.'

Eve's mouth opened and closed soundlessly, and she finally found her voice.

'But…' She paused and started again. 'Why would you want to do that?'

'Why not?' he countered.

'Well, for a start, you don't know Tassie, or her family,' she pointed out, and he shrugged.

'No, but I do know you, and if you think the child deserves help, then that's good enough for me.'

'But, Tom, have you considered the cost?' she protested. 'If Tassie stays on at school until she's eighteen, you'll be paying for her education for the next eight years.'

'A bit longer, probably,' he said, the colour on his cheeks darkening, 'because I said I'd keep paying if she wants to go to university. Look, I can afford it,' he continued as Eve tried to interrupt. 'It's no big deal.'

But it was, she thought. It was rather a large deal, and a sudden suspicion crept into her mind.

'When did you suggest this to Amanda?' she demanded.

'Yesterday morning.' He shot her a cool look. 'Long before I told you how I feel about you so this is not, in any shape or form, a bribe, Eve.'

In truth, that had been exactly what she'd been thinking, and she felt her cheeks redden.

'I'm sorry,' she murmured. 'I deserved that.'

'Yes, you did.'

She glanced at him hesitantly.

'It's very generous of you, Tom. More than generous, in fact, though I don't know how you managed to get Amanda to agree. She may not have much money, but she's a proud woman, and I would have thought she'd have considered it charity.'

'She did at first,' Tom admitted, 'but I talked her round.'

Eve's lips curved. 'In other words, you used the famous Tom Cornish charm. Well, I suppose it's never failed you yet.'

'Yes, it has,' he said, a wry smile appearing in his green eyes. 'With one very important person.'

'Tom…'

'I won't give up, you know.'

She opened her mouth to tell him she wished he would, but she didn't get the chance to say the words. The surgery door had opened with a bang, and Dragan stood there looking dishevelled, exhausted and absolutely elated.

'I have a son!' he exclaimed. 'I have a beautiful son, and

Melinda—she was terrific—much calmer than I was—and I…'
The smile on his face widened. 'I just had to come and tell you
all.'

Hazel let out a shriek of delight, and within seconds every
member of the Penhally practice had converged on the waiting
room.

'What weight is the baby?' Kate asked, as Nick pulled the
cork out of a bottle of champagne, and began filling some
glasses.

Dragan looked comically dismayed.

'I've no idea. The midwife did tell me, but I was just so
relieved my son had arrived safely, with the correct number of
fingers and toes, I didn't take it in.'

'Have you and Melinda decided on a name?' Chloe asked,
taking the glass of champagne Nick was holding out to her, and
the Croatian doctor shook his head.

'We didn't decide on a name or buy any baby clothes either,
or a cot,' he replied. 'We felt we might be somehow tempting
the gods if we did.'

'Then you'd better start hitting the shops in Truro fast.' Eve
laughed. 'New mums and babies are lucky if they're kept in
hospital for forty-eight hours these days.'

'I hadn't thought of that,' Dragan said, aghast. 'You're right,
I'd better go shopping right away.'

'But not until we've all toasted the new arrival,' Nick said.
'I always keep a bottle of champagne in the surgery for special
moments, and I think the birth of Melinda and Dragan's son certainly qualifies as one of those.'

'Hear! Hear!' Oliver called, and everyone laughed.

'Does everyone have a glass of champagne?' Nick asked,
and, when a chorus of assent rang out, he said, 'Then I want
you all to raise your glasses to the new arrival. May he have a
long and happy life, and have inherited his mother's looks,
and—' he winked across at Dragan '—his mother's brains, too.'

More laughter rippled round the room and, as everyone raised their glasses, Tom leant closer to Eve.

'Are you OK?' he murmured so low nobody else could hear him. 'I mean, if you'd rather not be here I can cover for you.'

She looked up at him, both surprised and touched he would realise occasions like this could be painful for her, and shook her head.

'I'm fine,' she said. 'Dragan… He had so little sunshine in his life until he met Melinda, and he deserves to be happy.'

'Eve…'

'Shush,' she whispered. 'I don't think Nick's finished yet.'

'Nick could talk for Cornwall,' Tom muttered, and Eve choked over her champagne, and waved an admonishing hand at him.

'I would also like to take this opportunity to say these last few days have been very difficult for everyone,' the senior partner continued. 'We've been through the kind of flood I never want to see again in my lifetime, and lost some good, decent people, but… *But,*' Nick added with emphasis, 'in the middle of the catastrophe my staff rose to the occasion magnificently, and I just want to thank you all, and say you were incredible.'

'You were pretty wonderful yourself, boss,' Oliver observed. 'Managing to assist at a breech birth with no electricity, and damn few medical instruments, takes some doing.'

A chorus of agreement met that comment, and Nick's cheeks flushed slightly, then he held up his hand, clearly calling for silence again.

'There is, however, one person who deserves my very special thanks,' he said. 'One person who I admit I have not made welcome since he came back to the village, and yet it is that one person without whose help things would most certainly have been considerably worse, so can I ask you to raise your glasses once more, and drink a toast to Tom Cornish? Penhally's very own, home-grown hero.'

'Tom Cornish!' everyone exclaimed, but when the toast had been drunk and Dragan was, yet again, being bombarded with more questions about his son, Tom looked down at Eve quizzically.

'Did you know he was going to say that?' he asked.

'I'm as surprised as you are,' she replied. 'Considering how unfriendly he's been towards you since you came back, I'd have thought you were the last person he would have wanted to thank.'

And not just thank, Eve discovered as Nick eased his way through the throng towards them, with Kate at his side.

'I owe you an apology,' the senior partner declared the moment he drew level with Tom.

'Forget it, Nick,' Tom said, and Nick shook his head.

'I can't,' he declared. 'I know I have a brusque tongue—'

'You can say that again,' Kate murmured, and Nick gave her a hard stare.

'And sometimes speak before I think,' the senior partner continued, 'but I will be eternally grateful for everything you did for the village. If you hadn't been here, I don't know what would have happened.'

'I just wish there could have been no fatalities,' Tom observed. 'Reverend Kenner seems to have been a well-liked man, and Mrs Baxter… She and I may not have seen eye to eye, but I'm sorry she's dead.'

'Did you know that Lauren is giving Foxy a home?' Kate said as Nick walked away in answer to Oliver's beckoning wave. 'The dog knows her, you see, from when she used to do Audrey's physio, so he's not scared of her, and she actually got him to eat something yesterday which the RSPCA says is a miracle because he's point-blank refused to take food from anybody else.'

'I just wish we could find Chloe's cats,' Tom declared,

glancing across to where the midwife was talking animatedly to Dragan. 'But there's no sign of them—not even their bodies. In fact, I was wondering—'

'Tom, I think Mitch wants a word with you,' Eve interrupted, seeing the redheaded pilot hovering in the waiting-room doorway pointing silently at Tom and then at himself.

'I'll be back in a minute,' Tom said, half turning to go, then he stopped. 'Don't go anywhere. Stay here.'

'Yes, sir.' Eve laughed.

But he was going somewhere, she thought, feeling her smile slip sideways when Tom reached Mitch and the pilot ruefully handed him a sheaf of papers.

They were leaving. She could see it in Tom's face. Mitch must have received a fax from their headquarters, and they were leaving.

Well, she'd known it was going to happen eventually, she thought as she took a sip of champagne then put her glass down. She'd just hoped—stupidly—that he might have been able to stay for a few more days.

'What's up?' Kate asked, gesturing towards Mitch and Tom.

'I think Tom's just received a call from Deltaron,' Eve replied.

'But that means he'll be leaving,' Kate said with dismay, and Eve forced a smile to her lips.

'He was never going to stay, Kate. His work—his life—isn't here.'

'But I thought…'

Eve didn't give the midwife the chance to tell her what she'd thought. Instead, she made her way towards Oliver, Lauren and Chloe who were standing by the window.

'Isn't it marvellous news?' Lauren beamed when she saw her. 'Melinda and Dragan must be so happy.'

'Christenings and weddings.' Chloe laughed. 'Reverend Kenner is going to be…' She came to an abrupt halt, and bit her lip. 'Sorry. Force of habit. It's so hard to believe he's gone, isn't it?'

'How is Rachel?' Eve asked. 'I thought I might call in on her this afternoon, see how she is.'

'She's gone to Plymouth with her aunt and uncle,' Lauren replied. 'She'll come back for the funeral, of course, but I think she wanted out of the village with all its memories.'

'She's a very brave girl—braver than I would be in the circumstances,' Chloe observed. 'To be left with no mother, no father, and expecting a baby… It's going to be tough for her.'

'She'll cope,' Eve said, her eyes following Tom as he scanned the waiting room, clearly looking for her. 'We all have to cope in different ways with what life throws at us, and she'll cope.'

'I thought I told you to stay where you were,' Tom declared with a frown when he reached her side. 'Give a woman a simple order, and what does she do? Completely ignores it.'

'I can see why you've never married, Tom.' Chloe laughed, and he gazed at her severely.

'You know, for that remark, I should refuse to give you the present one of my men has just brought in for you.'

'What present?' she said, looking puzzled.

'Actually, I'm more interested in meeting the bloke who thinks he can give my fiancée presents,' Oliver said, his voice mock stern, and Tom grinned.

'It's two presents actually,' he said. 'One is ginger and has only one eye, and one is white with a black patch over its eye.'

'You've found Cyclops and Pirate?' Chloe gasped, her face lighting up.

'One of my men has. They're outside in cat boxes if you want to see for yourself.'

Chloe was already halfway out of the room, and Oliver gripped Tom's hand fervently.

'Thanks, mate,' he said. 'I owe you. I owe you big time.'

'Are you sure your name isn't actually Santa Claus?' Eve said when the couple had gone, and Tom laughed.

'I didn't find them—Gregory did. He thinks they must have

decided to take shelter on top of one of the wardrobes because they weren't even a little bit dirty or wet.'

'Lucky cats,' Eve observed.

'Eve…'

He cleared his throat, and she knew what was coming. He was going to tell her he was leaving. She could see it in his face, and she didn't want to say goodbye to him. She'd said it to him once before, and she didn't want to say it again.

'I think Nick is trying to attract your attention,' she said quickly, and, when Tom groaned, she nudged him firmly with her hand. 'Look, if he wants to thank you again, just smile and accept it with good grace.'

He went reluctantly, and she waited only until he was deep in conversation with the senior partner then quietly slipped out of the surgery. He would be angry—perhaps even upset—when he found out she had gone, but she'd much rather he just disappeared out of her life as silently as he'd reappeared in it. To say goodbye to him, knowing she would never see him again… She didn't have that much courage.

'Lovely day, isn't it?' a woman called from outside one of the shops as Eve walked quickly past.

'Beautiful, yes,' Eve managed to reply.

'You and your gentleman friend must come back once we've redecorated,' the woman continued. 'You never did get your lemon meringue pies.'

It was the woman from the café, and Eve should have recognised her immediately but she hadn't.

'We'll do that,' she said, but of course they wouldn't.

By this time tomorrow Tom would be somewhere overseas, and she would have her work, and Tassie, to fill her days, and maybe, in time, she might forget this brief interlude. Though never completely, she thought as she crossed Harbour Bridge, and heard the chug of the firemen's hoses as they continued to pump water out of the houses. No matter how hard she tried, the day of the flood would be forever etched on her memory, whether she wanted it to be or not.

But she would survive, she told herself as she headed towards the lighthouse. She had survived before, and she would survive again.

'Kate, have you seen Eve anywhere?' Tom said with a frown as he walked towards her.

'She's gone, Tom,' the midwife replied. 'While you were talking to Nick she just slipped away. I imagine she's gone home.'

'Not home, no,' Tom said thoughtfully, 'but I think I might know where she is.'

He turned to leave, and Kate put her hand out to stay him.

'I hear you're off on another mission?' she said, and he nodded.

'Earthquake in China. We're flying out tonight, but I need to return to Switzerland first to finalise a team.'

'You be careful, you hear?' Kate declared, and he grinned.

'Hey, I'm always careful,' he said, and she shook her head.

'I don't mean in China. I mean with Eve.' On impulse, Kate stood on her toes and kissed him lightly on the cheek. 'That's for luck,' she whispered, 'and now go after her.'

'You'll make my apologies to the others?' he said.

'Of course, I will,' the midwife said. 'Now, *go*.'

He did.

'First Eve disappears, then Tom,' Nick declared when he joined Kate. 'What's going on between that pair? Are they an item again, or what?'

'I think whatever Tom says to her when he finds her will decide what their futures are going to be,' Kate murmured.

The senior partner frowned as stared down at her.

'I'm sorry, but you've lost me.'

Kate smiled.

'Let's just keep your fingers crossed for them, Nick. They both deserve to be happy, and that was a very nice apology you made to Tom.'

'Well, I had to give credit where credit was due,' Nick replied, 'and I think I was wrong about him.'

'I think you were, too,' Kate replied, but as she made to move away Nick caught her by the elbow.

'Kate, on the night of the flood...' He looked uncomfortable, ill at ease, then he firmed his jaw. 'What you said—about Jem. I can't make you any promises, but I will try.'

She looked up at him, her eyes very bright, then nodded.

'That's all I want, Nick,' she said, her voice husky. 'It's all I've ever wanted.'

She should have brought her jacket, Eve thought as she sat on the grass below the lighthouse, and hugged her knees. She was wearing her cherry-red sweater and a heavy tweed skirt, but there was no denying that autumn had well and truly arrived. There was a chill in the air, a feeling of darker nights approaching, and the scent of dried leaves now mingled with the tang of seaweed.

'I could see you shivering from all the way back at the church.'

Eve glanced over her shoulder to see Tom standing behind her, and sighed. She might have known she wouldn't be able to get away from him so easily.

'How did you know I would be here?' she asked as he took off his jacket, and put it round her shoulders before she could prevent him.

'No great mystery,' he said. 'I knew you would want to think, and this is where you always used to come if you had a problem.'

'It's amazing how many unimportant things you seem to remember about me,' she replied.

'I remember everything about you—I told you that.'

She gazed back out at the sea.

'Water… It's so very beautiful isn't it?' she said. 'And yet it can be so cruel and deadly, too.'

He sat down beside her on the grass.

'Mankind thinks itself so smart, so clever,' he said, 'but it's Nature that wields the real power. It can be a horrifying power at times, a terrifying power, but Nature also has the ability to heal. I've seen whole forests reduced to a smoking ruin and yet, within a year, wildflowers will have appeared, and the first shoots of new trees.'

She picked at the grass beside her for a few moments, then took a deep breath.

'How soon are you leaving?'

'I should be on my way now, but I didn't want to leave without saying goodbye.'

She stared down at the grass again, knowing that if she turned her head slightly she would see all of Penhally Bay spread out before her. The lifeboat station, St Mark's on the hill, the houses clustered round the harbour, and the newer bungalows higher on the hill. Everything would look just the same, but not quite the same any more, and it never would be because of the man sitting beside her.

'Have you decided what you're going to do?' she asked. 'I mean, are you staying with Deltaron, or…'

'I think you're right, that Deltaron is where I'm supposed to be,' he replied, 'but only if…'

She waited for him to finish, but when he didn't she turned to face him.

'If what, Tom?'

'Before I answer that question, I have something to give you. I bought…' Awkwardly he held out the plastic carrier bag he was clutching. 'I don't know whether this will help, or if I've got this wrong again, but I was thinking about what you said yesterday, and I thought… But maybe it's not a good idea, maybe you might think…'

'Tom, what are you trying to say?' she demanded, and when for an answer he produced a small nosegay of flowers from his bag she stared at them blankly. 'You bought me flowers?'

'I bought them for her,' he said, his voice half-muffled, his head lowered as though he was afraid to meet her eyes. 'For our daughter. You said yesterday that what upset you most was there being no grave, nowhere you could go and say you were sorry. Well, I want…' She saw him swallow. 'I want to tell her I'm sorry, too. Sorry for letting her mother down, for not being there for her when she needed me.'

'Tom—'

'Eve, I want our baby to know I'm thinking of her, and I thought…' His head came up, and when his eyes met hers she saw the pain and anguish she knew were in her own eyes mirrored in his. 'I thought maybe I could put this in the sea— if you wouldn't mind if I did that—in…in memory of her.'

Tears began to trickle down her cheeks and into her mouth.

'You really want to do that?' she said, scarcely able to see him through her tears.

'She was my baby, too, Eve. My daughter, too, and maybe…' His voice broke. 'Maybe…if I do this she might know that though she's not here with me—with us—we will never forget her, and we will always, always love her.'

'Tom… I…'

Eve couldn't say another word and when he hesitantly, awk-wardly, held out his arms to her, she reached for him, too, and clung to him and felt him shudder, and knew he was crying as much as she was for the child they might have had and who they would never forget.

And, when they were calmer, they walked together to the headland, and threw the little nosegay Tom had bought up into the air, watched it soar for a few seconds, a myriad of bright colours in the blue sky, then land with a gentle splash in the water, and clung to one another again and cried again.

'I know this is too soon,' Tom said with difficulty when their grief was spent. 'So much has happened—and you're fragile right now—and I...I'm pretty shaky myself—but do you think—is there any possibility—that we might start again?'

'I don't know, Tom,' she said uncertainly. 'We have so much history. Maybe too much.'

'You said...' He caught her hands, and held them tightly. 'When you first told me about the baby—you said you loved me all those years ago. Has it all gone—that love?'

'I think...' She stared up into the face she knew so well, at the lines which seemed to have become even more deeply etched around his eyes and on his forehead over the past few days. 'I think I will always love you, Tom, but I don't know whether loving you would be enough. What happened—the baby—I think it might always come between us. Not spoken about, but always there, and when we argued—and we would argue because all couples do— my fear is we'd use it as a weapon against one another.'

'I wouldn't.'

She smiled unevenly.

'You can't be sure of that, Tom.'

'Eve, no one can be sure of anything,' he insisted. 'We might have years of happiness together, or our lives could be snuffed out in a second by some pointless car crash. You said I wasn't to blame for Charlie's death, and for the deaths of those people in India, because I did what I thought was right at the time— that it was all anyone could do. Well, the decision you made about the baby was right for you at the time, it was all *you* could do, and you have to see that, accept that.'

'I hear what you're saying, Tom,' she murmured, 'and my head tells me you're right, but my heart...'

'Eve, I have loved you for so long,' he said, his voice constricted. 'I was in love with you even when we were at school.'

'No, you weren't,' she said. 'Starchy Dwyer, remember?'

'Do you want to know why I called you that?' he said. 'It was because I fancied you like mad but I was the no-hoper, Tom Cornish's son, whereas you… You were the one who always got the good grades, the one whose parents were respectable, acceptable, and I'd have looked a proper fool in front of my friends if I'd asked you out, and you'd said no, so it was easier to act like I thought you were the prat.'

'It was a pretty good act,' she said with feeling, and his lips curved into a slight smile, then the smile disappeared.

'Eve, I want to spend the rest of my life with you. Yes, we've made mistakes, and I made the biggest one of all, but I need you, Eve. It's not just the wanting—though God knows I want you so much—but…' He let go of her hands and thrust his fingers through his hair, his face taut, strained. 'I *need* you.'

'Tom—'

'No, please, let me finish,' he pressed. 'All these years I've been chasing dreams, and nothing brought me any happiness, any contentment, because you weren't in my life. When I think of all the years we could have had together, the memories we could have made and shared. I lost them. Me. Not you. Me, always on the move, thinking excitement was the answer, when all the time what I really wanted was here, in my own back yard, because, you see…' His voice cracked. 'You are my dreams, Eve, you always have been.'

There was honesty and truth in his face, and she knew she would never love anyone as much as she loved him, but so much had happened over the last few days, and she felt raw, exposed, vulnerable.

'Twenty years, Tom,' she said slowly. 'It's a lot of years to forget.'

'I'm not asking you to forget them,' he said, his voice soft with understanding. 'I know you can't, just as I know I can't go back and give myself the knowledge I have now. I wish I could. I wish I hadn't been the stupid, blind, selfish person I was then, but all the wishing in the world can't make that happen, but if we can both—somehow—forgive ourselves, then maybe we won't just have a shared past. Maybe we can have a future, together.'

'But, you're leaving,' she said. 'You're going to China.'

'Yes, I'm leaving.' He nodded. 'But what I want to know is, if I come back to Penhally, when all of this upheaval is over, would you want to see me again?'

She gazed out to sea to where the little nosegay was floating away towards the horizon, and then she looked up at him. Up into the face that had once haunted her dreams, the face she'd once loved, and then hated, and saw the entreaty in his eyes, the desperate hope, and though she didn't know what the future was going to bring she did know that the fates had given her another chance at happiness and she would be foolish to let it go.

'Yes,' she said, her voice a little wobbly, a little tremulous. 'I'd want to see you again, Tom.'

And a blinding smile illuminated his face, and he caught her hand, and pressed her knuckles to his lips.

'One day at a time, Eve,' he said. 'We'll take this one day at a time, and no matter how long it takes I will wait for you.'

And she smiled back at him, and nodded, and together they walked back down into Penhally Bay.

EPILOGUE

Six months later

DUSK. A magical time, a perfect time for a wedding. That's what any guest staying at the exclusive Lake Lausanne hotel would have said if they'd looked out of the dining-room windows onto the lawn and seen a clergyman and two other men standing beside an archway of spring blossom, clearly waiting for a bride to arrive. However, if those guests had looked a little closer, they would have seen that one of the men looked distinctly nervous.

'Mitch, are you quite sure this morning suit doesn't make me look like a complete prat?'

'Well, now you come to mention it…' the pilot began, then grinned as Tom gazed at him in dismay. 'You look fine.'

Tom tugged at his tie. 'Shouldn't Eve be here by now?'

'Tom, Eve is not going to do a runner, although I will if you keep on stressing.'

'Right. Sorry,' Tom muttered, glancing down at his watch.

'Eight minutes,' Mitch observed.

'What?'

'The ceremony is due to begin in eight minutes,' the pilot declared. 'Which is exactly two minutes less than the time was when you last checked your watch.'

'Right.'

Mitch shot Tom a mischievous glance.

'Wouldn't it just be typical if we were to get a call from Deltaron?' he said, then guffawed when Tom's mouth fell open in horror. 'Just kidding. They know you're not available. Know I'm not, too. No way was I going to miss out on being your best man.'

'I really appreciate you agreeing to do this, Mitch,' Tom said awkwardly. 'It's…well…it's very good of you.'

The big pilot looked equally embarrassed.

'Me miss out on the opportunity of seeing the head of operations at Deltaron in a complete panic? No chance.'

'I guess not.' Tom smiled, then glanced down at his watch again.

'Seven minutes,' Mitch said, 'and if you look at your watch one more time I'll ram it down your throat.'

'Amanda, are you sure we're not late?' Eve said as she glanced out of the French windows of the hotel. 'Tom's walking up and down out there like he's scared I'm not going to turn up or something.'

'Of course you're not late,' Amanda insisted as Tassie pirouetted past them, clearly revelling in her pale blue bridesmaid's dress. 'And, even if you were, it's the bride's prerogative.'

'Not this bride,' Eve said with a shaky laugh. 'This bride's been waiting twenty years for this moment.'

'No doubts, then?' Tassie's mother said, and Eve shook her head.

'None at all,' she replied, and she didn't have, not now.

Bit by bit, over the last six months, Tom had chipped away at her worries, emailing or phoning her every day, but it was when he had returned to Penhally for both Melinda and Rachel's little boys' christenings that she had finally been convinced. She knew he would never feel comfortable in Penhally, and yet he'd come back because she'd wanted him to. Come back to make her happy, and it was that which convinced her to say yes when he'd asked her to marry him, and that night, after Rachel's baby's christening…

Her face softened. She'd been so nervous and self-conscious that night, and he'd been so gentle, so tender, making her laugh, relaxing her, so their joining had been even more wonderful, even more perfect, than it had been the last time they'd made love twenty years ago.

'I still can't believe you're actually going to be living here,' Amanda continued. 'I thought you were like me—destined always to stay in Penhally.'

'I thought so, too,' Eve admitted, 'but it makes sense for us to live in Switzerland when most of Tom's team have homes here, and…' She shrugged. 'I think it's maybe way past time I spread my wings.'

'Tassie and I wouldn't be here at all if Tom hadn't paid our air fares,' Amanda said. 'We owe you so—'

'You owe us nothing,' Eve interrupted, putting her fingers to the woman's lips quickly to silence her. 'We wanted you at our wedding, and I'll be very cross if you don't use those other air tickets Tom gave you to come and visit us regularly.'

'But—'

'No buts,' Eve insisted. 'Tassie's special, and so are you.'

'I don't know about us being special,' Amanda said, blowing her nose vigorously, 'but you certainly look lovely today. That colour really suits you.'

Eve uncertainly smoothed down the folds of the long crimson skirt and matching embroidered bolero jacket she was wearing.

'You don't think it looks odd, me wearing red?' she said. 'It's just Tom likes this colour—'

'I think you look gorgeous,' Amanda insisted. 'Like you have a candle inside you, burning with happiness.'

It was how Eve felt as she stepped out of the French windows and saw Mitch nudge Tom, and Tom's whole face light up when he turned and saw her. It was how she felt throughout the whole ceremony as Tom repeated his vows, his voice a little husky, and she made her own pledges, her voice just as uneven, and his fingers tightened round hers as though he never wanted to let her go.

She didn't want to let go of him either. All she wanted was to be alone with him, but Mitch had organised a wedding supper for them and she knew it would have seemed ungrateful if she and Tom had slipped away the minute they'd finished eating.

Mitch obviously didn't agree. In fact, the second their plates were cleared, the pilot gave Amanda a very decided wink, then glanced at his watch.

'Half past nine already,' he said. 'I think it's time some folk should be in their beds.'

'But I don't normally go to bed until ten o'clock,' Tassie protested and, as Amanda laughed, and Eve blushed, Tom got to his feet.

'I couldn't agree with you more, Mitch,' he said, 'but there's something I want to do first.'

Eve's eyebrows rose as he strode across to the quartet who had been playing a medley of tunes throughout the evening.

'What he's up to, Mitch?' she asked and the pilot shook his head.

'Haven't a clue, love.'

Neither did she until the quartet began to play the opening bars of a tune she recognised instantly, and when Tom held out his arms to her, she had to blink very rapidly before she could walk out onto the small dance floor and join him.

'My very own Lady in Red,' he murmured into her hair as he drew her into his arms. 'And you are mine now, for always, aren't you?'

And she was, she thought as he whirled her round the small dance floor, holding her closer, and closer, moulding his body to hers, so she could feel the uneven throb of his heartbeat, could see his eyes growing darker and more intense with every passing second and, when the music ended, and he kissed her, she never wanted the kiss to end.

Neither, it seemed, did the other diners if the eruption of applause, and the sound of Mitch whooping enthusiastically, was anything to go by when they finally drew apart.

'I think maybe Mitch was right,' Tom said, leaning his forehead against hers, his cheeks flushed, his breathing uneven. 'Maybe it *is* time we go to bed before I completely forget we're not alone.'

'Definitely,' she said, chuckling shakily as the leader of the quartet shook her hand, and said something incomprehensible in Swiss, and the diners applauded again.

She thought it even more when Tom drew her back into his arms the second they reached their hotel room.

'Oh, Tom, I am so happy.' She sighed, as he slid his hands up her sides so she felt the heat of his fingers through the fine satin of her jacket. 'I keep thinking I'm going to wake up, find this is all a dream, that no one has the right to be as happy as I am right now.'

'You do,' he said, tracing the outline of her jaw with his lips. 'You deserve everything you've ever wanted, and I'm going to make it my life's ambition to ensure you get it.'

'You already have,' she said huskily. 'In fact…' She took a deep breath. 'There's something I have to tell you.'

'Later,' he said, his eyes liquid with desire as he began unbuttoning her jacket. 'Later we talk, but right now…'

She wanted the 'right now', too, she thought as he eased her jacket off, then her bra, and when he caressed her breasts with his fingers and lips she felt the heat flare everywhere. Every part of her body seemed so much more sensitive tonight, she thought as he removed the rest of her clothing, then his, and she knew why but it would keep. Just for a little while it would keep, she decided as she clung to him, revelling in his hardness as he whispered words of love, and touched her, and kissed her, telling her over and over how beautiful she was, how desirable, until she was shaking with need.

'Tom, please—*please*,' she gasped, wanting more, even more.

And he laughed, and kissed her again, and just when she thought she wouldn't be able to bear it any longer, he finally entered her, hot and slick, and she rose up to join him, wanting to give him the same joy he was giving her, and felt her heart clutch with happiness when he carried her over the edge and his cry matched hers as they spiralled and shuddered and climaxed together.

'My wife,' he said, gathering her, spoon-like, against his chest. 'You're all I've ever wanted Eve, all I'll ever need.'

She gazed down at his arms encircling her, and cleared her throat.

'Tom…do you remember when you told me how much you would like to have children?'

His grip on her tightened.

'Eve, I'm happy simply having you,' he said softly. 'I'm not saying it wouldn't be a great joy to me if we were so blessed, but…' He turned her round in his arms so he could look at her. 'For such a long time I thought I'd lost you. For an even longer time I thought I'd messed things up completely. If we should have a baby then it would be wonderful because you deserve so much to be a mother, but if we're not lucky—if it doesn't happen— you've already made my life complete, just by being you.'

'You've made my life complete, too,' she said unevenly, 'but what I meant…' She could feel her cheeks darkening which was ridiculous because she had nothing to feel embarrassed about, but she so wanted him to feel the same way she did. 'When I asked whether you still wanted to be a father I was thinking of… perhaps in about six months?'

'Six months?' he repeated with a frown. 'Eve—'

'Tom, when did we first make love again?' she interrupted, and saw his frown deepen.

'It was when I came back for Rachel's son's christening. When I asked you to marry me, and you…' He smiled. 'You said yes, and made me the happiest man on the planet.'

'That was three months ago, Tom.' He still looked confused and she chuckled softly. 'And you call yourself a doctor. Think about it. Tom. If I'm asking whether you would like to be a father in six months' time, and we made love three months ago…'

He stared at her silently for a second, then sat up so fast she had to catch hold of him to prevent herself landing face down in the pillow.

'You're pregnant?' He gasped.

'Yes.' She nodded, watching his face anxiously.

A smile tugged at his lips. A smile that grew, and grew, and tentatively he reached out and gently put his fingers on her stomach.

'A baby,' he said, wonder plain in his voice. 'We're going to have a baby.'

'Are…are you pleased?' she said, and he dashed his hand across his eyes.

'Oh, Eve,' he said, his voice husky. 'Oh, my love, my *love.*'

And he clasped her to him, his eyes as bright and shimmering as she knew hers must be, then released her abruptly, concern plain on his face, and gently touched her tummy again, and she laughed, a hiccuping laugh that was halfway towards a sob.

'Tom, I'm not made of glass,' she said. 'I won't break.'

'No, but I think I might,' he said. 'Break with happiness, and joy.'

And he drew her to him again and kissed her so tenderly, and she felt the wetness on his cheeks, knew her own cheeks were tear-stained, too, but they were tears of happiness. That at last—at long last—she and Tom would have not just a past together, but a glorious, wonderful future.

* * * *

Dr Devereux's Proposal

MARGARET McDONAGH

Margaret McDonagh says of herself: "I began losing myself in the magical world of books from a very young age and I always knew that I had to write—pursuing the dream for over twenty years, often with cussed stubbornness in the face of rejection letters! Despite having numerous romance novellas, short stories and serials published, the news that my first 'proper book' had been accepted by Mills & Boon for their Medical Romance™ line brought indescribable joy! Having a passion for learning makes researching an involving pleasure, and I love developing new characters, getting to know them, setting them challenges to overcome. The hardest part is saying goodbye to them, because they become so real to me. And I always fall in love with my heroes! Writing and reading books, keeping in touch with friends, watching sport and meeting the demands of my four-legged companions keeps me well occupied. I hope you enjoy reading this book as much as I loved writing it."

With special thanks…

To those who helped with my research on retinitis pigmentosa …your courage is humbling www.brps.org.uk…and on Duchenne muscular dystrophy www.muscular-dystrophy.org

To my fellow Medical Romance™ authors involved in this exciting series

And to the wonderful editorial team who conceived the Penhally project—thank you for believing in me.

CHAPTER ONE

'*QUE L'ENFER?*' Shocked by the sight that greeted him as his destination came into view, Dr Gabriel Devereux drew his car to a halt at the side of the cliff road and stepped out. '*Mon Dieu!*'

What had happened to the small Cornish town of Penhally Bay? His one previous visit had been in the summer when he had spent a weekend looking around and finalising details for his year-long contract to work as a GP in the local practice. Penhally had recently been twinned with St Ouen-sur-Mer in Normandy, France, where he had been filling in for the last ten months at his friend François Amiot's busy medical clinic.

As part of the twinning process, people from different occupations and ways of life were crossing the Channel, exchanging jobs and skills, building bridges and friendships, bringing the communities of the two towns together, socially, commercially and culturally. None of the other doctors in St Ouen-sur-Mer had been prepared to move their families for a year, but for Gabriel it had been too good an opportunity to miss. Taking this post in Cornwall was a heaven-sent chance to put even more distance between himself and the unresolved issues that had seen him leave Paris for St Ouen-sur-Mer in the first place.

Ruthlessly banishing any thoughts of home, Gabriel's gaze narrowed as he concentrated on the scene of devastation below him. In the summer, Penhally Bay had been an attractive, hilly, seaside town bustling with tourists and basking under sunshine and clear blue skies. The rows of houses, shops and businesses along the curving seafront, painted in an array of pastel colours, had watched over the boats that had bobbed gently in the harbour. Now… He shook his head in disbelief. This cloudy late October day, the scene could not have been more different.

When his new boss, Nick Tremayne, the senior partner at the Penhally practice, had emailed a week ago to confirm the date to begin work, he had mentioned a flash flood, but Gabriel had not fully grasped the seriousness of what had occurred. A man of few words, Nick had not gone into detail, but Gabriel could see that the event had been far more cataclysmic than that one brief email had implied.

After breathing in a lungful of fresh, salty, Cornish air, Gabriel climbed back in the car and drove down the hill to the town. He passed the promontory on which the church and the lighthouse stood, before heading along the seafront that formed a horseshoe round the harbour. At the far western end of the arc were the lifeboat station and the surgery where he would be working from Monday. Halfway around the seafront, he slowed as he neared the bridge. Here, the river Lanson, which flowed down the hill between Bridge Street and Gull Close, effectively cutting the town in two, spilled its waters into the harbour.

This central area appeared to have borne the brunt of the flooding with damage obvious to houses in Bridge Street and around the seafront. The end wall of the Anchor Hotel—on the corner of Gull Close and Harbour Road—had come down under the force of the water. Standing forlorn and closed for business, the remains of the building were shored up with scaffolding, and demolition notices warned that the property was unsafe.

Twelve days on, the waters had receded and the clean-up operation had begun, but the empty houses and shops were all too apparent, as was the debris that had washed down the angry river in full spate. Ruined and discarded belongings sat forlornly outside abandoned properties, full skips awaited collection and disposal, while redundant sandbags remained by doors and gateways.

The town bustled with life, however. These people clearly had spirit, banding together and refusing to allow the difficult circumstances to defeat them. It was past lunchtime and the Saturday market was thriving. People were shopping in the stores that had evaded damage, a few were fishing off the harbour wall or working on their boats, while dedicated parties were continuing the task of restoring order after the flood. Gabriel planned to do all he could to help in the days and weeks ahead…but first he needed to find the house that was to be his base for the next year, move in and find his feet.

As he reached the outskirts of town, his memory guiding him down a narrow, hedge-lined lane, he experienced a flicker of uncharacteristic nervousness. He hoped he would settle here, that he would be accepted…a stranger and a foreigner in this tight community. Penhally Bay was not the cosmopolitan metropolis of London where he had spent time during his medical training. Would the people here judge him on his skills as a doctor or on being different? He hoped the former…was wary of the latter.

Half a mile farther along the lane, he came to the turning he was seeking and steered the car between the twin gateposts that marked the unpaved driveway. To one side was Gatehouse Cottage, the single-storey thatched lodge which Nick Tremayne had told him belonged to the physiotherapist at the surgery. Gabriel frowned, unable to remember her name. There were no signs of life from the cottage so he hoped his arrival had gone unnoticed. The drive curved away from the lodge and fifty yards farther on the impressive but not-too-large Manor House came into view, sheltered and surrounded by mature shrubs and trees. Gabriel paused, admiring the traditional fifteenth-century building, feeling now the same contentment he had experienced when he had first been here in late July.

Symbolically, the clouds overhead cleared, and low autumn sunshine filtered down from a patch of pale blue sky, highlighting myriad colours in the old, lichen-spotted granite blocks and dark roof slates from which the Manor House was built. Instinct told him he had been right to come here. This was what he needed. A place where he could work with his customary enthusiasm for the job he loved…a refuge where he could be alone and decide what he was going to do about the rest of his life.

He parked his car at the rear of the building, out of sight should anyone approach up the drive. He had arrived a day early and planned to take time to himself before announcing his presence. After finding the keys to the house—left for him by the solicitor acting for the owners, who were working abroad long term—he collected together his essential belongings and let himself in. He knew the house had been empty since the last tenants had departed at the end of August, so he was surprised to find the air smelling fresh and the surfaces clean of dust. Someone had been thoughtful enough to make preparations for his arrival. The knowledge warmed him.

Upstairs, he selected a bedroom with a lovely view over the surrounding countryside. Whoever had taken care of the house had anticipated his choice, because clean linen was folded neatly on the huge four-poster bed and fresh towels were hanging on the heated rail in the *en suite* bathroom. Bars of unfussy, masculine soap, still in their wrappers, sat on the basin and in the generous shower cubicle. Appreciating the welcoming touches, and making a mental note to discover the identity of and thank the unknown cleaner, Gabriel stripped off his clothes and headed for the shower.

Hot water jetted down, easing the kinks out of his body, soothing his muscles and restoring his jaded spirit, making him realise how much tension remained coiled inside him.

'You're sure this is what you want?' François had asked him as he had come to see him off the day before. 'I don't want you to feel obligated to go to Cornwall because none of the rest of us are willing to uproot ourselves.'

'It's not that,' Gabriel had reassured his friend.

Frowning, François had helped him load his bags into the car. 'You're worried about interference from home?'

'Always.' His smile had been wry, hiding the inner turmoil that had plagued him for months. 'I need the distance, the space to make some decisions.'

'You know I'll watch your back. I won't be giving out details of your whereabouts to anyone. Especially now we know what Yvette is capable of to achieve her ends.'

Gabriel had nodded in gratitude. 'Thanks, *mon ami*. But you and I will keep in touch.'

'Try to get rid of me! I want regular texts and emails.'

He would miss François and his wife, having stayed with the couple for the last ten months. 'You and Celeste take care.'

'We will—and we really appreciate the way you stepped in when we needed you,' Francois had told him.

'That's what friends are for.'

After shaking hands and exchanging a brief hug, Gabriel had driven away from St Ouen-sur-Mer filled with nervous anticipation for what lay ahead. One chapter was over—a new one was about to begin.

Now, remembering that conversation, he closed his eyes and tipped his face to the shower spray. Today was the first day of the rest of his life. It was up to him what he made of it…whether he went his own way or allowed old ghosts and new pressures to trap him into something he knew he didn't want. This posting to Cornwall had bought him some extra time. Time he intended to use wisely, making the decisions that would set the course of his future.

Shutting off the water, he stepped out of the cubicle and reached for a towel, hesitating when he heard a noise downstairs. It had sounded like the front door closing. Frowning, Gabriel waited, listening. Yes, there was definitely someone moving around inside the house. More curious than concerned, he wrapped the towel around his waist and left his bedroom, moving silently down the stairs to investigate the trespass into his new domain. The noises were louder now. He tiptoed in the direction from which they came, pausing in the shadows of the unlit passageway to look through the door into a large, homely farmhouse kitchen.

A brindle-and-white greyhound lay on the stone-flagged floor, its head on its paws, solemnly watching the movements of the woman who was moving about as if she owned the place. Guessing her age to be in the late twenties, Gabriel's gaze lingered on her with as much intensity as the dog's, warmth and pure masculine appreciation spearing through him, catching him by surprise.

A bunch of home-cut flowers, dahlias and chrysanthemums amongst them, were arranged haphazardly in an old stoneware jug on the table, while several carrier bags littered the polished wooden work surfaces. Humming an unrecognisable tune, the woman busied herself stocking the kitchen cupboards with her purchases, her movements athletically graceful. Tight white jeans accentuated the length of her legs and lovingly moulded the rounded swell of her derrière. As she turned round, still unaware of his presence, he could see how the super-soft angora jumper she wore skimmed her shapely frame, outlining the curves of full, firm breasts. The lavender colour set off the natural paler highlights in her light brown hair and lent an amethyst glow to what he could see, even from this distance, were gorgeous grey eyes. Gabriel was mesmerised. Who was this woman?

Picking up a carton of milk and a box of eggs, she twirled her way to the fridge on trainer-clad feet, presenting him with a delectable view of her feminine curves as she bent over, her hips swaying provocatively to the music she heard in her head. Left loose, her wavy hair cascaded round her shoulders in a darkly golden curtain. She flicked it back with one hand as she rose and returned to the counter, still humming to herself as she delved into the carrier bags once more.

Intrigued, Gabriel stepped into the room. The dog was the first to acknowledge him. Anxious brown eyes turned his way, then the too-thin creature whined and all but crawled towards the woman, who leaned down to stroke it with gentle care.

'What's wrong, Foxy?'

Knowing whatever he did was going to startle her, Gabriel cleared his throat, announcing his presence as he walked forward. 'Hello.'

With a shocked cry, the woman swung round, the pack of pasta shells in her hands dropping to the floor. Beautiful smoky grey eyes widened between long, dark lashes as she stared at him, and lushly kissable lips parted in surprise. Her tongue-tip peeped out to moisten them as she stepped back a pace, one hand dropping to calm the fretful dog pressed against her legs, the other curled to a fist at her throat. Gabriel felt her gaze skim over his scantily clad frame and an unexpected but immediate wave of attraction crashed through him.

'I'm sorry.' He offered a smile with the apology, unable to look away from her. 'I didn't mean to scare you. I heard a noise down here and had no idea anyone was around.'

'OK. Um…hello,' she greeted after a moment, her voice melodious but with a husky undertone that appealed to him. Hell, everything about her appealed to him. 'You must be Dr Devereux. I wasn't expecting you until tomorrow,' she continued, bending to pick up the fallen pasta, fumbling briefly as she set it awkwardly back on the counter. With a sudden smile that had the same effect on him as a punch to the solar plexus, she held out her hand. 'I'm Lauren Nightingale…your neighbour at Gatehouse Cottage and also physiotherapist at the Penhally Bay Surgery.'

This was the woman Nick Tremayne had spoken of? *Ooh la la!* 'Lauren, it is a pleasure to meet you. Please, call me Gabriel,' he invited, trying to pull himself together and remember his manners.

Closing the remaining gap between them, he took her graceful hand in his. Her grip was strong, her fingers slender but capable. Looking down, he noted how much paler her warm, satiny skin was than his, how her bones were far more delicate. A jolt of electricity zinged up his arm and along his nerve endings at the contact between them. That Lauren felt it, too, was apparent by the way she bit her lip, her pupils dilating, her body momentarily swaying towards him before she caught herself and pulled back, withdrawing her hand. Gabriel released her with reluctance.

Close to, she was taller than he had realised, five-seven or -eight, he judged, and even more attractive than he had first thought. She had an earthy allure quite unlike the sophisti-cated, deliberate beauty of some of the Parisian women he had dated in the past but vastly more entrancing and natural. A subtle, floral scent—sweet peas, he recognised—mingled with her unique femininity, teasing and enticing him. No make-up was needed to enhance her flawless skin. Pale gold from a fading summer tan, it looked as smooth as silk. His fingers longed to touch, to discover if she was as warm and soft all over as her hand had felt in his. He struggled to rein back the runaway thoughts but it wasn't easy when every particle of his being hummed with awareness while she studied him as closely as he had regarded her.

Dr Gabriel Devereux was the most delicious surprise!

Fearing that her legs would not hold her upright much

longer, Lauren leaned against the kitchen counter and affected what she hoped was a nonchalant pose. She didn't *feel* remotely nonchalant. Any minute now she was going to do something uncharacteristically shocking, impulsive and embarrassing…like throw herself wantonly into his arms and ravish him.

Gabriel's sudden arrival had taken her off guard. She was disconcerted that she had not been aware of his presence and wondered how long he had stood there watching her. But the fact that she had not seen him in the shadows and had only formed a distinct visual impression when he had stepped into the brightly lit kitchen stirred inner anxieties she was unwilling to deal with. That he was wearing only an ivory towel was a suitable diversion, however, and she grabbed the excuse to ignore her disturbing concerns, unable to resist the temptation to observe him in detail.

She saw bare bodies, or bits of bodies, every working day, but she had never seen one that made her heart hammer, her mouth water and that robbed her of breath as Gabriel's did. Goodness! Her hands clung to the counter as she greedily inspected him. She feared she was about to melt into a puddle at his feet. Nice feet, too, she couldn't help but notice. Very nice. Like the rest of him. Her gaze slowly climbed back up his scrumptious frame.

Strong, lean legs were braced hip-width apart and the towel slung low around his hips revealed a tantalising glimpse of pleasingly muscled, hair-brushed thighs. A narrow line of dark hair in the centre of his flat stomach dipped past his navel and disappeared below the towel. She licked her lips, resisting the urge to touch as she looked over his perfect athletic body, toned abdomen, well-defined chest and broad shoulders, all supple flesh and rippling muscle. He'd clearly just stepped out of the shower as droplets of water glistened on his delicious dark caramel skin, its colour hinting at a French

Caribbean ancestry. Lauren swallowed, battling against the overwhelming desire to press her lips to that warm, damp masculine flesh. She still remembered the faint scent of him when they had been close and shaken hands…tangy citrus soap and clean male, heady and earthy and arousing.

Topping six feet, he was more than impressive. The close-cropped dark hair suited him, accentuating the classically beautiful but supremely masculine bone structure of his face, the slash of high cheekbones, the straight nose and the carved lines of his jaw. Her palm itched to smooth over his head, to feel if the razor-short hair was rough or soft to the touch. His mouth was undeniably sexy, his bronze lips sensually curved and designed for kissing. She yearned to press her own against them, to learn the shape and feel and taste of him.

Twin dimples creased his cheeks when he smiled, while laughter lines fanned out from the corners of his eyes, adding character and hinting at an active sense of humour. Finally, she looked into those thickly lashed eyes. They were the richest brown she had ever seen. As Gabriel met and held her gaze, his pupils dilated, darkening the irises to the colour of finest coffee. The flare of masculine interest was unmistakable and caused a tightening ache of want in the pit of her stomach that was so strong and so sudden she barely suppressed a gasp.

What in the world had come over her? Yes, it had been a while since she had enjoyed male companionship. She had broken up with her long-term boyfriend, Martin Bennett, six months ago, but to all intents and purposes they had been apart a long time before that. They had gone their separate ways amicably, both knowing their lingering on-again-off-again relationship had been based more on old friendship than grand passion and had been leading nowhere. Martin was desperate to get out of Cornwall, to explore and experience new things, while Lauren was content to remain in Penhally, enjoying her job, her friends and her hobbies, including her painting.

Unwelcome and worrying thoughts intruded once more. She hadn't painted much lately and she wasn't anywhere near ready to face the reasons why. Determinedly, she returned her full attention to the exquisite man before her, a quiver running through her at his thorough inspection, as if he had touched her physically.

Since midwife Kate Althorp had met Gabriel at Nick's house in the summer, she had reported that Penhally was in for a treat when the French doctor arrived in their midst. Kate's comments had caused some of their colleagues to tease Lauren about her soon-to-be neighbour. Lauren had ignored the ribbing. But now she could acknowledge first hand that Kate had not been exaggerating. Dear heaven, the man was *gorgeous*!

That Gabriel Devereux would be close by, at home and at work, for the next twelve months was wonderfully thrilling. Already the year ahead was filled with new and unexpected possibilities. Everything feminine within her stood to attention and all the hormones that had been switched off and un-interested since long before her split from Martin now started doing a happy dance like over-enthusiastic cheerleaders. She looked into Gabriel's eyes, excited by the answering desire she saw there. Oh, yes! She was most definitely interested! She just hoped he was in England alone, uninvolved, and had no wife or girlfriend tucked away at home in France.

'It is kind of you to bring things for the kitchen, Lauren,' Gabriel said, the dimples forming in his lean cheeks, his eyes crinkling as he smiled.

She could drown in that smile. And as for his accent, the way he said her name… He made her tingle all over. His English was perfect but delivered with a soft burr and all the Gallic charm imaginable. There was so much she wanted to learn about him but she reined in her rush of questions, scared that she would frighten him away before he'd even properly arrived. There would be time in the days and weeks ahead to explore the inexplicable and immediate connection she felt with this man. Or so she hoped. Better to play it cool for now.

'It's no trouble,' she answered, not sure how she managed to form any words at all, let alone sensible ones. 'I promised Nick I would make sure you had all you needed.'

Relaxed and at ease, he folded his arms across his chest, the play of muscle distracting her. 'Thank you. I am sorry I took you by surprise arriving early.'

'No problem.' Returning his smile, she couldn't prevent herself looking over his superb body once more. Oh, it was no problem at all!

'Are you also responsible for airing the house and providing the clean linen and towels?'

'Yes.' Almost overcome with nervous anticipation, she tucked some strands of hair behind one ear, her hand unsteady. 'Is everything all right?'

'Very much so. I was planning to ask the solicitor who to thank for making the house feel so welcoming.'

'I'm glad to help,' she assured him, warmed through and pleased by his thoughtfulness.

He watched her for a long moment, then glanced at the greyhound who whined and nudged against her legs. 'And who is your companion?'

'This is Foxy. He lost his owner in the flood and was found distressed after searching the rubble,' she explained, a catch in her voice as she gently stroked the dog. 'Both the RSPCA and Lizzie Chamberlain, who runs the local kennels, were overrun with extra work and animals needing help during the crisis. Foxy was always nervous of people, but he knew me and we bonded, so I was happy to give him a home. He's adjusting but still wary. At least he's started eating again. He needs time and lots of love.'

The approval and flash of admiration in Gabriel's eyes made her feel good. She held her breath as he turned his attention to

Foxy. Speaking softly, he hunkered down and held out his hand for the dog to sniff. Calm and patient, he waited for the dog to be comfortable, making no sudden moves. Lauren was surprised and delighted when Foxy inched forward and allowed Gabriel to touch him, something he had permitted few people but her to do in the last ten days. Slowly he was forming a tentative bond with her friends Chloe and Oliver. Foxy's current reaction and his instinct to trust Gabriel was more than interesting and told her much about this intriguing man.

As if satisfied with the early progress, Gabriel didn't push things, moving carefully back and rising before returning his attention to her, causing her heart to pound once more.

'Nick mentioned the flood in an email but I had no idea how bad things were. I was shocked when I drove through town.' He paused, a pout of consideration shaping his mouth and giving her all manner of wicked ideas. 'Are you busy this afternoon, Lauren? Do you have plans?'

'No. Why?' She was filled with sudden hope that she might be able to spend more time with Gabriel. She wasn't ready to leave just yet.

'I was going to make myself a late lunch. Will you join me? It would be good to talk, to learn more about Penhally and the surgery…and what has gone on in the last couple of weeks.'

Not wanting to appear as shamefully eager as she felt, she forced herself not to rush her agreement. Maybe Gabriel's reasons for asking her to linger weren't all she had hoped for, but at this point she would accept any opportunity to enjoy his company. Who knew where things might lead?

'OK.' She cursed the breathlessness of her voice but could do nothing to temper her excitement. 'I can stay a while longer.'

At Lauren's confirmation, Gabriel felt a wash of relief course through him and he expelled the breath he had not realised he had been holding. He was nowhere near ready to let her go.

This was ridiculous. He felt like some gauche sixteen-year-old boy with a crush, rather than the thirty-six-year-old man he really was. Then Lauren looked over him once more and his body instantly heated and tightened in response, as if her touch had been an actual caress. He hoped the loose towel hid the evidence of the arousing effect she had on him.

'Give me five minutes to get dressed,' he requested as he turned away and headed to the door.

'Gabriel?'

Her soft voice halted him and he glanced back. 'Yes?'

'I could prepare a quick meal while you're gone,' she offered.

'Are you sure?'

Her head bobbed in assent. 'It's no trouble. Is there anything you don't like?'

Dieu! He couldn't imagine anything Lauren could suggest that he wouldn't like, but he managed to focus his attention on food. 'Mushrooms, shellfish and red meat,' he informed her, catching her surprised smile.

'Me, too.' Mischief gleamed in her eyes. 'And I confess I'm not keen on boiled cabbage, tapioca or mushy peas either.'

'Believe me, Lauren, you are not alone!' Chuckling, he left the room.

'I certainly hope not—not any more.'

Had he really heard those final whispered words? And could they mean what he hoped they did? He was confused by his instinctive response to this woman. It was unlike him. And that was disturbing. He'd not been so spontaneously attracted to anyone for years—if ever. The timing was unfortunate. He had never considered such a thing happening to him, especially not while part of his world was in turmoil and he had decisions to make about his future. Coming here was meant to give him space to declutter his life, not add more complications to it.

But he couldn't deny the way his body had reacted to the

sight, scent and sound of Lauren Nightingale. Anxious to dress and return to the kitchen as quickly as possible, Gabriel hurried up the stairs. Had he dreamed it all? What if the sizzle of electricity between himself and Lauren had been a figment of his overactive imagination? What if it wasn't? He was here for a year. To work. To think. Did he even want to consider any kind of involvement? He hadn't been at the Manor House an hour and already he was feeling alive at an unexpected awareness, filled with a sense of wary excitement at the possibilities that might lie ahead.

Perhaps it had just been too long since he had dated a woman. After his most recent experience with Adèle, and with his mother's continued interference, he had become cautious, untrusting. But that had been a year ago. And Lauren knew nothing about his life—or his family circumstances. More importantly, Yvette, his mother, knew nothing about Lauren. If anything happened between them, it would be because of who and what they were…no ulterior motives, no deception, no scheming.

Unzipping a suitcase, he pulled out fresh clothes and dressed in record time, favouring casual jeans and a warm cashmere jumper. As he made his way out of his bedroom, tantalising aromas teased his senses and sharpened his hunger, and he increased his pace, keen to discover both the food awaiting him and the intriguing woman who was preparing it.

Lauren occupied his thoughts. He would be cautious about rushing into anything, but he wanted to spend time with her, to get to know her better. If the connection and charge of desire he had felt between them *was* real…

CHAPTER TWO

LAUREN set the plate of food she had prepared on the table in the rustic kitchen and tried very hard not to stare at Gabriel. An impossible feat. He looked almost as gorgeous with his clothes *on*...and just as impressive. The sweater he wore—over the kind of faded, body-hugging jeans that ought to be made illegal, so lethal were they to a woman's blood pressure—looked expensive, the mulberry colour warming and flattering the espresso-coffee tones of his skin.

He sat down, a quizzical expression on his face as he noted she had only laid one place. 'You are not eating, Lauren?'

'No.' The breathlessness was back in her voice—an uncharacteristic reaction that seemed to afflict her at every sight and sound of Gabriel Devereux. 'I met up with friends in town. We had soup and sandwiches at the farmers' market.'

'But you will join me here, yes?' He drew out the chair nearest to him before extending a hand and inviting her to sit.

Gratified by his suggestion to be near him, Lauren hastened to take her seat, hoping she looked far less flustered than she felt. 'Thank you.' For goodness' sake. She was a thirty-year-old woman, not some blushing schoolgirl!

'Forgive me tucking right in, I'm hungrier than I thought.' The appreciative look he sent her, and the readiness of his smile, heated her right through. So much for cool, calm maturity. 'This looks and smells wonderful.'

Cooking was not her greatest talent, but Gabriel gave every evidence of liking her food. She'd made him a simple omelette with cheese and chives, serving it with a warmed granary roll, plus a tomato, rocket and watercress salad…all fresh ingredients she had picked up on her shopping trip that morning. He was eating with relish, his enjoyment making her smile with relief. And she had even more to be grateful for, she admitted to herself—she'd not had any accidents or set fire to the kitchen which, given her current run of clumsy *faux pas*, was a major achievement.

Foxy, having quenched his thirst from the bowl of water she had set down for him, now sprawled his long, too-skinny body beside her chair, his paws twitching in his sleep, blissfully unconcerned by the electrically charged atmosphere crackling between the two humans. Lauren couldn't help but be aware of it. Aware of Gabriel. She was glad she had made herself some tea. It gave her something to do with her hands. Anything to avoid the temptation—the compulsion—to touch him. She cupped the mug, watching from beneath her lashes as he finished his meal. When she raised the mug to her lips and took a sip of her drink, she looked up to find mocha eyes watching her intently, and a fresh dart of feminine recognition zinged through her body.

'That was delicious.' Gabriel's smile and sexy accent undid her every time. 'Thank you, Lauren.'

'My pleasure.'

After taking a drink from his glass of water, he turned so he was facing her, giving her his undivided attention. She could feel fresh heat tinge her cheeks. 'It seems a long time since breakfast.'

'Did you come over from France this morning?' she ventured, struggling to appear cool and composed.

'I took the chance of an earlier ferry from Cherbourg to Poole yesterday, then I stayed the night with an old friend in Bournemouth before driving down here today.'

A bleakness shadowed his eyes, so fleeting it was gone before she could be sure. But she was left with a sense that there was more to Gabriel's departure from France than he had let on. She wondered what had happened, and whether there was a woman involved.

Instead of satisfying her curiosity and asking outright, she endeavoured to be more subtle. 'Wouldn't getting a ferry to Plymouth have been easier?'

'Not really. Cherbourg is only about thirty or forty minutes from where I was based in St Ouen-sur-Mer. If I had gone to Plymouth, it would have meant a long drive through France to Roscoff and almost twice as long for the Channel crossing.' His eyes twinkled as he sent her a wry smile. 'I am not the best traveller on ferries! And I prefer to be in control of my own destiny. Besides, the drive down from Dorset to Cornwall today gave me the opportunity to reaccustom myself to English roads.'

'How did you come to take this job?' she asked, propping her chin in one hand as she looked at him.

'I volunteered.' Pushing his empty plate aside, he leaned closer and rested one forearm on the table. 'I was only working in St Ouen-sur-Mer on a temporary basis to help out a friend from medical school. François is head of the clinic and his wife, Celeste, is also a doctor there. Another of the partners, Marianne, had a baby last Christmas and was on maternity leave. Then, in early January, François badly broke his leg in a skiing accident. He was having trouble finding a replacement doctor, so he called me. As I had reason to leave Paris for a while, I was happy to provide cover. I've been there ever since. But now François is back on his feet and Marianne is ready to return to work. It was time for me to move on.'

'I see,' Lauren murmured, toying with the handle of her mug. Clearly Gabriel was loyal to his friends and ready to help in a crisis, but she wondered what had made him so eager to leave Paris in a hurry at the start of the year. He had sounded relieved to have received François's initial call…and now to be in Cornwall.

'When the position came up to work here for a year, I was interested in taking it,' he continued, and she lost herself in the sound of his huskily accented voice, captivated by the way he looked at her, maintaining eye contact as though she was interesting and important to him. 'I speak English—'

'Perfect English,' she interjected, halting his explanation.

An amused smile curved his mouth at her praise. 'Thank you, *chérie.*'

'Sorry, I interrupted you.' She smothered a groan of embarrassment.

'That's all right.' Her skin tingled as Gabriel briefly reached out and whispered his fingertips across the back of her hand. She sucked in a shaky breath and struggled to concentrate as he continued to speak about his reasons for moving to Penhally. 'I was the only doctor at the clinic who was single and without commitments…the others did not want to uproot their families to come here. And I've worked in England before—in London. I enjoyed it, but I was eager to experience small-town, rural medicine, too.'

Again Lauren thought there was more to the story than he had told her, but she was exceedingly glad he was here. She had also noted with a shiver of hopeful anticipation his comment that he was single and had no commitments. Surely that was a good sign? She had no idea why, but she had felt a deep connection with and recognition of this man from the outset.

'So, Lauren, tell me about the flood.' Gabriel broke the silence, drawing her from her thoughts. 'What happened?

How much damage has there been? You said Foxy's owner was tragically killed but was anyone else hurt?'

Lauren huffed out a breath, taking a few moments as she wondered where to begin recounting the events of that never-to-be-forgotten and emotional day.

As Gabriel waited for Lauren to speak, he resisted the fierce urge to keep touching her, remembering how silky her skin had felt beneath his fingers. Instead, he reflected on what he had told her about himself and his reasons for coming to Cornwall, hoping he had said enough to curb her interest without giving away any of his secrets…or his inner turmoil.

It was true that the request from François in January to help out in his clinic on Normandy's west coast could not have come at a better time. He had been deeply sorry for the injury that had caused François so many problems, but his friend's need had provided Gabriel with the chance to leave Paris—and Yvette—far behind. Time away to come to terms with all he had suddenly learned about his family, and to put space between himself and home, had been exactly what he had needed. But that space had not proved great enough, so the offer to work in Penhally Bay had been even more welcome. The width of the English Channel would surely be a suitable barrier. Here in Cornwall he felt he could breathe again and hear himself think.

His early departure from France had been sparked by another summons from home—one more demand, one more threat he had chosen to ignore. Things were increasingly strained with his mother. Not that Yvette Devereux had ever been particularly *motherly* towards him, he reflected with a cynical twist of his lips. She had never been the warm, nurturing and understanding type, but always stiff, distant, with her rigid view of duty and propriety. Now he knew why.

A light touch on his arm startled him from his disturbing

thoughts and he glanced up to find Lauren watching him with a frown on her face.

'Are you all right, Gabriel?'

'Yes, of course.' His skin felt warm and alive long after her fingers had been withdrawn. He managed a smile, grateful for the interruption and thankful to push family troubles to the back of his mind again. 'I was miles away. Please, you were going to explain the events of the last couple of weeks.'

'You hear about these things happening, but you never expect them to affect your own community,' she began, a serious tone to her voice. 'We had no warning. The sky went black, there was thunder and lightning, and the most torrential rain I've ever seen or heard. It poured off everything. Combined with the run-off inland, something collapsed upstream and the deluge swelled watercourses, causing a flash flood that swept away everything in its path. The river Lanson burst its banks, funnelling massive amounts of earthy-black water laden with debris down through the centre of Penhally, hitting us full force.'

'What happened to you?' Gabriel asked with concern, noting how Lauren shivered, rubbing her forearms in reaction. 'Were you caught out in it?'

'I was lucky. I was visiting a patient at the time. The power went out, the telephone lines were down and mobile phone coverage was patchy, but I received a message to go to one of the two evacuation points. I spent the rest of the time at the school, helping out.' She raised her gaze to his, her eyes registering grief. 'It was really frightening. People were missing, we didn't know what had happened to friends. There were a number of minor injuries, some more serious ones…and two people died.'

Gabriel listened to Lauren's explanation of the disaster with shock. '*Dieu*. I had no idea things were so bad,' he murmured, taking one of her trembling hands in his, needing to comfort, to touch her. 'I am so sorry. It must have been horribly traumatic and such a loss for the whole community.'

'Yes, it was. Is.' Hearing the waver in her voice, he tightened his hold on her hand, linking their fingers and brushing the pad of his thumb across her wrist. 'Audrey Baxter was one of our regular patients at the surgery. Elderly and with health problems, she was a bit of a busybody but she meant well. She had recently taken Foxy in as a companion from the rescue centre and having him helped her emotional well-being considerably. They helped each other, I suppose. Anyway, Audrey was caught outside when the flash flood came. She never stood a chance with that wall of water. The local vicar, Reverend Kenner, plunged in to try to save her, but he was lost, too, when the end of the Anchor Hotel collapsed on them. He was such a good man. He did a great deal for this community. And it was tragic for his daughter, Rachel. She's just a teenager, and with her mother dying a few years ago her father was all she had. They were very close. Now she's pregnant and alone. Her aunt and uncle in Plymouth are caring for her.'

'Lauren,' he murmured, wishing he had the words to ease the pain and horror of what she and the rest of the town had been through.

'It's all so unfair!'

'I know.' He stroked her arm, aware of the softness of her skin and the beat of her pulse. 'Sometimes it is impossible to understand why these things happen.'

Her fingers returned the pressure of his and she looked at him with a sorrowful smile. 'That's the truth.' She shook her head, a sigh escaping.

'Thank goodness you had such excellent rescue aid or things could have been even worse for the town.'

'Yes, we were very grateful. I think people are finding it hard to accept we've been affected like this again. It's not that long since Penhally's last great tragedy. The big storm ten years ago took many lives, including those of Kate Althorp's husband James and Nick Tremayne's father and brother.'

'How are people coping now?' Gabriel asked after a short silence, one that saw them both lost in thought.

'A lot are still displaced after the flood. The caravan park above the cliffs on Mevagissey Road has taken in several families, while others are staying with relatives and friends or renting temporary accommodation.'

'It looked as though much has been done to begin clearing up.'

Lauren nodded, her voice stronger again now. 'Everyone has worked very hard. It's amazing the mess and damage water can cause. I think it will be months before some of the homes are fit to be lived in again.'

'Many of your patients must be needing extra care and understanding,' Gabriel allowed, looking down at their joined hands, thankful that Lauren had not pulled away.

'Yes, there's been trauma and anxiety. And it's hard for some to come to terms with losing irreplaceable and senti-mental possessions. We also had to be careful because of things like polluted water and so on as some people failed to heed the safety advice in the aftermath.'

Gabriel watched as she tucked a couple of wayward strands of hair behind her ear. Adjusting his hold on her hand, he played with her fingers and traced a circle on her palm with his thumb, aware of the growing connection between them.

'So, tell me about your regular patients,' he suggested after a few moments, relieved to see a lightening of her expression.

He listened with interest as Lauren talked of little Timmy Morrison, nearly five months old and diagnosed at birth with cystic fibrosis, of eleven-year-old Paul Mitchell, coping spir-itedly with Duchenne muscular dystrophy, and of older patients like Harry Biscombe in sheltered accommodation at

Gow Court, with osteoporosis, whom she had been visiting when the flood had hit, and Stella Chamberlain, currently in the Harbour View Nursing Home with Parkinson's disease.

'Stella's desperate to go home but it's becoming impossible for her daughter Lizzie to cope. It's very sad. We're all doing the best we can to find the best solution for both Stella and Lizzie.'

Every word Lauren spoke, both about the regulars she visited at home and her more mobile and short-term patients who came to the surgery, revealed how dedicated she was and just how much she cared about each and every person. Minute by minute Gabriel was more impressed with Lauren Nightingale. Her natural beauty had first appealed to him and he had been unable to ignore the sparks of attraction that had crackled between them from the first moment. He had only just met her and yet the more he knew about her, the longer they talked, the more he respected and admired her as a person. She was funny, intelligent and caring. Genuine, without any airs or graces.

Meeting Lauren put an interesting and unexpected slant on his time in Cornwall. Her eyes reflected a feminine interest she made no effort to hide and he felt the answering response rise within him, one he had not felt in a long time. This might well turn out to be an even more interesting year than he had ever imagined.

'I'm not sure which patients you'll be seeing,' Lauren told him now, explaining about the staffing at the surgery and how GP Dragan Lovak was taking time off to be with his wife after the recent birth of their baby boy. 'I expect Nick will suggest you spend time with one of the other doctors this week—if you are lucky, it will be Oliver Fawkner.' The affection in her voice as she mentioned the other doctor brought a flash of unexpected jealousy. 'If Nick agrees, it would also be good if you could come out on house calls with various members of staff.'

'Including you?'

'Probably.'

His gaze caught hers. 'I hope so.'

'Me, too.' She bit her lip, her eyes widening as she realised she had spoken aloud. He felt the kick of her pulse beneath his fingers as she hurried on. 'There have been some changes due to the surgery expansion—you'll see those when you look around on Monday. Immediately after the flood, Nick asked us all not to go out on calls after dark unless it was an emergency, because of all the debris and possible danger of unsafe buildings and falling masonry.' Gabriel nodded, knowing it made sense not to put more people at risk than necessary. 'That ban has been lifted since the clean-up started,' Lauren continued. 'But I've kept to the new schedule. It works for me and my patients now we have the new physiotherapy room. With Nick's agreement, I do house calls that are required in the mornings and see patients at the surgery in the afternoons.'

'So I'll keep at least one morning free to go on visits with you.'

Gabriel's statement brought fresh warmth to her cheeks. 'OK,' she agreed, already eager for the time they would spend together, even if it was work related. That he was so keen and interested in her patients and the work she did brought her a glow of pleasure.

He asked more questions about the surgery, staff and the town in general, and she was happy to answer them, to help him fit into his new role in a different country. They had clicked from the first and got on so well she felt she had known him for ever. Yet all the time there was the undercurrent of sexual tension, the hum of desire between them, and excitement bubbled inside her at what might happen.

She had not forgotten for a moment that her hand was still in his, their fingers entwined, but she had no desire to let go until he did. They talked about local activities and their hobbies, discovering shared interests in books and music. They both loved sport, but while Lauren was keen on running, swimming and cycling, Gabriel favoured team sports like football. She could listen to him for ever with that sexy accent and soft huskiness edging his voice.

'So you jog every morning?' he asked now, pulling her from her thoughts.

'Yes, I try to do between three and five miles a day.'

'I can see it keeps you fit.'

The knot in her stomach tightened as he looked her over, the expression in his melting brown eyes letting her know that he liked what he saw. 'I try.' She swallowed the restriction in her throat, a tingle running through her as his thumb began to brush across her palm and wrist once more. 'I've done a few triathlons in the past but I don't get the chance to compete much these days.'

'Do you prefer to run alone, or do you enjoy company?'

'Company is good,' she murmured, hoping that meant he might join her one day. 'If you still play football, you should talk to Oliver. He's organising a charity match next weekend to raise money for the flood relief fund.'

'That's an excellent idea, I'll do that. Lauren—'

Whatever Gabriel had been about to say was halted by the sudden beep of her mobile phone announcing an incoming text message. Lauren jumped at the intrusion, disappointed when her hand was released. Already she missed the contact between them. Beside her, Foxy stirred at the noise, stretching and yawning before rising to his feet and nudging her leg. Absently, she stroked his head with one hand while rummaging in her bag with the other to find her phone.

'Sorry about this.'

'Don't worry,' Gabriel reassured her, but he looked as regretful for the interruption as she was.

Sighing, Lauren tilted the phone, frowning as she concentrated on reading the message, aware it was harder to see the small letters illuminated on the screen than it had once been. Again, she pushed the concern away, unable to face the implications. The text, she discovered, was from her friend Chloe MacKinnon.

'Worried you aren't home yet. Any problems? Oliver says supper ready in an hour. Love C x'

Shocked, Lauren looked towards the windows and saw how dark it was outside. She glanced at her watch, stunned to discover the time. 'Oh, my gosh!'

'Everything all right?' Gabriel asked.

'I'd no idea it was this late. I'm so sorry, I've taken up all your afternoon!'

Laughing, his hand brushed her arm. 'I've enjoyed every moment with you, Lauren. Thank you. I am the one who should apologise for detaining you.'

'It's fine. I just didn't say I was delayed. I was expected home ages ago.'

'I see.' Gabriel moved back from her, disappointment dulling his eyes.

Her breath caught as she realised what he thought. 'I've told you about my friends Chloe and Oliver, midwife and GP at the surgery?' she asked, and he nodded. 'They're engaged and Oliver's been living at Chloe's cottage in Fisherman's Row since the end of July. They were flooded out and have been staying with me since then,' she rushed to explain, gratified to see relief lighten his expression.

'So there's no boyfriend waiting for you?'

'No. There's no one.' She responded to his blunt question with equal clarity. 'But I'd better get back.'

'Of course.'

Reluctantly, she rose to her feet, unhooked her bag from the back of the chair and looped the strap over her shoulder. 'Is there anything else I can do? Do you have all you need?'

She looked around the kitchen, hoping she had remembered everything.

'It's fine, Lauren. You have done so much and I appreciate it.'

'If you think of anything…'

'I'll let you know,' he promised with a smile.

'I wrote out some phone numbers for you.' Including her own, she added silently, pointing to the fridge where a piece of paper was held firm by a colourful Penhally magnet. With nothing else to prevent her leaving, she slipped on Foxy's lead and turned towards the door. 'I'd better go, then.'

She was acutely conscious of Gabriel following close behind her as she walked out of the kitchen. Pausing a moment, she formed a picture in her mind of the dim, unlit hallway and the route to the front door, trying to remember if there was anything in the way. She didn't think so…provided she avoided the bottom tread of the stairs that stuck out a few inches on her left. Anxiety gripped her as she was faced with her failing night vision. She could fumble for an unseen light switch and risk drawing attention to her problem, or take a chance the hall was clear. She chose the latter.

A short while ago she had breezily told Gabriel about her altered working hours. What she had not told him was how she had used the cover of the flood disaster and completion of the new physio room to make her changed schedule permanent. A flicker of guilt assailed her for the deception and for hiding her real reasons from Nick and everyone else. She was afraid to venture out after dark and, with each passing autumn day, dusk was falling earlier. The only journey she felt able to make at night was from the surgery to her cottage, a route she knew so well she could cover every inch of the short distance with her eyes closed. Which was how it had felt lately in the dark. She was scared what it meant, but was unable to face the fact that something strange was happening to her sight. At some point, if it got worse, she would have to. She would never put other people in danger. But for now she could still cover it up.

After she had negotiated the hallway slowly but safely, Gabriel reached round her to open the door, momentarily bringing their bodies into close proximity and firing her blood once more. Before he could put on the outside light, she moved forward, missing her step, unable to see. For a second, she teetered off balance, then Gabriel's arm was there to steady her. The light came on and she blinked, disoriented for a second, aware, when her vision sharpened, of the frown on his face.

'Are you OK?'

'Yes, fine,' she assured him breathlessly. With caution, she stepped out of his hold and down the steps to the gravel drive. Needing to disguise her latest mishap, she turned back to smile at him. 'There is something you should know about me before you hear it from anyone else.'

The wariness returned to his eyes and she could sense his tension. 'What's that?'

'I'm renowned for being impossibly clumsy.' She managed a passable laugh, trying not to think of her catalogue of stupid incidents. Unfortunately they seemed to be happening more and more often, her most recent examples being the moment she had inexplicably reversed into a parked car at the church after Jack and Alison's wedding, and the way she had stumbled and fallen in the rubble the day after the flood. 'Everyone teases me for being an accident waiting to happen.'

'I'll consider myself warned,' Gabriel replied, his answering laugh not completely masking his confusion.

Eager to leave on a more positive note, Lauren lingered. 'If you have nothing else planned, would you like to come for lunch tomorrow? You can meet Chloe and Oliver…get to know them before work on Monday.'

'I'd love to.' A teasing glint flickered in his eyes. 'Not the roast beef?'

'No! Chicken and all the trimmings. And Chloe is doing one of her special puddings,' she told him, laughing back.

'What time?'

'About noon?' She tried to sound casual, but already she was brimming with excitement at seeing him again.

'I'll be there,' he promised, making her pulse race. 'Would you like me to walk you back?'

She would, but she didn't want him witnessing her tripping again. 'Thanks, but there's no need.'

'Until tomorrow, then.' His voice dropped to a rough murmur. *'Au revoir, chérie.'*

'Bye.'

She felt him watching her as she walked carefully down the drive, Foxy well behaved at her side. Silently, she counted her steps, having made this journey before. She knew that when she reached the curve, the lights in her cottage would guide her home, but the knowledge that she was seeing less and less at night filled her with silent fear. How long could she hide her secret?

A sigh of relief escaped when her cottage came into view and she picked up her pace, more sure of herself, keen to tell Chloe and Oliver about the exciting new doctor. It was awful that the flood had driven her friends from their home. Chloe had been more upset at her missing cats, but one of the members of the rescue team had found Pirate and Cyclops unscathed on top of a wardrobe upstairs as the waters receded. In the days since they had moved in, Foxy and the cats had negotiated a cautious stand-off.

Until Chloe and Oliver found a suitable new home, Lauren was happy for them to stay with her. She enjoyed their company. But she wondered if things might get a bit awkward should anything develop between herself and Gabriel. There was plenty of time to worry about that, she reassured herself, knowing she shouldn't get too excited even though their first meeting had left her in no doubt about the connection between them. However foolish, she sensed that something unusual and important could evolve in the days and weeks ahead.

'We were going to send out a search party!' Chloe teased when Lauren let herself in, took off Foxy's lead and walked into the living room.

Her friend was cuddled up in Oliver's lap on the sofa in front of a roaring log fire. It didn't take a genius to know from their rumpled clothes and tousled hair what they had been doing with their extra time alone. Lauren was delighted for Chloe but it was ironic that her friend—who had suffered an abusive past at the hands of her brutal father, and who had remained a virgin until Oliver had come into her life—had enjoyed a more varied and extensive sex life in three months than Lauren had in ten years. She didn't begrudge Chloe her happiness and pleasure for a moment, but she wouldn't half mind being as lucky.

An image of a certain scrumptious French doctor filled her mind. Oh, yes! Now, there was a man with va-va-voom, one who would surely know how to make a woman feel special. Unable to stop smiling, Lauren sank into an armchair. Her heart was still pounding.

'Sorry you were concerned. I got held up. Dr Devereux had just arrived when I took the shopping up to the Manor House. I stayed for a chat.'

'Some chat,' Chloe commented with a meaningful grin that had Oliver laughing and Lauren's cheeks warming. 'Come on, tell us what happened.'

Nothing…and yet everything. But Lauren didn't know how to explain that. 'We talked about the surgery, Penhally and the flood. Gabriel's coming here for lunch tomorrow. I told him about your football match, Oliver, and he's keen to play.'

'Great! Thanks, Lauren. Nick has suggested that Gabriel shadow me next week, so it will be good to meet him in advance.'

'But what's he like?' Chloe persisted.

Lauren leaned back and sighed, unable to keep her smile from broadening. 'Absolutely *divine*.'

No way was she going to last out Gabriel's time here without being a *very* bad girl.

Hopefully.

CHAPTER THREE

'THANKS again for coming in early this morning, Gabriel. I think we've covered everything,' Nick Tremayne decided, leading the way back to his consulting room after a tour of the revamped surgery. He returned to his chair and rubbed his hands together. 'Do you have any other questions?'

'Is the expansion work nearly complete?' Gabriel had been impressed with the improvements that had taken place since his previous weekend visit in July.

'It won't be long now. Hopefully no more than a week. My daughter Lucy originally worked on the plans for the changes and devised a way to use the dead space we had here to make more room. We've rearranged the layout, adding extra facilities as well as increasing consulting-room availability upstairs and down,' Nick explained. 'There are a few minor jobs to finish, mostly outside, but we've been very lucky…the builders have worked around us so that patient disruption has been kept to a minimum.'

'The new X-ray and plaster rooms on the ground floor must make life much easier.'

'Indeed,' Nick agreed. 'It means we can handle the less serious breaks and injuries here now, rather than having to send everyone on the half-hour journey to the hospital in St Piran. It benefits the hospital, the patients and ourselves. As does having the new physiotherapy room for Lauren,' he added. 'Our workload is increasing all the time—and not just during the tourist season—so your presence here is even more welcome.'

'Thank you.'

Nick shuffled some papers on his desk. 'I've arranged for you to spend a few days working with Oliver Fawkner. You can take your own consultations, of course—we've assigned you one of the new rooms next to Lauren's—but Oliver will help you learn your way around the district. Is that all right with you?'

'But, yes, I appreciate it. I have already met Oliver, Chloe and Lauren—we had lunch together yesterday.'

'Good, good. I'm sure you'll get on well.' Nick nodded with approval, then handed over a sheet of paper. 'Here is this week's roster. We take turns doing out-of-hours cover so no one is unduly burdened, but we won't expect you to do your own evening and weekend calls until you are settled in. Again, as Oliver is temporarily living so close to the Manor House, you can share duties with him for a week or two before we add you to the list to do calls alone.'

'That sounds fine. Maybe I could also make some visits out with other staff?' Gabriel suggested, following up on the idea Lauren had given him.

Nick glanced up, an eyebrow raised in question. 'What did you have in mind?'

'I would be interested in learning how the various disciplines interact here. And it would give me a chance to meet some of the regular patients. Maybe if I spent a morning with the nurses, and also go out on a few home visits with Chloe and Lauren during my first couple of weeks?'

'An excellent idea,' his new boss agreed. His smile of approval stripped some of the characteristic sternness from his face. 'The more familiarisation you can gain, the better. I'll leave you to arrange the details with the staff concerned. You can sort things out to fit your own schedules. I'll mention it when we all meet and—' The phone buzzed and Nick frowned, momentarily distracted. 'Excuse me,' he murmured. 'Yes? Of course, Hazel. We'll be there directly.'

Gabriel visualised Hazel, the practice manager, whom he had met a short while ago during his wander around with Nick. The older woman had been polite while giving him the once-over but appeared to be reserving her judgement about him. He could understand that. Hopefully he would pass muster with her, and the rest of the staff, in time. He was thinking of all he had been told about his new colleagues when Nick set down the phone and reclaimed his attention.

'Pretty much everyone on duty is here now. Come on up to the staffroom, Gabriel, and I'll introduce you,' he invited, rising to his feet.

Glad that their chat had gone well, and looking forward to starting work, Gabriel followed Nick towards the stairs. Although reserved and serious, the senior partner had been welcoming, their discussion informative. Even so, Gabriel was thankful to have had the chance to meet Oliver and Chloe in more informal and relaxed circumstances at Lauren's cottage the previous day. He had thoroughly enjoyed himself. They had lingered over a delicious lunch and talked long into the afternoon. It had been dark by the time he had walked the short distance back to the Manor House feeling content and more comfortable about his new job.

With dark hair and green eyes, Chloe was kind and gentle, as dedicated to her role as a midwife as Lauren was to hers as a physiotherapist. As for Oliver, dark-eyed and with over-long dark hair, Gabriel had liked him from the first, forming an instant friendship with the handsome, charismatic doctor. Oliver was only three years younger than himself and they had quickly established that they shared many interests in common besides their careers, especially a love of sport. Gabriel did not share Oliver's and Chloe's love of motorbikes, however. It hadn't needed Lauren to tell him that Oliver and Chloe were a couple…that they were madly in love was obvious to anyone who saw them together.

And then there was Lauren herself.

She had been a complete surprise to him and he had not been able to stop thinking about her since finding her in his kitchen on Saturday afternoon. He'd been intrigued to learn she was an accomplished artist. There hadn't been an opportunity to look around her studio the day before but he had seen a couple of her landscapes hanging in the surgery's reception area during his tour with Nick. He had found himself drawn to the paintings even before he had realised they were Lauren's. She had real talent. He was looking forward to working with her—and to getting to know her better socially. Only his early meeting with Nick had prevented him from joining Lauren for her morning jog. There would be time for that in the days ahead. And, he hoped, for much more. He still intended to be cautious, but any resolve to remain uninvolved had wavered on Saturday and melted entirely on Sunday.

The sound of chatter coming from the staffroom became louder and drew him from his thoughts. As Nick led the way inside and an anticipatory silence descended, Gabriel's nervousness at the prospect of meeting his colleagues returned. He'd never experienced this self-doubt about acceptance until recently—until his world had turned upside down after his father's death and things he had thought he had known about his life, his family, his very identity—had proved to be a lie. Gabriel swallowed the rush of emotions, forcing his private issues to the back of his mind. It was good to know there would be at least a couple of familiar faces here. A quick glance around the room told him that Lauren had yet to arrive and he struggled to mask his disappointment. However, Oliver and Chloe were there, their smiles reassuring him.

Uncomfortable at being the centre of attention, he hoped

his own smile was natural and that he came across as being more relaxed than he felt under the scrutiny he was being subjected to. Thankfully the atmosphere was welcoming, although he imagined some people had similar reservations to those Hazel had exhibited earlier. He remained silent as Nick made the introductions and turned to draw him forward.

'Come on in and join us. Everyone, this is Gabriel Devereux.' His manner benevolent and paternal, Nick gestured around the room. 'You already know Oliver and Chloe. And you remember Kate Althorp, our other midwife, from your visit in the summer?'

'But of course. It's good to see you again, Kate.' As the older woman rose to greet him, he gave her a Gallic kiss on both cheeks. 'How is your son Jem?'

Kate's smile revealed her pleasure. 'He's well. Thank you, Gabriel. Welcome back to Penhally Bay! We are so pleased to have you with us.'

'I am excited to be here.' He smiled back, grateful for Kate's warm approach.

Nick made the other introductions and Gabriel shook hands with the rest of the team. When the formalities were over, Gabriel sat on an empty chair opposite Oliver and Chloe, and accepted the mug Eve Dwyer, one of the practice nurses, handed him.

'We usually start the day with a coffee and a chat,' she explained, her manner friendly. 'Milk and sugar?'

'Just a dash of milk, please.'

As Eve added the milk to his mug and then turned to replace the carton in the fridge, a crash sounded out on the stairway, followed by a string of muffled curses. Gabriel looked round in time to see Nick shaking his head and moving towards the door.

'That must be Lauren.'

Everyone laughed in response to Nick's wry comment, but

the amusement was affectionate, Gabriel realised with some relief, already feeling protective of Lauren. Then he noted the concern on Oliver's face, along with the way Chloe's smile dimmed when she exchanged a glance with her fiancé. Gabriel shared a look with Oliver and as a silent acknowledgement passed between them he felt a shiver of unease. He had known Lauren less than forty-eight hours, but it appeared he was not alone in his impression that something more might lie behind her clumsiness. Gabriel filed the moment away. He would keep his own counsel for now, but Oliver could be the man to talk to if his initial worrying suspicions came to anything.

Looking adorably flustered, and dressed in a uniform of navy blue tunic and trousers, her hair tied back in a ponytail, Lauren hurried into the room. She was carrying a haphazard stack of files and balancing a round tin precariously on top.

'Sorry I'm late. I was delayed downstairs talking with a patient on the phone,' she explained, sounding a touch breathless. 'The waiting room is starting to fill up early—the usual collection of post-weekend crises, no doubt. Hazel is holding the fort and says to carry on without her.'

'Are those some of Hazel's biscuits?' someone asked.

Gabriel watched as Lauren awkwardly juggled the files and manoeuvred the tin so she could prise open the lid. 'Her Cornish fairings,' she announced once she had peeped inside. A twinkle of mischief in her smoky grey eyes, she offered him the tin. 'All Hazel's home-made food treats are favourites here, Gabriel, so I advise you to take what you can before the rest of this unruly lot devour them.'

'Thank you.' It was a bit early in the day for him, but Gabriel accepted one of the biscuits to please Lauren. He tried it with his coffee, surprised how much he enjoyed the ginger-flavoured local delicacy. 'They're excellent.'

'Tell Hazel that and you'll be in her good books for life.' Kate laughed.

'Come on, Lauren, don't hog the tin. I missed breakfast and I'm starving,' GP Adam Donnelly called, growling in mock complaint as others grabbed their share of the biscuits before the tin reached him.

Gabriel was gratified when Lauren chose the chair next to him, her smile and the look in her eyes setting off the zing of awareness he felt every time he saw her.

'A word of warning, Gabriel,' one of the district nurses joked. 'Make sure you park your car well away from Lauren's—if you want to find it in one piece when you go back to it!'

As the tale of her reversing into a car at a recent wedding was recounted, Lauren smiled, taking the ribbing in good part, but Gabriel could see the flash of hurt and worry in her eyes. The belief that there was something more than Lauren just being clumsy nagged at him but he hadn't yet put his finger on what it was that disturbed him. Frowning, he remembered her uneasiness leaving the Manor House on Saturday night and the way she had tripped in the dark. She had explained away her stumble by telling him how accident prone she was, but he had sensed she was covering up for something else. More than once in their short acquaintance he had noticed the way she squinted at her mobile phone screen, tilting it around before reading the message. Then there were the moments she displayed an apparent lack of spatial awareness and misjudgement of distances.

As Nick reclaimed the attention of those in the room, the teasing ceased and Gabriel had to set his considerations about Lauren aside. Instead, he listened with interest as the discussion turned to items of surgery business and any noteworthy out-of-hours incidents with patients. Adam had been called out the previous day to a thirteen-year-old girl with appendicitis who had been admitted to St Piran Hospital, while Kate had attended a mum-to-be who had reported some abdominal pain.

'I'm convinced it is nothing serious but, given her level of anxiety, I've arranged for her to see the consultant at the hospital today instead of next week.'

'Better to be safe than sorry,' Nick remarked, to murmurs of agreement.

Gabriel watched the interaction between Nick and Kate with interest. The tension between the two had been glaringly apparent during the barbecue at Nick's house back in July. He had no idea of their history but he thought it went beyond the doctor-midwife dynamic. Thankfully, the atmosphere between them today was less fraught.

'Gabriel is going to be shadowing Oliver this week, especially on home visits and out-of-hours work,' Nick outlined as the patient reviews came to an end. 'I've also supported his request to spend some time with other staff and will leave you to organise convenient days between you…Lauren, Chloe and the district nurses in particular. Gabriel, enjoy your time here and speak up if you have any queries. I am sure everyone will do all they can to make you welcome and help you settle in for this year-long stay with us.'

Smiling his thanks, Gabriel's attention lingered on Lauren beside him. She had done more than anyone to make him feel comfortable, both at home and work, and her insights and advice had been invaluable. As everyone rose to their feet and began to file out, heading off to attend to their respective duties, Oliver hung back with Chloe.

'We can do a joint list this morning, Gabriel. And when we come back from the house calls, we'll get you set up in your own room. You can take your own surgery slots from this afternoon if you'd care to,' his new friend suggested.

'That suits me.'

'Great.' Oliver smiled and ushered Chloe ahead of him. 'I'll see you downstairs in a few minutes, then.'

Left alone in the staffroom, Gabriel felt Lauren's hand slide into his. Palm to palm. A perfect fit. Delicate yet strong.

And her skin was satin soft. Not at all sorry to be touching her but surprised by her actions, he looked into warm grey eyes.

'Lauren?'

'I just wanted to wish you an enjoyable first day.' Her fingers squeezed his before letting go. He felt the loss of their contact. Then she caught him unawares again, leaning in to press a gentle but all-too-fleeting kiss on his cheek. 'Good luck, Gabriel.'

His skin prickled from the brush of her mouth. Unable to let her go, he caught her hand as she drew away. Her thoughtfulness and caring touched him on an emotional level, while inflaming the physical desire he had felt from the first moment they had met. His body tightened with need for her. He wanted to haul her into his arms and kiss her senseless. Unfortunately he didn't think Nick would be impressed to find the new doctor passionately making out with the physiotherapist in the staffroom on his first day at work!

'Thank you, *chérie*.' He cupped her face with his free hand, relishing the feel of her and the instinctive way she pressed her cheek to his palm. He grazed his thumb across her parted lips, the pad briefly catching on the fullness of the lower one. Her breath hitched, and he watched as her eyes darkened, the desire in them unmistakable. 'I'll see you later.'

'Yes. OK,' she agreed, the husky edge returning to her voice.

He regretted letting her go but he had to. If he kissed her now he wouldn't want to stop. Oliver and their patients were waiting for him downstairs. It was time for him to start work. Time to concentrate on the first day of his new job and think about something other than Lauren…before he lost his head entirely.

Come Friday, Lauren was convinced her lips were still tingling. She licked them, sure she could taste a hint of the masculine tang of Gabriel's skin even now. He'd felt so good. And had smelt delicious, too…earthy and citrusy and all male. She had never been so drawn to and aware of a man before.

The attraction was fierce. Immediate. Scary but incredibly exciting in its intensity.

On Monday morning, dressed in a dark suit, crisp white shirt and ocean-blue tie, Gabriel had looked as if he had just stepped off the catwalk—a star model for the finest Parisian fashion house. She hadn't thought he could look any better than he did in his figure-hugging jeans—or that ivory towel— but suited up for work he'd taken her breath away all over again. He had an aristocratic bearing, one that hinted that he had origins in wealth and status, yet he was completely natural, down-to-earth and unpretentious.

Gabriel's reaction to her good-luck gesture had taken her by surprise. She could still feel the warmth of his palm cupping her face, the stroke of his thumb across her lips, the desire that had flared in his eyes as he had looked deep into her own. She desperately wanted to know what it would be like to kiss him. It was all she had thought about for days. How would it feel? How would he taste? She wanted to touch him. Wanted to feel his hands on her body.

It had been such a hectic week that she hadn't seen Gabriel anywhere near as much as she had hoped to. Not alone, anyway. He had joined her for her morning jog before work on a couple of occasions and he'd come to Gatehouse Cottage for an evening meal some nights. But Oliver and Chloe had been there, too, and there had been far too much talk about work for Lauren's liking. Tomorrow, Saturday, marked the first-week anniversary of when she had met him. Gabriel had morning surgery and then was on call with Oliver for the rest of the day, so there was not going to be much chance for her to see him then. And Sunday was the day of the charity football match. Yet another missed opportunity for some time alone with him. She knew she was behaving like a foolish, thwarted schoolgirl, but she couldn't seem to help herself.

'Are you all right, Lauren?'

Embarrassment made her cheeks turn pink as Mike Trevellyan's voice jolted her from her thoughts. 'I'm so sorry, Mike, I was…distracted.' Guilt surged through her because she had been daydreaming about Gabriel instead of focusing on her patient.

'So I gathered.' Amusement shone in his eyes. 'Anything to do with the new French doctor I've been hearing about?'

'Why would you think that?' Goodness, had the rumour mill started already?

'Kate has mentioned Dr Devereux to Fran several times since meeting him in the summer. She said Penhally was in for a treat when he finally arrived here to work,' Mike explained, his tone teasing. 'And there's been some envy that you are his nearest neighbour. The whisper has gone around that he's impressed many people during his first week here.'

'Gabriel is an excellent doctor,' she allowed, trying to keep her comments professional and hide the pride she was experiencing at the news.

'I'm not sure his medical skills are what interests most of the ladies!'

A wave of possessiveness surged through her. She was unaccustomed to jealousy, but she felt territorial and protective of Gabriel, and she didn't want to think of other women lusting after him. Refusing to react to Mike's comments and add more fuel to fire any possible local gossip, she forced a smile and got them back to the matter at hand.

'Now then, how are things going with you, Mike? How is your leg?'

'I've been doing all the exercises you gave me. Mostly the ankle is fine, although I do get some pain at times,' he admitted grudgingly.

Lauren nodded, knowing what a rough time Mike had been through and how important it was for him as a busy farmer to keep mobile and working. 'No doubt you've been overdoing things, though.'

'I've tried to increase my workload slowly, but I can't do as much as I'd like. There is still a bit of weakness and stiffness in the ankle.'

'That's to be expected,' she reminded him.

Lauren ran through some of the exercises and checked his range of movement. The offending leg bore the marks of the breaks and subsequent surgery he had sustained when part of a tree he had been cutting with a chainsaw had fallen on him, pinning him to the ground.

'Any problems from the bruised ribs?'

Mike shook his head. 'Not any more. The doctors tell me I healed quickly.'

'Just not quickly enough for you,' she filled in with an understanding smile. 'I know it seems a long haul, Mike, especially when you're used to physical activity. You've done so well. We don't want any setbacks. Let your brother help you.'

'Joe's picked up enough of the slack. But you're not alone…Fran tells me I'm too impatient,' he conceded wryly, speaking of his wife with affection.

'Thankfully you didn't tear the ligaments, but the two fractures to your fibula—one above the ankle and one at the bottom, the lateral maleolus, where it joins the tibia—were serious. As you well know from your time in a cast after the operation to fit the plates and screws.' She gave him a sympathetic pat on the shoulder. 'You've worked hard to build up the strength in the muscles and to remobilise the joint. It must be frustrating, but keep up the exercises, don't try to do too much too soon, and you'll continue to improve.'

Mike nodded his agreement. 'Thanks, Lauren. I'll do my best. I've got so much to be grateful for.'

'You have indeed!' While he put his socks and shoes back

on, she reflected on how delighted the whole of Penhally had been at the news that Fran Trevellyan was expecting naturally after a previous miscarriage and an unsuccessful attempt at IVF. 'It's so exciting about the pregnancy. When is the baby due?'

'Late spring.' Mike positively glowed with joy. 'We're just praying everything goes without a hitch this time.'

'I'm sure it will,' she reassured him, happy for the couple.

'Things definitely seem different with this pregnancy. It's nearly November now, past the danger point in terms of the number of weeks when we lost the baby before. Kate is keeping a close eye on Fran and she says everything is fine.'

'So we have to make sure you are fit to run around changing nappies and chasing after an active toddler!' Lauren teased. 'Come back and see me in a month, Mike, but phone any time if you have questions, swelling or discomfort.'

After showing Mike out, she welcomed her next patient, a woman in her late forties who had presented with pain and associated symptoms in the C5 and C6 region of her neck. The classic 'poking-chin posture' evident at their first appointment had been caused by over-activity in the levetator scapulae and stermocleidomastoid muscles, along with a weakness of the cervical flexor muscles. This was Zena's third visit and she was showing excellent signs of improvement in her range of movement and her posture.

'The pain and stiffness are much less and I've had no more headaches or dizziness,' Zena reported, her relief evident. 'I'm finding the exercises easier now.'

'That's great.' Lauren was pleased that the combination of manipulation therapy she had used at the surgery and the corrective exercises Zena had done at home had resulted in the woman's progress. 'We'll make another appointment, but keep up the programme. It's helping correct your posture as well as increase your range of movement and strengthen the muscles.'

Happy that Zena was following her advice and had no more questions, Lauren sent her on her way and welcomed patient number three of the afternoon.

It turned out to be a busy Friday clinic, one that overran as she had a couple of new cases and time was needed to make a thorough assessment and take a complete history. Consequently it was late by the time she had finished her list. When her last patient had left, she sat down and adjusted her desk light so she could see more clearly to type up all her case notes and make comprehensive profiles of her new patients. She didn't anticipate being able to leave for home any time soon. Stifling a yawn with one hand, she switched on her computer and set to work, ignoring the noises coming from the workmen who were putting the finishing touches to alterations outside the building.

She was engrossed in updating her files when all the power suddenly went off, shutting down her computer and plunging her room into darkness. Losing any unsaved work was the least of her problems. Disoriented, she sat still, but her eyes didn't adjust to the gloom. She could see nothing. This was the realisation of one of her worst fears. Her heart started thudding under her ribs and she felt tense, her throat tightening. After sitting in the dark for a while, increasingly concerned, Lauren rose gingerly to her feet and, one hand extended out in front of her, slowly, awkwardly edged her way towards the door, thankful that her mental map of her new room was accurate. Judging each step with care, she found the door without bumping into anything, but opening it brought no relief.

It was pitch black throughout the whole surgery.

She strained to hear, but no sounds came. How late was it? Had everyone else gone home? She didn't recall hearing the workmen for a while. Pulling out her mobile phone, she tried to read the time on the screen, but the luminous glow provided scant light and failed to aid her vision. Increasingly alarmed, she pressed herself against the wall, not wanting to lose her bearings.

What should she do? Wait a bit to see what happened? Or call someone? She clutched her mobile phone tighter in her hand. How could she ring without alerting the person to her predicament? She wasn't ready to face the issue of her diminishing night vision herself, let alone confide in anyone else. Fear chilled her at the knowledge that she might not be able to ignore or hide the subtle but insidious changes to her sight for much longer.

A noise from upstairs made her jump. Her pulse throbbed.

'Hello?' Was that her voice sounding so uncharacteristically shaky and feeble? She hated this. What was happening to her? Silence descended again, enveloping her. Cursing herself for being feeble, battling the inner panic rising within her, she raised her voice. 'Is anyone there?'

Several moments later, footsteps sounded on the stairs. 'Lauren?'

'Gabriel!' Relief flooded through her and she blinked back a stupid threat of tears.

'Where are you, *chérie*?'

She pressed a hand to her chest, trying to calm her ragged breathing. 'Outside the physiotherapy room.'

'Stay there.' Gabriel's accented voice calmed her nerves. 'I'll find you.'

Seconds later, Lauren squinted at a pinpoint of light wavering in the darkness. Sensing Gabriel's nearness but misjudging the distance, she stepped out from the wall and bumped into his solid frame.

'Oomph!' she gasped.

His hands came out to steady her. 'Are you all right, Lauren?'

'Yes.' She was now. 'Thanks.'

It was brazen but she couldn't help snuggling closer, welcoming the feel of his arms coming around her. She absorbed his strength, scared of her lack of vision but unable to explain to him.

'I finished my surgery half an hour ago and Nick had just

called me up to the staffroom to talk about my first week when the power went off,' he explained, one hand soothing as it stroked up and down her spine.

'What's happened, do you think?'

'The contractors were finishing off some work outside and one of them cut a cable by mistake. Nick has gone to see them. I knew you were still here and was coming to find you when you called.'

Reassured by his presence and the knowledge he had thought of her, Lauren allowed herself to relax, some of the tension draining from her.

'Come and sit in my consulting room while we wait.'

'Um…' Lauren hesitated. Unfamiliar with the layout of his room, she didn't want to fall over anything or make even more of a fool of herself in front of him. How could he see with just a penlight? Had he guessed her problem? Not wanting to alert his suspicions by asking if they could just stand where they were, she reluctantly agreed to his suggestion. 'OK.'

His arm around her made her feel safe as he led her back down the corridor to the next doorway. Unable to see him, all her other senses seemed heightened, and his warmth wrapped around her like a comfort blanket in the dark. The citrusy male scent of him was familiar and exciting. Putting her trust in him, she was thankful that he guided her to a chair without any fuss. She sat down, disappointed when he released her. But then she heard the sounds of him dragging another chair closer, and he sat beside her, taking her hand in his, linking their fingers. She tried not to cling too tightly and reveal the extent of her unease.

'I want to thank you for all you have done helping me to fit in and making me welcome in Penhally,' he told her with warm sincerity.

'I don't think I'm responsible for much, but I'm glad that

you've settled so well. Word is you've made a great impression.' She wished there was enough light for her to see his face.

'I just want to be a good doctor for the people here,' he responded with simple but genuine modesty. 'Perhaps we can arrange a morning next week for me to come out on your home visits?'

'Yes, of course,' she agreed, delighted at the prospect.

Gabriel's thumb stroked across the inside of her wrist, making her shiver. 'Oliver and Chloe plan to go to Plymouth next weekend to see Rachel Kenner. Will you spend some time with me while they are gone? We can be alone…get to know one another better.'

'I'd like that.' Which was a massive understatement! She felt breathless with anticipation. The week ahead would be a long one…waiting. 'Gabriel—'

Before she could speak further, the lights flashed back on. Startled, Lauren blinked several times, her eyes taking a few moments to adjust and refocus. Then the fog cleared and Gabriel's gorgeous face swam clearly into view. She noticed his look of concern as he watched her, then he smiled, dimples creasing lean cheeks, and her stomach turned over.

'Lauren? Gabriel?' Nick's voice sounded from the front of the surgery.

With a wry grimace, Gabriel squeezed her fingers before he released her and stood up. Moving to the door, he called out to Nick, and a few moments later the older man arrived in the room.

'Here you both are.' Looking harassed, Nick ran a hand through his hair. 'I'm sorry about the disruption. I've been assured the problem is now resolved. Gabriel, perhaps we can have our informal debrief over a drink and something to eat?'

'Of course.' Gabriel's consent and smile were polite, but Lauren sensed his reluctance.

Nick turned to her. 'Are you heading home now, Lauren?'

'Yes, I am.' She could finish updating her computer files from her written notes another time, she decided, disappointed that she wouldn't be seeing Gabriel again this evening.

'Good. Right, then.' Nick rubbed his hands together and smiled. 'I'll meet you out front in a few moments.'

When he had gone, Lauren rose and walked towards the door, pausing to look at Gabriel. 'Thanks for being here.'

'No problem. If I don't catch up with you tomorrow, I'll see you at the football on Sunday.'

'All right.' She returned his smile, warmed through by the huskiness of his voice and the promise in his eyes. 'Goodnight, Gabriel.'

'Goodnight. Sleep well, *chérie*.'

After a short but tense and cautious drive, the lights of her cottage welcomed her home. The cars outside announced that both Oliver and Chloe were in, and she parked her own with extra care not to hit anything. As much as she loved her friends and valued their company, it was someone else who dominated her thoughts and whom she wished she was with right now.

Sleep well, Gabriel had said...

As had been the case every night since she had met him, she knew her sleep would be filled with dreams of a sexy Frenchman.

CHAPTER FOUR

SUNDAY dawned a perfect warm and sunny autumn day. The whole of Penhally had turned out to support the charity football match, along with many outsiders and autograph-hunters who had been drawn by the impressive number of sporting and television personalities in attendance. The media were also out in force, capturing the action from the school playing fields. Given the size of the crowd, plus the interest in the snap auction of items donated by the celebrities, there was going to be a very healthy sum of money added to the relief fund.

Kate didn't want to think about the flood. Almost three weeks on and the memories of being stuck in an upstairs flat in Bridge Street with Nick, the water rising beneath them, still left her feeling shaky. They had struggled successfully to deliver Stephanie Richards's breech baby, and then had come the frightening experience of being winched up to the rescue helicopter. Kate shivered despite the mild temperature.

'Are you all right, Mum?'

'Yes, my love. I'm fine.' Smiling, she ruffled Jem's hair. He'd found her at half-time and was taking advantage of the refreshments she'd brought. 'Are you enjoying yourself?'

'It's cool! I've got some great autographs,' he added, pointing to all the signatures he'd collected on his football jersey, then his eyes went round in alarm. 'You won't wash them off, will you?'

'Never, I promise.' She hid her amusement as she reassured him, watching as he drained his fruit drink and wiped the back of his hand across his mouth.

'It was good of Uncle Nick to arrange for me be a ballboy.'

Uncle Nick. Pain lanced through her. Jem had no idea that Nick was his natural father. Would the man she had loved for ever one day claim his son? Or were old hurts and the weight of guilt too much to be overcome? While they had been trapped during the flood, they had talked about that long-ago night when they had lost their heads…a night of great stress and emotion that had resulted in Jem's conception. Nick had promised to try to make an effort to come to terms with the situation, and at least be more attentive to Jem, even if he couldn't go as far as making a public declaration of father-hood. Kate wasn't holding her breath that anything would come of it but she could not help but hope—for Jem's sake if not her own. So far Nick had kept his word and things were less tense between them.

'The second half is starting soon. Will you come and watch me?' Jem asked, returning after throwing the empty drink carton into a nearby litter bin.

'Of course, my love.'

He caught her hand and tugged. 'Come on, then.'

Kate allowed her son to lead her towards the touchline, pleased that he was so happy. Nick had already returned from the half-time break, acting as team doctor for the celebrity side. Jem released her hand and ran to him. Kate saw Nick's guarded smile as he greeted the boy and heard the modulated tones of his voice.

'Back to help again?' he asked, and Jem nodded enthusias-tically. 'Good lad.'

Sharing a look with the most enigmatic of men, Kate

mouthed, 'Thank you,' understanding how difficult it was for Nick to confront his own demons. Not wanting to push things or make a scene in public, she saw Lauren and Chloe returning to the side of the pitch and went to join them.

'Everything OK, Kate?' Chloe asked.

She nodded in response to the gentle query, seeing the understanding in the younger woman's green eyes. Her fellow midwife was one of only two other people, besides herself and Nick, who knew the secret about the identity of Jem's father.

'It's been an excellent day and Jem is having fun being part of it.' Again, Kate's gaze strayed to where her son waited impatiently for the game to restart. Nick was watching him, too, and she wondered what was going through his mind. Aware she was on dangerous ground, she turned her attention back to her two colleagues. 'Oliver did a brilliant job organising this. It's a huge success.'

Chloe glowed with pleasure at the praise for her fiancé. 'I know. He worked so hard. Jack Tremayne helped, too. Both of them were able to call in favours from their days in London, securing the support of several national celebrities as well as the Cornish ones.'

'Everyone's really got behind the event,' Lauren added with approval. 'Despite the arrival of his baby boy, Dragan worked hard behind the scenes for today.'

'I think he would have liked to play, but it's understandable that he and Melinda wanted to keep out of public view after the press intrusions last spring,' Chloe pointed out, and Kate nodded in agreement, remembering what it had been like in the village when Melinda had been identified as a member of European royalty.

As both sets of players jogged out for the second half, cheers echoed around the playing fields.

'Gabriel has been a star, jumping in to give support the

moment he arrived here,' Kate commented, glancing at Lauren. 'He scored an excellent goal, too.'

'All our guys have been great.'

Kate smiled at Lauren's reply, noting the wink Gabriel sent the young physiotherapist as he ran past and the flush that warmed her cheeks in response. It was clear where those two were heading! And Kate couldn't be more pleased for them. Her smile broadened as Oliver detoured to give Chloe a kiss. Leaving the two friends to focus on the match—and the men who held their interest—Kate wandered farther along the side of the pitch so she could keep a better eye on Jem.

The flood had been terrible for the whole village, causing physical and emotional trauma. The damage to property would take many months to overcome, while the loss of Audrey Baxter and Reverend Kenner was a tragedy never to be forgotten. But the aftermath, including the mass support for today's event, showed what could happen when the community pulled together.

Penhally's previous disaster, the big storm a decade ago, had been the catalyst that had caused the moment of madness between herself and Nick which had led to Jem's existence. Maybe the flood could have done some good if it sparked a turning point for the future…if Nick found a way to move on from the past and accept his son.

'You really like Gabriel, don't you?' Chloe asked Lauren as Kate walked away from them.

Lauren nodded, although 'like' was an insipid word to describe the complexity of her feelings and the extent of her attraction. 'I do.'

'The electricity the two of you generate when you're together could power the whole of Cornwall,' her friend proclaimed, giving her a quick hug. 'I hope everything works out. I want you to be as happy as I am—and around Gabriel you look how I feel when I'm with Oliver.' She hesitated a moment, then added more soberly, 'I know we rarely mention it, but I'll never forget all you've done for me, Lauren.'

Chloe was such a sweetheart. That she was now blossoming was wonderful. Lauren still vividly recalled the state in which she had found Chloe eleven and a half years ago when the girl, then sixteen, had been beaten by her father. She had helped Chloe get away that night and was so proud of the success she had gone on to make of her life. Even so, for a long while Chloe had shut herself off from love because of her past—until Oliver had arrived. The perfect man to be understanding, gentle and loving, he'd taught Chloe all about being a woman in the fullest sense of the word.

'You've come such a long way and I'm so delighted for you,' she said, hugging Chloe back.

'Thank you. Ooh, sorry, I didn't mean to get all sentimental!' Chloe's smile was wobbly, her eyes bright with a suspicion of tears. Doggedly, she changed the subject. 'Can you believe Vicky taking off like that after the flood?'

Lauren had been friends with Vicky Clements since junior school. They were close but she acknowledged Vicky's faults—primary amongst them being her propensity for gossip. Vicky didn't mean any harm, but she often hurt people's feelings and said thoughtless things she shouldn't. And working at her mother's hair and beauty salon, Vicky heard a lot of tales she was only too keen to pass on. They'd had a lot of fun together over the years, and Lauren enjoyed the flighty woman's company, but it was to Chloe that Lauren turned for advice and to share confidences. Chloe was discreet and kind and totally selfless.

'It will be a while until the salon is up and running again after the flood damage. Vicky's mother is going to keep up her regular clients by doing home visits until the salon can reopen,' she explained now. 'Vicky's been restless since embarking on her hot new romance with the guitarist of that up-and-coming band she met in a nightclub in Rock. When the band asked her to go with them on their world tour, to do all the styling and hair for them and the backing singers, she felt it was too good an opportunity to miss.'

'A real adventure, for sure,' Chloe agreed.

'Vicky's never been so committed to a man before…maybe this will change her.'

'It'll seem quiet around here with her gone.' A twinkle of mischief appeared in her friend's green eyes. 'At least Vicky is too busy with her own love life to gossip about or interfere in ours!'

'Amen to that.'

Lauren remembered how Vicky's tactless meddling had caused problems—thankfully temporary ones—for Chloe and Oliver back in the summer. It was a good thing that Vicky was away for the next few months, she decided. She didn't need her nosy friend making wisecracks or involving herself in what Lauren hoped was her own budding new relationship with a certain sexy French doctor.

'The second half is about to start.' Chloe's comment drew Lauren from her thoughts. 'It's been competitive but friendly so far—I hope no one gets hurt.'

'Me, too.'

The famous, top-flight referee, who had agreed to officiate for the charity match, blew his whistle and the game began again in earnest with the celebrities leading the locals by four goals to three. Lauren, as Penhally team physio, was kept busy as the game went on, with various muscle pulls and a couple of sprains. Then Jack Tremayne received a nasty cut to his knee, one that was suspiciously shaped like a stud mark from a misplaced football boot.

'You need stitches in this,' Adam Donnelly declared, examining the wound and stemming the bleeding.

'It can wait until after the game.' Jack ignored the combined medical opinion and insisted on rejoining the fray once he had been bandaged up. 'If we win, I'll let you at me with a needle.'

Adam turned away with a good-natured grin. 'Gee, thanks. Perhaps I'll misplace the local anaesthetic. That or sew your lips together,' he called back, making everyone laugh.

The game continued and the goals kept coming for both sides. Lauren cheered loudest of all when Gabriel scored another spectacular goal to put the home team in the lead with only ten minutes left to play. Standing on the sidelines, enjoying the action, she couldn't stop watching Gabriel. He had a wonderful physique, strong but leanly athletic, and his sleeveless top—part of the players' kit donated by a national sportswear chain for the occasion—showed off the roped, corded muscles of his arms to perfection. Oliver had a good body, too, but looking at him did nothing for her in terms of attraction. Neither did any of the other men here. Only Gabriel. Just one sight of him stole her breath and set a fire of need smouldering inside her, clenching her stomach and leaving her giddy with excited anticipation.

Watching him so closely, she was aware the instant something went wrong. She was already reaching for her bag when Gabriel collapsed as if he had been poleaxed. Seeing him fall scared her witless. Then she was running towards him, even before the referee had given her permission to cross the pitch. Gabriel needed her. Her heart in her mouth, Lauren dropped to her knees beside the prone figure on the ground.

'Gabe, what's wrong?' Her voice shook with emotion and she didn't consciously realise she had shortened his name. 'Where are you hurt?'

'Cramp,' he managed through teeth gritted with pain.

His right leg was rigid with vicious spasms. Lauren got to her feet and grasped his ankle, holding his leg up straight and pushing back against his foot to try to ease the locked muscles. By the time the referee, Oliver and a few of the other Penhally players had jogged across to see what was going on, some of the knotted tension in Gabriel's leg was beginning to dissipate.

'You'll have to carry out any other treatment off the pitch,' the referee insisted, for all the world like this was a major professional match rather than a fundraising one.

'I can play on,' Gabriel insisted, trying to get to his feet. 'There's not much longer to go. I want to see it out.'

Lauren held on to him as he took a few faltering steps only for his leg to give out and cramp up again. 'Gabe, you can't. We need to get you rehydrated and your leg dealt with.'

'She's right, my friend.' As Oliver backed her up, she sent him a grateful smile. 'Let Lauren take care of you.'

'You've given your all and scored two goals,' she reminded him.

Coffee-coloured eyes, threaded with pain, looked into hers. After a moment, he nodded. 'All right.'

'Thank you.' She turned to Oliver. 'I'll take him down to the treatment room.'

'Good idea. We'll ferry down any other walking wounded when we're done.'

As Oliver went to organise a substitute for the last part of the game, Lauren grabbed her bag with one hand and slid her free arm around Gabriel's waist, helping him balance as he limped to the sidelines. He put an arm around her shoulders, accepting the support, and she welcomed the weight of it. Even given the circumstances, she couldn't help but be aware of how it felt to be so close. She could feel the heat of him and scent his earthy maleness.

Chloe and Kate awaited them on the touchline, looking worried.

'Is there anything we can do?' Kate asked.

'Can you keep an eye on him while I get my car?' She hated to leave him but no way could he walk all the way to the car park. 'If you have water or a sports drink, Gabriel needs them.'

'Of course.'

Knowing Gabriel was being cared for, Lauren ran for the car. Soon she was driving as close as she could to the pitch, pleased to find that Chloe and Kate had helped to guide Gabriel to her through the crowds. She jumped out and hurried round to open the passenger door, noting the tension on his face as his leg tightened again when he sat in the restricted space.

'Thanks.' She smiled at her friends and slid back behind the wheel, grateful it was only a very short distance to the surgery.

She threw him a quick glance, pleased to see he was continuing to drink. His eyes were closed and he was stretching out his leg as much as the confines of the car would allow. 'Are you OK?'

'I'm getting too old for this,' he joked. 'Don't worry, *chérie*, the cramp will ease.'

It certainly would once she had a chance to work on those calf and thigh muscles. But she made no comment as she parked outside the surgery, unlocked the door and helped Gabriel inside. The problem with her plan only hit her once they were in the physio room.

Alone.

And Gabriel had gone behind the curtain to take off his football boots, socks and shorts.

Oh, sweet mercy.

Now he was lying face down on the treatment table. True, he was still wearing his football top but the towel covering his lower half reminded her of the day they had met. Lauren swallowed. She was a professional. She could do this. She could put hands on Gabriel's scrumptious body and give him a therapeutic massage without thinking about or acting on any of the salacious and erotic fantasies running through her mind.

Of course she could. And would. If she kept telling herself enough, she might even believe it.

Ignoring the way her hands were shaking, she took out a bottle of the embrocation she favoured for working on tired, cramped muscles and approached the table. Biting her lip, she pushed the hem of the towel up to mid-thigh. His legs were beautifully sculpted, all toned muscle and supple, dark skin.

'L-let's get these knots sorted out,' she murmured, cursing her lack of control. 'Ready?'

'Do your worst, Lauren.'

'Right.'

She poured oil into her hands and rubbed them together to warm it, telling herself to forget all the 'worst' things she really wanted to do to him and focus on the professional massage. Sucking in a steadying breath, she touched him for the first time. Her hands settled low on his calf, feeling the tightness of the muscles in spasm as she pressed upwards with deft strokes to the back of the knee. She forced herself to concentrate on what she was doing. She couldn't allow herself to dwell on how wonderful it was to touch him, or let her gaze to move any farther up to where the towel brushed his thighs and draped across the enticing shape of his rear.

Gabriel groaned as her thumbs circled deeply into his flesh. '*Mon Dieu*, that feels good.'

The sultry roughness of his voice shimmered to every nerve ending. *He* certainly felt good, his skin warm and male beneath her fingers. She worked slowly up his leg, relaxing the muscles of the calf and thigh, feeling his tension ease while her own magnified. No matter how hard she tried to remain professional, to keep her touch neutral and impersonal, she had never been so intensely aware in her life. She wanted this man as she had never wanted anyone before. The temptation to caress, to glide her hands higher and allow her fingers to explore his body was overwhelming.

Lauren was relieved that Gabriel didn't talk. She didn't think she could. Indeed, he seemed unaffected, his head turned to one side, resting on his crossed forearms. His eyes were closed, and he gave every impression of being relaxed and at ease, while she was on red alert, aroused and aching. It was mortifying.

'Turn over now, please,' she directed, injecting as much calm unconcern into her voice as she could manage.

'Lauren…'

She reached for the bottle of oil. 'Hmm?'

'I think it is fine now, *chérie*,' he stated, sounding oddly wary.

'Nonsense,' she riposted briskly. If he could do this without batting an eyelid, so could she. 'I haven't finished massaging the leg.'

'But—'

'Please, Gabriel.'

He huffed out a breath, and she frowned, wondering what the problem was as he continued to hesitate. She waited endless moments before he slowly rolled over. Her pulse rate rocketed and her throat closed as the reason for his reticence became apparent…the tented towel gave evidence to the fact that the extent of his arousal matched her own. She couldn't look away. Her stomach knotted with an ache of need, her heart pounded, and she could feel her nipples pucker even further in response, sensitive against the lacy fabric of her bra.

Gabriel sat up and swung his legs off the table. 'Lauren.' His hands cupped her face, raising it until she was looking into eyes so dark and hot with desire she felt singed from the fire.

'Gabe…'

His name had barely whispered from her lips before his mouth met hers, firm, demanding, delicious. The plastic bottle she was holding fell forgotten to the floor, her fingers trailing up the leanly muscled contours of his arms before clinging to the strength of his shoulders. She had longed for this moment.

Had yearned to taste him. And now, at last, she was. There was no hesitancy, no awkwardness of a first kiss. It was as if their mouths, their bodies, already knew each other.

Her lips parted in welcome and she moaned as he accepted the invitation with barely restrained hunger, sweeping inside, taking and giving, stroking and sliding. One arm wrapped around her waist, pulling her closer, and she stepped up between his thighs. The fingers of his other hand sank into her hair, tilting the angle of her head to deepen the contact between them. His touch was electric, his kiss explosive. Lauren felt as if all the cells and molecules in her body bonded with his, their genes homing in on each other.

The kiss melted her, stealing her reason. Her legs threatened to give way and she tightened her hold, leaning into him for support. She had never felt like this before. The intense, thorough kiss was even more than she had imagined and dreamed about in the time she had known him. She met and matched Gabriel's every move, never wanting this to end. Her tongue twined with his, and she sucked on him, excited when he nibbled at her lips, teasing and tormenting before deepening the kiss again and sucking back at her. She wanted more, needed everything, revelled in his immediate response, the passion between them intensifying.

Gabriel lost himself in the sweet heat of Lauren's kiss. The firm softness of her breasts pressed against his chest and he could feel the hardened crests of her aroused nipples through the thin barrier of their clothes. His hand grazed down her back to cup the enticing swell of her rear, and he shaped her, pulling her tighter, swallowing her involuntary whimper as she met the fullness of his erection. An answering groan escaped him as she wriggled closer, rubbing herself against him.

He'd never felt this out of control from a kiss, but the wild chemistry between them had him on the ragged edge already.

A kiss was never going to be enough. He wanted her. Wanted her as he had never wanted any other woman in his life. Needed to see her and touch her and taste her all over. Couldn't wait to unite their bodies, to possess her fully, to lose himself deep and tight inside her. Lauren and this incredible passion they shared could make him forget all about the problems awaiting him back in France.

A loud knock on the door brought them sharply back to reality. They broke apart, panting for breath. How could he have forgotten where they were? Lauren's eyes opened, dark grey and smoky with unfulfilled passion, her regret at the interruption matching his own. They stared at each other and he watched as she stepped back a pace, raising shaky fingers to lips that were moist and plump from the incendiary kiss that had taken him to paradise. He could see the pulse beating wildly at her throat, mimicking the way his own heart pounded a frantic rhythm beneath his ribs.

'*Damnez-le,*' he cursed, drawing in a ragged breath. 'Wrong time, wrong place.'

'Yes. Gabe…'

No one had ever shortened his name before. He liked it. Liked it that Lauren was the only one who used it, who spoke it with such husky intimacy. Renewed heat prickled through him as they looked at each other, her eyes dark with an answering desire and need. Another knock at the door had Lauren moving farther away, adjusting her clothes and smoothing down the hair he had tousled.

'Just a minute,' she called out, her voice sounding shaky and rough.

He licked his lips, still able to taste her. Her subtle sweet-pea scent had invaded him, familiar, arousing, sensual. His whole body was charged with excitement. There was bitter disappointment that they'd had to stop, yet raging anticipation at the thought of how explosive the experience of making love was going to be for them when the time came. As it in-evitably would.

'I'd better get that.' She forced the words out but they sounded hoarse.

Knowing he couldn't delay things now, Gabriel sighed. 'I know.'

He retreated behind the curtain, listening as she opened the door and had a conversation with Adam.

'Sorry to bother you, Lauren. I hope Gabriel's OK. We've brought down two more team players needing treatment,' Adam explained. 'I'm just going to stitch Jack's cut—we won, so I'm at him with the needle!—and Dan Somers has pulled his hamstring. It looks a bad one so he's going to need follow-up treatment. Can you see what you can do for him?'

'Of course.'

Gabriel heard the thread of reluctance at being interrupted mingle with genuine concern in her voice as she agreed. The son of one of the local farmers, Dan had played for the Penhally team and Gabriel had met him for the first time that day. Hurrying so as not to embarrass Lauren in any way, Gabriel pulled on his shorts then sat down to sort out his socks and football boots. Once he was done, he drew back the curtain in time to see Lauren glance over her shoulder at him, her expression flustered.

'We're just about finished here,' she told Adam. 'Give me a few moments to make sure Gabriel is all right and I'll be happy to help Dan.'

'Thanks, Lauren. He's in the waiting room. We'll help him through.'

When Adam had gone, Gabriel moved up behind her and, hidden by the door, turned her to face him, cupping her cheek with one palm, enjoying the feel of her warm, soft skin.

'I'm sorry,' she whispered, and it was an effort to drag his gaze away from the temptation of her mouth.

'It's not your fault. Next weekend we'll have some privacy. I don't want to rush things and have to steal odd moments like this.' He felt the tremor run through her in response to his words. 'Thank you for making my leg feel so much better.'

Her smile held a spark of mischief and he chuckled, not sure if it was the expert massage or the fiery kiss that had most eased the pain in his cramping leg. Hearing people approaching along the corridor, Gabriel released her and stepped back, allowing her to open the door again so that Adam and Oliver could assist Dan Somers into the room.

'How are you feeling Gabriel?' Oliver asked as Lauren and Adam settled Dan on the treatment table.

'Like a new man, thanks to Lauren.'

Gabriel noticed the warmth bloom on Lauren's cheeks as she rejoined them. 'He should be fine,' she said.

'I'm heading home with Chloe,' Oliver continued, apparently oblivious to the charged atmosphere. 'Do you want a lift as Lauren's going to be busy for a while?'

'Sure. Thanks, Oliver.'

'Thank *you* for all your help. The match was a huge success. And we won—thanks to our secret weapon in our French star!' Oliver smiled, his humour infectious.

'We'll leave you to get on, Lauren,' Adam decreed. 'I have an appointment with Jack and a needle!'

Lauren walked them to the door, and Gabriel hung back, allowing Adam and Oliver to leave ahead of him. He paused, leaning in to whisper in her ear. 'Later, *chérie*. Next weekend we'll have time for us,' he promised, gratified by the flare of desire in her eyes.

Filled with impatience at the wait and disappointed to be leaving her, Gabriel walked away. The time until they could be alone together with no threat of interruptions couldn't come soon enough.

* * *

The frustration and anticipation was every bit as bad as he expected as the following week unfolded and he had little time alone with Lauren. One bright spot on the horizon was the arrangement to spend a morning accompanying her on her home visits. He was happy to give up his time off on Thursday because it meant being with her.

Finally it was Wednesday. His late-afternoon surgery was typically mixed, with cases including a young man with psoriasis, a fifty-two-year-old woman with menopausal symptoms, a teenage girl with a nasty stye, who needed some antibiotic eyedrops, an elderly man with signs of blood in his urine, who needed further tests to rule out infection and determine the source of the bleeding, a toddler with earache and several cases of colds, sore throats and influenza.

'You done for the day?' Oliver asked, tapping on the open consulting-room door and stepping inside.

'Yes.' Gabriel smiled, waving Oliver to a chair and saving the notes he had written up on his computer to back up his handwritten ones. 'What can I do for you?'

'I hear you are going out on home visits with Lauren tomorrow.'

And the time couldn't come soon enough, Gabriel thought, nodding at his friend. 'That's right.'

'You'll be visiting one of our regular patients, Gertrude Stanbury. She's quite a character, as I am sure Lauren will explain to you!' With a bad-boy smile, Oliver sat back in the chair and hooked one ankle over the opposite knee. 'Would you mind giving her a flu jab? I found out today that the district nurses missed her off their schedule by mistake, and I'm not due to see her for a fortnight. I don't want her to wait that long. I'd go myself, but I have a full list tomorrow and I'm off on Friday. I could get one of the nurses to fit her in, but as you'll be there anyway…'

'No problem, Oliver.'

'Great. Thanks. Chloe's free on Friday, too, so we're planning to get off early for our weekend in Plymouth.'

'I hope Rachel Kenner is coping.' Having heard the full story of how the troublesome youth Gary Lovelace had targeted the vicar's daughter so cruelly, he felt sad for the girl. 'I'm sure she will be delighted to see you.'

Concern shadowed Oliver's expression. 'Chloe is fretting about her. It will set our minds at rest if she's settled in as happily as possible with her aunt and uncle, as well as managing her pregnancy. Goodness knows how she is dealing with all that on top of losing her father.'

'Grief affects people in different ways.' Realising that his tone of voice had revealed more than he had intended and had roused Oliver's interest, Gabriel cleared his throat and changed the subject, unwilling to think of home and family. 'Don't worry about anything here. I'll see to Ms Stanbury's flu vaccination tomorrow. And I know Lauren will take care of the cats for Chloe while you are gone.'

A knowing gleam shone in Oliver's dark eyes. 'Somehow I doubt that you and Lauren will be sorry to have us out of the way for a while. We've cramped your style a bit, having to move into Gatehouse Cottage after the flood.'

'It's fine.'

'You look much more relaxed than when you first arrived,' Oliver continued after a moment.

Gabriel nodded. 'I feel it. It's been enjoyable and I've learned a great deal. I'm glad I came here.'

'Moving to Penhally Bay certainly changed *my* life.'

'How so?' he prompted, interested to know more about the man who had become a close friend in such a short time.

'I was dissatisfied with my life in London and knew I wanted something different. I'd planned to take time to settle in and establish myself before I started thinking about the future and a family. But then I met Chloe. I knew from the first moment that she was the one for me.' He glanced across with a smile that was both reminiscent and wicked. 'It took me a while to acknowledge the truth of it to myself—and a bit longer to persuade Chloe I was serious. She's the best thing that's ever happened to me. I've never been this contented.'

'I'm pleased for you. Anyone can see how great you are as a couple.'

'I hope Penhally will bring you the same contentment.'

Gabriel hesitated a moment, finding it surprisingly easy to share confidences with Oliver—something that was uncharacteristic for him. 'I have issues to work out from home… things to consider about my future. And a year here in which to decide on the direction of my life.'

'Penhally is a good place to think. If you want to talk, I'm here. And there's Lauren,' he added, a teasing glint in his eyes. 'The sparks between you are obvious. I hope you'll find your time in Cornwall brings you the same happiness and direction it gave to me.'

'Thank you, *mon ami*.'

Gabriel wondered the same thing. Would his time in Penhally not only lead him to some answers about his family dilemma but also open up a whole new world of opportunity with Lauren? Their friendship had established and deepened from the first moment. It had happened quickly, but there was no denying the connection between them. The heightened awareness and desire fizzing through him whenever he so much as thought of Lauren could not be ignored.

He was looking forward to finding out what the next weeks and months held in store for him.

CHAPTER FIVE

'WE JUST have Gertrude Stanbury left to visit,' Lauren informed Gabriel as she steered the car away from the Mitchell family's home and headed towards Trelissa Road.

Despite hearing good things from others, this morning was the first time she had seen Gabriel in action as a doctor for herself. She was even more impressed than she had anticipated. He had an innate warmth that set people at their ease and evoked their trust. He was interested and genuine, compassionate without being patronising. Combined with everything else she knew about him, it made her admire and care about him even more.

'Paul Mitchell is an inspiring youngster,' Gabriel said, and Lauren smiled.

'He is. I always feel humbled by his bravery,' she admitted, shaking her head at the way the eleven-year-old coped with the limits Duchenne muscular dystrophy placed on his life. 'Paul's faced each new challenge and stage of the disease with good humour and fortitude, although he hates having to use the wheelchair now. He loves school but doesn't attend full time because of the difficulties, so has some lessons at home, like today. Thankfully he's a genius with a computer…it's his pride and joy. The family don't have much materially but they do all they can to meet Paul's needs with home adaptations and equipment. They are very close and wonderfully supportive of each other, not to mention grateful for whatever back-up we can give them.'

Gabriel nodded, his admiration evident. 'They are certainly devoted to Paul and take his exercise regime seriously.'

'Paul's willingness to keep trying, to do the stretching exercises for his muscles and the breathing ones to keep his lungs clear, expel the mucus and reduce the risk of infections, makes my job much easier. He's determined not to let it beat him. And we are all determined to work as a team to ensure that Paul has the fullest and most enjoyable life possible.'

'I think you are amazing.' Gabriel's compliment warmed her inside. 'I've seen you today helping a variety of people— Harry Biscombe with his osteoporosis, Edith Jones with her minor stroke, the after-effects of her broken knee and assorted health problems, Stella Chamberlain with her onset of Parkinson's disease, the Morrisons with young baby Timmy's cystic fibrosis, and now Paul.' He paused and she could feel his gaze on her. 'You have a special rapport with your patients, Lauren. You give so much of yourself. It's not just a job to you.'

His praise touched her, his opinion mattering a great deal. But his own dedication and giftedness as a doctor was unsurpassed. 'You're the same. Medicine—caring for people in need—is part of the very fabric of who you are.'

'Yes.'

There was a thread of sadness and confusion in his voice, along with a weary sigh. She glanced at him, wondering what lay behind his change of tone. Did it have something to do with why he had been so keen to leave France? There was so much she wanted to discover about this man.

'Gabriel—'

'Tell me about Gertrude Stanbury,' he suggested, interrupting her. 'Oliver tells me she is something of a character.'

Reluctantly, Lauren allowed the change of subject…for

now. 'You can say that again. Gertrude is retired now but she was an institution as long-time headmistress at the secondary school here in Penhally. She has a bungalow in Gull Close and suffers badly from arthritis, especially in the knees and hands, although other joints are becoming affected more seriously. She had her first knee replacement recently but is still not very mobile. Her recovery wasn't helped by the flood, but at least she was safe. Thankfully one of the young local girls, Tassie Lovelace, was visiting her at the time, and as the water started coming in she was able to encourage Gertrude into the attic, from where they were rescued by one of the helicopter crews.'

'How on earth did Gertrude manage to get up there?'

'I've no idea, but it didn't do her joints much good.' Lauren shook her head, pausing a moment as she parked in Trelissa Road, taking extra care to make sure she didn't have a repeat of reversing into anything…not with Gabriel as a witness. 'Until her home is fit to live in again, Dr Tom Cornish has insisted she live in this house—it used to belong to his father and Tom inherited it. A former Penhally resident, he happened to be here, dealing with the house, when the flood hit. He's head of Deltaron, the international rescue agency, and his team were marvellous during the emergency.'

Gabriel unclipped his seat belt and glanced at the house. 'Why would Dr Cornish loan Gertrude his house?'

'Apparently Tom was a bit wild when he was young and, although a formidable adversary, Gertrude always believed in him. Tom was glad to help her now and repay her faith in him.' She chuckled at her own memories of the feisty woman who had watched over the school and its pupils with an all-seeing eye. 'She scared the life out of most of us!'

'I shall look forward to hearing all about your misspent youth!'

Lauren laughed. 'The trouble is, Gertrude will be all too keen to tell you.'

'Now I'm even more intrigued.' He smiled back at her, and she felt the faint wash of pink that tinged her cheeks.

'Just don't believe everything you hear.'

'Maybe that depends what *everything* is.'

His teasing deepened her blush. She was aware of him following close behind as she walked towards the house and opened the front door with the spare key they kept at the surgery. Rotund, white-haired Gertrude was propped up on pillows in a comfortable recliner in the living room. Age and crippling arthritis had brought an end to her working life, but had done nothing to dim the sharp expression in her steely grey gaze or take the edge off her shrewd watchfulness. A sense of humour and keen interest still lurked behind her outward bark and bluster.

'Oh, it's you, Lauren. Come in, then, if I have to be poked and prodded,' she grumbled, a sparkle dancing in her eyes as she took her first look at Gabriel. 'Who is this handsome creature?'

'I've brought Dr Devereux to meet you, Ms Stanbury.'

Lauren introduced them and watched with amusement as the elderly lady regally extended her hand, a pink glow washing pale, papery cheeks at Gabriel's gallant greeting. She was surprised, however, when Gertrude began speaking rapidly to him in his own language.

'I'd forgotten that you used to teach French, Ms Stanbury.'

'I did have a life before becoming a headmistress, you know,' she barked in response.

Lauren saw the laughter in Gabriel's eyes and struggled to contain a giggle. 'How have you been since I last saw you? Have you been managing the exercises I gave you?'

'Pure torture, they are.'

'I'm sorry to hear that.' Lauren smiled, not fooled for a moment by Gertrude's mock complaints. As she carried out a gentle examination and encouraged her to try a few more movements and exercises, both standing and sitting, she could see the improvement in the knee that had been replaced. 'You are doing so well, Ms Stanbury. Once your other knee is done, you'll find your mobility will be much better. How are your hands? Are you finding the new combination of pills Dr Oliver put you on helping at all?'

An affectionate expression crossed the elderly lady's face at the mention of Oliver, for whom it was well-known she had a soft spot. 'These pills are an improvement.'

'I'm so glad. We'll run through a few more gentle exercises to keep you moving, then Dr Devereux is going to see to your flu jab.'

A groan greeted the news and Lauren shared another smile with Gabriel. When she had finished, she sat back on her heels and packed away her things while Gabriel dealt with the vaccination and chatted with Gertrude in French. Lauren didn't catch much of the conversation, but hearing the names of Martin and her parents mentioned, she smothered a groan of her own. Maybe it was a good thing she couldn't remember much of her schoolgirl French or she would likely be mortified at whatever Gertrude was telling Gabriel. The former headmistress possessed an encyclopaedic knowledge about her past students and embarrassing moments were recounted with glee. Feeling Gabriel watching her, she looked up. The interested speculation evident in his mocha-brown eyes made her wonder what questions she would face once they were alone.

'You didn't understand much of that, did you, Lauren? You would remember your French had *I* been your teacher,' Ms Stanbury rebuked, reverting to English, mischief in her eyes. 'As I recall, it was always art and sport with you. When you weren't tripping over and dropping things. Still,' her tormentor continued, her knowing gaze moving from Lauren to Gabriel and back again, 'it seems to me that your interest in things French has increased considerably of late.'

As Gabriel chuckled, Lauren fought another blush. The

woman was a menace! Fortunately, they were soon able to escape. Unfortunately, her time with Gabriel was over for today and she dropped him back at the Manor House.

'Gertrude Stanbury was everything I expected and more,' he teased, silencing her grunt of disgust with a parting kiss that left her breathless. He drew back and stroked the fingers of one hand down her cheek. 'Thank you for this morning, *chérie*. I learned a lot.' Lauren feared he had learned rather more than she had intended, thanks to Gertrude's runaway tongue. 'We'll talk at the weekend.'

With his enigmatic promise ringing in her ears, Lauren returned to the surgery for her afternoon list of appointments, wondering what the weekend held in store and if, once finally alone, they would succumb to the charge of desire that hummed between them.

Today had been his most enjoyable day in Cornwall so far, Gabriel reflected, lingering over coffee after the meal he had cooked and shared with Lauren in the kitchen at the Manor House on Saturday evening.

The weather had continued to be kind and they had spent the day exploring, Lauren showing him Bodmin Moor and parts of the coast. They had also indulged in a number of increasingly heated kisses that had whetted his appetite for more. From the look in her eyes and the responses of her body, he was pretty sure Lauren felt the same. Foxy had accompanied them on their walks, growing in confidence all the time, and the sleek greyhound now lay asleep in the basket Lauren had brought up for him. Returning from their outing as dusk had descended, they had stopped off at Gatehouse Cottage to check on and feed Chloe's cats.

He had noticed once again Lauren's nervousness and caution in the dark, the care she took, the way she sometimes counted to herself as if she was measuring her steps because she couldn't see. He wasn't even sure she was aware of the habit. Once the lights went on, she reverted to her usual self. Again, her actions puzzled and concerned him, but he was wary of mentioning anything to her until he had a clearer idea if there was, indeed, anything wrong…and until she knew him well enough to trust him. Was he making something out of nothing? Maybe, if everyone else accepted her as clumsy and she had always been this way, he was seeing something that wasn't there and Lauren just had bad night vision. Gertrude Stanbury had confirmed Lauren had been renowned for being accident prone even in her schooldays. He planned to keep a watch on her until he was more certain of the facts.

Looking at Lauren now, Gabriel marvelled again at her natural beauty. Her skin glowed with freshness, her hair, left loose around her shoulders, shone with life—myriad shades of light browns and golds—and her womanly figure was shown off to perfection in dark jeans and a lilac button-through top that hugged the fullness of her breasts. Long, sooty lashes rose and beautiful grey eyes stared into his own.

'What?' she asked, her voice husky, rosy lips parting slightly as her tongue-tip peeped out to moisten them, tightening his gut with need.

He edged his chair closer and reached out to take one of her hands in both of his, holding her palm up in one hand and stroking her soft skin with the fingers of the other, feeling the way her flesh quivered in response to his touch.

'I had a great time today, Lauren.'

'Me, too.'

He forced himself to look away from the temptation of her mouth for the moment. They had talked about so much today but had not touched on any of the things that were contentious or difficult, like family and past relationships. Gabriel thought of all the well-meaning but meddling gossip Gertrude had told him on Thursday. Knowing how he felt about having his own privacy invaded, he didn't want to pressure Lauren, yet he knew they had reached a point where an exchange of confidences was needed if they were to take the simmering passion that only grew hotter and more intense between them to its logical conclusion.

'Will you tell me about Martin?' he asked after a long moment of silence. He watched Lauren carefully but saw nothing in her reaction to worry him, no sign she was still in love with the man Gertrude had mentioned.

'Martin and I had an on-off relationship for a long time,' she explained, no inflection in her voice. 'We grew up together, went out as teenagers, then broke up when I went away to do my physiotherapy training. I had a couple of casual boyfriends while we were apart and I know Martin dated other people. He stayed in Penhally, apprenticed to his father's construction business, but he was never happy there.' Gabriel waited when she paused again, welcoming the way she twined her fingers with his. 'When I moved back here to work, neither of us were involved with anyone and we started seeing each other again. I suppose we drifted into it for lack of other options. That sounds bad, but we were good friends first and foremost. We just became comfortable with each other, like an old habit. Things were wrong for a long time but neither of us faced up to what was happening.'

'And what did happen?'

'Martin became increasingly restless and withdrawn. He felt stifled by a job he hated, a town he wanted to escape from and a relationship I'm sure he knew deep down was going nowhere. I was settled—I love my job, my friends, my hobbies. But he needed to go off and explore new things and places. And to find someone he could share more than friendship with.'

She sounded understanding and not too sorry that things had ended, Gabriel thought. 'So he left.'

'It was the right decision. We were both relieved.' She smiled, her expression clear. 'A lot of people were shocked— a few had presumed we would marry. That was *never* on the cards. We didn't even live together. It was only once we'd made the final break that I realised how dull and predictable and restricting things had become, and how long it had been since we had been together in any real sense of the word. Our friendship was important but anything more was wrong for us both. Martin needed to leave. We couldn't provide what each other wanted.'

Smiling, she rose to her feet and began to clear the table, moving to the sink to wash up the plates. Thoughtful, under-standing the rut she had found herself in, Gabriel drained the last of his wine and crossed the kitchen to join her, working silently by her side for a moment. The atmosphere was thick with the ever-present awareness and desire that rippled between them.

When the last plate had been washed and dried, Gabriel turned her to face him. 'And what did you want, Lauren, that you never got from your relationship?'

Gabriel's smoky, accented voice sent shivers down Lauren's spine. Did she dare admit her secret yearnings? She sensed that with Gabriel she could experience all the things she now knew she had been missing. His compelling gaze drew her in, mesmerised her. The last two weeks had been leading up to this point and they both knew it. Taking her courage in both hands, she looked into his eyes, holding nothing back.

'I wanted things to be more passionate, more spontaneous, less boring.'

'You'd like to be adventurous, *chérie*?'

'Yes,' she whispered, her own voice low and throaty in response to the dark sensuality lacing his.

He didn't move. He wasn't touching her in any way but it

felt as if he was. 'You want to experiment, to be fully satisfied.' It was a statement, not a question, and Lauren swallowed, a shiver of desire skimming down her spine.

'Yes.' The admission was torn from her.

'You want a partner to be your equal, to explore the full scope of your sexuality, to surprise you and challenge you. To give and to take. To break rules and test boundaries.'

Speech was now impossible. He was seducing her with his words, his voice, the promise that remained as yet unspoken. Excitement fired her blood. The wicked glint in his sexy dark eyes made her breathless. She had no doubt that making love with Gabriel would never be boring or predictable or lacking in passion. Her heart pounded beneath her ribs. Unable to wrest her gaze from his, she nodded her answer, aroused beyond bearing, unable to look away from the flare of desire that turned his brown eyes almost black.

He stepped closer, reaching out to take her hands in his. It was their only point of contact and yet her whole body vibrated with sensation. His arms encircled her, his fingers linked with hers so that their joined hands fisted at the small of her back. The movement caused her body to arch and press against his. Every thud of her heart sounded loud in the silence of the kitchen and her breathing sped up, matching the uneven rate of his.

A gasp escaped unchecked as his lips whispered over hers, the tip of his tongue teasing as he circled it round the outline of her mouth, pausing to stroke each corner. It was incredibly erotic. She moaned, opening involuntarily, seeking closer contact, her lips clinging to his as he gave her what she needed. From the first second the kiss flared out of control, deep and demanding as they all but devoured each other, exploring, tongues duelling and entwining. His teeth nibbled at her, inflaming her senses. He pulled on her lips, then sucked on her tongue, drawing her into him. She couldn't get close enough, intoxicated by the male taste of him and his warm, citrusy, masculine scent.

The next moment, she found both her hands restrained behind her by one of his, leaving his other hand free to explore her. And explore her he did. His fingers trailed her face and down her throat, setting little fires wherever he touched, making every particle of her skin tingle. She whimpered when his mouth abandoned hers. Forcing heavy lids to open, her eyes focused to find him watching her, following the path of his fingertips over her flesh. As he bent her back, his palm splayed over her skin, stroking across from one collar-bone to the other before slowly grazing lower. Lauren held her breath as his thumb dipped down her cleavage, tantalisingly brushing against the swell of her breasts, setting her aflame, making her ache for a firmer touch.

'Gabe...'

Her breath rasped out again as his fingers went to work on her buttons, peeling back her top and freeing one breast from the confinement of her lacy red bra. The sight of his darker skin against her paler tones enthralled and excited her. Her nipple, already peaked and flushed with arousal, tightened further under his hungry gaze. She quivered as the pad of his thumb brushed around the outside edge of her areola before gliding once over the proud crest, making her cry out at the sweet ache. After an agonising delay, when she thought she would die of anticipation, his palm cupped the firm fullness of her breast, shaping, testing, before plumping it up as his head lowered. She tried unsuccessfully to free her hands, desperate to touch him, but he kept her captive to his will. Her knees turned to jelly as the moist warmth of his mouth closed over her swollen flesh and he suckled her deeply.

'Oh, my!' She sobbed, shocked by the powerful sensations crashing through her, more intense and incredible than she had ever felt before. Her body arched further in response to his sensual caresses, the rhythmic, hot, heavy pull of his mouth at her breast spearing a devastating ache of need straight to her womb. 'Please. Gabe, please!'

He finally released her hands and she clutched at his shoulders to keep from melting to the floor. Cupping her rear, his fingers flexing, shaping her through the denim as he sank to a chair, he drew her down so she was straddling his lap. Swiftly he dispensed with her shirt and bra. He arched her back, supporting her spine with one hand as the fingers of his other hand traced her skin, learning the contours and textures of her body.

'*Tu es parfait, ma belle,*' he praised huskily, his accent more pronounced. 'Perfect.'

His mouth moved to lavish attention on her neglected breast, bringing the nipple to an aching ripeness to rival its twin. Lauren wriggled on his lap, making him groan as she rubbed herself against the hard thickness of his arousal. She glided one hand up his neck to the back of his head, holding him to her. His close-cropped hair tickled her palm, feeling softly spiky to her touch. Unable to wait any longer to see him, to feel more of him, her fingers tugged at his cable-knit jumper, and he drew back just long enough for her to wrench it over his head. As her fingers traced his upper arms, he returned his avid attention to her breasts, driving her insane with the devastating skill of his hands and mouth, tormenting with his lips and teeth before salving with his tongue. Again he suckled strongly, taking her flesh deep inside, rolling her swollen nipple against the roof of his mouth with his tongue. She cried out, already on the ragged edge, shocked by the urgency of her need.

'I can't bear it!'

He chuckled, the huff of his breath against her over-stimulated flesh nearly sending her past the point of no return. She had never responded to any man the way she did to Gabriel.

He only had to look at her to arouse her. One touch and she was primed, ready. Now she was a whisper away from climaxing and they still had most of their clothes on!

'Hold on, *chérie*.'

Taking her by surprise, he stood up, lifting her with him. She curled her legs around his hips and her arms around his neck, as he headed out of the room towards the stairs. She wanted this with a fierceness that shocked her. They had been heading here since the first moment they had seen each other. Excited anticipation rippled through her. Her hands explored his shoulders and back, delighting in the smoothness of his warm supple skin, the feel of hard muscles rippling beneath.

The rest of the house was in darkness and she pressed her face to his neck, not wanting to acknowledge how little she could see. Instead, she lost herself in his scent, the feel of him, the rightness of her body against his. His hand on her rear tightened, one finger wickedly dipping down to stroke the seam of her jeans over her most sensitive flesh. She moaned, her body reacting instantly, and she wriggled, trying to assuage the terrible ache, desperate for release.

When they reached his bedroom, he set her on her feet, keeping hold of her as he leaned over and switched on the twin bedside lights, casting their welcome glow in the room, easing her anxiety and helping her to see.

He cupped her face with his hands, his expression serious. 'Things in my life are unsettled at the moment, Lauren, and I need to make decisions about my future.'

'Is this about why you left France?' she ventured, nerves tightening her insides.

'Yes. There are family issues.' He hesitated, his uncertainty evident. 'I'm not ready to talk about it. When I am, it will be to you.'

She nodded. 'I understand.' And she did. She wasn't ready to get into her whole family situation either, or face the scary subject of her changing sight. No way would she push him but she would be there if and when he needed her.

'I hadn't planned on or expected to get involved in anything here.'

Terrified he was going to call a halt, she began to protest. 'I—'

'However…' The pad of his thumb pressed gently against her mouth and silenced her. 'I cannot deny the connection that sparked between us from the first moment, or the attraction and longing I have for you. I want you…badly.' Her body tingled, her legs felt weak, and hopeful excitement stirred within her. 'I've not dated at all since my last relationship ended a year ago.'

She was surprised. 'Because you still love her?' she dared to ask.

'No. I didn't love her.' Gabriel smiled and she read the truth in his eyes. 'Like you and Martin, Adèle and I had no grand passion. One day I'll explain, but it ended because of deceit and manipulation. I was angry. It's made me cautious, and I have not been interested in a woman since. Until you.' He paused a moment, then continued. 'I can't make any promises at the moment, Lauren. I—'

'Let's not worry about the future or waste time assessing what this is. I'm not expecting anything or asking for commitment, Gabe, but I don't do one-night stands.'

'Neither do I. I don't embark on things lightly.' His thumbs brushed across her cheekbones. 'I can't give you any guarantees now but this is a hell of a lot more than one night for me. If that's what you want, too.'

'It is.'

Lauren knew the decision had been made the instant she had met him. She meant what she said. She wasn't holding him to anything, but she couldn't deny the hope flaring within her or quell the sense that the chemistry between them was special. She planned to explore it to the fullest and see where this exciting journey took them.

'Why don't we enjoy what we have and see what happens down the line?' she suggested. It had been a long time for her—for him, too, apparently—and she craved Gabriel with an intensity that was almost scary. 'Later will take care of itself.'

'I agree. We live for the here and now.'

She sucked in a breath as his touch became caressing and the flare of sultry desire returned to his eyes. His fingers whispered down her throat, stroking her skin as they trailed between her breasts, neglecting for the moment the flesh that most craved his caresses. Instead, he journeyed down, over and around her navel, making her muscles clench, before grazing down to the waistband of her jeans and working all too slowly to unfasten them.

Lauren was glad he had left the light on. She wanted to see him, to experience everything of their time together. Heat flared inside her as his fingers slid inside the loosened waistband of her jeans, moving down to cuddle her rear. Her own hands settled against his bare chest, enjoying the freedom to touch him. She wanted to linger, to learn every inch of him, but she was too impatient, too needy. She ran her nails lightly over his bronze nipples, smiling at his reaction as he groaned, his body trembling. Moving closer, she set her mouth to him, nipping, licking and teasing, heady from the male taste of him.

Gabriel fisted a hand in her hair, drawing her mouth away from his chest, his eyes dark with a hunger that drove her wild. She sought his kiss, but he denied her, kneeling in front of her to remove her ankle boots and strip off her jeans, revealing the French knickers she favoured, the red lace matching her discarded bra.

'Very nice,' he murmured, nuzzling against her, taking her back to the edge of reason.

Oh, so slowly, he eased the lingerie away. His fingers tormented her, skimming up the backs of her legs, stroking her inner thighs, withholding the touch she most needed. Instead he set his mouth to her navel and used his lips, teeth and tongue to drive her crazy with want.

Just as her legs became too shaky to hold her upright any longer, Gabriel swept her off her feet and tumbled her to the huge four-poster bed that had featured in so many of her dreams in the last two weeks. Dreams that were becoming a reality. She lay there, breathless with expectation, watching hungrily as he kicked off his shoes then took off his faded jeans and black briefs. The breath locked in her lungs as she took in his wonderful physique, the blatant, beautiful male-ness of him, her stomach tightening and her mouth watering as she looked at his impressive erection.

'All right?'

Way more than all right. She nodded at his husky query, involuntarily licking her lips. *'Magnifique,'* she whispered with anticipatory delight.

Smiling, he took an unopened box of condoms from a drawer and put them on the bedside chest after ripping off the outer plastic covering. Then he unsnapped the watch on his right wrist and set it aside. Unable to wait any longer, she held out her hand and he took it, joining her on the bed, drawing her into a deeply intense and arousing kiss. Gabriel rolled them over until she was beneath him and she welcomed the weight of his body on hers. She lost all ability to think as his hands and his mouth laid claim to her body, rapidly taking her to a fever-pitch of need.

'Please,' she demanded, uncaring that she was begging.

'All in good time.'

'Now!'

Gabe chuckled at her plea, sending another stimulating huff of warm air across her taut nipple. 'There's no hurry.'

'There is,' she whimpered, part of her craving release at

once, part of her never wanting the delicious torture to end. 'Gabe, I can't.'

'Trust me, you can…and you will.'

'Wait until it's your turn,' she threatened, making him chuckle again, the throaty, seductive sound tightening everything feminine inside her.

'I'm looking forward to it, *chérie*. Now be still and let me enjoy you.'

No way could she be still! Her body arched and bowed and writhed to his intensely sensual and skilful caresses as he journeyed slowly down to settle between her thighs and use his mouth to take her to paradise. She was the instrument and he was the virtuoso musician and conductor, orchestrating her downfall, playing her to a shattering orgasmic crescendo. Gabriel unleashed a depth of passion and sexuality from within her that she'd had no idea was there. She had enjoyed making love in the past, but she had never experienced this all-consuming, out-of-control explosion of earthy desire and searing need before.

She had barely re-established a tentative grip on reality when he eased two fingers inside her, setting up a rhythmic stroking that threatened to turn the aftershocks still rippling through her into an earthquake of unprecedented proportions. Her heart pounded, her lungs burned, and every nerve ending zinged with sensation. She couldn't bear it. It was incredible, terrible, wonderful. Far too much and yet nowhere near enough. Shaken by her total abandonment, she tried to rein in the litany of cries and moans and whimpers clamouring for escape. She'd never been noisy before. Now, on the point of another explosive climax, she pressed a hand to her mouth to bank down the uncharacteristic scream rising inside her.

'No. Let it go, *ma belle*,' Gabriel demanded huskily against her ear, his tongue teasing her before he sucked on her lobe.

Her hand dropped away as he encouraged her, pushing her to shed any remaining inhibitions. 'Gabe!'

'I want to hear your pleasure.' His fingers intensified their erotic torment, joined by his thumb that circled her clitoris, sending her shooting back into orbit, his rough, accented voice urging her for more. 'That's it. Again. Come for me.'

Gabriel relentlessly took her from peak to impossible peak. Just as she was sure she was totally spent and satisfied, he protected them with a condom, then his hands found hers, their fingers linking, grasping, holding on tightly as he finally united his body with hers. Any remaining breath she had struggled to maintain was stolen as she cried out at the blissful reality of his slow, deep, total penetration.

Lauren couldn't look away from him, trapped by the searing heat in his eyes. She had never felt so taken, so possessed, so complete. Had never shared such intense intimacy—laid bare, as if he could see into her soul. For endless moments he remained still and she savoured his delicious invasion. But she didn't want him to wait. He *had* to move. *Now.* Her hips lifted and rotated in encouragement, demanding a response, and he needed no further invitation. As he slowly withdrew, only to return with more urgency, laying claim to her in a way she had never experienced before, her grip tightened on his hands. His fingers returned the pressure of hers and they anchored each other, swept along on an unstoppable tide.

Lauren surrendered herself totally to Gabriel and the unparalleled joy of making love with him. The friction and pressure were exquisite, the sense of fullness unbelievable. She drew her legs higher, wrapping them around him, taking all of him, drawing him deeper still. He groaned, his control slipping as his movements intensified, harder, heavier, faster.

'Yes, yes.' She sobbed, matching his rhythm, losing all sense of reality as the unimaginable pleasure built wave after wave, threatening to swamp her. 'Please, Gabe. More.'

He gave everything, took everything, demanded everything. She did the same. Together they drove each other higher and further, caught in a raging firestorm of passion that engulfed them and carried them over the edge, consumed by the flames, surrendering to the ecstasy, tumbling into oblivion.

They collapsed together, fighting for breath, their hearts thundering in unison. As Gabriel released her hands and wrapped his arms around her, Lauren clung to him, shaking, shattered, rapturous, scared to let go in case she never found her way back to earth again. An aeon later Gabriel eased his weight from her. She protested, not wanting him to go, but he drew her with him, pulling her even closer and burying his face in her neck. Lauren tightened her hold, inhaling his scent, stunned by the incredible experience they had shared.

'*Mon Dieu.*' Gabriel's voice was throaty and raw. He sounded as overwhelmed as she felt. Slumberous dark eyes looked into hers, his fingers shaking as he brushed damp tendrils of hair back from her cheek. 'Are you all right?'

Lauren licked lips still plump and tingly from his deliciously erotic kisses. 'I don't know. You?'

'Not sure.'

'That was…' Still dazed, she searched for the right word. 'It was…'

'Wow,' Gabriel volunteered huskily, cradling her against him.

That pretty much covered it in any language, Lauren decided. 'Exactly.'

She was never going to get enough of this man. He did things to her she had never imagined, made her feel things she had never thought possible and took her to places she had never been before. She had no idea what the future held in store for them beyond his stay in Penhally, but she wanted Gabriel to be part of her days…and her nights…for as long as possible.

CHAPTER SIX

THE weeks leading up to Christmas sped by and Gabriel had never felt so content...settled both at work and in his private life. Being with Lauren was the most amazing thing that had ever happened to him. A smile curved his mouth just thinking about her. The first patient for his Saturday morning surgery having cancelled, he had a few moments before the next person arrived, so he leaned back in his chair, his hands linked behind his head, and thought back to that first night he and Lauren had spent together.

He had known from the moment that they had met that there was an inexplicable and special connection between them, one that transcended the undeniable physical attraction. The first time they had made love had proved him right. He'd never experienced anything like it before. Incredibly, it had just got better and better since...not only in the intensity of their passion but in the deepening of their close bond and instinctive trust. In bed they matched each other in adventurousness, pushing each other to explore the boundaries of their desire and sensuality. Their rapport and innate friendship meant they were perfect companions personally and fully supportive and complementary colleagues professionally.

The only subjects that remained taboo were their family histories—his in particular—and Lauren's sight. A frown creased his brow. After lingeringly making love a second time that first night, they had fallen into an exhausted sleep, only for him to wake in the early hours when Lauren had slipped out of bed. Unknown to her, he had watched as she had tried to find her way to the bathroom through the unfamiliar room, one hand extended out in front of her, feeling her way in the dark, taking cautious, baby steps, bumping into things. He'd waited until she had been in the *en suite* before switching the bedside lamps back on, noting the way she hesitated when she came out, looking uncertain. Not wanting to spoil things or to confront her about the issues with her vision, he had smiled and pulled back the duvet.

'I missed you, *chérie.*'

More sure of her footing with the lamps casting a glow in the room, she had hurried back to bed and he had given himself up to the blissful magic of her mouth and her hands on his body. But the incident had convinced him that Lauren was exhibiting night blindness. There had been several more moments over the weeks, little things he had noticed but which Lauren had brushed aside, and he had not found the right moment to talk to her about it. In truth he was scared of saying or doing anything to spoil what they had, so he kept putting it off, telling himself he would wait until something happened that could not be ignored. But Lauren's problem nagged at him. Had she always been lost in the dark? Was there some simple cause? Or was her night blindness a symptom of something more serious?

His fears had been compounded following a conversation with Chloe last week. Worried about Diane Bailey, one of her mums-to-be, Chloe had asked for a doctor to accompany her to the woman's home and, with Oliver unavailable, Gabriel had been happy to help. Having had a terrible time delivering her first baby, the young mother had been understandably terrified at facing the birth of her second child. She was de-

termined to have a home birth, refusing to go to St Piran's for
the delivery in case she suffered as she had at another hospital
whose overstretched staff had failed to give her proper care
and consideration. Between them, he and Chloe—the best
midwife he had ever worked with—had allayed many of the
woman's fears and promised to work together as a team to
give her the safest birth possible and ensuring her their
constant support.

On the way back to the surgery Chloe had surprised him
by pulling over to the side of the road. 'Gabriel, can I talk to
you for a moment?'

'Yes, of course.' Concerned, he'd turned to study her. 'Is
something wrong?'

'Lauren saved my life,' she had told him softly after a
long pause.

Gabriel had listened in horror as Chloe confided in him
about her past with her abusive father, her green eyes
shadowed with remembered pain as she had told him of the
last beating and how Lauren had rescued her and helped her
escape. '*Mon Dieu*, Chloe. I am so sorry. I had no idea.'

'No one but Lauren and Oliver know the full story. And
now you.'

'Your secret is safe with me,' he'd assured her.

'She saved my life back then…now Oliver is teaching me
to live it to the fullest. I'd do anything for her.' She paused a
moment, nibbling her lower lip in indecision. 'Gabriel, have
you noticed anything, I don't know…*off*…about Lauren?'

He felt his own guard slipping into place. 'What do you
mean?'

'I'm probably being silly.'

'Go on,' he encouraged when she hesitated.

'Everybody has always teased Lauren because of her clumsiness, her habit of doing daft things and having minor accidents. She has terrible hand-eye co-ordination.' Anxiety and

confusion had replaced her earlier indecision. 'The incidents seem to be happening more often these days. When Oliver first came here in June, he didn't know of Lauren's reputation for mishaps and I had the feeling he believed there was more to what was happening than her just being clumsy. He wouldn't say more and I'm scared to bring the subject up again. It's just…' Again Chloe paused, her worry for her friend evident.

'Just what? Tell me.'

'I don't know how to explain.' Sighing, she shook her head. 'Spending more time with Lauren at Gatehouse Cottage because of the flood damage to my place in Fisherman's Row, I've noticed little things I'd never been aware of before. Odd things. And then there's her painting. She's so talented and she loves her art. In the summer I bought a picture for Oliver's birthday present and was looking around her studio—it was the first time I'd been there in a while. I noticed subtle differences in her newer works, less detail, more fuzziness, but Lauren denied it. Shortly after that she stopped painting altogether. I tried to ask her about it and she got defensive, made excuses.'

She looked away from him for a moment and took a deep breath before rushing on. 'Plus she seems reluctant to go out at night. Not that we've had many opportunities lately with the other girls in our circle of friends busy with new babies and husbands, Vicky away and myself being with Oliver. But Lauren doesn't even seem keen on going to the cinema now.'

'Is that new? Has she been confident in the dark until recently?' he probed, concerned that Lauren's lack of night vision was not a long-standing issue after all.

'I've never noticed that nervousness in the dark before. It's like the way she used the chance to change her work hours so she does her home visits in the mornings. I sense something is wrong, Gabriel, but I don't know what to do. I'm so delighted you and Lauren are together…' she flashed him a sweet smile '…but I wondered if you saw whatever Oliver did, what the rest of us who have known her for years have missed because it's always been there or worsened slowly.'

'Chloe, I—' He broke off, unsure what to say.

She rested a hand on his arm. 'I don't want to put you in a difficult position. But I care about Lauren and I *am* worried. Can I just ask that if you have any doubts or concerns in future, you'll talk to Oliver to see if you both think the same and if there is anything you can do to help her?'

'I can promise you that, Chloe, yes.'

He would keep the promise he had made but not yet. Not until something more specific happened that gave him real evidence of a problem. Part of him was relieved to know he was not alone in noticing the odd, erratic and worrying things about Lauren's poor night vision. But the rest of him was wary of invading her privacy, unsure how to get Lauren to talk about something she had so clearly not even acknowledged for herself. He *would* talk to Oliver—if and when the time came that he had to intervene.

In the meantime, scared about Lauren driving at night—even though the only time she took the car out after dark was for the short drive home from the surgery—he had managed to contrive a new routine. They now went home together, leaving her car at work where it was ready for her morning house calls. He wasn't sure how long he could get away with it without arousing Lauren's suspicions.

Since their first night together Lauren had virtually moved into the Manor House with him, leaving Oliver and Chloe at Gatehouse Cottage, although they got together often for meals and the occasional trip out when they were all off duty at the same time. At work he and Lauren were totally professional, keeping their private life separate from the surgery, but their relationship had never been a secret. Without exception, everyone had accepted them as a couple and were happy for them, especially Oliver, Chloe and Kate. Even Hazel had warmed to him.

As the days and weeks went by, they had enjoyed time alone as well as taking part in community events. They had been to the local firework display on Guy Fawkes night, eating toffee-apples and cuddling up in front of the bonfire to keep warm. They had explored the local environment, walking with Foxy who was growing more confident all the time. They had jogged, listened to music, spent time with Oliver and Chloe, and had talked for hours about everything and anything but their taboo subjects. Most of all, they had made love…everywhere, every way and as frequently as possible. A smile replaced his frown. By rights he should be worn out! But he was energised, happier than he ever remembered being. Any doubts and worries about what was going to happen when his time in Penhally was over, he forcibly set from his mind.

The ringing of the telephone brought an end to his reverie and he leaned forward, reaching for the receiver. 'Yes, Sue?' he asked of the head receptionist.

'Adrian Westcott is here, Gabriel,' the friendly, efficient woman informed him. 'He's a few minutes early but I thought you would like to know—it isn't every day we're ahead of schedule.'

Gabriel chuckled. 'Indeed not. Thanks, Sue. Please, send him through.'

After hanging up, he pulled the notes out of the tray and had a quick glance at them before rising to greet his patient. In his early forties, with thinning blond hair and pale blue eyes, the man looked tired and dejected.

'Hello, Adrian,' he said, shaking the man's hand. 'Please, take a seat.' He waited a moment as Adrian made himself comfortable. 'What can I do for you today?'

'It's about my tinnitus, Doctor. It's worsening all the time, as is my hearing, and affecting my work. Things are really getting me down.'

'What work do you do?'

'I'm a teacher at the secondary school.' Adrian grimaced and shook his head. 'I love my job but it's harder to cope with the noise levels or several people talking at once, not to mention making sure I'm hearing my students properly.'

Gabriel glanced again at the notes to see what history and previous advice had been recorded. 'You saw a specialist ten years ago and you were told you had otosclerosis?'

'That's right. I lived in the north of England then. I moved here for the job with my family eight years ago. No one really explained what it meant to have otosclerosis, just that I had to live with the tinnitus, that there was nothing much to be done.'

'Tinnitus is a symptom that has many causes and is experienced in different ways. For most types there isn't a cure. Otosclerosis means that the bones in the middle ear harden and this affects the hearing as it prevents the bones vibrating. It can lead to deafness. What kind of noises do you hear with your tinnitus?' he asked, making notes as his patient explained.

'It's a whooshing noise but throbs and thumps like my pulse, as if I'm hearing my heartbeat all the time. I've had it for fifteen years or more. For a while I tried to follow the advice to cover up the sounds, but it's progressively got worse, to the point I can't ignore it. And my hearing is diminishing.' Adrian paused, a deep sigh escaping. 'One on one with people I'm not too bad, I'm learning to lipread, but in a gathering or with other noises, it's becoming impossible. My wife encouraged me to come, to try again, even though I doubt there is much you can do.'

Gabriel considered the options, feeling for the man and his situation. 'What you describe is pulsatile tinnitus. It's many years since you saw the specialist and things may have changed since then, so I'd like to refer you to a consultant at the audiology department at St Piran's. He'll do a thorough reassessment.' He paused a moment, not wanting to give any false hope. 'There is an operation that works for some sufferers of otosclerosis that involves removing the stapes and replacing it with an artificial plastic bone. It's high risk and carries a chance of deafness during the operation, but if successful it gives improved hearing and a reduction in the tinnitus. They do the worst ear first. But all this is dependent on what the surgeon has to say when he sees you—and on what risk you want to take.'

'I certainly want to find out about it,' Adrian enthused, looking much happier than he had when he'd arrived.

'I can't promise that you will qualify, or that it would work.'

The man nodded at the warning. 'I understand. But it's worth exploring…better than doing nothing and just going on as I am. You live with something for so long and the changes creep up on you slowly, so you learn to live with it. Often it's only when something unusual or big happens that you realise just how bad things have become and how much you have deteriorated,' he added and Gabriel frowned, thinking of Lauren and what could be a similar pattern with her sight.

'I'll write to the consultant and arrange for him to see you,' Gabriel reassured him, focusing back on his patient. 'I'm not sure what the waiting time is but we'll get things moving as quickly as we can in the new year.'

As Gabriel rose to show Adrian out a few moments later, the man turned at the door and shook his hand. 'Whatever happens, I can't tell you what a difference it makes to have someone understand and take me seriously. Thank you so much, Dr Devereux.'

'No problem. Call me any time if you need anything explained or have any problems.'

His appointments continued smoothly for the rest of the morning and, after tackling some of the mountain of paperwork, he was able to leave and meet up with Oliver for a pub lunch. Lauren had gone out with Chloe for the day to do some last-minute Christmas shopping. He couldn't wait for her to come home.

It was the last weekend before Christmas and the shops in Newquay had been manic. Thankful to escape the crowds, Lauren wedged her purchases with Chloe's in the back of her friend's car before sinking thankfully into the passenger seat.

'Oh, boy, my feet are killing me.'

'Tell me about it.' Chloe slid behind the wheel and sighed. 'I can't believe we got everything done.'

'I don't want to see another shop or hear another tinny carol ever again.'

Chloe chuckled, steering the car out of the parking zone and heading out of town towards home. 'You'll get a second wind. Let's hope Oliver and Gabriel have managed to pick out decent trees. Do you think we were right to entrust the job to them?'

'They'll be fine.' Lauren wasn't so fussed about all the Christmas paraphernalia as Chloe but she kept her thoughts to herself, knowing how miserable Chloe's childhood had been and how much she wanted this first Christmas with Oliver to be perfect. 'That set of baby clothes you got for Rachel Kenner's little boy are so cute.'

'Thanks. I can't wait to see him. I'm just so relieved both she and the baby are well after the birth. Rachel's naming the baby Daniel after her father,' Chloe added, a wobble in her voice.

Lauren smiled in sympathy. 'She's been through so much, the poor girl, but she's remarkable, the way she's handled everything.'

'She is. And her aunt and uncle have been wonderfully supportive.'

Dusk was falling as they arrived back at Gatehouse Cottage and Lauren wasted no time in switching on plenty of lights as soon as she went inside. Foxy greeted her enthusiastically. After she and Chloe had unloaded the car and hidden away their packages, they sank down for a reviving cup of tea while they waited for Gabriel and Oliver to come back. Foxy laid his head on her knee and she stroked him.

'Lauren?'

'Hmm?'

'I want to tell you something.'

Alerted by the uncertainty mixed with excitement in her friend's voice, Lauren opened her eyes and looked over at Chloe. 'Is anything wrong?'

'Nothing, it's just…' A blush pinkened Chloe's cheeks.

'You're pregnant!'

'No! No, that's not it.'

'Sorry.' She sent Chloe a rueful smile. 'Everyone in Penhally seems to have been breeding like rabbits this year! I wouldn't have been surprised.'

'I know! And I do want children one day. We both do. For now all this is so new to me and I just want time to be alone with Oliver, to enjoy being a couple,' she explained, her blush deepening.

Lauren fought a grin. 'Of course you do.' Chloe was such a sweetheart and it was obvious that she was more than well loved—and satisfied—thanks to Oliver. As she deserved to be.

'The thing is…' Chloe's green eyes sparkled with delight. 'This is a secret and you can't tell anyone. Except Gabriel.'

'OK, I promise,' she agreed, reaching for her tea.

'Oliver and I are eloping.'

'What?' Lauren nearly dropped her mug she was so surprised at Chloe's rushed announcement. Setting it safely on the table, she faced her friend. She felt Foxy's tension at her sudden movements and soothed him. 'You're eloping? When?'

Chloe positively bounced with excitement. 'Over Christmas. But we don't want to spoil anything for you.' Worry momentarily dulled the gleam in her eyes. 'Gabriel isn't going back to France for the holiday, is he?'

'I don't know. We've not discussed it,' Lauren admitted with a frown.

'Well, I know it's an awful cheek, but Oliver's asking Gabriel today if he'd mind covering for him. Kate knows I'm taking my remaining week's holiday, but not why. We're hoping not to have to tell Nick. You know he can be a bit starchy about things.'

'He does have set ideas,' Lauren agreed. 'It's so exciting, but why all the cloak-and-dagger stuff?'

It was Chloe's turn to frown. 'We're getting a lot of interference from Oliver's family. It's well meant,' she hastened to explain, 'but neither Oliver nor I want some huge fuss and production made of it. And with Reverend Kenner gone and no permanent replacement here in Penhally, I'd feel weird getting married in the local church,' she finished, and Lauren felt a shiver of empathy.

'I can understand that. So what's the plan? Can you tell me?'

'Oliver has a friend he trained with in London who has a glorious cottage in southern Scotland. He's loaning it to us. We found out all about it three months ago and got the necessary permissions. We've sent the papers back to the registrar and we're getting married at Gretna in the traditional Old Blacksmith's Shop! We'll be back the day after New Year,' she confided, bubbling over with happiness.

Chloe's enthusiasm was infectious and Lauren was thrilled for her. 'How romantic!'

'I can't wait! I hope everyone will understand. We plan to have a party for all our friends later in January.'

'Do what's right for you and don't worry about anyone else,' Lauren urged, reaching out to take her hand. 'You know I'll support you. I just want you to be happy—and I know Oliver is the man for you. It's wonderful seeing you together.'

Tears shimmered in Chloe's eyes. 'Thanks.'

As they talked more about the secret wedding plans it was impossible not to share Chloe's excitement. Although nothing had been said about Christmas and New Year, Lauren was certain Gabriel would do all he could to cover for Oliver. She'd miss her friends over the holiday, but the thought of being alone with Gabriel held its own appeal. The man was amazing! His dimpled smile pulled at something inside her. And she could listen to him for ever. That softly husky voice with the delicious accent always made her stomach turn over and sent a tingle of awareness down her spine.

The bond had formed quickly between them. Friendship, respect and trust mingled with instant attraction and high-octane passion deepening and swelling her swiftly growing feelings for him. She tried to live every moment, as they had agreed, and not think about what was going to happen in the future, but it was impossible to imagine not having Gabriel in her life.

He was a wonderfully inventive lover, exciting, erotic, wicked, challenging her to really let go and experiment. She had never experienced such pleasure, such closeness, such utter bliss as she did with him. He brought all her secret fantasies to life. The desire and passion between them seemed to increase, not diminish, blazing ever hotter with every passing day.

The only black moments came as she tried to cover up her increasingly scary sight problems. The night blindness was now a major and permanent problem. She was pretty sure that Gabriel had noticed her difficulties, her clumsy moments when her sight failed her, but he'd not brought the subject up and she was grateful. Equally grateful that they had fallen into going home together most nights so she didn't have to drive. She suspected Gabriel was doing it on purpose but she was too thankful to make an issue of it.

That Chloe and Oliver were aware of some changes was obvious. Several times Chloe had mentioned painting and Lauren hadn't been able to explain why she had stopped the thing she had loved so much for so long. In the summer Chloe had noticed changes in the new paintings, changes Lauren herself didn't want to face up to. When her sight problems had been confined to the dark, she had been able to pretend it didn't matter, but in the last weeks she had noticed that it took longer for her eyes to adjust to changing light, and it was starting to become difficult to distinguish contrasts, even in daylight or under bright light indoors. In the last few days she'd had odd moments when she'd thought her peripheral vision wasn't as sharp as usual. She was frightened, unsure what to do.

'You are the only one, apart from Oliver, I can confide in like this,' Chloe said, and Lauren tried to push her own worries aside. Her friend paused a moment, nibbling her lower lip, the expression in her green eyes serious. 'You know you can always talk to me about anything, too, don't you, Lauren?'

She forced a smile and kept her voice steady, unable to speak aloud the fears that grew more troublesome as the weeks went by. 'Sure.' How much longer could she pretend that nothing was wrong?

Thankfully, Gabriel and Oliver arrived back then, a blast of wintry air sweeping through the cottage as they propped the door open to wrestle a huge, sweetly scented pine tree into the cosy living room. Diverted from her questions, Chloe jumped to her feet, hovering eagerly as the tree, already potted, was positioned, then she threw herself into Oliver's arms.

'Hi, babe,' he welcomed her, enfolding her in a hug. Lauren saw him glance at Gabriel before he looked at her. 'Have you told Lauren?'

Beaming, Chloe nodded. 'Yes.'

'Gabriel's happy to help out and he's going to cover my

shifts for me the week we're away—and look after Pirate and Cyclops,' Oliver informed his bride-to-be, laughing as she rushed to hug Gabriel, too.

'Thank you so much!'

'My pleasure, Chloe,' Gabriel reassured her.

Lauren stroked Foxy before she, too, rose to her feet. 'Congratulations, Oliver.' Smiling, she kissed his cheek. 'I'm so happy for you both,' she added, hugging Chloe.

After enjoying a celebratory glass of wine, Lauren happily agreed when Gabriel suggested they return to the Manor House. 'I'm sure you and Chloe would like some time alone and I still have another Christmas tree to wrestle with,' he joked.

'Do you want me to come and help?' Oliver offered, walking with them towards the front door, Foxy trotting ahead.

'We'll be fine.'

It felt odd, standing in the small hallway of her own house, leaving her friends there, as if she were the visitor, and going back with Gabriel to the Manor House where she felt so right and content. She was about to step outside, grateful the lights were illuminating the short pathway, when Oliver stopped her.

'Sorry, Lauren, I forgot. There's a pile of mail for you,' he told her, handing her a stack of envelopes held together by an elastic band.

'Thanks.'

Once at the Manor House, Lauren switched on the lights downstairs and settled Foxy in the kitchen with his food while Gabriel managed to manoeuvre a beautifully shaped tree that smelled as delicious as the one Oliver had bought, into the living room. Lauren joined him. While she may not be as excited about the festivities as Chloe, she was looking forward to decorating the tree with Gabriel and to them spending time together. She thought of the presents she had bought him, now hidden safely away until she had some time alone to wrap them, and hoped he would like them, that she had found the right balance and hadn't gone too over the top.

'I didn't see the elopement coming.' Kneeling on the floor to light the log fire, Gabriel chuckled. 'Did you?'

Lauren sat on the sofa, the pile of unopened mail in her lap. 'No. But I'm not surprised. In fact, I'm delighted for them, they're so perfect together.'

'Indeed.'

'You're sure you are OK with taking on the extra shifts? You weren't planning to go back to France for the holiday?' she probed cautiously.

'Hell, no.' Gabriel paused, glancing over his shoulder. 'I know I've been close-mouthed about it, but I'm not in any hurry to go home.'

Unsure of the issues but having every faith that he not only had his reasons but had done nothing wrong, she placed a hand on his shoulder. 'It's OK. I'm certainly not complaining about having the chance to spend the holiday with you— even if we are working for part of it.'

'There's no one I want to spend Christmas with but you, *chérie*.'

The husky words warmed her right through. Smiling, Lauren watched for a moment as Gabriel turned back to tend to the fire, putting some larger logs on as the kindling took hold. She turned her attention to the mail and sorted through the mixture of bills, letters and cards, including an oversized postcard of Cologne cathedral from Vicky, full of excited news and typical Vicky-isms. Her smile faded, to be replaced by a knot of tension in her stomach when she recognised the Australian stamps and familiar handwriting on an air-mail envelope. For a moment she sat and stared at it then, fingers shaking, she forced herself to open it. A stupid threat of tears pricked her eyes as she looked at the plain card. There was no accompanying letter and nothing written on the inside but two names.

'I know we've avoided talking about our families, Lauren, mine in particular,' Gabriel said, but she barely heard him, focused as she was on the card. 'Lauren?' She jumped when Gabriel's hand settled on her knee and looked up, finding him watching her with concern. 'What is wrong, *ma belle*?'

'You said we avoided families—perhaps that's because family often isn't all it's cracked up to be,' she whispered, sucking in a breath and handing him the card.

Gabriel opened it, then glanced at her with a frown. 'Who are John and Betty?'

'The people I called Mum and Dad for the first twenty-five years of my life.' She managed to say the words without betraying the emotion roiling within her. 'They became John and Betty the moment they told me I was adopted and the pretence of being my parents ended.'

Gabriel cursed, taking one of her hands in his. 'You had no idea until five years ago?'

'No. Don't get me wrong, they were always kind to me. I had everything I needed in terms of a safe and secure home, guidance, the freedom to go my own way…'

'But not the love and cherishing,' he suggested when her words trailed off.

She sighed and ran the fingers of her free hand through her hair. 'I never felt as if I belonged. Like a cuckoo in the nest, I didn't fit. I still don't understand why they waited so long to tell me. Worse was the realisation that had they known they could have their own children after all, they would never have adopted me. I was always second best. Clive was born after I had been with them for two years and they couldn't exactly give me back.'

Gabriel swore again, his fingers linking with hers. 'That's horrible. It must have been a huge shock and very confusing.'

'Yes.' She'd been so unsettled, so angry and hurt when the truth had come out. Yet it had explained so many things. 'I was three months old when they adopted me as a last resort, believing Betty couldn't conceive. It was a big surprise to them when she fell pregnant. They doted on Clive. He was terribly spoiled. We never got on. He knew he was the favourite, the golden boy who could do no wrong. I envied him his special place in their lives, unable to understand what was wrong with me. I think I sensed even at a young age that I was less somehow.'

'Lauren—'

'No, really. All Clive's needs came first. Everything was geared to him and his success. He went off to Australia seven years ago and settled there, marrying a local girl and starting a family. Two years later, wanting to be near their grandchildren, my parents—' she stumbled over the words '—decided to take early retirement and emigrate. Before they left, they told me the whole story, explained their need to go and gave me Gatehouse Cottage as a gift, a pay-off to salve their consciences and feel they had done right by me, I guess.' A part of her, a part of that child she had once been, craved to be loved for herself…to be really wanted. But she didn't say that aloud. 'Fortunately, I'm happy here—I love my friends and my job.'

'So they just cut you loose? They left you alone to deal with the shock, having told you the truth about your life?' Gabriel protested, his anger on her behalf clear.

'Yes.'

He shook his head and huffed out a breath. 'Do you know anything about your birth parents?'

'Only that they died in an accident shortly after I was born. There weren't any grandparents or siblings to take me in…' not who wanted her, anyway, she added silently '…so I was taken into care and put up for adoption.'

Gabriel didn't say anything for a few moments but Lauren hardly noticed as she was lost in thought. There was so much she wanted to know about the family she had originally come from, not least details of her medical history. Was there any clue among her birth relatives that could explain the weird things happening with her eyesight?

'I understand how disruptive and unsettling learning the truth about your identity can be, Lauren.'

Startled from her reverie, she looked up and saw that the pain in Gabriel's eyes matched that lacing his voice. 'You, too?'

'Yes.'

Hurting for him, she returned the pressure of his fingers. 'Can you tell me now?'

The only sound in the room was the crackling of the flames as they ate into the wood in the fireplace. Lauren held her breath. Was the time right for Gabriel to open up and trust her with the demons that had driven him from his home?

CHAPTER SEVEN

'YOU are not alone in learning late on that everything you thought you knew about yourself, your family, your life is a lie, Lauren. Or in wondering where you fit in.'

As he spoke the words, Gabriel found it easier than he had imagined to confide in Lauren. He had been so contented these last weeks in Penhally Bay that he had largely succeeded in pushing France and the unresolved issues there from his mind. The approach of Christmas had brought them to the fore again. At least this year promised to be more settled and happier. Last year had been the first Christmas without his father, bringing back the pain of his loss and the anger and uncertainty at the secrets that had come to light after his death, leading to a widening of the rift with Yvette and the row about his future.

Lauren had shared her background with him and he more than understood how shocked and hurt she must have felt, learning about her adoption in such a way and then being cut off by the couple who had raised her. The strength of his desire to have been here to support and protect her through such a difficult time took him by surprise and made him realise just how involved his feelings for her had become. He knew with utter conviction that he trusted Lauren completely. Without giving himself any more time to consider his actions, he sat back on his heels in front of the fire and told her things he had never shared with anyone else, laying bare the skeletons in the Devereux family cupboard.

'My father, Pierre, died twenty months ago. He was fifty-eight. It was sudden and unexpected…a big shock. We were very close,' he explained, shying away from the knowledge that his father had kept such an important truth from him. 'I was working at a practice in Paris at the time, in an area that served a poor community and a large immigrant population.'

Lauren edged closer and he was happy to let her take his hand in hers to return the understanding and comfort he had tried to offer her a short while ago. 'Gabe, I'm so sorry about your father.'

'Thank you. The trouble began shortly afterwards.'

'Trouble?' Lauren queried with a frown.

'The exposing of family secrets and lies.' He stared into the flickering flames of the fire and sighed. 'I have always had a difficult relationship with Maman. She was cold, unforgiving, dictatorial, and mostly I was raised by a nanny. I spent a lot of time with Papa, but never with Maman. Now I know why. And why my skin is darker than most of the other members of the family. Yvette Devereux is *not* my mother. She did not give birth to me and she resented it that she had to raise me.'

'Oh, Gabe… How could she?'

He shot Lauren a quick glance but saw nothing but concern and understanding in her slate-grey eyes. 'I only have her side of the story—a story she took vicious delight in telling me after the funeral. Part of me feels betrayed that my father never explained to me himself but, despite that, I did know him and love him and the things Yvette said just don't make sense. I have the feeling she has embellished the truth at best and lied at worst to serve her own ends.'

'What was her explanation?' Lauren asked, encouraging him to talk it out.

'She said that my father had an affair with a lowly woman from Martinique, a *servant*—it infuriated me the way she used that word. He took me away from this woman and demanded Yvette bring me up as her own, using her obsessive sense of duty and fear of sullying the family name to force her to agree. Now she expects me to pay her back for all the years she had to be humiliated and put up with me.'

'That's absurd,' Lauren exploded, gripping his hand. 'You are not to blame for anything. Whatever the truth of your birth, your father—who must have been very young at the time—took you, loved you and raised you. Yvette had choices of her own. Choices that are not your responsibility. What does she expect you to do?'

'The first demand is that I stop playing at being a doctor and—'

'Playing?' she interrupted with outrage.

'To Yvette my career and lifestyle are not good enough for the family name and she sees it as my duty to take my father's place in the running of the family estates, safeguarding her position. She doesn't feel secure that the decisions and the control of finances are left in the hands of my uncle's side of the family, despite the provisions made for her in my father's will.' His cynicism deepened as he thought of Yvette's other plans for him. 'She also expects me to marry someone socially acceptable of her choosing.'

Lauren stared at him, wide-eyed. 'No way. That's archaic and ridiculous.'

'Exactly. But so determined was she that she sent Adèle to Paris to lure me.'

'Lure you?'

'Yes. We went out for a while, but then I found out about the deceit, that Yvette had set me up and was using Adèle to try to ensure I gave up medicine and returned home, especially that I left what Yvette considered an unacceptable job. She made a lot of trouble for me at the practice. Adèle was to be handsomely rewarded with my name…plus the family money and standing, of course, which interested her far more than I did.' He sighed before continuing. 'That's why I needed the space away. First in St Ouen-sur-Mer and now here in Penhally Bay. No matter what levels of guilt my mother tries to lay on me, I have no intention of marrying for convenience.'

'Nor should you. And you can't give up medicine either. It's your *life*.' Lauren squeezed his hand, her gaze earnest. 'You are an amazing doctor, Gabe. You have to live your own life in whatever way is right for you. Don't let Yvette's schemes and any misplaced guilt force you into something that would make you unhappy and change the person you are.'

It felt amazing to have someone believe in him. Cupping her face, he kissed her before drawing her close and wrapping his arms around her. 'Thank you. I think Yvette is bitter that she could never have children of her own and give my father a legitimate heir. Not that I believe theirs was ever a love match—she was as distant to my father as she was to me. She's an attractive woman in a polished, icy kind of way. Everything was, and remains, about duty and appearances to her.' He slid Lauren off the sofa and nestled her more snugly into his embrace, breathing in her scent. 'What hurts is that Papa never explained any of this. I don't know his side of it, what is the whole truth and what is exaggerated. He wasn't a man to avoid anything, no matter how awkward, which makes me more confused that he kept it from me. I thought he approved of my career, that he was proud of me.'

'Of course he was proud of you,' she protested heatedly. 'How could he not be?'

Lauren's loyal support and fierce protectiveness eased some of the tension inside him and he found it easier to continue his story. 'My father and his brother inherited a big estate that includes a vineyard, a farm and assorted business holdings, all funded by my ancestors who made their fortunes in the Caribbean. I find it hard to come to terms with that part of my family history. I feel ashamed that my family's money and success was built on the disenfranchisement and misery of others, even if it was generations ago. I had so many privileges and took them for granted, not knowing it was based on the hard work and sacrifices of those who'd had nothing, often not even their freedom,' he told her, his emotions scarcely held in check.

'You are not accountable for the actions others took years ago. Many businesses and families today are founded on regrettable things from times past. What matters is how *you* act and what you do with those things in your own control.'

'Logically I know that, but…' He hesitated, brushing his free hand over his face. 'It's just been a confusing time with much to try to come to terms with. The identity of my birth mother explains my darker skin—something I share with a couple of distant cousins, which was explained away by the past involvements and dalliances of my great-grandfather and grandfather in the Caribbean. Nothing was said about my father. I want to learn more about my true heritage and find out more about my real mother, but I don't even know her name.'

Lauren's arms tightened around him. 'So many things go through your mind, so many questions that have no answers.'

'Yes.' He stroked her hair, knowing from what she had told him of her own adoption and family circumstances that she understood the sense of rootlessness and uncertainty. 'I never questioned my ethnicity and very identity before. Now…'

An aching vulnerability laced Gabriel's voice, cutting Lauren deep inside. She felt his pain and confusion, knew exactly where he was coming from, and wished she could do more to reassure him and help him find a solution, a *resolution*, to his past. She'd had five years to get her head around who she was and how her perceptions had changed. Gabriel had known for less than two years. And she had not suffered a bereavement. He had lost the father he had loved and who he now questioned. That had to be impossibly hard. If there were things she needed to know, she could ask—it wouldn't be pleasant, but she had the choice. Gabriel didn't. She wished she could ease his heartache, make things right for him, but all she could do was be there to listen and comfort and understand.

As well as mourning his father and dealing with the revelations about his true birth mother, Gabriel still had Yvette to contend with. The woman sounded awful. It was bad enough that she had been emotionally cold to a child in her care, worse that she wanted to change Gabriel and tie him to something so wrong for him. But to insinuate a woman into his life, one who cared nothing for him, with the purpose of influencing him, lying to him, deceiving him was unforgivable. No wonder Gabriel was loath to return to France or have contact with Yvette.

'Never before has the colour of my skin been an issue.'

Startled from her thoughts and shocked by Gabriel's words, Lauren frowned, pulling back to look at him, seeing the shadows dulling his eyes. 'What do you mean?'

'I never questioned my ancestry. If anyone mentioned my skin colour, it didn't bother me. Now comments about it make me feel uncomfortable.'

'Why would anyone mention it? No one in Penhally has said anything, have they?' she asked, unable to imagine anyone being so narrow-minded.

'One or two. Not in a prejudicial way,' he added, and Lauren tamped down her anger on his behalf. 'But I'm conscious of being different…the cuckoo in *my* family, to follow your analogy. That's probably because of the derisive way Yvette spoke of my birth mother, as if the woman was beneath contempt, as if I was worth nothing.'

'Your father didn't think so. He cared about your mother and he loved you.'

'I think so. I hope so. I wish I knew the circumstances, how Papa really felt, if he *did* have feelings for my mother or if I was a mistake,' he murmured.

'I understand the need to uncover your missing roots, to find answers to your questions, but *you* are the same person you've always been.'

As Gabriel released her and moved to put another couple of logs on the fire, Lauren's heart cried out for the uncertainty he was feeling. She studied his handsome profile, the leanly sculpted body outlined under his shirt by the flickering flames, the play of muscle along hair-dusted forearms.

'What?' he asked, a quizzical smile on his face as he turned back to her.

She shook her head, raising a hand to cup his jaw. The end-of-the-day stubble there prickled against her palm, reminding her how exciting and arousing the rasp of it felt on her body as he caressed and explored her with his mouth. Realising he was waiting for her answer, she returned her gaze to his.

'The colour of your skin is not what I see when I look at you.'

'What *do* you see, Lauren?' he asked huskily, taking her hand and moving it so he could kiss her palm, his tongue tracing teasing circles, igniting the fiery need for him that always simmered inside her.

'I see *you*. All that makes you the man you are. An excellent doctor…one who shows great care and consideration for his patients, and…'

He nibbled on her fingers, momentarily stealing her breath and her words as he slowly sucked each one in turn into his mouth, distracting her. 'And?'

'And,' she continued, trying to force the words past the constriction in her throat, every part of her trembling with desire, 'I see a gorgeous man who is warm and intelligent, funny and generous. A man who is great to be with, who is a loyal friend, who makes me feel good…and who is incredibly sexy.' Her breath ragged, her voice rough with emotion, she looked deep into his eyes, seeing how they darkened with answering passion. 'Gabe, you are beautiful just as you are.'

She gasped in surprise as he caught her to him, one hand threading through her hair to hold her still for his inflaming, hungry kiss. Kneeling in front of him, she opened her mouth hotly in welcome. His free hand slid down her back to shape her rear and pull her against him, leaving her in no doubt of his growing arousal. With Gabriel she felt truly alive, aware of every sensation. The fierceness of his desire was a powerful aphrodisiac, heightening her own. He made her feel whole, complete, and so wanted. Needing to make him feel the same way, to reassure him and prove to him how special he was, she took over, pushing him back until he was lying on the floor beneath her.

She sat up and went to work on his clothes, glad they had left lamps on in the room so she could see him as she slipped each button free before he impatiently pulled off his shirt and tossed it aside. Bending to him, she took her time working down his torso with her mouth and fingers, lingering over his nipples, then his navel, his muscles rippling and tautening, before licking down to the waistband of his jeans.

'No. Let me,' she demanded, pushing his hands away when he moved to undo his belt.

With a groan, Gabriel surrendered to her and she teased him, fondling the hard length of him through the soft, worn denim. 'Lauren,' he growled in warning.

Smiling, she unfastened his belt, then unsnapped the jeans and lowered the zip as slowly as she could, her own aching desire increasing with every moment. He raised his hips to aid her as she skimmed down his jeans and briefs. Once he was naked, she revelled in enjoying his body, in bringing him pleasure, encouraged by the sounds he made, the way his body shifted restlessly beneath her.

'Lauren…'

This time her name was a plea on his lips as she took him to the brink of his control. Nuzzling against him, she breathed in his warm, earthy male scent. She wanted to savour him for hours, as he did with her, but already she was as impatient as he was and could no longer deny herself. She needed him so badly. Hastily dispensing with her own clothes, she took the condom he'd carried in the pocket of his jeans, controlling her eagerness long enough to torment him as she rolled it on, earning herself another threat of retribution. The kind of sensual threat she loved. Sliding over him, she wasted no more time and welcomed him fully inside her.

His hands stroked her with a reverence and tenderness that brought a rush of emotion, making her acknowledge how deep her feelings for this special man had become. Taking her by surprise, Gabriel sat up, pulling her close. Sitting in his lap, she wrapped her legs around his hips, pressing her body against him. They rocked together, sharing slow, deep kisses, their hands caressing. The firelight flickered over their joined bodies as they moved in unison, their rhythm increasingly urgent. When, eventually, they drifted down from the giddying height of passion, reaching a new pinnacle of pleasure, they remained locked in each other's arms, cuddled up in front of the fire under the fleecy throw Gabriel had pulled off the sofa to cover them.

The evening had been the most intimate she had ever known, not only in the intenseness of their love-making but in the sharing of confidences and baring of souls. They had each revealed a part of themselves in a way they had never done with anyone else, which said much about the level of trust between them. She had told people about the adoption thing, it wasn't a secret, but she had never discussed her innermost feelings about it, not even with Chloe. Only with Gabriel.

Holding him tight, she nestled against him, turning her face into his neck. She had never felt closer to him than she did at this moment. Gabriel cared about her, she knew that, but she could no longer pretend to herself that her own feelings stopped there. She loved this man, totally and completely. Knowing what he faced in France, what decisions he had to make about his future, troubled her…both for his own peace of mind and for whatever might lie ahead for them as a couple.

But she couldn't afford to think about that now. She had agreed the terms. No commitments. Live for today. And she would. She loved him, would cherish every moment with him, would show him in every way she could without words what he meant to her, but she couldn't and wouldn't put pressure on him for more than he could give. For now they had the promise of Christmas alone together and she planned to make it as special and unforgettable as possible. She could only wish with all her heart that the new year and beyond would bring hope and happiness.

Christmas Day brought winter sunshine, pale blue skies and cool temperatures. Kate stifled a yawn and took a sip of strong coffee, hoping it would help her wake up. Jem had been on the go for ages. Although he no longer believed in Father Christmas, he still had all the youthful enthusiasm for the day and had opened his presents with breathless excitement. Fearing her son was missing out without his father—and maybe salving her own inner guilt over his true parentage— she tended to spoil him at this time of year, no matter how hard she tried not to overdo it.

Having wolfed down his breakfast, Jem had raced upstairs eager to try on the new football shirt of his favourite Premiership team that Oliver and Chloe had given him. Kate smiled. Her friends were so generous and always remembered Jem, usually giving him books and CDs which he enjoyed immensely. Her smile faded as she thought of Nick. So far he had not given Jem anything. Not that he was obligated to do so, of course, but she had hoped the effort he had been making to be more friendly to Jem since the flood would continue.

She knew that the whole Tremayne clan were getting together for a big family Christmas this year—the first for a long time. With Jack and Edward now back in Cornwall and settled with their respective partners, and with Lucy and Ben celebrating Annabel's first birthday over the holiday, it was a special time for the Tremaynes. Had it only been a year since she had helped deliver that precious baby in difficult circumstances in a deserted barn during a snowstorm?

A wave of sadness swept through her. She wished Jem could be a part of all that Tremayne love and laughter. But she doubted it would ever happen. If only Nick would acknowledge Jem she would be content. She would even be able to force herself to ignore her own needs, her loneliness, the unrequited love she had harboured for Nick for so many years—as long as her son was happy and secure.

This morning, the plan was for a walk along the beach as Jem was eager to fly the Rhombus Entry stunt kite she had bought him, an inexpensive but longed-for item that had been top of his Christmas wish list since they had watched a display in the summer. The fliers doing elaborate stunts and tricks had allowed Jem to have a go and had recommended the Rombus as an excellent beginner's kite.

Kate was about to go upstairs to get dressed for their outing when the doorbell rang. Puzzled as to who would be calling on Christmas Day, she tightened the belt of her robe, pushed some wayward strands of hair back from her face, and left the kitchen. Chloe and Oliver were away—if her suspicions proved correct, Kate believed they would return with some exciting news—so she was on call for any midwifery emergencies over the holiday. But that would entail a phone call, not a visit to her house.

'Nick!' she exclaimed, shocked to discover who awaited her when she opened the door. She could feel the blush warm her cheeks and cursed herself for responding like some flustered teenager to the very sight of him. It didn't help that she was still in her robe. 'Sorry, I wasn't expecting anyone. Merry Christmas.'

'Good morning, Kate. Merry Christmas to you, too.'

Noting the wrapped gifts he held, she moved back. 'Would you like to come in?'

'Please.' He stepped into the hallway and she closed the door. 'I hope I'm not too early. I wanted to call in before going to Lucy and Ben's.'

'Not at all. Jem's been up for hours, excited to open his presents.'

A smile softened the characteristic sternness on Nick's face. 'I imagine. I hope you don't mind. I've bought him a couple of things.'

'No. That's lovely. Thank you.' Surprised and delighted that Nick had unbent enough to remember his son and think to bring him gifts, she led the way to the kitchen. 'Would you care for a cup of coffee? I'll run upstairs and fetch Jem.'

'All right.'

Her pulse racing, Kate hurried upstairs and dressed hastily, pausing a moment to brush her hair and apply some lipstick and mascara before going to Jem's room. She found him wearing his new red-and-white Arsenal top, absorbed in the football annual that had been a present from Lauren and Gabriel.

'Jem, we have a visitor,' she told him with a smile. 'Can you come down, my love? Then we can take your kite and go for our walk.'

'OK.'

Downstairs, Kate smiled at Jem's excitement when he discovered the identity of their guest and the unexpected presents that awaited him.

'Uncle Nick!'

'Hello, Jeremiah.' Setting down his mug of coffee, Nick held out two neatly wrapped parcels. 'These are for you.'

'Gee, thanks!'

A lump lodged in Kate's throat as man and boy exchanged smiles and she noticed the similarities between them. The same eyes. The same shape to the mouth. The same frown of concentration. Would those likenesses become more pronounced as Jem grew older? Would people begin to suspect who his real father was? Hiding her concerns, she watched as Jem tore off the paper to reveal a fun book of science facts and two of the latest computer games.

'Wow! I love them. Thanks, Uncle Nick,' he gushed, taking the older man by surprise and giving him a hug.

'Happy Christmas, Jem.'

Nick's voice was hoarse as he responded to his son's engaging and instinctive reaction. Looking stiff and uncertain, he rested a hand on the boy's head for a moment, and Kate met his gaze, her own eyes stinging with unshed tears at the confusion and emotion in Nick's. This was more than she had expected and she knew it was greedy of her to wish for more.

'Do you have to leave already?' Jem asked with disappointment as Nick rose to his feet.

'Yes, I'm afraid so.' Nick cleared his throat . 'Um… We're having a get-together at my house on New Year's Eve,' he announced after a moment. 'It will be family and a few friends, including children, so it won't be a late night. If you and Jem would like to come, Kate, you'd be welcome.'

Her heart fluttered at the surprise invitation. 'We'd love to, wouldn't we, Jem?'

'Yeah, that would be great!'

Walking with Nick to the front door a few moments later, Kate hesitated and looked up at him, unable to read the expression on his face. 'Thank you, Nick,' she said, fearing the welter of emotions *she* was feeling were all too apparent.

Nick nodded and stepped outside. Kate tightened her hold on the door as she watched him climb into his car, not looking back before he drove away to be with his proper family. He'd thought of Jem, had made him happy, she told herself as she closed the door. That was the important thing to remember right now.

Half an hour later, they had walked around the harbour and reached the nearly deserted beach. While Jem concentrated on sending his colourful delta-wing kite soaring into the sky for the first time, Kate's thoughts remained grounded and on Nick. He had thought to include them in his gathering to mark the end of a year that had been eventful personally, professionally and for the town as a whole, and for that she was grateful. What, she wondered, would the new year hold for them all?

'Lauren?'

Receiving no answer when he walked into the Manor House shortly after midnight, Gabriel headed to the kitchen, washed his hands and then poured himself a glass of water. Reflecting on the last couple of hours, he gave a rueful shake of his head. This had not been the way he would have chosen to spend New Year's Eve.

His first callout had come late in the evening to a four-year-old girl who had experienced her second severe acute asthma attack in less than a week. Her breathing had finally been eased with the administration of oxygen, nebulised salbutamol and oral prednisolone but, given the child's distress, along the frequency and severity of her symptoms, he'd arranged for hospital admission.

He'd only just arrived home when he had been asked to attend an emergency at the Penhally Arms on the harbour front, where a fight had broken out between two groups of revellers who'd had too much to drink. Taunts had turned to threats and, uncharacteristically for Penhally Bay, a running battle had ensued in the street when the guilty parties had been evicted from the pub. Several people had suffered minor injuries, while two had received more serious stab wounds from broken glass. It had taken a while to sort everything out and to stabilise one of the patients, who had lost a great deal of blood and gone into hypovolaemic shock, for ambulance transport to hospital in St Piran. Gabriel had been thankful to come home and leave the police to handle the aftermath of the trouble.

As promised, he had stopped off at Gatehouse Cottage on the way back to check again that the cats, Cyclops and Pirate, were fine. Oliver and Chloe—who had rung a couple of times during the week, sounding blissfully happy with married life—were due back in a couple of days, ready to face the music about their secret wedding. Gabriel felt sure that everyone would be delighted for them.

Foxy, who was curled up on his beanbag by the range in the Manor House kitchen, stretched and snuffled in his sleep. Gabriel washed up his glass, checked all was secure downstairs and that the log fire had safely burned down with the guard around it before he jogged up the stairs in search of Lauren. Light spilled out from his bedroom across the landing, drawing him onwards. His heart swelled and emotion gripped him at the sight he found when he walked into the room.

Dressed in lilac French knickers and matching camisole— the satin and lace creations far more alluring and feminine in his view than blatant, obvious items like G-strings—Lauren was sprawled face down across the four-poster bed. The lavishly illustrated book he had given her on her favourite artist, Claude Monet, and his stunning garden at Giverny in France, was open in front of her. Smiling, he recalled her reaction when she had unwrapped the book on Christmas morning and discovered the promise that had accompanied it…

'What's this?' she had asked, holding up the sticky note he had stuck on the front with 'IOU' written on it.

'Do you have a valid passport?'

A frown had creased the smoothness of her brow. 'Yes, I think it has another two or three years before it's due for renewal. Why?'

'Maybe we could have a long weekend away together in the spring.' Grey eyes had widened with surprised delight at his suggestion. 'I want to take you to see Giverny for yourself.'

'Do you mean it?'

'Of course, *ma belle*. I've been once. It's beautiful.' It meant returning to France far sooner than expected, but it would be worth it to make Lauren happy, and he wouldn't be near the family home. 'I want to share it with you. We'll go when the gardens reopen in April.'

Tears shimmering in her eyes, she had thrown herself into his arms. 'Thank you, thank you, thank you! It's the best gift ever!' She'd kissed him...then shown her gratitude in wickedly enjoyable ways.

Now he crossed slowly to the side of the bed and discovered that she was fast asleep. She looked adorable. Gently, he eased the book out from under her outstretched hand, marked her page and set it on the bedside chest. He hesitated, looking down at her, loath to wake her but needing her with as much desperation as ever.

She had made this Christmas so special for him. Aside from the Monet book, they had exchanged several gifts, each of them finding a mix of things that were either funny, touching, saucy or thoughtful. But it was the time with Lauren, her warmth, her understanding, her passion, her generosity of spirit, that had been the greatest gift of all. The issues with Yvette, his heritage and his future remained unresolved, but some of his heartache had eased by sharing his fears and his hurt with Lauren.

Turning off the main light, leaving the room illuminated by the rosy glow of the bedside lamps so Lauren could get her bearings, Gabriel stripped off his clothes and returned to the bed. Desire rippled through him as he began kissing his way softly up her silky smooth legs, whispering along her calves and lingering at the back of her knees before skimming over her creamy thighs. Lauren murmured, moving gracefully under him as she gradually came awake. He allowed her to roll over and, sleepy-eyed, she looked up at him with a smile...a smile that was so beautiful, so welcoming and so sexy it almost overwhelmed him.

'Gabe.'

'Hey, sleepyhead,' he whispered, his voice rough with emotion and arousal. 'Sorry I was so long.'

'Are you all right? Was it bad?' she asked, her concern evident.

'It wasn't pretty but I'm fine.'

He sat back on his heels and indulged himself, running his hands up and down her body, his fingertips catching on the lace covering nipples that peaked to his touch. Lauren pulled him back down to her, her kiss hot and intense, matching his own hunger. Her hands glided over him, her touch tender, reverent, setting him on fire. He forced himself to slow down, concentrating on removing her camisole and French knickers, kissing each fragment of flesh he exposed. He felt as if he was unwrapping the most precious gift he had ever been given.

'Please,' she begged, moving against him. 'I want you.'

'Soon.'

He nuzzled against her, wanting to take his time and cherish every inch of her but as needy and impatient as her. The subtle, flowery scent of sweet peas, mingled with her own womanliness, intoxicated him. She was so responsive to his touch. Her body quivered beneath his lips and fingers, and the little purring sounds of pleasure in the back of her throat drove him crazy with want.

'Now, Gabe…'

Succumbing to her pleas, unable to resist her or deny her anything, he gave himself up to the magical passion that grew more intense and fiery and special every time they came together.

An age later, sated and relaxed, Gabriel held Lauren close, arms and legs entwined, as she slept. They had gone into this with the pledge of no ties and no commitments. At one time he would have felt relieved that a woman made no demands, but with Lauren he was disappointed and felt a flicker of unease. He had not been looking for any kind of relationship when he had come to Cornwall but what he'd found with Lauren was unique, and he very much feared that nothing between them was ever going to be as simple as they had both vocalised at the start. Instead, he had the sense that he was at a crossroads in his life and what happened here was going to be far more important and life-changing than he could ever have foreseen.

Each day he fell more in love with her. But he hadn't told her. She'd made it clear there were no expectations and she'd given no indication that what they shared meant any more to her, that she felt more for him. He had ten months left in Penhally…ten months to convince Lauren that they were right together. But before he could pledge himself to her, he needed to settle the family issues that dogged him, as well as decide what to do about Yvette and her demands.

Confiding in Lauren, knowing she believed in him and supported him, had helped him rationalise that he could never give up medicine. She had told him about her adoption but he needed her to show the same level of trust, to face up to the problems with her sight and share it with him. Could she ever do that? Would she?

Hugging her tighter, he let out a shaky breath. As they headed into a new year, filled with new hopes and endless possibilities, he vowed to show her in every way how much he loved her. One day, when the time was right, he would tell her how permanently he wanted them to commit to each other. Until then he could only pray that the future would be kind to them and that Lauren would come to love and trust him, too.

CHAPTER EIGHT

LAUREN stood on the pavement by the construction site where the demolished Anchor Hotel was in the process of being rebuilt and gave her details to the policeman beside her. How did her voice sound so calm when inside she was shaking? She looked at her beloved Renault as it sat by the kerb, the driver's side dented and crumpled. A few yards farther along Harbour Road was another car, its front caved in, its angry and foul-mouthed driver arguing with two other policemen.

'I'm sorry about this,' she murmured as the constable put his notebook away.

'It's not your fault, Ms Nightingale, not according to all the witnesses.' He gestured to the gathered crowds and then to the young man who had hit her. 'Luckily there was an off-duty policeman on the scene or the other driver would have driven off. Turns out he has no insurance and was driving while disqualified.'

Lauren didn't know what that would mean in terms of a claim to repair or replace her car, but apparently everyone was satisfied that she had not been to blame for the accident. Everyone but her. She had finished her morning home visits—her final appointment having been with Harry Biscombe at Gow Court, whose osteoporosis was increasingly trouble-some—and had been returning to the surgery for lunch before her afternoon clinic when the crash had happened. Having stopped at the junction of Bridge Street and Harbour Road, she had pulled out into a gap in the traffic, only to have an oncoming car plough into the side of her. Apart from a few bruises she was unharmed but shaken…and she felt impossibly guilty.

The witnesses all attested to the fact that the young man had been speeding and driving erratically, having almost hit a pedestrian and a parked car farther along the seafront before colliding with her. What Lauren hadn't said, but could not ignore, was the simple fact that she had never seen the car at all. It had come out of nowhere and sideswiped her. Her explanations had been silenced by the behaviour of the young man, his unsuccessful efforts to flee the scene and the discovery that he had no business driving at all taking precedence with the police.

'Lauren!'

Hearing her name and the sound of running feet, she looked round to see Gabriel and Oliver hurrying towards her. Someone must have phoned the surgery, she realised, stifling a groan. The last thing she needed was to have people fussing over her and asking her more uncomfortable questions. However, she couldn't deny how comforting it felt to be enfolded in Gabriel's embrace, and she allowed herself a few moments to lean against him and absorb his strength.

These first months of the new year had been the happiest she had ever known. Everything would have been one hundred percent perfect if only she hadn't had to hide two things…how much she loved Gabe and how frightened she was that her sight was deteriorating further. The night blindness she had managed to excuse and cover up, but the fuzziness, the blind spots and decreasing peripheral vision that had begun to occur in recent weeks terrified her.

'Lauren, *ma belle*, what happened? Are you all right?'

Gabriel demanded, holding her slightly away from him so he could look her over, one hand stroking her hair before his fingers trailed down her cheek. He tilted up her chin and looked into her eyes. 'Are you hurt?'

'I'm fine.'

Gabriel frowned, clearly disbelieving her, and glanced over his shoulder. 'Oliver?'

'Here.' The smile curving Oliver's mouth failed to mask the concern in his brown eyes as he stepped forward. 'Hi, Lauren, how are you?'

'She says she's fine,' Gabriel answered for her, increasing her annoyance.

'I'm perfectly all right and able to speak for myself.'

'OK.' Oliver smiled, but she wanted to stamp her foot as the two men shared a glance before Oliver eased Gabriel aside. 'Let me take a look at you to be sure.'

'For goodness' sake,' she muttered ungraciously, aware that the shock of the crash and the fright about her eyes was making her uncharacteristically grumpy.

'Did you bump your head at all?' he asked her.

'No.'

With a gentle but impersonal touch, Oliver carefully checked her neck for any pain or stiffness. After assessing her pulse and her breathing, he cupped her face and she noted his slight frown as he studied her. What had he seen? She bit her lip to keep from asking, not ready for the answer.

'Do you have any discomfort with this bruising?' Oliver queried, moving on to check her arms and discovering the marks beginning to colour along her right forearm that had taken the brunt of the bang as the driver's door had distorted inwards. 'Any nausea or dizziness?'

'Nothing, really. My arm isn't even sore. Honestly, I'm OK. I was just a bit shaken up.'

'I'm not surprised.' Gabriel stepped close again and slid an arm around her waist, his angry gaze on the young man who was being arrested and put into a police car. 'I'd like a few moments with that driver myself.'

Oliver rested a hand on Gabriel's shoulder. 'Let the police take care of him. There are enough witnesses to make sure he doesn't get away with it and from what I hear, he has no licence or insurance, so he will definitely be charged.'

'I should hope so. He could have hurt or killed someone.' Gabriel drew her closer and she could feel the tension in him. 'Come on, I'll take you home.'

'No, it's OK. I need to go back to the surgery,' she insisted, determined to carry on as if nothing had happened.

Gabriel turned her to face him. 'Lauren, be sensible, you've had a shock. You need to rest, *chérie*—'

'What I need,' she stressed, her anger mounting as she pulled away from his hold, 'is not to be babied and told what to do. I make my own decisions. And I'm going back to work to attend to my patients.'

'Lauren…'

Aware that Gabriel and Oliver were staring after her, she picked up the belongings that had been rescued from her car and walked purposefully along the pavement towards the surgery. She was not yet ready to deal with the consequences of what had happened today—or to face the horrifying truth that the problems with her eyesight were getting worse.

'Leave her for a while,' Oliver advised.

Angry, confused and scared, Gabriel wanted to shake off his friend's hand and rush after Lauren, needing to cuddle her and satisfy himself that she was really all right. The rational part of him accepted the sense of Oliver's words, so he fell into step with him and followed Lauren back to the surgery at a discreet distance. At least he was keeping her in sight.

Her outburst had been so unlike her. She had been genuinely irritated by his concern, while all he had wanted to do was take care of her. The day was mild and the March sunshine gleamed off the lighter streaks in her hair as she moved on ahead of them. Another three weeks and they would be in France for their long weekend. He couldn't wait for them to be alone, away from the usual distractions and demands on their time and energy.

Professionally, things had been hectic since the new year, with the surgery busier than ever. Oliver and Chloe had returned from Scotland to much fuss and celebration of their marriage. Only Nick had displayed any sign of disapproval about the elopement, not that anyone had taken much notice of him because it was clear to everyone how happy the couple were and how perfect for each other.

Some of the pressure had been taken off for all the doctors, the workload easing, especially for out-of-hours and weekend calls, with Dragan Lovak back from paternity leave. Gabriel admired the calm, quiet Croatian and was enjoying getting to know him.

Adrian Wescott, the local schoolteacher with long-term tinnitus, had seen the specialist at St Piran and had been declared a suitable candidate for surgery. The operation to remove the stapes and implant an artificial plastic bone was scheduled for the Easter holiday when Adrian would have time off school to recover and, if all was successful, to accustom himself to his altered hearing before the new term began.

Personally, things between himself and Lauren had been just as blissful as they had at the end of the previous year. If anything they were even closer physically, their relationship more intense, but still neither of them had spoken of the future or their feelings, and Gabriel was becoming edgy as almost half his time here in Cornwall was already over. He'd noticed more small moments of concern with Lauren's sight but she refused to confide in him and that lack of trust hurt.

Gabriel thought back to his talk with Chloe in December and her request that he talk to Oliver if he became worried about Lauren. He'd been worried for a while but… He let out a rough sigh. Maybe now was the time to consult his friend and get some advice.

'Did you notice Lauren's eye?'

Oliver glanced at him. 'The right one?'

'Yes.' Gabriel paused, a frown on his face as he watched Lauren disappear through the entrance to the surgery a few yards ahead of them. 'What did you see?'

'Her eyelid was a bit droopy and I thought I detected a squint I'd not noticed before,' Oliver admitted, his voice serious and concerned.

As if by mutual consent, they slowed their pace, coming to a halt outside the car park and turning to look out over the harbour. 'But you've noticed other things before—about Lauren's sight, I mean—since you've been here?' Gabriel asked, sliding his hands into his trouser pockets.

'Nothing I could be definite about, Gabriel.' Oliver sighed and leaned against the wall. 'As an outsider coming in, I was suspicious about Lauren's supposed clumsiness. Everyone laughed at her mishaps and said she had always been that way. I had a hunch there was more to it…but no facts.'

'Me, too,' Gabriel agreed. 'From the first day I met her I knew she was having trouble with her night vision, but I didn't know if it was a long-standing problem or a symptom of something else.'

'And now?'

Gabriel shook his head. 'I'm still worried. She's definitely night blind but copes well and manages to cover it. I'm sure that's why she changed her work hours. And she never drives after dark now. There have been a few other incidents lately and over the last couple of days I saw what you did with her right eye.' He hesitated but decided to keep his nagging suspicions about today's accident to himself.

'Have you spoken to her about it?' his friend asked, meeting his gaze.

'No. Once or twice I've tried to mention the night blindness, as well as the fact that she's stopped painting, but she gets defensive and changes the subject.' Shifting with restless impatience, he let out a shaky breath. 'I'm scared of rocking the boat, Oliver, of pushing her away if I press too hard. I have a feeling that Lauren is increasingly worried but she's not facing up to the problem.'

Oliver gave his shoulder a reassuring pat. 'I never said anything either, even though I noticed that Lauren didn't judge distances well, that she tripped on kerbs and didn't see things in shadow. I didn't know that had progressed to such serious night blindness, though.'

'So should I wait a while longer?' He looked up and saw the answering worry in Oliver's eyes, as if neither of them wanted to voice out loud the various and increasingly frightening explanations that could be the underlying cause of Lauren's sight problems. 'You think it's right that I don't confront her about it?'

'Until Lauren admits it to herself, she's not going to appreciate or accept anyone else challenging her on it. Especially you.'

'Would *you* try to talk to her?' he asked, knowing he was expecting a lot of his friend.

Letting out a heavy sigh, Oliver ran his fingers through his hair and moved away. 'Damn, Gabriel.'

'Please. I'm worried about her.'

'If the opportunity presents itself, I'll see what I can do,' he agreed with evident reluctance, a warning in his eyes when he turned back to face him. 'But I have to tell you, Gabriel, that if Lauren confides in me as a doctor, I'm not going to break her trust and divulge anything if she asks me not to. Not even to you.'

Gabriel felt rigid with tension, his hands clenched to fists. He wanted to argue, but he knew Oliver was right, knew he would do the same if the situation were reversed—their oath allowed them no other option. 'On a personal level I don't like it, but I understand. And I'd just be relieved to know that Lauren was getting some help.'

'I know it's difficult.' Oliver's smile was sympathetic. 'If the chance arises, I'll be advising her to talk to you—count on that.'

'Thanks.'

Knowing there was little more he could do right now, Gabriel tried to be satisfied with the progress he had made. At least now he had voiced his fears to Oliver and he knew his friend would do his best. But knowing he wasn't alone in recognising Lauren's problems was a double-edged sword— while it confirmed it wasn't his imagination, it increased the real possibility that there was, indeed, something wrong. Filled with a mix of emotions, he walked back into the surgery with Oliver, planning to check on Lauren before taking his afternoon appointments. For now his most important job was to be there for her, to love her…and hope that she would trust in him.

Lauren hesitated outside Oliver's consulting room, her hand poised to knock on the closed door.

It was early Friday evening at the end of March and the surgery was quiet. Most of the staff were having a farewell drink with practice nurse Eve Dwyer, who was leaving not only the surgery but the country, too, and heading out to Switzerland to marry Dr Tom Cornish. Lauren didn't know the whole story but apparently the couple had been reunited at the time of the October flood and had spent the last few months rekindling their relationship. Now they were getting married in Tom's adopted country where he was based for his work with the international rescue organisation, Deltraron.

Lauren had been for a drink and had said her goodbyes. Oliver, too, had been at the pub but had returned to the surgery to finish some paperwork while waiting for his wife. Chloe was out with Gabriel attending Diane Bailey, the mother-to-be who had been under their joint care since the autumn and who was determined to have her baby at home—a baby that was now on its way. It was the perfect time to see Oliver alone and confide in him. If she could pluck up the nerve.

It was two weeks since the car accident. Two weeks in which Gabriel had been supportive, caring and concerned. He hadn't pressured her at all, had asked no questions, but she feared he suspected things were not right. It had made things tense between them. Physically things were as wonderful as ever, but she'd been more reserved, concerned about what was wrong with her and trying hard to hide it. She felt guilty. Gabriel would be hurt if he thought she didn't trust him. It wasn't that. It wasn't him. She was scared…terrified. How long could she continue to deny the problems with her sight? It was one thing to fool herself, quite another to put other people at risk.

The young driver who had crashed into her was being prosecuted. Not only had he been driving while disqualified and without insurance, but it turned out he had taken the car without permission. Crashing into her had been a minor sideshow compared to the other charges against him. Her car had been towed to a garage and, as nothing vital had been damaged with the chassis frame or alignment, it was being repaired. While she waited for the work to be done, the insurance company had arranged for a rental car for her.

Although the days continued to lengthen and the nights became shorter, she refused to venture out after dark. During daylight hours, she had been too nervous to do more than the basic local travel she needed to see those patients who relied on her for home visits. Even then she was taking extra care and time. It was an impossible situation and one she knew could not continue.

However scared she was, she had to talk to someone—a doctor—and find out once and for all what was wrong with her eyes. She admired Nick, but she couldn't feel comfortable seeing him and discussing something like this. Dragan and Adam were delightful colleagues, but she knew it would be Oliver to whom she would turn. She trusted him. Despite being aware she was putting him in a difficult position, she knew he would not tell Gabriel, Chloe or anyone else anything she told him in confidence.

She was still undecided what to do when the door in front of her suddenly opened and she stepped back with a gasp of shock, her hand dropping to her side and her startled gaze clashing with Oliver's.

'Hi, Lauren. Were you coming to see me?' His easy smile faded as he looked at her. 'Is something wrong, sweetheart?'

Much to her dismay, she felt an uncharacteristic welling of tears. She *never* cried. What was the matter with her lately? 'No, I— Sorry…' Horrified, she heard her voice break and felt the moisture on her cheeks.

'Come here.'

Oliver gently drew her inside his consulting room and closed the door. He led her to a chair and sat her down, pulling another up so he could sit beside her, his arm around her shoulders as he held her close. After pressing a tissue into her hand, he waited in silence while she gathered her composure.

'Sorry,' she whispered again.

'There's nothing to apologise for.' He took her hand, making her feel comforted, safe, less lonely. 'Lauren, anything you tell me in this room is strictly between us.'

His reassurance gave her the courage to speak up, but

also alerted her to the fact that maybe she hadn't hidden her problems as well as she had thought. 'You know why I'm here.' It was a statement, not a question, and he met her gaze steadily.

'I think maybe you are ready to talk about your eyes.'

The words were gentle but she flinched nonetheless. 'How long have you known?'

'I suspected when I first came here last summer that there was more to your mishaps than clumsiness.' He paused a moment, his touch gentle as he brushed her hand. 'There was nothing I could put my finger on at the time.'

'Does everyone else know?'

'I very much doubt it. No one has said anything…except Gabriel,' he added, watching her.

Lauren swallowed against the sudden restriction in her throat. 'What did he say?'

'Just that he'd noticed a few things, including how you have trouble seeing in the dark.' His expression was sympathetic, understanding. 'He's worried because he cares about you, but he knew it would be wrong to pressure you, that you needed to come to terms and ask for help yourself.'

'I see.'

She pulled her hand away and looked down at her lap, toying with the damp tissue. Part of her was relieved, grateful that Gabriel had given her space and not nagged her, but the knowledge that he had guessed all along, had apparently spoken to Oliver about her, made her uncomfortable.

'Gabriel didn't betray any confidences, Lauren. It was a one-off conversation after your crash when we both noticed that your right eye appeared…different.'

'Different how?' She remembered the way Oliver had looked her over, his frown when he had studied her face. At the time she hadn't wanted to know—now she did. 'What did you see?'

'Your eyelid was unusually droopy and you had a squint.'

'Do you think it was caused by the accident?' she asked after a short pause.

Oliver shook his head. 'Gabriel said he had seen it a few days before.' Sitting forward, he rested his forearms on his knees. 'He also knows that, should you ever decide to speak to me, I would never break my word to you, as a doctor and a friend, and tell him anything you asked me not to. Are you going to talk to me, Lauren? I want to help if I can,' he told her, his voice encouraging, cajoling.

'Yes,' she whispered, knowing she had little choice but to see this through. 'But I'm scared.'

'I'm sure you are, sweetheart, but we'll take things a step at a time together. OK?'

She nodded. 'OK,' she agreed, barely managing to get the word out.

'Good girl.' Oliver's smile carried both relief and gratitude for her trust. He crossed the room, returning after a moment to hand her a glass of water before sitting down again and picking up a notepad and pen. 'Now, in your own time, tell me what's bothering you and what's been happening with your sight.'

After taking a few sips of water, Lauren leaned back in the chair and drew in a steadying breath. 'I don't know exactly when I started to notice things or to equate being clumsy with vision problems. It happened so gradually that it crept up on me over years,' she explained, finding it easier to talk as she found her stride and released so many things she had bottled up and hidden for so long.

She was grateful for Oliver's patience. He listened without interrupting, silent yet supportive, as she recalled her clumsiness, her lack of hand-eye co-ordination, which had made her bad at team sports at school, and how the visual problems had grown worse in the last few years, how it was only in recent months that the night blindness had deteriorated so disastrously and how she had stopped painting since the summer when Chloe had noticed differences in her work.

'I couldn't even see it at first.' A fresh wave of emotion hit and she took a few moments to regroup. 'It was only in good light when I really studied the pictures that I saw the new ones were less sharp, less detailed, that I'd missed things not in the centre of my vision, and that there were subtle changes in depth perception.'

'And you can't see anything in the dark now?' Oliver prompted.

'No. It's becoming difficult in shadow, too, even during the day, and my eyes take a while to adjust to sudden changes in light. Even some colours of text on certain backgrounds are hard to distinguish, including the display on my mobile phone.'

He nodded, resting a hand on her arm and giving her a gentle squeeze. 'Can you tell me what it's like now? What can you see? How do the visual disturbances happen and affect you? Are they there all the time?'

'Not all the time. Things come and go, but gradually worsen.' She frowned, trying to explain, to put the vague impressions into words. 'Sometimes it's like a hazy veil is slowly closing in from the sides and I can't detect things on the periphery of my vision. Things are fuzzy at the edges. The central area is really clear, though, and I can see perfectly. I went to the optician last year and things were fine—but he only checked the basic things like reading the charts and I didn't mention the other problems I was having. I know it was silly but I was in denial.'

'Did he check the pressures in your eyes?' Oliver queried, making a few notes.

'Is that the little puff of air that makes you jump?'

Oliver chuckled. 'Yeah. It's a weird feeling, isn't it?'

'Yes, it is.' Grateful for the easing of the tension, Lauren smiled back. 'He said the pressures were normal.'

'Right. That's fine. And these changes you've noticed have been happening over a long time?'

Lauren nodded in confirmation as they recapped. 'For years the differences were so tiny that they scarcely registered and I guess I deceived myself into believing nothing was wrong. And I found ways of working around things, made excuses for misjudging distances or bumping into things. But I'm worried, Oliver. I can't keep ignoring it. I'm frightened I'm going to make mistakes.' She paused and bit her lip. 'Having found out recently that I was adopted, I have no family medical history to draw on. I don't know what's happening to me or what I should do,' she finished, her voice breaking again as she battled a new threat of tears.

'It's all right, sweetheart,' Oliver soothed, drawing her close for a hug. 'You've taken a huge step, and a very brave one, by admitting it and talking about it. You are not alone in this, I promise. We'll find out what's going on.'

'What do you think it is?' she asked, voicing the fearful question.

Oliver hesitated a moment, raising her concern it might be serious. 'It could be one of several things, so let's not get ahead of ourselves. I'm going to refer you to an excellent consultant at St Piran. Professor Murchison is one of the best. He'll talk things over with you and then he'll do some tests and assessments. When we know what he has to say, we can discuss it again and decide what to do. All right?'

'All right.' She accepted a fresh tissue and blew her nose. 'How long do you think it will be before I can see him?'

'I'll arrange it as soon as possible, but the appointment won't be until after your holiday.'

Lauren bit her lip. 'We're meant to leave next Thursday, but—'

'I know it's difficult when you're worried, and you can't

forget about your eyes, but I want you and Gabriel to go to Giverny and have a wonderful, relaxing time,' Oliver insisted.

She wanted that, too, so she nodded her agreement. 'I'll try. Are you sure you and Chloe don't mind looking after Foxy?'

'Of course not. He's much more comfortable with us now,' he reassured her with a smile. 'And he'll be on familiar territory, too. I know none of us meant for our stay at Gatehouse Cottage to last for so long, but it's worked out well so far. You just tell us if you want your space back.'

'No, it's fine. I know all the repair and renovation work after the flood is taking ages, but we agreed it was important to get those in temporary accommodation at the caravan park back into their homes first.'

'Not to mention people like Gertie Stanbury,' Oliver added with an affectionate grin.

Lauren smiled back. 'Yes. She's done well at Tom's place but I know she'll be much happier when she can return to her bungalow.'

'I hear it should be ready in another couple of weeks.'

'Good.' She paused a moment. While not regretting a moment of her time with Gabriel, living with him at the Manor House meant she had seen less of Chloe and Oliver at home. 'There's no hurry on my account for you to move on. I know the cottage in Fisherman's Row won't be habitable for a while yet.'

'I'm not sure we'll move back there. It's a bit small. But we've not found anywhere else we like. We're just very grateful to share with you.'

'Well, I've rather neglected you,' she admitted, colour staining her cheeks.

Oliver chuckled. 'With good reason. Both Chloe and I are delighted to see you and Gabriel so happy.'

'Thanks.' But mention of the man she loved brought a

return of her anxiety. 'You won't tell him anything about my eyes or the appointment, will you?'

'No, of course not.' Frowning, Oliver closed his notebook. 'You have to decide what is right for you but, for what it's worth, my advice is to confide in Gabriel. I know you care about each other. He's already worried and he'll want to support you. You need that support, sweetheart.'

But what if there was something seriously wrong? She and Gabriel had made no commitment to each other and she didn't want him feeling trapped. He had worries of his own, decisions he had to make about his future, and she couldn't add to his burdens.

'Lauren?'

'I'd rather wait, Oliver. Please. I need to have all the facts first, to know where I stand, before I decide what to do.'

'If that's what you want,' he allowed, but she could tell he was disappointed and that he disagreed with her decision. 'I'll contact the consultant on Monday and make the arrangements for you to be assessed as early as possible. As soon as I have a date, I'll let you know.'

A sliver of fear iced her spine. 'OK.'

'The appointment and tests might last a while, so you should be prepared to be at the hospital for a few hours. You'll likely have some drops in your eyes that could temporarily affect your vision, so you shouldn't travel alone.' He paused a moment, watching her. 'If you haven't told Gabriel or Chloe by then—but I hope you will—I'll come with you to the hospital myself. You don't have to handle this on your own.'

What had she done to deserve such wonderful friends? 'Thank you, Oliver—for everything.'

CHAPTER NINE

'IT's even more amazing than I ever imagined! I can't believe I'm really here!' Spinning round, a huge smile on her face, Lauren launched herself into Gabriel's arms and he caught her in a tight hug. 'Thank you *so* much for this.'

'My pleasure.'

And it was. Seeing Lauren so relaxed and happy and engaged was all the reward he needed. With reluctance, Gabriel released her, contented to follow when she took his hand and led him off around Monet's famous garden. This was her moment, her day, and it was a joy to share it with her.

They had flown from Bristol to Charles de Gaulle airport in Paris on Thursday morning. After spending a couple of hours in the city so Lauren could enjoy some of the sights, they had driven their hire car north-east to the hotel where they were staying for their long weekend. Situated in a stunning eighteenth-century chateau an hour from Paris and twenty minutes from Giverny, the hotel was in a beautiful and peaceful setting, the staff friendly and discreet.

Today, Friday, with the weather exceptionally mild for early April, they were enjoying their visit to Claude Monet's home. Parts of the restored pink-painted house with its green shutters had canopies along the veranda covered in swathes of lushly leaved climbing roses that would look spectacular when in flower. The main gardens were full of spring colour, the borders packed with tulips, narcissi, forget-me-nots, aubretia, fritilaries and pansies, with irises, geraniums and other perennials coming through, along with the soon-to-flower wisterias, clematis, rambling roses and yellow laburnums, which draped over arches and pergolas. Cherry and crab-apple trees were also in bloom and looked magnificent.

Lauren chattered freely and he was happy to listen, to live the experience through her. As she made notes and sketches and took endless photos on her digital camera, he indulged himself and watched her, unable to banish his concern about her behaviour since the crash. Physically she appeared fine, but... He frowned. She'd been different these last days, distracted and distant.

Things had been hectic at the surgery. He'd been out almost all night the previous Friday, missing Eve Dwyer's farewell as he and Chloe had worked together to bring Diane Bailey's second daughter safely into the world. He'd arrived home in the early hours to be welcomed to bed by Lauren who had made love to him with an almost frantic urgency. He still sensed that desperation and restlessness in her and he hoped their few days away would enable him to get to the bottom of what was driving her.

'Can we go and find the Japanese water garden?' Lauren asked, pausing to consult her map of the site.

'Of course.' He brushed a few strands of caramel-coloured hair—the natural blonder streaks shimmering under the spring sunshine—back behind her ear, then dropped a quick kiss on her smiling mouth. 'We have to go through the underground passage to the other side of the road.'

'Great!'

Her enthusiasm was infectious and her delight at finding the famous waterlily pool with its weeping willow trees and the graceful wooden bridge, so familiar from Monet's paintings, filled him with warmth and love.

'It's a shame we're too early for the waterlilies themselves, but it's just magical here, Gabe,' she murmured, awe in her voice as she snuggled close to him.

'We can come again at a different time of year.'

She didn't respond to the promise with the pleasure he expected. Instead, he felt her tense. She withdrew, using the pretext of taking more photos, but he experienced a real sense of fear, an inner chill, that in some intangible way he couldn't understand, Lauren was slipping away from him.

Giverny was as magical as Lauren had imagined it would be and it was even better to be sharing the experience with Gabriel. He was puzzled by her, she knew, and she tried her best to hide the fact that she was distracted by following Oliver's advice to make the most of this short holiday and set her worries to one side. It wasn't easy.

How ironic that she should be here at this time. The place inspired her to paint but her nerve had failed her because of her vision problems and she had made excuses not to pick up a brush since the previous summer. For the first time, faced with the reality that she might never paint again, she felt grief at the loss of the activity that had been such a part of her. And yet Monet, one of the world's greatest artists, had produced some of his best and most well-known works while living here amidst this landscape he had created and when he'd been suffering from his own loss of sight.

Aside from never-to-be-forgotten memories, she took endless photographs which she would download to her computer so she could share them with Chloe, who was excited and envious of her trip. She would also email some to Vicky, who was currently in California, the latest stop on the band's tour. Not that Lauren had divulged much to her curious and gossipy friend about Gabriel and, with the worrying issue of her eyes coming to the fore, she was even more glad now that Vicky was away and otherwise occupied.

The whole weekend was wonderful. They breakfasted on chilled fruit juice and fresh warm chocolate croissants at the hotel, and she wondered how many miles she would have to jog to burn off all the extra calories when they went back home.

On Saturday they went to the nearby town of Vernon. As well as visiting the museum, which held some of Monet's paintings as well as many other interesting exhibits, they also enjoyed seeing the old mill on the Seine and Bizy castle.

While she savoured every moment of being with Gabriel, exploring the local area or relaxing at the hotel, and making love with fervour every night, Lauren couldn't shake off her edginess. She was aware all the time of the sword of Damocles hanging over her. When she returned to Cornwall on Tuesday, this special time out of time would be over and she would have to face reality…the appointment with the consultant which Oliver had scheduled for the end of the week. An appointment which could reveal the true state of her visual problems.

She loved Gabriel so much, but she couldn't tell him so until she knew what was wrong with her and what, if anything, she had to offer him. For now she would not burden him with her worries and confusion. Not until she knew exactly where she stood and what the future held for her. What if she had some kind of tumour or something? If things were bad, she knew he wouldn't desert her, but that was part of the problem. She wouldn't want him to stay for the wrong reasons, couldn't bind him to her out of pity. Despite how her feelings had changed, they had made no promises to each other and were taking things one day at a time until his contract in Penhally Bay came to an end. *If* her situation proved to be bleak, she would have to set Gabriel free. He had his own issues to face. But the very thought of him no longer being in her life, of never being able to touch him, kiss him or make love with him again, was too painful to contemplate.

On Monday morning, after a lingering shared shower, they were enjoying a walk in the hotel grounds before breakfast and discussing their plans for their last full day in France when Gabriel's mobile rang. Lauren noted the frown on his face when he took out the phone and looked at the display.

'It's François,' he explained, surprise evident in the huskily accented voice that still sent tingles down her spine. 'Sorry, *chérie*, I'd forgotten I had left the phone on. Is it OK if I speak with him?'

'Of course.'

She knew the two men kept in touch but it was unusual for his friend to call at this time of the day, especially when François knew they were having a few days away. Despite Gabriel teaching her some French these last months, she didn't follow much of the conversation, but the changing expressions on his face made it clear that whatever news his friend was imparting was unexpected and of some importance. A flicker of unease rippled through her.

'Is everything all right?' she asked as he hung up but remained rooted to the spot, looking stunned. Closing the gap between them, she took his free hand. 'Gabe?'

He shook himself, his fingers linking with hers as if he needed the contact. 'I don't know what to say,' he murmured, sounding shaken.

'Come and sit down.' Concerned, Lauren led him to a rustic seat on the edge of the woodland path. 'What's happened?'

'I had not told anyone but François my address in England. As you know, I needed space from Yvette and her scheming,' he explained and Lauren nodded, still gripping his hand. 'François had a letter this morning from the firm of solicitors in Paris who did work for my father. They have been trying to find me.'

Lauren frowned. 'Does François know why?'

'Yes…in part.'

'And?' she whispered, the tension growing with every passing second.

Dark eyes focused on her and she saw the whirl of emotion in them. 'And they have found something I should have received two years ago. It was mislaid.'

'Mislaid?' Lauren swallowed, barely managing to force the words out. 'What is it?'

'A letter—to me—from Papa. He didn't forget me, Lauren.'

His shaky smile and the roughness of his voice undid her, and she wrapped him in her arms, holding him tight, hoping and praying that his father's last words would help to ease the pain inside him and provide answers to some of his questions.

'Are you sure you don't mind doing this?' Gabriel asked for the umpteenth time.

They sat in the foyer at the solicitors' office in Paris. He shifted restlessly, anxious about what was to come yet filled with gratitude for Lauren's support. From the moment he had received the news from François, she had been adamant that they change their plans and return to the capital straight away. After a hasty breakfast, they had packed their things and settled their bill with the chateau owner, apologising for their premature departure.

'I don't mind at all. This is important, Gabe,' she reassured him now, her hand resting on his thigh. 'We've had a wonderful time and now we need to be here.'

The sudden events had distracted him from his worries about Lauren, the feeling he had that something was wrong and that, despite their physical closeness, she was emotionally withdrawing from him.

'Dr Devereux?' The receptionist, a trim brunette, claimed their attention. 'Monsieur Picard will see you now. You go up the stairs and take the second door on the left.'

'Thank you.'

'Do you want me to wait here?' Lauren asked.

Feeling uncharacteristically vulnerable and uncertain, he shook his head. 'I'd like you to come with me.'

'No problem.' Rising to her feet, she slipped her hand into his and gave an encouraging squeeze. 'Let's go.'

All too soon they had reached the designated room and were greeted by Monsieur Picard, a dapper man in his early sixties, who welcomed them with a gracious smile, switching to English with ease when Gabriel informed him that Lauren's French was not proficient.

'Please, sit down and make yourselves comfortable. Can I offer you some refreshment?' the man enquired as he took his own chair behind a vast leather-topped desk laden with folders.

'No, thank you.' Gabriel hoped Lauren wouldn't mind him speaking for them. He felt on edge, wanting only to take possession of his father's letter. 'It is pure chance that I happened to be in France when the message came through. I understand you have something that belongs to me.'

The solicitor's expression turned grave with apology and discomfort. 'Yes. And I cannot say how sorry I am. The fault was entirely ours. The envelope was misfiled and only came to light in the last week. We did not have your current address on file, hence the further delay in contacting you,' the man explained.

'And this letter…it is from my father?' Gabriel asked, cursing the unsteadiness of his voice but drawing strength from the way Lauren's fingers tightened on his.

'Yes,' Monsieur Picard continued, opening the file in front of him and withdrawing a white envelope. 'This was meant to be given to you in the event of your father's death.'

Gabriel's hand shook as he took the envelope the solicitor handed to him. 'Thank you.'

He looked down at it, saw his name typed on the front, and

was filled with a mix of fear, hope and curiosity about what it might contain. The next moments passed in a blur. He signed a release form, then Lauren handled the pleasantries of departure before guiding him out of the building and encouraging him on the short walk back to the hotel they had booked into for their final night in France. Once there, Gabriel sat on the bed and stared at the envelope in his hand.

'Would you like me to leave you alone for a while?'

'No!' Surprised by Lauren's question, he looked up at her and shook his head. 'Please, stay.'

With care, he finally slit open the sealed envelope and withdrew several sheets of thick cream paper. His heart lurched at the sight of his father's familiar large, sweeping handwriting in the dark maroon ink he had always favoured for his fountain pen. A few photographs fell out and he picked them up, shocked to find himself staring at an attractive young woman with long dark hair, a laughing face and wide dark eyes. He turned one over and read the note, name and the date written on the back before passing it to Lauren.

'My mother,' he managed, staring at the other pictures of the same woman with his father as a young man.

'She's beautiful, Gabe.' Lauren's whispered words and the emotion in them brought a lump to his throat. 'You have her eyes…and her smile.'

Scared he wasn't going to hold things together, he sucked in a steadying breath, returned his attention to the letter and read it through. By the end, he was feeling awed and immensely grateful, as well as emotional. He looked back at Lauren, saw the concern and care in her grey eyes, and desperately needed to share with her, and her alone, what he had just learned about his father and himself.

'It's in French,' he told her. 'I'll translate it for you.'

'If you're sure.'

He just hoped he could reach the end without making a fool of himself. 'I am.' That said, he read the letter again, this time aloud…

'My dear son,
'If you are reading this, I am gone, and I did not find the courage or right time to explain things to you in person. I regret that more than words can say.

'Whatever you may have heard by now from Yvette, I hope you will read my side of the story and find it in your heart to forgive me. I loved Angelique, your birth mother, with all my heart. We were so young, barely twenty, yet she was everything to me. She truly was my angel. Despite all the obstacles my family put in the way, we married as soon as we knew you were to be part of our lives. I would have given up everything for Angelique but she died just days after you were born. I refused to lose you, too, but I couldn't manage alone.

'Beside myself with grief, I stupidly allowed my family to take over and railroad me into marrying Yvette—a good business and social match. Yvette promised to raise you as her own in return for the wealth and position the marriage afforded her. There is enough mixed blood in our ancestry that no one questioned your skin being darker than ours. Your grandfather and some of your cousins carry the same Caribbean heritage, as you know.

'The family placed a condition—you were not to be told about Angelique. I was uneasy but weak. I agreed…but have long wished I had not. Yvette was never a good mother and I am so sorry for her coldness to you. She resented you, hated me and the situation. She will try to use my death to tie you to a life not of your choosing. Do not yield, my son. You are a doctor through and through. The estate will survive well in the hands of your cousins and Yvette's welfare needs are guaranteed for life.

'Please…follow your heart. Do not repeat my mistakes and be bound by a false sense of duty to something that will never make you happy or fulfilled. Live your life your way. You have my love and my blessing always. You have so much to give to the sick who need you. Medicine is your destiny.

'Enclosed with this letter are details about Angelique and her origins, as well as some photographs. Although she had no immediate family left when she came to France, I am sure you will wish to learn more of your heritage and that side of the family. She was an amazing young woman, full of goodness and love. We both wanted you desperately.

'There is much of her in you. I am so proud of you, Gabriel, and Angelique would be, too. Be true to yourself, my son, and be happy.

'Love always, Papa'

His voice cracking, Gabriel set the letter aside and looked up to see tears streaming down Lauren's cheeks. She rushed across the room and wrapped her arms around him. Taking her down with him to the mattress, Gabriel held on tight, burying his face in her hair, breathing in her scent, giving thanks that she was here.

He felt a huge weight lifting off his shoulders and a new sense of freedom welled within him, a peace he had not known for a long time. It was nearly two years since his father had died, two years in which he had struggled to come to terms with all Yvette had told him. Now he knew the truth. His father had not had an affair. He had loved Angelique. Both his natural parents had wanted him. Thanks to his father's loving words, the road ahead was clear to him. Being a doctor was a fundamental part of who he was. His father had known that, had released him from any misplaced family duty and urged him to follow his own path.

Despite Yvette's belief, family responsibility was not something he took lightly. He valued his upbringing, the benefits he'd enjoyed, his father's love. Learning that his father had been proud of him and respected his choices brought a rush of emotion to his heart. His father had known what would happen, had wanted to prepare him, to protect him in death, as he had in life, from Yvette's bitterness and spite.

Thank goodness Lauren was here with him. Natural, earthy, intelligent and genuine, she had given him so much in every way. And she responded to his touch like no other woman he had ever known. She shifted, pulling back to meet his gaze. Touched by her concern for him, he brushed away the tears that showed how much she cared. He loved her so much and valued her opinion above all others. She accepted him for who and what he was, the whole person, not his family name or his bank balance or the ancestral estate. From the first he had sensed Lauren was a kindred spirit. It had been like a meeting of souls.

'I'm so glad for you, Gabe,' she told him, her voice thick with emotion. 'Listen to your father—and to your heart.'

It was good advice. And he planned to follow it. 'Right now my heart is telling me to take you to bed,' he murmured huskily, delighting in the way her eyes flared with answering desire.

Late that night, cocooned in the privacy of their room, the noises of the city filtering up from the streets below, Gabriel held Lauren close, their bodies tangled together, limbs entwined. It had been an unforgettable day…a day in which he had been given a new lease of life and had recaptured his true memories of his father.

His thoughts turned to Lauren. Their love-making remained as passionate and explosive as ever and yet he still sensed that new desperation in her. He needed to tell her how special she was and how much she meant to him. He had held back for so long, scared to push too soon or too hard—in the same way he had given her space to come to terms with the problems with her sight.

Stroking her satiny hair, breathing in her scent, he tightened his hold. 'I love you, Lauren, *ma belle*,' he whispered against her skin, knowing she was not yet asleep.

He fought against the heartache that gripped him when there was no response to his admission bar the tensing of her body. Fear clenched his stomach. Today Lauren's support and reactions had proved that she cared, too, and yet she refused to acknowledge what was between them. Why? What was holding her back? For days he had sensed the times when she had been distancing herself, backing off from him emotionally, and he didn't know how to stop it.

He couldn't force her to trust in him, to love him, but he wanted so much more than the commitment-free relationship they had discussed at the beginning. He *wanted* commitment, *needed* Lauren in his life—for ever. How ironic that at the very time he should have rediscovered his father and be in a position to not only understand his mother's heritage but to be free to plan his future, the one person he wanted most to share it with him was slipping out of his reach.

Lauren sat in Oliver's car on the journey back from St Piran Hospital on Friday afternoon frozen with shock and despair. She bit her lip, trying not to think of the last hours and all the tests she had undergone—a battery of assorted eye-function tests and examinations, including visual field, acuity and colour assessments. There had been a blood test, an electro-retinograph—which determined the function of the photoreceptors in the eye—and endless questions. Unfortunately, due to her adoption, she had not been able to provide any details of her family medical history.

Oliver had reassured her several times about Professor Kieran Murchison's reputation and the rotund, balding and jovial man had lived up to his billing today, showing a kindness that matched his thoroughness. Yet he had held her fate in his hands and she had felt sick to her stomach when he had finally delivered his verdict.

'I'm sorry to keep you waiting so long, my dear, but I wanted to be very sure of the results,' he had told her when she had been shown into his office, leaving Oliver—who had stuck with her throughout and had borne the delays and boredom with amazing fortitude—sitting outside in the waiting area.

'But you have the results now?' Her voice had wavered alarmingly. 'What's wrong with me?'

His expression serious, the professor had looked down at her notes before speaking. 'I'm afraid you have a condition called retinitis pigmentosa.'

'What does that mean?'

'It's a group of related, inherited disorders—a genetic disease of the retina—the majority of which have no known genetic cause. The most common cases of RP result from abnormalities of the photoreceptors—the rods and the cones,' he had explained. 'The presentation of your symptoms suggests that you have autosomal dominant RP, which means that you fall into the group who have rod-cone dystrophy, affecting the rods more than the cones. This explains the problems you have reported, including those with your night vision, peripheral vision, bumping into things, slow adjustment to light and so on.'

Struggling to take it all in, Lauren had forced herself to ask the next question. 'What about treatment?'

'There is much we can do to help you manage the condition, and to prepare and cope for the changes that lie ahead. There are various genetic and stem-cell studies ongoing around the world which might have positive results in future, even a bionic eye project. For now, though, Lauren, there is no treatment and no cure. Progression of RP is different for everyone. Yours has been slow so far. Hopefully it will continue to follow the same pattern. You have a challenging time ahead, but it's not a death sentence. And it's not going to happen overnight. So much will still be open to you.'

The words rang in her ears even now. She had a whole stack of advice leaflets to read, a list of recommended books and website addresses to gain further information, but the appalling and impossible truth could not be ignored. Retinitis pigmentosa was a progressive disease. She would continue to lose her vision and, ultimately, could become totally blind.

Her mind in turmoil, she leaned back and closed eyes still blurry from the drops Oliver had warned her would be administered. Aside from the utter terror of today, of facing up to the reality that all was not well with her eyes, she couldn't get Gabriel out of her thoughts. France had been amazing, she'd loved her time away with him. The icing on the cake had been learning about the letter and seeing the difference his father's words, love and pride had made to him, to his sense of identity and his thoughts for the future.

On Monday night in Paris she had frozen when Gabriel had told her he loved her. She had wanted to turn in his arms and kiss him, to shout from the rooftops that she loved him, too, but instead she had pretended to be asleep and had ignored his longed-for words. If only they had come at a different time and not while she'd had this problem hanging over her and had been rigid with fear for her future. A future that now stretched ahead of her, painful and lonely, because Gabriel could not be part of it.

He had been hurt by her silence and there had been an uncharacteristic tension between them on their journey back to Cornwall the next day—a tension that had continued throughout the rest of a busy week. No matter how much she told herself she was doing the right thing, guilt weighed heavily upon her. She hated deceiving Gabriel and keeping things from him. He'd be so upset if he knew where she had been today. And he'd believe she'd kept it from him because she didn't trust him. Which wasn't true. Far from it. She was just so terribly scared about what was happening to her and devastated now that the diagnosis confirmed the worst.

'Lauren? Talk to me,' Oliver cajoled, taking her ice-cold hand in his as he drew the car to a halt outside Gatehouse Cottage. 'What do you want me to do?'

'I don't know. I can't think at the moment.'

His fingers squeezed hers and she heard the shock and upset in his voice. 'I'm so sorry, sweetheart. I'm here for you. We all will be...if only you will let us.'

'I need some time to decide what to do,' she whispered after a long, uncomfortable pause. 'Promise me that you won't say anything to anyone. Not even Chloe. Especially not Gabriel.'

'I've already told you I won't break your confidence, Lauren. But I have to say I think you are wrong to shut out those who care so much about you,' he advised gently.

Shock, anger and fear made thought and reason impossible. Withdrawing her hand from his, Lauren gathered up her things and reached to open the door. 'I can't thank you enough for all you have done for me. I'm more grateful than you can know. But I need to handle this my own way, Oliver,' she told him, her voice quiet but firm.

'All right.' He sighed, running his fingers through his hair, his frustration and concern clear. 'You can always come to me at any time if you want to talk about things, or if there is anything at all I can do. Promise me that much.'

'I know. I promise.'

'I don't like to leave you alone,' he protested, his voice

heavy with worry. 'But Adam swapped with me and I have to get back to the clinic to take evening surgery.'

'Go. Please. I'll be fine. I need to read up, to absorb all the professor said,' she reassured him, holding on to her composure by a tenuous thread.

After Oliver had finally been persuaded to leave, Lauren went inside and wandered around the cottage that no longer felt like home. Home was with Gabriel. A place she could no longer be. She sat down on her bed, Foxy's head in her lap, the booklets describing her disease spread around her, and cried for all that was lost. Everything seemed too monumental to cope with. How long could she continue to do her job? What was going to happen to her one, five or ten years down the line? Would she be totally blind?

The first most pressing and impossible thing she had to do was to distance herself from Gabriel, to begin the terrible process of withdrawing and ending their magical relationship. Even thinking about it brought more pain and sadness than she had ever known. It cut deep inside her. But she had to do it. For his sake. Because he deserved someone who could be his equal, someone with whom he could have a family. With her condition, genetic testing might show she could never risk having children of her own.

Hearing Gabriel's car going past in the drive, Lauren left Foxy behind at Gatehouse Cottage and walked slowly to the Manor House. For endless moments, scared of what was to come, she hesitated on the steps, shivering despite the mildness of the late afternoon. Finally, unable to delay the inevitable, she rang the doorbell. After a few moments, she heard Gabriel's steps jogging down the stairs, then the front door swung open. All the breath left her lungs in a rush at the sight of him. He was so gorgeous. More than anything she wanted to throw herself into his arms, confess all, tell him she loved him, but it wasn't fair to him.

'*Chérie*, what are you doing?' he asked with a laugh, reaching for her. 'Did you lose your key?'

Evading his touch, she stepped back and shook her head. 'No. I—' She broke off before her voice cracked, seeing the smile leave his face, doubt and fear dimming the light in those glorious dark eyes.

'You are scaring me, Lauren. What is it?'

'I need some space—some time to think,' she began, cursing her lack of decisiveness.

Gabriel frowned. 'Space?'

'Yes.' Wringing her hands together, she took another step away, trying to find the strength to do what she believed was right.

'To think about what?'

'I'm going back to the cottage, Gabriel. We've had a great time, but we said no promises, no ties, and I think we need to cool things. You've sorted the situation out now about your father,' she rushed on, her heart breaking at the hurt disbelief on his face. 'You're free to plan your future, to find out about your mother's heritage, to go where you like with your work. The last thing you need is to be shackled to anything or anyone.'

Anger mingled with the pain in his eyes as he looked at her, roughly thrusting his hands into his trouser pockets. 'Don't make this about me, Lauren. Don't make excuses. You had to know how much more this had become. It was never some casual fling. Not for me. I had thought not for you either,' he challenged, his accent more pronounced with his hurt disappointment. 'Or have the last months been nothing but a game to you?'

'No, but…' He had cut her to the quick and she had no way to defend herself so she fell silent.

'I love you, Lauren. I want to make a commitment to you, to marry you. But that clearly means nothing to you and you don't feel the same for me. You've been pulling away emotionally for days. Just have the guts to say so.'

'OK.' She swayed, fearing she was going to collapse in a pit of pain. Nothing had ever been this difficult and she couldn't bring herself to look him in the eye. 'You're right. I can't commit like that.' Her voice wavered as she told that fragment of truth. She couldn't commit but she couldn't tell him why…because she loved him heart, body and soul and couldn't burden him with a blind wife. 'I'm sorry.'

'You're sorry? Is that meant to make this right?' he demanded with an anger she had never heard from him before.

Tears stung her eyes. 'No.'

'You've made your decision, Lauren. There's nothing else to be said.'

Rigid with tension and with a quiet dignity that cried out with his pain and twisted the knife inside her, Gabriel closed the door, shutting her out of the house and his life. The tears fell then, hot and heavy. Selfishly, she wanted to call him back, to pound on the door, to tell him it was all a mistake and explain everything. She needed him, wanted him, couldn't face this without him—but she couldn't manipulate him that way, not after all he had been through with Yvette.

She thought of all he had said, words that should have made her joyous, not despairing. Gabriel loved her. It was what she'd wanted most. But for his sake she had had to reject that love—the most precious of gifts. She didn't deserve him. Pressing a hand to her mouth to mask the sound of the sobs that racked her body, she turned and stumbled back down the driveway, praying that Oliver and Chloe would not be back yet.

She had achieved what she had set out to do. Now her future stretched ahead of her—cold, dark and full of fear. A future that was going to take her sight, her job, her hobbies, her independence. Even that didn't seem to matter as much as what she had already lost. Gabriel…the only man she had ever loved.

CHAPTER TEN

'I'M GOING for a walk,' Lauren announced, unable to bear the atmosphere in the cottage any longer and needing to be alone with her thoughts. 'I'll take Foxy down to the beach.'

'Whatever.'

Chloe's response, while not unfriendly, left Lauren in no doubt that she remained in her friend's bad books and was not to be forgiven any time soon. Smothering a sigh, knowing it was her own fault for not following Oliver's advice and confiding in the people who cared for her, she attached Foxy's lead and let herself out, the Saturday morning sunshine failing to raise her spirits.

She had no idea how she had lived through the last week. Nothing had been this painful and no matter how much she told herself that hurting Gabriel now was better than condemning him to a hopeless future with her, it didn't help. She couldn't sleep, couldn't eat. People were shocked and surprised by the break-up. However many times Lauren trotted out the same excuse—that things had run their course and she and Gabriel had decided to go their separate ways—the telling never became easier, the lie sticking in her throat, multiplying her agony.

She couldn't avoid contact with Gabriel at the surgery. The sight of him, proudly dignified yet so obviously unhappy, ripped at her shredded heart. How she was going to bear the situation for the remainder of his time in Penhally she didn't know—seeing him every day, not being able to touch him, barely speaking unless it was with strained politeness about work. But the very thought of him leaving for good, of never seeing him again, or hearing his softly accented voice and rumbly laugh, was impossible to contemplate. No matter how much she kept convincing herself she was doing the right thing for Gabriel's sake, the temptation to be selfish and go to him to confess all never diminished. Indeed, it increased with every hour that passed.

Desperate to escape the pain of losing Gabriel and the anxiety over her diagnosis, she had thrown herself into her work, all the time wondering how long she would be able to do her job and how soon she would have to stop driving completely. Yesterday she had taken Paul Mitchell and his mother on their once-a-month trip to a local private spa that made their hydrotherapy pool available by appointment for patients with special needs. The water-based exercise she was able to do with him was good for Paul with his Duchenne muscular dystrophy.

Some long-term patients she had seen during the last twelve months had been signed off, Mike Trevellyan among them. As well as cases which turned around fairly quickly, like Zena with her sore neck and Dan Somers with his hamstring injury, she had all her regulars, including Harry, Edith and baby Timmy Morrison. Stella Chamberlain's Parkinson's disease was still keeping her in the Harbour View Nursing Home, while Gertrude Stanbury was looking forward to returning to her bungalow in Gull Close in the next week. Neither the anticipation of going home nor her painful arthritis diverted Gertrude from commenting on what she viewed as Lauren's stupidity in letting Gabriel get away.

At home she had Chloe on her case and she recalled her

friend's initial reaction when she had learned of the break-up. 'You said to me in the summer to grasp what I had with Oliver, that something that special, some*one* that special, doesn't come along often in life. You and Gabriel are special, Lauren. He loves you, and I'm sure you love him. Why are you throwing it all away?'

'You don't understand.' And she hadn't been able to explain.

'No, I don't. Neither does Gabriel. He's confused and distressed. You've really hurt him. You owe him more than that.'

Lauren had spent as much time in her room as she could, avoiding Oliver and Chloe. She'd studied the leaflets the professor had given her, looked up information on the Internet and read a couple of biographies written by people who were living with retinitis pigmentosa. It was all depressing but moving. She hoped she could be even as fractionally as brave and resourceful as those whose stories she had read—stories which had scarily mirrored many of her own experiences. With time she hoped to come to terms with it, to make plans, to find some courage to cope with whatever was thrown at her, but the shock still lingered, as did the gut-wrenching ache of missing Gabriel every minute of every day.

Leaving the quiet country roads, she headed down through the town towards the harbour front. All she could do was tell herself she was making the best choice for Gabriel in the long run. He'd had enough of manipulative women in his life. She couldn't tie him to her out of duty or because he felt sorry for her. But it was almost impossible to let go. Nothing had hurt this much. When his time here was over, he would go back to France and no doubt settle down one day and have a family of his own. She couldn't allow him to take on a wife who was slowly but surely losing her sight, who might be a genetic risk and unable to have children, and who, at some time down the line, could be blind and dependent in more ways than she could bear to comprehend.

Despite feeling as if she was slowly but surely unravelling, somehow she had to try to survive this torment. One day at a time.

With one more house call left to make on Saturday morning, Gabriel sat in his car outside the patient's home, his arms folded on the steering-wheel, his head resting on them. A week and a day on and he had still not recovered from the shock of Lauren's words. One day he had been given the gift of his father's love and approval, the identity of his birth mother, and had felt his life was finally getting back on track again, but shortly afterwards Lauren had dropped her bombshell, rejecting his love and breaking his heart in the process.

What had he done wrong? Had he taken Lauren for granted? Had he been mistaken that she returned his feelings? He still didn't understand how she could have walked away as if there was nothing at all between them. It hadn't been just sex. Lauren could deny it all she liked but he wouldn't, couldn't, believe she felt nothing, that all they had shared had been meaningless fun. He was sure he hadn't misjudged things that badly. What they had was special, explosive, a once-in-a-lifetime connection…a connection that had hit them both the moment they had met. He had never felt like this about anyone else. Had never hurt so much. He couldn't sleep without Lauren in his arms, couldn't eat, was barely getting through each day.

Even the letter from his father had failed to distract him for long, despite the searches he had done on the Internet to learn about Martinique, where his mother had come from. One day he hoped to go there, to find out more about his roots, but he couldn't get excited about it now, could do nothing but yearn for Lauren.

With a deep sigh, he climbed out of the car, collected his medical bag, and walked to the front door, reviewing what he knew about the woman he was going to see. Delia Rocco was only thirty-two and had suffered a serious stroke ten days ago. She had been discharged from hospital the previous day and he was doing a follow-up visit to ensure she and her husband were coping. He hadn't wanted to leave them all weekend without support, and he needed to discuss Delia's needs—which would include physiotherapy and necessitate him facing Lauren. His gut tightened with pain.

Delia's husband, Neil, answered the door and invited him in, a tired smile on his face. 'Thanks for coming, Dr Devereux.'

'No problem. How are you both doing?' he asked, knowing that Neil was going to need as much understanding and support as Delia. 'Relieved to be home?'

'Very. But it's scary, too, not having the nurses on hand,' the man admitted.

'That's understandable, but I'm sure you'll do fine, and don't forget you have the doctors, district nurses and physiotherapist from the surgery willing to step in whenever you need us.'

Looking reassured, Neil relaxed. 'Thank you. Well, I expect you want to see Delia first?'

'Yes, please. Then we can have a chat.'

Talking with and examining Delia revealed that she had been left with weakness and reduced movement down one side of her body and her speech was slurred. Given the severity of her stroke, she had done well to make so much improvement so quickly, although she had a long haul ahead of her. She was brave but clearly bewildered at having been struck down at such a young age, scared about what the future would hold for her. Gabriel determined to do the best he could for the couple to ensure they had something positive to look forward to.

'I'm just so grateful Delia is still here and recovering,' Neil said a while later, holding his wife's good hand. 'Life without her would be intolerable. She tried to send me away, of course, but I wasn't having any of it.'

Puzzled, Gabriel frowned. 'Sorry? Send you away?'

'I was so scared, so confused. I got it into my head that Neil would be better off without me, that I would be a burden to him and prevent him having a normal, happy life,' Delia explained, taking time to try to enunciate each word.

'She said she didn't love me any more, that she didn't want me,' Neil confirmed with a rueful smile. 'I almost believed her at first, I was under so much stress and so worried about her, but thankfully I saw through what she was doing.'

With a start, Gabriel sat back, his thoughts on Lauren. Frowning, he thought over the sudden way she had ended things with him. Was there more behind it than he was seeing? Unsettled, he began packing his things away and returned his attention to Delia and Neil.

'I'll see you again next week. But call any time if there is anything you need,' he advised them. 'Our physiotherapist, Lauren Nightingale, will come to see you on a regular basis and work out an exercise and therapy schedule with you.'

'Thanks. How is Lauren?' Neil asked.

Pain lanced through his heart. 'Fine, as far as I know. She's an excellent physio, so you'll be in good hands.'

'Oh, I know that,' Delia confirmed with a lopsided smile. 'I was a couple of years ahead of her at school. She was always very caring to people.'

'I was just concerned because I saw her at St Piran Hospital last week when I was waiting for Delia. Lauren didn't see me, but she looked upset,' Neil clarified.

Lauren had been at the hospital? Upset? Every part of him went on high alert. 'When was this?' he asked, trying to keep his tone casual.

'Last Friday afternoon. They'd taken Delia down for some

eye tests,' he added, clearly unaware of the turmoil Gabriel was experiencing.

Dieu! Why hadn't he considered it before? He thought of the timing. Lauren had been to the hospital and that same night she had broken up with him. What on earth had she found out? Fear gripped him. Had Lauren reacted to the shock as Delia had, pushing away those close to her because she felt she would be a burden? He had to know, had to find out.

Taking his leave of the Roccos with as much speed as was polite, he rushed back to the surgery where Oliver was taking the Saturday morning clinic. Hippocratic oath or no Hippocratic oath, he was going to get some information from his friend.

'Is Oliver still with patients?' he asked Sue when he arrived back at the surgery and handed over his tray of patient notes.

'No, the last one left about five minutes ago,' she confirmed. 'Everything OK?'

'Mmm? Oh, fine. I need to see Oliver.'

Leaving a surprised Sue behind him, he hurried to his friend's consulting room. The door was closed, so he knocked and waited impatiently, just in case Sue was wrong. Despite his urgency, he wouldn't embarrass or upset a patient.

'Come in.'

Oliver was alone, he discovered, writing up his notes. He swung his chair round, a wary expression on his face as Gabriel closed the door and crossed to the desk.

'I know you can't break a confidence, Oliver, but I want to know what's going on with Lauren,' he began, pacing out his frustration. 'I love her, I want to marry her. When she broke things off, it nearly killed me. Someone told me they saw Lauren at the eye clinic last week. That same day she told me it was over. I don't believe that's a coincidence.' He paused, considering how much to tell Oliver. 'It's taken a

while to get my head together but I think she has some misplaced idea she's going to be a burden and has to let me go.'

'Gabriel—'

'I *know*,' he cut in with irritation, rubbing a hand across the
back of his neck, feeling the tightness of the tension gripping
his muscles. 'I know you can't tell me outright. But you can
give me a clue.'

Oliver regarded him for a few moments in silence. 'For what
it's worth, I've tried several times to get Lauren to confide in
both you and Chloe, but I have to respect her wishes.'

'Whatever it is, however bad, I'm not leaving her, not
giving up on her. Am I on the right track? Or does she really
feel nothing for me? Give me something to work on. Please.'

'You don't make things easy, Gabriel.'

'How would you feel if it was Chloe?' OK, he wasn't
playing fair, but he was desperate. 'If Lauren thinks she's
doing this for my benefit, she's wrong. If she cares about me,
she'll thank you in the long run.'

Oliver closed his eyes and sighed, running his fingers
through his over-long hair. 'I can't give you any details, but
you're right, Lauren's pushing everyone away because she
thinks it's the right thing to do.'

Sitting down because his legs felt too shaky to hold him
up, Gabriel met Oliver's troubled dark gaze. 'She's not dying?
It's not a tumour?' He forced the words out, the relief indescribable when his friend shook his head. Sucking in a steadying breath, he pressed a hand over his sternum as he
acknowledged how frightened he had been. 'OK. It doesn't
matter what it is, I want to be there for her. I just wish she had
told me so she hadn't had to face all this alone.'

'She wasn't alone,' Oliver admitted after a moment.

Gabriel glanced up, a mix of emotions rushing through him—
disappointment and annoyance at being shut out, but gratitude
to Oliver for being such a good friend. 'You went with her?'

'Yes. I thought it was the lesser evil. Lauren refused to tell you or Chloe and I knew none of us would want her to go on her own.'

'Thank you for being there for her. Now, it's time I found her and discussed a few things,' he finished, rising to his feet.

'Good luck.' Oliver's smile was wry. 'She can be stubborn when she sets her mind to something.'

'So can I. And now I know what she's up to, I'm not going to let her sideline me again.'

He left the surgery for home, needing to change clothes and then track down Lauren. A shiver went through him as he imagined all she had been through this last week or more. He realised now that the worry of facing up to her sight problems had led to her withdrawal, to her being distracted and to her urgency for physical closeness—especially if she'd feared things would be over when she had a diagnosis. While it pained him that she hadn't spoken to him about it, he understood how fear and anxiety could affect someone's decision-making. Thinking of her frightened and confused and alone brought a lump to his throat. He wished more than anything that he had been there to help her through what must have been a shocking and scary experience. His heart ached for her.

Lauren touched something deep inside him, filling an empty space he hadn't realised he'd had until he'd met her. She grounded him, made him laugh. The last months with her had been the happiest of his life—breaking up more painful than anything he had ever experienced. But now he knew what lay behind her actions and her misguided thoughts he wasn't letting her go—not while he had breath in his body.

'I can do all kinds of tricks with my kite now, Uncle Nick.'

'I'm sure you can,' Nick responded, voice gruff. 'Show me some of them.'

Kate smiled as Jem rushed ahead of them on to the surfing beach below the cliffs and beyond the promontory on which the lighthouse and the church stood. She glanced back at the latter building, wondering what the new permanent vicar would be like, an appointment finally having been made. Whoever took up the role next month would have a difficult act to follow. Reverend Kenner was still much missed.

It was a perfect spring morning, sunny and with a hint of freshness in the air. Nick's suggestion of a walk on the beach had been a pleasant surprise and she had been happy to put off her visit to the Saturday farmers' market so that the three of them could spend time together. Since Christmas, and the successful New Year's Eve party at his house, Nick had made a real effort to play a part in Jem's life. For that Kate was grateful. That he'd made no mention of claiming his son still pained her, but she tried not to be impatient.

They stood side by side, watching in silence as Jem skilfully had his kite soaring into the sky and began performing some stunts.

'He's good,' Nick commented after a while, an enigmatic expression on his face, his hands buried in his trouser pockets.

'Yes.' Kate pulled her gaze away from his profile and looked back at her son with pride. 'He took to it straight away. I'm thinking of getting him a more advanced kite for his birthday.'

'Good idea.'

Nick's tone was cool and she worried that mentioning Jem's birthday had touched on forbidden ground and brought back memories of his conception. She sighed, weary of having to be careful what she said in case Nick took exception to it. Before she could decide whether to call him on it or change the subject, they were approached by an older couple.

'Are you folks local?' the woman asked with a broad smile, her American accent thick with Deep South tones.

'We are.' Aware of Nick's reserve, Kate smiled back. 'Can we help you?'

'Would you be kind enough to take a photograph of us with the lighthouse in the background?'

'Of course.'

Kate was surprised when Nick stepped forward and took the digital camera. While he snapped a few photographs, the man chattered about the legend of the wreck of the seventeenth-century Spanish treasure ship, the *Corazon del Oro*, which lay off the rocks to the north of the lighthouse. Keen not to be left out, Jem ran up to join them just as Nick handed back the camera.

'Thank y'all so much! What a cute family you make,' the woman gushed, beaming at them as she linked arms with her husband. 'Why, the little man is just the image of his daddy!'

The American tourists left and Kate smothered a groan as she glanced at Nick and saw him stony-faced and rigid with tension. Jem, however, laughed.

'She thought you were my dad, Uncle Nick,' he joked, oblivious of the atmosphere as he picked up his kite and prepared to run off again. 'Cool, or what?'

Anxiety gripped her at Nick's expression. She sucked in a breath. 'Look, Nick—'

'No.' He held up a hand and backed away. 'I'm sorry, Kate. I tried. But I can't do this. It's too much.'

Tears stung her eyes, pain lancing through her as he turned and strode off in the direction of his house, leaving her and Jem alone. Again. All the progress of these last months, the new closeness, the joy for Jem, had been stolen in an instant by a stranger's unwitting comments. Clearly Nick wasn't ready. Maybe he never would be.

The knowledge tore at her heart and made her unutterably sad for herself and deeply hurt and angry for Jem, who had asked for none of this. How could Nick reject the boy? She wanted to chase after Nick and make him see reason, but she knew him of old and he wouldn't change his view unless he wanted to. Pushing him further would get nowhere. He had to come to terms and make the decision for himself. And if he didn't? If he could never accept Jem and have any kind of role in his life?

If that were the case, maybe the time had come for her to make a complete break, to think about leaving Penhally Bay and the man she had secretly and hopelessly loved for so long. For Jem's sake she couldn't risk Nick flitting in and out of his life as the mood took him. It would be too confusing for her son. And unfair. Maybe she should admit defeat and make a new life for herself and Jem elsewhere. A life without Nick. As he disappeared from view, her heart ached, and she feared this might well be the end to all her hopes and dreams.

A familiar car drew her attention as it approached the church and parked. Gabriel climbed out and she watched as he walked towards the solitary figure sitting hunched and alone on the rocks by the lighthouse at the end of the promontory. Lauren. With all her heart Kate prayed that the young couple, so right for each other, could find a solution to whatever had caused them to part last week. Their hurt had been palpable. She sent up a wish that Lauren and Gabriel could enjoy the kind of happy ending and life-long love that she herself had been denied.

Her mind full of the tough decisions that lay ahead, Kate turned and went to find her son.

Lauren sat on the rocks by the lighthouse—a favourite place she had often come to paint—and stared sightlessly out to sea. She wore sunglasses, as advised by the professor, to protect her eyes from damaging UV rays…eyes currently blurred and puffy from her tears. She despised self-pity, but she felt so overwhelmed at the moment and liable to cry at the merest provocation. It was very unlike her. But the future seemed so scary, so lonely, so bleak. She was worried about her eyes, about how she would cope when she could no longer work or maintain her independence. And her heart ached for Gabriel and what could never be.

Foxy sat beside her and she hugged him close. When he began whining and struggling against her hold, she pulled back in puzzlement. He strained at his lead, panting as he stared fixedly at something behind her. Lauren glanced round, a gasp of shock escaping, her heart lurching and her body tensing as she saw Gabriel striding towards her. He looked impossibly sexy in well-worn, figure-hugging jeans and his mulberry jumper. The lead slipped through her suddenly nerveless fingers, and Foxy's paws scrabbled for purchase on the rocks as he charged to greet the man whose every step inexorably closed the distance between them.

She watched as Foxy greeted Gabriel with enthusiasm. Clearly the dog had missed him as much as she had. Gabriel hunkered down and she could hear his huskily accented voice, if not his words. She saw him stroke the smooth brindle-and-white coat and her stomach clenched as she vividly recalled what it was like to feel those hands caress her bare skin.

Unable to bear it, she stifled a sob and swung round to face the sea again, trying to tune out Gabriel's voice by focusing on the sound of the waves against the rocks. But the sea was fairly calm today, providing poor entertainment for the surfers and failing to distract her from the man she could sense approaching. She stiffened as he sat beside her, far too close, far too tempting. What was going on? Why had he sought her out?

'Hi. Chloe said you might be here.'

His voice betrayed none of his previous anger and hurt. Indeed, he seemed impossibly relaxed. The same could not be said for herself. She was too aware of Gabriel. His earthy, citrusy fragrance tantalised her. Even across the small gap that separated him she felt the warmth of his body—a body every fibre of her being longed to hold again. Gabriel knew just where to touch, to stroke, to lick to send her to madness, as she did with him. Her heart yearned for what she could never have. Shifting restlessly, she kept her gaze averted, watching as Foxy turned a couple of times and lay down on a rock in front of them, dozing in the sunshine. She jumped when Gabriel reached out and captured one of her hands in both of his, panic rising as he refused to allow her to pull free.

'It's not going to work, you know, *chérie*.'

The sound of his voice tightened her insides with longing and his touch made her shiver. Her control deserted her. 'W-what isn't?'

'You…trying to push me away,' he told her, his tone calm and conversational. 'Pretending you don't feel the same as I do about what we have.'

'You don't understand. I can't offer you anything,' she whispered, failing once more to remove her hand from his, his touch setting of ripples of sensation, weakening her resolve.

'I understand more than you think. And you can offer me everything, *ma belle*, if only you believe and trust me.'

'Gabriel…'

'It took me a while to work out what you were doing.' He raised her hand to his mouth, his lips whispering over her skin, stealing her breath. 'This has been the worst week of my life. I cannot describe how much I have missed looking at you, talking with you, making love to you, holding you in my arms as I sleep.' His tongue-tip teased circles on her palm and she bit back a whimper, fighting with everything she had to hold on to her resolve. 'I'm not prepared to be without you for another minute.' He took off her sunglasses, dark mocha eyes gazing deep into her own. 'Look at me and say you don't love me. I know you think you're doing the right thing, but you're not. Tell me the truth, Lauren, once and for all. Lay it on the line.'

Every part of her was shaking and a tear breached the barrier of her lashes and trickled down her cheek. His thumb caught it, brushing the salty wetness away. It had been impossible enough to end it and send him away that evening outside the Manor House. There was no way she could force the lies out a second time. She felt trapped, desperately wanting to avoid this confrontation but unable to escape.

'I'm losing my sight! Is that what you want to hear?' she cried, all the fear, anger and despair welling up inside her and seeking release in an unstoppable tide. 'I have retinitis pigmentosa. I'm going blind, Gabe.'

'Shh. Come here, *mon amour*.'

Turning to face her, he pulled her close and she collapsed into his arms, sobbing as she buried her face against him. His warm strength enfolded her and she breathed in his scent. One arm held her tight while his free hand stroked her hair, his soothing words calming her. Weak, she allowed herself a few moments to believe everything could be all right, but reality intruded and she pulled back. He allowed her some space but he didn't let her go.

'Gabriel, we can't do this. I—'

'Yes, we can,' he interrupted with steely determination, his fingers gentle as they wiped her cheeks. 'I've known from the first that there was something wrong. The way you walked into things or missed what was in shadow right in front of you. How you unconsciously count your steps in the dark. You stopped painting, sought routines that were familiar, had trouble judging distances.'

'Why didn't you say anything?' she challenged, shocked and upset.

He frowned, a furrow creasing his brow. 'Because I didn't want to lose you by nagging. And you had to come to terms yourself, to recognise and accept, to ask for help.'

'But—'

'Lauren, it doesn't change how I feel about you. It matters to me in the sense of what it means for you and your joy in life, but not for any of the reasons you think.' He cupped her face, forcing her to look at him, to see and hear his sincerity. 'I don't feel pity or duty. Far less trapped. I love you, *ma belle*, no matter what. As the vows say…in sickness and in health, in good times and in bad, for better and worse.'

'You can't want me! I can't let you be burdened with this,' she cried.

For the first time a thread of anger returned. 'What gives you the right to make my decisions for me? To take away my choices? I'm an adult, Lauren, and capable of knowing my own mind.'

'I can't ask you to be tied to this. To me.'

'You are not asking. I am choosing. Of my own free will. Because I love you.' He paused a moment, watching her, considering, thoughtful. 'If it was the other way round, what would you do?'

Lauren licked lips that felt dry and struggled to find her voice. 'I don't understand.'

'If I were the one who faced some kind of illness or had RP, or if I had an accident and faced the rest of my life in a wheelchair, would you walk away and leave me? Would you stop loving me?'

'No!' she exclaimed, fury rising within her. 'Of course not.'

'Then do not expect that of me.'

Her heart stopped. With those words, she truly understood. 'Gabe…'

'I can no more live without you than I can without oxygen,' he told her huskily, drawing her back into his arms. 'You give meaning and joy to my life. You're my friend, my confidante, my lover. I will always love you, no matter what, and I will *not* walk away from you.'

'I don't know what's going to happen to me,' she sobbed, fresh tears threatening.

'I know you are frightened. And angry. It's all so new and confusing and scary. That is normal, human,' he reassured her, hugging her close. 'But I also know your courage and humour and intelligence. Your spirit will see you through. And you won't be alone, *mon amour*. We'll face this together. And together we can do anything.'

She cried again then, releasing all the tension and the fear and loneliness of the last days and weeks as she clung to him. 'RP is degenerative and incurable.'

'No one knows what the future holds. Already there are advances, possible new treatments, encouraging research with stem cells, even prosthetic retinas. However bleak things seem now, a few years down the line it may be different, there may be much that can be done to save, maintain or even improve sight for those with RP. But whether or not that happens, we have our love, our passion, our friendship. Life waits for no one, Lauren. We grasp what we have. We've been blessed to have each other.'

Accepting a tissue, she blew her nose and allowed him to cradle her against him. 'What about a family?' she asked, broaching a subject that disturbed her greatly. 'Professor Murchison said I could have genetic screening but what if the results show I can't risk having children? I don't want you to give things up for me.'

'We'll cross each bridge as we come to it, *chérie*,' he encouraged, and she marvelled at his calmness, his acceptance. 'You are the person who matters most to me. If we can't have children, so be it. If you wanted to, we could consider adoption—and do it properly so any child knows he or she is loved and all about their roots.'

'I really don't deserve you,' she whispered, overwhelmed by his love and understanding and innate goodness.

With a mock growl he gave her a gentle shake. 'Don't say silly things like that. You are the best thing to ever happen to me.'

'But what about your search for your own roots, Gabe? You can't give up on that, on finding out more about your mother,' she insisted, knowing how important it was to him. 'I don't want to hold you back. And don't you want to go back to France? What about your work?'

'Stop inventing obstacles,' he chided with the kind of rumbly chuckle that warmed her right through.

'I—'

His fingers stroked her face as he hushed her. 'I'm still going to research my mother. I've not decided what to do when my contract here ends, but we'll make that choice together. There are all kinds of options. I just heard this week that Lucy is about to give birth again,' he informed her. 'She wants to stay at home with the children and may not come back to work at the surgery for some while, and then only part time. Maybe I can stay on in Penhally.'

'Really?'

'I love it here.' He dropped a kiss on her forehead. 'The solicitor says that the Bartons have decided not to return to England after all. They are going to put the Manor House on the market when my tenancy ends. We could buy it—leaving Oliver and Chloe to buy Gatehouse Cottage, where they are happy. There are a range of possibilities, Lauren. We can do whatever we want.'

Filled with new hope, she pressed closer to him. 'I don't care where we go or what we do—as long as I'm with you. I'm sorry, Gabe. I thought I was doing the right thing. I love you so much and I thought it was unfair to trap you, that you would have a better life without me being a burden and dependent on you. You'd already been so manipulated by Yvette, I didn't want to do the same thing.'

'I know. You temporarily lost your judgement,' he teased,

nipping her earlobe. 'But I forgive you. We put that behind us now and move on. OK?'

'OK.' A rush of peace flowed through her and she allowed herself to believe that maybe it was going to be all right.

Gabriel smiled and drew her to her feet, taking Foxy's lead in his other hand. 'Good. Now, come with me.'

'Where are we going?'

'Home. To bed. We have a week of loving to catch up on and I intend to make the most of every moment.' The sensual promise in his sexily accented voice sent needy desire coursing through her. 'When we come up for air,' he continued with a wicked smile, 'we can start planning our wedding. We can elope like Oliver and Chloe or we can have a big shindig. Whatever you want. Just so long as it is soon.'

'Is that a proposal, Dr Devereux?'

'It is, Ms Nightingale.' He sent her a mock glare in warning. 'And I don't plan to take no for an answer.'

'Just as well I'm going to say yes, then.'

He caught her to him and swung her round, tangling them up with Foxy. Lauren laughed through her tears—happy tears—beyond grateful that Gabriel loved her, believed in her and hadn't given up on her. The fingers of one hand sank into her hair, tilting her head for his kiss. A hungry, deep, thorough kiss that was full of the passion and desire that had flashed between them from the first moment and the love that had grown with each day that had passed.

Gabriel broke off, his breathing as ragged as hers. She could feel his heart thundering as madly as her own. She could also feel the effect their kiss had had on him as she rocked her hips against his. Sweet mercy she had missed this…missed him…so much.

'Home,' he growled with pleasing desperation.

She wasn't at all sure she could wait to get back to the Manor House. Excitement fired her blood and an ache of need clenched deep in her womb. Some time in the next decade or two she might even manage to breathe again. Filled with the same urgency that drove him, she allowed Gabriel to take her hand, linking their fingers, as they all but ran back to his car.

Anticipation clamoured inside her. How could she have gone from despair to blissful joy in such a short time? The sexual tension crackled between them as they drove back through town—a town that had been through so much in the last year or two but which had only grown stronger and more together because of it.

Just like Gabriel and herself.

The future of her eyesight was uncertain, but with Gabriel by her side and secure in their once-in-a-lifetime love, she would no longer be afraid. Wherever they went, whatever they did, together they had everything they would ever need. Each other…united in body, heart and soul.

Don't miss Pink Tuesday
One day. 10 hours. 10 deals.

PINK TUESDAY
IS COMING!

10 hours...10 unmissable deals!

This Valentine's Day we will be bringing
you fantastic offers across a range of
our titles—each hour, on the hour!

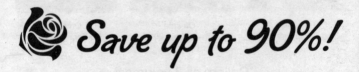

Pink Tuesday starts
9am Tuesday 14th February